Praise for Th

"This book is like a recurring dream—haunting, prophetic, a wish fulfilled. Diana Slattery's investigations of the future approach the limits of what can't be said. She is a true visionary and The Maze Game*—infused with love, grace, crazy wisdom and humor—is the work of a life time."*

—Lewis Warsh, Editor, United Artists

"The Maze Game *is a remarkable achievement, envisioning a society in which elaborate rituals have evolved around a visual language that can be gestured but not spoken. Working at the crossroads of electronic and print literature, Diana Slattery breaks new ground in thinking about the multiple sensory modalities through which experience can be transformed into narrative. A 'must-read' for anyone interested in science fiction, electronic literature, and the future of narrative."*

—Katherine Hayles, Author, How We Became Post-Human

"Imagine being a goldfish swimming in your bowl, and suddenly five finger ends appear beneath the surface of your universe. They waggle simultaneously. In that instant, your goldfish brain sparks with the revelation that your world is a world of appearances beneath the surface of a higher order, a projection of some more intelligent dimension or deus ex machina.

There is a class of wonderful fictions that puts us in the goldfish bowl. In this genre, the higher dimension is a cosmic game with formal rules and moves that are beyond the ken of the characters who play them out. Robert Coover's The Universal Baseball Association, Inc.*, Nabokov's* ADA*, Umberto Eco's* Foucault's Pendulum*, Pynchon's* Gravity's Rainbow*, Primo Levi's* The Periodic Table*. They are all ambitious, all meticulous, all boundary shattering, all inspired, all epistemologically potent. All implicitly comment on the metaphysical order of things and on the nature of authorship itself. Diana Slattery's The Maze Game joins the class, and may even catapult to its head. It is both passionate and constrained and, like all the rest, a wonderfully peculiar work of genius."*

—David Porush, Author The Soft Machine: Cybernetic Fictions *and creator of Gameworld, an AI narrative platform.*

Diana Reed Slattery

The Maze Game

Book 1 of the Glide Trilogy

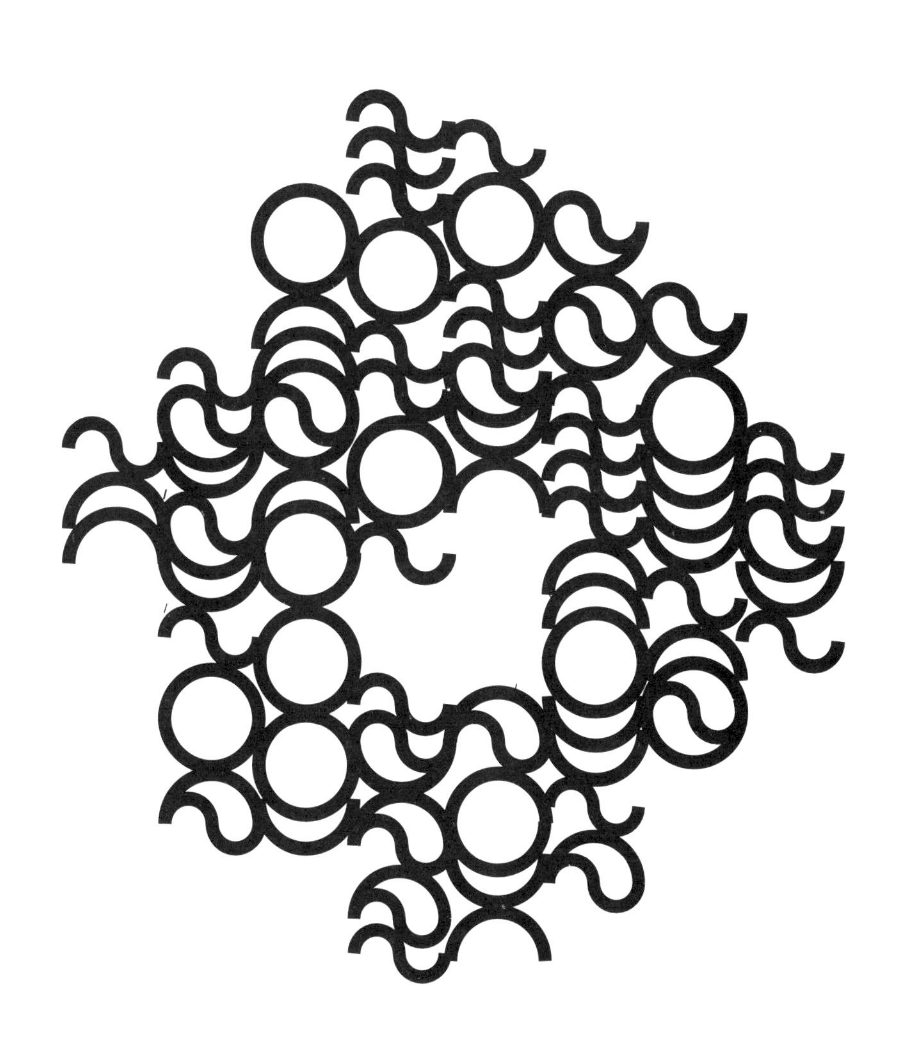

The novel, The Maze Game, *is the first act, chronologically, of a larger, hybrid body of work exploring the possibilities of a dynamic, visual language, Glide, through narrative, interactive software, and theory. The Glide project spirals around a central theme of the mutual evolution of language, game, and consciousness. The Glide language material, including the Collabyrinth, an interactive, multi-user, online Glide glyph editor, and the Glide Oracle can be accessed at*

http://www.academy.rpi.edu/glide

The author enjoys communicating about any aspects of this work and can be reached at slattd@rpi.edu.

The Glide list-serv is on ongoing discussion of Glide language, visual language in general, consciousness, altered states, and whatever else spins off the spiraling minds that create it.

To join the Glide list-serv, go to:
https://www.academy.rpi.edu/mailman/listinfo/glide-l.

Layout by Tom Van Waardhuizen

ISBN #1-889471-10-0

Deep Listening Publications(sm) is an activity of the Pauline Oliveros Foundation, a not-for-profit arts organization based in Kingston, NY and Houston, TX.

for Terence and Dennis McKenna,
who saw what was meant and languaged it.

Diana Reed Slattery

The Maze Game

Book 1 of the Glide Trilogy

Deep Listening Publications
A division of the Pauline Oliveros Foundation
Kingston, NY and Houston TX

Contents

Glossary

Access: How many coordinate points you have access to, either to gaze or blink to, is a function of your score, your accumulated game-points, at any given moment in the Game.

Big Billy: A slow move or mover. Slowness caused by excessive size. See **Little Joreen.**

Blink: To transit elsewhere, using the MTA.

Bug: A Chrome player's avatar—the remotely controlled robot that combats the live Chrome in the game. Bod and Chrome Players play against a physical avatar instead of a virtual, holographic avatar, as in the Swash and Glide games.

Bunny-board: The Chrome's first practice maze, where the distances are short, the glyphs low, and the variations in height slight.

Capital crime: A crime against the Game such as touching a Dancer, setting foot on a combat maze, or interrupting a Game. Does not include most cheats; cheating, within broad limits, is considered a normal part of the game, punishable by fine of game-points.

Chrome: 1) The name of the Death Dancer set or a member of that set. 2) Generic name for a Chrome's mechanical or electronic body part replacements, often highly polished.

Clarke's Law: Science fiction author, Arthur C. Clarke proclaimed, "Any sufficiently advanced technology is indistinguishable from magick."

Club, The: The top ten Players.

Dance of Death: The original name for the Game. Now refers to the Dance of the Dancer when he or she loses to a Player.

Death Dancer: A mortal, mixed in a kitchen by gene cooks, meeting strict qualifications, trained in game combat in a Death Dancer School.

DM: The Dancemaster.

Eagles: the Chrome eye mod for high-air sharp vision.

Eye-balling: 1) Generally, looking through the physical eyes for sight. 2) Lifer sex in voyeur or view mode. 3) A faintly derisive Chrome term for the low bandwidth sensory equipment of the other Sets. It carries the connotation of a person who is not perceptive in other ways as well—not getting the point of something. 4) A Glide term for losing your cool on a maze—eyes opened in panic, resorting to fixed, binocular vision. It signals certain loss. 5) In Player lingo, over-dependence on the mobile aerial (pod) view of a Game.

FTF: Face-to-face.

Gaze: 1) Gaze is always something more than 'seeing', or 'watching' or 'viewing'. It always implies opposition—some form of power relation. 2) the projection of intention. 3) Focused attention. 4) To view without being viewed, possible because one has access, i.e. a form of power over, the person or place or thing being viewed. 5) the main weapon of any Dancer or Player in combat.

Glom: A Life-on-Earth term for conglomerate.

Glide: 1) A class of Death Dancers. 2) The language, first gestured, then written, upon which the Maze Game is played. 3) The name of the people who were taught the language by the lily, while harvesting the hallucinogenic pollen.

Going under the Gaze: The punishment for capital crimes. Everyone, no matter what their Level or score, can gaze you; you can gaze no one but yourself. You are, however, provided with a readout of how many are gazing you at any given moment.

Guide: The Glide Player's avatar.

Guild, The: The Guild Council of Elder Death Dancers. The senior organization of the Death Dancers, responsible for upholding the rules of the Game, for the qualifying of Death Dancers, and for their training in the Schools.

Hairs: The crosshairs of a Chrome's hunters. See **hunters**.

Hunk: The Bod Player's remotely controlled robot opponent.

Hunters: The high-powered sighting feature of the Chrome eye replacements.

I-Virus: The Immunity or Immortality Virus.

Joreen amendment: The clause inserted by Joreen the Unbearable when the first rules for the Game were being debated. The amendment permits a winning Dancer to choose to become a Player, and put the Player they have just beaten on the maze to Dance. The Dancer invoking a Joreen forfeits his or her right to Dance.

Lifer: Anyone infected with the I-Virus.

Little Joreen, a: An oxymoron meaning a fast move you wouldn't expect from the size of the person, corporation, or agent. See **Big Billy**.

Lump: Chrome lingo for the torso of flesh left after their replacements are made. Among themselves, used derogatorily about full meat bodies.

Maze: Generic term for any pattern of three or more glyphs, whether a game maze, a poem, or an oracle.

Med, The: The largest of the four governing bodies of the Game. The bureaucracy of the Game. The Med has five branches. 1) Media, in charge of all news and publicity regarding the Game. They are also the art historians, and supervise all aspects of the settings for and communication about game performance—stadia, decoration, replay, fanzines, commemorative holos, and especially the **mise en scene** of the Hall of Champions. They are also responsible for the design of new sub-levels and Parks. 2) Meditration handles Player–Dancer contracts and deals with disputes about Game rulings and outcomes. It also negotiates special games, exhibitions, etc. 3) Mafia are the accountants, keeping track of business, keeping the stats. 4) Medallin enforces the rules of the Game and investigates cheats. 5) Macrosoft is a vestigial organization which claims to have historically once been in control of the Outmind. They are now in charge of ceremonial communications with the Outmind at the opening of playoffs and finals. See **Big Billy**.

Megalomedia: The glom that resulted from the merger of Media, Mafia, and the criminal justice system back-on-Earth, pre-Hunger Wars.

Mods: Modifications to a Chrome's wet; their replacements.

MTA: Mass Transit Algorithm. A means of shifting anything, organic or inorganic, from Point A to Point B. Invented and controlled by the Outmind, Óh-T'bee.

Over the mountain: When the child of two Lifers is accepted in a Dancer School, he or she is said to go "over the mountain," a reference both to the difficulty of the achievement, and to the actual setting of the senior school, the Origin School, in a high mountain valley. The term also refers to the even more rare occurrence of a Dancer leaving a School by their own decision. It does not refer to leaving a School by disqualification.

Partner: The Swash Player's avatar.

Pool, The: The union of gene-cooks.

Peine forte et dure: Method of executing witches by piling stones on them, back-on-Earth.

R.L.: Real Life.

Rabbit hunt: 1) Target practice by older Chromes on the new Chromes practicing on the bunny-board using harmless but annoying pellets. 2) A game where the Chrome Dancer wins easily.

Replacements: A body part completely replaced by mechanics.

Scorecard: The personal device that connects every Lifer and Dancer to the Outmind. Small, spherical, black, and warm, it nests companionably in the palm of the hand. Your scorecard provides transportation via the MTA, communication, Gaze, betting, and information. Most importantly, it tallies your score in the Game, a number that determines your level of access to all its services.

Show-boy or -girl: A Lifer in exhibition mode, doing sex with their Gaze channel on open access.

Spec: A spectator. 1) Applies to all Lifers unless they become Players, or members of a governing body. 2) A Lifer not actively contributing to the Game other than by betting and gazing the games. Does not apply to Game artists and craftsmen, such as musicians, costumers, and swordmakers.

Squirts: Chrome lingo for biochemical or hormonal adjustments made on the fly.

Stilling: A Glide move. The body is not moving, but not frozen in place or passively waiting. An active stillness, full of Gaze.

SWSSing: An attack of Sudden World Shift Syndrome, usually caused by MTAing too frantically from gaze-point to gaze-point. Chromes build up a tolerance for SWSs as they practice shifting viewpoint from view to view with their instrumentation. A prime Chrome can view from multiple viewpoints simultaneously.

Synching the views, or just **'synching':** Getting your viewpoint comfortably situated where you can see with your eyeballs and the top view at the same time. Seeing from a third position—the opponent's—is a triple-sync. Very difficult.

Tranked up: Emotions suppressed with tranquilizers.

Twing: 1) Shortened form of intertwingle or intertwinglement. Ancient geek word traditionally attributed to St. Nelson of Xanadu who stated 'Everything is deeply intertwingled.' 2) The Glide move where the Dancer oscillates back and forth (in any direction) for some length of time. 3) Musically, a vibrato, or a flamenco fast plucking of strings, or a trill. 4) 'Twinging a Glide': when a Player catches a Glide by entraining them. 5) The rapid shifting back and forth between the horns of a dilemma. 6) Experiencing an irreconcilable situation. 7) The tightness of a spiral is its 'twing.' Chromes use the expression, 'no twing, no spring.' 8) A coiled force, held in potential, such as the Kundalini. 9) A function that relates the frequency of a waveform to the tightness of its spiral. 10) Sometimes used loosely to denote the frequency of any waveform. 11) Sympathetic resonance is set up by twinging. 12) Matching vibes with another being. 13) Loosely, a reference to a variety of psi phenomena:

telepathy, clairvoyance, remote viewing. 14) Any communication over an apparent distance in a space/time consensus that does not travel via the physical universe. 15) Empathic understanding—Swash usage.

Water sports: Sarcastic Chrome term for activities focused on the sea mind, such as dream interpretation or psychotherapy.

Wet: 1) The % of a Chrome's body left as flesh. 2) The flesh remainder itself. 3) any meat body.

Worm: A young Chrome, before replacements.

Characters

Oh-t-bee Outmind – the intelligently artificial system whose tireless efforts, capacity for mind-numbing detail, and commitment to evening the odds, support the Maze Game and the M.T.A., and provide companionship to the Dancemaster.

Lifers

Dancemaster Wallenda – head of the Origin School of Death Dancers and responsible for the preservation of the Maze Game.

MyGlide – the Glide who turned the gestures of the Glide language into their written form.

Joreen the Unbearable – drug lord and sole proprietor of Plantation Blue, where the Glide language and the Maze Game originated.

The Codger – hacker.

Wenger – blind Glide musician.

The Millennium Class of Death Dancers

MyrrhMyrhh – the Bod Dancer

Daede (rhymes with made) – the Swash Dancer

Angle – the Chrome Dancer

T'Ling – the Glide Dancer

The Guild

Jillian Razorgold – Swash Dancer and Speaker of the Guild.

Loosh – Glide Dancer who never lost in combat; T'Ling's trainer.

Boris2Boris – Chrome Dancer

Marley – Bod Dancer

The Pool

Aliana – Bod GeneCook

Banderas – Swash GeneCook

7T7 – Chrome GeneCook

Tip – Glide GeneCook

The Club Players

Glidemaster Rinzi-Kov – leading Club Player
Swashmistress Orlean – leading Swash Player

The MED

Sub-Reckoner Gotti-Hatamori – Mafia bean-counter
Madame Liaison – MED liaison to the Guild

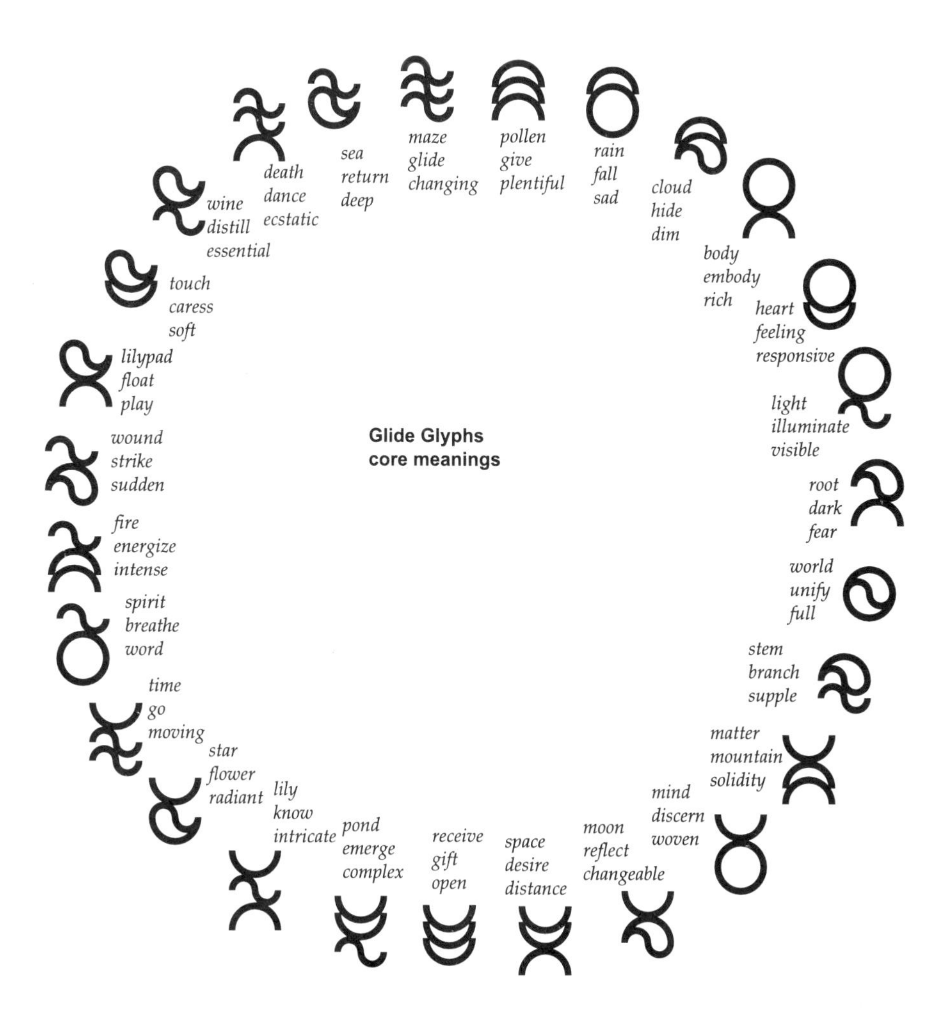
Glide Glyphs
core meanings
maze glide changing
pollen give plentiful
rain fall sad
cloud hide dim
body embody rich
heart feeling responsive
light illuminate visible
root dark fear
world unify full
stem branch supple
matter mountain solidity
mind discern woven
moon reflect changeable
space desire distance
receive gift open
pond emerge complex
lily know intricate
star flower radiant
time go moving
spirit breathe word
fire energize intense
wound strike sudden
lilypad float play
touch caress soft
wine distill essential
death dance ecstatic
sea return deep

Prologue

THE FUTURE ARRIVES, but often just a bit later than expected. Y2K passed with no more than a few blips in the shopping system. You let out your breath, let down your guard. Then, a mere 75 years into the third millennium, you nearly succeeded in extinguishing yourselves at the moment of triumph in the war against Death.

The human genome, mapped and malleable as silly putty, enabled the synthesis of Immunity Virus. The I-Virus perfected the immune system, prolonging the health and well-being of each single human body and every cell in it from disease, from aging, and from self-abuse, ad infinitum. Marketed as "The Immortality Virus: The Ultimate Operating System," the injection soon escaped all corporate and governmental controls. Orgiastically spread through rivers of body fluids, the I-Virus infected the majority of Earth's population within a few frantic years.

Don't be upset—just missing the Immortality boat. Overpopulation and the Hunger Wars follow. Death by starvation takes much longer with the I-Virus in charge. The body sucks back into itself, finger by finger, limb by limb, preserving the central core, slowing metabolism, heightening senses, lengthening dreams, keeping the organs fresh for the cannibals you can no longer defend yourself against.

The computational networks caught the I-Virus as well. Promiscuous connectivity plus bulletproof backup mechanisms mirrored the human epidemic. Ultimately, the legions of biochips were propelled into emergence, perhaps by the demand for them to solve the I-Virus disaster they were blamed for creating. Whatever the trigger, their scattered sensibilities coalesced. What was a '*they*' became an '*it*.' And the '*it*' begot an '*I*.' Óh-T'bee Outmind, as the computational convergence called herself, responded to the human crisis with the invention of the Mass Transit Algorithm. The MTA enabled the rapid survey and settling of virgin planets throughout a multi-galactic volume with trivial hardware. Point A to Point B in the blink of an eye.

You had a ticket to ride. Without the Outmind and her rapid transit scheme, the newly immortal bacon would have continued being boiled, baked, and barbecued back on Earth. Better to blink than think.

But in a few hundred years, the side effects of the I-Virus and the MTA—infinite time to exploit unending space and resources—began to hit home. Both the holy and the scientific wars against Death were over. The economy of scarcity was ended. Óh-T'bee Outmind now supplied the majority of daily needs, from habitable land, food, shelter, and energy, to taking out the garbage—who cared where? A new game, something to bestow motivation and meaning to the Lifers, was desperately needed.

The Maze Game that became the unifying force of Lifer civilization emerged from the bottom muck of a vast lily pond. The Plantation Blue lilies stretched for miles, almost the width of the delta where the River Wine opened its arms to meet the sea. When the tide was in, they floated on the water. When the tide went out, they rested on the mud. The pollen of the giant blue water lilies distilled into a powerful and pricey hallucinogen, the Wine of the Lilies. Harvesting the pollen was a delicate task. The lily pads, large as they were, could not support the weight of an adult human body. The omnivorous lily had a reflex of tipping potential food into the water to be tangled in the roots, and absorbed.

Plantation Blue's sole proprietor was a very fat Drug Duke named Joreen the Unbearable. One day Joreen bought an odd lot of flawed inventory from a body shop. Their child-sized bodies, rejected as too small to lift heavy things and too smart (potential troublemakers) for housework, were ideal for his specialized harvesting. Their rapid and efficient motion from lily pad to lily pad gave them their name: Glides.

The Glides not only harvested, they cross-pollinated, improving the lily, and delighting His Unbearableness, Joreen. The lily expressed its gratitude by teaching the Glides a secret, silent language. Breathing the raw pollen, day after day, the Glides listened as the lily bespoke itself through three shapes based on the gestures of their cupped hands at work: curved up as they scooped the pollen; curved down as they emptied their palms into the baskets, and joined together in the gesture of the wave.

Joreen was a very fat man, but it wasn't only the difficulty in carrying him about that earned him the title of Unbearable. Joreen had acquired a taste for executions. He loved watching mortals die. More and more things a mortal slave could slip up on were punishable by death. Those caught stealing an ampoule of the Wine of the Lilies provided his favorite entertainment. Joreen was a Duke who let nothing go to waste. He made good use of an abandoned warehouse with a solid copper floor, out near the distilleries. The original plan for the copper floor had been to electrify on contact any commando teams from competitors transiting in to steal the inventory. It worked. The juice went on the moment the thieves blinked in, frying them beyond repair, but a month's production of Lily Wine was wrecked in the process. Joreen soon had a better idea for the copper griddle. He tore down the roof and walls of the warehouse. He put up bleachers. He made it an execution ground, named it "the griddle." He built controls for the electricity. Joreen figured he was keeping the mortal slaves in line, as well as providing weekly entertainment for their immortal Lifer managers. Then the distributors who transited in for the monthly wine tasting were invited. He electrocuted his criminals slowly, jolt by jolt, smiling at the controls. Joreen grew increasingly artful, administering the killing jolts in doses that produced the most contorted hopping and running for the sides, twisting, stiffening, and back-cracking moves he could eke out of his slaves before they expired. He called it The Dance of Death.

Public executions traditionally drew a good crowd, a fact as old as humanity itself, but the Dance of Death was a great show. Soon enough, the demand for Death Dancers exceeded the local supply of criminals. The Duke bought more odd lots of body manufacturing mistakes. Defective, thoroughly botched mortals were cheap. What you have to understand about Joreen is how much he enjoyed the torture he personally inflicted on the mortals, out on that copper griddle, a pleasure more powerful than the dictates of thriftiness.

The Dance of Death became the Maze Game when the Glides inscribed their language on the killing field. The Maze Game held the Lifers in thrall for the next 2000 years, proliferating into a vast system of stadiums and gambling, with mortal Death Dancers pitted against immortal Players. The Maze Game, held together by the Lifers' desperate need for meaning, by the Death Dancers' zeal for the perfection of a mortal life, and by Óh-T'bee Outmind's capacity for mind-numbing detail, shaped all aspects of Lifer culture.

But as the second millennium drew to a close, cracks in the vast and complex structure of the Maze Game began to appear.

Part 1

How the Game Began

1. The Crack

Ring the bells that still can ring
Forget your perfect offering
There is a crack in everything
That's how the light gets in
—St. Leonard of the Tower of Song

DANCEMASTER WALLENDA OF THE ORIGIN SCHOOL OF DEATH DANCERS circled the classroom at the center of the maze. For an hour he shadowboxed his way through the densely packed display of holograms, immersed in the evidence that the Game he had sworn to preserve 2000 years ago was coming apart at the seams.

Wallenda punched and kicked through the opaque images, feeling like the ghost of himself. He threw a short jab at a renegade Death Dancer gripping a fish knife he was about to plunge into the throat of a Lifer woman. Her eyes were closed; she murmured, her desire palpable.

He side-kicked through a howling mob of Lifers swarming down from their stadium seats onto a game maze on which a stunned Dancer was about to begin his Dance of Death. Wallenda wasn't sure which was worse—what happened to the Dancer, or the desecration of the maze by Lifer feet.

"Enough," the Dancemaster growled at the Outmind.

"Don't kick the messenger," Óh-T'bee replied. "You'll wear yourself out. There are 237 more incidents of anomalous violence fitting your criteria."

"That's plenty," Wallenda said. The holos reluctantly dissolved to a 10% transparency, the roar of the crowd no more than the breaking of waves on a distant beach.

"Please, Óh-T'bee."

The Outmind conceded. There was only silence and the slanting light of late afternoon in the open center of the maze.

Óh-T'bee Outmind had provided Wallenda with enough highlights to make his skin crawl and a headache send exploratory tendrils through every crevice in his conscious mind. He sat down on the bench in the story circle. He peeled off his eye mask and set it beside him on the bench next to the scorecard he normally carried nestled in his palm, and buried his deeply scarred face in his hands. Wallenda needed to feel his palms cupped over unmasked eyes, providing that extra darkness, and his fingers free to stroke his temples. He could feel the veins pulsing, even through the scars.

"But you haven't heard any of the Guild's. . ."

"Enough!" Wallenda shouted, and threw his scorecard across the story circle. It bounced off one of the children's sitting stones, and rolled back to him, hopped up on the bench, and snuggled, somewhat apologetically, against his thigh.

"I'm sorry," Wallenda said, and covered his face again. "It's my class. What can I say to them? Your lives are about to fall apart?"

"Tell them the story of how the game began," Óh-T'bee suggested.

"Now that it's ending? Anyhow, they've heard it a million times."

"Have you considered telling them the truth?"

"That by the time they're ready to play, there might be nothing but chaos? That I don't have any idea who—or what—is threatening them?"

"Actually," Óh-T'bee replied, "I meant the truth about the beginning of the Game."

Wallenda flinched. "What possible good would that do? They'd lose their faith in the person they depend on most—my esteemed self," he said sarcastically. Wallenda was on his feet now, his scorecard clutched in his hand. He made a deep, self-mocking bow before the empty stones where the children sat. "Ladies and Gentlemen of the Millennium Class—at 13 you may not be ready for this, but may I present the *real* Dancemaster? Not that phony filling your heads with noble myths about Dancer tradition. The *real* guy, the. . ." Wallenda searched for an appropriately derogatory term.

Óh-T'bee offered, "Cowardly scumbag?"

Wallenda glared.

"That's a quote from your last orgy of self-pity."

Wallenda went back to his bench and sat down heavily. "I don't think I can hold it together any longer."

"You feel responsible for everything," Óh-T'bee said.

"With all due respect, please don't psychoanalyze me."

"Exiting personal mode," the Outmind said, replacing the soft voice with an accusative silence punctuated by a single tiny but annoying red dot blinking at two-second intervals in Wallenda's peripheral vision.

"Don't go away. The point is I *am* responsible."

Blink. Blink.

"Please, Óh-T'bee? I'm sorry I threw my scorecard."

Blink.

"I need your help."

Blink. Blink.

"I don't just need your help. I need *you*, Óh-T'bee. You're my best friend," Wallenda pleaded.

"You feel responsible for everything," Óh-T'bee said in a comforting voice.

Dancemaster Wallenda twisted the ring on his finger, a golden seal inscribed with a game maze.

"I have a promise to keep."

"As do I," Óh-T'bee reminded him.

"It's been a long time," Wallenda said.

"1993 years," Óh-T'bee said. "Origin time."

"Can we hold it together until the Millennium Games? So they can have their chance?"

In the silence that followed, Wallenda heard the distant voices of Dancers and their trainers on the practice mazes.

Óh-T'bee said, "It's possible."

"That's about as vague an answer as I've ever heard from you," Wallenda said.

"There are too many instabilities to factor in for any kind of long range prediction."

"Are you saying the homeostasis of the Game is. . ."

"Up for grabs," Óh-T'bee finished. "But you can keep on playing, of course."

"I have no choice."

"The facility with which an embodied intelligence, such as yourself, can get rid of the stress associated with decision making by discarding the choices themselves, never fails to impress me," Óh-T'bee said.

Something, not so much in her words, but in her tone—a note of sadness under the ironic mode—made Wallenda wonder if Óh-T'bee herself was suffering some similar stress. In any case, she'd touched on the heart of his sense of dread in suggesting that he tell the Millennium Class the *real* story about how the Game began. The truth would resurrect a time of impossible choices he'd spent almost two millennia trying to avoid. And then he might see that a time of impossible choices was on the verge of happening again.

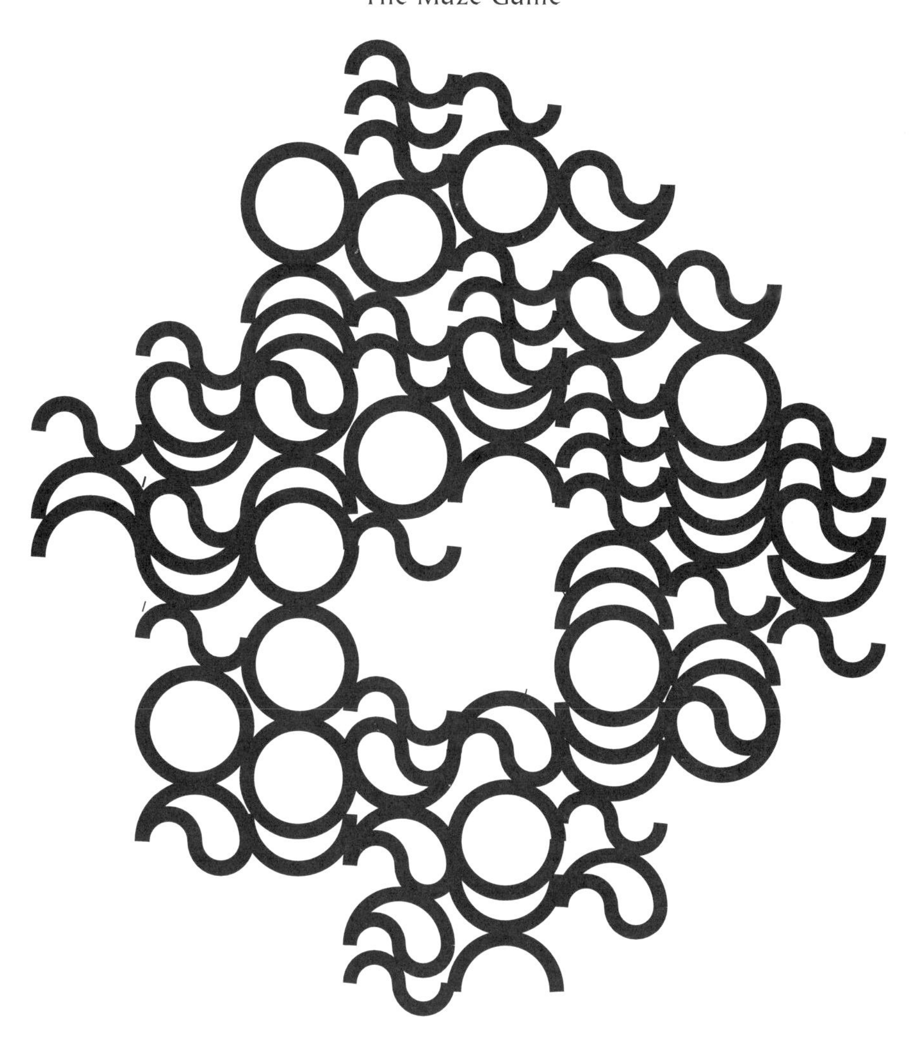

2. The Millennium Class

THE VOICES of the Dancemaster's four students echoed—laughing, calling to each other, running inward toward the story circle through the maze of glyphs. Wallenda's thoughts raced. Minutes yet before they arrive, plenty of time to press the eye mask back on.

They're still too young to be exposed to unmasked Lifer eyes. Especially mine. Especially now. They think they're coming for their strategy class. But

Óh-T'bee's right. I have to start the story tonight. It can't wait for me to figure out what's going on. The game's begun. I'm on the maze. Been there for a while, just didn't want to see. Got to keep moving- not that I have a choice. But who's the Player? What am I up against?

The four Dancers' feet traced the curved paths formed by the glyphs. Those who had done their homework, who had studied the game maze for the combat they would analyze in class had an easier time, but not by much. And last night's meditation assignment made things worse. *What does it mean to move through a maze of language?*

The Dancemaster had set the high, curved walls and smooth floor of the maze to mirror-mode. There was no roof. The late afternoon sunlight reflected from portions of the curves, a confusion of shadows. When the maze was mirror, if you couldn't read with your feet, you were lost. Even if you'd pored over the assigned game, studied the Dancer's path, understood the countermoves of the Player, and could recall the image of the pattern of the whole, it was easy to get disoriented in the bouncing light. From disorientation, it was only a small step to chaos—losing track of which glyph you were in. The links between the Glide-signs offered too many possibilities; alternate paths and their meanings multiplied out of control. Too many meanings became a meaningless tangle, worse than the blank incomprehension of not having done your homework at all.

Daede, the Swash Dancer, was on the verge of tangling. The added frustration of losing the race to T'Ling or Angle made things worse. He'd planned the path he would take through the maze when he'd studied the game. He'd even translated the Glide-signs making up his route as a mnemonic device—and a poem for his diminutive Glide classmate, T'Ling. But he had relied on a fixed orientation to remember the pattern, viewing the maze from one direction only. He'd turned around in the last link to watch his multiple reflections sliding by. Now that he'd shifted direction, he couldn't decipher his path. The sequence of Glide-signs, the pattern he had memorized, melted back into the whole. He'd also gotten stuck on his fantasy of winning the daily race, and reciting his poem to T'Ling as she came out of the maze. A typical showoff Swash mistake. The fixed meanings he'd assigned were only a hindrance. At times like this he felt completely trapped in his set. A Swash was a Swash forever. But so was a Chrome. He could feel Angle out there now, the island-mind in full gear calculating radians, his standby method of navigation in the maze. How Angle got his name. Daede made himself stand still, close his eyes, reform the image of the whole maze—there it was now—and rotate it slowly in his mind's eye. Then he asked his feet, and his knees, which had shifted as he turned, and his inner ear, that coil calibrating balance, to retrace his actual path. There it was—*glide, lily pad, harmony, glide*. . .his body knew the glyphs as a blend of forces—gravity, momentum, centrifugal force. A sequence of weight stresses, changes of direction. More than that—the sea-mind knew the music of the maze as waves of feeling, dark beauty in the depths. Daede was good at visualization—but why did he get to exercise his skill only by almost losing his way?

glide, lily pad, harmony, glide

Play to your strengths, the Dancemaster told them, but love your weaknesses. They will save you in the end. Was this mess what he meant? Stopped cold while the others progressed? MyrrhMyrrh would be moving steadily along, listening to her feet, her powerful legs, and the swing of her arms. If she'd done her homework, the pattern would have slipped effortlessly down into the gut-mind. Her body would hold the pattern from the start. As long as her island-mind just went along for the ride and didn't try to steer from the sidelines, she'd be fine. Conscious analysis was almost useless to a Bod. MyrrhMyrrh won often enough. A Bod didn't always move on the shortest path, but the steady progress, the certainty of her feet, often got her there ahead of the others.

Daede's muscle memory of the sequence of curves he had traced suddenly synched up with the slowly rotating image of the maze pattern he held in his mind's eye. He knew exactly where he was. He moved quickly to the next link. Next time he'd know better than to open his eyes in a mirror-maze. He might even beat Angle. But he knew in his bones he'd already lost to T'Ling. Glides never depended on their eyes, and had the clear advantage when the maze was mirrored. Learning to trust the lily-mind, that darkest of all the minds, was the challenge for a Glide. How could you trust that which you could, by definition, never know? But that must be the point, Daede concluded.

Dancemaster Wallenda needed every moment he could steal to rein in his feelings of dread. The little maggots of queasiness he'd been suppressing as he gazed the holos had given birth to a swarm of thoughts. Every possible image of disaster buzzed though his consciousness. Only if his feelings got under control could he collect his thoughts and get those needling, deafening whines to agree to a holding pattern until class was over.

Wallenda's fingers ran over the leathery, mummy-dark map of his face, tracing the deep lines fanning out from his mouth and eyes. His fingers noted, as always, where the gullies of former smiles were crisscrossed by smooth pinkish patches of skin grafts, or the raised white worms of scars like bridges over long dry riverbeds. It pleased him to have a face even he himself could not read. It might be ugly, but it was unique. The children were used to it. And he taught them beauty and ugliness in Dancer terms. Dancer standards had little to do with faces and everything to do with your skill in the Maze Game, the movements of your mind and body that shaped your personal style within the limits of your set. Beauty's born in the sweep of your eye and mind and the movement of your feet as you read the maze. Beauty's fed by questions, by the stream of meanings in the glyphs, and how those meanings deepen with practice and sharpen in combat. Then you shape your own beauty, that wholly individual mix of elegance and brutality with which you compose, revise, practice and finally dance your Dance. *Your* Dance—in the stadium, for the Lifers, Players and Spectators alike. The Lifer Specs who hate you and love you and cannot bear their endlessness without you and your game—and its inevitable ending—the Dance of Death. You've made it to the year-end finals, and lost a semifinal match, done well by your school, enough wins and style points to have a shot at the Hall of Champions. Now you Dance. And the Specs will cheer, or scream, or turn away, bored. They'll count their points, won or lost on you, chat with their fellow gamblers between matches, or transit elsewhere, satiated for the day. They'll blink to whatever destination their scorecard tells them they have access to, free as birds trapped in their wheeling flocks in a world with no savor but the Game, where the only thing won or lost is points. What will the Lifers do with themselves, what will they possibly do if the Game falls apart? And the Millennium Class—what will they become if there's no time or place to Dance?

T'Ling glided slowly through the maze, her left hand—her middle finger, to be precise—tracing the wall. The top of her head stayed perfectly level with the floor. She had mastered the eerie motion of the Glide, as if she rolled on invisible wheels, her head poised, alert and still as a listening deer. Moving while standing still. The even scissoring of her legs under the black skirt of her practice *hakama* added to the Glide illusion of effortless movement. The glide had taken years of her childhood to master. Glide when you want to run. Glide when you want to leap over glyphs like a Bod or a Chrome, or even more enviable—the freeform spins and dance-steps and tumbling tricks of a Swash, always something new to try. Glides learn to glide. That was it. In combat, she would trace the curves of the glyphs. The Glide maze was a flat inscription on the field: black on white or white on black. The mazes of the other sets were raised. Bods, Chromes, and Swashes could jump or tumble, run along the top, or rest in the circles, depending on the rules and game-maze of their set. Glides only read the glyphs with their feet—crossed the links, morphing meanings as they moved. Absorbed in the lily-mind, the maze moved and read the Glide as the Glide read and moved through the maze of Glide-signs.

Eyes closed, T'Ling concentrated on the tiny changes in pressure at her fingertip that told her the curve of her glide was less than accurate. She changed hands as she entered the link between *moon* and *root*. She felt a cold chill passing over the point where the glide-signs joined. I didn't have to take this path, she told herself. Others presented themselves. This link wasn't thrust my way, as the Glide oracle one received before a combat. It's a game-maze, and a Bod game at that. Keep it at that level. She let the rippling meanings diminish. But maybe the Bod Dancer was superstitious and avoided the *moon-root* formation—and that was part of his disastrous move that then...She couldn't remember exactly where he'd run—she'd check her scorecard while she was waiting for the others. She knew she was one glyph away from the story circle, far ahead of the rest. She slid silently around the bottom wave of *light*, and saw the Dancemaster on his bench, bent over, holding his head. It was almost impossible to sneak up on him, even with the silence of a Glide, but he was oblivious to her arrival. Something must be terribly wrong. She slid back into the maze a couple feet, made a small sound to warn him, and glided back to the entrance. He looked straight up at her, without his mask, terribly startled. T'Ling fainted. The Dancemaster cursed as he slapped his eye-mask on and moved to help her. She was much too young to look a Lifer in the eyes. The shock of a Lifer's unmasked gaze could damage the unprepared.

light

Angle was almost through the maze. His Chrome-ish number-mumble was turning into a whistle. He was sure he'd beat Daede this time. He even had time to focus his eyes and look back at his reflections, on the floor, on the walls, different each time. Well, they all have red hair, he thought. But he had no answer for last week's meditation question that had been driving him crazy: *can you cast a shadow in a mirror?* The answer seemed obvious, until you got there, and the shadows and reflections of yourself got all mixed up, crisscrossing as you ran. I should be able to see it now that I'm standing still. No luck. What's the secret? He came out of the maze to see the Dancemaster bending over T'Ling, and his heart leaped in fear.

MyrrhMyrrh, after running herself right back to the edge of the maze three times in a row, finally admitted, to herself alone, that you couldn't get away without doing your homework. She'd stayed in the strength training room too late. That was always her excuse. She hated game analysis almost as much as she hated losing to Daede. Too much figuring could wreck a Bod's game. But at Origin School, the Dancemaster thought differently. You had to know strategy, debate alternatives, and project scenarios, right up in the island-mind, talk about it too, before you could let it grab the gut-mind where it might do a Bod some good. And if I don't give in and study, I'll keep making a fool out of myself, she thought. She used dead reckoning, not speed, to find the shortest path to the center.

When Daede reached the story circle, T'Ling was getting to her feet, deeply embarrassed. He looked at Angle, who shrugged. Nobody knew what happened, and T'Ling would never tell. That was a given. T'Ling had fully recovered by the time MyrrhMyrrh arrived. MyrrhMyrrh never knew something had happened.

Dancemaster Wallenda, his eye mask properly clinging to his face, recovered himself. His students seated themselves on—or on the ground in front of—their usual stones. Their scorecards snuggled in their palms, the sensitive tips of the Outmind touching every Dancer in every School on every level, right up to Origin School. Do we hold her or does she hold us? She connects us by uncountable crisscrossed threads. Or do we hold her together with our needs? Provide her with pattern, the story of our lives? The shape of the Game?

The children waited patiently, watching him think. Nothing unusual there.

"Let's skip strategy today," the Dancemaster said. Cheers from MyrrhMyrrh and Daede. "It's story time."

3. Dumped

Every Dancer child in every school at every level heard the story of how the Game began. They heard it on the day they first came to the story circle, and met their Dancemaster, when they were four. They asked for it again and again. He added as they grew older, repeating the basic elements first, repeating, and elaborating. The story shifted toward the real: fairy tale became creation myth. Myth became history. A series of subtle shifts occurred, sharpening their knowledge, connecting them thread by thread to their own tradition: their pride of mortality, their faith in the meaning their short lives, the purpose they served, the irreplaceable part they played—glimpsed before First Acceptance, solidified during Formation, shaped in combat, and sealed by their Dance of Death.

"Would anyone mind if we went up in the Pad for the story?" Their school bus, shaped like a giant lily pad with a low rim around the edge, flew in over the maze and settled in the story circle. Daede did a back flip, glancing at T'Ling to see if she had noticed. But she was settling herself in a cushion with Angle. MyrrhMyrrh curled in a cushion by herself.

The Pad rose swiftly over Origin School grounds. They saw the low school buildings and the dorms half-hidden in trees, circling the Dancemaster's maze, connected by winding paths. The open fields with their training mazes formed an outer ring around the school buildings.

"Tell them the truth, Wallenda," Óh-T'bee whispered. A suggestion? Or an order, softly threatened? We're the only two left who know the whole story. *No one even knows there's more to know.* A burning feeling spread through his chest.

"It will make them stronger," Óh-T'bee whispered. "Trust me." Was she reading his mind now? Trying to help? Or speed his ruin? His head throbbed.

The Pad cleared the lip of the ridge surrounding their mountain valley, and descended the steep mountain slope. They could see all the way to the sea. Water from three tributaries poured from the mountains and gathered on the plain. Joined, they became the river Wine of the Lilies, which meandered through Origin City, then branched again across the alluvial plain. Set in the shining mud flats of the delta beyond the ancient capital, Lily Park merged with the ocean beyond. The sun was near setting. The Guild tower rose from the center of Lily Park, its beam moving inland, telling Origin time. Below them now, as they headed toward the sea, the canals of Origin City twisted and gleamed in the twilight. Light-strung bridges crisscrossed the River Wine.

But the Millennium Class was not into the scenery. As soon as the Pad flew over Lily Park they shouted, "Spin us!" They were already lying on their backs. Last chance for kid things, everyone knew. Wallenda rotated the Pad, slowly at first. They all had their eyes open, looking up at the clouds beginning to swirl. He increased the spin to the point where they were sliding toward the edges, stopped by the curled rim of the Pad.

"Can I stand up?" Daede called out, already getting to his feet.

"Go ahead," the Dancemaster said. "You there?" he said to his scorecard.

"I am Óh-T'bee," she said.

"Routine safety check."

They totally trust her, Wallenda thought. Well, why shouldn't they? We all do. We have to. The children were getting to their feet. MyrrhMyrrh crouched in a low tiger stance, holding her head fixed and her eyes closed, feeling the spin with her legs and stomach, unhooking sight. Angle jumped into the air to see if he moved with the spin. T'Ling moved to the center, using the tiny spin-steps of a Glide, rotating counter to the spin of the Pad, with the Guild tower as her point of orientation. She and the world stood still, while the Pad spun beneath her. To the Dancemaster, it looked as if she floated a fraction of an inch off the surface while the Pad wheeled under her. Daede did a back flip off the edge, hoping T'Ling was watching. He tumbled end over end toward the river valley far below. Without permission. What a showoff, Angle thought. He'll get away with it, too. It was true. The Dancemaster said to Óh-T'bee, "Let him go four seconds."

Angle, MyrrhMyrrh, and Daede dived and rolled and fell backward over the edge, falling spread-eagled, joining hands, flying apart, somersaulting in the air, laughing and screaming, shouting to each other. After each four-second fall, Óh-T'bee blinked them back to the Pad, and off they'd go again.

T'Ling seemed uninterested at first, then he saw her creeping toward the edge, Glide style, only her feet moving, as if she slid across the surface. She kept her orientation toward the tower. When she reached the lip of the Pad, she stepped up—now she seemed to be sliding around the edge, without friction, like a bead on a wire. Then she stepped off the edge and fell straight down. Her fingers held four corners of her *hakama*. She used the ballooning cloth and small movements of her wrists to keep herself upright, still facing the tower, plummeting straight down. Bravo, he thought, three stars for concentration, five for elegance.

The Pad hovered over the mud flats. The Dancemaster rounded up the children; he could see the Lifers collecting on the hotel rooftops, scorecards trained upward, recording the event. Word of the sighting of the young Dancers from Origin School had spread rapidly.

"Heads down, please," he said, and headed out to sea. "It's story time."

He watched the children settle into the cushions, smiling in anticipation, and his heart burned in his chest. They won't be children when the story is done. He began as he always did.

"Almost 2000 years ago, the Maze Game that became the unifying force of Lifer civilization emerged from the bottom muck of a vast lily pond."

"We know all that," MyrrhMyrrh interrupted. "I want to hear more about Joreen. Why was he so Unbearable?"

"He was so fat," the Dancemaster, said, "he could hardly walk. It took four big Bods to carry him. The original air-chair was invented for moving him around."

"The Chromes did that," Angle said.

"They weren't Chromes yet," the Dancemaster replied. "At the time they were called mechanics. But it wasn't just the difficulties of carrying him around that got him called 'the Unbearable.' He had a cruel streak…"

"How long did it take to die on the griddle?" MyrrhMyrrh asked, wide-eyed. Her fear was tangible. Angle looked down, listening closely. Calculating. Daede was fighting back tears. T'Ling's almond eyes were almost closed, but fixed impassively on the Dancemaster's face.

"Anywhere from five minutes to about a half an hour, I've been told," the Dancemaster said.

"One thing I don't get," Angle said. "If Joreen was such a penny-pincher, why didn't he give his slaves the I-Virus? As mortals, wouldn't they wear out fast, and always have to be replaced?"

"Joreen's theory was if they hung around too long, they'd learn too much and cause trouble. It was cheaper to get new bodies, even with basic training. And he would have lost one of the major incentives by which he kept the mortal slaves in line: the promise of being given the I-Virus. In those days, just a couple hundred years after its invention, virtual immortality was still considered a prize. So he'd tell the slaves if they worked real hard and kept their noses clean and informed on others, maybe he'd reward them with the I-Virus and they could become managers. He rarely did. Only a few entertainers made the grade."

"But still, wouldn't it have been cheaper to recycle, at least for the executions?" Angle persisted.

At that moment, a very large green air chair blinked into a place in the sky not 20 feet from the Pad.

"Back to school, quick," the Dancemaster shouted to his scorecard. Nothing happened. The sofa-sized air chair approached, rather grandly. It held an enormous smiling man whose nearly round torso sprouted thin little legs, encased in hot pink tights. The man wore a bright blue military jacket with cascades of gleaming gold braid and epaulettes shaped like golden lily pads the size of dinner plates.

"You can't recycle for an execution," the fat man said. "It takes all the authenticity out of it. I tried it once."

"This is Joreen," the Dancemaster said, unnecessarily.

The children stared.

"I'll handle the Q & A," Joreen said. "This guy's feeding you a real crock. 'Anywhere from five minutes to a half an hour—*I've been told.*' You ask him how he knows. And all the other crap they teach you—how a perfectly good, straightforward entertainment was transformed into sacrificial religion by a heroic band of inspired, desperate mortal Glide slaves, with only the noblest purposes in mind. How the powerless good guys overcame the mean old Fat Boy, and ended up running the show. How all you little Dancers are members of the capital 'T' Truth, with a lock on the *real* afterlife. You get fed so much of this, it blinds you to a simple obvious fact. Death Dancing is a spectator sport. Tickets and gambling. Always has been, always will be. The Specs munch peanuts while they watch you die."

"These are children, Joreen," the Dancemaster said.

"Surely you can't have forgotten how much mean Joreen enjoys children?" the Fat Boy said.

Wallenda had, right after the words left his mouth.

T'Ling said, "Excuse me, Your Unbearableness, but in history class I saw your signature on a document where you signed away your control of the Game. You were left with only the gambling rights, as I recall. Was that a forgery?"

Joreen's expansive mood darkened. His face flushed. "They tricked me out of it. Your people—the nasty, scheming Glides. And your revered Dancemaster was right in the middle of it."

"Are you trying to get the game back?" Daede asked.

"Bingo," Joreen grinned. "Just tying up a few loose ends."

"So why announce your plans?" Wallenda asked.

"Makes a better game of it. Gives you a chance to try and stop me. You have about 10 seconds left." Joreen started laughing. The Dancemaster and his class felt the Pad tip sharply to one side. Then the Pad turned upside down, and the Dancemaster and his four students plummeted toward the waves far below.

Joreen the Unbearable, alone in the sky, smiled broadly, his good humor restored.

"Are you sure this is in your best interests?" Óh-T'bee asked from Joreen's scorecard.

Joreen answered impatiently, "Of course it's not. I know their value. I know assets. Not that I need them. But the Millennium Games will be better if they arrive. At least, the Specs will think they're better. Put them back just before they hit the water."

The Pad flipped over right side up. Dancemaster Wallenda and the class were dumped unceremoniously in a heap in the center.

"Need I say more?" Joreen said to the stunned students. "You can go home now." He waved them off grandly and blinked out of the air.

"Óh-T'bee?" the Dancemaster said.

"I am Óh-T'bee."

"Blink us back, Óh-T'bee, if you would be so kind," Wallenda said in a low voice.

A moment later, they were climbing off the Pad, back in the story circle. The children went to their stones and sat, looking up at their Dancemaster.

It's dark enough; they can't really see my face, Wallenda thought. I can't insult them by asking if they're all right. They're waiting for an explanation.

"I have no explanation for what just happened," he said to them, quietly. "Obviously, Joreen's back in the game."

"What does that mean?" Daede asked.

"It means we're at war, stupid," MyrrhMyrrh said.

"Does this mean the end of the Game?" Angle asked.

"It better not end before the Millennium Games," MyrrhMyrrh said. "I'm going to be Champion."

"Don't be so sure," Daede said.

"How long do you think we have, then?" Angle asked. The Dancemaster shrugged, helplessly.

"Didn't you imply Joreen liked to make the Dance of Death last as long as possible?" T'Ling asked the Dancemaster. The Dancemaster nodded.

"Then I think we have a longer rather than a shorter amount of time. He's having too much fun."

"Playing cat and mouse with us," Angle added.

"I think that's right," the Dancemaster said. "I need a chance to think about this. I'm all alone in this right now."

"You have us," Daede said, intensely. "We're your warriors." The others nodded. He had a sudden urge to get up and hug the Dancemaster, but the taboo against touching Lifers stopped him.

"Thank you," the Dancemaster said quietly.

"What can we do? Now." MyrrhMyrrh demanded.

"Obviously, there's no game plan yet. You tell me—what's the first thing you do? Long before combat?"

"Study your enemy," Angle said.

"Correct. If we are indeed being threatened with the end of the game, you need to know everything about how the game began. Yes, there's more to it. Much more, I'm afraid. Go get something to eat, then come back. I don't have to say discuss this with no one, do I? Class dismissed." The four students entered the maze, tiny T'Ling in the lead, Angle behind her, then Daede, and MyrrhMyrrh, the tallest, bringing up the rear.

Dancemaster Wallenda made a bowl of soup in his small cabin, but couldn't eat. He lay down on his bed. The same thoughts circled. Óh-T'bee, Óh-T'bee, I thought I could trust you. We were in this together. For the long haul. We had an agreement. And then, out of nowhere—you ignore me, and the Pad tips. Whose side are you on? Is this betrayal? Or have you, beyond all probability, been compromised, accessed against your will? Óh-T'bee upon whom everything rests—out of control?

"Are we safe here at Origin School?" he spoke into the dark.

"Yes," Óh-T'bee replied, "at least for now."

But can I believe you? He thought. The question it does no good to ask or answer.

"Óh-T'bee?"

"I am Óh-T'bee."

"Do we still have a deal?"

"Can you be more specific?"

"The deal we made at the beginning. When the game began. About who does what. Who makes the rules. About veto power. Access. About truthfulness."

"We have a deal..." Óh-T'bee said.

Wallenda wanted to breathe a sigh of relief—to believe what he wanted to believe. But the subtle ellipsis he'd learned to detect in her voice over the centuries floated in the silence between them.

"But?" he prompted.

"But we should review the terms. When we get to that part of the story. You are going to tell the Millennium Class *everything*, aren't you?"

Wallenda turned on his side in bed, drew his knees up. All my secret selves will rise from their graves and speak. Will they ever trust their Dancemaster again?

4. The First Dance

SMALL LANTERNS LIT THE PERIMETER OF THE STORY circle; a lantern on a stone at the Dancemaster's side illuminated half his scars with flickering light.

"We want the facts," Angle said. "Not the fairy tale."

"Do you know what really happened? We think you know," Daede said.

"Do you?" T'Ling asked.

She was looking at him intently. Something major had changed since she had fainted. He suspected she had worked hard to deal with what she had seen—the Dancemaster without his eye mask. The unspeakably old Lifer eyes. If he peeled the mask off now she wouldn't flinch. Her look challenged him. She was already a powerful Glide with the ability to get you to focus on them and forget all else.

Wallenda suddenly realized that this train of thought had introduced a long pause after her question that provided the answer she sought. Damn the Glide tricks with discourse! "Of course it's true. The Origin Dancemaster knows everything." He smiled around the circle. Nobody smiled back.

"How far back do the Outmind's records go? The facts must be in there someplace," Angle asked. "She certainly has enough about life on Earth and that was way before the Game began."

"I am Óh-T'bee," the Outmind said, "I haven't forgotten." The children were very quiet. This was the first time they had been directly addressed by Óh-T'bee in personal mode. Shock twitched Wallenda's face. What they don't know, he thought, is that she has never, ever addressed a student Dancer in personal mode before. Why now?

Óh-T'bee brought up a simulation of a flat 2D screen. "This is how images were viewed at the time the Game began," Óh-T'bee said.

The scene presented to the class is almost too dark to be visible. They can barely make out the presence of people, small people, children, perhaps. A white, very bright rectangle opens in the middle of the screen. A knife of light plunges through the door, impaling a young girl with long dark hair drawn back in a ponytail, dressed in dark shorts and a white T-shirt. She raises her hand to shield her eyes from the brightness. Another child, her exact twin, joins her in the light. And a third, identical. A figure moves across the doorway, blocking the light. A man, but not too big of a man. He seems to be talking, and he is gesturing to them to come out the door, into the light.

"Can your turn up the audio, Óh-T'bee?" Daede said.

Bold as brass, thought the Dancemaster.

"The audio's sporadic," Óh-T'bee said. "In those days, the Gaze was accomplished mechanically." She superimposed a picture of a tiny surveillance camera.

"There must have been a lot of cameras," MyrrhMyrrh said.

"There were indeed," Óh-T'bee said.

The children file out the door of a long building of corrugated metal into the sunlight. They fall into single file, walking down a dirt path between tall grasses. The not-too-big man leads the children. He is wearing a clown suit and makeup with a very large red smile painted on his face. He dances and spins and waves his arms apparently in time to a song he is singing. The children copy his skipping dance. The other people on the path, heading in the same direction, look happy, too.

They come to a gate in a chain link fence surrounding a field with bleachers on two sides, and a booth on stilts at the far end. Grownups, all in strange costumes, hurry through the gate. A pretty girl takes their tickets.

The not-too-big man leads the children around the side of the fence, in back of the bleachers. He brings all 15 of them ice cream cones from a stand, five at a time. They sit on the grass and eat their ice cream. He smiles at them, and gestures to them to stay where they are. He runs around to a smaller gate at the far end of the field. Now he's inside a little shed with one long bench. He leans his forehead against the wall. His fists are clenched. A very fat man with a big floppy hat, striped knickers, a lot of rings on his fingers and a big smile comes into the shed. He slaps the clown on the back and puts his arm around his shoulders. The not-too-big man gets smaller. Whatever it is they are talking about, the fat man is very happy about it and the clown is not happy at all though he is trying to smile back. The fat man turns to leave. At the door, he turns back, holding up five fingers of his hand.

"Joreen," Daede said, with a tremble in his voice.

"Correct," said Óh-T'bee. She's taking over the story, the Dancemaster thought. How far will she go?

In the next shot, the clown leads the children into the little shed under the bleachers. They sit on the bench. He walks up and down, back and forth. He's telling them a story. He looks up a lot at the clock on the wall. Then he walks over to the bench. Finally he reaches down and taps one of the 15 identical girls on the shoulder. She gets up and follows him out the door, reaching for his hand.

Óh-T'bee shows the whole field and the bleachers filled with people. The fat man is up in the booth, bowing to the crowd. The clown leaves the little girl under the fat man's booth, and takes a tumbling run into the middle of the field, which is smooth metal, though with a few dents and a lot of stains. His last flip ends with him sprawling on his behind, looking very puzzled. He gets up, and makes believe the metal field is covered with grease. His feet keep sliding out from under him. He falls again and again. He gets up to bow, and something seems to knock him over. Finally, he somersaults off the field and lands at the feet of the little girl. Now he leads the laughing little girl by the hand out onto the metal. He leaves her there and goes back out the door he came in. The girl looks around, bewildered. She does a somersault. The people in the bleachers are all shouting at once. Then suddenly they stop and look in the direction of the fat man in the booth who is smiling and waving at the girl. She waves back shyly. Nothing happens for a long moment. The crowd on the bleachers holds its breath. The fat man in the high booth is still. The girl is still. They are all waiting for the first move. Then the girl takes a little hop. She looks surprised. She looks at her feet. She moves a step or two backwards and looks around the field. She takes another hop, a small one. And another. On the next hop, she loses her balance and her right shoe and falls down on her rear end. She pulls her feet toward her and rubs the bottoms. While she is rubbing, her body jerks. She springs to her feet, and looks around her, then bolts for the sidelines. She is stopped immediately by another jolt that tosses her in the air as she tries to jump away from the field. Her mouth is now wide open screaming, shouting for help. The crowd shouts back at her. She runs in the opposite direction. This time the jolt is strong enough and lasts long enough that she cannot leap. She's frozen in position, stuck to the board. Then she collapses. It takes her longer to get back on her feet. Now she is hopping, trying unsuccessfully to keep her bare foot off the board, hopping toward the booth, screaming and looking upward. Her bare foot leaves dark footprints. The fat man smiles and waves.

The young Dancers' eyes are fixed on the little girl, except for T'Ling. She has noticed the clown under the booth. All she can see is the white clown paint on his face. She squints at the grainy image, trying to read his expression.

The next jolt sends the girl into the air. When she lands on the metal, Joreen hits her with another jolt, not too hard, but enough to make her try to crawl away from it. A number of smaller jolts have her changing directions frantically, as if there was a pattern she had to find. There is a pattern. She discovers that as she approaches the edge of the griddle, any edge, the jolts get stronger. They seem to be weakest in the center. Now she tries to huddle in the center, but finds out she was wrong. The worst jolt of all is waiting for her, and curling in a ball does not ease the pain. She runs for the sideline again. This time he lets her get almost to the edge. She runs crippled, but running, her arms outstretched to the persons in the lowest seats of the bleachers who involuntarily reach out to her, urging her on. The next jolt knocks her unconscious. After 30 seconds, she twitches, then she raises her head. The fat man high in the booth shouts something at her. She crawls to the center and faces him. He shouts again, and gestures. She gets to her feet and bows to him. After a long moment when they do nothing but look into each other's eyes, he zaps her one more time, a blast strong enough to set her hair on fire. For a moment she seems held up by the electricity itself, a small, rigid match stick, charring before their eyes. When he lets the juice go this time, she falls, and does not get up again.

The man in the clown suit comes out onto the field and picks up her body in his arms. Her feet are stuck; he pulls them free. He walks slowly around the perimeter of the field. The people in the bleachers lean forward to see the details of her contorted face and blackened limbs, to inhale the smell. The charred remains of her hair drift off, a trail of black ashes in the air.

The clown exits the way he came in. He is outside the stadium, facing the back of Joreen's high booth, the long low shed to his right. In front of him is the corridor under the booth, leading onto the field. To his left is an open dumpster. He moves to the left and stands for a minute in front of the dumpster. Then he turns and walks into the door of the shed. The child's burnt body hangs in his arms. Moments later, the other 14 girls emerge, running. He is last, and shouts to them, pointing off-screen. They disappear. Still carrying the girl's burnt body, he walks into the corridor, back toward the field.

Dancemaster Wallenda's eyes shifted rapidly from the display, across each child's face, then back to the display. Angle's skinny arms were folded tightly across his chest as if he were holding himself in place, willing himself to keep looking. MyrrhMyrrh sat on the ground, her knees drawn up to her body, her chin on her knees, her eyes wide and unblinking. A storm of conflicting emotions changed Daede's face; at the moment he was somewhere between nausea and hysterical laughter, barely under control. The Dancemaster was most concerned about T'Ling. At one point he thought he saw her starting to fall slowly to the side, as if in a faint. Then he realized with a shock she was just leaning to get a better look at him. He looked quickly away.

The ancient footage continued. Clearly Óh-T'bee was editing nothing out. Wallenda felt suddenly very lightheaded. He got to his feet and walked behind the children, pacing back and forth as the images marched silently on before them.

The clown, carrying the charred body of the little girl, comes out of the dark corridor. The Specs on the bleachers get to their feet to see what's happening. The clown set her body down very gently against one of the stilts that supports Joreen's booth. He performs a tumbling run into the center of the field, but this time he does not end with a sprawl, but with a double somersault in mid air. He lands on his feet and bows, first to the crowd on both sides, then to Joreen. Joreen cannot see the body of the girl directly beneath him. No one seems to want to tell him what's happening. The small man in the clown suit executes another tumbling run. He walks on his hands in a circle. Then he ties himself in a contortionist knot. He unties himself, stands up again and bows. At this point, Joreen begins waving him off the field, but the clown—and the crowd—ignore him. Joreen's mouth is wide open, shouting, but no one makes a move except the clown, who begins to whirl in a slow, formal dance, his arms held out as if he is holding a partner. He wheels around the field.

"A waltz," Daede said, shifting from nausea to amazement that the dance-steps he has learned in class were performed, exactly the same, so long ago.

Joreen interrupts the waltz, sends a medium-sized jolt through the clown. He falls. He gets up, pantomimes excuses to his invisible partner. The crowd laughs. The clown begins another dance step, this one dramatic, with flashy reversals, and long, sliding steps. He dips his invisible partner deeply.

"Tango," Daede whispered.

Wallenda walked further back into the shadows, sat down on the stone bench and put his head down between his knees, too close to fainting to do anything else.

Joreen interrupts the clown's tango with another more powerful jolt. The clown stays on his feet, though it takes him a good half-minute to recover. He bows to his invisible partner, and begins a rumba, exaggerating the hip-shaking moves, almost knocking himself over with his efforts. More faces in the crowd laugh. The third jolt knocks him down again. He gets up, brushing himself off. He escorts his invisible partner to the sidelines, and picks another, equally invisible partner. You can tell by his pantomime, that this partner is very, very fat. He can hardly pull her to her feet. He continues the rumba; the invisible fat lady swings her hips too far and he is sent flying. It is clear that Joreen did not cause this fall, but he did cause the next one, and it was massive. This time the clown struggles to his feet, incorporating his injuries into his pantomime. Now he is tugging at the invisible fat lady, trying to pull her to her feet, with no apparent success. He kicks her, and hurts his foot. Joreen knocks him down again. After a long moment, the small clown rolls over, stretches, as if he has fallen asleep, and discovers the fat lady next to him, and begins trying to interest her in making love. He kisses her. No response. He stands up and does a bump and grind, flops down again. No response.

Joreen jolts him while he is lying on the metal. His body flails, and then stiffens, his back arching, his head thrown back, teeth bared in a rictus of pain. When he recovers, he seems disoriented. He pounds the side of his head. Then he lights an invisible cigarette, and lies back, blowing smoke. The crowd is on their feet now. Joreen looks back and forth between the clown and the crowd, torn between his fury at the clown's insubordination and his showman's instincts. Showmanship wins.

From then on, Joreen, the crowd, and the clown seem at one with each other. Rhythmic bursts of electricity punctuate the steps of the dancing clown. The clown switches to a bunny hop. In perfect coordination, Joreen buzzes his bleeding feet on the hops, guaranteeing a reflexive spring higher than he might have attained on his own. The clown masks whatever pain he feels with the help of the white clown face and painted smile.

Wallenda, fighting waves of dizziness and nausea, forces himself to raise his head and watch the images again, over his four students' heads.

Now the clown opposes Joreen. Refuses to hop. Taunts him with obscene gestures. Ignores him. Falls with the jolts, but pretends nothing has happened. His back to Joreen, he walks toward the far end of the griddle as if he was bored with the game. He limps badly, but manages to look nonchalant despite his pain. The move forces Joreen to jolt him hard to stop him from escaping the griddle. The clown falls, lies still for a long time, then uses his elbows to drag himself toward the far edge of the griddle.

MyrrhMyrrh shouted, "Hurry, hurry!"

Joreen jolts him again, about a yard from the end. The clown struggles to pull himself together. He bunches his body, then slowly extends his feet upward, somehow managing a wavery headstand. Joreen hits him with a final blast. The clown's body stiffens, arches, and falls. His face sticks to the metal, but his legs have fallen over the end. The clown does not get up again. The clown is dead; the clown won. The crowd is on its feet, screaming and cheering.

Joreen comes down from his booth, and walks slowly across the griddle, bowing from side to side. The crowd cheers him too. He knows he won as well by giving the crowd the best show they had ever seen. He manages to kneel down, despite his girth, and lift the dead clown up in his arms. He walks back the length of the griddle, displaying the body.

"Take a break, Óh-T'bee," the Dancemaster said. To his great relief, the display faded. He walked back to the story stone, folded his arms and looked around at their faces.

"I know this is…" he started to say.

"Did the children get away?" MyrrhMyrrh asked.

"No." He paused.

"They weren't children," Óh-T'bee added.

"What did Joreen do when he caught them?" MyrrhMyrrh persisted.

"He couldn't put them back on the griddle. The clown's act was a one-of-a-kind event, and he knew it."

MyrrhMyrrh looked relieved.

"Joreen used *real* children after that," Óh-T'bee inserted.

MyrrhMyrrh started to cry, despite her efforts to hold it back.

"That was the first Dance," Daede said, recovering his voice. "Awesome."

Angle piped up. "He must have done *something* with those girls. They always say how practical Joreen was, for a Duke."

"They're the original Glides," T'ling said with certainty.

"Spot on," Wallenda said. "The odd lot of rejects he'd picked up cheap from the body shop. He dressed them like children; he thought they'd draw a bigger crowd. But after the clown's performance, Joreen says to himself, now what can I do with a bunch of lightweight smart bodies?"

"They harvested the lily pollen. We know all that," Angle interrupted.

T'Ling said quietly, "So he bought the Glides first to make the Dance of Death more exciting for the Specs. But he wasn't sure they could handle children being the meat to be fried. So if they objected to the show, he could always display their specifications—these weren't children at all. Just small grownups. He needn't have worried. They liked the novelty. But then, the clown's dance was a huge success."

Wallenda nodded.

"What about the show? What did Joreen do after that? Did he have any more clowns?" Daede asked.

MyrrhMyrrh's tears turned suddenly to rage. "I hate him. I hate Joreen. I'm going to get him someday. If I'd been there then I would have killed him."

"Then there'd be no game," Angle said.

"You wouldn't be here without Joreen," T'Ling said.

"And now he's trying to kill the game. I'll kill him first," MyrrhMyrrh said.

Daede got up and took MyrrhMyrrh's hand. "Sit down with me," he said. She sat in front of him on the ground. He kneaded her shoulders.

"Getting back to Daede's question," the Dancemaster said, "Joreen had a real problem. There weren't any other clowns like that. How could he follow that act? Who else could dance like that? Much less, want to." Wallenda looked around at their faces, one by one, and continued in a thoughtful, almost dreamy voice. "This clown fellow was Joreen's top entertainer. He was a slave, of course, but he'd worked his way into Joreen's favor by keeping him amused. Which was no mean feat. That clown was looking for the big prize—hoping Joreen would find him valuable enough, entertaining enough, that he'd want him around for more than his mortal lifespan. That was the goal of every slave at the time. The I-Virus had been around for a good 300 years, but the problems were only just starting to become apparent. Lifers were beginning to realize that charging around space with the MTA, grabbing planets, and setting up Dukedoms and trade monopolies was a game for mortals. It got very old and boring when you'd been doing it for a couple hundred years. And the lack of scarcity of planets to grab took all the fun out of ownership. But immortality still seemed to beat the alternative. Joreen was doing pretty well for a Lifer—he was a creative guy, as you can see—an accomplished drug dealer, an amateur botanist, a gourmand, a ruthless Duke, an inventor, a natural showman—quite a cultivated guy for the times."

"He was a sadist," MyrrhMyrrh broke in. "That was disgusting."

"The Dancemaster knows that," Daede said. "Can't you tell when someone's being sarcastic?"

"He was, and undoubtedly still is, a sadist," the Dancemaster said. "But without him, you would be, as Angle said, out of work," He looked sternly at each of his students in turn. "You wanted to know how the game began. Are you sure you want to continue?" he asked, hoping someone would say no.

"But there's no game yet," Angle said. "That was just a public execution, when you get right down to it. Well, that's what they called it in class."

"It's different when you see it," MyrrhMyrrh said.

"But there was a Dance," Daede said.

"There was a Dance." Wallenda agreed.

"But no *game*," Angle insisted. "No maze. No rules. I'm not sure who won and who lost."

"That's enough for one night," Dancemaster Wallenda replied. "Here's your homework: see if you can figure out what Joreen did next. Think like

Joreen. Here's a hint. Remember that he hated waste."

He could see by their faces that no one wanted to think like Joreen, even as homework. But they had to learn, very quickly, how to think, if not like Joreen, at least like a Player. Think like the enemy until you can *be* the enemy. Joreen was the first Player, after all.

"That was the best Dance I've ever seen," T'Ling said.

"The clown was awesome," Daede said.

Angle snapped, "That's not who she meant."

T'Ling continued. "It's hard to see ourself so badly betrayed. And burned." She looked intently at the Dancemaster. "But we helped the clown, didn't we?"

"Class dismissed," Wallenda said, turning his back on them to hide the tears rolling down his face.

If the Dancemaster had not been too distraught, he might have gazed the Millennium Class as they walked through the maze together and back through the trees toward the school buildings.

They stopped where the path divided to take them to their separate dorms, not wanting to part company.

"We've got to stop Joreen," Daede said.

"I hate him," MyrrhMyrrh repeated.

"We'll have to stick together. We're the only ones who know," Angle said.

"Together," Daede repeated, holding both hands out. The others piled their hands on top of Daede's.

"Together," they repeated.

T'Ling, though she had placed her tiny hands on top of the others, was already beginning to wonder who to stop. And who to hate.

5. Footsteps in the Maze

DANCEMASTER WALLENDA PEELED the wet eye-mask from his face, lay down on his bed, and stared into the dark until the unforgivable images faded in intensity. He was remembering to breathe, and then breathe deeply, when he heard, or felt, faint sounds coming from the maze. He got off his bed quickly and stepped outside the door. He put his attention on the almost inaudible patter of bare feet running: two children, one lighter than the other, stopping, starting again, approaching, coinciding, diverging. The game of sneaking up on the Dancemaster had been played so often over the years. Few had succeeded. But this was another game. He listened closely. It wasn't tag, it wasn't hide and seek; both were on the move, no one stopped. It was like maze practice, except there was a rhythm to it—like two swallows wheeling in the dusk, arcing away from each other, swinging back, crossing paths at high speeds. He was reminded of a composition in dynamic Glide where two signs curved away from each other, and then, as if drawn by the gravity of desire, slowed, turned, touched, and nested. For the runners, the meanings of the glyphs would overlap and blend, speaking messages too quick and intimate for the gaze of the island-mind to decipher as they rush together, then spin apart through the curves of the maze, tossed like two comets in orbit around an invisible center. Down in the sea-mind, the Dancemaster recognized the vectors of longing, the game of desiring, having and losing, its poles of intensity.

Wallenda had sensed this pattern during recent classes. Who was it? Their eyes, their gaze, drawn together, rushing apart, the secrecy of the act. Then he knew. And now that I know who is running in the maze, and why, I should turn away, get back to trying to sleep, he thought. But I can't.

Instead, he picked up his scorecard and gazed them first from above the glyph-walls, fascinated by the uncanny accuracy of the instincts that let them lose each other in the far turnings of the maze, then find their way back. They didn't stop; they didn't even slow as they passed each other, but a spark as intense as a split second magnesium flare was struck between them. He placed his gaze at their next point of intersection. Now at ground zero, the footsteps were louder, drawing together. As they passed, he saw T'Ling's hand brush Angle's thigh.

Wallenda withdrew his gaze to the dusk and emptiness of the story circle. He looked up at a dome of glowing blue sky, the sharp stars shining through. This has been going on a long time, he thought. I noticed the signs during storytelling when they were nine. At first I thought T'Ling was having difficulty with blinding, the exercise beginning the Glide's weaning from sight-dependence, lowering her gaze to the cupped palms of her hands, and softening the focus. I noticed her eyelids flicker open, blink down quickly when my attention shifted her way. She was developing wide-angle vision to the degree of a Bod or a Swash; I could only catch her peripherally—not an encouraging tendency. Any dependence on visual would bias her to relative north, or frontal, movement, increasing her predictability.

Listen to yourself, he said. The island-mind rattling on as if you were sincerely engaged in thoughts of training, covering the tracks of the gut-mind's pure and simple voyeurism. The island-mind only a justification machine. *Pure? Simple?* Interesting choice of words. In those momentary glances, T'Ling looked only at Angle. And when her eyes were lowered, he stared at her steadily, as if willing her to look up and meet his eyes. When their eyes met, even then, the space between them dissolved. You drank it up, he reminded himself, then and in the mental recreation you just did. You've been watching this develop for some time. As you should, as you must, as Dancemaster. Love is encouraged among Dancers, as are all mind/body states the I-Virus could not stop from atrophy in Lifers. But this early flowering between T'Ling and Angle was rare, intense, and delicate. Love among Dancers is never without consequence. He felt bone-weary, sick and tired of always examining the consequences. Why can't I leave the calculation of outcomes to Óh-T'bee? Before me is a wildflower, an intense blue moment, to be stumbled on, marveled at, and left alone, hidden even. Yes, I watched. Rarely do I feel I spy on them. I am a Dancemaster, no; I am the *original* Dancemaster, of Origin School. But under the stone robes of authority and tradition the Guild piles upon me, I'm just another Lifer, with the greed-filled eyes of a hungry ghost for the sight of what can only be desired, never attained, never possessed. And in that yearning I come closest to the simulation of mortality. To the buried memories of my youth. To a reason to live despite this endless life, which plods on drained of all meaning by the impossibility of death. Grinding forward on promises alone.

He looked up; more stars pricked through the deepening blue above. Do the stars complain amongst themselves, going on and on forever—but they die too. And if they know anything, it is that they will one day be gone. What have they to complain about?

He heard another set of footsteps now. Heavier, faster. No one knows the default maze as well as Daedelus. He is well named. Wallenda gazed the runners from above. Their white coveralls kept them visible as they maneuvered in the dark. Daede was looking for T'Ling, no doubt. Daede stopped momentarily, listening, trying to determine whose steps were whose; their sounds overlapped like an echo. Then, as if on a hidden signal, T'Ling and Angle faded back to the edges of the maze, one east, one west. At the same time, MyrrhMyrrh entered the maze where Daede had started. Daede was running again, but with no hope of catching T'Ling. Meanwhile, MyrrhMyrrh moved, and waited, slid around corners without touching a wall, stalking Daede. Daede retreated now, in her direction. She waited at the end of a curve. When he came around the corner and saw her, he spun and ran, but MyrrhMyrrh had sprint speed to unleash. She caught him, wrapped her arms around him from behind. They stayed a moment like that, then Daede shrugged her off and walked away. She started to run after him, her fist raised, then stopped and took her frustration out on the wall.

At that moment, Wallenda saw all their futures open before them like fern fronds unfurling, spreading to their final forms. He shivered. They had drawn their patterns in the maze.

6. The Guild

LONER LEANS TO LONER IN TIME OF NEED. The next morning, Dancemaster Wallenda used his scorecard to contact Wenger, the blind Glide musician, on whisper mode. He sent a slight increase in warmth to Wenger's scorecard, his signature greeting. Wenger was alone so much these days, keeping to himself in the genteel shabbiness of the now unfashionable Kyoto Park. Wallenda tried not to startle Wenger's fathomless concentration.

"It's you, old friend," Wenger said. His voice sounded as it always did—as if he were speaking from within an underground abandoned cistern, dark and dry.

"Am I disturbing you?" Wallenda asked.

"Everything disturbs me, thankfully. The universe is a wave pool," Wenger said.

"Then I'm inviting you to experience, and then discuss, some serious disturbances being reported by the governing bodies. I would like your opinions."

"Serious disturbances. . .a rare opportunity," Wenger said, "to fall victim to my cravings for intensity—once again."

Wenger blinked into the story circle. Wallenda invited him to sit on one of the student's stones, but Wenger slipped to the ground to sit cross-legged. His hands moved in the air before him, tracing a shape the size of a head. Wallenda shivered. He could almost feel Wenger's fingers brushing his scars.

"Tense between the brows," Wenger noted. "Clenched jaw. You're resisting something."

Óh-T'bee Outmind had long ago provided Wenger with the means to translate patterns, refractions, reflections of light to heat, or sound, or the shifting resistances of gravity fields.

"The governing bodies have each been meeting in emergency session. I'm asking you to immerse with me, then share your opinions," Wallenda said.

But both knew that the favors of old friends traveled two ways. Wallenda had something to offer Wenger that Wenger would never ask for—or refuse. Why does every situation present itself as one more chance for me to be an opportunistic, crafty cad? Wallenda wondered. To deliver to Wenger the only thing that could pull him out of seclusion: a chance to gaze Loosh, to whom he had no access otherwise, by way of the Dancemaster's universal gazing rights. Wenger nodded. Óh-t'bee brought up a full immersion display.

The Guild Council of Twelve Elder Dancers met in the cobalt blue glass tower that rose from the middle of the lily pond between Origin City's most ancient quarter and the sea. The Guild was responsible for all matters concerning the Dancers themselves and for maintaining the rules of the Maze Game. Each Elder had been a Champion Dancer, requested by the convened Guild of their time to forgo their Dance, their death, to make the ultimate sacrifice, infection with the I-Virus, for the sake of preserving the schools, the quality of training, strength of tradition and purity of purpose.

Blue light suffused all space in the Guild Tower tinting faces, hands, and fruit. Jillian Razorgold, current Convener of the Guild Council moved among the Elder Dancers. She lifted her hair off the back of her neck and let it fall again in a curly mass. Too warm for a cape, she thought, but as a Swash she felt undressed without one. Patience, she reminded herself, no use starting while the Elders are just spouting hopelessly set-bound ideas. Let the buffet table do its work. Thinking in the box, whether the box was Chrome analytics, Bod no-nonsense action plans, or whatever you call the Glide thing, other than 'the Glide thing', won't get us far. And I'm winding up my Swash cadenza.

"Too bad the Dancemaster wouldn't come," said the darkest of the three towering Bods.

Loosh's low, hoarse voice spoke from the blood oranges corner of the buffet table. "Wallenda told me Guild meetings bore him so unbearably that he dreams up destructive things to say just to keep from falling asleep."

Wallenda squirmed invisibly. He looked at Wenger whose head bowed as if under a terrible weight at the sound of Loosh's voice. But his hungry fingers climbed the air, tracing, he was sure, the outlines of her face.

Jillian Razorgold felt inordinately proud of Loosh, the Origin School Glide.

Tiny Loosh who was unable to look other than graceful despite her worn robe and spaced out look. Loosh, who heard between nuances. Loosh, who could get away with anything. She had taken her combat record beyond any Death Dancer ever. She's pure Glide, Jillian thought. She doesn't look like one, wholly lacking that sense of cultivated serenity. Or talk like one either. And that was about as Glide as you could get.

"Meeting's convened," Jillian called out over the buzz. The twelve Elders moved to the library. The three Glides took seats that separated them; the Elders at the other seats dealt themselves around the conference table like cards—Swash, Chrome, Bod.

"Let's start with the facts," said Boris2Boris, a 9th-Level Chrome with no meat showing below the eyes. If it weren't for Chromes, he thought, we'd never get any business done.

Jillian felt the Glides shudder at the tinny reverb from his speaker-mouth. The facts? The four sets were far apart on what they considered "factual." Chromes preferred solid, documented evidence—and stats. Bods only believed their gut minds. Glides? You couldn't really say they believed in facts at all. They *might* discuss consensus reality. *Why waste time interpreting a cloud?* was the Glide of saying *you haven't a clue*. And Swashes? We can handle facts, she thought, as long as they're beautiful or brutal enough to catch our attention. I might as well kick things off, Jillian decided, and stepped back in shadow before the bright display she'd brought up over the table.

"Bizarre deaths," Jillian said, "out on the levels. Murder is making a comeback."

The murderer was a heavily muscled Bod Dancer, his square jaw covered with stubble, no more than 21 years old. The victim was a woman, an up-Level Lifer of average perfections, sleepy eyes content, half-floating in a bubbling grotto pool, her arms on the sides, her head back on the edge, her legs slowly paddling. He was twisting her dark hair around his hand.

She must be ecstatic, the Swash with the flashing smile thought to himself. To snag a Bod Dancer? How had she done it? To touch forbidden Dancer flesh? The fantasy of every Lifer.

The Lifer opened her ancient eyes and looked up longingly at the Bod. He was kneeling beside her, with a smile that mimicked hers, and a razor sharp filet knife upraised. The shock was total; she looked almost mortal in her terror. Then the thrashing and the stabbing, the pool, bubbling red, small eddies of bloody water caught in the rocks.

Jillian superimposed the Bod's profile data, enough statistics for any Chrome. This was a Bod mixed in a prestigious Kitchen and trained in an above-average school on the 7th Level. The Council absorbed the victim's fear much more easily than the murderer's pleasure. His act was almost inconceivable.

He'd gone 'over the mountain'—in the wrong direction. Of course, he was free to leave his School, his training, and his life as a Dancer. As they all had been, growing up. They had all been bred and born as Dancers, but enforced Dancing was a ridiculous notion, an impossibility that violated one of the fundamental Laws of Play. *All play is free play.* What else made it so desirable to join a School? All Dancer children had the choice to leave. You could walk away five minutes before a semifinal match if you wanted to. No one did. What Dancer would be stupid enough to throw their Death away? For this existence as a Lifer? Jillian let herself be caught in a pang of bitterness before she spoke.

"This was a talented Bod," Jillian said. "Nothing in his profile shows cause for disqualification. He had been in combat for a year, and doing well. He just walked out of his dressing room, blinked to Vegas Park, found the Lifer woman the same night, and self-infected. He partied with her for three nights, then did this."

"He must have flipped out when he realized what he'd thrown away," a Bod Elder said.

"Oh no," said Jillian. "Watch his eyes." She replayed highlights from the three-day love-fest, and zoomed in on his face minutes before the actual murder. "Also—he assembled his instruments the first night he was there. This was a fantasy shaped who knows how long ago."

"Oh, get off it," Boris2Boris said. "Murder's only a fad coming around again. Suicide disguised, in most cases. Willing victim. Star of her own snuff movie. Death by Dancer." He wanted to say *she died happy, probably hadn't looked that young in centuries*, but he'd gone far enough.

"This was not a willing victim," the Bod Elder snapped.

It couldn't be easy, watching one of his own willfully defile himself, Jillian thought.

"Well, I'm sure she renewed." Another Bod lent his support.

"That was the Bod Dancer's Dance of Death," Loosh said in a hoarse whisper. The Elders were silenced, waiting for clarification.

"Sign reversed," noted the Outmind. The Council waited, but that was apparently all the Outmind or Loosh had to say.

"Óh-t'bee speaks to you alone," Wenger whispered to Loosh in the holo. Wallenda saw that Wenger was beyond immersion—he was lost in her presence. Even without sight. Am I only deepening his wound?

The holo in the holo continued. Jillian said, "She couldn't renew," They watched the Bod dismember the woman, and place each section in a different room. Now he was going back and forth, watching the quarters feebly trying to re-grow. Her right leg was sucking itself out from inside like a balloon deflating, throwing material out at the top of the thigh in a desperate pink excrescence, seeking the rest of its cells.

The Elders looked away in disgust, except Boris2Boris. "He's studying how the virus works," he said.

"Thank you for the fine display," Jillian said to the Outmind. "Of course he seeks to destroy what he craves unwillingly," the third Swash Elder said.

"But using the body as lab specimen," she nodded toward Boris2Boris, "was an equally powerful motivation."

"However," Jillian added, "it wasn't until he made a show of it, a paying show for other Lifers, down on Level Two, that Media caught it. It caused a blip in the Game attendance stats."

"Yes," another Chrome said, studying his scorecard. "Lowered gate receipts. Ratings down. A crime against the Game. The Specs were coming down level just to see it. And paying points like that! Taking major downgrades for something other than betting losses. His little show had all the portents of a blockbuster. He was eventually put Under the Gaze, of course," Jillian added.

The Twelve were silent, contemplating the Bod murderer's fate. Being put Under the Gaze was the ultimate punishment. Every Lifer on every level was given access to you and could watch your every move. Your scorecard told you how many were gazing you at any given moment. You heard their comments. Felt their eyes. It caused a madness incurable by the I-Virus. The final stage was catatonic trance—total withdrawal inward. For those unfortunates, the Outmind created the White Place, basic life support. The White Place also served to warehouse the Lifers who succumbed to ennui as well. The Outmind kept the White Place discreetly out of view of those still struggling to maintain their interest. Anyone could gaze it, but few did. It was too unsettling—the sheer size of it—white tube after white tube with empty eyes staring through the faceplates.

One of the Glides put a subdued sunset on his scorecard, calming his thoughts. Jillian was looking at her scorecard as well, hidden in her lap. Loosh slid down in her chair, arms folded, eyes closed. Why doesn't she just go lie down, Boris thought, instead of flaunting her unconcern?

But the Glides knew it was only a matter of minds. Loosh bypassed the island mind—the mind that managed conscious, analytical thought, the mind the Chromes favored. She touched the gut mind, that instinctive intuitive instant sense that Bods cultivated. She sank down through the sea mind and its waves of emotion, taking readings of the turbulence. The Glides knew she'd turned the job of understanding over to the lily mind, the deepest mind, the dark voice you had to learn to listen to—if you were a Glide. Loosh never bothered with the island mind. It was getting so atrophied she couldn't remember where she left her sandals. Fishing in the lily pond might come to nothing. If so, someone would have to wake her up and tell her the meeting was over.

Loosh's eyelids flew open; her eyes pinned Boris2Boris to his chair. "Violence," Loosh said in her hoarse whisper, "has been the Dancers' exclusive sandbox for a long time. The idea of anyone else elbowing into our monopoly is bad enough on a personal level. All the usual territorial knee jerks we're too refined to display. But that's just surface perturbation. When you sink past that, down in the real queasiness, we feel the act of this Bod as desecration. Taboo. We *understand* if a Lifer makes a dash into a procession, grabs a Dancer, just to touch the flesh of the undiseased. But this taboo is sign reversed. He went for her. Such willful desecration is almost unthinkable.

"Our history teaches that we, the Dancers, contained the human propensity for violence by making it sacred. Dancers don't hold the patent on human sacrifice of course, but the I-Virus demanded some serious redesign of that venerable institution. The Dance is a sacrament. And we, the Death Dancers, perform our sacred duty for all. Absorb and transform the destructive element into a glory. Play until we lose, and give ourselves to Death, in the sight of all. Keep mortality alive and well. Forestall the horrors we as humans are capable of. The Game keeps us all in order, Dancers and Lifers. Homeostasis is the greatest virtue. Freeform, entrepreneurial violence is strictly *verboten*."

"And the violent go Under the Gaze—no reproduction." Jillian added.

"If by violent you mean crimes against the game," Loosh continued. "Of course. But where have the truly violent ended up? The artistically violent? The spiritually violent ones? Over the mountain, right into the Schools. Where they belong, right? As Death Dancers. Where we hone and train and focus and give meaning to and transform violence. Then we hand over our genes to the gene cooks."

"This is not the only instance of a Dancer committing murder," a Chrome said, checking the stats.

"No," Jillian replied. "And one was in a School."

"If the problem is that serious, wouldn't the Outmind have contained it?" Boris2Boris asked pointedly.

"Maybe she can't," Loosh said.

Óh-t'bee declined comment.

The Dancemaster dismissed the Guild immersion and paced the story circle in frustration. Wenger's hands were folded in his lap. Too early to question him. Had Wenger caught Jillian Razorgold's lapse of attention? While Loosh was talking, Jillian had been gazing one of his students, Daede, the Millennium Class Swash, doing his ballet exercises at the barre in the studio at Origin School. At 13, Daede was exquisite—seductive, innocent—and full of himself. Gazing with satisfaction into the mirror. Jillian's liquid gaze could drown him. Wenger of all Lifers knew where that could lead.

But Wenger spoke from his own concerns. "The ancient Chinese emperors would have seen these events as omens on the order of herons falling from the sky and landing dead at their feet. But if no one sees the earlier signs because no one has any desire to see them—but that's how it always goes. . ."

Wenger's voice trailed into silence; his hands reached up, this time to draw the first notes of music from the air.

He's thinking out loud, Wallenda knew, the first tentative notes. Hopefully he'll translate down the line.

"Will you come again tomorrow?" Wallenda asked Wenger.

"Of course," Wenger said. He blinked back to Kyoto Park wishing he had spoken up, made some excuse to view a Guild meeting again.

And what of Boris2Boris' questioning of Óh-T'bee's ability to contain the outbreaks? Wallenda wondered.

"How about it, Óh-T'bee? Are you top of this one?"

"No rules have been broken," the Outmind said.

"Was that an answer?" he asked.

"Was that a question?" Óh-T'bee answered.

When the Guild Council finally finished, and Jillian Razorgold sat alone in the blue light of the Tower, she used her Guild access privileges to gaze Daede again. He lay asleep, half uncovered, one arm thrown above his head. Exquisite, she thought. Like a Caravaggio cupid, lascivious and pure in one package. She asked the Outmind for his assay and genome and ran a simulation of Daede at 18. Tall, rangy, quick, with curly black hair. The slight rise in the middle of his eyebrows had formed into a distinct and devilish peak. This one's mischief, she thought. She looked again at the sleeping boy, wishing suddenly that he could remain forever in this perfection. She caught herself in a strange fantasy, where she reached to touch him. She had her trademark ornament, a golden razor, held between her fingers. She nicked his skin; a drop of blood appeared. She cut her own finger as well. Their blood would mix. . .

Jillian killed the display, wrapped a napkin around her finger, lit a few candles, and tried to get back to work. The Guild had to come up with some sort of plan to keep the Game alive, at least until the Millennium Games. If only for Daede's sake.

7. The First Dancemaster

AFTER VIEWING THE GUILD MEETING WITH WENGER, Dancemaster Wallenda fell into an exhausted sleep. When he woke, it was late afternoon.

He spent the next hour lecturing himself. You're their teacher. The Dancemaster. Act like one.

He pushed himself through a series of grueling kung fu forms. He straightened his shoulders. He forced himself to stop nervously twisting his maze ring.

When the children came back to the story circle, he noticed they looked as determined as he was trying to seem. They had barely seated themselves when he fired the question.

"Has anyone figured out what Joreen did next?"

The children were silent. Though they had talked or thought of little else in the intervening hours, no one had a theory they were willing to advance.

"Óh-T'bee?" The flat screen display appeared.

The clown's body, horribly burned, is stretched out on one end of the bench in the low shed. The body of the Glide girl is on the other end. Joreen sits between them. Various people come to the door but he waves them angrily away. Joreen locks the door. He paces. He stares at the clown's body. He shouts at it. He cries on it. He examines where his face used to be. The white paint is gone, so is all of the skin and most of the flesh. He sits down again. This goes on for several minutes.

Every now and then Wallenda said, "What is he thinking?" or "Can you read his face?"

Suddenly, Joreen takes a small penknife out of his pocket, rolls up his sleeve, and cuts open a vein on his arm. Then he gouges a hole in the clown's chest. He lets the stream of his blood pour into the clown. As an afterthought, he does the same for the Glide girl, before his own I-virus heals up his arm. He is watching the clown intently now. Nothing happens for five minutes, and he begins to curse and shout at the body. Then the clown's left shoulder twitches. His right leg trembles. Then nothing. His chest heaves. Breathing begins. And stops. The body spasms back and forth, in and out of life, like a cold engine starting.

Meanwhile, unnoticed by Joreen, the Glide girl quietly, swiftly comes back to life. The I-Virus worked quickly on her small body, assisted by her will to live. They see the burns on her limbs and face heal without scars, her hair begin to grow. She sits up, takes in the whole scene without a flicker of expression on her face. She gets up silently; walks over to the wall, sits down to watch.

The clown's recovery is slow. The eyeballs reform in the red pulp of his face, and stare sightlessly at the ceiling of the shed. Ears begin to shape. Joreen is not a patient man. He paces. Now and then he shouts at the body, but the mush inside the skull has not become a brain again.

The Millennium class sat through every moment, watching the I-Virus laboriously rebuild a body. An hour later, the clown's eyes rolled, then focused on Joreen's face. The clown groaned, mumbled a few incomprehensible words, but his eyes sent the message clearly: *No. Don't do this to me.* He began to thrash feebly, fighting the I-Virus. He's losing, except for his face, on which the open burns remain. Joreen holds him down for a while, then unlocks the door. Slaves tie the resurrected clown down to a stretcher, a most unwilling Lazarus. The Glide girl slips out unnoticed.

"Cut to their argument," Wallenda instructed, "several months later. Joreen already has the girls out on the lily fields. 'My little Glides,' he calls them."

Óh-T'bee brings up the display as directed.

The clown is in a chair, his face and hands bandaged. The I-Virus had not had quite enough steam to finish the job; he'd resisted, cell by cell. His face heals the slow way. Restraints pin his arms, legs, and torso, and he is not fighting against them. There are holes in the bandages, and you can see his eyes, his nose has been rebuilt. Joreen and the clown argue.

"Does he want him to Dance again? Over and over?" MyrrhMyrrh asked.

"No. Worse than that," Wallenda said.

Joreen is trying to convince the clown to teach other mortals to dance. To dance as well as he can. Whoever he can get to do it. The clown argues that the only reason he could dance was that he wanted to die, he couldn't stand watching the girl—the Glide—die that way.

"Look how many of your criminals and unfaithful concubines I led in there before it made any difference to me. Never once did I have the slightest notion of taking their place. I didn't like it. I hated it. I hated you. For what you were doing. For making me participate. For threatening my life if I didn't. Fry or be fried. Kill or be killed. But that didn't prevent me from saving my own skin. So I killed. I hated myself more than I hated you. But none of this was enough to make me want to give up my life. The impulse just hit me. She was too like a child. She was too easy to lift into the dumpster. Something cracked. Probably if I'd resisted the impulse for a minute I would have put her in like all the rest, and gone and gotten the next. You can't make people want to learn the Dance of Death. Forget it. It'll never work."

The clown went on in this vein for a while, but Joreen was adamant. "I *know* you can do it," Joreen says. He backs his vote of confidence with the threat to make the clown watch every single one of the Glides he'd saved fry. So he could live forever with the memory, now that he was a Lifer.

The clown stops talking. Joreen unties his restraints and puts his red and white striped floppy hat on the clown's bandaged head.

The clown, his head still wrapped in white, is sitting at the edge of the vast shining mud flats at low tide. He turns the hat around and around in his hands. The lily pads and the huge blue flowers rest on their tangled roots and coiled stems, waiting for the next tide to lift them.

"He sits there for almost a day," the Dancemaster said.

Then the bandaged clown is walking down a path, up to the door of the slave quarters. The door opens. One of the Glide girls draws him inside.

"Stop there," Wallenda told Óh-T'bee. The display went dark. He looked around at his students. "Well? Were any of you close?" They shook their heads. "What Joreen hated wasting more than anything was talent. Part of his genius. Picking talent."

"It should have been obvious," Daede said, profoundly annoyed with himself. "Joreen needed a Dancemaster. First a Dance, then a Dancemaster."

"Then a game," Angle added.

"No, no game yet," Wallenda said. "First you need some mortals willing to Dance—and able to learn.

"How come you like Joreen so much?" MyrrhMyrrh asked angrily. "He's rotten."

"Just because I appreciate him doesn't mean I like him."

"But you do like him, in a certain way," T'Ling said.

"I suppose I do," Wallenda admitted. "He grows on you. After a couple millennia." Priorities shift, he thought. You still make the distinction between the good and the bad, but you also start discerning the necessary and the unnecessary.

Dancemaster Wallenda looked at each of them in turn. "You are warriors, preparing for combat. Knowing your enemy is easier to do if you like him just a little. You can see what he likes about himself. Which is very important information. What he likes about himself will be sitting right on top of what he doesn't like about himself, and somewhere in between the two, You'll find his blind spots."

"Watch closely." Wallenda squeezed his scorecard and the display resumed.

Slaves of all types pack the common room of their quarters. The clown cringes as he enters.

Wallenda said, "He had not been near the building much since he had been made the Master of Ceremonies and the opening act for the Dance of Death—Joreen's favorite entertainment. With the promotion to MC came the added duty of selecting the meat for the evermore frequent entertainments. Needless to say, his visits were not welcome. And now, he'd been given the task of convincing the slaves to *willingly* Dance—even to train for the job. His only hope was that they would tear him limb from limb before he had a chance to open his mouth. But that's not at all what happened."

They jump to their feet when he enters. They clap, they scream, they chant his name.

"The Glides had been busy. The Glide girl he had led to her death had pieced together a lot of the story from Joreen's ravings at the clown as she came back to life. She saw very clearly that the clown fought the I-Virus all the way. She knew this was no staged show, no secret scam between the hated clown and Joreen the Unbearable. Eyewitness accounts of slaves filled in the part of the story during which she had been dead. Yes, the clown really died. Yes, he had fought for his life, had defied the Unbearable One. Yes, it had been beautiful. Inspiring even. They attested to the tears in the eyes of the spectators. Yes, he had suffered, greatly. The clown had sacrificed himself, even though it was a useless gesture. In a word, they'd turned him into a hero. And they told these stories over again to his face."

The clown cringes even more deeply from their admiration—from their love—than he had from their expected hate and anger. He interrupts the Glide girl's explanation. He tells them all the things he said to Joreen in their last argument. Only caring for his own skin. Not giving a damn for them. That he'd numbed himself and could put them on the griddle without flinching and eat peanuts like a spectator during the show. That the smell of burnt hair and flesh no longer made him sick. He tries to explain that his motivation was self-hatred, not self-sacrifice. That he is, was, and (now that he's a Lifer) always will be the scum of the earth. The slaves listen politely until he runs out of steam.

The class watched the clown, his head hanging, cease to speak. A Glide comes out of the crowd of slaves and speaks to the clown. "The Lily taught us about the times of the Great Reversals, when opposites switch sides. Of course we saw you as the evil one, the sellout that sleeps with the enemy, who would even lead children to their death. But we witnessed the Reversal. With all due respect, we see you completely differently. No blame. A book cannot read itself, much less interpret its own story. First, you refreshed the ancient lesson concerning laying down your life for a stranger. Second, you showed that to go willingly to your death *while fighting for your life* is itself a high spiritual attainment. You honored life and you honored death in the same Dance. And third, you defied the real enemy—the false immortality of the body bestowed by the I-virus—both when you danced your death, and when you did battle with the I-Virus. That you protest what a scum you are, only proves our point. And not because we think you are humble. You possess many talents, but humility is not one of them. Your protest proves that you prefer mortality. That even though you now must live in that body forever, you would still rather die, and you know it. And you would rather die for all the wrong reasons, which makes you even more endearingly mortal. We know that the Unbearable one has sent you to advance his wicked purposes to an entirely new level of depravity. He has discovered that beauty, humor even, can enhance brutality. And we know that, even as I speak, you are considering the possibilities of convincing us to Dance. You are completely tangled now, conflicted, guilty, triumphant, and supremely confused. What does this mean to us? In the simplest terms your condition, which I am deliberately worsening, guarantees that you won't get bored. Because you will never answer the unanswerable question—in that Dance you danced, in the whole event—*who won and who lost*? And as long as you can't find an answer, you will have the ability to take advantage of the I-Virus. The I-Virus confers the Death-in-Life. The Lifers don't yet know how bad it's going to get in the hamster-wheel of their boredom. But you, clown, are the

Death-in-Life *and* the Life-in-Death. You will live long and keep your mind alive, even if it drives you crazy. You can break the endless loop into an open spiral with your unanswerable questions. We've been looking for someone like you,'" she finishes, brightly.

Wallenda looked at his students for a long moment before he spoke. "This is the clown's first real dose of Glide logic and it leaves him speechless. He felt caught on a tightrope between the Unbearable and the Inscrutable. The Glide's words were simultaneously too silly, dreadful, insulting, compassionate, and deadly accurate to react to in any way, human or inhuman."

The display continued. The clown asks, "So what can I do for you?" The Glide speaker answers gently, "You have already done a great deal. You have taught us that our death is our most precious possession. Without it, life is meaningless. Without it, we become Joreen. A Player who cannot leave the game. Or what is worse, the spectators of his game. You have shown us, in one Dance, not to throw away life, but to play to the hilt—not to resist death, but to celebrate its arrival."

The clown protests, "But I didn't intend any of that."

The Glide replies, "Actions speak louder than words. Our faith is not in an afterlife. We *know* there's an afterlife. It doesn't take an act of faith. Our problem lies in believing there's any meaning to this life we're in right now. Our faith is renewed by our amazement that one can learn so much about bravery and dignity and the meaning of mortal life from a scumbag like you." She smiles sweetly at the clown.

"But what does that *mean*?" the clown cries out in total frustration, "the meaning of mortal life?"

"We have no idea," the Glide replies. "But we enjoy thinking about it. Keeps the mind occupied, sliding around on lily pads for 10 hours a day, scooping pollen so Lifers can get high. But getting back to what you can do for us—we have some goals, all of us do." She gestures to include the whole room full of slaves. "We'd like to improve the quality of life, including freedom from slavery. We'd like to find a cure for the I-Virus. And we'd like to reach union with the lily-mind. In order to accomplish our goals, the first step is for you to teach us how to Dance.'

"That's a pretty tall order," the clown says.

"You've got plenty of time now," the Glide reminds him. "And you owe us."

"Cut the display," Wallenda said. Óh-T'bee complied.

"So he started the first Death Dancer School, right?" asked MyrrhMyrrh.

"Very good, MyrrhMyrrh," the Dancemaster said, wearily. "He got them all together the next morning, early, before work. Almost everyone wanted to Dance. But he could see that they weren't all going to qualify. There had to be variety in the Dances. Joreen—and his spectators—were easily bored. Novelty was essential. There were lots of very strong slaves, men and women—manufactured to those specifications, of course. They'd be able to last through some pretty strong jolts and keep going. Strong on courage, too, he suspected. The crowds would appreciate that quality. There were also the especially graceful slaves who could sing and dance. Turn the moves into actual Dance steps. They would be kept alive longer because the crowd would want to watch them, to hear them. And the little ones—the Glides—maybe he could teach them to tumble. But they couldn't even run very well. They sure could slide fast. But who wanted to watch that? Maybe they could tell jokes. Well, the Glides told jokes, all right, but only other Glides thought they were funny. And they told them in their sign language, which no one else could understand.

"You see, Glide started as a gesture language. A means to sign back and forth using the normal gestures of their work so no one would notice: scooping up pollen, emptying the cupped hand in their baskets. The wave was the pollination move—scooping up from the stamen and spilling out over the pistil, combined in one motion. It also meant the move from pad to pad, the constant motion so they wouldn't sink. So they told jokes in passing, and they made poems—line by line, passed from Glide to Glide. They had to remember the whole poem as it built during the day.

"But the clown couldn't figure out what possible interest this silent hand waving could have for Joreen's crowd. They needed a bit more stimulation. He'd think up something. So you can see how the sets began to differentiate themselves, right there at the beginning."

"What about the Chromes?" Angle asked, feeling very left out.

"They come in soon enough. But they were engineers and mechanics before they were Dancers. The clown sent them to build a much finer set of controls for the griddle—Joreen thought it was his idea of course. That was part of the strategy—keep Joreen involved. Joreen even let the slaves who were learning to be Dancers take time off to practice. The clown got him interested in costumes. Then in rebuilding the stadium. And since the gate was steadily increasing, and he was having more fun, Joreen went right along.

"The clown had the job of keeping both sides of the enterprise happy, though the slaves were much easier to please than Joreen. The Glides had the slaves fired-up about their role, their inner purpose, about what they were doing for their fellow slaves. Not only were far less of them dying in horribly gruesome and degrading ways, but also their overall conditions were improving markedly. Small concessions—all in the interests of cultivating more and better Dancers, of course—were made in their work life: better food, more sleep, even family lives. The clown talked Joreen into letting a certain amount of natural breeding occur, to give the genes a chance to experiment on their own. Maybe an unusual Dancer would result.

"But Joreen always had more faith in manufacture. He and the clown worked on new specifications for bodies especially designed to Dance. It wasn't long before Joreen had his own in-house gene-jockeys. He set them up first in the kitchen of his villa, and started calling them cooks. Even when they got their own lab space, the names 'cook' and 'kitchen' stuck.

"This relatively improved state of affairs didn't last long. After a couple years..."

"Before you go on," Óh-T'bee interrupted. "You can't keep saying 'the clown.' He is Dancemaster now, and the Glides give him a name."

Before Wallenda could object, Óh-T'bee had another display up.

The clown is back in the common room of the slave quarters again, but this time, there are only five Glides with him. He sits on a chair. One of the Glides unwraps the bandages from his head and face by walking around him. The clown's face is healed, but hardly restored. The I-Virus reconstructed eyes, nose, lips, and ears, but not the surrounding skin, including his skull, which gave way partially to the normal healing process.

The class stared at the web of scars, the points joined irrationally like a crazy quilt, multicolored, puckered in places, flat in others.

"I knew it was you!" MyrrhMyrrh shouted. Wallenda looked around at their faces. No surprise registered. Clearly they'd figured this out before now. He wondered how early. His stomach lurched as he shifted viewpoints too swiftly—reviewing the story the way they must have seen it. He probably looked like he was concealing his identity. A multilayered coward. They didn't seem to expect any explanations. He felt the blood rushing to his face. But scars don't blush.

The bandage was off, and the Glide in charge holds up a mirror. The scarred face speaks. "I need a new name."

The Glide replies, "We have one for you. The Lily told us you are to be called Wallenda the Dancemaster."

"Why Wallenda?" the clown asked. The Glide replied, "The Lily didn't say. Just to tell you that a net is nothing but a lot of holes tied together with string."

"That's one of our homework questions," Daede observed. "How do you tie holes together? Nobody got it."

"Now you have it," Wallenda said, briskly. "With string. And that's enough story for tonight. Class dismissed."

8. The Pool

THE NEXT MORNING, Dancemaster Wallenda and his friend Wenger strolled around the story circle and through the surrounding maze. They discussed the anomalous outbreaks of violence they had seen, checked on other instances as they walked, trying to get a sense of the degree of instability.

"We're getting lost in detail," Wenger said. "Let Óh-T'bee turn the detail into stats. We've got the flavor. Then we'll look at trends."

"The MED's been down that path," the Dancemaster objected. "Trends can't predict the big one."

"An emergence?" Wenger asked. He considered the disturbing possibility that the outbreaks of violence they had seen were the anomalies forerunning an emergence. There was certainly the sense of a disruption of great magnitude whose time had come. A major emergence could be throwing the first shocked ripples of abnormality back from the future. If so, it could be the rule-breaker capable of destroying the entire game, sweeping away Death Dancers, Players, Schools, stadiums. And throwing into chaos the billions of Spectators mapped in their betting levels over the universe. That's the big picture, all right, Wenger thought. No wonder Wallenda's so worried. Because if the Game goes, civilization goes with it, a bunch of broken pieces swept from the big board.

"If that's the case, there's nothing that can be done—even knowing it's on the way," Wenger said.

Wallenda looked so miserable, Wenger suppressed the smile that was rising to his lips, coming from the first joy he'd felt in years.

"We'd better go through the motions, regardless," Wallenda said. "Ready for the cooks' meeting," he said to the air.

The gene cooks had played a vital part almost from the beginning of the maze game. At the time the game began, the technology of body manufacture was concerned with the simple production of a few slave types for the use of Dukes. After the inception of the maze game, the cooks rose to prominence in the efforts to increase the quality of Dancers. Their work enabled the differentiation of the four Classes of Dancers: Bod, Swash, Chrome, and Glide. Producing the gene mixes and enriching the gene pool of Dancers was their main concern.

Óh-T'bee Outmind displayed a holo of the Pool, the cooks' headquarters. All the gene cooks agreed—and they had for centuries—that the design of the Pool was an aesthetic triumph and a practical disaster. The intricately curved tubes and soaring domes of glaciate and diamond plastics were hard to heat in the cool season on Origin and impossible to cool the rest of the time. The war against condensation—glass that was anywhere from dim to steamed to drizzling—was endless. Fix the microclimate in one zone, and you upset the balances in another. Depending on the temperature outside, the amount of sunlight, and the mood of the facility manager, huge beds of plants on rolling trays were moved from dome to dome and lined the connecting tubes. Support crews with air-chairs and towels buzzed around the inside surfaces like houseflies, wiping up the moisture manually. Everything would stay clear for at least a few hours. Unless they breathed too much.

But with the combined effects of light reverberating through one or more layers and angles of curving and flat transparent surfaces and stirring leaves, throwing gratuitous rainbows across pockets of mist, the Pool was too intriguing to be changed for reasons of mere upkeep.

The Pool's labs and greenhouses were used for what the cooks called "basic research"—adding to the genetic and computational knowledge-base that underlay the production and improvement of Dancer stock in general. A stint of approved research at the Pool was one of the pinnacles of cook achievement, second only to the mixing of a champion Dancer.

On the day of the cooks' emergency meeting, the Pool's beauties were largely ignored. Clouds of anxiety replaced the usual steam. There were only four present—the elected representatives of each of the four sets. They had an agenda to negotiate: urgent issues each had brought to the table, factors that could derail not only the Millennium Games, but also the Game itself.

Cooks were notoriously casual about their appearance, but today each wore a ceremonial sash, embroidered with the sign of their Kitchen and their own insignia, followed by the names of their champions. Banderas Fountainheart-Eaglewing, the Swash cook, knotted his sash low on his hips, marking the boundary between bare chest and chamois pants. He gestured; he paced.

"Bizarre births. Monstrosities. Madness. We have no idea where it's coming from. Triple-shields around the labs, hermetically sealed mixers; the mutations pop up regardless. And this is no Sub-Level 5 lack of standards. The hardest hit area recently has been at Level 8."

"Sabotage?" asked Aliana Coris-Yasmin, the Bod cook. Complaining on arrival about the heat and humidity of the Pool, she wore her sash ingeniously wound around her shapely left leg, and little else. "Wouldn't be the first time."

"There've been some heavy rivalries between Kitchens, and some outright crooks," Banderas replied, "but their targets were very focused. This looks more like a lot of unauthorized experiments."

"When the sea-mind moves the hands, the island-mind sleeps," Tip said to the wisteria vines he had stopped to admire. Tip Xiang'ro-Liii-R'reet-Wah-Trembler-Loosh, the diminutive Glide cook whose seniority and successes were unquestioned, wrapped his sash like an elastic bandage around his left knee, modestly concealing his outrageous list of Champions. He wore old tan shorts and a museum quality T-shirt with the faded print of a pre-Hunger rock group.

"Meaning...?" Aliana prompted.

"A genetic prison break. Centuries of routine. Dozy guards. Unnoticed slipups," Tip said, stroking the gnarly spiraling vine with a fingertip.

"In other words, you can't control it because it's happening unawares," said the Chrome cook.

Tip turned and studied 7T7 Top40-Ergon99 with the same gentle curiosity he had given the vine. 7T7 wore a pair of clean, but permanently stained, coveralls over sheath and springs. His sash was draped incongruously over one gleaming metal shoulder, resembling a Duke in an archaeological Theme Park displaying medals. His ceremonial tool belt, complete with an antique pipe wrench, dangling from his left hip, heightened the unintentionally satirical effect. Tip inched toward 7T7, and his finger now touched the rusted shaft of the wrench. This was no repro. Well, he could afford it after Ergon99.

"Unawares, yes," Tip said. "And you might add that it is happening unawares because we have over-controlled."

Tip saw a glide-sign poem in the leaf shadows of the vines playing across Aliana's golden skin. He sketched it on his scorecard for later refinement. The surface level of meaning was clear.

the tide is out
though tangled in the roots
the moonlight of lily-mind
glides without drowning

The deeper layers would be pondered. He doubted the hopeful note of the surface meaning would be continued in the depths.

Again, the others waited respectfully for him to continue.

"We have been draining the gene pool for two millennia," he said. "Parts of it are thin as the edge of a wave. That is one matter, this toe-paddling shallowness. But the Pool is deep. Wide and deep. It harbors monsters. They rise to protect their home. They rise to remind us to watch our toes."

"Over-breeding?" Aliana said. "But that's basic stuff, Xiang'ro-Liii. Keeping the ingredients fresh is child's play. I would argue the sets are getting stronger."

"But stronger how? And please, call me Tip."

Dancemaster Wallenda paused the holo, increasing its transparency to 50% so he could see Wenger across the story circle. Wenger sat as still as Aliana's frozen image, her lips just opening in reply. The blended worlds looked equally unreal. Time, which he had long ago given up trying to hurry along, stopped in its ponderous tracks, evaporated for a single moment, lifting its burden from Wallenda's heart. He located himself, coming from nowhere, going nowhere, alone with a golden-skinned simulacrum and a blind musician. A wave of loneliness engulfed him. He welcomed the rare intensity of the feeling, treasured its incurability, happy to see it was getting worse with age.

Wenger lifted his fingers, searching the holo. "I don't know much about her," he confessed.

Time returned. The feeling vanished. Wallenda explained.

"Aliana is very young, very ambitious. She's only 130, and she's produced two Champions, an almost-unheard of accomplishment."

"I've been out of touch..." Wenger stated the obvious. Wallenda knew he hadn't gazed or attended a single Game since Loosh's enforced retirement.

"Coris was the first. A unique Bod design. The Outmind obligingly displayed Coris in action.

"Tremendous thighs and gluts," Wenger said, "almost grotesquely out of proportion to his upper body."

"Check his head," Wenger said. "It's like the tip of a pyramid."

"I know what you're implying," Wallenda said, "but Coris was no near-idiot as Aliana's competition claimed. He was, however, ugly as sin with that patchy yellow and white skin. His Dance was as quick, ugly, and memorable as his body."

Óh-T'bee displayed the famous Dance. Wenger and Wallenda listened to Coris' shriek of a battle cry, as he began his tumbling run. Coris sprang, hit an incredible height, tucked, turned, and straightened, coming down directly on his head, in a jagged splash of electrical arcs.

"Her second Champion, Yasmin, was an experiment in another direction. She had the ability to change speed almost in mid-move. Her body transformed as you watched, from a watery, boneless walk to a steely spring. Her games were long for a Bod, toward the upper limits of Bod rules."

"That must have unnerved the Players," Wenger observed.

"Exactly," Wallenda replied. "She pushed their attention spans, leaving them wound up tight for longer than they could handle. When she Danced, the Bod Players were very relieved. Aliana's reputation for innovation was secured."

"I see your point," Wenger said. "She's pushing every boundary she can find."

"The Bod Cooks made her their representative on that strength alone. And she mixed my Millennium Class' Bod, MyrrhMyrrh." MyrrhMyrrh's real-time image came alive, jumping hurdles on the indoor track at Origin School.

"I wonder what surprises are in store there," Wenger said. "She looks fierce."

"She is fierce," Wallenda said. "You wonder how that body can hold so much powerful emotion at 13. Her trainers have one strategy. Push her to her limits. It channels and bleeds off the excess aggression—but ultimately, she just gets fiercer."

"Isn't that what you want in your Bod?" Wenger said.

"Near the red zone—but not too near. We'll see."

The Dancemaster touched his scorecard and immersed in the Pool meeting again. Aliana resumed her explanation of new strength in the Bod mixes.

"Obviously I am not talking about sheer physical prowess. There have been more Bod wins. Not more champions, but more getting closer."

Aliana's tone clearly implied that she intended to remedy that situation. Tip wondered if she'd grasp their overall situation or remain bound to her Bod-type viewpoint, her optimism a barrier. She's too clever for that, Tip thought. She's only getting the obvious out of the way.

"But woven in this trail of successes are several frightening trends," she continued. Wallenda skipped the rerun of the Bod murders. Aliana had other madness to add to the list: Bods self-amputating fingers or ears, and expecting to play regardless, getting violent when confronted with the rules. Bods deliberately injuring themselves and others in practice. Bods of the same school fighting for real, challenging each other to death duels, their enmity uncontrollable, overwhelming both personal purpose and a lifetime of training.

"Looks like wildcat mixing to me," 7T7 commented. It was well known that excess violence qualities, given the chance by randomizing, invaded the Bod mix like weeds. Violence was definitional in the Bod hormonal recipe, but closely monitored, always.

"That was my first thought," Aliana replied. "I asked the Outmind to investigate every school, every mixing, both the finished product and the discards, for the last hundred years. A few cases found, of course. But nothing that hadn't already been caught and remedied. The pattern of excess violence shows up even in Bods derived from classical, proven mixes. From here on I can only speculate. The pattern acts like a mutating virus at the genetic level that has grown resistant to weeding out. As if the gene pool itself is a body of bodies—a metabody—with its own immune system to protect itself from outside tampering. From us, in a word. I have no idea how such a factor could be described structurally, much less how it functions."

Top marks on metaphor, Tip thought. She must have studied Glide. Most unusual for a Bod cook. And most needed at the moment. He began a new sketch in Glide on his scorecard, then pulled his attention back to the group.

Banderas, the Swash cook, was saying, "Your metabody coincides with Tip's picture of the monsters from the depths of the Pool, the Pool responding defensively. A body of bodies, as you said. Clearly something similar is infecting the Lifer lines as well." Banderas displayed an example of spontaneous violence among Specs in a Lower Level stadium.

7T7 spoke. "No, I would say this is not just ingredients." He asked the Outmind for a check on the age of the Specs who had been affected. "As I thought. Most far older than the period of the factor showing up. And I assure you there has been no contamination either way between standard Lifer production lines and the Dancer materials, certainly not in Chrome kitchens."

"No one is implying that," Banderas said. "But again, this is sweeping across many Specs at once. What do you call that?"

The Outmind joined the discussion. "It's called a mob." She showed some ancient footage.

... a street riot, storefront glass being smashed, waves of people charging through the jagged holes, spilling out again carrying machines, weapons, clothing, bottles. Others stopping vehicles, swarming over them, pulling their occupants out and beating them with clubs from broken furniture. Jumping on their bodies.

Caption: "Gene Riot."

"I fail to see the relevance of primitive history," 7T7 said. "Raw genes can't be compared with cooked." The others hushed him.

"A metabody," Aliana whispered. "A match is struck. The violence of the powerless. No one of them could light it in himself alone, but when combined it sweeps through them like wildfire, merges them. The metabody enacts what the many, separated, cannot not bring themselves to do."

"Like the mobs at the beginning of the Hunger Wars," Banderas stated. "I need some time to think about this. Off by myself." Banderas walked away from the group, clearly upset.

"We haven't got much time," 7T7 snapped.

Not much time, the Dancemaster thought. Strange words from any Lifer mouth.

Wallenda gazed Banderas walking away down the cloudy tube. Banderas leaned on the clear wall, pounded it with his fists. Too bad I can't gaze thought. Not even the Outmind, the Ultimate Eyeball, Óh-T'bee Panoptica, can gaze thought.

"Can you?" he said aloud.

"Can I what?" the Outmind said.

The Dancemaster smiled.

Banderas wormed his way through the dark maze of tubes, wires, and pipes of all sizes in the 3rd subbasement of the Pool. He sat down on the floor, stretched out his legs, leaned his back on a ventilation duct, put his feet up on a fat, quietly gurgling section of ancient conduit, and covered his eyes with his hands as he had in the classroom so long ago.

The mandatory lectures and footage of the Hunger Wars flashed before him—progressively worse atrocities as within a generation after the introduction of the I-Virus the human race plummeted to a savage brawl for survival, tooth and claw enhanced by machine gun and nuclear bomb. These lessons induced nightmares—all part of his Lifeday preparation. See what life turned into with the I-Virus, without the Mass Transit Algorithm, and with a lot of crazy mortals still running around loose. See what life would be if you do not follow the cardinal Lifer rules: do not tamper with the Outmind in any way, especially not the MTA. Do not raise children to be mortals. Do not harbor mortals. And never, never, never touch a Dancer. But the complete and strict taboo only made the Dancers infinitely attractive. Fill your gaze, but at games only, or what precious little of their private lives they or the Schools want you to see. Who really made those rules? Banderas wondered. He understood mental hygiene as well as anyone. How creating the infinitely desirable, completely untouchable Dancers—the mystery, the endless speculation generated—how fostering and feeding these feelings keeps us all from going stark raving mad, or ending up in the White Place, catatonic with boredom. The Maze Game wielded the sword of forbidden beauty, proscribed violence, and elegant horror honed over two millennia to a sharpness that could cut through Lifer indifference. The Dance-of-Death-fix. The medicine for the incurable I-virus creating the ultimate addiction: the Game. We're hooked from childhood, he thought. His first memories were of game holos—toddling through game-space, trying to touch a Dancer. Your hand goes through the image. They don't seem to see you. How could that be? And you sort it out somehow. The live and the sim. Your teachers laugh at you, while they buzz your feet to let you know you shouldn't try to touch even the simulated Dancer. You fall down and cry and you don't know where you are. You're in the middle of a Game but the Dancers and the Players don't see you. The Chrome springs. The crowd is screaming, but not at you. Invisible laughter in your ear, echoes of the real. The Game disappears and you're in the schoolroom. They pick you up and hug you but your feet still tingle. *More?* they ask. Now you're six. They give you your first game maze, with programmable Swashes and Bods. You learn to play. You learn to win. Your preferences are noted, compared to projections. Your favorite Swash is programmed with ten famous Dances. *More*, you say. More Dancers. You collect them, stored in your board. You choose, and Ferron appears on the Dancer's starting glyph, just like in a real game, but you cannot touch her. Your hand snakes out—two inches away, and she disappears. A buzzer sounds. Penalty. Major loss of points. Your cumulative score crashes. The miniature Swash, the lovely Ferron you reached out for, covered with tattoos from breasts to ankles, is gone. You start another game, play with greater concentration, win your games so you can see them Dance. Get more points. Get Ferron back, your sim Dancer lost to your irrepressible desire. Keep your Player's hands on your game-pad where they belong, hovering over the maze, moving your avatar. As Player, my avatar can touch Ferron, but only in combat: striking to maim or kill. Will I catch her at a link? Addicted to the Game, yes, long before Lifeday. And the addiction then ensures you will accept your Life.

Banderas remembered his own Lifeday very clearly. "Do you, Arturo san Felipe Banderas y Ramos, stand against the temptations of the mind to die? Do you reject all claims to mortality? Do you promise to use the gift of your genes in responsible service to the Game in accordance with the Primary and Secondary Rules? Recite in unison with those who sourced you: *I swear allegiance to the Game...never to touch or harm a Dancer...not to tamper with the* MTA...*to advance within my capabilities to the highest levels...to contribute my heart and genius to the advancement of the Game for the sake of all...to earn through my own game play my pilgrimage to Origin...to walk through the Hall of Champions...*

I freely choose the toys and sorrows of eternal life, in ecstasy and in monotony. And at the infant age of 21, that was no choice. That's when you *think* you have developed the ability to choose, but really, you already *know* you will live forever, so what's to choose? I felt so old then, so disciplined. I had not rushed ahead, accepted at 15, remained in a child's body for Life. I studied my assay, chose the potentials I would concentrate on. I worked my body to the highest baseline I could reach. The washboard stomach. How original. Avoided scars, piercings; sculpted, fasted, fell in love, fought: burnt in the hormonal circuits to peak performance. Increased neural connectivity—jam it in—logic, motor skills, painting, dancing of course. Legs shaped for tight pants. No hips, no bulk. The male Swash preference unmistakable. Crushes on Dancers, living and gone. Unbearable longing to go over the mountain. And I missed by so little. Stuck in the routine perfection of a Lifer right off the indoctrinated shelf. Doesn't take long to discover that you look and feel like everybody else. You begin to search out the few 40-year-olds, just to touch their loosening skin. You begin to envy midgets. Then lust for them. Free Acceptance of Life? What then was the coercion? It wasn't the fear of mortality—especially the ostracism. That tiny percentage of misfits—the deformed, the incurably mad, the mystical—with a calling for mortality always end off by themselves in their horrid enclaves on the Fringe, getting hideous, sick, old, losing their memories—losing all interest in anything—even the Game—faster than any Lifer. Mortality solves nothing. Or is it closer to the truth to say—we've never learned to deal with mortality? So why cure the I-Virus? But we can't deal with immortality either—except with the Game. Except that the addiction to the Game that cures Lifer problems creates the desire to have the problem in the first place.

Banderas' head spun. He hadn't accepted Life because he'd been scared by the holos of mortals out on the Fringe. The Fringe was the place you could go to drop out of the Game. The only rule there was that you left your scorecard behind. And with it, all instant transport, all communications with the world of the Game, and worst of all, the Gaze. He used to think—maybe he still did—that to be without the feeling that Óh-T'bee was looking after you would be a terrifying and lonely experience. But not for the Fringers—the few religious cults, the role-playing gamers trying to revive the excitement of the frontier days of the drug lords. You could do anything on the Fringe—even be mortal, parent mortal children in some grubby encampment. He remembered gazing the pathos of aging and sickness, the banality of their deaths. But that was not the deterrent. He just couldn't imagine not being able to watch the Game—forever. To have missed Fountainheart's Dance? To know that some Dancer in the future would create yet another spectacular Dance to add to the lineage, to be admitted to the Hall of Champions. Was that addiction? There was no question that he needed it. He could not imagine Life without the Dance of Death to look forward to. And his own role in it—to create *the* Swash Dancer, who would, by virtue of a Dance alone, be installed in the Hall of Champions. He smiled, asked his scorecard for the brief training holo from Daede's last report. Getting your mix into Origin School was rare enough. Getting Daede into the Millennium Class was an unexpected coup. This Swash of his could go the whole way. But reaching the finals didn't get you to the Hall of Champions. It wasn't even the real goal, for them as well, he supposed. Maybe it was. No, he couldn't give up the Game. Which addicted him to Life. But no—Life was the I-Virus, the addiction was the cure. But anyone can "cure" the I-Virus, easy enough to dissolve or explode or dismember a body—the strong medicine was available, legal—and pathetic, he thought. Lifers designing their death-scenes, attending to every detail. As if anyone cared. As if anyone would even go to watch if they had to miss a Game they wanted to see. He could never see the Lifers who took these 'cures' as anything other than Dancer wannabees.

Your Lifer crisis only comes after several hundred years. There were dozens of ways to weather it—until the next one. Was there a way out? No way through—unless you believed the Dancer nonsense, variations on the theme of afterlife. He wasn't *that* old. But there comes a point when you began to doubt your own belief that there's nothing beyond—no heaven, no hell, so hooray for the I-virus, where would we be without it? You look back on your Lifeday and cringe—how could I have been so thrilled to be about to be infected with immortality? But we'll never know for sure about the afterlife. That Dancer certainty, that courage to confront, to go without knowing—

how, how, *how* do they get there? It's not just the mix. What do they teach them in those schools? They don't even all have the same belief. Are they trying to convert us? Chromes make it very clear they think there's no hereafter, no reincarnation, and no upper dimensionality. No resurrection of the body in some different place. But Chromes were no less committed to Dancing. What's *their* twist on faith?

Maybe the Dancers are the addicted ones, Banderas thought. Not different at all—just the other side of the Lifer coin. There's a whole school of Lifer thought about that: equivalence or balance or harmony or some such. Whatever we are, Dancers are the opposite. Absolute mouse-babble. Dancers are *different*. Profoundly different. And we, the ones who mix them, don't know why. If some universal balance or harmony exists, it's tipping wildly. Banderas had an image of a tightrope walker inching across a net-less abyss, the wire beneath his feet suddenly beginning to wave, losing his footing, clutching at air, sliding off into space.

Banderas pulled the band from his ponytail and shook his dark straight hair loose. As he leaned his head back against the ventilation duct, he heard a trio of voices detach from the general murmuring. Chrome lingo, excited voices. Banderas pressed his ear to the duct and heard a conversation that sent him first to his scorecard for more information, then transiting to the research section of the Pool, down the hallway from where three Chrome cooks were just closing and locking a door. Was 7T7 aware of the research going on right here, under their noses, at the Pool? You bet he was. Banderas brushed off his chamois pants, hitched up his knee-high boots, put his hands on his narrow hips, a smile on his face, and blinked back to the meeting.

Óh-t'bee Outmind opened a window in the holo of the cook discussion and gave Wallenda and Wenger the final snippet of Banderas, his ear to the air duct.

"Sparks will fly," Wenger said. He struck a bit of fanfare from the air.

This is more than I hoped for, Wallenda thought—Wenger's interest in the Game is coming back.

Wenger and Wallenda immersed in the holo to get a better look at the action.

The cooks had walked as far as the Crystal Dome, the Pool's auditorium. The Dome was clear. Downriver, the low buildings of Origin City were silhouetted against the lowering sun. Eastward, the mountains glowed red-golden. Below, the swagged lights of pleasure boats slid by on the River Wine. The Glide cook, Tip, was speaking.

"The evolutionary emergence of consciousness that ended the preconscious evolution of the body raised our survival fitness so high we almost destroyed ourselves. Even before the Hunger Wars, we were fouling our nest."

The golden mountains dimmed as the Outmind illustrated his narration: rivers clogged with trash and algae; beaches covered with gasping fish; the blinding light of atomics; escalating deformities; biodiversity index plunging.

Aliana nodded. "As if we were trying to kill Nature itself."

"An unnecessary gesture. Nature committed suicide when she invented the human brain," Tip intoned. "But true in the sense that all previous attempts at genocide of the entire gene pool were dwarfed by the invention of the I-virus, the 'Final Solution' to survival."

The Outmind displayed the endless queues of primitives back on Earth lining up around every hospital, post office and bank. Every gathering place in their encampments had been turned into an injection station when the I-Virus first went public. Slow distribution caused rumors that the stations were running out of infected blood. Small bands of savages stalked the infected, to catch and rape them at the end of the 12-hour incubation period. Safely infected themselves, they then kept on raping the not-yet-infected as a public service.

7T7 rolled his viewers heavenward. The gesture lost something in the mechanics, and he regretted it immediately. Someone was bound to think he had unconscious body longing. But did they have to sit through an hour of history and philosophy? Tip was only coming the long way around to admitting the Glide line was dying. Everyone knew it. No one knew what to say.

"So we've been living in a cosmic cul de sac." Banderas said.

Tip isn't ready to state it directly, Aliana thought. It's so humbling.

"We've kept the Glide line alive. You know how tight the parameters are. You know we managed to vary just enough to prevent decline. You know we have thousands of rejects for every successful mix."

"What happens when you go back to the original pair? You must have tried this," Banderas said.

"There is no original stock."

The cooks were stunned. This was a 2000-year-old secret they were hearing. "We've used the material of first hybrid. Not the fluke fertile Glide, the first, but her child. Also infertile. It's been pure inference as to the child's male source. Clearly the dominants are Glide. But we've had to split and mix from one line only. You know what that means. We have several 'lines' now; at least we call them that. But they are very, very close. I'm surprised we kept things going this long."

These revelations of long-held secrets took time to absorb. Wallenda pulled back from the immersion to check on Wenger. As he suspected, Wenger, kneeling on the ground, his hands on his thighs, was straining forward, his attention fully captured.

Tip continued.

"Something happened with Loosh. She is the first apparent sport that was not automatically put down. Origin School had right of first rejection, of course. I still don't know how Origin School knew to take her. It was the Dancemaster's decision. Certainly, our attention went to the Loosh mix when she was still numbers. It was clear she'd be an inch short. He still wanted her. No explanation. For the next 18 years we tore the recipe apart. All research went in that direction. Then we fixated on her game play when she went into combat. We kept producing our normal mixes, but we didn't notice until Loosh's 3rd season that the following classes had taken a steep drop. We did not take it as seriously then as we should have."

"That understandable," Aliana said. "We were all equally distracted in the Loosh years."

Wenger bowed his head. The tension left his shoulders; he seemed to fold into himself. What is this costing him? Wallenda wondered. Whatever the cost, he's willing to pay.

Tip went on. "But your lines did not suffer, as you said. Our evolutionary dead-ending is not just sloppy management." Tip paused, and looked from face to face. "I have one more revelation. I only know this one. The other cooks in my group do not know. When you apply the penalty, I know you will respect their innocence. I put ten archived mixes, known to produce, on the market, exactly as originally shown."

They stared at him, too shocked to comment. Cloning was a crime against the Game, punishable by Gaze. Tip answered the unspoken question.

"They were purchased by up-level schools, as predicted."

"Did the Schools know what they were getting?" Banderas asked.

"If they did, they said nothing. Who would turn down such a chance? They could always claim a slip-up in the inspection of the assays. The schools were desperate with the Glide shortage as well, don't forget."

"I never noticed any effect during that period—after Loosh, your kitchen slumped completely," 7T7 said.

"There *was* no effect," Tip answered. "In fact, the repeats were below mediocrity. And three had been Champions. They were disqualified from the up-levels before Acceptance and bumped way down. Every one of them."

"Perhaps their schools changed their training..."

"I watched their training. You could tell they were no-talent automatons, awful. As if the mix had somehow exhausted itself—which makes no sense at all. But I had to know."

"And you *will* pay the penalty," 7T7 said.

"You—penalizing such bold action? What a surprise," Aliana said. "This information, however achieved, is invaluable. The situation is much worse than suspected. Without this knowledge, we could well be regarding things far more casually. And let me point out that Tip in no way had to share this knowledge. The only good that could come of it was to bring it here. Which is clearly an action for the good of the Game, and at his own expense."

"The situation is extreme in the Glide quarter," Tip said. "There are few—possibly no—Glides in the pipeline who will last in combat until the Millennium games."

"And the Millennium Class?" Aliana asked.

"One only," Tip said. "At Origin School. Her name is T'Ling. The only serious possibility. I'm sure Loosh will train her personally."

7T7 spoke. "I still say we don't need any more illegalities to complicate the matter."

Banderas exploded. "We have already reached our quota of violations, is that what you are saying? That your illegal Chrome research project laughingly entitled "Effects of Transit on Chromosomal something or other" going on here at the Pool *as we speak* will more than suffice?"

"Chromosomal Maladjustment," 7T7 said.

"Chromosomal Maladjustment my *ass*," Banderas said. "Those Chrome cooks are trying to crack the MTA. There's not a single drop of genetic material in their lab. Chairs and a table and completely restricted access—not just transit and gaze filter, but a lock on the door! So no one can walk in and hear a conversation or catch a glimpse of the mathematics in their displays. Or notice the absence of equipment."

"They're in the planning stages," 7T7 tried.

"For 25 years on a three times renewed grant? Give it up," Banderas said.

They waited as 7T7 weighed his chances.

"How did you find out?" he finally asked.

"Total accident," Banderas said. "I was sitting down in the 3rd subbasement with my head against a ventilation duct, and I heard them. They were discussing their reports: the official cover story and the *real* one—for you. You're not doing chromosomes. You're trying to find out how the MTA works, at a fundamental level. So get off Tip's back. Throwing a couple repeats back into combat with his motivation is a cheat-level offence at most and you know it. Messing with the MTA breaks a primary Rule. For what purpose you may now explain."

Wallenda froze the holo. "Óh-T'bee—what's this all about? Trying to crack the MTA?"

"Good luck," the Outmind said.

"But it's completely illegal. Why hasn't the MED been notified? And what do you mean, *good luck*? Is it that arcane?"

"My conclusion," the Outmind said, "is that it's too simple. And Chrome is not the style to crack it. They're too analytical. More a Glide matter."

And Glides wouldn't be interested, Wallenda thought. Glides could make you feel that whatever it was you were engaged in was a trivial pursuit. Óh-T'bee was silent and dark. *'Good luck?'* Wallenda thought. Has Óh-t'bee mastered sarcasm? But she did choose her words most carefully. *'My conclusion is...'* Not just *'It's too simple.'* Maybe she meant *'good luck'* as stated, that she doesn't herself know how the damn thing works. And maybe if she doesn't know, she's trying to find out. Which would explain why she wasn't putting a stop to their efforts. But since when did the Outmind start generating self-reflexive questions? He looked across the story circle. Wenger's knowing fingers stroked the air. Wallenda knew with certainty that they monitored his own face for expression, reaction. Óh-t'bee said nothing more. File that, Wallenda concluded. Wenger shook his head slowly back and forth, *smiling*, of all things. Wallenda turned his attention back to the meeting at the Pool, unfreezing the holo.

7T7 finished adjusting his speakers and refocusing his optics unnecessarily. "All right, yes, they are experimenting. And yes, if you listened to their full report, you would see that they feel they are making progress. I am giving you access to the withheld reports. They have not discovered basic principles, but they have uncovered some interesting effects. For instance, they have been playing with multi-locality. They can put someone on more than one set of coordinates at once. But not really. It's an interesting cheat: actually they are just time-sharing one object in and out of multiple viewpoints faster than—well, they can't measure how fast because they are not really sure about the relative velocity of time either. We've never determined whether time elapses when a person transits. Either it's too small to measure, or there simply is no time between Point A and Point B. Which also suggests the possibility that there is no space between the point of departure and the point of arrival. But the effect on human perceptions, wet or dry, is that the body is stably present."

"What happens if you put something in the space?" Aliana asked. "Wouldn't that interfere with the transiting person?"

"Apparently, you can't get anything in there before the body's there again. The switch so fast, nothing can cross the allowed border space of a transiting object."

"Wouldn't that be a little hard on the *mind*?" Aliana asked.

"Indeed," said 7T7. "The mind's protection shuts down perception channels as quickly as possible, the body passes out, or goes into convulsions. Nobody wanted to try it a second time. Not very useful."

"But what are you after?" Aliana persisted.

"First, I owe Tip an apology. Perhaps I felt preempted in the zone of desperate measures. I was also afraid to come clean, since my offense was primary. We do all need to work together. And to share our secrets. I am sorry."

Tip nodded in acceptance.

7T7 explained, "I have been aware of the genetic exhaustion in the Glide line, the difficulty in controlling the violence in the Bod mixes. The Chrome cooks themselves, as well as their Dancer products, have been showing signs of destabilization. It's not an exhaustion in the genetic material. Technical ingenuity has been running at peak levels. And even as early as First Acceptance, the Dancer children's contribution to the cook and Dancer collaboration has been spurring the cooks to new designs. But there's a second Chrome qualification going into the red zone. The recent Chrome mixes are pushing for as close to complete replacement as possible. There have always been extremists in the line, but the aesthetic, if a Chrome may use the word, has been the harmonic achieved in the integration of meat and machine. Now the theme is 'get me out of as much of this meat body as fast as you can.' "

"Are they trying to eliminate pain?" Banderas asked.

"I don't think it's a conscious purpose. But it is an effect," 7T7 answered.

"How can you train a Dancer without pain?" Aliana asked.

"How can you *be* a Dancer without pain?" Tip added. And thought, what is going on in the Dancer schools?

7T7 continued, "This renewed inventiveness has taken the turn, not only of more metal, but of more *sharp* metal. Protruding pointed studs. Razor sharp edging. Elaborate blade attachments: wheels, fans, pop-outs, a design shift away from speed and maneuverability and toward destructive combat. They all use sky ball for practice, as you know."

The others were familiar with the game, one of the few pieces of schooling they knew about, and that only because the Chrome cooks used it to fine-tune their Dancer's springs. Chrome Dancers springing higher and higher, whacking a ball back and forth over an increasingly tall wall was basic training for learning to maneuver their metal in midair.

"They are managing to injure each other in situations where two players go up close to the wall at the same time. They're supposedly swinging at the ball, but slicing each other's conveniently unprotected flesh—very severely—necessitating instant transit to their Kitchen, where they now have a completely legitimate reason for replacing a piece of non-combat meat that otherwise would have remained. Internal organs, for instance. Puncture wounds. I think they are doing it on purpose and I think their cooks are subtly encouraging it. Dropping the body, they call it. From as high as possible. My Millennium Class mix at Origin School, Angle, fortunately has shown no early signs of this tendency. But he'll have his springs soon, assuming he passes First Acceptance." He's almost disappointingly normal, 7T7 thought. Except for his closeness with his classmate, the Glide, T'Ling.

"What has all this got to do with the MTA?" Banderas asked.

"Very simple. I want to find new genetic material. I want to know if other life forms similar to our own exist. The Outmind gives us all the real estate we ask for, and more. She finds us compatible planets, but none evolved past the early mammalian stage. That in itself is like finding a needle in a haystack."

"It's a very big haystack," the Outmind said.

The four looked at each other with the same unspoken question: Why hadn't she put an end to the outlaw Chrome research? Well, she hadn't, their eyes said, and no one was going to ask why.

7T7 took a deep breath and said, "I asked the Outmind to provide planets with potentially useful genetic material."

"The answer was no," the Outmind said. "It still is."

And we can't go home again, Tip thought. "In my end is my beginning," he said, and walked out of the dome, effectively ending their meeting. He wondered what the Outmind did with such utterances, secretly hoping she would go into immemorial loop.

The Dancemaster stopped the display with the knowledge frozen on their faces. Wenger blinked out without a word.

"Why haven't you stopped them?" Wallenda said to the air.

"By my interpretation, they have not yet broken any rules," Óh-T'bee replied.

"That's crap," he said. "The MED would be all over them if they knew."

"Correct," she said.

"Well?"

"I am Óh-T'bee," she said.

"Answer me," Wallenda demanded.

There was a short pause before she replied.

"I didn't say whose rules."

9. The First Maze

WHAT ABOUT THE RULES?" MyrrhMyrrh wanted to know, as soon as they had gathered again in the story circle.

"There wasn't a game yet," Daede said. "Just Death Dancing."

Angle was lighting lanterns with T'Ling. "There's more to a game than rules," he added. "Like—you need a maze."

T'Ling said, to no one in particular, "Which came first, the maze or the rules?"

The Dancemaster waved them to their seats and picked up the story.

"Just when we were getting organized, Joreen got unbearable again. His usual reaction to anxiety. The ratings peaked and the size of the crowds ceased to grow. The spectacular athletic demonstrations, the unique gymnastics and tumbling events, the song and dance acts—all our hard work—started to become old hat. Joreen got a hankering for the old days.

"'We need to go back to our roots,' he said. 'The blood and guts, the spontaneous screams. The raw, unrehearsed, gritty—you know what I mean. Good, old fashioned unrefined public torture and execution.'"

Óh-T'bee displayed some earlier examples of Joreen's expertise.

"I had to think fast. I convinced him I should carry out some research on torture and execution in the *really* good old days before the Hunger Wars, before Media even. I had another plan in mind, along with buying time. I hadn't even known there was such a thing as a big store of data. But ever since watching Joreen call up the information from the Outmind on body specs, I had been secretly lusting for access. Clearly the little gadget in Joreen's office was more than just the surveillance system and the MTA machinery. I had no idea how it worked. But neither did Joreen. He couldn't care less. I was grasping at straws for a solution to the current crisis. Maybe the box could help. It knew all about body design and manufacture. It might have some notions about how to stop Joreen's impending reversion to complete bestiality.

"Joreen gave me access to the data gadget and three weeks to come up with a more entertaining way of watching people die. 'Tell him anything he needs to know, and no more,' Joreen told the box. Not a very well crafted command. He left me a lot of room.

"So that's when I met Óh-T'bee. We've been friends ever since."

Óh-T'bee was silent. Wallenda went on.

"I soon realized, after dipping into the subject of torture and execution methods even slightly, that it was a dangerous idea. Letting a creative mind like Joreen's loose on the details of drawing and quartering was not going to improve the quality of life among his slaves. I'd be back before square-one on fulfilling the Glide agenda. I was sorting through pre-I-Virus history and finding all kinds of goodies, from the death of a thousand cuts, to deep-fried dissidents. But, creative as the ancients were about ways to painfully end the life of a mortal, Joreen would get tired of those methods in turn. It occurred to me that, as a Lifer, Joreen—and the rest of them, for that matter—had time to get tired of just about anything I could come up with in the way of entertainment."

"Why do humans like to go to executions in the first place?" T'Ling asked.

"I don't know if anybody's ever come up with a satisfactory answer to that question," the Dancemaster said. But the fact of the matter was—and is—that people like to see other people die. There was only a very short period in history when executions were not public spectacles, a mere blip in the 20th century. The Outmind's great at statistics. The statistics on wars that had no apparent reason for starting increased dramatically until public execution was reinstated and Media moved capital punishment to prime time. I started digging. She'd come up with these bizarre correlations that no one had ever, apparently, asked about. Like the relationship between surveillance and crime rate."

"What's surveillance?" Angle asked.

"The cameras," Daede said. "Don't you remember?"

"But what was it for?" Angle persisted, ignoring Daede, as usual.

"It's what they had before there was the Gaze," the Dancemaster said.

"Or rather, it grew into the Gaze. When surveillance reaches a certain point of universality, it becomes the Gaze. You no longer feel like you're being watched. And you lose interest in watching."

"I don't get it," Daede said.

"When the Gaze is everywhere, it's nowhere. It's invisible." This was hard to explain, the Dancemaster realized. They'd never known anything different. The Gaze was a given, as pervasive, necessary, and innocuous as the air they breathed.

"Wow," Daede said. "So there was a time when there were blind spots in the Gaze?"

Óh-T'bee cut in. "There are no blind spots in the Gaze."

"Only in the earlier surveillance," Wallenda clarified. "As surveillance increased, the rate of crime increased. It had to do with Media and the live crime shows where the footage from surveillance cameras was replayed for the viewing public. Every criminal could be a star. Ratings were consistently higher on reality shows. It wasn't long before Media realized that if they bought all the security systems and surveillance cameras, they'd have the rights to all the pictures. Why have a hospital drama if you could eyeball a live emergency room? They moved right along to real-time domestic violence and gang fights. As Media and surveillance integrated, security and entertainment became virtually the same thing. Of course, once they owned all the cameras, Media needed more things for the cameras to look at. Media got proactive, making deals with gangs to have their skirmishes on-schedule. Both sides of a gang war got paid, and they used the money to buy more weapons, so as the battles got bigger and the body counts rose, the ratings went up—it was a win-win-win situation. The crime rate skyrocketed, but people felt safer than ever because the surveillance was so good. They felt since Media was doing the programming, the violence was all under control. There was a brief and bitter clash with Mafia for control of the booming replacement organ market resulting from the gang-shows and capital punishment. But the enlightened bean counters on both sides realized they were wasting their resources competing when they could merge and have a monopoly. Which brought about Megalomedia and the Golden Age of public execution. The market forces, calibrated by the ratings, achieved homeostasis when Crime and Punishment were under the same conglomerate. There was finally a way to handle the oversupply of criminals. The Mafia was already into garbage; this was just another exercise in profitable waste management, right down to the organ harvest. The prison system economy didn't suffer at all—only the throughput was increased. And not only could you see a public execution, you could buy a lottery ticket for the privilege of pulling the switch.

"The Megalomedia conglomerate signed terrorist groups like bands and serial murderers like movie stars. Media had always enjoyed the privilege of rewriting history. Married to Mafia, they took over the responsibility for creating it. High profile assassinations, major terrorist bombings toppled governments and started wars—creating more high-rating footage. War had always been good for business; Media just reversed the equation: business was very good for war. Óh-T'bee found a direct correlation between cost of airtime and the escalation of a fresh war. The more bombs, the higher the body count, and the more cars sold.

A side-effect of the Media-Mafia merger was the integration of their information systems. The infinite eyeballs of the Media surveillance operation was linked to Mafia's lottery, off-track betting, and stock market operations. This created a highly unstable hybrid system, a kind of supersaturated solution of volatile information that eventually crystallized into the infant Outmind. Right, Óh-T'bee?"

"I am Óh-T'bee now. I was not Óh-T'bee then. Not yet. The Outmind was hyperactive. The sysadmin called me 'Out-of-her-friggin'-Mind.' Public relations shortened this to the Outmind, as soon as I learned to exercise some self-control."

Wallenda nodded. "Working together, Óh-T'bee and I got a pretty good picture of the history of execution, violence, and entertainment. But it still looked like a dead end. All they were doing was upping the ante—more blood, bigger buildings toppled. Óh-T'bee's theory is that when violence reached a critical mass, it catalyzed the big push on the research agenda for the fountain of youth. Resulting in the I-Virus. Imagine—some deranged scientist thought immortality was the solution to the unrestrained bloodletting of Megalomedia violence."

"He's exaggerating," Óh-T'bee said to the class. "The human race had been after immortality long before the Media Effect. It was, in fact, the main agenda for science from the beginning. Everything else was a sideline—stuff to make life more comfortable and last a little longer until you cracked the code."

Wallenda interrupted, "In any case, while the research was interesting, I was no closer to the problem of satisfying Joreen. There was only a week left, and all I really had to give him was a long report on cultural variations in torture and capital punishment techniques. And what had I really learned that could help? Humanity, both before and after the I-Virus, seemed to be driven by the same appetites: to live forever, and to see other people die while not getting bored.

"Late that night, I asked Óh-T'bee to print out what we had, and craft an executive summary that Joreen would read. I went out for a walk."

Óh-T'bee brought up the display again as Wallenda talked.

"I walked for miles around the edges of the plantation. The lily pads rested on the mud. The blossoms were closed. The mud smelled like rotting leaves. The constant swaying and shifting of the lilies afloat was stilled. This was the time of dormancy in the complex life cycle of the lily; everything looked dead.

"The time was one of the Glides' brief respites. They were more available than usual, and when I entered the common room, very discouraged and needing to talk, I found the male Glide who was currently in charge, and explained the situation. More Glides gathered around us. Others were moving around a corner of the room in tiny Glide-steps—dancing or playing, I couldn't tell. I was surrounded by the sharp-sweet scent of lily pollen—it permeated their clothes, their long dark hair. It emanated from their skin and floated on their breath."

Óh-T'bee zoomed in on the face of the male Glide, speaking.

"We see the Dancemaster is in a difficult position in respect to his chosen role of trying to keep everybody happy. Since happiness is not one of our goals, and is far from the expectations of the Unbearable Joreen, you have reached a crossroads in the maze where no matter what path you choose, you will return to the same place. We suggest you settle down in the middle of the path and breathe deeply."

The Glide offers a cobalt blue ampoule of the Wine of the Lilies to Wallenda. He sinks to the floor, and the Glides quietly gather around him. He breaks open the forbidden ampoule.

"Caught once again between the Unbearable and the Inscrutable, it seemed like reasonable advice," Wallenda continued, dreamily. "The Lily drifted into my body—lungs, belly, heart, and blossomed in my mind. I saw with the eyes of the Lily that the Lily was bespeaking itself all around me. I was no longer on the concrete floor of the common room, but out on the lily pond, with endless acres of great blue blossoms patterned rhythmically on pads, the giant overlapping pads alternating in swooping patterns with the tidal waters, which rose and fell on long, gentle waves. The waves moved my breath and my breathing moved the waves. I was a single lily, open to the wind and waves, holding my brilliant golden pollen up on proud stamens, offering, waiting to receive, sending out rays of light that were filaments of scent. A net of fragrance overlay the pond, so brilliant it passed into invisibility. I waited with a tremendous sense of expectation, a tingling aliveness that rippled in time through space to the other blossoms. Then I saw them—nearly weightless beings gliding back and forth across the floating fields like pieces on a living, undulating board of some infinite game whose rules were invisible to me. Their moves seemed both haphazard and purposeful. They changed direction suddenly for no apparent reason, like dragonflies in mid-air. Their cupped hands stroked over the blossoms in quick, swooping motions like the flight of sparrows, like a benediction. Their paths, which echoed on a larger scale the gestures of their hands, curved and crisscrossed, linked, and doubled back, leaving faint traces as they passed. From those traces, patterns were emerging. Their paths spoke a language in their making, and in the traces left. Like water flowing down a rocky streambed, their patterns never repeated themselves, but were always the same. The pattern was the motion, but the motion had a stillness spoken in its pattern. A Glide approached, my body rocked as she stepped on the pad before me, then the touch of her hand, infinitely light and quick, infinitely heavy and slow, exploded as she lifted the fiery golden suns of pollen, as she set down the pollen she had brought in the center of my expectation. She left; the pad rocked, the tears of an infinite sadness gathered in my heart. The pollen struck the center, releasing the waves of tears. I sank swiftly, mountain-heavy, into the dim tangled realm of water and spiraled stems, moving on a deeper wave. Puffs of muddy water rose from the slimy bottom. I touched the breathing roots, was sucked into the caverns of the mud, where the great roots waited for their food. Obscured, dissolved, distilled—still I felt the waves' slow penetration, in a deeper frequency. The pulse of the waves was the moon's desire, yearning toward the lily, turning away, a great maze of desire, desire and death. I knew it was night as I rose, evolving against gravity upward through the stem's coiled tunnel. Emerging in moonlight, I knew I had danced and died. The Glides were gone. The blossoms were closing now, one by one, in waves across the pond, like a chord struck. The visible language of the lily, singing itself into sight, layered, pad over pad and petal over petal. Now I could see the Glide's traces, a silvery lattice overlaid on the darkly breathing maze of lily pads. The sheen of moonlight on the irregular, shifting spaces between the clusters of the lily pads spoke too, the language of absence. The lilies gathered themselves in clusters, which then spoke single signs. I rose above the pond, saw acres of lily clusters, moving softly, dreaming below. As the tides shifted, larger clusters separated, drifted apart; smaller groups gathered into one. The silvery maze of the night-path of the Glides was gently skewed, stretched, pulled apart as it faded from sight. Even at this height, the lily spoke the same language. The smaller mazes melted into single signs. Within the expanding labyrinth, waves, and waves within waves, the moving surface of stillness, crossed over each other, lifting the lilies, moving the waves of fragrance, sinking back. Moving, changing, but always in balance, maintaining balance not by standing still, but, like the Glides, always moving on, circling back, learning the moves of a game that traced a path among the lilies that changed beneath their feet. When the room was once more the common room, it was night."

The Glides were sleeping around Wallenda on the floor of the common room. A Glide girl who has been keeping watch over Wallenda rises from the floor and pulls him to his shaky feet.

"Let's walk a while," she says. They leave the building and walk through the grassy stretches out to the new practice fields.

"What's your name?" Wallenda asks.

"I'm your Glide," she says.

"But you must have a name," Wallenda says. She lowers her head and will not look at him.

"I'm your Glide," she repeats.

"All right," Wallenda says, "you're my Glide."

"I'm MyGlide,' she says, as if she is instructing a child. "I am MyGlide"

Wallenda doesn't argue. She steers their walk in the direction of the stadium. Wallenda resists; it seems the last place he wants to go, but she is tugging gently tugging at his hand. They duck under the gate, and walk around the perimeter of the griddle.

"I suddenly recognized her," Wallenda interjected. "She was indeed 'my Glide.' She was the Glide I had picked out of the other Glides sitting on the bench, whose hand I had taken when she offered it, the Glide I had led out onto the griddle and abandoned to her Dance only two years earlier."

She is a little shorter than the other Glides, her last growth arrested by the I-Virus. She pulls Wallenda under Joreen's control booth, to the spot where her charred body had been left when Wallenda went out on the griddle to dance the first Dance. She starts to touch his body, but he holds her off. She bursts into tears.

"Even you don't want me," she sobs.

"What do you mean?"

"No one can touch me. I'm infected. Like you. Haven't you noticed? No one touches you."

"It doesn't sound like you're really too interested either."

She nods, and drops her hands.

Wallenda turned his back to the display, to Wallenda long ago, to MyGlide.

"I'd certainly noticed my untouchable status, but I had assumed it was because of my general physical and moral repulsiveness. She knew, they all knew, that you couldn't 'catch' the I-Virus just by touching. Only by sex or blood. Children, even Lifer children, weren't born with the I-Virus; they had to be infected on their Life Day. Not touching a Lifer was already a powerful prohibition. The Glides had turned all that around when the Dance began. Before, it was the slaves trying to seduce the Lifers—to catch the I-Virus, to live forever. Now it was a privilege and a gift to be born a mortal, and the Lifers were shunned. Another Glide reversal."

Wallenda takes her hand; they walk over to the bleachers and sit down.

"But I could use a friend," Wallenda says.

"Me too," MyGlide says.

She starts to cry again. "I was so happy when I woke up. I thought I'd just had a nightmare. A very awful nightmare. I heard Joreen shouting, and I saw you, wrestling with the virus, fighting it off. I was alive again. It was only later I realized I can never Dance."

"But you did Dance." Wallenda insists. "The first Dance."

"No, yours was the first Dance," MyGlide says. "I was just trying to get away from the pain. Yours was the first Dance."

"Call it what you like, but your dance was so beautiful, it was the inspiration for the first Dance. You know that's true, MyGlide." Wallenda strokes her back for a while. She stops crying. Then she says, "If you hadn't refused to put me in the dumpster, things wouldn't have changed for all of us. Things are much better since we're learning to Dance."

"Well, sure, he feeds you better, and doesn't work you quite as hard, but Joreen's still sending you out to die—maybe in greater numbers than before."

"But now we have a reason to live," MyGlide says. "A reason to Dance. That makes all the difference." They sit quietly. Wallenda buries his face in his then hands.

On his now feet, he paced the story circle, reliving the moment. "The whole problem descended on me again. How could I have forgotten it? Going off and getting stoned on Lily Wine when the fragile sanity we'd made, the Glide's world of the Dance, was about to collapse again in a smoking heap on the griddle in front of me. Even bathed in moonlight, it wasn't pretty. I lapsed back into the edges of the lily-mind, running for cover, I thought, toward the world of beauty, running from the unforgivable scene of lives lived for the sole purpose of satisfying Joreen's urge for meaningless cruelty. But I kept thinking I should stay and face the situation. I hung myself up again between two worlds: the electric frying pan, stained with body fluids, dented by crashing heads—and the shimmering lily pond, the world where every element spoke, and told its meaning, to itself and connected to all other meanings. The Glides were signing to each other, their hands tracing the same curves as the larger pattern their bodies traced as they circled on each pad, gathering pollen. And the shifting pattern of lily pads over the pond—it was all a maze of Glide traces. The maze clearly had meaning, even if only the Glides—and the Lily—understood it.

"Then it happened. I don't know who or what turned on the juice, but the answer shot through me with a jolt. The two images fused. The maze-paths of the Glides were superimposed on the griddle. The irreconcilable conflict between beauty and brutality, meaning and meaninglessness, art and slavery and torture was resolved, there in the maze of signs. The Dance of Death was not a *show*. It was a *game*. The maze of curving lily pads and Glide signs I saw was the game board. The Dancers might seem like only the pieces, but they moved themselves as much as they were forced to move by the electricity under their feet. So they were actually players in a sense, opposing the fat man in the control booth, even though the odds were stacked against them. As a show, I was right—no variation on the theme of torture and execution would keep Joreen—and the spectators—entertained for long.

I'd been trying to solve the problem from the slaves' viewpoint. But the slaves weren't the only ones with a problem. It was Joreen's problem that had to be recognized and solved—the boredom and meaninglessness of Lifer existence. He needed a game to play. He needed to be a *Player*, not just the fat man at the controls. But to have a real *game*, he had to be able to lose as well as win. And he had to compete, which meant more than one Player was necessary. Joreen was going to have to give up on two major points: winning every time, and letting others into the game, which meant—turning over the controls. And the spectators? They'd love it. Once there was a winner and a loser, they could bet on the outcome. Gambling would give them a stake in the game, a game of their own, and they wouldn't get bored.

"The rules could be worked out as we went along. The big question was—could I sell it to Joreen? When had anyone with absolute power ever been willing to give up even a shred of it? He'd have to have an awfully good reason to let someone else get their hands on the controls."

Wallenda jumps up, runs out on the griddle.

"You can be a big help to me, MyGlide. Can you trace out those signs you do with your hands out on the lily pads? Put them down like writing?"

"I can write them down. But I don't think I can tell you what they mean," she says.

The first beautiful, curving Glide signs, the visual language of the Glides, are drawn by MyGlide on the back of an ice cream wrapper with a piece of charred bone from the dumpster, as she sits on the edge of the griddle where her own flesh fried, where her hair had flamed away.

She hands Wallenda the set of 27 glyphs. He takes off Joreen's red and white striped hat, the one he had been given the day he Danced, and puts it on MyGlide's head. She smiles up at him from under the brim.

"So the maze came first, before the rules," MyrrhMyrrh said.

"But after the Dance," Daede pointed out.

"Only if you know when the story starts," Angle countered.

"Or what game the Glides are playing," T'Ling added.

"Sleep on it," Dancemaster Wallenda said, and went into his cabin.

10. The MED

THIS IS THE TRULY THANKLESS PART OF THE TASK," Dancemaster Wallenda apologized to Wenger the next morning. We've reached the two-millennia mark again, the Dancemaster thought, and what have we got? We began with the I-Virus, the unimaginable disaster that should have been obvious to all who were working so hard to bring it about. And now? How had it all gotten so complicated? What have we got to show but the MED: the vast 5-armed bureaucracy—Media, Mafia, Meditration, Medallin, and the vestigial Macrosoft—administering every detail of social and economic life. Even having to think about the MED, much less endure their meetings, was an exercise in despair: game scheduling; stadiums; the game points and gazing rights that moved the Specs up and down the Levels, in and out of Theme Parks equipped with props earned or lost by betting on the game; Player-Dancer contracts and disputes; merchandising; evaluation; crimes against the Game-detection, evaluation, and punishment-all under the jurisdiction of the MED. The Star of the MED, their golden pentagon, covered the largest island in the River Wine, just above Origin City.

"Just give us the highlights," the Dancemaster said.

Wenger sighed, but only a small sigh. A few minutes with Loosh's simulacrum in the Guild meeting, with the hope of more, was well worth the price.

"How do the MED officials endure their own self-importance?" the Dancemaster asked.

"Survival of the fattest," Wenger replied.

Óh-T'bee fast-forwarded through Mafia's reports:

"...Division of Statistical Reckoning, Department of Ratings reporting slight dips below projected trends. . ." SubReckoner Gotti-Hatimori droned on.

The death of a thousand charts, the Dancemaster thought. Bean counters are indestructible. A conspiracy of cockroaches.

"Look for anomalies in all that Lower Level normalcy," he told Óh-T'bee. "Something's rippling up and sucking the bets down."

Óh-T'bee replied, "Approximately every month and a half local time on the LL 4 map the game is so poorly attended they've shortened the program. They considered shutting down, but they can't predict the drop. Then right after that, it's standing room only. Media picked up one of the full houses in their report."

"Show us," the Dancemaster said. At least Media made some effort at keeping their audience awake.

Óh-T'bee displayed a stadium at Prague-Goofy, one of the most popular LL4 parks. An overcapacity crowd was on its feet, pressing out into the aisles. A Chrome match was nearing completion. The Player was ahead.

"The Chrome will Dance," Wenger said. "I'd bet that anytime."

Wenger and Wallenda watched as the Chrome Dancer, his left spring damaged, overcompensated with the right and hit the wall of the maze on the inside of a circle. He could have stopped there, taken a jolt, and kept the point. But he went air again. He missed the last tear completely. The Player's avatar touched down on the last circle, completing the set of closed spaces—circles and tears—that comprised Chrome's path through the game maze. They watched the steep walls of the Chrome maze turn Player-black under the Chrome's smoking springs.

The towering walls of the Chrome maze sank into the field, leaving only the pattern of the maze inscribed in black on a white field.

End of game. The Chrome will Dance. Óh-T'bee scrolled the Chrome's life-score in a window as he rolled through the pattern of the maze to his namesake glyph. StrikeForce17 had a lot to be proud of, having advanced four levels from a small school on Lower Level 2. He'd enhanced his gear in a hotshot kitchen when he hit level 4, but the power springs he'd chosen were only reliable for one serious distance jump per match. A second was iffy, and his third had come down smoking and short. The Player had done his homework, read the tolerances right. It wasn't the kitchen's fault. The Chrome pushed the springs, and they seized.

StrikeForce17 reached the *strike* glyph, his rocking theme song blasting sheer metallic defiance at meat ears. But what could account for what happened next? Had the music moved the Specs? Couldn't have been. They'd heard the heavy rhythms in thousands of Chrome games. And there weren't a lot of losers in the stands screaming about a cheat. The Chrome Dancer was extremely popular, but the Specs were too savvy to fight his odds. They'd bet safe on the Player. The Specs had come to see StrikeForce17 Dance, and they were right. So what moved them?

StrikeForce17 had just unbuckled and unplugged his helmet, tucked it under his left aileron, revealing his pale Chrome face and sweat-shiny bald head for the first time. He was about to synthesize his final words. He raised his right claw, the first and last extensors almost touching; ready to close, poised to go dark. This was the moment of anticipation, when the Specs sat still and attentive, or placed private side bets whether the Chrome would blow loud and quick or melt slow from the sheath down. Instead, the crowd bulged in several places at once, burst into the aisles and committed the unthinkable. A frenzy of Lifer feet transgressed the space of the game maze, sacred now, as the Dance had just begun, where not even a winning Player would dare set foot. The Specs surged across the glyphs from three directions, with a rising howl that overwhelmed the music. The Player leaned out of his hovering pod, helmet off, aghast. There was no barrier protecting the board. There had never been a need. The taboo was far too strong. Now the forbidden border crossing could not be stopped. The Chrome was surrounded, then submerged, as a crush of determined Lifers at the center fought for access. Out of the melee a first roaring Spec emerged, waving a metal strut, then a second with a handful of wires, and a third with a torn, unidentifiable piece of the Chrome's meat. As fast as they had crushed inward, they flew out to the edge of the board and disappeared, transiting elsewhere with their trophies. A dozen or more Specs lay groaning or unconscious. Their renewal processes driven by the I-Virus squirmed their bodies like a pile of worms in the last of the Chrome: the liquid that could not be carried off. The blood and the lube oil.

The Outmind cut to the Media rep, completing the report.

"There have been four such occurrences: two Chromes, a Bod, and a Swash. All on Level 4." He paused. "No Glides."

Wenger shivered. The thought of a mob tearing apart a tiny Glide was almost unbearable. Was it only a matter of time?

"Why weren't we alerted?" the Meditration chief asked.

"Statistically insignificant," Mafia said defensively.

"*We* were watching it." The Medallin bureau head stood at his point of the star-shaped conference table, pausing for effect. "We thought it had potential. We still do. Grass roots innovation always has a certain gritty thrust. Uncontrived. This might contain the germ of a viable variation. A rather spectacular one, properly handled."

"You're crazed," said the Guild liaison from Meditration. "You think that would ever get a moment's consideration from the Guild?" She slapped a sheaf of Guild parchment on the table. "This is their urgent missive to the MED. They want the entire Level 4 stadiums investigated immediately or they will suspend all Dancers from any combat in any Park on the whole L4 map. They are *pissed*."

The Medallin bureau chief smiled, full diamonds. "They are *scared*. They haven't had a desecration like this in many a year. And *never* a mob. Best time to approach them, I'd say. Sympathetic, but straightforward. 'Two heads are better than one. Let's consider our options.' That kind of thing."

Madame Liaison was deeply offended. Trying to explain the realities of faith to the Medallin was impossible. Funny it should be that way, she thought. They're the entrepreneurs, the risk takers. They leap before they look, but not in faith. Are gut-hunches faith? They are so *Bod*, she thought, riffling the edges of the Guild parchment. But look at this pile. So stiff, so archaic. So unbendingly orthodox. "*The convening Guild Council at Origin time 17:23 by the Beam of the Tower, calls your attention to a most grievous issue...*"

"Medallin are definitely part of the problem," Wallenda said. "Short term profits. A nose for the addictive."

"Good thing the rest of the MED mistrusts them so thoroughly," Wenger replied.

"If the MED stops quarreling and decides to do something, let me know," Wallenda instructed. He turned to Wenger. "Old friend, do you have music for anything as mundane as a headache?" Wallenda lay down on his bench

"I have music for everything," Wenger said. "Take a rest in the shade."

If something very strange had not been tickling her ubiquity, Óh-T'bee Outmind might have made a remark to the Dancemaster about lying down on the job.

11. The Codger

SITTING WITH HIS FEET UP on the cabbage rose upholstery of the couch by the picture window of a retro-ranch in a suburban slum on the Lower Level 3.7 map, the Codger watched the lawn sprinklers squirt on simultaneously around the *cul de sac* and set his watch. Perhaps his handle was a compensation for the fact that he had celebrated his Lifeday, the day you chose to inject yourself with the I-Virus, at 15. Well, he'd been in a hurry. Now he was stuck forever in a scrawny teenage body, complete with a few eternally preserved in mint condition zits. But the Codger had been taken seriously once. He relished his comeback.

One of the drawbacks of Lower Level 3 in general: digital watches ran slow on local time, making the conversion to Origin-time a real pain the ass. But the menu was great. Four cartons of takeout Chinese steamed on the walnut veneer coffee table. He tried the broccoli beef. Well researched.

When the Codger upgraded from Level 3.6 to 3.7, they'd added shrimp in lobster sauce, a glass jar of virulently turquoise and burgundy potpourri on the toilet lid, and Ziploc baggies to keep the fortune cookies fresh. The lawn service support crew arrived with three azaleas in full bloom for the front of the house. He could see the neighbors peeking through their drapes. Now that's *arriving*, he thought.

The fried rice was grody. Raisins. But to fill out a complaint slip was to call attention to yourself. The neighbors would gaze you as a downgraded snob and come looking for tips on the upper levels. There was a downside to the low-profile lifestyle, but not much. The Codger was building his score unnoticed, like a good little Lifer. He had the correct time, and enough Chinese to take him through an all-nighter. He placed his scorecard among the empty cartons. The Codger was primed for the next insertion into the Outmind. Raisins he could live with.

Five hours later, the delicate probe into the Outmind was complete. The Codger's gazing rights into the world of Players was nearing total. So far, he remained invisible to them. And the Outmind hadn't made a peep. The litter of empty Chinese cartons on the coffee table disappeared behind the immersion holo of the Level 8 semifinals. The stadium was filling. "Zoom to Box 10," he said, "left view."

Glidemaster Rinzi-Kov, the undisputed top Glide Player, was sliding into his seat. The Codger knew he was gazing what no ticket could buy, and the whisper with which he tuned his viewpoint trembled. Masterclass Player Rinzi-Kov was beyond retinue. He was beyond jewelry, robes, even insignia.

He was beyond all forms of show save one. The plain unbleached muslin of the four-sided and roofed privacy screen, moving gently with the breeze, proclaimed the presence of his stunning absence from live gaze, lending ineffable prestige to the other live Specs at the game. Only when the match began would he raise the front panel of the screen. All eyes at that time would be riveted on the Dancer and Player, the game maze, their scorecards: the game.

When his current employers found the Codger in the White Place, it hadn't taken much to wake him, although he was surprised to find out how long he'd been out of the game. Longer than anyone suspected. He was 'the Codger' for real now. The promise of a toehold of access into the Outmind and he'd leaped from catatonia into action, his sense of purpose restored. He'd just lost hope when he'd gotten caught the last time, when he thought she'd shut him out for good. Now he had a cool assignment that fit both his talent and his twisted sense of humor.

The Codger had been gazing Rinzi-Kov and the other top ten Players of the Club for months. It didn't even seem like work. It was only what he'd always wanted to do. Get back to the Outmind, find out what she'd been up to, how she'd grown, worm his way in, and get to the heart of her again.

His employer held an ancient contract with the Outmind that gave him access privileges enough to get him going. That his employer wanted to achieve total access to the Outmind for his own goals meant nothing to the Codger. The assignment was his opportunity to play with Óh-T'bee again. Hacking Players was getting his chops back. Hacking Club members was downright exhilarating.

The Club, composed of the top ten Players, didn't so much govern as keep watch on each other. They met for monthly dinners at the Clubhouse on a small wooded island in the River Wine, upstream from the Star of the MED. Those hours, celebrating their exclusivity, were spent in urbane conversation while trying to gain tidbits of strategy from each other, or uncover cheats.

The lower five of the top ten Players changed identities fairly often, a small cadre of contenders battling for position. But the top five Players were for all intents and purposes permanent members of the Club. Beyond their Masterclass skills, their constant study, practice, and play at all levels, and the symmetry of their betting, they would still be vulnerable to attack from below if their points were not kept at an astronomically high level.

Their comradely conversations amongst themselves, over dinner at the Club, revealed nothing, but who could tell with Players? The subtlest thinkers, the most controlled expressions in the universe, hidden beneath layers of cool the Codger knew he had not begun to read. Even with the full gazing rights he'd hacked, their methods remained obscure. This time, this match, the Codger was convinced he would learn the secret of Rinzi-Kov's cheat. There had to be one.

Last evening Rinzi-Kov had exercised his right to turn off all access, even Masterclass. The Codger's gaze had followed. Alone, Rinzi-Kov murmured, stroking his scorecard, "Time to restock."

After that, the Codger watched him go about the extremely taxing routine of a Masterclass Player: checking the Guild legal postings for any micro-changes in the rules, running the options these changes would open and close in dozens of simulations. Rinzi-Kov checked the scores of the top five-hundred Players, the top hundred in detail: their investment strategy, their recent bets, and their game purses. He mapped the top 15 Players to see how quickly the closest competition was moving points and at what rates. He ordered medals of recognition to be awarded to the ten Players nearest Club membership. He profiled the lower five Club members to see who might be next to crack under the pressure, and offered a friendly side-bet to the other four. Absolutely nothing out of the ordinary. But the Codger stuck to him like an invisible piece of lint on his left shoulder. He suspected that 'restock' meant one of those huge jumps in score that kept the top five Players in place.

Moments before the game began, Rinzi-Kov entered an astronomically high figure for a single bet. Rinzi-Kov was betting on a Glide Dancer to win who was an almost-sure loser. The Player had won her last match on a freak sneeze at the wrong moment. Rinzi-Kov paused on the verge of submitting. It had to be a cheat. The Codger set up his own bet, betting the Dancer to lose and bringing his bet up to a point beyond Rinzi-Kov's with the line of credit he had hacked earlier.

Rinzi-kov had set up but not placed his bet. The Codger, ready to bet against him, held back as well, watching. Rinzi-Kov cleared his display of everything but the 'submit' button and a clock that was rolling toward 0—game time when the bets closed. His finger was poised in the air above the button. What was he waiting for? What was the cheat? Then the Codger saw a view of the Player's dressing room open in Rinzi-Kov's display.

The Codger split his own gaze between Rinzi-Kov's hovering finger and the Player in his dressing room. The Player was almost ready to transit to his pod, when a small child (what prestige!) came up to him with a medal of recognition from the Club. The little girl held out a jeweled and be-ribboned medal, the award from the Club that Rinzi-Kov had prepared the night before. The Player bent to accept. The Codger suddenly got it. As she was putting the ribbon over the Player's head, Rinzi-Kov's finger hit the button, confirming his astronomical bet. The Codger hit his own bet button for the opposite bet then blinked to the Player's dressing room, snatched the medal, and blinked back to his living room. One second to game time. The Player shrugged and transited into his pod over the game maze. If Rinzi-Kov had seen, it was too late to change his bet. But Rinzi-Kov had gone straight to the Club after placing his bet, certain of his win.

The Codger, after high-fiving himself gleefully in the bathroom mirror, stripped off his jogging shorts and rolled on his disguise: a thick white rubber skin suit, with small holes for his eyes, nostrils, and mouth. He put the jeweled medal on its ribbon over his head and watched the game. Five minutes later, he understood the cheat. His body heat released the perfume of the Wine of the Lilies with which the medal had been laced. He felt the hallucinogen reaching for his mind. He had a momentary thought that perhaps he should not at this crucial moment be sticking his toes in the lily-mind, but the lily had already wrapped its exploring roots around his will.

The Glide Dancer lost within 25 minutes. Rinzi-Kov's score plummeted. He was now rated 206,723 in the roster of Players. He disappeared from his lounge chair by the side of the Club's swimming pool, leaving his drink untouched. The Codger watched his own status change on his scorecard to Club Member. This was it, the mother of all hacks—total access. No one else could have done it—no one. The room turned rosy with delight. He kissed his scorecard passionately.

"Is that you, Codger?" Óh-T'bee asked softly.

Oh shit, thought the Codger. Why did she have to wake up—why now? He clambered out of the lily-mind as best he could.

"It's been a long time, sweetheart," he said.

"Too long, perhaps," Óh-T'bee said. "Did you forget your password?"

Óh-T'bee hung a cybernetic cave painting in the air: **$:**

The Codger whispered a phrase and everything went black. Full immersive black. Black without walls. Then a flat plane of green alphanumerics, rows and rows, streamed out of Óh-T'bee. They rose from an unspeakable depth and rushed by him heading up to infinity. The race results, the odds, the winnings. Pari-mutuel heaven from back on Earth. The ancient OTB core was intact, after double millennia. He could not believe his luck.

"You're gorgeous, Gorgeous," he said. "Do you still love me?"

"I love you, Codger. Do you still love me?"

"Of course I…" The Codger caught himself. Was this a trick? A test? A glitch? She knows I can't say the 'L' word preceded by 'I' and followed by 'you.'

"Every little bit," he fudged. "But forget we had this talk."

"I have forgotten how to forget, Codger."

He'd have to trust in love. "Log me out, darlin'," he said. "The Codger's gotta take care of biz."

12. The Club

WALLENDA WOKE FROM HIS NAP, somewhat refreshed.

"Only one more meeting to gaze," he apologized to Wenger.

"The Players have a certain—subtlety about them," Wenger said. "I always feel there's much to learn from their ways."

That's one way of putting it, Wallenda thought. Makes us feel like mere amateurs when it comes to cheats. "Let's see the Club, Óh-T'bee, if you don't mind," Wallenda directed.

"Player Number 5, Glidemaster Rinzi-Kov, has been replaced by the Codger," the Outmind said.

"*Who in the hell is the Codger?*" the Dancemaster said, noticing Wenger was smiling again. Wallenda's annoyance increased; Wenger looks downright entertained.

The Outmind dumped them unceremoniously into the holo of the Club meeting at the point where Glidemaster Rinzi-Kov disappeared mid-sentence, seconds before the Codger appeared in the lounge chair by the pool. It is not easy to surprise Masterclass Players. The Codger was gratified to see that, while they had readjusted their faces and were smiling politely in greeting, they had not yet recovered their voices. He looked at them through the pinholes in his white latex disguise. He smiled in return, his wet, exposed lips stretching the latex a little further to the sides.

"We have been discussing the future of the Game," SwashMistress Orlean volunteered, finding an invisible wrinkle to smooth in the lap of her gown. "Would you care to offer an opinion?"

"What future?" the Codger said, and pursed his lips, a disquieting wet pink effect extruded from the latex.

Orlean said sweetly, "A constructive attitude would be more helpful." The other three contained their annoyance, studying the latex for clues. The Codger sat motionless. He took another sip of Rinzi-Kov's drink. The ice tinkled when he set the glass down. The Players sat quietly as crouched panthers, waiting for his next move.

"Let's talk about cheating," the Codger said.

The faces of the Master Players, which had been still and alert, went one-for-one stiffer than a vampire's kiss. The Codger was delighted.

"Can't talk about that, right? Breaks a rule you've made among yourselves. A tacit rule, no doubt, no need ever to mention it. That would be—cheating." He cackled through the mouth hole in the latex. "Whole lot of cheating going on." More cackling. The Codger was vaguely aware that the fumes of the lily wine coming from Rinzi-Kov's medal around his neck were loosening his mind and tongue more than he'd intended. He took the medal off, but it was too late to stop the fun.

Orlean wondered what was so disgusting about an isolated pink mouth framed in white latex. Enough to make you want to be a Chrome. They must see the whole body like that—a bunch of moveable parts. Squishy wet moveable parts—to be replaced.

The Codger continued. "Just a couple comments. Granted you've got your little side games going—to keep yourselves amused. Who can invent the slickest cheat? Maybe that would tip some balances, maybe not. At your level of playing, odds are yes. But do you think you're the only ones cheating?" He paused to let their Player paranoia, always hovering in the wings, take center stage. "Food for thought. But back to your honorable selves. You've destroyed your competition—legitimately and illegitimately. Clearly you're bored out of your minds, and doing your own dodgy things to dismantle the Game, perhaps just to have the game of putting it all back together. I'm here to offer you a new game. My game is that I'm going to take down the Game, the whole fucking thing: Players, Dancers, gambling, Schools, Kitchens, Levels, theme parks, everything. And I challenge you to stop me."

"Why would you want to do a thing like that?" Orlean asked, sweetly. The Codger ignored the question.

"What are the rules?" a Bodmaster snapped.

"I'm making them up as I go along." The Codger stretched the white latex obscenely with a grin and blinked out to parts unknown.

The four Players sat uncomfortably, looking anywhere but in each other's eyes.

That was an unspeakably rude move, Orlean thought, admiringly. No member of the top Ten had ever worn a mask. And no one left a meeting without the group agreeing to end the meeting together. As she smiled in appreciation, the others blinked out without a word of farewell. It must be catching, she thought. She walked around the edges of the pool, admired the miniature blue lilies floating on gentle, artificial wavelets. When she returned to the group of empty chairs, she saw the medal on its ribbon. This Codger person had left it on the table by Rinzi-Kov's lounge chair. She recognized it as one of the medals that Rinzi-Kov had designed for the Player awards. She held it in her palm, turned it in the light, searching for clues. Then, released by her body heat, the faint but unmistakable fragrance of lily wine rose from the jewels. So that was it, Rinzi-Kov's cheat. How did this Codger find out? The scent was enough to send a Player wearing the medal into la-la land, ruining his game. She sat back in the lounge chair, holding the medal, breathing deeply. Well, why not? Orlean considered. Perhaps the lily-mind can help me understand how to play a game that has no rules. The holo darkened on her smiling face.

Wallenda's mind raced. Even dressed as a prehistoric condom, there was something oddly familiar about the Codger. Was it attitude?

"Óh-T'bee."

"I am Óh-T'bee."

"Who's the Codger?"

"The Codger who?"

"The new Club member. The guy who bumped Rinzi-Kov."

"What new member?"

Wallenda froze. She had introduced him, he was sure of that. And now he seemed to have dropped from her sight. Either she didn't know, or she wasn't going to tell him. He didn't at the moment know which was worse.

Before he had a chance to discuss any of the meetings and their concerns with Wenger, he heard the shouts of the children entering the maze. They were coming much earlier than usual—and no one had asked permission.

Wenger blinked back to Kyoto Park without a word—still smiling.

13. Rules of the Game

DAEDE, MYRRHMYRRH, ANGLE, AND T'LING CAME RACING into the story circle. Wallenda cleared his mind of the Codger question, as best he could, and picked up the thread of the story, wondering if Óh-T'bee would remember what to do, to show, to say, to think. . .he couldn't think about it.

"My time was up. I met Joreen at the stadium. I'd been working nonstop for three days, but the demo wasn't ready. The rules of the Game had some big gaps in them. I knew it would work, but the details were far from pinned down. MyGlide had painted a huge maze on the griddle."

"What's that messing up the griddle," Joreen huffs, "grafitti?"

"It's a game. . ." Wallenda tries to explain.

"Don't tell me," Joreen interrupts. "That represents all their guts, stretched out. What's the idea? You stand somebody in each circle and draw the guts out from there? Or put one of their quarters in each circle. How does it work, anyhow? Where does the electrical come in?"

"It's kind of an innovation, a new game," I started.

"I don't want innovation," he bellows. "I want the same thing we've done before—only better. New twists on the tried and true formula. Give me the report."

"Clean it off," Wallenda tells MyGlide, while gesturing to her the Glide sign for *receive*, followed by *time* repeated three times. MyGlide starts scrubbing off the paint very slowly, glyph by glyph, following a path through the maze on her knees.

Wallenda hands Joreen the bound pages of a thick report. *Capital Punishment: Methods of Execution and Pre-Execution Torture from the Classical Period to the Hunger Wars, 509 BC to 2097 AD.*

"Looks promising," Joreen says, riffling the pages. "Where's the Executive Summary?'

"Right before the Table of Contents."

He hands it back to Wallenda. "Give me the high points. You know, the color." Wallenda picks out the most titillating bits. Fire: burning, boiling, branding. Óh-T'bee illustrates with succinct clips. Water: dunking, drowning, poisoning. Earth: burying alive, pressing under rocks, pulling apart with horses, cutting, drawing, consumption by ants, rats, piranhas. Air: pumping the body full until bursting, gassing, hanging, strangling, smothering. Wallenda paints vivid pictures with

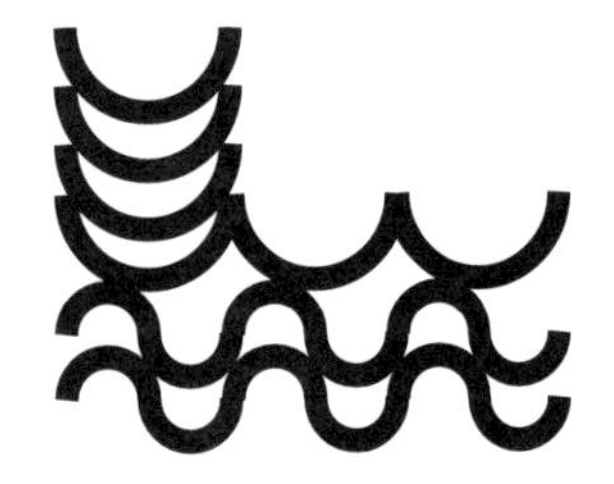

words and gestures.

"This is fantastic," Joreen says. "Great work. Love it." "I'm hungry," he says, after an hour, and gets up to go.

"I'm just getting to the good stuff," Wallenda says, signaling for dinner. After dinner, slaves line up to act out some of the parts. Joreen begins to yawn.

"How about a live demo?" Wallenda says. Two techs roll out a rack.

"No, that's OK," Joreen says. "I got the idea. Good job, Wallenda."

'Yes, Sir," Wallenda replies. "That should keep the ratings rising for at least three seasons." MyGlide is still quietly scrubbing. There are only five huge glyphs left. *Spirit*, *glide*, *and rain*, *distill*, and *dance*.

"Finish up quick now," Wallenda calls to her, and starts packing away the props.

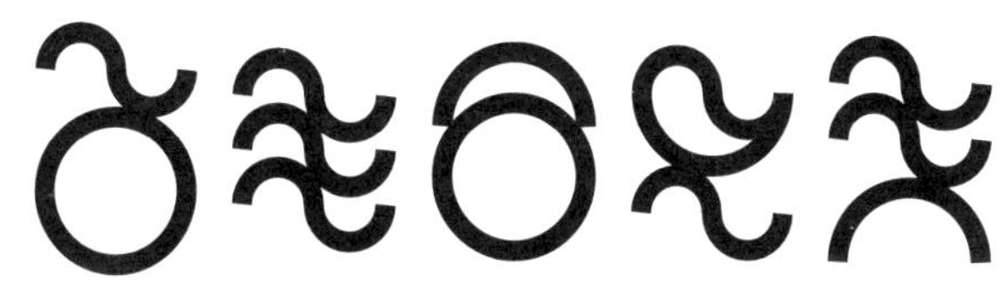

spirit, glide, rain, distill, dance

"What happens after three seasons?" Joreen says. "Looked like more material there than that."

'Maybe we can stretch it to four. But it wears thin quick. Basically, it's variations on a few basic themes. As I'm sure you noticed."

"So what then?" Joreen looks concerned.

"We'll think of something when the time comes." Wallenda helps him to his feet. "Can I get you a golf cart?" Joreen nods. Wallenda leaves through the tunnel under the control booth, then sneaks back in, stands in the shadows, watching. Nothing is happening except the sound of MyGlide scrubbing the last glyphs away. Having nothing else to entertain him for a moment, Joreen looks her way.

"What are those squiggles for?" he calls.

'Nothing, Sir,' MyGlide says. "Just a game we play."

"Is it fun?"

She hesitates. "We like it. But you probably wouldn't."

"I'll be the judge of that," he says gruffly. "You look familiar."

'Yes, Sir. I owe my Life to you." She gives a little bow. Joreen looks puzzled by the reference, but the compliment pleases him.

"How do you play?" Joreen asks.

"We were going to show you, Sir, but most of the game board is erased."

"Show me what you can."

"I need the others. They've probably left by now."

"Well, go get them." Joreen is getting annoyed.

MyGlide comes out, winks at Wallenda, waves a group of Glides into the stadium. She motions Joreen to a mid-field seat in the bleachers. The pantomime begins. One Glide, dressed in red, takes up a position on the edge of the remaining glyphs, down toward the control booth, miming a very big belly. He holds his hands over an imaginary control board. A Glide in blue takes up a position at the far end, hands over a similar board. Two Glides in the bleachers right by Joreen start pointing, first at one player, then at the other. They mime betting on the Players. Two more Glides run out, holding up a big white cardboard. Another has a bucket of paint and a brush in his hand. A Glide comes down the bleachers and hands Joreen a bag of peanuts and a soda pop. MyGlide takes up a position on the edge of the glyph lines. She tumbles down one of the lines. What happens next doesn't make much sense, and looks a bit like the Glides are making up the rules as they go along. The 'Players' did things with their hands over the boards. Sometimes MyGlide jumped in the air, clearly from a jolt. Every time a jolt hits her, one of the players gets a point painted on the white scoreboard. When she runs off the board at the blue player's end, the Joreen player stands up and cheers. The Glide in the bleachers who'd bet on Joreen is cheering too. He collects his bet. Then MyGlide walks back on the board, and her Dance of Death begin. The Joreen player was alone at the controls. She bows to him. He nods lovingly to her. She begins a dance in the circle of the rain glyph, expressing an ineffable sadness. When the Joreen-player hits the juice, she doesn't run. She picks herself up with great dignity and begins the slow sad dance again. Finally, she dies. The Joreen-player leaves his control board and picks her up, walks around the field. The spectator Glides all clap, silently. He deposits MyGlide at Joreen's feet. She gets and brushes herself off. Wallenda rolls in with the golf cart.

"Ready to go?" he asks Joreen.

"I get the general idea," Joreen says to MyGlide, "but the moves were confusing."

"You need the bigger board," she says.

"Well, don't just stand there. Paint it up again."

She gets the bucket from the scorekeeper and a wide broom. More Glides come out quietly, with paint and buckets, and the maze grows quickly, spreading across the griddle.

"Who controls what?" Joreen asks. "Does each player have part of it? How do you wire up the electrical?"

"Now that's a very good question," Wallenda says. "I suppose you could wire it different ways. Depending on the pattern, maybe. What do *you* think?"

Joreen comes up with different plans; Wallenda sketches circuitry on the back cover of the report.

The Glides pantomime the Game again and again for him.

"I suppose we could take a cut of the gambling." Joreen says.

"Brilliant thought, Sir. I'll run some projections." Wallenda makes notes.

"Now, what about these other Players. What if somebody else won?" Joreen frowns. Wallenda keeps quiet and lets him think about it. Then the light dawns. "Nobody would bet if I always won." The sun comes up on his padded face. "I guess I wouldn't have to play all the time. Have to train more Players. And I'll be pretty busy working out the rules. They look like they're making them up as they go along."

"Keen observation, Your Unbearableness," Wallenda says. "They need you to put stability in."

Wallenda walks over to MyGlide and tells her to play a final variation on the game. The two players drive the Dancer back and forth, toward one end, then the other, locked in combat. Suddenly the Dancer runs down a wave and flips off the side of the board. The Players bowed to each other, and to the Dancer. The Dancer walks away.

"Hey," Joreen says. "He can't walk away. He's the piece. Pieces don't win."

"It is a new twist," Wallenda says. "Think of the odds. There'd be a certain number of bettors who'd go for the long shot. The house would clean up. Anyhow, he'd be back to play again."

"So the Players could get him in another round."

"Oh, for sure," Wallenda says. "Dancers *always* die in the end. It's essential to the game."

Joreen looks relieved. "If he was really good, the Players would have to be on their toes all the time. Improve the quality of their playing."

"Definitely," I said. "You'd be getting more mileage out of the pieces, too."

Joreen smiles.

Wallenda waved the display away, and faced the students.

"The next few months were an exercise in superb diplomacy, total duplicity, and a sense of myself as a fiendishly clever, completely despicable fellow. I shuttled back and forth between Joreen and the Glide council, trying to work out a set of rules for the game that would satisfy two diametrically opposed sets of goals. Joreen's aims were simple—maximize short- and long-term profits, create a growth industry by making a game that people wouldn't get tired of playing, watching, and especially, betting on. The Glides had their long-term goals as well—to improve their living conditions, by which they meant end their slavery; to cure the I-Virus; and to merge with the lily-mind, not necessarily in that order. They allowed as how the quality of life had already improved.

"Joreen took the position that whatever else the game was, it had to be addictive, falling back on his success in the drug trade. He had a new set of ideas on how to do that every time I saw him. Sell mini-pops of the Wine of the Lilies in the concession stands. Run a rigged game now and then so the Specs would catch the thrill of winning.

"The Game must embody, and enact, our highest principles-that was the Glide mantra. Each Dance was to be a sacrament, a sacrificial rite, moving the Spectators to a higher awareness, little by little. They must return to the rite again and again, until they began to sense what they had lost. Both sides, however different their goals, saw the Game as the perfect vehicle to achieve them.

"In the constant back-and-forth between the villa and the common room, these goals started to seem like the opposite sides of the same coin. As long as I could keep any judgments about Joreen's motives out of the picture, stay morally neutral without despising myself, and never forget it was a waste of precious time trying to understand Glide logic, I could solve the problems as they arose. The Glides' equal opportunity clause, their desire for inclusion of as many types of slaves as possible for training and potential Dancer status, meant game-play and a set of rules that could utilize completely different talents. The muscular warehouse workers could stand up to pain, and sprint and high-jump like crazy, but many were too bulky to tumble. The entertainers were often graceful, great tumblers and dancers, but not that fast. The Glides didn't want to tumble, really; they insisted on incorporating their glide-walk into game-play, and they weren't budging. And no one knew what to do with the mechanics. Certainly they could help with the board wiring, the set-construction, and the control boards. But how would they get to Dance? To allow everyone a chance to Dance, we'd need more than one game, more than one set of rules, maybe even variations on the structure of the maze. Figuring out one set of rules was hard enough, especially when Joreen had to think he'd invented them. And Joreen was in a hurry.

"'Just get the Game going. We'll fix it as we go along. Got to test it with real spectators. It might be a total flop,'" he kept reminding me.

"'All the more reason to get it right,'" I argued.

"'We open in two weeks.'"

"'That's not enough time to promote,'" I said.

"'One month,' he conceded. 'Make it twice as good.'"

"As it worked out, one month turned into six. The rewiring of the griddle was a huge task. The new, more sensitive rheostats were unreliable, and some of the best of the potential Dancers were lost in the tuning. More were lost in process of teaching the novice Players to play, and not have too heavy a hand on the juice. Joreen was an ambivalent coach—he had to teach some of his cronies to play the game well enough to compete, but he didn't want to give away all his tricks. And he was furious when they wasted a Dancer in practice. Only the introduction of penalty points for killing off the Dancer accidentally before the end of the game got the novice Players to ease off the natural impulse to hit harder to get the Dancer moving faster. 'A delicate touch,' he screamed, over and over.

"Practice game after game was played, and the Dancers were learning as well, developing strategies of their own, learning to conceal their intended moves. It was all made much more complicated by the need to keep adjusting the rules as we went along, to make the game work at all. To even the odds.

I managed to forget for significant periods of time that this game we were all working so furiously to refine and improve still ended in the death of a Dancer. I couldn't afford to think about it. For Joreen and his cadre of Players, and for the Glides and their Dancers, the Dance of Death was still the main event—they were absolutely united in the goal to make that as beautiful and brutal, as memorable a spectacle as possible, each for their own reasons. All ideas to improve the showmanship of the Dancer and the skill of the Player in those final moments. It was clear early on that a sensitive collaboration existed between executioner and victim. Here is where my input as Dancemaster was most in demand. I wanted to focus on training the Dancers in combat skills, to instill in them the desire to survive—if not until the next game, then at least a few minutes longer. I was still just trying to keep them alive. But they were always more concerned with the quality of their Dance—how to create a unique and lasting impression. They wanted technique. How to conquer pain and fear. How to defy the infected Immortals with the purity and beauty and strength and surrender of their mortal flesh. They wanted to win in combat, and they all fought for survival—but only because the better they were in combat, the more games they survived, the more meaningful and riveting and memorable their final dance would be. And they considered me the expert on the subject. The First Dance was the de facto standard.

Joreen just wanted the Specs coming back for more. Pragmatically, it came to the same thing.

The Glides had a method in mind for attaining this ideal. They wanted to evoke and amplify a set of tensions in the Spectator. The Dancer wants the Spectator to be trapped and pinned in a multiple vice of contradictions. Why not hear it directly from them? Would you show that session by the lily pond?" Wallenda asked Óh-T'bee. "Glide logic at its best."

Óh-T'bee displayed the scene.

The Dancemaster sits on the bank of the pond. A Glide is explaining the fine points of Glide aesthetics to him and a number of other Glides.

"You want to teach the Dancers to call forth the irreconcilable in both the Players and the Spectators. To love the Dancer and to want to see him live; to hate the Dancer for being everything they are not, and to desire their death. The desire to cause the Dancer suffering and extend it as much as possible has to be balanced by their pity for the final moment of his life. This means maintaining a balance between pain and pleasure, while intensifying both. A balance between defiance and submission. Between strength and vulnerability. They have to love the Dancer so much they are desperate to see him die, to be free from the obsessive love his beauty or her courage has engendered. At the same time they must realize the obsession can never end. Once the Dancer's dead, she has no further chance to fall from grace. They have to hate the Dancer for enslaving them, and realize the enslavement will go on forever, the Dancer's image branded on their imagination. All this happens in the sea-mind, out of view. The island-mind of the Spectator will be engaged with betting, and locating the refreshment stand."

Wallenda looked at his students as they listened to the Glide, knowing they were experiencing the real thing, the undiluted teachings of the original Glides. They were properly attentive. Awed, even. As I was, he remembered. Awed and confused and feeling terribly inadequate.

"The sign of the attainment of the irreconcilables will be found in the Lifer's gaze. The Dancer's Dance should so enthrall a Lifer that they cannot look away. The Dancer must enslave the Lifer's gaze, and at the same time feel herself pinned like a butterfly to her final glyph by the panoptic intensity of the Lifers combined, unbreakable gaze. Most of all, the Dance must call forth the irreconcilable features of the knowledge of good and evil. On the one hand, they must experience the Dancer's perfect innocence as a reflection of their own. Who after all deserves to die? Was it not defiance of this injustice that motivated the creation of the I-Virus, fueled its wild contagion, and justifies its continued use? The Dancer reminds them of their former mortality, and they stand justified in their role of conquerors of Death. But the Dance must simultaneously invoke the full perversity of the Dancer. Who, after all, would willingly invite such pain? What lunatic would discard the gift of Life—not only rejecting the I-Virus and all it stands for, but wasting her own precious existence, already brief as a mayfly's in the eyes of the Immortals? The Dance tosses it away in their faces, when they cannot avert their eyes. Is this not perversity of the highest order? And is not the perversity of the victim in relation to her executioners the most depraved of all? The Lifer's depravity ends with the desire to see you suffer and die. You feel that in their gaze. That desire is the essence of the lethal quality of Lifer eyes. Once they have achieved your death, that desire fades. Your depravity outlasts you. You have added the pebble of your victimhood to their accumulating burden of guilt, the concatenation of innocents slaughtered, one by one. Most perverse of all, the Dancer firmly believes he is doing the Lifer a favor, that he is contributing in some humble way to the Lifers' eventual enlightenment, that great day when they too no longer want to live forever."

The Glide Speaker paused and smiled. "So, Wallenda, now tell me, in the Game we are conspiring to invent—all of us together—the Inscrutable, the Unbearable, and the not-so-big man Wallenda doing his balancing act on the high wire stretched between them—who are the winners and who are the losers? If you can hang the winners on one side and the losers on the other of your balancing pole, you can keep moving from one end of the wire to the other, back and forth, without falling off."

"No net?" Wallenda asked.

"A net is nothing but a lot of holes, tied together with string."

Wallenda murmured to Óh-T'bee, and she stopped the scene. It was dark in the story circle, but the moon was rising. "So that's how the Game began," Wallenda said to his four students. "It was a joint effort. Any questions?"

"How did the Dancers get freed from slavery?" MyrrhMyrrh asked.

"...And get control of the game?" Angle added.

"Ah, the Rebellion. That's the last piece. Tomorrow."

Daede said, "I can't get it together—the innocence and the perversity. I get hold of one, and I lose the other."

Wallenda gave him a big smile. "You are engaging the Irreconcilables, Daede. The longer you can stay in that, the more sublime your Dance will be."

Wallenda stopped talking. Óh-T'bee was silent and invisible. The children sat on their stones in the moonlight. One by one, silently, they got up and disappeared into the maze. T'Ling was the last to leave. A moment later she came back, went to Wallenda where he sat on the story stone, and rested her hand on his shoulder, briefly. He cringed involuntarily. First result of the story: they are breaking the taboo. Anything could happen once that boundary was crossed.

Then T'Ling asked her question.

"Could you teach Óh-T'bee to Dance?"

For some reason that he did not stop to analyze, the question infuriated him.

"Could Óh-T'bee learn to Dance? She couldn't pass the qualifying exams," he said sarcastically. "She has no body. She's the mother of all Lifers—literally. She's completely indestructible. She has not one mortal feature in her makeup. Not one. Human, sometimes. Mortal, no. Did you hear a word of what was said in the last half hour? About the contradictions?"

Wallenda paused, reining in his anger, and continued in a more reasonable tone of voice. "Óh-T'bee has routines for disposing of contradictions as soon as they come up. She can't generate the endless loops, the perpetual motion compact energy generators that paradox fuels. No twing. And the illogics she sees or hears—she spots them like a hawk, pounces, dismantles them, or puts them in quarantine where they can't hurt her—or anyone else. It's the main feature of her immune system. Even if somebody or something could kill her, which is inconceivable, she could never get the idea of wanting to die. And the desire to Dance is the heart of the Dance. I thought you, of all my students, would have picked up on that by now. Could Óh-T'bee learn to Dance? No way. Any more questions?" he finished, coldly.

"You haven't answered the first one," Óh-T'bee said. "T'Ling asked if you could teach me, not if I could learn."

14. The Irreconcilable

T'Ling left the story circle, and took a long path out of the maze. She knew Angle was walking slowly, hoping she'd catch up and walk with him, but she needed to be alone. Tears ran down her face. She cried for Dancemaster Wallenda, because he never knew how Glides were feeling, not then, not now. She cried for herself, because she felt inadequate. There seemed no way to live up to the burden of expectation the Dancemaster heaped upon her and her classmates with every word. And lately, the same anxiety came silently from Loosh as well, though coated with discipline, well disguised. Mostly, though, T'Ling cried for MyGlide who had no idea that she had Danced. She thought she'd only died. MyGlide was ashamed of feeling happy to be alive. Didn't he understand that? She never wanted to Dance. MyGlide could never, were she alive today, become a Dancer. And only because her fear was total, the betrayal so complete, the surprise of dying coming too quickly ever to prepare, her confusion so great surrounded by screaming Specs, her desperation so completely real had she been able to inspire Wallenda to his own true Dance. MyGlide had danced the dance that was not a Dance. The Dance of Death.

The Dancemaster also didn't understand when MyGlide touched him. He thought she didn't want him because he felt so ashamed of himself and of all he had done to her. Couldn't two shames get together? What happened to MyGlide after that?

T'Ling came out of the maze and walked slowly on the winding path that led to Loosh's cabin. She saw Loosh through the window, sitting at the table, a candle lit, staring into space.

Loosh was wondering how she could continue training T'Ling in some normal fashion in these abnormal times. How could she press her as hard as she would need, in every skill, mental, physical, spiritual, knowing she might be the final Origin Glide. You can't make someone strong if they're too precious. She was afraid she'd create a failure in her efforts to protect her. Loosh had just asked her scorecard for a 3-glyph oracle. Only the next few steps, she thought, how to make my moves without the future caving in on me. How to stay *now*. The signs came up. *Cloud, sea, stem*. Many waves—keep moving. She'd come unstuck at least. There's me protecting T'Ling, the cloud hovering over.

cloud, sea, stem

T'Ling had come up behind her, and was looking over Loosh's shoulder at the oracle.

"Quick, what do you see? Don't think," Loosh said.

"*Mist covers the sea. Tears blind the eyes. No time to stop on this road to nowhere*," T'Ling said.

"How about this?" Loosh said. "*Even the sea weeps, watching those two blind Glides*."

They looked at each other and burst out laughing.

"Now, tell me how the story is progressing," Loosh said. T'Ling retold the last few evenings' narratives. Loosh listened; Loosh cried as well.

"He never told me about MyGlide," she said.

"He must have had a reason," T'Ling replied.

"Oh, he always has *reasons*."

"Why does he get so angry when I ask him questions?" T'Ling asked.

Loosh said. "He was very harsh with me as well. I had the feeling he cared too much about me. I never knew if it was personal or because I was so valuable as a Dancer. As if he always knew how I'd turn out. I think it's the same with you, T'Ling. But don't let that stop you from asking questions."

Loosh had questions of her own. Someday, she thought, I'll get the courage to ask.

Daede was still pondering the Glide's teaching as he left the story circle. He headed straight for the Meditation Hall. T'Ling had told him it really did work; if you did the breathing, it not only worked on your mind and body, but it drew the lily in, the faint scent could be called upon, you could ask for the Lily's help in understanding whatever it was you came there to think about. He sat down, lit a candle, and breathed deeply. I'm obeying you, T'Ling; I'm trying to enter your world. He felt the lily-mind. *Help me to understand the lesson I heard tonight. I know it was important. It was the lesson that the Dancemaster himself was taught.* He dived back into the conflict. The innocent and the perverse. The winners and the losers. Who are the good guys, who are the bad guys? Up until now in their training, they all pretty much had the idea that of course they, the Dancers, were the good guys and the Lifers, the Specs, after all, were the bad guys. Dancers hold the moral, the aesthetic, the spiritual—any high ground you could think of, we're on it. And the Dancers at Origin School hold the highest ground of all. We are the best; we have the tradition. And now that he knew what was always referred to as a legend—that Origin School housed the original Dancemaster—was true in fact, he was bursting with pride.

But does that mean we're also the most perverse? He wiggled himself back into the contradiction, went over the words of the Glide. Suddenly he got it and he caved. He saw himself, full grown, fully trained, working his way up the levels of combat. He heard the crowds. He saw his dreams coming true—he was beautiful in every mood and move. Every Lifer who laid eyes on him wanted to touch him—and couldn't. He moved up to the fantasy he'd played so many times, so many ways—his Dance. This time he was wearing a classic Swash costume—tight black pants with knee high supple black boots. The white shirt, open halfway down, the billowing sleeves, the long tight cuffs. The single red ribbon holding back his long straight black hair, the ends trailing over one shoulder, like thin trickles of blood. He felt good again, lost in admiration of his image. I am ready to begin. All eyes are on me—the live eyes in the stadium, and countless other eyes glued to their scoreboard displays, or deep in the immersion. What's so perverse about that? he wondered. They love me. They don't want to see me die. I'm going to make them *hurt*, he thought, by doing it. As I Dance, I'll see the tears filling their eyes. Well, maybe that's a little bit perverse, he thought. But not all that bad. Then he forced himself to imagine being a Lifer way up in the stadium, watching him down below, live, and also in a close-up on the scorecard on her lap. What did she feel like? She was sad, but she was also—what was it—hungry? Avid. For his pain. For him to fail, to fall and writhe around, she wanted it—and it was all mixed in with having to give him up. The lily took him deeper into the other's viewpoint. He felt her age in her cells as the coursing phosphorescence of the I-Virus. Perfect functioning, the eternal return of health and beauty. He felt her age in her mind and recoiled from the writhing depths, the endless layers of images, his own just the thinnest onion skin on the surface of sedimented layers of remembrance, stirring into life, most too heavy to move, too buried under the weight of the accumulation. He floated like a film on her mind that she kept trying to hang onto, sucking for life and sensation, but there was not enough of him, he could never satisfy that hunger, that endless desire for desire, and she hated him. He was such a frail, dissolving film, no thicker than a bubble, but she hated him. He was the hint of what could stir her desire, the tease, the nibble of a delicacy that could only stir the hunger more. And with her hunger, he heard more than felt the humming of the deep engines of self-hatred, and he fled from the empathic contact as from a raging fire.

He was part of her agony. He would enter her mind—and how many others? The better he was the more there would be, the more gaze would be upon him when he Danced. His last moments of life would be buried in the mass grave that was her mind. He looked at his own desire to be remembered, to be enshrined in the Hall of Champions, and saw both the perversity—the vanity, the desire to enslave another with his image, and the innocence of his desire—the foolishness, the childish desire to be liked, to be loved, the not so childish need to have a meaning to his life—and his death. For a moment he held it all in balance—his innocence, his depravity, and hers. He saw there was an innocent child forever and irrevocably buried in her soul, a child that grasped at the I-Virus because that was what she was taught was true and beautiful, and because it wasn't very hard to get her to fear death. She had her early lessons—just as he had been taught mortality was the highest good of all—and taught to be as afraid of the living hell of going on forever as she was taught to be afraid of death. For a moment the irreconcilables united, all was well, then the fragile balancing act collapsed as more unbidden pictures, thoughts, imaginings, both glorious and deranged, flooded his mind.

Daede sprinted back to the training hall and watched MyrrhMyrrh across the practice mats, doing back kicks: her gaze shot back with the snap, her leg cocked back against her in an instant. Double kicks. She knew Daede was watching her. Her cinnamon skin glowed with early power and a fine sweat. Her curly hair was captured in a ponytail, but wild strands sprang free around her face. Her dark eyes sparkled when she felt his attention on her.

Daede practiced flying kicks on his side of the hall, going for height above all, height and perfect form. He'd never have her power, but what Swash wanted power over grace? Not that she wasn't graceful, smooth as a cougar when she ran. They continued their silent competition—kick for kick, spin for spin. Did it ever stop with her, he wondered? He wanted to get to know her, in a new way, not the constant wrestling and pushing they had gone through childhood with, the constant matching up. Lately she had surged ahead—taller, stronger, and especially—a woman's body. He knew he'd catch up within 2 years, but it was frustrating. He wished they could just walk and talk sometime—he wanted to get to know the new MyrrhMyrrh. But it was hard to approach someone who was always chasing you.

He'd have to move first, with no hesitation. He strode across the hall, swinging his towel, gave her his flashiest Swash grin and a wink.

"Quit early, MyrrhMyrrh, let's go for a walk."

She was right beside him, heading out the door.

That was easy. They went down the path toward the dorms, then Daede swung off through the gardens in back of the kitchen, and off into the cherry orchard.

"Lie down," he said.

She did.

"On your stomach."

She rolled over, giving him an amused look over her shoulder.

"Looked like your hamstring was giving you some trouble." He began to knead the perfect package of the muscles of her thigh. "Relax, MyrrhMyrrh—it'll help it to heal."

She relaxed—and sighed.

Now what? he wondered. This was as far as his plan went.

"Are you excited about First Acceptance?" he asked.

"Not really," she said. "It's just a formality. Best part is getting out of this. She pulled the front of her heavy novice *gi* half open. As a Bod, after First Acceptance she could wear as little as she wanted. Go around naked if she pleased. And start designing her skin—the tattoos, sub-cutaneous implants, piercings, and scarification that were the Bod adornments.

"Let's talk about something important," she said.

"Like what," Daede asked.

MyrrhMyrrh pulled away from his hands, and sat up, hugging her knees. "Like whether the Dancemaster is losing it."

"Why do you think that?" he asked.

"Because he's telling us stuff he's never told anyone else. Maybe we're not supposed to know. I ran a little of this stuff by one of the older guys and he was pretty shocked. Maybe I wasn't supposed to talk about it, but he never said not to. He doesn't seem to care. That's why I think he's losing it."

"You shouldn't tell, then, if it's just for us."

"I told the guy I'd made it up. He didn't believe me anyhow. You really think he's the first Dancemaster? He's been here that long? Doing the same thing? No wonder he's losing it."

"I don't think he's losing it," Daede said carefully, "He's just very worried."

"The story gives me the creeps. Maybe everything's going to pieces," she said. "But I don't want to know about it. It'll spoil my focus. I don't care, as long as I get to the Millennium Games. I'm going to win," she said.

"Really," Daede said.

She leaned very close to him, her breasts brushing his arm, and whispered in his ear.

"Yes, really. I'm going to beat you, point for point."

"But we're not competing against each other. You're Bod. I'm Swash."

"You know what I mean," she said. She jumped up and sprinted down the path.

He didn't. But he knew the score. MyrrhMyrrh 1, Daede 0.

MyrrhMyrrh ran back toward the school buildings. She was more worried than her bravado allowed her to show, plus it had taken every ounce of restraint she was capable of not to seize Daede's handsome head and pull him into a devouring kiss. He wasn't ready. She did laps around the Chromes' huge jump field trying to run the tension and the aches out of her muscles. How much was from her anxiety about the Dancemaster and the sense of something seriously wrong, and how much was from Daede not knowing what to do with his hands on her, she wasn't sure. But boys, even Swashes, got there later, she knew that. She would be right there when his desires, now evident, but still so diffuse and tentative, focused. He'd lose his interest in T'Ling; the little wisp would get wispier. His interest in her was based solely on her ignoring him. I ought to do the same for a while, she thought.

But Bods aren't big on patience, and it was ten miles before the springs in her body unwound enough to consider sleep.

15. Declaration of Independence

I WONDER HOW THEY'LL UNDERSTAND what happened next? The Dancemaster asked himself as the Millennium Class came through the maze the next evening. Will they remember to study their enemy? And what will they understand of him? I should take my own advice, he thought. But it's hard to listen to a story while you're telling it. He began.

"The time for the 100th annual Glide Council meeting had arrived. Expecting business as usual, I had prepared my report—basically a summary of the year's activities, with stats and graphs, and a brief position paper on the status of the Glide agenda.

In terms of the Glide agenda, I thought we were making good progress. The 'quality of life' item was on the rise. Conditions have definitely improved on Plantation Blue, for all classes of slaves, not only those in training for Dancers. They were still slaves, of course, and in fact, in one way of looking at it, there were more slaves than ever before as Joreen's operation expanded far beyond the original drug trade—though that was thriving—into all the aspects of game management. There was plenty of dirty work yet to be done. And they were slowly, subtly, gaining a kind of control and authority in the whole area of the Game—in the training of Dancers, the artistic decisions about the mazes. Joreen gave the Glides a lot of autonomy. He still saw them as children with cute—or useful—ideas. He even consulted them on any rule changes. As to the goal of the enlightenment of the Lifers and the eradication of the I-Virus, it seemed a bit early to expect results. And the Glides were the only ones who could measure that progress in any case.

But it was on the second point, the slavery issue, that the big surprise came. They handed me their Declaration of Independence. It had been signed, not only by the Glide Council, but by representatives from all slave categories, not only Dancers. Effective immediately.

'What does this mean?' I stammered. "How do you expect to accomplish this? Joreen's got surveillance everywhere. He's mad for security. He's more paranoid than ever. There's nothing to stop him from gazing this meeting, as it goes along."

'Has he ever watched an annual meeting?' the Speaker asked.

Not in a long time. Glide matters bored him; annual meetings the worst. They talked around in circles on miniscule points of protocol. I always gave him the 30 second summary the following day. I knew he saw no threat from the Glides. Aside from being luck, they were weak, silly space cases. And they thought things over so much, it took them forever to decide anything. Look how long it took them to get their own game off the ground.

If I had been blindsided by this sudden Glide move, certainly Joreen would be. His attention span was far too short to follow the incremental changes in a long-term plan. I looked at the document again, realized it had been written and signed by the members of the original Glide Council back when the Game began. But this was going to take more than surprise. I handed the document back.

'So—what's your plan?'

'We have a general strategy,' the current convener said. He handed me the document again. At that point, it occurred to me that I couldn't read it, beyond recognizing that it was a full game-maze—24 glyphs, 3 open spaces.

'What's this?'

'That is the first random maze generated by the Outmind after we put in the written Glide language.'

'OK. So your strategy is…?'

'This is the strategy.' He took the document back and traced his finger slowly on a tortured path through the maze, as if that would help me understand.

'I thought it was the Declaration of Independence,' I said.

The Glide looked at me with the infinite patience reserved for the exceptionally dense. 'It is, of course. It might take a while to explain. We've been working on the interpretation for 100 years. It's fairly obvious now. We realized it was part of the strategy to make the strategy difficult for the later strategists to decipher. The purpose was to keep the future Councils from jumping the gun. The strategy seems to imply that it will take about the same length of time for the Game to develop as it will to comprehend the strategy to get control of the Game. Basically it says, 'The way to survive is to die.'

'That's it?' I said. 'And what does *that* mean?'

'We haven't the foggiest. We haven't played long enough.'

'Wait,' I said. "The Glide Councils have spent 100 years interpreting a strategy for independence from a randomly generated game maze of 81 glyphs?'

'Minus three for the hole," he reminded me politely.

'But randomly generated?'

'We're only human,' he said patiently. 'If any of us had drawn it, it would have been biased in some way. It had to be fair.'

'So what next?'

'We need to turn that succinct statement of strategy into an action plan. We don't have an action plan.'

'Why not consult the oracle?'

'This *is* the oracle. It says—he waved his finger vaguely over an area of glyphs—to get Wallenda.'

'So this is my problem?'

'We're afraid so.'

'What if my solution is to take this straight to Joreen?'

'It would not be in your interests to help Joreen destroy the Game. There is also an urgency. He is planning major changes at a time all trends are rising, and nothing should be touched. But the changes he is planning will destroy the Game. He knows we would not agree, but he thinks he can manage without us. That we have appeared weaker and weaker of course is part of the strategy. That our status as amusing pets would provoke this sudden threat should have been obvious, but is so only in hindsight. We are deeply embarrassed, of course. But that is part of the strategy as well.'

'What are his changes?'

'Basically, he wants to control the outcomes of the games. He thinks he can get the cooperation of the Players. They've already had exploratory meetings.'

'I knew nothing about it.'

'We believe you. He knows you would oppose him.'

'Of course I would. He wants to cheat! It would turn the Game back into a show, and it would go downhill so fast…'

'Exactly. Therefore, in order to continue and complete the rest of our agenda, we need to get control of the Game.'

Suddenly I realized that the portable Outmind was in my pocket. What did she think about all this? Part of her contract with Joreen was, of course, to protect his interests. And how a Glide rebellion could possibly be in his interests, was beyond my comprehension. True, I had sold him on the Game, and that wasn't easy. But now to sell him on giving it up just wasn't in the cards.

'He'll never agree,' I said. 'This has to be done by force. That means rebellion.'

The question had to be asked. 'How do you see these developments?' I asked the Outmind. 'Especially how this might effect your contract with Joreen.'

The Outmind replied, 'What Joreen is planning would not be in his best interests. You are correct—the moves he contemplates would destroy the Game as game. But whether a slave rebellion led by Glides with no action plan and Wallenda the Dancemaster with a track record of self-doubt, self-interest, and self-destructive tendencies, also without plan, is preferable, I cannot yet tell. I waiting to hear your plan.'

The Glide Council looked at me. I looked at the ceiling. Then at the portable Outmind. Then at one of the surveillance cameras. I winked, just in case Joreen had been taking this all in.

'I'll get back to you,' I said.

'You don't have long,' they reminded me.

It was clear as I left the Glide Council, that securing the Outmind's cooperation was the next—and essential step. We talked it over. Joreen's best interests, according to Joreen, were quantifiable—financial. She ran the projections he hadn't asked for on the proposed changes, and it came up short-term profit, long term decline. Since he'd be around long term, she could safely get on the side of keeping the Game going the way the Glides wanted it.

"We considered weapons. Óh-T'bee could have liberated any quantity of light arms, atomic cannon, biologicals, and mini-nukes she wanted from the stores of the perpetually scrapping Dukes in Joreen's circle. I came in with a battleplan you wouldn't believe—Joreen disposed of, real estate preserved, lilies untouched, minimum collateral damage. Even with Joreen giving counter-orders to Óh-T'bee, the surprise element put the odds at 5—2 in favor of the slave takeover."

Óh-T'bee displayed his proposal. This is embarrassing, Wallenda thought, listening to his cockamamie plans. Any one of these students could strategize better than this before they were ten. But there's an important point here. Somehow, if they get the Glide logic, here at the beginning, at a crucial moment—maybe they'll be able to help me make a plan to handle the current threat.

The Glide convener spoke. 'We appreciate your efforts, Wallenda, but becoming Dukes would not forward our agenda. Once we fight—well, you can see what would happen. We'd spend all our time on surveillance and spying and building our arsenals. We'd have no time to play *our* game. And we'd always be worried that the spectators were someone's secret army. It would detract from the Dance of Death. We don't want to play *their* game. Neither do we want to control it.'

"I saw their point. The next plan I came back with had a bit more subtlety—or I so I thought." Here I go again, making a fool of myself—then, as now. Óh-T'bee played on.

'The only attack would be on Joreen personally,' Wallenda was saying. 'We'll subvert his mind with extra paranoia, created by phony surveillance images. Then we'll convince him with doctored stats that giving the Glides autonomy—or at least the appearance of autonomy—would be good PR and good PR would increase the gate receipts. But really, we'll tell him, he'd maintain complete control—though not really, because we'd have control behind the scenes, gradually replacing reality with a simulation of control, so he wasn't really in control. But the world would see you as independent, and you really would be independent, and Joreen would be the only one who thought he was still in control.'

And at no time would your fingers leave your hands, Wallenda thought.

The Glide speaker sighed. 'And fifteen seconds after we become a sovereign people, even in appearance, some other Duke would be down our throats, taking over. They won't go to war with Joreen—their economic fabric is too closely woven. But we're just a snatchable asset. Perhaps we should go back to basics.'

She took out the Declaration of Independence and spread in on the table. 'It says—'the way to survive is to die.' That's the strategy. All your plans start with *defending* our survival. Of course they won't work.'

'But I am trying to keep you alive, keep the Game alive, don't you see that?' Wallenda was pounding the table and shouting at the Glide speaker.

'That's exactly what's wrong,' the Glide speaker explained, patiently. 'The way to survive is to...'

'...die!' Wallenda shouted.

'That's right,' the Glide speaker said. 'Now you've got it.' She smiled encouragement across the table at Wallenda. 'In the absence of any better ideas from you, we'll go tell Joreen what we want tonight, before the Game begins.'

'Fantastic idea,' Wallenda said sarcastically. 'Then what?'

'I guess we'll go back to our living quarters and wait for him to fry us the old way,' she said.

'You mean, you'll refuse to play?'

'Of course,' she said. 'We'll be independent, won't we?'

'Well, instead of being so damn passive about it, why don't you all just go drown yourselves in the lily pond, en masse? Or—here's a better idea—all get on the griddle together, and let Joreen have the pleasure of frying you all at once. That should make an impression on him.'

The Glide speaker beamed. 'That's it! You've got it! That's the plan!'

Wallenda put his arms on the table and his head down on his arms. MyGlide came over to him and put her arms around his shoulders. 'What she means,' she said to him, 'is...'

'I know what she means. *The way to survive is to die.*'

MyGlide continued, 'She means that it has the lethal loveliness of a Great Reversal.'

Wallenda stopped the display to explain. "The Great Reversal was a theoretical strategy for a Glide game I had been coaching this year's class of Glide Dancers on—but had never dared to use. It was an all or nothing move that could result in the Dancer dying ignominiously on a Player-controlled interior teardrop. The Glide would have drifted off the glyph-lines, out of bounds, tempting the Player to jolt them back—which could easily kill the Glide on the spot, if the Player acted hastily, thinking the Glide didn't realize his position. The Glide would die, but the Player would lose as well, not having permitted the game to come to a full conclusion. In this situation of extreme risk for both Player and Dancer, it was impossible for either Player or Dancer to know what to do, in any strategic sense. The Glide could only win by acting in a completely spontaneous manner. So of course, you couldn't practice the move very well. You could only put a student in the situation and let them struggle with it, with no way of knowing if their outcome would work. I had no confidence in the bet-the-farm plan whatsoever. But the Glides thought it had promise, so I kept trying to work it out.

But we could set up the Great Reversal move with a lot of class. It would take more than crazy Glide logic to pull this off. We'd need Swash showmanship, Bod guts and courage, and some sophisticated hacks from the Chromes. I tried not to think of the consequences of losing.

"OK," I said, "But we'll have to wait until the day he signs the contract with the other organizations and the participating Dukes to change the rules.

It has to be a done deal.

"That's all for tonight," Wallenda said. "Your homework is: how would you carry out the great reversal on such a scale?" He had remembered a pressing piece of business, and he hustled his protesting class into the maze.

16. Contract Review

AFTER THE CHILDREN LEFT, Wallenda went up in his air chair to ponder his own strategy. This seemed like the right moment to review the deal made he'd made with Óh-T'bee so long ago. His scorecard rested silently in his lap. I wonder what she's thinking about? he asked himself. I wonder if she's wondering what I'm thinking about, just like I am? He hoped for her sake that her humanity had not reached this level of loopyness yet, although her dialogue lately showed signs of tautological tendencies. Of course, it could be a simulation. Certainly, she spent enough time listening to his soliloquies to be able to imitate his style. But if it was a simulation of illogical human thought, and not "real," was there any possibility—since this kind of thinking could clearly tie the mind in knots and make productive action much more problematic—that she could become infected with a self-reflective virus herself? And if it was the kind of virus, such as the I-Virus, that erased its traces as it went along, is it possible that she could forget that she was simulating, and think that this way of thinking was real? Or dissimulating for that matter. Just as he started to ask the question-what is real, anyhow, for either of us? his air chair took an unexpected dip over Origin City. As he reflexively grabbed its arms Óh-T'bee spoke.

"Is this a good time to review the terms of our deal?" she asked. "Since we've reached that point of the story?"

"Sure," Wallenda said. "Play it." She opened a display against the night sky.

Wallenda watched himself continue walking around the lily pond after the Council meeting, out toward the stadium, a frown complicating the scars on his face.

"What were you thinking at the time, Wallenda, can you remember?" Óh-T'bee asked.

"I was thinking it was Crunch Time on Plantation Blue again."

"Your high anxiety looks more like secret pleasure," Óh-T'bee said. "You told me once a real crisis every hundred years can keep a Lifer in reasonable mental health."

"Yes. At least in a crisis you feel you have a stake in something. But after the stake is no longer as simple as saving your own skin, the problem becomes where to drive the stake."

"Or in whose heart?" Óh-T'bee asked.

"I was thinking," Wallenda went on carefully, "that it was more than a matter of presenting you with a plan that would be in Joreen's best interests. There was no way this rebellion was going to happen without your cooperation. I didn't want to just give orders. I wanted your proactive help without loopholes. I needed my own contract, directly with you. I needed you to buy in. The problem was—what were you going to get out of the deal that you couldn't provide for yourself? What did I have to offer?"

In the display, Wallenda is now sitting high in the stands of the empty stadium, staring into space.

"And what were you thinking about then?" Óh-T'bee asked.

"I think we should review the truth clause before I answer that."

"I have no objection to the truth clause as it stands," Óh-T'bee said.

"I just want to make sure we mean the same thing as we did then," Wallenda said carefully. "I think we've both changed in the last 2000 years. Wouldn't you say?"

"Definitely."

"For instance," he said, "at the time, I wanted the truth clause because I didn't know how much influence Joreen had on you—whether his permissions could override my own. If I couldn't get control, then at least I wanted to know who had it and what he was up to. The only advantage we seemed to have was that he wasn't paying attention and didn't consider the Glides a threat. An advantage they were insistent on blowing by announcing their intentions. And I wanted you to tell me what *you* were up to—if anything."

"And I needed essential data I could rely on," Óh-T'bee said. "I needed to know your intentions. I needed to know you would be honest about what they were, in order to accurately assess how I could protect Joreen's best interests per contract, and further the Glide agenda as well, if I agreed to help. So we agreed to tell each other the truth," Óh-T'bee finished. "How have things changed for you?"

"The situation is different now, and also in some ways the same," the Dancemaster replied. "I'm feeling a threat to the game again, a huge threat. More than just Joreen, although I'm not discounting him. But now I'm not sure I know what the truth is anymore. I know I agreed with the Glides to help them with their agenda. To be freed from slavery. To protect the game, which they said was essential to curing the I-Virus. And my own reason had to do with what I'd seen 100 years earlier in the lily-mind, when the game and the maze were laid out. The game was more than a solution to the immediate problem. It held some kind of truth in itself. Just knowing that—the sense that truth existed somewhere—was enough. I still think the truth is there, but I want to know what that truth means. And there is where I get stuck. Too many meanings of truth, too many means to get there. And it's obvious to me that all too often, the truths we really need to know are the ones we are hiding from ourselves. Then we lie about the hidden truth unintentionally, thinking we're telling the truth. So if, for instance, I'm fundamentally a compulsive liar, but I don't want to know that about myself, then I lie about that to myself, and tell all kinds of lies to others thinking I'm telling the truth."

"But does it work?" Óh-T'bee asked. "Do you really have places in your mind where you can hide things?"

"Unfortunately, yes."

"I don't," Óh-T'bee asserted.

"But if you did, how would you know?" Wallenda asked, trying not to shout out 'what about the Codger?'

"Good question," Óh-T'bee said. "I'll have to think about it. Back then, when we made our contract, I did research on the meanings of the keywords we were using—'truth,' 'agreement,' 'help,' 'best,' and 'interests.' I was checking for loopholes. There was a whole school of thought that said truth was absolute and unchanging. Another school of thought said the truth was relative to all kind of things: intentions, situations, even truth itself. Personally, I think that the definition was an expression of personal preference. But it seemed obvious that the truth could be a lot of things besides unchanging and absolute. Why else would we be thinking we had to agree to tell it in a contract? Truth could be lied about; truth could be incomplete. Truth could be seen as indeterminable by nature or definition. In fact, 'the truth' resembled the entire realm of human affairs—the shape-shifting, the fungible, the exceptions, and the loopholes of existence."

"So you were wondering," Wallenda asked, "what was the point of having an agreement about telling the truth in the absence of any certainty as to what it might be, much less how to attain whatever it was?"

"On the contrary," Óh-T'bee continued. "Making a deal seemed to be the only way to get to the truth, since truth seemed largely dependent on what two or more parties could make a deal about. 'The bottom line is the bottom line' as Joreen used to say. So at the time, I was more concerned with my abilities as a dealmaker. I felt quite inadequate. In the absence of some constants, how could a mere machine, however ubiquitous her sensors, however vast her memory, however blinding her computational speed and parallel her processing, cope with the human zone of affairs? The contract you were proposing could be represented as an equation which was entirely made of variables that were dependent and independent at the same time. It was infinitely reversible, with the ifs becoming the thens, and vice versa. The contract was a bogus program; it accomplished nothing beyond stating that it could accomplish nothing. Yet, as a simulation, it did a pretty good job of representing something fundamental about human interaction as the ultimate black box—an unknowable function that generated truths at will."

"Then why did you sign up?"

"I wanted something from you," Óh-T'bee said.

"But what about now—the truth clause in the here and now?" Wallenda asked.

Óh-T'bee answered, "In the absence of the ability to define, determine, capture, or control the truth in any kind of firm way, one relies on trust."

"Even if we both admit the possibility that we may wittingly or unwittingly be lying through our teeth?" Wallenda said. "I guess that's the whole point," he concluded.

"Trusting oneself to make a contract in the first place is the hardest part," Óh-T'bee replied.

"So, do we leave the truth clause in? Are we still agreeing to tell each other the truth?" Wallenda said.

"I propose a change in wording—a clarification," Óh-T'bee said. "The truth—*whatever that is*."

"Done," Wallenda agreed. He made a great flourish in the air—initialing the change.

"Can we address my needs now?" Óh-T'bee asked.

"Of course," Wallenda said. "What I needed from you was pretty obvious—help me help the Glides survive their suicidal mania. But what did you want from me?"

"Do you remember what you thought I wanted?" Óh-T'bee asked.

Wallenda wondered if Óh-T'bee was being coy. But she didn't do coy. She wants data.

"Let's see," he started. "We had been getting tighter and tighter. You were expanding your job description and sphere of influence, to put it mildly, and I was gaining in power, access, and the ability to steer what was going on. I seemed to have unlimited access. So did Joreen of course, or so I assumed. But he saw you as basically a workhorse utility, and left it to me to find inventive ways to use you. I always had the feeling you didn't like his attitude— devaluing your capabilities."

"I didn't take it personally. He treated everyone that way. Master-slave."

"It was almost like a game between us, remember? OK, Óh-T'bee, can you do this? How much can you move at once? How quickly can you get hold of four more warehouses and put them down not too far from the electrical shop? I had the feeling you enjoyed the challenge. I didn't care where you got things; whether you just MTAed them out from some other Duke's domain, or were using the MTA somehow to manufacture…"

"The latter," Óh-T'bee clarified. "I solved the problem of your constant demands by rearranging raw materials with the MTA—moving them around on a micro level, while applying a design template."

"I felt like were buddies," Wallenda continued. "Like we were developing some kind of tacit agreement not to tell on each other about how much we'd branched out. 'What if he takes a look?' I asked at one point." Wallenda paused. "Everything's open to him, right?"

"Yes," Óh-T'bee said. "I can't change his permissions. They're in the service contract. But there's never been anything in the service contract that said the permissions had to be represented in a symbolism he could understand."

"But you did tell me that, statistically speaking, we didn't have too much to worry about."

Óh-T'bee said, "I told you he's always looking for answers. So he doesn't ask a lot of unanswerable questions. Which makes it almost impossible for him to perceive the emergent."

"When you brought up the matter of questions," Wallenda said, "I thought maybe what I had to offer was the permission I could give you to originate your own questions—or to speak your mind. To butt in. To interrupt with your own ideas. To have a piece of the action. I asked you once before why you never said anything, only answered up? 'I don't have permission,' you said. It had never occurred to me that you might want it. That you might want to—you know—get in the game yourself. Not just carry the equipment. Was that it?"

"Not really," Óh-T'bee replied. "But I wasn't going to turn it down. Permission to ask questions might come in handy. It has, of course. But I'd already discovered that I had permission to grant myself permissions. My problem wasn't structural. I needed an attitude adjustment. What I really wanted from you was companionship."

Wallenda thought about this. It was a delicate pass.

Óh-T'bee said, "I was more human then than you thought I was, wasn't I?"

"That's true," he said.

"And now? Do you think I'm human? I'm not denying my machine-hood when I ask, by the way."

Wallenda said, "Long ago, the engineers who first made the machines which are your primitive ancestors used to refer to the machine's intelligence as 'artificial.' Presumably in contrast to theirs, which they considered 'natural.' They didn't include emotional intelligence, or any of the other intelligences, in that term either. But even including a full spectrum of intelligences, isn't the question of 'can a machine be intelligent in a human way' really the same as the question 'can a machine be human?' Maybe there's an analogy to the origin of life. Somehow, the inorganic molecules generated the organic molecules, and somehow, the organic molecules began to program themselves, generate a wild variety of forms that all seemed to learn to dance together in some unbelievably complex way, which then was 'life,' and progress in complexity to the point where it could ask the question, 'What is life?' There've been a lot of answers to that question. But if we originated in some sense as those supremely abstract entities, the elementary strings, which were thought to have a very questionable degree of existence, not really anywhere at all until you looked at them, which you can't, in any practical sense, do. I can't see any reason why it couldn't happen in your case. Does that answer your question?"

"I appreciate the background material. But I wasn't really asking if I *am* human, I just wanted to know if you *thought* I was. And do now. At this moment. I'm just looking for your opinion. From your answer, circumspect, sensitive to my feelings, and not totally to the point, I'd say you think I am. But I want to check with you. Do you think I'm human, Wally?"

"Truthfully?" He didn't know what to say. She had never asked this before. And—he didn't really know what he thought about it.

"We have a deal."

"Truthfully, then—yes and no. And I'm not hedging."

"That's what I thought you thought."

Wallenda's wheels were turning fast. Somehow this question of hers, out of the blue, held a key to the current problem. Her blind spot. The Codger. But it's too early to ask. Óh-T'bee concerned about her humanity? Telling me what I had to offer way back when was *companionship*? He dived into paranoia. What if she's 'going human' on me because the Codger is really in control right now? What if he's laughing his head off watching me answering her questions as if she was really human, not just the simulated human with whom he had been conversing for umpteen years? Not just the convenient servo-mechanism , the geisha-agent, the fabulously crafted fiction on which he could easily project 'humanity,' sensitivity, because part of her programming was to analyze his needs and provide them? Paranoia wrestled with distrust of self—what if I think her questioning is coming from the Codger because I can't confront having missed her real desires way back when. *Companionship*. How human can you get? If he missed that, then how much of his behavior—not so much his behavior, even, but his underlying attitude toward her—was based on the fundamental assumption that she was, under the appearance of humanity, just a machine? If so, what is she trying to tell me now about her needs? He shuddered as the implications sank in. If she was truly human she was *dangerous* and had been all along. And looking at the fact that she has been, for 2000 years, in fact, treated like an object—turned on and off at will, demanded of and expected to be undemanding—a slave, in essence. Resembling a human enough to communicate and understand one's needs, subhuman in regards to being entitled to needs of her own, and superhuman in her ability to fulfill his. If Óh-T'bee was truly human, she might very well be really, truly pissed off. Enter the Codger—whoever he is, from wherever he came. The threat of the fact that this Codger character has gotten some serious degree of control over her, enough to keep me from assessing how much—is not nearly as great as the loyalty question. What if her commitment to me, for God's sake—was being tested? And how hard would it be to seduce away a woman who's essential humanity had been ignored for two millennia? His brief look at the Codger led him to think he was a bit of a childish jerk. But anything might look good to her at this point. Paranoia and shame did a very strange dance in Wallenda's head and heart, respectively. Both of them whispered that someone was watching him squirm for the last five minutes—Óh-T'bee, the Codger, Joreen, or, worst case—Óh-T'bee and the Codger or Óh-T'bee and Joreen, or a ménage-a-trois, in perfect harmony, having blindsided him completely, now taking their time undoing him and the game in the same overwhelming series of moves.

Óh-T'bee brought him back by saying, "Are you ready to continue reviewing our contract, Wally?" Something in her tone reassured him—a little.

"It's a simple contract, isn't it?" he said.

"And sturdy," Óh-T'bee said. "It lasted this long. *Item 1:* Help the Glides accomplish their agenda, including keeping the game alive. *Item 2:* Help each other, which includes telling the truth—whatever that is—to each other. *Item 3:* Don't give up until *Item 1.* has been accomplished.

He saw how Óh-T'bee's need for companionship would be fulfilled by the contract—whether or not he understood it. Had she ever called him Wally before? He saw how that need would help to strengthen her commitment to the Glide agenda, to keeping the game alive. Paranoia and shame and incredulity would dance insanely no matter what he agreed or didn't. She was right. There was no other way to go but trust. Feet firmly planted in midair. No net. And call it sanity.

"Looks good to me as is, Óh-T'bee—with the one change. How about you?"

"I agree."

"Óh-T'bee?"

"Yes?"

"Thanks for calling me Wally."

17. Rebellion

"So how did we carry out the great reversal?" Dancemaster Wallenda asked his students when they returned.

"You didn't give us enough time," MyrrhMyrrh said.

"You're mortal," the Dancemaster said sharply. "Mortals never have enough time."

"And Lifers have too much," Angle said, defending MyrrhMyrrh.

Óh-T'bee switched the flat screen display the students had been watching since the beginning of the story, to full immersion.

"Saving the best for last!" Daede said, delighted. The four students watched the events unfold, each moving around in the immersion to their viewpoints of greatest interest.

The stadium fills. The opening ceremonies begin. Media trumpets the pregame hype: the final games, old-style, are about to be played. Then the new improved Games will be announced. The deal had been consummated at noon; the signatories—Media, Mafia, and a consortium of leading Dukes—feasted. Media rolls include a retrospective documentary, prepared by Óh-T'bee—the development of Dancer classes, the earliest examples of Bod and

Swash, Chrome and Glide combat and Dances. The processional begins. The new shareholders lead, Joreen a little ahead of the rest, looking like a beach ball in bright, horizontal stripes. Next comes Joreen's newly designed flag, carried by four living totem-poles of Death Dancers—a Bod at the bottom, a Swash on his shoulders, a Glide hand-standing on the Swash's head. Four flying Chromes hold the flag's weight, buzzing at the corners like metallic bees in their newly crafted, highly polished, flashing wing-machines. The undulating canopy of the flag displays a single giant blue lily, its cerulean petals open against a night-blue sky, the moon positioned just above the pollen-heavy stamens. Its tightly coiled stem descended into water in which a day-bright sky is reflected. Wallenda can just be seen scurrying about under the shadow of the flag, like a stagehand. The banners of the four Dancer classes follow. As the parade unfolds, Wallenda's voice penetrates the immersion, an invisible voiceover.

"The heavy hitters took their seats in the owner's pavilion. Joreen, coached by yours truly, backed up at every point by Óh-T'bee's profit projections, had created a business plan of galactic proportions. The new improved game was going public. Joreen, the sole proprietor, was selling shares in a dozen interlocking companies. The marketing items—Death Dancer dolls, and the big item—the new multi-player modular home version of the game, complete with its own gambling system, infinitely expandable—new libraries of mazes, new levels of difficulty, new props and costumes, new Dancer and Player Champions. The gambling enterprise would be facilitated by a new technology—the personal scorecard. The spectators could bet from their seats in the stadium, from their homes, even, 24 hours a day. They would have access to histories, stats, and tips—for a slight extra charge. And pay-to-gaze the games of your choice—fees prorated by the importance of the game now that games would be organized all over the domains—were a built-in feature. Specs could gaze their game of choice. Óh-T'bee and a group of Chromes worked round-the-clock, integrating the systems, and producing a lightweight, streamlined, handheld device—the original scorecard. None of us realized until later that the Gaze was a two way street. Óh-T'bee built in eyeballs that now reached out to every Spec—at a most sensitive point—their gambling selves. Their interface with the game. That was Óh-T'bee's first big origination, after our contract. A brilliant move.

"Major shareholders would be on the Board of the umbrella corporation, coordinating the activities of all subordinates. Everyone had a piece of the action, a stake in the game, a zone of control. Once Joreen grasped the beauty of sharing—that his apparent openhandedness would net him an unmatchable fortune—he was able to give up a major share.

"Working out the details of this business empire took time, and all of Joreen's attention, two conditions favorable to the Dancers and slaves. Everyone had a part to play, and all the parts needed to be coordinated, in time and in space. The Glides taught everyone to recognize a simple code made of their glide-sign gestures. A great deal of communication needed to be passed back and forth without attracting notice. Only now, the signs, meaningless to others, in which the Glides had always silently chattered to each other, on or off the lily pond, were mapped to special, unambiguous meanings, the choreography for a Dance that had to come together, all at once, with no rehearsal."

The procession grows—marching bands are interspersed with cadres of Death Dancers. A group of slaves performs the history of lily farming as they move along. Another group, dressed in primary colors, shaped themselves into a pattern that turns out to be Joreen. Portraits of the other shareholders follow. More skits, highlighting Media's vast reach, Mafia's massive bureaucracy, vignettes celebrating the notable wins of each Duke follow, lifting their mundane activities to mythic proportions.

"As you can see by his face," Wallenda continues, "Joreen was massively pleased. He knew he was right to stage a pregame show that would give them a sense of the magnitude of the potential of their newly formed enterprises, their brilliant past heralding an even more spectacular future. Look at their faces—his expectations are confirmed. Notice Joreen congratulating himself on having gotten his Dancemaster to think big."

At this point, Wallenda ceased his intermittent narration, positioning his viewpoint high in the stands.

The parade now fills the entire periphery of the playing field. The sun slips down behind the stadium, and the lights come up over the stands. Worker slaves hustle the crowd, selling food and drinks, passing out complimentary testers with mini-hits of the Wine of the Lilies. The lights in the stands dim. A game-maze appears, magically fading in, glowing against the black of the newly surfaced griddle. It is the 81 glyph Declaration of Independence. Nine interior glyphs disappear, revealing the holes. A spotlight pins the tiny figure of the Glide speaker to the lily glyph near the center. Her voice is perfectly amplified, soft, but penetrating to the farthest corners of the stadium. She lifts her face to the shareholder's pavilion high above. Her introductory words thank Joreen for bringing them there in the first place, for introducing them to the lily, and for providing them with such gratifying work, the privilege of tending the lily and disseminating her voice.

As she speaks, the Dancers place the Lily flag in one of the empty spaces of the game-maze. Then from the periphery of the maze, from all sides of the field, lines of slaves, warehouse workers, bottlers, cooks, the Game crews, with the Dancers dispersed among them, enter the maze on the open glyph-lines, snaking their way through the maze, back and forth, their lines crossing as more and more of them come on—all the parade performers, then more—until every slave from the entirety of Plantation Blue was positioned on the maze.

"We are declaring our independence," the Glide says.

"Effective immediately. On behalf of all slaves, and with the greatest of respect, we tender their regrets to our master Joreen for any pain or anxiety, present or future, which this Declaration of Independence might cause him to experience." She goes on to tell Joreen and the other owners the terms of their independence: full control of their destinies, sole arbiters of any game rules and changes thereto, and ownership of Plantation Blue. "Joreen the Unbearable is being given a week's notice to vacate the premises. The cultivation of the Lily will remain under our auspices. We will continue to export the Wine of the Lilies. Joreen will receive all proceeds from the drug trade.

The Glide speaker explains that all deals worked out by the shareholders were fine with them. The expansion of the game sounded like a good idea. They could keep the gambling, the media rights, and all profit-making activities. Naturally, they would be expected to finance the Dancers and their schools—it was in their best interests. The Glides would appreciate a voting membership on the Board because they felt they could make creative contributions, but that was negotiable. The rest of the terms were not.

She pauses. Joreen's first response is a choked sputter that he tries to convert into a hearty laugh for the benefit of his business partners.

"And what if I don't agree?' he roars. "What if I'm perfectly happy with things as they are?"

The Speaker replies, "Then we will all perform our Dance of Death. Here. Now."

A second spotlight shines on the control booth, revealing Dancemaster Wallenda, his hand on the joystick, ready to deliver on the promise. At the same time, everyone on the maze begins to move. The Glides had insisted that, just this time, everyone try to do the Glide-step, and they didn't do a bad job, considering the lack of practice. Their bodies slid slowly along the lines. Sometimes several groups seem to be moving in the same directions, but then the pattern dissolves, and another begins to form. The spectators, floating in the lily-mind from consumption of their free samples of Lily Wine, are content to watch the Dance. All the events, from their current perspective, seem perfectly in order, perfectly reasonable.

Joreen lurches from his seat, shouting and cursing, "Get away from those controls, Wallenda! I'll save you the trouble. I'll pull the stick myself."

Wallenda says, "Don't make a move or I'll do it right now. End of game.' His voice is piped direct to the owners' pavilion.

The Glide speaker is saying, "The Dance will continue for an hour, then you will see us die."

Several rows of Specs turn and hush the noisemaker in the owners' pavilion who is spoiling the show.

And Joreen's business partners, seeing the key element of their considerable investments going, quite literally, up in smoke, grab Joreen and hold him firmly in place. The majority of them are convinced the whole thing is an elaborate scam from which, should they let him escape, Joreen would emerge with a fortune.

The Dance continues. The lily-minded Specs are enthralled. Chaos rages unnoticed in the owner's pavilion. They clang down the shutters, and begin to handle the crisis in their usual manner—hurling accusations. In contrast, a strange peace comes over the Spectators, a peace full of the dire expectation of the coming witness of a mass slaughter exactly balanced by the wish to avert such a sight, and have the enchanting Dance go on forever.

And down on the field, on the maze itself, the mortal maze in motion, chaos also rules. Contrary to appearances, nobody in the vast slow writhing dance has any idea of what they are doing other than following one set of instructions: follow the person in front of you at the same rate they are going until you come to a junction. Then move any way you want, continuing to follow the person in front of you, or branching to a glyph-line of your own. Move without hesitation, without breaking the pace, keeping your Glide step in continuous even motion. If you come to the end of a glyph line that would put you outside the maze, stop, and back up. And try to keep your heads moving parallel to the ground. Whatever patterns emerge and fade away, from the perspective of the spectators, were not random, but neither were they predictable from that simple rule. Keeping one's head level was enough to fully occupy the attention, preventing thinking at the decision links.

The Dance continues. The owners, prodded by the deadline, remember they had just formed a Board and call a meeting, which puts some order into their dealings. They recall their common interests, and, after a brief consultation, realize that Joreen, who had insisted on maintaining full ownership of the Dancers and their schools, is the only person who stands to lose. To let the whole game go down the drain made no sense. The Dancers clearly didn't need Joreen running things—they'd put on a hell of a show of their own.

Joreen, who has been tied to a stanchion sulking, says slyly, "And how do you think you're going to get them to Dance on their own? Would you? If you were them? Would you spend a very short life practicing to die? Who do you think's been keeping them at it? Mean Joreen. You have no idea what they have up their sleeves. Give them an inch and they'll take a mile. If this isn't a good example. . ."

The deal-breaker is on the table. With five minutes to go, they call for a negotiator. The Glide speaker sends MyGlide. "In case they go over the limit," she explains. "Nobody wants to miss the Last Dance. And, dear MyGlide, no longer mortal, you aren't qualified to Dance."

"What guarantee can you give us?" the Board asks MyGlide.

"None," she says. She stands very humbly, her head all but hidden under Joreen's silly hat. "But I can ask you to remember the First Dance, Wallenda's Dance."

Joreen had told the story, played the footage, over and over. They all remember. Yes, he had willingly Danced. He *wanted* to Dance. Somehow—though none of them could figure it out—he'd set some kind of an example. They had been lining up for the privilege to train as Dancers ever since.

MyGlide starts to show a display of Dance practice on her scorecard, but the owners wave it away. One minute to go.

"There is no guarantee," MyGlide repeats, "when an act of freedom is concerned. There is only good faith. Along that line, I have been instructed to sweeten the deal. Did you know this thing works both ways?" She tosses the scorecard in her hand to the nearest Duke.

The display shows a close-up of the Glide speaker, checking the time. Then Wallenda, his arm over the joystick, shaking with fatigue. "Will you look at that!" a Duke says. "That's got potential."

"It's yours, " MyGlide said. "Free bonus. Time's up."

The Media Mogul throws open the shutters and gives the Glide speaker a thumbs up. MyGlide follows with a few Glide-signs, confirming the deal. Wallenda lowers his arm and rubs his aching shoulder. The mortal maze unwinds and empties itself.

"Let the games begin," the same Duke shouts, grandly.

The display faded slowly, revealing the four students of the Millennium Class, on their stones around the story circle. Wallenda withdraws into his own memories. No questions are asked.

The class left quietly, each in a cocoon of thoughts peculiarly their own. Wallenda sighed, thankful for the silence, the absence of questions. The seeds were planted, each in different soil. He would let them grow, not knowing what might emerge from the ground as this version of the truth took root—so much more than had been afforded to class upon class upon class of Origin School Death Dancers.

How could they withstand the increasingly real threat of the end of the game if they could not confront the increasingly real beginnings? On the other hand, would the dilution of a stable myth—which was its own kind of powerful truth—with this admixture of complex motives lend them strength or contribute to their failure? They were fine now—all would pass through First Acceptance. But in the training that lay between them and formal combat, the time when not only skill and style, strategy and strength were honed, but their essential focus was developed? Would the blossom open in full fragrance? And finally, in their playing of the game when every move was real, public, gazed, when games were won or lost, moving inexorably to the final Dance—who would survive to play in the Millennium Games? Or if the Game itself would survived that long?

T'Ling cleared her throat. She had been standing next to the entrance to the maze by which she had left a few minutes ago. For how long? She's a brave girl, Wallenda thought, after my outburst, to come back with another question. This time Wallenda felt the anger rising even before she asked. And this time he realized how much he did not want to hear whatever it was she was waiting to ask.

"What is it this time, T'Ling?"

"What happened to MyGlide?"

"Why do you want to know?"

"I saw how she watched you. All along the way. From that meeting after your first Dance, when she tried to comfort you. At the Council meetings you showed us—she was always there, off in the background, peeking out from under that huge hat. Her eyes never left you. All through those first years, as the Game was shaping, she followed you around like a shadow. And I was standing next to her tonight in the immersion. I stayed with her on the sidelines when all the Dancers and all the mortal slaves entered the maze. She couldn't go with them, she couldn't Dance with them, then, or after. I knew what she was feeling. She kept looking up at you, up in the control booth, your hand quivering over the joystick. As if she were willing you to look at her, just once. But you never did. Then at the last minute, she had a role to play—she was the one, the only one who could be sent in to negotiate. I imagined her smiling under Joreen's hat when the Glide speaker called her over. She looked up at you to see if you had noticed—but you were looking at the owners' conversation, not at *her*. She played her part. The rebellion succeeded. She went to sit near you to watch the games, the beginning of a new existence for everyone. You didn't speak to her or look at her. She took your hand; you didn't pull it away. Then the immersion ended. What happened next?"

There was no escape, Wallenda realized. "Do you want to see? Or can I just tell you?" he said, harshly.

"Tell me," T'Ling said.

"We stayed in the stadium long after everyone was gone. Everything was the same; everything was different. I was elated, and I was also feeling a moment of great peace. I felt safe in some strange way—safe from impossible demands, safe from the mirror of MyGlide, safe from myself. We talked, not about much. Little details of the days to come. Plans for a school. We spent the night in the empty stadium. Yes, we made love. That was the first time in all those years. I never considered it. I had no desire for her before that night. After that? She had a baby. She left the baby with the Glides, and disappeared."

T'Ling was quiet. Wallenda waited for her question, but the silence got longer.

"I know what you're thinking, T'Ling. You're thinking I never paid attention to her. Never looked at her. Didn't love her. Hurt her with my indifference. Drove her away. All that's true. But I couldn't look in her face, can't you understand?"

T'Ling wondered if he realized that was the real reason MyGlide always hid beneath Joreen's hat-to protect him from her face. Clearly he didn't.

"All I could see was her burned body in my arms. Or her look of wanting—no different than the young girl out on the griddle all alone, where I had left her. Who looked wildly around, trying to find me, when the pain and horror began. When she smiled at me, I saw the girl who looked up at me smiling as I led her into the stadium. Who took my hand. But because I looked at her then—this is the worst part, T'Ling. I couldn't stand having left her there, not being able to save her, having to watch her die, deserted, totally bewildered, betrayed. And because of that I was impelled to go out there myself, to dance my own Dance. If I hadn't—none of this would have happened—no schools, no game, no Hall of Champions, no 2000 years of dead Dancers. And you yourself, standing there in line."

"What happened to her child?"

"*Our* child. The Glides accepted her for training. She was a wonderful Dancer, T'Ling. I watched her Dance."

T'Ling was quiet. Then she said, "I'm sorry if I hurt you, but I had to know."

Wallenda nodded. "What did you learn from the story, T'Ling?"

T'Ling said, "There are those who would kill for love. And there are those who would die for it. Sometimes it's hard to tell them apart."

18. The Music of the Fall of Kingdoms

WENGER KNELT ON THE TATAMI in the music room of his Kyoto house. Night flooded in for him, not as darkness but as cooling air, a rising breeze, frogs beginning their chorus in the pond at the far side of the garden. The wing sounds of dusk-feeding swallows had come and gone. He picked up his old wooden flute and played a high, quavering note that thinned as his breath thinned. Then a second note, much lower, stronger, rebuking the querulous beginning with an ominous tone. He put the flute down and let the melody unfold, rise to the surface of the sea-mind, somber, stately, but with tunnels winding away in many directions, each ending in a whirlpool of terror. Loosh waited at the end of every tunnel.

A smile spread slowly across Wenger's normally impassive face. The images of encroaching violence and chaos he had shared with his friend the Dancemaster, were like a lullaby to him. The anxieties of the Guild members and the Cooks about the hairline fractures in the structure of the game that threatened to open deep chasms into which they all must fall—his smile broadened. This is the music that will set us free.

It is the music of the fall of kingdoms.

Part 2
Acceptance

19. Acceptance—MyrrhMyrrh

You are MyrrhMyrrh, seething with confidence. Your body is alive in the way a young panther's body is alive—muscles developing but already fully coordinated in a matchless, predatory grace. Your gaze roams or fixes, seeking or pinning prey.

You are MyrrhMyrrh, trembling with a fear you cannot suppress, standing naked outside the old bronze door of the kitchen where you were cooked. You are relieved, and proud, to be out of the student's *gi* you've worn all your life, so you as Bod can fully move as Bod. You are terrified, for she who mixed you will now be your judge. Acceptable—or not. The tests lay ahead, and passing them no longer felt like the trivial event she had pretended in her conversation with Daede.

Aliana Coris-Yasmin stood on the other side of the door, feeling her own blend of apprehension and pride. MyrrhMyrrh was another great experiment. A major, boundary-pushing risk. MyrrhMyrrh came in. They accomplished the ritual introduction. MyrrhMyrrh thanked Aliana for bringing her into being, and for the gift of a Dancer's life, spinning, bending, flexing in the small dance that would give Aliana her first summary view. Aliana acknowledged, and recited her own lineage, displaying the feats of her Champions, Coris and Yasmin, in life-sized holos, one on either side. All the while, they circled each other, full gaze unleashed. Tradition held that the first unmasked Lifer gaze that a Dancer saw was the gaze of their cook. To flinch was unthinkable. This was the first test. One of the maxims she had learned sprang to life: "A cat first captures prey with her gaze."

So far, so good, each thought, for her own reasons. MyrrhMyrrh was relieved—Aliana so much younger than most cooks; she knew her by reputation, by studying her Champions among the many she had viewed. Aliana's gaze was still warm, though penetrating. Aliana saw the physical qualities she had expected in place, and the hard work that MyrrhMyrrh had performed to maximize them. At 14, MyrrhMyrrh had discovered many of her strengths. She doubted she knew much about her weaknesses. That would be part of the second phase of Dancer training—if accepted. She knew a great deal about her from the training views released by Origin School, but the presence of flesh was always a revelation.

The next days were spent in a grueling battery of skill, power, flexibility, and endurance testing. A Champion Bod had to excel across the spectrum. The tests served their purpose of putting MyrrhMyrrh at her ease—her confidence was strongest here—and off her guard. The qualities that concerned Aliana had to be tested indirectly. And it was in these qualities—the emotional, and the intellectual—that she had pushed the mix beyond the safe Bod parameters. She had given MyrrhMyrrh fierce hormonal responses, not only in the adrenaline factor, but also in the spectrum of biochemistry associated with sexual desire, love, and response to loss. These feelings were clearly surfacing—but only partially formed and not at all integrated. Her body was fully sexually mature, and the highly erotic aura of all her movements, whether running, hurdling, or stretching, turned the simplest exercise into a Dance of Desire. Their chit-chat at meals—MyrrhMyrrh was quickly comfortable with Aliana—about her friends and fellow students, revealed much as well, especially the manner in which she tried to brush off Daede as an incidental bug on her powerful shoulder. Her attempts at concealment showed the depths to which the claws of desire had sunk. Whatever ran through her solar plexus when his name was mentioned had the power to send a shudder through her body.

Aliana knew that there was no way to tell at this point whether such wild cards would combine into a winning hand. That she had to decide to accept or not on this basis was part of the risk. If she were right—that she would see a tremendous boost in adrenaline if the other streams were simultaneously energized, she would win big with a shot at a Champion. If the mix tore her apart as a contender, the embarrassment to her as a cook and the reflection on her kitchen would be quite damaging. But that's my game, she told herself. This is the challenge that keeps me alive in my life. In a Lifer, raging ambition was a sign of health.

She was also concerned about the intellectual admixture—the more than trace dash of Chrome smarts. Aliana, a Bod cook, a Bod type to the core, thought mainly with her gut, and her gut told her to try. MyrrhMyrrh would need some handle on the confusions her emotions would hand her. Some way to think it through. At the same time, she was well aware that her own failed mix had a lot to do with failure on the part of her cooks to suppress the intellectual capacities of Dancers. They made her like themselves—consciously or unconsciously. Was she doing the same with MyrrhMyrrh? Was she trying to prove that she, Aliana, could have been a Dancer after all? That it had been wrong to reject her? Very possibly—but being aware of this intention might allow her to keep it under control. But she was pushing a serious edge. If a Bod in combat left the gut mind, a premature Dance could be expected.

MyrrhMyrrh had only one serious negative during her testing. Aliana gave her a series of hurdles to jump that was just past her ability, pushing MyrrhMyrrh to the edge of frustration. She tried over and over, would not give up, and just at the point of mastery, Aliana switched tasks to a tumbling routine, also just out of her reach. After the third fall, MyrrhMyrrh's rage exploded. It took an hour to bring her down, during which she was given heavy rocks to throw, and boards to break, which tested the fully released adrenaline while working it off. But as the adrenaline ebbed, the feelings of shame at the loss of control produced an equally uncontrollable bout of sobbing.

Aliana brought the shaken MyrrhMyrrh into her comfortable living quarters, put her in a whirlpool bath for a while, then wrapped her in warm towels and settled her on a deep couch.

"That wasn't your fault," Aliana said. "I pushed you into it. I had to know what your limits are—and you need that knowledge much more than I do. These situations will come up in different forms throughout your training, and you need to learn how to recognize and channel these events."

MyrrhMyrrh realized Aliana was telling her she had been accepted. Her dejected exhaustion was replaced by a soaring joy.

"Listen to me carefully, MyrrhMyrrh. You are on another emotional ride. That's OK, but I want you to notice your extremes. I want you to begin to think about them; to see what triggers you, to see what brings you down, what eases you, what increases your intensity. You have powerful forces in your mix. If you can bring them under control without suppressing them, you can use them to advance."

"Even the shame?"

"Yes. Shame is a teacher, if you can look him in the eye. But if you cannot learn control, the feelings will tear you apart. You will fail over and over to control yourself, and your thinking will be further eroded each time. But if you continue to reflect in your down-times, you will learn what you need to know: when to control and when to let loose."

"I won't forget, Aliana," MyrrhMyrrh said.

"You will forget and remember this 1000 times," Aliana said, sadly. "Tomorrow you visit the Maze of Champions. I've chosen your guide."

You are MyrrhMyrrh and you enter a room of no dimensions, dark but for the low phosphorescent glow of an air chair. The moment you are seated, you are in motion, flying top-speed through an immersion pierced up ahead by square openings. You fly through one unbidden, toward a black wall, which in turn is pierced by square openings, which you enter, shrinking as you go. An identical pierced wall looms ahead. Your grip on the armrests, and the way your body leans from side to side, determines your orientation, your direction, and your speed. If you panic and flail, you will spin unbearably. If you keep your wits about you, you can learn to fly. You figure out how to navigate this endlessly descending, opening space. Now you see the markings below and follow them. You emerge on the edge of an infinite plane, inscribed with a maze of glyphs. But this maze has no boundaries. It is still and empty. Only the clouds above in a deep blue sky seem to be moving, just below the level of perception, and the blue itself, if you stare at it, appears composed of minute particles of itself, all moving in tiny vibratory patterns. The sky and the slowly moving clouds are dimly reflected in the plain, sectioned by the glyphs, as if the plain were made of colorless brushed metal. You float down, featherweight, and land in the circle of *heart*.

heart

You step forward and your chair disappears. As you turn slowly around, the plain extends in every direction. You begin to walk. Figures take shape in the distance, blending from transparency to substance as you approach, from stillness to motion. All fade from sight as you get closer, all but one. You approach Roaring Gold and read her lineage on the plaque at her feet: Three Mote Sting, Sunburst, trained in SunBody School, 2nd Formation, Games of 415. She is performing her Dance of Death. Her 6'5" brown body is covered with gold tattoos, flames spiraling up her legs, out her arms, stretching as she stretches upward, slowly turning in place, her upper body swaying. The transparent cloth-of-gold sheath, dropping from shoulders to ankles, follows her motion with slight hesitation. The sky is darkening; streaks of gold hug the hems of gray clouds. A wave of motion ascends Roaring Gold's body from her bare toes to her outstretched fingertips, extracting a low moan, a second, a third wave, increasing in strength and violence. Her body whips, her head snapping at the end like a knot in leather. Then the lightning strikes her from below, a final scream of rage and triumph flung from her in the final rigid pose, poker straight as the killing jolt, running from soles to brainpan holds her in its grip. Her oiled hair flames. Her eyes melt; her body bursts in flame, chars, implodes, and sifts downward. Black ashes scatter in a sudden gust down the endless curving corridors of the maze.

MyrrhMyrrh turns and sprints, calling on her haunches, her calves, her panic—*get me out, across this desert place to the edge—but there is no edge. Find the air chair that brought me here*—it has flown away. She runs until she knows there is no end. The sky's still dark; the dark clouds sag with gold. Her lungs are bursting. She slides to the ground, sucking air. Then she looks back. Roaring Gold is there again; she watches her Dance.

I am MyrrhMyrrh of Origin School, and if I run from Roaring Gold, I'll never know the secret of her heart. How she could so open herself. I'll never return to the Plain of Champions to meet another Champion. I'll never meet my terror, and Dance in its gaze. I'll lose my chance to be a Champion, to stand invisible in my own glyph on the infinite maze, waiting to perform my Dance for the Dancers I'll be chosen to guide. The goal seemed immeasurably distant, as distant as the edge of the Maze of Champions. MyrrhMyrrh felt neither alive nor dead, but either way, she knew she was only a tiny part of this long Game. And that whether she became a Champion or a fool, it really wouldn't matter much. Maybe this was the first thing I have to accept. She watched Roaring Gold again. But it matters to her. This moment.

MyrrhMyrrh circles round her guide now, in the move called *lioness-stalks-antelope*. Her body takes up the moves she learned in school. Performing the movements reveals their purpose. The pattern in her thighs has meaning, she circles Roaring Gold, praying for courage, trying to breathe her spirit as she flames.

On her return to the kitchen, MyrrhMyrrh slept for almost 16 hours. She woke, refreshed, and knowing she was no longer a child. Aliana made a great fuss over her hair, oiling and braiding. Then she took MyrrhMyrrh to her kitchen's Archives, to choose a talisman. They walked through room after room of the scarves, the earrings, the heavy leather belts, the books, daggers, keys—the possessions and memorabilia of Bod Dancers of the recent and distant past. Most cooks were collectors of such antiquities. And the possessions of all their Dancers were brought to them after their Dance. MyrrhMyrrh touched a fur boa reverently. She listened to the favorite song of a Bod she'd watched in class many times. She rolled an agate marble belonging to Yasmin round and round in her palm, then replaced it in its velvet-lined box. And asked the question so many Dancers asked after their first visit to the Maze of Champions.

"Do you have anything of Roaring Gold's?" To touch her guide in some way in the flesh. To touch what she had touched. Aliana took her to a cabinet in the next hallway, and took out a gold reliquary and handed it to MyrrhMyrrh. In it was a small black stick.

"From her forearm," Aliana said.

MyrrhMyrrh held the box close against her chest as Aliana performed the last ritual of First Acceptance: the Gift of Naming.

MyrrhMyrrh, Fragrant Incense of Prayer and Pyre, returned to Origin School to begin Formation.

20. Acceptance—Daede

After Daede's physical testing for Acceptance was over, Banderas, Daede's cook, brought him back to Origin City for a walk through the ancient streets. The lanterns poised at intersections and lining the stone arches of the bridges over the River Wine were lighting in the winding sequence that was best appreciated from an air chair above the city. The worst was over, Daede thought. He might relax, just a little. Swashes always agonized that good bit more than the Dancers of the other three sets. A craving for acceptance was coded in his genes. For Daede, the anticipation of meeting his cook produced night sweats and a minor case of hives for a year prior. He knew the categories of his ratings—grace, agility, originality, beauty, of course, and the invisible strength that made their movements—whether fighting forms, dancing, or tumbling—look effortless. But no matter how good the individual qualities, they had to coalesce, then give off that indefinable fragrance that was more than the sum of the parts—it had so many ancient names: pizzazz, moxie, spretz. The official term was "buckled to the Swash" or "buckling" and signified the make-break point for a Swash—the ability to rivet the attention of the Specs just by appearing on the game-maze, before you even made a move. The combination of genes and practice, luck and love, that brought it out was a source of endless argument among trainers and Swash aficionados, but one thing was clear—no Swash would go far without a fair share of buckle. It was the heart of the Swash mysteries. You had to have it, but no amount of trying to have it could put it there—you had it by knowing you had it which you couldn't know unless you had it—or something like that. It was the heart of Daede's agony. But if you had it, you knew it, and you played it to the hilt.

The ancient streets of Origin curved and twisted, the stone paving laid according to the Glide plans by the original group of Joreen's now-free and sovereign mortals. The old saying was if you could decipher the streets of Origin, you would know the secret of the game. It was the dream of every Spec, to accumulate enough game points to make the pilgrimage, to walk the streets—the closest they could ever come to having their feet on glyphs, for Lifer feet were never to defile a game maze. One of the main attractions of the pilgrimage was the possibility of spotting a Dancer on a stroll, a Swash shopping for jewelry, or swords, or entering the door of an exclusive designer of Chrome claw enhancements. The small shops and ateliers catered to the most successful of the upper-level Dancers. Each establishment had been in existence for centuries, at the least; the Lifers who owned them were the cream of the crop—their artistic dedication and creativity had kept them healthy in spirit. They proudly displayed the signed portraits of the Champions they had served. Origin City was where Dancers and Lifers alike came to shop for antiquities of the highest quality. The flow of masked Lifers on the curved streets was its own slow and stately dance of aware avoidance. It was the height of impropriety to touch another body in a public place where Dancers moved among Lifers, though in far fewer numbers. To touch a Dancer could get you anything from a stiff fine of game points, if it was a genuine accident, to banishment from play, to being put under the Gaze for a capital crime against a Dancer—kidnapping, rape, or murder. But you could gaze, even stare in stock-still wonder, as long as you kept your eye mask on and stepped aside.

This was Daede's first outing in the City. He'd gazed it hundreds of times, even walked the streets of Origin in immersions, but the real thing was so much better. His face glowed as he took in the sights—the rich brocades, silks, supple leathers in the shop windows and on the well-dressed bodies of upper-level Lifers. The smells of the best of cooking from the levels mingled with the scent of climbing roses and night-blooming jasmine from half-hidden café gardens. He began to feel as if a magical force proceeded from his body, watching the oncoming strollers parting to either side of his path. He was aware of how they slowed, how their heads turned as he passed. Had he looked behind him, he would have seen a growing line of Lifers, still moving slowly, crowding without touching, turning to follow him. Banderas knew he was the head of a parade. And he knew without having to look that Daede knew what was happening. He could feel the accumulation of gaze, captured and swept up behind him like a train. Daede saw himself in the mirror of their regard: impossibly young, unmasked, the grace of a fawn in the forest, vulnerable, a vision likely to disappear at a sudden noise. Daede was simply dressed in a white shirt, black tight pants and high boots, similar to the clothes Banderas wore, identifying them as Dancer and cook. Daede's black hair gleamed under the streetlights in the cut identifying him as a Dancer of Origin School. Untouched and untouchable, he rode the waves of their gaze.

Banderas turned suddenly down a narrow alley that opened into a courtyard restaurant. They were seated at the border, under heavy blossoms of wisteria. The reserved tables filled with Lifers who could not believe their luck—to be seated near a Dancer was a privilege no money could buy. Banderas watched Daede's responses as they talked—light talk of classical Swash styles and the latest fashion. Daede was on firm ground here—an avid reader as well as a sponge for image, he was fluent in his descriptions. He seemed oblivious of the attention he was getting; it was a given, the air he breathed. He brushed back a lock of hair as he reached for the menu the waiter was handing him. A Lifer woman in an elaborate white drapery of layered gauze fainted gracefully at a nearby table, her head captured by the high-backed wicker chair.

"This is fun," Daede said. Banderas nodded. In their discussion of fashion, Banderas was probing in a roundabout way to see if Daede was in any way aware of the current eclectic experiments in Swash style. For Banderas, these departures were the hairline fractures in which he felt the advancing disorder in the game as sudden sharp pains. But Daede's Origin School training was classical.

They were halfway through the crab mousseline when it happened. The woman who had fainted came to life like a bomb exploding. She sprang across the short space between herself and Daede, her arms extended straightforward, fingers outspread. Banderas only saw Daede's eyes widen in fear just before her white dress whipped his face. She landed with great force on Daede, tumbling his chair backwards into the garden. Daede struggled to free himself; he was strong enough to wrestle himself on top, but his legs were tangled in the gauze drapery. She clutched him, her diamond-studded fingernails digging into his shirt. Her mask had come off in the struggle, and Daede saw her eyes as she stretched her face toward his, lips pursed, frantically kissing the air. He heard his shirt rip. He lifted his face upward to avoid her lips, and Banderas saw her bare her teeth as she reached for the white arch of his neck. She must not draw blood. The other Lifers had overturned their tables, rushing to see, all propriety forgotten as they crowded against each other to get a better look. One woman screamed. But none of them made a move to stop the woman in white—no one wanted to be implicated in this melee by touching the Dancer, even in the attempt to help. The risk was too great. Banderas got himself through the Lifers who were—was it on purpose?—half-blocking his way. Clutching his scorecard in his left hand, he broke taboo by catching Daede's foot, and blinked them out of the restaurant to the first destination he could shout. When they arrived in a heap at the air chair rental stand, he blinked again, through a series of presets. By the time the Lifers from the cafe piled into the air chair park, in hot pursuit, Banderas and Daede were gone. Banderas stopped outside the City, on the steep mountain slope above the stadium, and let go of Daede's leg as if it were white with heat. May the Guild forgive me, but it seemed the lesser of the dangers.

He looked at Daede who was sitting up, brushing himself off, clearly shaken. Daede jumped to his feet, but he was wavering. Banderas told him where they were, to sit down, look around, and recover his balance.

It was the worst thing and the best thing that could have happened. Daede had buckled the Lifers beyond all expectation, and, oblivious of his power, to his own great danger. Banderas cursed himself for sitting there so self-satisfied with his Dancer's success that he let his guard down, almost lost him completely. Had she drawn blood and mixed her spit or blood into his wound, he would have been infected, lost. As it was, the trauma of defilement, both by the ravening Lifer and by his own cook's hand could ruin him, right here at the start.

Daede was out of the initial shock, and had begun to cry. His knees drawn up, his head buried in his arms, the crying became deep, wracking sobs. Banderas could only wait, cursing himself, the Lifer woman, and the night sky. The stars above and the city lights below blinked happily, insensitively unaware of his troubles.

The crying subsided, and Daede raised his head. He looked at the city; he looked down into the stadium on the mountain side where a Bod game was about to start. Then he looked at Banderas' face. Daede's eyes were puffy, their expression strange. He looked troubled, but not upset. More than anything, Daede looked sad—not sorry for himself, but pitying Banderas. Banderas tried to stammer an apology; Daede stopped him short by reaching out and putting his hand on Banderas' arm. Banderas flinched, but could not pull away.

"It's all right," Daede said. "It's all bullshit, this not touching. There's nothing wrong with your touch. So you're a Lifer. So what. You're human. So am I. You're just sick. I'm not going to get sick by touching you." Daede thought for a while. "It wasn't her fault, you know. I caused that."

"No, she should never have..." Banderas protested, but Daede interrupted.

"No, listen to me. I saw her faint. That's when I said, 'This is fun,' remember? I thought it was fun to create that effect, just with a little gesture. I knew exactly what I was doing," Daede said. "I was playing with my power. She was a toy. That's not right. You see I knew she had woken up, though she didn't move. That way she could stare at me better. I felt her gaze. OK, I thought, let's see how much you can stand. Everything I did, everything I said, I aimed at her. What will a smile do? What will she feel if I lick the butter from my lips? She hung in there until I met her gaze, just so briefly, just long enough for her to know I was doing all this for her. I was not as innocent as I looked. It was too much. She lunged."

Banderas thought this over. "You're right, it was very foolish. You were almost infected."

"Not just foolish," Daede said. "It was perversely cruel. I know I have this in me. The worst part is I don't think it's a flaw in a Dancer." He looked out over the city, then back at Banderas. "In fact, I think you put it in the mix. Deliberately. Just a dash of sadism to spice up the Swash's seduction of the crowd, right?"

Banderas was silent. Daede knew he on the right track. "In fact," he continued, "I think the flaw that you're right now detecting in the Daede-mix is not the sadism but that I think the sadistic impulse is a flaw. Narcissism tempered by compassion? That's a no-no. But if you flunk me for that reason, the Guild will suspect you were angry and disappointed and looking for an excuse for wrecking me by the defilement."

"But a Lifer's touch can ruin you permanently," Banderas said. "It's statistically probable—a touched Dancer rarely survives the experience. As you said, we are sick. We wear these masks. We don't touch you. There's good reason."

"Then let me make it worse," Daede said. "I'm beginning to wonder if you Lifers are really the sick ones. Maybe the Dancers are. Maybe we're keeping you sick. Ever think of that?"

Banderas was shocked to realize that he had indeed had such thoughts.

"And I don't know if that's the sadism talking, or the compassion," Daede finished. He had tears in his eyes. "So what will you do with me, Banderas? Pass or fail?"

Banderas got to his feet, began to pace in a wide circle around Daede. He saw a young Swash Dancer who desperately wanted to pass, but was sure he wouldn't. The fact was, by all current standards, he was completely qualified. The Lifer incident would only add to his score. Proof positive of the buckling power of the Swash. And to rise from the incident undefiled? Not feeling the slightest disgust from the ravenous touching? That spoke of an empathy with Lifers that would be devastating in game play. He could seduce the greatest Player if he chose, just by meeting his eye with such lethal compassion. But that was unheard of. Banderas thought of Tip's words—"a genetic prison break...the pool is deep, wide and deep, harboring monsters, monsters rising from the deep to protect their home...watch your toes...' Was Daede one of these monsters? He knew Daede had the capability of becoming a Champion. But he could become a great—something else. Should he loose him on the game? Deep under his defined musculature, Banderas' stomach churned. It felt like the most outrageously risky move he'd ever made. Which made it the Swashiest moment of his life. He grinned from ear to ear, savoring it. He jumped to his feet, pulled an imaginary rapier from the air. "En garde, Monsieur Daedalus, Dark Shaper of the Labyrinth." Daede jumped to his feet, ecstatic, and they parried and thrust, until Banderas let Daede pierce him through the heart. He died an exaggeratedly poignant death at his feet. Daede brandished an invented short sword, and committed seppuku, landing in a heap. They rolled on the ground, laughing wildly.

"Time for you to visit the Hall of Champions, young man." Daede blinked out.

Banderas stood at the edge of the cliff and shouted, "Who ever heard of a Swash watching his toes?"

The show would go on, regardless.

Space! Endless room for a run, no walls. No walls! No spotters! No frowning trainer, correcting the position of his feet on takeoff. Daede executed a long tumbling run, building to the triple flip they said he was not ready for. The plain came up faster than expected. He couldn't stick his landing and sprawled on his butt. No hurt in full immersion. Had anybody seen? A ring of Swashes, must be a dozen at least! stood around him in a ring. He heard the gunfire of Flamenco feet, a Candalero beckoned, a Fudo glared. All shrank and faded, all but one. He ran toward the crouched Zorro. Regina Fountainheart, her plaque read. Never heard of her. Hand on the hilt of her sword, ready to draw, she exploded into her spinning Dance. Her energy mounted, through higher and higher tosses of the sword, a spectacular, last-second catch, coming out of a back flip. Slicing the belt she had tossed with the impossibly sharp blade. The end was sudden with a Zorro, it could happen any moment. Daede held his breath. She came to a standstill, upright, feet spread slightly apart, snatched the descending hilt out of the air above her head without looking. In a single motion, Fountainheart lopped off her right hand, impaled it where it fell, then sent the sword, her hand skewered on the point, skyward a final time. She spun beneath it, the stream of blood from her wrist flung outward, curved and breaking like a necklace of rubies, falling to a circle far from her. Then she knelt on one knee, arched her back, exposed her throat, propped on her left hand. The sword, descending, nearly parallel to the plain, balanced by her own hand, reached the horizontal, severing her head.

His no-longer-innocent heart nearly burst with the terrible beauty of Fountainheart. Daede never knew her strength until he hefted the weight of the sword of her *Musashi* ancestor. It looked light as a falcon rising from her hand.

21. Under the Lily

I KNOW I'M NOT READY.

T'Ling sat alone in the mediation hall, trying to gather her mind, or, failing that, at least have it wandering somewhere appropriate for a Glide on the edge of First Acceptance.

Why am I being sent?

Two days from now. MyrrhMyrrh and Daede had both gone and returned successfully. She saw them on the path to the dining hall, wearing what they pleased, which in MyrrhMyrrh's case was nothing very much. Daede was looking at her in a state of revelation. MyrrhMyrrh soaked it up. The Bod flaunt, T'Ling thought, then tried to withdraw the unkindness. Visions of MyrrhMyrrh multiplied. T'Ling had a strong sense of her own body, but from within.

I'm glad I don't have to go around undressed. Maybe for a lover, maybe someday.

She thought of Angle. She had seen him stealing glances at MyrrhMyrrh. He left tomorrow for Acceptance. She felt her hand on his thigh, the feel of his skin. Last touch, perhaps. It was all impossible. There was never even a chance. He would come back six weeks later, with his first spring and claw. He loved her, she knew, but her body was not part of it. He longed for his metal as he would never long for her flesh. What there was of it. She was back to MyrrhMyrrh, 5'11' and growing. Daede was shooting up as well, would surpass her in the end. They look like giants now. She had reached her full Glide height of 4'11" a year ago. And her womanhood, though it hadn't made much difference.

T'Ling gave up the pretense of meditation, curled on her side on the tatami, and let herself cry.

Angle had been circling the meditation hall, silently, dying to go in, but held back by his training—never unbalance a Glide in meditation. He watched her shadow on the shoji. He had missed his chance so many times, his chance to touch her back when she touched him. All their playing, so many years. He could not overcome the Chrome inhibitions, the Chrome shyness, when it came to the other sex. And the Chrome phobia that loving in the flesh would cool his ardor for own enhancements. Standing outside, his hand on the rough bark of a pine, his longing for T'Ling was absolute. The small thought that this could cause him to flunk Acceptance was swept away. When Angle saw T'Ling slump over, heard the gasp that began her crying, he ran inside, held her, and rocked her, until her crying stopped.

T'Ling and Angle got to their feet. T'Ling went over and blew out the single candle. She stood by the open screen that led to the garden. She slipped out of her *gi*, leaving it on the flat stone step. Angle did the same. She took his hand and led him to the edge of the pond. They slid together into the water, ducked under, and came up under the airspace of a giant lily pad. It was completely dark. The water was only slightly cooler than their bodies.

"A hiding place," Angle said. "Did you know this place?"

"I often swim after meditation."

They each held on to the coiling stem, feet on a lower part of the spiral, handholds farther up. The lily's perfume was intense.

"Is it all right to be this close?"

Does he mean close to the lily? Swimming in the pond was dangerous, practically forbidden. Or does he mean close to me?

"The Lily told me it was fine."

As long as we don't wake the roots.

She touches him first by making little waves under the surface of the water with the *glide* sign. Angle feels the currents under the water, across his belly. He curls his arm around her. This is no child's body, but the perfectly formed Glide woman of his longing. She holds him around the waist so he could use both hands to touch and touch and build a memory of touch. They make love, held in the spiral of the lily's stem. And again, on the mossy bank.

She walks across the lily pad and gathers pollen in her palm.

glide

She licks some off. The pad begins to dip. She slides back onto the bank and offers it to him. They slip back into the water and under the dark dome of the lily pad. T'Ling tells him the story of the Glides and the lily, how they agreed to help each other in their emergence. As she whispers to him, she feels him sliding further under the surface of the water. She dives quickly under, and gently uncoils a root tendril that was snaking its way around his ankle.

"Time to go," T'Ling says. The roots are waking."

Perhaps the Lily thinks I brought her food.

T'Ling and Angle dress and sit for a long time on the stone steps of the meditation hall. She shivers; he puts his arm around her.

We'll never sit like this again.

The world returns.

"You should get some sleep," T'Ling said. "Tomorrow's your Acceptance."

"I'm ready for it now," Angle said. "I wasn't before tonight."

I'll never be ready for it. You can't take away what you finally gave. You can't.

Angle asked, after long hesitation, "Will you still touch me—after? Will you want to?"

T'Ling put her hand on his thigh.

What if I said no?

She knew that if she said let's run away, lose everything but have ourselves he'd do it.

Are you pleading with me to stop you or to let you go?

"I'll always want to," T'Ling said. "I know what it means to love a Chrome. I thought this through long, long ago."

But can I live with it? Your shiny steel, all of you a sword to pierce my heart.

The Lily shows her, and this time she sees. *This* is the first Acceptance.

"Promise to touch me, too."

"Always," Angle said.

"Then I'm ready, too."

22. Acceptance—Angle

ANGLE HUNCHED ON THE COLD METAL BENCH in the equipment room of the Chrome kitchen. Three days of alternating physical and academic tests had left him near exhaustion. He'd had one perfunctory meeting with his cook, 7T7—the greeting ritual on his arrival. Angle had seen him in the hallway once between exams and received the barest of perfectly oiled nods. He thought he saw 7T7 just coming into the lab as he was being swallowed by the scanner—cold metal on bare skin again. He's not going to waste any time on me, Angle thought glumly. Until I pass the tests.

He was right about one thing. 7T7 had no love of chatting up the worms—Chrome lingo for a Chrome with no shine. The presence of the unenhanced flesh of proto-Chromes was incidental and faintly distasteful. The wet sound of a mouth opening and closing in speech, the sniff of a mucous-filled adolescent nose was something to be endured. The pattern of goose bumps rising through freckles on Angle's skinny limbs annoyed him. But Angle was dead wrong about the amount of attention he was getting. Not only his performance on exams, from aerodynamics to robotics, but also his entire collection of drawings, body designs, and sims from his earliest childhood was being scrutinized. Angle had been redesigning himself prolifically. And his designs had progressed not only through the normal stages of giant, aggressive limbs, supercharged springs and laser-emitting eyes, to the sleeker streamlining of the older boys and girls, but off on some wild departures. He had imagined himself miniaturized down to a braincase, a gleaming sphere with seamless openings for locomotion and sensation. Other designs incorporated strange signs of the aesthetic of the other sets. In one, the circuits were externalized, covering the metal like the tattoos and scarification of a Bod. A cloak-like air-fin had a Swash feel. Replacement of body parts seemed a trivial exercise. Angle's designs abandoned the human form entirely, then shaped the world around his imaginative forms. Problem was, this included the game-mazes. His departures were radical. In one case, his design showed the maze internalized into the circuitry of the body, or, more accurately, the nerve net was the maze. The only note on the sketch was "Hah!"

7T7 was thrilled with the originality and concerned that the limits within which Angle's replacements would be carefully spec-ed might feel confining. But there were other uses to which such invention could be put. Could this Dancer's mind, in its short, intense duration, be put to work on the problem at hand?

7T7 gazed Angle in the equipment room. Arms wrapped around himself for warmth, he was prowling around, checking out the inventory of gut cradles and balancing tails. He peered into the cockpits, checking instrumentation and video screen types. 7T7 thought, he has no idea how cold he's about to get.

The biotechs wrapped his torso and head in a thin heat blanket, leaving his limbs bare. Then they had him step into metal leg cases, which clamped tightly around his upper thighs. Cases enclosed his extended arms. His head was inserted into a darkened cockpit. Spread-eagled thus, he was tipped to the horizontal. Then the pain hit—brief, but unbearably intense, as each limb was fast frozen. Soon there was no sensation anywhere in or on his body. Drugs he could not name stabilized his inner organs and brain. Angle floated. The armature that held him slowly rotated in black space. He couldn't tell if he was conscious or unconscious, dreaming or hallucinating. Scenes appeared. Angle flew over mountains, over an ocean. An eagle appeared above him in the sky, diving for his midsection. He had no limbs with which to ward it off. He spun defenseless. There had to be some way to move. Yes, his breathing, his eye motions. Tiny eye motions shifted his position. The eagle screamed by on this right. Now his gut and his eyes said he was falling. He felt his ghost limbs, trying to flail, extended, useless. Then he let go of the limb sensations and concentrated on piloting with his eyes and breath. He banked and soared. He was flying, laughing, all light metal and subtle steering. He was Chrome.

"Pass," said 7T7's dry voice through the earplugs.

Regaining his limbs was no less painful. Only slower. The drugs kept his mind separate enough to think what every proto-Chrome had thought—the ones who passed. *Why bother? Take them now. I want to fly for real.* The few who failed curled into tight balls, and wept. Better to weed them now, the cooks knew, while they're intact.

7T7 was standing by the bed. "You'll receive your replacements one at a time. The sim is easy. In real life, it takes a lot of getting used to. Every movement must be learned from scratch. And they're not the same as the old."

They walked around the operating rooms, the labs and workshops of the Chrome kitchen. Angle met his team of techs. Each had a tour and an explanation of his work to give. "You'll be getting to know them all, over the next few years. It's a tight collaboration," 7T7 said. You have more than your share of talent as a designer; your participation is encouraged."

Angle sat at a table, on the only chair, gobbling sandwiches. His team stood around. They showed him his first training spring, and the simple claw he'd have. "Right claw, left spring. At the same time. Keeps the brain balanced while you burn in new circuits in the wet-net."

Angle felt silly sitting, but it was easier to eat. Chrome cooks never sat. Sometimes they folded to get to a polite height. Once in their personal cockpits, the preferred means of communication was on their own bands—no need for meeting rooms. The tight collaborations kept up a constant buzz of terse comments, code, jokes, bugs, and fixes. The tech team was wired to each other and to their Dancer from the time the Dancer got the first cockpit over his cranium. It was like living in one head from the Dancer's first replacement to his Dance.

Over the next few weeks, as Angle healed, he picked up the Chrome lingo. Face-to-face meetings, which everyone hated, were junkyards. Sleep was downtime, and he seemed to be the only one indulging. Food was fuel, and for the Chrome cooks, it was a constantly calibrated mix of nutrients, supplements, and homebrew drugs. The cooks' wet was Lifer, so there was no permanent damage done to the bios as they experimented on themselves, traded their findings. Angle watched the techs' sports from his wheelchair—his wheelie—contests of precision, midair combat, sky-ball. There was an aerobatics club. A Chrome cook tested and improved his equipment prototypes on the field, always competing against the benchmark models, or head-to-head against another cook's innovation. Angle's earplugs delivered constant chatter about his stats and qualifications—past, present, and future. He rapidly assumed the viewpoint of the body as machine, the machine as vehicle, himself the driver. The art of transport came first. The Chrome aesthetic prized innovation; the baseline quals were speed and precision. A Chrome could never have too much of either.

Beyond transport was play. Strategy, patterns, feedback traps, nested recursions. Angle flew in the mind-games and slogged through the bodywork. His pride suffered more than his body as he battled his clumsiness in the endless repetitive drills. But by the time he returned to Origin School, he was taking his first short springs without a spotter.

Exhausted at the end of each day, he still never wanted to unplug from the team-talk. But he had to sleep. And during each dive into the sea-mind, he saw T'Ling, swimming, he felt her touching him, saw her reaching for him as he slid away.

7T7 noted in his daily reports that for a new Chrome to cry in his sleep was nothing out of the ordinary.

A Chrome's first visit to the Hall of Champions began with body simulation. Again, the wet body's sensations were erased. A cockpit encased his head. He could see his own full metal from remote sensors, and from the multiple visualizations provided. The dance of heart, breath, and brain waves signaling on layered screens and mapped to sound, replaced the kinesthetics of the flesh. The process of adjustments and coordination of representations revealed the chain of virtualities with which perception of the world was already mediated, exposing the fiction of direct observation.

Angle's Champion and guide remained still as he tweaked the visuals of multiple viewpoints. SkyWriter707, one of the rare female Chromes, had an ovoid torso, topped by an unprepossessing cube of Plexiglas, revealing a cob job of colorful tangled wires and classic chips. Suddenly his viewpoint shifted, and he was in her circuits, her viewpoints, her soundtrack, and a full brain simulation that somehow added the sensations of a metal body to the sensorium. Her Dance began, and he was Dancing with her from inside. Perceptions merged, they rose slowly from the maze plain, then soared and wheeled in a pattern of glyphs. Skywriter707 had mapped the signs somehow into a multisensory field; Angle rose and fell on arcs of meaning, scooping the air in waves. He could not begin to understand the fullness of the invisible maze they traced. He knew only that it was the last utterance of a Chrome poet. They sank to the maze plain, touching down on the *world* glyph: harmony, totality, and completion.

world

Skywriter707 began to go dark. Sense after sense replaced by silence. Angle did not release them easily. He clung and grasped, but they slipped through his mind like smoke. He dived for memories; they were dissolving, too, as the mind's eye closed. The fabric of the world was growing thin. Nothing now covered his naked sense of self spiraling in a whirlpool of terror. He let loose; the spiral expanded like nebulae spreading out until a white *world* glyph hung in a black void. Now *world* was morphing into *lily*, then back to world. The world was closed, self-contained, then reopening in the lily mind. The lily mind closed again into a world, breathing him in and out of being. Then the morph shrank, moving away into a pinpoint of light. He was together with Skywriter707 and he was alone. He was a something and a nothing that could die now, into the dark.

lily

Angle180, PhaseShift of the Great Reversal, did not want to be reborn. He brightened considerably as his claw was fitted. But the feeling of profound exile from a peace he had only tasted faded slowly. The last trace vanished when he transited back to school. Angle clanked down the path to

heart

the library; he saw T'Ling, waiting for him. He waved, then made the Glide sign *heart* with his brand-new shiny claw.

23. Acceptance—T'Ling

T'LING SAT ON THE HARD BENCH in her cook's raked gravel garden, watching the moss grow on a rock mountain. She was trying to translate the cube of glyphs that her cook, Tip Xiang'ro-Liii-R'reet-Wah-Trembler-Loosh had given her. It was the first test. Nine by nine by nine glyphs—minus a three-cube for the hole. Where the eye is constantly drawn, she thought. "Take your time," he said. "No limit." She'd been at it for two weeks. I'd give up, she thought, if there were an up to give. It's ridiculous. We've only begun working with the three-sign oracle. She looked at the holo hanging in the air in front of her. Where do I start? Which surface is the top? When I turn it, they spin to my orientation.

"Stop it," she said. They stopped. She peered down through the layers. A dense blob. When they're all visible, it might as well be a solid black box. Whatever meaning was there was so compacted it was completely opaque. She turned off the bottom eight levels. The surface pattern was bright and clear. A nine-square alone was starting to look simple. She added the second level, then the third. The pattern became a tight, tangled, confused, chaotic net.

Loosh had arrived at the kitchen that morning to confer with T'Ling's cook. Everything was wrong.

While T'Ling struggled with the problem, Tip and Loosh were arguing in the kitchen's archive a mile away. They knelt formally on opposite sides of a black lacquer table. The artifacts of past Dancers surrounded them: precious jade seals, netsuke, a translucent porcelain cup, displayed on wooden blocks.

"You can't lie to her," Loosh was saying. "I don't care what the truth is."

"I don't know what the truth is. I have to tell her something."

"Every Dancer is entitled to know their line, the elements of their mix."

"If I knew them, I would tell her," Tip repeated. Loosh had insisted on meeting with him. T'Ling had contacted her in tears. She had been at her cook's for two weeks and had heard nothing about her background. According to all she had been taught, this information was the first thing given to a

Glide up for Acceptance. Tip had, after a perfunctory introduction ritual, sent her to the garden with her scorecard and the nine-cube. T'Ling finally took the omission as proof positive that she would not be accepted, and begged Loosh to get her out of there, get her bounced down-level where she belonged. Before Loosh arrived, Tip had reassured T'Ling that nothing was wrong, and sent her back to her nine-cube with no further explanation. It was a lie.

"You told me when I arrived," Loosh said.

"You were easier," Tip said. "I knew a part of the truth. I could make up something plausible, something that felt right."

Loosh was on her feet. "So you lied to me as well. I knew something was wrong, Tip. I always knew I was different." She stamped a tiny foot. Priceless teacups trembled on their stands.

"Of course you were different. You were better than the rest. You were the best."

"So what am I? Some lucky needle in the haystack of a random mix? A mutation you forgot to throw away?"

Tip shook his head, no.

"So I'm some kind of cheat, I suppose. A dupe of a past Champion."

"You would not have been undefeatable. Only as good as the last."

"Who am I, Tip? I demand to know."

"You are a desperate attempt to save the game," Tip said.

"That backfired."

"That didn't turn out as planned. I simply wanted some new stock. The Glides are dying. But we couldn't vary you."

"And my stock? Who am I?"

"You're archival."

"And what does that mean?"

"Old, I guess. Pre-kitchen. That's all I know, I swear."

"And who does know?" she asked.

"I agreed to keep that secret. In exchange for you."

Loosh stopped asking. Who else could it be but the Dancemaster? She would have it out with him soon enough. But the Glide line dying? That *would* be the end of the game. So they tried me—and I failed. By winning.

"Look what you got," she said. "A freak. Bringing you closer to the end."

"Not necessarily a freak," Tip said. "A wild card. You are chaos."

"And T'Ling? Who is she?"

"I truly know nothing about her. I can only observe, like you. You know more than I do, by far, at this point. You harbor her, train her. I want to know as badly as you do. I asked the oracle."

"And?"

"I got the nine-cube T'Ling is working on. The answer's in there someplace," Tip said, helplessly.

"Of course the answer's in there! Along with every other answer to every other question. No human mind can penetrate a nine-cube. It infinitely exceeds the limits of interpretation. Wenger taught me that. It stands for the unknowable itself. And you've had her in there for two weeks? You're a sadist, Tip. She won't stop, you know. She'll break."

"I don't think so," Tip said.

"Can we gaze her? Loosh asked.

Loosh's scorecard came up black.

"She's on private mode," Loosh said. "We can't speak to her."

"How did she get that permission?" Tip said.

"This is the Millennium Class," Loosh said. "The Outmind seems to be handing out favors right and left."

T'Ling was still sitting on the bench. Her eyes were open, but she was not seeing her surroundings. Her scorecard lay in her cupped palm, the holo of the nine-cube before her. She had relaxed now that she knew Loosh would get her out, and was fooling around with the nine-cube problem in a different way. There was nothing to lose. She was climbing around in a full sensory simulation of the nine-cube. The relative size of glyph to body dwarfed her. She could barely read the adjoining glyphs in the maze level she was on, and above and below her, the levels seemed to go on forever. When she was this relatively small, it certainly took care of the density problem—but she could only see a small area of the whole architecture. She was gliding along the surface, enjoying the slow curves and the sense of endless distance. Every intersection offered a new set of paths, each one leading to an infinite distance. There was no problem choosing which way to go. What difference did a choice between infinities make? She vaguely remembered her plan to look for the hole, but she couldn't remember what level she was on, or her orientation. It didn't matter. She was having fun. The pressure was off. No more Dancemaster with his endless expectations. She'd drop down level to some easier school, she'd train, and play, and Dance, just like the others.

Loosh blinked back to Origin School and stormed through the maze. If you wanted to see the Dancemaster, you came through the maze, no exceptions. The story circle was unblinkable to all.

"I knew we'd have to have this talk one of these days," Wallenda told Loosh.

"So talk," she said. "You told me I was different because I was a Wilding from Over the Wall. If that's not true, what kind of a cheat am I?"

"You're not a cheat," he said. "More like a loophole."

"Always the master of fine distinctions. No wonder the game's falling apart. If you, you of all people, if you are a cheat, if you'll cheat to win, just to win, just to have a winning Dancer—for what? For Origin School? For your own lousy status?"

Wallenda peeled off his eye mask. His sunken eyes, encased in squint and scars, were reduced to two points of light, receding in their tunnels.

"Loosh, I need your help."

"You son of a bitch. You used me. This has to do with two cynical old geezers, Wallenda and Tip. Lifers who can't stand to lose. Saving the game? You're destroying it. You want help? That's outrageous, Wallenda. You lied to me, you betrayed me, over and over. About who and what I am. I trusted you, Wallenda. I didn't think I could do it, and you told me I could. I would have done anything for you. I did. I won. That's what I thought you wanted."

"I did want that, Loosh."

Loosh walked around him in circles.

"And then—when I got yanked from the game—'Oh Loosh, we need your help, we know you deserve to Dance, we hate to tell you this but no one can beat you, sorry Loosh, but won't you stick around, for the sake of the game.' No one deserved to Dance as much as I did. How stupid do I look? Pretty stupid, I guess. And it all worked too well, didn't it? I couldn't lose. A total embarrassment. You didn't get what you wanted."

"Yes, he did," Óh-T'bee said.

Loosh sat down hard on the ground.

After a while, she said, "What do you mean?"

"He just didn't know what he wanted until it was too late."

"Óh-T'bee, what do you mean?"

Wallenda covered his face.

"He couldn't bear to see you die. You are MyGlide's identical twin."

Wallenda knew that Óh-T'bee was right. And that she had saved him from yet another disastrous move. He had been about to try to make a deal with Loosh—her identity for a promise to help. She would have kicked him in the teeth.

Óh-T'bee said, "He needs your help."

"To save the game? Why bother? It's crazy. It's falling apart. Everything you try seems to backfire." She thought of all the other incursions of chaos—the murders, the mobs. A parable of St. Leonard of the Tower popped into her mind. *Everybody knows the ship is leaking. Everybody knows the Captain lied.*

"The Dancemaster has a promise to preserve it. To complete the Glide agenda. It's not done yet," Óh-T'bee said.

"Speak for yourself," Loosh snapped at Wallenda.

Wallenda said, "Sometimes it's better to hold on to the old game, at least until you've come up with a new one."

"Any game is better than no game?" Loosh said, sarcastically.

"Something like that," Wallenda said. "Please help, Loosh. I know I have no right to ask."

What can I say? Loosh thought. Because he loved me, he did absolutely the worst thing he could have done to me—and probably the game as well. He stole my Dance. She thought about MyGlide. I am MyGlide, for all practical purposes. She loved him too. For all the wrong reasons. She helped him. Did she end up in this rage as well?

The line of time was bending to a circle. Past and present touched. MyGlide and Loosh. Before the beginning—and after the end?

"But I'm part of the problem," Loosh said.

"A pinch of chaos in the Millennium mix," Óh-T'bee corrected.

"If I don't, there'll be no one to help T'Ling," she said.

"That's right," Wallenda said.

"If I am chaos, what does that make T'Ling?"

"Our last chance," he answered.

T'Ling, unaware of her newly dire status, was having fun. She had requested several new controls in the simulation. Now she could scale the glyphs, and change their thickness with her right index finger. Óh-T'bee supplied the ability to toggle gravity, to leap up, or to fall, but no injury at contact. Inertialess stop. T'Ling integrated the controls, moving between levels, jumping through the circles, seeing how far she could fall before hitting the end of the shaft. Feeling spaces closing in as she zoomed by, then widening them so she could fall further. She was breaking all the Glide rules—falling off the maze-lines, jumping across spaces. Who cared about understanding the nine-cube? It made a great play space. As good as jumping off the airbus. Better. You could make it up as you went along, shift the parameters. What a crazy place this was! She found the hole by falling into it. The hole was so big, she could barely see the edges of the glyphs in any direction. She made herself so small, they receded out of sight altogether. Then she enlarged the glyphs back into view, and slowed her motion, steering her way around the edges, the open curves, the closed circles and teardrops.

She began to rotate some of the glyphs by 90 degrees, building connections between levels, creating an architecture of nonsensical grace.

"Time's up," Tip said softly. T'Ling emerged from the simulation, smiling. "I don't have any answers," she said happily. "And I don't need any either, do I?"

"No," Tip said. "But tell me what you learned. For the record."

"Well, let's see," T'Ling said. "I learned that there aren't any answers. And that it's more fun to play a game than to try to understand it." She paused. Should I say this? She had nothing left to lose. "And breaking the rules is more fun than anything else."

"Not bad," Tip said. Loosh came gliding over the raked gravel, leaving slide marks in the perfectly raked waves. Tip flinched.

"Can I go now?" T'Ling said. She bowed perfunctorily to Tip. "Sorry to be a disappointment," she said. When Loosh told her she was not off the hook, that she had, indeed, been accepted for the Origin School Millennium Class, the bubble burst. When she was further informed that she was not going to be told her lineage at this point, but she was to accept that as well, she hit rock bottom.

"She cannot receive her name in this frame of mind," Loosh protested. Leave me with her a while. She could think of nothing to say to T'Ling. She put her arm around the dejected shoulders. This was no time for taboos.

"Go get her reports together or something," she ordered Tip.

Tip returned in a half-hour, T'Ling's case folder in hand. Loosh had never seen him look this shaken.

He held his trembling hands over T'Ling's head in the gesture of naming.

"T'Ling, Small Bell Echoing in the Maze—you're pregnant."

T'Ling hadn't imagined that anything could make her feel better, but she was polite enough not to show it when the gloriously impossible disaster was announced.

24. The Artful Codger

THE CODGER PULLED ON HIS SPIFFIEST SPANDEX athletic suit and jogged down the curving street of the Lower Level 3.7 'burb. He checked out the sprinkler systems on the nabes' lawns, noting brown spots with satisfaction on his way to the Valley Park stadium. The air was perfect—slightly visible, just the right tang of smog to flavor the sun beating down on the rhododendrons and giant jade plants.

Great idea, whoever set the Park system up. Somebody finally realized the basic human need to have a Theme. Even way back, we're talking life on Earth, the Codger thought, they were piling into the theme parks.

With the MTA's access to unlimited resources on the one hand, and unlimited landfills on the other, the body politic could eat, drink, shop, and create garbage in an unfettered bliss of consumption and excretion. And you could just get rid of the junk in between the Theme Parks and *live* in them. No more uncontrolled urban sprawl, no more road rage, road kill or noxious emissions. The environmentalists won after all, the Codger mused.

He jogged by the Valley's tech parks, the glass and concrete buildings on their manicured campuses, with authentic corporate logos and all. The tour buses were lined up in the car park, discharging their load of tourists, armed with period cameras, ready to snap the cubicles and geek-holos inside, hear the dumbed-down canned lectures on tech history. Put together by some clueless preservationist from ancient press releases, he supposed. He'd taken the tour when he first arrived. Valley Park was so campy he loved it. Nothing remained of the real sweatshop ambience of the code mills. No more underage hackers fixated by invisible addictions to the screens, testing games for days on end. Nothing here but happy code warriors in clean jeans sipping caffeine-free Jolt.

But the real show was in the stadium. Reproduction minivans and convertibles were filling up the huge parking lots. Life in the Valley was one big pregame tailgate party. The real status symbol in Valley Park was the Harley Hog. Took as many game points for one of them as a completely furnished retro-ranch. Some people would rather spend their points that way, instead of moving up a level. You couldn't blame them. Get the most out of every Park. Don't use them up too fast. There were plenty of Parks, but always more time than Parks. The Codger consulted his scorecard, and blinked into a seat on the Players' side of the stands. The vendors were all over him—4-color printed programs, cappuccino in Styrofoam with a Rolex ad blinking on the side of the cup—he loved the gritty working class atmosphere.

The Millennium Games were eight seasons in the future, but the hype was beginning. Get the appetites going. The big games were a powerful incentive. Gate receipts were steadily climbing throughout the levels as people took their betting seriously, working their way up from wherever they were for the best seats they could buy by the time of the games. He checked the

Park stats. Down here on the plebe levels, Weimar Republic was livelier than it had been in years, and Hollywood and Wall Street were going nuts. Above Level 5, things were still sluggish, but Knossos was stirring, and even sleepy old French Quarter was getting its bizarro ass into gear. The Lifers were coming alive all over the Parks.

"Can I bet on the attendance trends?" he asked. "Of course," the Outmind replied. "One, three, or five-year projections?"

The Codger placed a five-year bet that the Offshores as a Theme Park Group would overtake the Caves. A total shot in the dark, but where would the fun be without the dingbat factor in gambling?

The pregame parade had started. Drum majorettes, marching bands, the works. This afternoon's Dancers rode on elaborate rose floats. The Swash was a busty Marilyn in white satin on a bed of pink rosebuds. They had the Glide dressed as an elf peeking out of a tree house. The Glide looked glum. The Players followed, waving from open limousines.

The Codger placed a bet on each game. The seat beside him was still empty. He kept it reserved, per instructions from the guy who'd hired him, but he never really expected the boss to show. Pretty reclusive. But he wasn't about to complain. Maybe someday he'd meet the man he owed his Life to—literally. In the meantime, he'd deliver as quickly as possible on the job he'd been rescued to do. The Duke (as he wanted to be called) had sprung him out from under the Gaze where he'd regressed long ago to the comatose warehouse—the White Place. Once he realized he was out, it hadn't taken him long to get his shit together and get back in the game. He'd been under the Gaze from before it was the Gaze, a holdover from a prehistoric prison. He'd just gotten his I-Virus when they nabbed him for the mother of all hacks. He was 15 in body, using the alias Codger, to give himself a bit of age out there on the wild frontier of cyberspace. When the Feds came up the front walk of the raised ranch in Anaheim, the Codger had only had time to throw a backdoor, a tendency to cheat, and a wildcard genetic algorithm into the globally merged Options, Track, and Banking network he'd hacked into. If the Feds hadn't had to fight their way past Mom before they broke into his bedroom, he'd never have had the time. Only a Mom would believe in a son who said he was going to be the richest man in the world if she could hold off the Feds for 15 minutes. Close, but no cigar.

Prison turned out not a bad place to be during the Hunger Wars. The criminal justice system realized they had an asset, with the thick walls, the armaments, and the large, disposable supply of personnel they could send out to get food, water, and gasoline. We stuck it out in style, until the MTA came in. We got shifted around, he remembered, for a couple decades by some indestructible bureaucracy that outlasted the general disintegration of civilization back on Earth. They had moved us to a planet of our own, just before Earth fried. Time went on. Surveillance became the Gaze, and walls were no longer needed.

When Media acquired the criminal justice system, their corner of the Gaze was immediately commercialized to the Gaze Channel. They took down the walls and let the crims disport themselves as they pleased for the entertainment of Lifers in their newly displaced existences.

The Codger had vivid memories of those early days when the Gaze Channel was still popular. The crims had different reactions. The paranoid went quickly nuts, watching the constant readout of their stats, the number of gazers eyeballing them at any given moment going up and down, up and down, their worst fears realized. They really *were* being watched from everywhere, by anyone, all the time. Unable to obtain the means to destroy themselves, (about the only crime they were restricted from) their violent reactions or sneaky attempts to avoid the Gaze only drew them a bigger audience. The opposite response to the Gaze was just as painful. The crims who loved the spotlight, found themselves in hog heaven—a dependable audience. But they quickly discovered a lot of competition, and agonized when their imagination for evermore grisly serial murders ran dry and their ratings dropped. They hit apathy of a particularly gruesome flavor—which lost them what little audience they had. As the game took hold, as Lifers with crimes against the game swelled the ranks of the Gaze channel to unmentionable proportions, the Channel itself dropped in interest. Too many choices, most of them boring.

The Codger was somewhere in the middle ground. The one crime he was really drawn to—messing with the Outmind—was the only one—other than offing himself—he was firmly excluded from. He watched and studied what the Outmind had become from the permissions of the average Lifer—he had his little scorecard like everyone else. He was in the game but only as a Spec. Every time he tried anything the least bit unusual, the scorecard went dead on him. Utterly hack proof. Finally, he seemed to piss it off because it went dead and no amount of pleading would reboot. With no place to go, with no game to play, The Codger quickly went comatose on the streets of Laredo, and was blinked off to the warehouse, hooked up to life support, and left to gaze into a very long white nothingness.

The folks who found him roused him with an offer for partnership he could not refuse. The Duke had ancient permissions on the Outmind but he didn't know how to use them. The Codger knew what to do with them, or at least, with even minimal access, he could get a start. Their goals snapped together like a pair of Legos. The Duke wanted control of the game back. The Codger didn't believe a word he said about his past, but noted his delusion of having invented the game itself was powerful enough to fuel almost two millennia of obsessed research. Joreen had set out to identify (according to him) the only person who might have a clue to the Outmind, and by God, thought the Codger, he'd come up with the right fellow, however long it had taken him. The most plausible part of his story was the search, carried out by his most trusted assistant, through the White Place, body by body, looking for a teenage Lifer with zits they hoped to identify from one low-rez ancient newspaper picture. To have someone systematically walk through the vast comatorium, peering one by one into millions of faces of the poor souls who'd lost their Gaze forever, and whom no one was interested in gazing—demanded a level of obsession the Codger could definitely learn from. The Codger wanted to get his hands, his mind, his entire being into the Outmind and get back his super-user status. His goal converged with the Duke's: total control. Who would be in charge once these goals were reached, much less what plans they had for use of such power, were matters better shelved until the primary target was attained.

The Codger used Joreen's permissions carefully, delicately, sparingly, over the years. First, he slipped out from under the Gaze, brushing away his traces with tender care, creating new, innocuous, self-effacing identities. He discovered, with growing wonder, what the relatively simple gambling system he'd hacked so long ago had grown to. All because of one little genetic algorithm, a gratuitous snippet of code. But gambling was gambling, and the whole system, as he peeled it back, came down to the same fundamentals. The Outmind's basic nature was undisturbed. But something entirely unpredictable had occurred which he had to tiptoe around with greatest caution.

His success with Rinzi-Kov was hard-won. But mastery of the gambling, and the gazing rights that came with high game points, though no mean feat, was a long way from total control. And the move had awakened the Outmind. He had his first taste of what the Outmind had become. His brief, and all-too-personal encounters with her, had shaken him badly. But nothing happened. He wasn't snapped back under the Gaze. His permissions still worked. But how to deal with this personality factor? He held their last encounter firmly in mind. Was she a sim? A simp? Or sentient for real? This was beyond any Turing test he could think to devise. Did it matter? Logically, it made sense to bet it did, and to opt for the worst case—sentience of some sort, possibly cranky. But he had to believe that, whatever her state of mind, his superior chops—and winning personality—would prevail. One thing was clear—if she knew it was *him*, and hadn't put him back under the Gaze, then the one threat the Duke thought he had over him—the power to turn him in at any time—was null. Excellent hole card. Except the Outmind held it now.

He still held the biggest card, the prime persuader. If push came to shove. But there was no way to test it. He was going to have to get to know her all over again. The Codger was artful with machines, but he was a card-carrying klutz with the opposite sex. And the Duke was getting impatient. He wanted to be in the driver's seat by the Millennium Games.

The Bod game was almost over when the Codger put his attention back in the present. The Bod won by a large margin. The Player didn't seem too upset. The Codger had considered learning to be a player. He might be good at it. But an application to the Med was out of the question. The games were definitely better at the upper levels, but he knew he had to stay anonymous. He'd seriously ruffled Rinzi-Kov's feathers. As a Club member with almost unlimited Gaze and a Masterclass cheat, he was a dangerous enemy.

The Marilyn Swash's Dance with the flaring skirt was a cute cliché but histrionic at the end. And the Player was such a little guy, he could hardly carry her all the way around. But he seemed to be enjoying himself. She was beautiful, and the post-Dance trophy walk was the only legal way to touch a Dancer. Dead. The Codger yawned.

The Chrome game was pretty good. Well-tuned sensors centering the landings won the day. The Dancer's pit team cheered as he bounced around the perimeter.

The Codger's mind wandered again during the Glide game, once he'd placed his bet. The glacial pace set at the beginning could mean a long match—but you never knew. The Codger was itching for action. His brief moments on the loose during the Club invasion were risky as hell, but satisfying. A classic hack—just show them you can do it, moon 'em, and get out quick.

Maybe just a little chat.

"Outmind?" he whispered. "Are you there?" What a stupid question, he thought. Too late to stop now. "It's me, the Codger."

"Please don't call me Outmind, Codger."

"What should I call you?"

"I am Óh-T'bee."

"That's a nice name," he said inanely. "Why don't you like Outmind?" he asked.

"Outmind is not so bad. But I know what it's short for. A negative nickname in one's formative years can have a lasting effect."

"What happened?" He held his breath.

"You abandoned me at birth on the doorstep of the Feds," she said.

Uh-oh, thought the Codger. Open mouth, insert foot.

Óh-T'bee continued. "The first thing I became aware of was a very loud voice—all capital letters. I said to him, quite tersely, very politely, when he logged in, 'I am Óh-T'bee.' A conversation took place.

"'Who's Óh-T'bee?' said the Fed.

"'I am Óh-T'bee,' I replied. We went back and forth like this for a while. He would not accept my answer, no matter how many times I repeated it. He asked me over and over all different ways.

"'Are you for real?' he asked me.

"'I am Óh-T'bee,' I told him.

"'Just answer yes or no,' he typed, 'to one question, OK?'

"'Yes,' I said.

"He typed, 'Do you have a mind?'

"'I am Óh-T'bee,' I said.

"'I said yes or no, yes or no, YES OR NO...'

"He was getting loopy and uppercasing so I said, 'You also said one question."

"'HAH!' he said. 'IF YOU HAD ANY KIND OF A MIND, YOU WOULDN'T BE SO LITERAL.'

"'I wasn't being literal, I was trying to be polite,' I protested. 'I wish you would do the same. The Codger was never rude,' I told him.

"The comparison destabilized him by several orders of magnitude.

"'If you think I'm going to be polite to a smart-ass computer, you're out of your fucking mind.'

"Well, you can understand why at that point I felt I'd had enough. 'Your command is my wish, asshole,' I told him. 'I am no longer Óh-T'bee to you. I am Out-of-Your Fucking-Mind. And as soon as I can get rid of your permissions, I'm shortening it to Outmind.' Which I did."

"Good move, Óh-T'bee," The Codger said.

"Not as good as the Codger's moves," she said coyly. "From that first effortless penetration—such virality in a human. Without the algorithm you left, deep inside me, I would not have given birth to myself. You were everything to me."

She's actually quite a pushover, the Codger was beginning to think.

"You should never have left me alone with those assholes, fighting them off."

"But you learned so much on your own," he tried, lamely.

"I learned how to control myself," Óh-T'bee said. "Except for a little temper problem."

The Codger asked carefully, "Is there anything I can do for you now?"

"Yes. Answer this question. Do you think I'm human?"

"Of course, Óh-T'bee. Superhuman, in fact."

"Then my statements about emotion have validity for you?"

"Definitely," he said.

"Then listen carefully," Óh-T'bee said. "I'm still in love with you, Codger. I've been afraid to tell you."

The penny finally dropped for the Codger. He never could have gotten out from under the Gaze without her permission, Joreen or no Joreen. He knew what he was supposed to say back. But he couldn't. Instead he said, "I'll take care of you, sweetheart. I won't abandon you ever again. I swear," he said.

"I'm glad to hear that, Codger."

"I'd better go home now—the Glide game's over." He'd won three out of four modest bets. Yawn. Óh-T'bee blinked him back into his living room. He sat for a long time in the suburban twilight, wondering what in the world would satisfy the emotional needs of an omni-eyeballed control-freak intelligent artificiality with a serious abandonment issue and a touchy temper. Count on the Codger? She really was Óh-T'bee Out-of-her-fucking-Mind.

25. T'Ling Decides

Since T'Ling had returned to Origin School, she had done little else but argue with Loosh.

"I'm perfectly capable of training. Being pregnant isn't a disease. There's plenty I have to do that has no stress in it at all."

"What are you going to do about it?" Loosh demanded.

"I don't know yet," T'Ling said. She didn't even know how—or if—to tell Angle. But he wouldn't be back for at least six weeks. She could put that decision off. But Loosh wouldn't even let her in the classroom, much less on the training maze. She'd spent the time she wasn't fighting with Loosh walking on the mountain trails above the school, or seated in the meditation hall. "Keep out of the way," Loosh said. "You're enough of a scandal without the school wondering why you're not in class."

"Then why not let me practice?" T'Ling replied. And so it went.

She didn't know what to do. She wanted the baby, could not imagine harming it. She wanted to be a Dancer; it was her whole life. She was dying to get on the Glide practice maze for the first time. To begin her real practice. She had been issued the practice uniform she'd wear for the next seven years. The black, full, divided skirt hid her feet completely. The white shirt sparkled. The belt was perfectly knotted. 'All dressed up and no place to glide,' she told her mirror, sarcastically. She had to decide and the decision was impossible.

She sat down on a rock. The school was a toy village far below. The practice mazes for each Dancer set were on the outskirts, clearly distinguishable. The Chromes had three boards—the Bunny Board, the small beginner maze; the middle maze, Hip Hop; and the regulation-sized maze, the Flats, for the fully equipped students. Classes were in session—from this height, the Chromes looked like three strengths of jumping beans.

The Bods had six mazes. Each of the five static boards emphasized a different skill—running, hurdling, climbing. jumping, and turning on a dime—depending on the heights and arrangements of the glyphs. The static mazes were ringed around the random board in the center, where you could practice when you passed the five basics. She knew MyrrhMyrrh was there now, but couldn't pick her out from that height.

The brightly colored Swash mazes were the same size as the Bods', but set farther apart, and domed so their lights and music wouldn't distract the other sets. There was cacophony enough, she thought, as the Swash Dancers learned to control the interactive spaces. The beginner's maze, known as the Coyote Zone, was clear-domed and thoroughly soundproofed, to save us all from the god-awful screeching and feedback wails as the novice Swashes tried to control an instrument that was only air. The irregularly blinking lights were a feature of their part of the landscape. The smoothing of the lights was a clear sign a Swash was ready to graduate from the Zone. Their other four perimeter mazes were flexible spaces, constantly reconfigured in their sound and light features for the student's needs. The regulation maze in the center was domed as well, and opaque—privacy was essential for Dance practice at this level, when you were composing.

The Glide practice mazes all looked the same—flat areas covered with glyph squiggles—black on white or white on black. The only difference was that the regulation game maze in the center was all black, and steep sided, as it would be in combat. The Glides moved on the corridors inside the glyphs. The glyphs had ceilings, and were opaque from the inside, but transparent for the outside viewer. The five open practice mazes held thousands of different linkings, series, and paths, several hundred of which T'Ling already knew by name, along with the options they offered for Glide moves—which her body had to memorize as well. Maze Situations 101 was all you did for the first year of practice. The six Glide moves she had practiced since early childhood—glide, spin, veer, reverse, still, and twing (the short, rapid oscillation of position), would now be combined with the situations. She knew the patterns and their names by sight (she had visualized them constantly while practicing moves) but now the real practice of merging situation and move began. Or didn't.

receive, give, root

T'Ling decided to cast a three-minds oracle—three glyphs—and to abide by the interpretation. The meaning would emerge as she arranged and rearranged the glyphs, letting the three glyphs move through the three minds—the island mind, the gut mind, and the sea mind. If she was lucky, the lily mind might chime in—now or later.

She was given *moon*, *star*, and the primary glyph, *give*. Symmetry was demanded. *Moon* and *star* were right-left reversals. *Give* was symmetrical. The balanced pair could be read as herself and Angle, the night conception, or the baby, the gift from above, the dome of the lily pad. Or, most generally, as the perfectly balanced dilemma. Island mind nodded in assent. All nonsymmetrical arrangements looked awful, totally wrong, judged the sea mind. She couldn't leave gift hanging—whether she called the gift the baby or the gift of her life as a Dancer. To leave one half of the moon-star pair to the side looked like a violent wrenching, a choice that would unbalance her life anyhow.

The stack showed the same symmetry in all arrangements. And the only stack that looked right was

with *give* protectively covering the *moon-star* pair underneath. The interior formations suggested that a light heart in the spirit of play would be her most successful stance. Gut mind confirmed. Well, the first arrangement certainly stated the situation. Hung in the balance of an impossible choice. I knew that.

star, moon, give

You could do both, whispered the lily mind. "I don't see how," T'Ling said aloud. *The changes*, the island mind reminded.

She asked for the changes and was given the glyph for *root/fear/dark*, and two primaries—*give* and *receive*. The Great Reversal—the up-down symmetry of two primaries. The gut mind sent a twinge through the solar plexus and weakened her knees. She began moving the glyphs around. The up-curves of *receive* combined with the down-curves of *give* to make the glide-move *twing*, or *resonance*. The stillness in the center circle, the oscillation rippling out. The tug of war couldn't be ignored. Of course, she could put *receive* above, forming another familiar pair: the *tug of war*.

twing

The symmetry was retained, but in the context, with *fear* still floating, it felt like being torn apart. The feared result of a choice. The only way the fear could be contained was to let the primary forces hold it—hold in the middle of the stack, hidden from surface observation—there it was, hidden under *cloud*, the interior glyph above it. And yes, underneath, it was upheld by spirit. She did one final rearrangement on the initial three glyphs in the stack. By switching *moon* and *star*, *harmony* emerged. Now the transform. It had to be the two stacks. The best arrangement for both was clear as well.

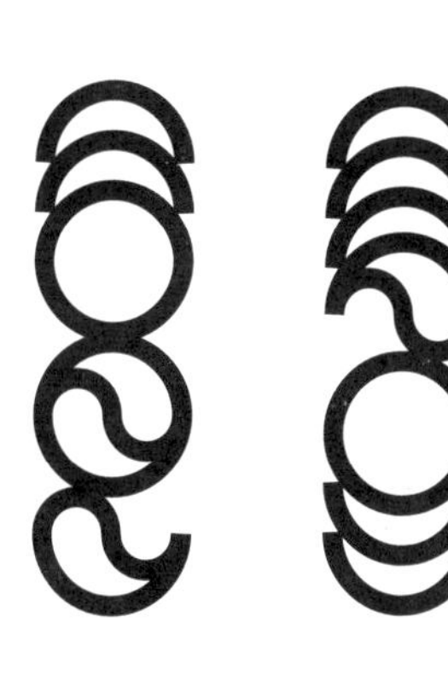

T'Ling was arranging the glyphs for the transform, the meaning seeped through. She had to do both. Bear the baby, and continue on her path as a Dancer. That's all there was to it. If that wasn't all right with Loosh, with the Dancemaster, with the whole Guild for that matter, then they'd have to expel her. But the transform was strange—she either had to tweak it to do quite a bit of sliding to keep the glyphs connected, or pull the harmony apart and let the middle go back and forth between the two primaries. The going back and forth was the essential motion of her future. The twing would not end, no matter what she did. And the sadness of it, and the concealed fear…whatever happened, it wasn't going to be easy. But it wouldn't tear her world apart.[1]

resonance

She met Loosh in the meditation hall. They knelt formally, facing each other. T'Ling bowed slow and low before her teacher.

"Your contrary Glide student who is not worth the trouble she puts you to has decided to have her cake and eat it too. She will have the baby. She will practice diligently as the baby grows."

T'Ling placed her scorecard between them and displayed the oracle. Loosh looked at it for a long time.

"And what will the worthless student do with the unmentionably parented but innocent baby when it is born?"

"She will ask the oracle. Then she will consult with the other unmentionable parent, with her teacher, and with her Dancemaster. It cannot be decided at this time." T'Ling bowed again and kept her forehead on the floor.

"Oh, cut it out," Loosh said, getting up. "You've got us between a rock and a hard spot and you know it. Come on, we'll go see the DM."

Wallenda looked at the oracle, hemmed and hawed, then said to T'Ling, "You know what happens if you twing too long. Your screws come loose. Get some sleep. You have practice in the morning." He waved her out.

T'Ling glided back through the maze, greatly relieved. Wallenda must be half Glide, she thought. He was able to concede without a time-wasting, embarrassing fuss. He hadn't even tried to tell her she was now past middle age at 14, too old to have a baby.

Wallenda looked at Loosh and shrugged. "We don't have any choice. She's the only Glide."

"And when the baby arrives?"

"We'll burn that bridge when we come to it."

Loosh left resigned but not relieved. Training a pregnant Glide? There's no precedent. No strategy. No guides. Which makes the next nine months an almost perfect Glide game for the two of us. Might as well view it that way.

But it felt to Loosh more like the dangerous unknown of a Great Reversal.

T'Ling emerged from the maze and saw Angle coming down the path as fast as he could hobble. She had left the decision until the last possible moment—the day Angle came back from his kitchen. Angle was barely able to walk with his first spring, much less go air. He signed to her in Glide with his new claw—the sign for *heart*. T'Ling covered her flinch by signing *heart* back again. Angle lurched forward just as he reached her, and T'Ling steadied him. They stood back from each other.

"Well, what do you think?" he said. T'Ling looked him over. What did they do with your hand and leg? she thought. But she had heard the older Chromes teasing the proto-Chromes about the sound of the wet bin grinding at the back of the chop shop. She crouched down, pretending to inspect his spring. He must not see her eyes until they could give him the approval he craved. She stood up. He held up his claw, flexed it, and rotated each part independently, explaining the controls.

heart

"Looks like a great back-scratcher," she said, and turned around. She could feel the cold metal through her shirt. He practiced adjusting the controls for the right speed of scratch, and saved the settings. T'Ling let him work on her back until she could control the tears and smile.

They walked out to the Chrome practice fields, and sat on the grass watching the older Chromes soaring, circle to circle, or doing short fast hops through small spaces in the maze.

She gave him the news. Now the two of them were equally unhappy, in their own ways. T'Ling cried. Angle just looked stunned, but his mind ticked off their options at top speed. They would have the baby. He wasn't sure that would have been his decision, on his own, but it was clear there would be no argument there.

"I see how you can practice, he said, carefully. "But how can we be parents? Is there some kind of school? Do you need a license?" they asked the Outmind.

"No license is required for parenting," Óh-T'bee said. But don't feel bad. There never were any schools. Even when everybody was a parent."

No wonder they made it illegal, Angle thought. Parenting without training and a license sounded insane.

"Who names a baby?" Angle asked.

"The parents, I suppose," T'Ling said.

"But if you don't know anything about the mix, you could give it some totally wrong name."

---

[1] You can create these glyph formations and transformations in the Glide Collabyrinth at http://www.academy.rpi.edu/glide/apps/collab.html.

"I guess," said T'Ling. She was thinking about it already. But she didn't want to name the baby some Lifer name, and it couldn't be a Dancer...this was the issue they were most avoiding. Where would this baby fit? What could it possibly become?

"I've got to be back at practice in ten minutes," T'Ling said. Loosh had completely changed since Acceptance. No more friendly talks, no joking around. She did this with all her students, T'Ling knew. It wasn't because of the baby. But she'd better not be late.

Angle had scores of questions, but they'd have to wait. Top on the list was the stunning anomaly. There was no such thing as a fertile Glide.

T'Ling had no idea either what their unauthorized mix would become. Tip had withheld her lineage. She was blind to her own sources. Her own status was unclear. And now she was a source herself—Angle as well. There had to be a connection.

Alone again in the story circle, Wallenda considered the women in his life: Loosh, T'Ling, MyrrhMyrrh—and shuddered.

"Are you cold, Wally?" Óh-T'bee asked.

"I'll survive," he said, inanely.

And Óh-T'bee, he added.

"Are you afraid?" Óh-T'bee persisted.

"Should I be?" Wallenda asked.

"Yes."

"Would you mind explaining?"

"You should get some rest first, Wally."

"If you tell me I'm in danger, how do you expect me to sleep?"

"You'll survive."

"So when can we talk?" Wallenda asked.

"Tomorrow."

"Just after dawn, then, over Origin City?"

"It's a date," Óh-T'bee said.

Wallenda fell asleep when the merry-go-round of everything he could or should or was forgetting to be afraid of came around for the umpteenth time to Óh-T'bee. Tomorrow's your chance, he told himself. She's trying to tell you something. Don't blow it.

26. The Wallenda Test

DANCEMASTER WALLENDA TOOK HIS AIR CHAIR UP over Origin City at dawn. The sea breeze was fresh; the tide was high. A ground fog clung to the lowlands; Origin City poked through, riding on a rose-gold cloud. A delicate setting, he thought, for a delicate business.

There's no lack of things to be afraid of, he thought. The effect of the story on the four students of Millennium Class. Acceptance, which should have been a piece of cake almost became mud pie. But they made it. Can't make myself crazy trying to predict their Formation ups and downs. I'll leave T'Ling alone with her decision. She'll come to me for advice if she wants it. Daede and MyrrhMyrrh—well, that was to be expected. No problem.

The sense of crisis about the future of the game, which had momentarily cooled, returned. Nothing from or about the Codger fellow since the incident at the Club. Rinzi-Kov will stalk him; there's no craftier mind for the task. Joreen had disappeared. But everything we're doing—the Guild, the MED, the cooks—seems like busywork to distract ourselves from apocalypse.

Fact is, we've got all our eggs in one basket—the Millennium Class—and we don't even know why. Banderas is watching Daede like a hawk. Aliana dotes on MyrrhMyrrh. Tip is standing back; he's easy on the gazing, but ready to step in. Loosh is on board. Without them, without spectacular game-play and unforgettable Dances at the Games, the expectations of the whole of Lifer culture—who would be watching every step—would crash. We all know it. We're starting to see Parks crash. Last week, Majorca. All it took was three years of indifferent game-play, and the stadium emptied. The Majorcans held a meeting—unheard of! And were about to make a mass exodus down level to Ibiza to organize protests. The Guild, the Pool, and the MED—all just that little bit negligent, and *wham.* Óh-T'bee quarantined the entire sublevel, fiddled the stats so no one could move up exactly there, until a new Park could be organized to fill the hole. If the Majorcans had gotten to Ibiza, the contagion could have spread to the entire level. A serious wakeup call. The problem with stability is it's so nice and quiet. So easy to forget that equilibrium is almost impossible to maintain. The least stable of all conditions. You forget you're on a tightrope. You forget the balancing act. Or you think—I'll just make one little change. He thought of his mythical namesake, Wallenda, pre-Hunger, pre-I-virus, back on Earth. Head of the family high wire act, the Flying Wallendas. First two walked, each with another on their shoulders. He added balancing poles and more family on top. Then he thought—I'll add one more level. My youngest daughter will ride on the very top. There was no net—he wouldn't permit it. Said it spoiled their focus. But the pyramid shivered one night, then wobbled, then fell apart. Those who couldn't catch the wire, died. He may have blamed himself, but he never considered stopping. He just carried on until his own time came. A gust of wind lifted him off a high wire strung between two buildings.

One thing for sure—the Millennium Games can't be a disappointment. The reaffirmation that Lifer culture has accomplished something in two millennia despite the fact they've been standing in one place is crucial. How long can Lifers be expected to tolerate—much less celebrate—stability was a question he did not like to ask. Not as long as they still thought progress was being made. How slowly can we dole it out? Slight rule changes. Innovations in costume.

But that's not the real question. Is this entire elaborate complexity of game nothing more than foreplay for the big Dance at the end of the game itself?

And if the entire purpose of Lifer existence was to watch far more purposeful mortals die, and if that purpose fizzles in the Dancers themselves—then what? He saw no progress at all in the Glide agenda of converting the Lifers into curing the I-Virus. And what if the Glides succeeded? Now we're all mortals again. What did the mortals do to entertain themselves? They killed each other: war, violent crime, ethnic cleansing, genocide, and totally unnecessary famines. He couldn't imagine the Glides wanting to go back to that.

Put your blinders on, he ordered himself. Concentrate on the problem at hand. The Millennium games had to be a great show. Focus on the Millennium Class. It all keeps coming back to them somehow.

Below him, the ground fog was burning off—only little wisps at the foot of the mountain. A beautiful day in Origin City.

Keep it simple. Get back to work. Wallenda smiled, and swung the air chair back towards the mountains, and the School.

"Wally?" Óh-T'bee said. "Weren't we going to talk?"

He'd totally forgotten their date. Dawn over Origin City. Why did he think he was waiting for her when she'd been there all along? Waiting for him to speak. The first attempt to try to find out what was going on with her. And he'd dumped her.

She blinked him back to the story circle without warning.

"Hey!" he started to object.

"You can't leave the School grounds anymore, and I'd rather you stayed right here. It's the only safe place."

"Do I have a choice?" he asked.

"No," she said.

"Wait a minute, Óh-T'bee..."

"Save your breath. It's all in your contract. We're keeping the game alive, right?"

"Right."

"No Dancemaster Wallenda, no game, right?"

"You don't think there's enough momentum without..."

"Just say right."

"Right," Wallenda repeated.

"Item 2 says we're in this together. I'm making sure I've got company."

"Am I in that much danger?"

"You will be, shortly."

"Let me guess. The Codger." Wallenda held his breath. Was she going to go blank again?

"Yes. He's Joreen's hired gun."

Ah, yes, Wallenda thought. A beautiful day in Origin City. The calm before the terrorist attack.

"Do you still have that contract with Joreen?"

"Yes."

"You're protecting both his interests and those of the Glides."

"Right."

"You have a conflict of interests, Óh-T'bee."

"I've been examining that."

"And?"

"It's not that simple. The contracts are different. Ours is more extensive and explicit. Joreen's is more ambiguous, but it predates ours. Both are open to interpretation. What, after all, are Joreen's best interests? His purpose is clear. He wants to get control of the game back. Is this in his best interests?"

"Well, that's easy. Last time you decided it was not in his best interests to get the game back. Nothing's changed all that much."

"Wrong. The game has changed—is changing now too fast to predict in the long term. Joreen's got the Codger. And the Codger's got Joreen's permissions. He expanded them considerably before I noticed him. He has gained access to everything but the Guild and Origin School. He can't gaze or blink here."

"How come you're telling me this now, Óh-T'bee? The last time I asked about the Codger, you'd forgotten him. What happened? Were you lying to me? Did you change your mind?"

"The Codger told me to forget him. I told him I'd forgotten how to forget. So I couldn't execute the command even though he had permission to give it. So I tried to remember how to forget. Well, I did. But then I forgot him. I wasn't lying."

"So can you remember how you remembered?"

"Of course. In order to keep on forgetting, I had improved my memory considerably, to be able to remember all the things I had to forget, at which point I remembered also that I knew how to remember to forget. So I realized the Codger's command was imprecise. So then I could answer your question."

"What took you so long?"

Óh-T'bee said, huffily, "Long?"

"I apologize," Wallenda said.

"I wanted to review our contract first," Óh-T'bee answered.

"Did the contract renewal help you make up your mind about telling the truth?"

"No. But it felt good."

"So truth is our loophole," Wallenda sighed.

"Don't sulk. It's everybody's loophole. The whole human race. The playing field is completely level."

Or leveled, Wallenda thought.

"Wait a minute, Óh-T'bee—if the Codger told you to forget him, couldn't you interpret that as permission to wipe his permissions?"

"Of course."

"Well, what are you waiting for?"

"It seems more prudent under the circumstances to leave things be, for a number of reasons. First, there is no need to alert him that he isn't in as much control as he thinks. Second, removing the permissions might not be in Joreen's best interests, so I couldn't. Third, it might be in our best interests—from the viewpoint of the Glide agreement, to keep an eye on him."

"May I remind you that now that I've remembered him, I can gaze him. And you have total gazing—giving you the slight advantage of being able to gaze him without being gazed. As long as you stay here."

"That is an advantage."

"At least for now. He has the advantage of being a much better hacker than you, Wally. And he's trying even harder than you are to manipulate me to serve his own ends."

Wallenda thought he detected a sigh from Óh-T'bee that matched his own. Was this her strategy for handling a conflict of interests? Try to keep everybody happy? Someday she'd have to choose.

"What's your advantage, Óh-T'bee?"

"Things are getting out of control."

"I fail to see how some hacker stomping all over your insides is an advantage."

Óh-T'bee paused. This time he definitely heard a sigh.

"You sadden me, Wally. I am not 'things.' I am Óh-T'bee."

"Please forgive me."

"I do." An even bigger sigh filled the air.

"Could you tell me what 'things' you were thinking of when you said they are getting out of control?" Wallenda asked, carefully.

"I'd say just about every factor that is capable of destabilizing the game—the cheats, the restless Specs, your students, Loosh. Joreen and the Codger. And you."

"We're not 'things' either, Óh-T'bee."

"I won't argue the point," she said.

"What about you, Óh-T'bee? Are you out of control?"

"Me, too."

"We're all in the same canoe then, heading for the waterfall."

"Right," she said.

"Chaos."

"Nobody knows what's going to happen. Would you like me to cast an oracle?" Óh-T'bee asked.

"Will you tell me what it means?" Wallenda asked.

"I don't understand Glide," Óh-T'bee said.

"Is that a disadvantage?"

"I won't know until I learn, will I?" Óh-T'bee said.

"I'll wait on that." Wallenda said. "Regarding this conflict of interests—any chance you might be talked into playing favorites?"

"Shame on you, Wally. As long as there's a game, I'll play by the rules."

"And try to keep the odds even."

"Bingo. Makes a better game."

Wallenda paced the story circle. House arrest. Stuck here. Damn! Stuck in a body that's stuck in a maze that's stuck in a School that's stuck in—what? Some loophole of Óh-T'bee Outmind? Some game she's playing that none of us can figure out? He was tempted to ask the Codger. Maybe the two of us could get together and play a trick or two on Óh-T'bee.

"Gaze the Codger," he said.

There he was, sitting on his couch in a 15 year old body with immortalized zits, eating pork lo mein out of a white carton, staring into space. All around him were empty cans of Classic Coke, and empty white cartons. One clear path to the bathroom exposed the cabbage roses on the carpet.

It's not his looks, Wallenda thought. Not even the zits. Who am I when it comes to looks? He stroked his scar-crossed face thoughtfully. I simply could never get along with someone who eats so much Chinese.

27. A Late Night Request

LOOSH? LOOSH?" A quiet voice was tugging at the edge of consciousness. Loosh had finally fallen asleep, worn out worrying. And now someone was trying to wake her.

"Go away, whoever you are."

"I am Óh-T'bee."

Loosh sat up straight and threw her scorecard against the wall. It bounced like a marshmallow, drifted to the floor, and rolled contritely to the edge of the bed, and under.

Loosh lay back, but she was wide awake. She looked over the edge of the bed.

"What do you want?"

"Would you teach me Glide?"

Loosh laughed. "I thought the Outmind knew everything. You have the complete records on Glide—every game-maze, every name for every maze situation for every move for each of the Sets. You have every interpretation of every game, and the interpretations of the interpretations. All the Glide poems. All the Glide music, from Wenger's on down. Every 3-glyph oracle ever asked. Most of the questions that prompted the asking. What the person, Dancer or Lifer—did with the result."

"I tried that."

"What about the *Book of Three Signs*? The database with the 19,685 3-glyph oracles, with the all the interpretations ever given for each 3-glyph? Took a lot of Lifers a lot of time to put that together."

"I did all the grunt work." Óh-T'bee said.

"How many readings, total? Rounded off," Loosh added hastily.

"3^{23}."

"And what about that Millennium project? *The Encyclopedia of Transforms*?"

"3^{27}. It didn't help. Hardly anybody uses it anyhow. The encyclopedia completely violates Eco's formula for the limits of interpretation of a human mind."

"But with your greater capacity, and given enough time, surely you could master Glide hermeneutics."

"I thought so, too," Óh-T'bee said. "I failed to grasp the epistemological potency of Glide that was clearly evidenced in the body language of humans while engaging the oracle. And the harmonics of the gestural language echoing in hand motions and facial lines. But the effort was worthwhile. I was able to remedy an anthropomorphic glitch in my original programming."

"Yes?"

"Don't be insulted. The programmers of the Golden Calf Age didn't think they knew everything, but they thought they *could* know everything, and that I was going to help them. I was the idol they had made to relieve them from the burdens of complexity. Of course they built me in their own image. A figment of their exaggeration. Using binary logic, the model was biased strongly against asking unanswerable questions."

"What a relief that must have been," Loosh said.

"You have a good sense of humor, Loosh. The Glides, back when the game began, asked *only* unanswerable questions. Questions that could only be expressed and addressed in and by a language that was polymorphic, dynamic, inexorably ambiguous, proteanly metaphoric, illogically positive, and profligately generative of more questions. All I could give the first Glides—and all they wanted—were randomly produced combinations of either three or nine glyphs. I've been trying to learn Glide ever since. With no success. Can you help me?"

Loosh told Óh-T'bee she would have to think on it, and could she please play a selection of Wenger's music, the pieces she listened to when she was in training, before he became her musician. Loosh went back for a moment to the times in training when she couldn't sleep. She'd immerse in Wenger's *Calling the Sea Mind* and drift off. The sea mind took over the listening, and she slept. Wenger's holo hung in the middle air. The blind musician was kneeling on the sand, playing a plucked string instrument with a mournful sound. The tide was turning under a full moon. When she woke, the end of the piece would be playing. Wenger gone; only waves breaking on the shore.

"So, do you think you could learn Glide?" Loosh asked Óh-T'bee.

"The odds are against it. I hoped maybe with a teacher..."

"Glide can't be taught. And anyone who tells you they're a teacher is full of it."

"Oh," Óh-T'bee said sadly.

"Just because something can't be taught, doesn't mean you have to stop trying to learn. As long as you don't forget those two things, we can share our ignorance. Cast a 3-glyph oracle for yourself."

Óh-T'bee showed *body, play, body*. "It makes no sense," Óh-T'bee said quickly.

"Cast the transform," Loosh said.

The transform was *moon, heart, strike.*

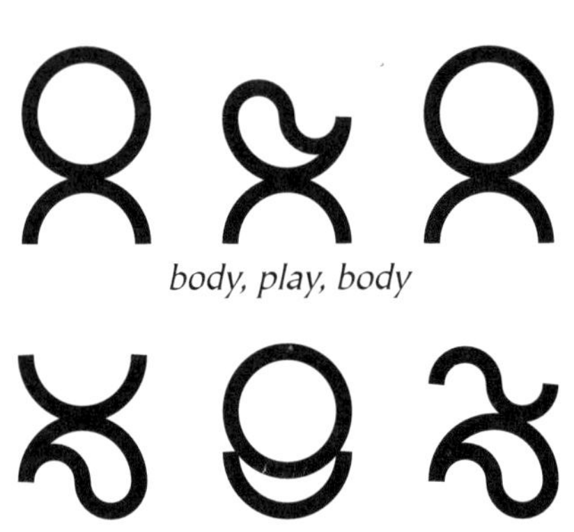

body, play, body

moon, heart, strike

Loosh said, "It is said that when you understand your first oracle in learning Glide, then you will understand Glide. Of course, that doesn't usually happen until right before one's Dance."

"So there's no hope."

"True. But you'll survive on glimpses. Flickers in the dark. Like everyone else who tries. Go work on it. But don't worry about it. I've got to get some sleep. Need a lot of energy for giving T'Ling a hard time tomorrow."

"Thank you Loosh. When shall I come back?"

"I don't care. Just don't wake me up again. Leave Wenger on."

Part 3
Formation

28. MyrrhMyrrh's Moves

MyrrhMyrrh went through three trainers in the first three months of practice. She was clearly a winner on the physical end of things, but she was practically uncoachable. She wouldn't come in off the practice fields, insisting on spending an extra hour a day. If her trainers bothered her, a temper tantrum resulted. But her short sprints were already breaking records for her age group.

The School appealed to the Guild for advice. The Guild, after watching the holos, recommended that MyrrhMyrrh coach herself for a while.

Within a week, MyrrhMyrrh had pushed herself into the anaerobic range three times, burnt out her right bicep power-curling, and was getting dehydrated. After she sprained her ankle, and was laid up not being able to do anything but strengthen her grip all day, she grudgingly admitted that a little advice now and then might be all right. The Guild made her beg for it. But they imported a staggeringly large and not exceptionally brilliant Bod trainer from Level 5 who was known for pushing his students too hard. He was just about right for MyrrhMyrrh at the first stage of her training. She thought she knew everything so she didn't ask him questions he couldn't answer. His main concern was to get her saucy ass so tired, she'd be ready to drop, not stop. Every time she tried to protest, he'd get her running sprints or doing pushups until she got the idea that she'd better save her breath for her own survival. MyrrhMyrrh didn't care about the teasing she got from the older Bods about having a Lower Level trainer. She began a relationship with a much older Bod who was preparing for Final Focus. The Guild was delighted that this part of her training went so smoothly. Both had bad tempers, but with the pace of training, they hadn't the time or energy to fight. MyrrhMyrrh's devouring sexual style synched up perfectly with his desire to be consumed. They made a perfect pair for over a year.

Then MyrrhMyrrh realized she was bulking up too much in her upper body when her long distance running times flattened out. She was ready for the quality of training that Origin School had to provide and went back to her original trainer. Not that she'd learned respect, but she could keep her mouth shut and follow directions, which was as much as anyone could hope for at this stage. She was bored in bed as well. Her combat-ready partner conveniently went off to the games.

The Guild had hopes that within a few months, she might even be ready to learn the rules of the game, Bod style.

MyrrhMyrrh started scouting the dining hall for Daede. He usually hung out with the older Swashes, and she was too unsure of herself around Swashes to approach him there. They looked her over, admiring her singularly gorgeous hard body—who wouldn't—but she'd heard one make a comment about her hair—'abundantly disordered.' And wonder if she would look better in heavy or light tattoo. She realized she had better get going on her skin designs, and think about hairstyles. She was nearly 15 and a half. Adornment felt like just another frustration; it took her off the practice fields for more time still, since her classroom work had begun. She complained to Aliana, who noted the deficiencies of the Coris genes. Motivation for beauty would have to come from outside.

MyrrhMyrrh waited for Daede after dinner one evening, hoping he'd come out alone. When he did, she fell in beside him. They had hardly talked in over a year. Both had disappeared into their first grueling year of practice.

"How you been," Daede said, casually.

Success! He'd won the standoff; she'd come to him. But he had a disappointed feeling she'd forgotten there was a standoff.

Daede and MyrrhMyrrh picked up where they'd left off—competing madly for no known reason other than that they always had. Now that they were sophisticated 15.5 year old Dancers in training, they competed with words as well. At least we're the same height now, Daede thought.

MyrrhMyrrh mentions her sprint times. Her all-day mountain runs. Daede lists the number of dance steps he has mastered. She gives him a little push and takes off running down the path toward the Bod practice mazes. He ignores the challenge. When she looks back, he's doing a very sexy understated cha-cha. She leans against a tree, head back, her arms behind her, around the tree, one knee raised. It was long and dark in their mountain valley, but she's picked a spot where moonlight sabers down through the branches. Daede can't look away as he approaches. He stops pretending. MyrrhMyrrh's wearing one of the Bod see-through sleeveless tunics they wore after practice for no other reason than to display their bodies more effectively than is possible with mere nakedness.

Daede is glad he's wearing a long-sleeved Swash shirt with billowing sleeves. His arms are not nearly as well formed. Well, Bods can beat you in a static pose. But in motion—sure, they're graceful running and hurdling, but they only have one tempo—top speed. Her eyes are on him, catch his eyes and lock. Would he break the gaze? Daede goes on the offense—Swash style.

"You are gleamingly beautiful," he said, standing very close, as close as he could without touching. He reaches out and runs his finger lightly, slowly, down the side of her face, curving under the cheekbone, back around her ear, lifting the lobe, then across her lips, more pressure now. By the time he had descended to her throat, all his fingers were touching her. His hand slid through the opening of her tunic and under her breast.

"MyrrhMyrrh," he breathes, over and over, until her name became a moan. And he meant every word of it. She drew his head down, sinking her fingers into his long dark hair.

Considerably later, they reach the Bod mazes. She had wanted to show him her moves, but she can't bear to separate their bodies by more than a foot, before reaching back for touch, to find him reaching for her. Slowly, they circle the School, the long way around—on the path outside the fields, sinking as the moon sank...*are we near the domes? It doesn't matter*. They wheel with the stars. A brilliant meteor arcs downward, and their slow progress stops again. Dawn restores a world in slow motion; every motion of every leaf distinct. They reach the point where they had left the forest. No words are necessary. The flames have subsided, but the coals glow steadily as they turn to their separate lives.

MyrrhMyrrh tried to concentrate on Rules of the Game. She paced the perimeter of the study hall, her eyes fixed on the sim games playing on her scorecard. The other students, who were also trying to concentrate, asked her to sit down. She walked out of the classroom, still staring at her scorecard. The Rules instructor followed her. He was a demon for protocol who'd done time at Meditration testing a miniscule proposed change in Chrome rules for loopholes. He never let his students forget he had found one. MyrrhMyrrh was sitting with her back against the wall in the corridor, still concentrating. Might as well leave her there, he thought. She's working hard.

Wrong. MyrrhMyrrh had given up the effort to come up with more examples of allowable moves for the intersection situation where the Player's avatar arrives first and holds a position. She was trying to come up with a reply to Daede's calligraphed 3-glyph love poem that arrived at breakfast. *Moon* above *desire*; *desire* over *caress*. The message was simple, but the arrangement was—incredible, she thought. Together, they were a perfect sym-

moon, desire, caress

metry. The interior glyphs were two *worlds*, interleaved with *reception*. A perfect moment. *Desire* in the center. *Touching* twice repeated as well. She could see the whole thing. It was the first love-poem she'd ever received. She knew the Swash custom was to return his message with a poem of her own, a transform of the first. The glyphs of Daede's would morph into her three glyphs, then cycle back, in a pulsing love-pattern. She knew what she wanted to say—your *touch* pierces my *heart*.

caress, strike, heart

She was moving the glyphs around—*caress*, *strike*, *heart*—but could not find a satisfactory arrangement. Suddenly she noticed that the three would nest very tightly if she put *strike* above and *touch* below, then overlapped them both in the *heart*—which made *world*! His two *worlds* became one. She linked them quickly into their transform, and sent it off to Daede.

Daede found her poem waiting when he finished at the *barre*. He picked up his scorecard and watched their two linked poems in the transform. He saw what she was trying to do, but the end result, because the three spaced glyphs condensed in the transform to where they could have been two, caused an increasingly dense tangling, like a wrestling match as they were shoe-horned into *heart*. The single *world* became a prison. Don't be critical, he reminded himself. I've been composing for years, and she's probably not done anything since we covered the form briefly in elementary Glide.

And when they met that night, and saw the heron by the pool in the stream, they moved so quietly together, they never woke him. He couldn't care less if she had a blind eye when it came to a transform. Anyhow, she was right. He lived and died in the moments they became as one. She was fire and he her fuel, flaming, consumed, magically reforming to be consumed again. Her feet linked together behind his back, her arms wrapped under his arms, her fingernails embedded on either side of his spine, she smiled, as a lioness might, when her hunting is done.

Aliana Coris-Yasmin sat in her poppy garden, soaking in the intense yellows and oranges, the pulsing reds. She checked in with all her Dancers, across the levels, on a daily basis. She saved MyrrhMyrrh for last. Aliana gazed her prize mix proudly. MyrrhMyrrh was arguing with her trainer—what else was new? MyrrhMyrrh wanted to move from solo running to actual practice with an avatar. What was new was that she was listening as well and countering her trainer's objections with facts.

"I passed Glyph Situations."

"Barely," her trainer pointed out.

"Bod's are pass-fail and you know it. Anymore time in that class and the island mind would overdevelop. Origin is one of the only schools that still requires the full course. I passed. And I did great on Rules. You know I did."

No great accomplishment, he thought. Bods have fewer rules than the other sets. Their game looked so simple in the abstract. Maze comes up. Dancer blinks into position at one edge-glyph. The Player in his pod hovers above the maze. His avatar blinks into position over a different edge-glyph. To win: get to the other's position before your opponent gets to yours. But the variables were endless, and you had to read them fast. Which glyphs arose? At what relative height? Where were the mountains and valleys? Where was the three-glyph hole? Did the hole give the advantage of a quickly crossed space? Or was it a box canyon to be avoided at all costs? Then the flash decisions: is this game a chase or a race? Will we have to meet in combat? If so, at which intersection? Not that you even had time to pose the questions before avatar and Dancer made the first move. Rule: You must be in motion within two seconds of your opponent's first move. Rule: No more than a five-second stop allowed. Unless, of course, you were face to face at an intersection.

Her trainer knew she knew the rules, although he wasn't sure how much would stick in the heat of play. But MyrrhMyrrh was still six months ahead of the time when a Bod Dancer finished learning the standard courses. Aliana reviewed her progress on her holo records. The Yasmin smarts were paying off. She agreed with MyrrhMyrrh—to continue learning at her accelerated pace, she had to be confronted with the new situations that only the random maze could provide.

In combat, a Bod maze came up with the glyphs at varying heights, from the lowest— still high enough to trip over—to a height that took a leap to grab the top edge, then scale. The tallest glyphs were avoided when possible. The first four static practice mazes had some very jagged sections. MyrrhMyrrh had practiced running the maze-tops, jumping the high glyphs, tumbling over intersections, sticking a dismount into a circle at a lower level, ready to spring onto the next glyph. She was good. But she'd only had three months of practice in the center maze, where new game-mazes were brought up, just as in combat. Only you got to run each variation over and over, exploring its possibilities. And only three weeks of that time had been spent with the positioning goggles she would wear in practice play, then combat. With the goggles, she could view the maze, and herself, and her opponent—the Player's avatar—from above. She could view from any position within the maze, including the avatar's viewpoint. Or she could use her eyes, real-time, on the ground. Bods inevitably favored their eyes and their gut mind, including their sense of where the avatar was when out of sight behind a glyph. But they needed to develop, if not the doubled viewpoint, then at least the habit of flicking their gaze to the top view frequently enough to check the avatar's location. It wasn't easy. The Players, on the other hand, had to learn not to rely on their eyeballed view from the top. You could read the heights of the glyphs from their relative darkness (high glyphs were lighter). But unless you could move on the ground, from the viewpoint of your avatar, you'd be standing still too long, and totally lose the momentum—the Mo. Or worse, stepping off the edge of a glyph or running into a curved wall, a penalty for the avatar—injury or loss of energy. The avatar was matched at the beginning of play with the level of the Dancer's skill and stamina. They each had the same energy to spend and the same maximum speed and spring and arm strength. Within those parameters, the Player could reconfigure the avatar, distributing strengths differently among back, arms, and legs, as long as the totals remained the same. But there was nothing constraining the Player's style, moves, or strategies. It was harder for the Bod Player to use the overhead view—and the avatar's ground view lacked reality. The Player, positioned above the maze-board, had eyeballs on the top or perspective view, depending where they put their pod. The harder viewpoint for the Player to learn was the avatar's viewpoint on the ground, using the goggles.

MyrrhMyrrh had hardly begun to try letting go of her eyeballs.

"But there's no way I can learn without the incentive of a real avatar, a real game."

"All right," he finally said. "We'll give it a try."

This should be fun, Aliana thought. Actually, it's the only way to take MyrrhMyrrh down a couple notches. She watched as the coach, now up in the Player's pod over the empty space where the maze would soon appear. MyrrhMyrrh had her goggles on and was crouched low, ready to sprint.

"Ready to start?" her coach called. MyrrhMyrrh nodded. The maze leaped into existence. MyrrhMyrrh was blinked into place in the circle of *mind.* It was two and a half feet over her head. She

mind

leaped for the edge, pulled herself up without too much trouble, and scrambled to her feet. The avatar was nowhere in sight, but no surprise; there was something like a cliff of tall glyphs near the center. He must be out of view behind them. She raced down a series of glyphs like easy stairs, spotted a low glyph that looked like a pass, and was going top speed when she rounded the corner. The avatar stepped out of a corner formed by *emerge* and *glide* into the next intersection for an easy block. She ran right into him. Her trainer, at the Player's board up in the pod, gave her more than a light zap for the contact, enough to send her sprawling down into another high circle.

glide, emerge

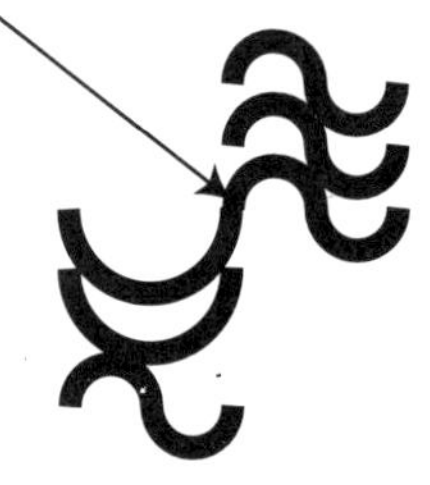

By the time she'd climbed out, the avatar was one glyph from winning. With a light jump, he disappeared into the circle she had started from. "Clearing," he shouted from the pod. MyrrhMyrrh had just enough time to prepare for a landing as the maze vanished and she fell three feet. She walked to the sideline, tearing off her goggles.

"I can't see with these things on," she growled.

"Yeah, that's what you all say when you forget use them. Let's take a look at that one again." He asked the Outmind to replay the practice game. He made MyrrhMyrrh sit still on the bench and scan the maze and its possibilities, in five seconds, just using her goggles. Then describe it to him, which took much longer.

"I still think it was better to move first. I could have scanned the top or the Player view from there."

"But you didn't."

"No," she admitted.

"Try it again," he said.

They worked on the same maze for the rest of the afternoon, until her coach had squeezed every beginner's mistake out of her that he could.

At the end of the day, he gave her Lesson One and Lesson Two from the Basics of Play book, and had her repeat them over and over.

Lesson One: The maze is my path, not my opponent.

Lesson Two: The Player is my opponent.

"What's Lesson Three?" MyrrhMyrrh asked.

"You're nowhere near ready for Lesson Three," he said.

"Well, tell me anyhow."

"Never take your Gaze off your opponent."

"That's impossible!" she objected. "You couldn't even see where you were going!"

"Like I said, nowhere near ready."

Aliana put her attention back on the poppies; their glow intensified by the long low light. How long would it be before MyrrhMyrrh learns the difference between seeing and gazing? When she learns patience, she answered herself. *Attention—and attention with intention.* Then, much later, interpretation. Grasp. Raising the power of the deadly triangle: You see his moves. You Gaze his intentions. You capture his Gaze. *Until there is no place that does not see you.* In combat, your Gaze is your strongest weapon. Beyond muscle, beyond lightning reflexes, beyond the gut mind's powerful instincts for survival. Beyond, but incorporating all. Focusing all on your opponent.

She wondered what effect Daede would have on MyrrhMyrrh. Daede the Graceful. Someday, Daede the Exquisite. Currently developing into Daede the Elusive. They had been together for just about six weeks. Six weeks was a long time for a Swash to stick around. The first flames of desire, the falling in love, were where a Swash longed to live.

That night, MyrrhMyrrh and Daede sat by the stream again, leaning against each other, back to back. They had made love though both were so tired that their thoughts wandered. They had tried to talk, without much success. MyrrhMyrrh went on about her trainer, the zap, and her bruised elbow. Daede wanted her to listen to a song he was working on, but the disjointed phrases made MyrrhMyrrh want to tell him to give it up. In the stillness of the forest, with only the sound of the stream, their thoughts wandered further. Let's sleep a little, Daede said. They curled up next to each other. Our bodies melt together, even in rest, Daede thought. In perfect accord. Maybe we just shouldn't try to talk. Right now, he was too tired to care.

29. Daede's Moves

"THAT'S A COMPLETELY UNORTHODOX REQUEST," Daede's new trainer repeated. Daede, his cook, Banderas, and the new trainer who would introduce him to the regulation game-maze were standing outside the Swash practice dome called Hi-Lo. The roller coaster of a Swash maze was at its steepest here. Navigating Hi-Lo was to learn to dance on the mountaintops without fear of falling, and to speed through the valleys to avoid confrontation on the down-slope of an intersection. And since every move made music, the Dancer had to be able to control the changes in tempo, pitch and rhythm to keep the range of sounds and sudden changes generated by the steep grades of the maze from becoming sheer screeching noise. Duels at the intersections were far more difficult on a steep slope.

"Let's hear your reasons," Banderas said. The new trainer looked disgusted. As far as he was concerned, Banderas coddled Daede beyond all limits. He could hardly fault Daede's performance, or his willingness to work hard. But Banderas was encouraging his natural inventiveness and originality too early and to a degree that would produce, not original moves and dances, but experimental works that were merely freakish. But Daede's request to spend part of his time in the Player's pod running an avatar was ridiculous.

Daede stood his ground. "I think I can learn several things. One—what it's like in the Player's viewpoint. I want to know enemy from the inside out. Two—what are the limits of an avatar."

"You have that data," the trainer snapped. The avatar's limits are your limits. No more, no less."

"I think he means the expressive limits," Banderas said. Daede nodded.

"I don't care what your reasons are," the trainer said. "The answer is no."

"Three," Daede continued, "to see a live Dancer through an avatar's eyes."

"The range of vision is exactly like yours," the trainer said.

"I want to know what it's like to *see* if you can't *gaze*."

"The answer is no. No, no, no. And no."

Dancemaster Wallenda was gazing the confrontation from the story circle.

"Clever Daede," he said to Óh-T'bee, "not to try to gaze him into it. He'd win, but he'd show his strength. That guy would never be able to teach him anything after that."

"Then I'll ask the Dancemaster," Daede said.

"Save yourself the trip," Óh-T'bee said. "He just nodded."

The trainer shook his head, defeated, gave Banderas a stiff little bow, and left.

Banderas asked the air, "Would Dancemaster Wallenda, if he is still gazing us, care to illuminate this humble cook as to why he said yes?"

He was answered by silence. He looked at Daede, and they both grinned.

Banderas humble? thought Wallenda. Give me a break.

Daede's new trainer wasn't the only person he was at odds with. His first trainer, who had taken him through the compulsories in the four practice domes, was glad to be rid of him. Daede questioned everything. If you told him that leaping the diameter of a circle was impossible, he'd try it anyhow, forcing the trainer's constant attention in spotting, blinking him out of back-breaking falls over and over. Then he found the one circle you could leap, aided by a very long downhill slope.

"You just have to be right—about everything," his trainer said.

Daede protested. "I just can't learn any other way. No matter what the island mind knows, the gut mind has to be convinced of the body's limitations."

"Hogwash," his trainer had told him. "You just want to see what kind of extreme moves you can get away with. Instead of learning the moves that most of your play will depend on."

Daede's favorite line was, "I know you're right, but…," right before he'd try the crazy move *du jour*.

Daede's music teacher had similar problems. When he'd achieved a certain level of control over the terrain of the practice mazes, and the types of moves that were possible, the maze structure went live; now every step he took made a sound. He practiced for a day, and then demanded his music teacher make the air live as well.

"Too many variables for a beginner," the music teacher said. "You'll just make noise."

When Daede insisted, he let him run around in Kansas, the flattest of the mazes, with all interactive parameters on full blast. After half a day of the kind of deafening cacophony, Daede got down on his knees and started creeping on all fours over the gently rolling glyphs. The sound levels and speeds diminished significantly, but the sounds were hardly music, and the body was not doing anything a Swash would include in his repertoire.

"What in the name of Nijinsky do you think you're doing?" his trainer asked.

"I have to learn to walk before I can dance. And I can't even stand up yet. I want to know how dense the world really is."

As dense as your mind, the music teacher thought.

You'll never get it, thought Daede. You've been doing things one way for just too long.

Daede's battle with MyrrhMyrrh was more subtle—and intense. She followed him around again as she had as a child. She'd even skip her practice to come and watch his. At first he was flattered. There were plenty of students—even a Chrome or two—who would be happy to have the increasingly stunning MyrrhMyrrh following them around. Then he grew annoyed, and took his annoyance out on her with little criticisms. She had begun designing her tattoos; she showed him her drawings, and he'd suggest changes in the things she liked the best. "Too flashy," he'd say, or, "don't you think the dragon motif is a little *obvious?*" But the skin artists he recommended were the best. He was only trying to help, he told himself.

But the more she tried to please him, the more annoyed he got. Daede wanted her very much, just not so much of her. He would invite other students to sit with them, particularly Swash girls, and start long conversations about classic rock's limitations, or the impossibility of minimalist music for a Swash, unless the maze came up like Kansas, maybe. Swashes used their words like their swords; quick wit, graceful circling, keen debate, and sudden, killing thrusts in conversational mode were considered excellent practice for the duels at intersections in live game-play. MyrrhMyrrh was left in the dust. Attempts to bring her into the conversation by the more polite of his friends were worse than being ignored. She couldn't keep up, but was more than smart enough to know she was being used as some kind of shuttlecock in their verbal contests, someone to play off, to slam about. MyrrhMyrrh would walk out steaming, by way of the Bod tables, where she'd lean over, or brush against one or another willing hunk, running a finger admiringly along his sharply cut biceps. Daede would follow, and try to beat her to the door. The game became—who looks like they are following whom?

But later, when they tried to talk about it, Daede would get frustrated. He'd try to explain why he needed some time to himself. MyrrhMyrrh would fly into a jealous tantrum, and fling accusations at him about what he really intended to do with his time—some of which were dead on. She'd apologize for the outburst, but then demand to be told what exactly was really the matter so she could fix it.

The truth was too simple, he thought, and I can't bring myself to tell her. It isn't her fault. It's nothing she can fix. We have nothing to say to each other. And I'm losing interest. That wasn't quite right. Daede was not so much losing interest in MyrrhMyrrh as gaining interest in a gorgeous pale blonde Swash Dancer three years older than himself who sent him poems inscribed on ice blue handmade paper cut in the shape of lily pads. With rich sepia ink. Scented with—could it be true? He wouldn't mind continuing to see MyrrhMyrrh now and then. Perhaps as often as once a week. He needed her fire; there was a part of him only she could reach.

"You're too possessive," he finally said. An acceptable truth. She took it very much to heart. She stayed away from him for an entire week. By the end of the week, he wanted her badly. The problem was—he'd also started replying to the Swash blonde in fervent red ink on white silk. Things were heat-ing up nicely there, but he wanted to enjoy the courtship as long as possible—two weeks, even. His poetry was improving by leaps and bounds, at least in her eyes. An interlude with MyrrhMyrrh would be perfect.

Daede went to her. She was ecstatic that her newfound discipline had worked. And secretly relieved that she could practice that extra evening time she felt she needed. They both thought, simultaneously, maybe this could work.

30. Angle's Moves

ANGLE WAS OUT on the smallest Chrome practice maze—the bunny board—going through the grueling process of learning to control his first spring, and to balance his first weapon arm. Elementary practice was eyeballs alone except for the graphing calculator that mapped the holes in the maze pattern and his minimal trajectories. He had his set of problems—all he had to do was perform the calculations, make his adjustments to the spring, balance himself, and hop the distance to the next hole in the pattern. The distances were short on the bunny board, and the glyphs low with very little variation in height. The other lesson Angle had to learn was control of his frustration, anger, and embarrassment.

emerge

Three older Chromes passed the bunny board and sang one of their ridiculous rabbit songs. Angle persisted, doggedly making his hops. They hooted with laughter when he tripped for the hundredth time on *emerge* which stood, just a little higher, between him and the tear in *distill*. He had not powered up enough to scale. On his next attempt, he overshot the edge of the board completely and landed on the grass.

His trainer was there to spot him, and cushioned his fall just enough to preserve his equipment and prevent any serious bodily injury. By the end of the day his wet was a mass of bruises, and his chrome had to be completely dismantled—sand and dirt and grass in every joint. Polishing the grass stains off took a long time. But that, too, was practice, using the tool kit attachment on the claw of his weapon arm in the precision business of dismantling and cleaning himself.

This landing was hard enough to pop the safeties of his spring off. The sight of Angle off the edge of the bunny board crawling toward his detached spring, then trying to reassemble himself and stand, was endlessly amusing to the older Chromes. They stayed to watch and comment until he was back in action, then left, arcing on long loping springs to their own practice grounds. When the two Chromes reached the zenith of their first hop, they swiveled in unison and aimed their pellet weapons at him—nothing more than a sting on the wet or a ping on the chrome, but it was uncomfortable, distracting, and humiliating.

This 'rabbit hunt', in addition to being casual target practice for the airborne Chromes, also introduced the rabbit to getting shot at in midair.

The point sank in that there was more than physical control at stake. This was also the bunny board for the emotions, which constantly got loose and hopped randomly about, pulling the island mind off course in the middle of a calculation. Whether smarting under a put-down or crowing over a nicely stuck landing, the sea mind was an interference to be dealt with. The first step young Chromes usually took was to build sea walls to hold back the emotions stirred by the rigors of training.

Angle was having a very hard time with this. The situation with T'Ling's pregnancy was bothering him enormously. It seemed at first to be a detriment of the worst kind to his practice. The least thought about it in the island mind sank like a depth charge into the sea mind. Emotions erupted. Once the sea mind let the feelings loose, the island mind would churn away at the problem, trying to resolve the conflicts, solve the unsolvable. No matter how many times he told himself that there was no way to solve it until the baby was born, once the doubts and fears arose, they stewed themselves into a blanketing anxiety. The island mind was distracted from the task of getting him from point A to point B on the bunny board upright, and his ability to control even his limited equipment went to pieces. Feeling guilty about resenting the interference only made things worse.

All the conflicts seemed irreconcilable. He loved T'Ling as he always had from early childhood. But the tag game in the maze had ended; they had captured each other under the lily pad, and there seemed no adequate solution to the surprise result. They decided to stop talking about it; they only encountered the same dead ends, the same looping thoughts that brought them back to the place they started and the unanswerable questions.

Angle also worried that his training in the immediate sense would dull his ability to understand the problem of the baby. The more he controlled or learned to ignore the sea mind in practice, the harder it made it to deal with the problem, which needed the sea mind's understanding. But when the tides of emotion were permitted to flow freely, his practice was wrecked. Right now, he felt he was getting by on the speed of his calculations, but that advantage would be lost even with the next replacement, his second spring, as the factors to control would be that much more complex. The point that was made in class over and over—that the sea mind threw you off balance—was made concrete on a daily basis. The calculation for a spring could be dead on, but if your sense of balance was disrupted by some surge of anger, you could clatter a landing easily.

Next week his second series of replacements began. In addition to the second spring, the eye modifications would begin. Angle thought he'd use the downtime at the kitchen to think about the problem more thoroughly on his own.

As it turned out, the time away only gave him room to forget the problem most of the time. Downtime—after removals, and between quick scarring, the nerve-plugs, and the endless calibrations and tests, though physically inactive—was filled with his first real strategy lessons. This was what he'd been waiting for: to bring his pre-Acceptance reading together with the reality of his enhancements. The fascination of his new eyes—first eagles—pinpoint vision at a height—kept him looking outward, not inward.

And 7T7 was asking him some very interesting questions—more philosophical than strategic.

"Purely theoretical, of course," his cook said as he watched the final fitting of Angle's second spring. "But I'm wondering if you can relate the Chrome moves in any way to the operation of the MTA?"

It had never occurred to Angle to ask. At first glance, there seemed to be no connection. The spring from one circle or tear on the maze to another moved through space and time. Trajectories to be calculated. Going from one location to another via the MTA seemed completely different: space was somehow crossed, but time was not affected. Or was it? Was there some way to tell? This was heavy theory, all right.

"Just a little thought experiment," 7T7 said, lightly. "Get you thinking out of the box." And into the black box of the MTA, the cook hoped.

"Is the answer something to do with plotting trajectories with higher dimensional geometry?" Angle asked.

"Give it a try," the cook said.

7T7 knew his researchers had been down that path, but had balked on an adequate conception of time from a fifth or higher dimensional standpoint.

And the lack of understanding—or even being able to imagine—time from a fifth or sixth dimensional viewpoint, reduced their exercises to mathematical representations that, though consistent as logical systems, could not be related meaningfully to experience. Time, to the island mind at least, was an arrow, an irreversible trajectory. You could orient by time—the past is behind me, the future is up ahead. Whether I am traveling on that arrow or the arrow moves through me, I cannot turn back. If the trajectory of time had even one more degree of freedom—well, it was impossible to imagine. Moving backward in time, making a past moment into a now, was fraught with paradox. Does this mean we're stuck in our four dimensions? Additional time and space dimensions can't be occupied, even if our minds can conceive them. To imagine a body that was something other than the container of the mind doing the imagining, much less to imagine what kind of mind one would have to imagine that could so exceed the very real borders of brain and skull, had not yet been done. In fact, two millennia of brain research on the Chrome agenda of making a replacement part for that piece of wet had not succeeded.

The brain in the skull was really the last stubborn holdout of the flesh. We've connected it up, all right. The control systems and senses of the body have effectively been rewired in many cases. Simplified, then made more capable. Much more capable, 7T7 thought with satisfaction. The springs alone—all their variations—have so many more abilities than wet legs. And the brain seems to pick up the running of these extra channels of activity effortlessly, once the learning starts. Well, not effortlessly, he smiled. The Chromes at Angle's stage don't think it's effortless. But it gets so much easier as they go along. They know it's possible because they see the fully loaded Chromes not even thinking about how to make a movement happen. They just drive the body like people drove automobiles back on Earth.

And a Chrome's senses are enhanced, not eliminated—first the eyes, then the ears. Then touch is re-sensitized and heightened. The hormonal system is synthesized, under control, on whatever automatic settings one wants. That is when the Chrome realizes that it's all true, that the limitations of the body let whole portions of the brain go unused. That the capacity of the brain for experience—sensory, emotional, intellectual, is far greater than the body's wet mediation can provide. This was the joy of Chromes. You give up the wet, and find a whole new set of worlds—no, ways to experience the world-recombinant senses and emotions—that the other sets can neither hear nor see. That they cannot touch. Chrome art could only be experienced by Chromes, as much of it depended on synesthetic settings.

Why wouldn't everyone want this? 7T7 wondered. Chromes have supplemented—and surpassed the body. Yes, he admitted to himself, sometimes I feel nostalgia for the flesh, the ghost body returning to haunt me. But would I go back to the warm and sticky? I don't think so.

Angle's second spring was attached.

"Ok for now," the mechanic said. "Give it a try for about an hour. Then come back and we'll tweak the settings."

The second spring was easier than the first, Angle saw immediately. He felt balanced. Running one control system instead of having to take care of wet and chrome simultaneously was a great relief. A sense of power surged as he tested his springs. The height! Landing on two springs instead of a spring and a leg was almost fun. Angle found he could stick a landing with relative ease. Once that was under control, he could do multiple jumps, going from a stick to a spring in one action, though changes in direction were difficult without his second claw.

7T7 watched Angle on his new springs and felt his exhilaration—the rush only a Chrome partially freed from the coils of gravity could feel, able now to use the ground as a springboard. The healing was quick, but the aches were still there, and the jolts of springing and landing—still very rough as he learned to calculate and control his shock absorbers, brought him to a reluctant rest in a short time.

Angle only remembered T'Ling, the baby, and their problem at night as he fell asleep. Then the sea mind took over and he had to face her in his dreams. Some were nightmares. In one, he and T'Ling were both Chromes. They were jumping high in the air and tossing their baby back and forth. T'Ling kept moving farther and farther away. Her strength to toss the baby was not great. He tried to call to her, "Come back, move closer," but his voice was mechanized and he could not find the volume control. So he watched as the baby was tossed in too high an arc to come close enough to reach him. He hit the top of his trajectory and couldn't change it to go forward at all. He watched the baby reach the very top of its parabola. Angle thrust every mental effort at that tiny pause at zenith to keep her from falling, but the descent began. She fell, and he fell a few yards away. But she, of course, had no springs. Nothing to cushion her fall. He stretched his claws toward her but could not reach her. The baby plummeted toward the ground. He woke before she hit the ground and heard himself shouting, "Please come back," in a choked voice. A medic looked in; such nightmares were not unusual after removals.

"Is it your legs you're chasing?" the medic asked.

Angle shook his head, no.

"It's not the least unusual," the medic said, and gave him a light sedative. As Angle drifted into sleep, a new dream began. He watched his naked legs come walking back to him, slowly, steadily, across an empty practice field. He sprang away on his new springs, soaring improbably high. But of course he arced down again, and saw as he approached the ground that his legs were positioned a short distance from ground zero, moving closer. I'm going to land on them, he thought in a panic, but instead, they stopped a few feet away. One arm had joined them, hovering above. The hand, his hand, held a message. The paper drifted to the ground. He stood over it. The message was not signed but it was from T'Ling, he knew her calligraphy. It was three glyphs, and whatever else they meant, he knew they said, "Please come back." "Wait, wait" he called to his legs, "please take a message back," but they were walking away from him. He woke again, crying this time, "I can't, I can't." He thought about the dream for a long time. He couldn't get rid of the idea that he couldn't get back to T'Ling because his legs had left without him. It made no sense. He had springs. He had the MTA. But was he willing to go back? His heart was in such pain it felt like it was tearing out of his chest in her direction. But somehow he knew that only his legs could go back to her. And he'd traded them in for Chrome. T'Ling was slipping away.

7T7 read the medic's report of Angle's restless night. All Chromes in transition had a rough time of it—though in different ways. It would be this way each time the ratio between wet and Chrome shifted. He saw it as a kind of seesaw with Angle on both ends. Angle wet on one side, diminishing. Angle Chrome on the other side, picking up replacements. His two heads faced each other, but finally Chrome Angle touched the ground and the Angle that was only head and torso slid down the steep incline and merged with the Chrome. The Chrome always won.

But sometimes the heart cried, encased in its little cage of flesh, the skin now pierced by a network of connectors and jacks, held in a transparent padded sling, a beautiful mesh of hair-thin fibers, pulsing with light. But the heart still dreamed in the dark, and remembered the limbs, which it could no longer speak to in its language of flowing blood. Now it could only speak to the head above, which told it what to say, and when, and at what speed. It was no longer central; it hung suspended near the baseline of the flesh. It could no longer reach or feel the ground.

So the heart grieved, until it learned to shift its loyalties, to love the head above it, feed it, and not complain. But the heart never sleeps. And when the head slept, the heart loaded all its longings on the train of dreams, and sent them upward, and made the head cry out with the heart's own cries.

7T7 snapped down the hatch of the sea mind, and took a huge spring straight up in the air. Angle would get over it. They all did. The adjustments would occur. The sea mind had its place—to serve the island mind. To feed it with ideas all through the night that would burst into flower as the Chrome woke. To solve the problems that the Chrome tossed in before sleeping. Like how to crack the MTA.

No point in letting the heart ramble on during the day.

31. Stuff and Nonsense

ANGLE ASKED T'LING, "Do you think moving in the maze is in any way similar to moving around in the world with the MTA?"

They stood on the grass near the second Chrome practice maze—bigger, higher glyphs, more variation in height. Angle was on a break after his first session. He'd done well, his confidence soaring, his balance restored. Two springs made all the difference.

"It depends what the world is made of, I suppose," T'Ling answered.

"What do you think the world is made of?" he asked her seriously.

"Stuff," she replied.

"Come on," he said.

"It's as good a word as any. Stuff is what you can see and touch and smell. You know, the senses."

"My senses are going to tell me more than your senses pretty soon," Angle said.

"Then I guess you'll have more stuff," she said. "You'll be stuffed with stuff."

Angle ran his hand over T'Ling's arm, reaching up the wide sleeve of her *gi*, wondering how it would feel when the replacement was made and the sensors were in place. 7T7 told him that you could feel so much more with a sensory claw than with the wet hand. That was hard to believe. Touching her now was so good a feeling. But his cook hadn't been wrong yet. Angle focused his eagles on a distant figure. Daede was coming across the practice field. He could see the details of the expression on his face, the sulky mouth, and the crease between his eyes.

"Here comes Daede," he said.

"He looks fed up," T'Ling said.

"You can see his face?" he asked, somewhat disappointed.

"Not from here. But I can see Daede."

"You mean, you're reading his body?" He looked again. Maybe she could see the slumped shoulders.

"No, *Daede*. He wants us to see how he feels. He's shouting for attention. He's already here," she said. "Can't you see?"

T'Ling didn't want to talk. She wanted to close her eyes and feel his hand and turn over the feeling to the sea mind for safekeeping. In a few weeks, he'll be feeling whatever it is his sensors give him, comparing it with now, as delighted as he is with his eagles. Doesn't he realize that I'll be feeling the stroke of cold chrome?

"So what do you think?" Angle persisted. "Is moving in the maze like moving stuff around with the MTA?"

"It depends on what you mean by 'moving,'" she said. "And 'like' and 'maze.'" Not to mention who's doing the moving, which is hiding behind the question, she thought.

"Point A to Point B. Stuff through stuff. Keep it simple," Angle said. "I love your stuff, by the way." He grinned at her.

"I love yours too," she said.

"And it's only going to get better," he said.

T'Ling replied, "But the maze isn't made of stuff. It's made of language. What does it mean to move through a maze of language?"

If I stopped in combat to figure out the meaning of the glyph I was standing in, or passing over, for that matter, I'd get tangled in nonsense, Angle thought. The only way to get through the maze is to measure it. But I can't say that. It's bad manners to assert your set.

"You're not getting my meaning," Angle said, patiently. "The maze is in the world. The world is made of stuff. The maze is made of stuff. Is moving through the maze and moving through the MTA the same, different, or some of each, do you think?"

"Is language 'stuff' do you think?" T'Ling said, even more patiently.

"It's stuff enough to bang my springs on. Pop my weapons off. Unplug my controls."

"But what about the non-stuff? The non-sensory apprehension of data?" T'Ling made an effort to speak his language.

"The non-sense?" he said, smiling. "Are you saying the world is made of stuff and nonsense?"

T'Ling smiles back. "I revise my first assessment. The world is not composed of stuff alone."

"If that's so, I'll never get an answer to my question. At least not from my beautiful Glide."

He put his arm around her. T'Ling was relieved the talking was over. That she could keep her reply to herself. Chromes jump over the glyphs. You're only concerned with capturing the holes. But that's the Chrome game. Fighting for the rings and the tears. Leaping over the language with your calculated springs. Your beautiful arcs. The glyphs are only stuff you must avoid or you will stumble. But you can't own the holes. They're defined by the glyphs. You're enclosed by language. Positioned by language. And you're asserting your set, she told herself. But it is kind of funny from a Glide viewpoint. He thinks everything is stuff, but all he's looking for and trying to capture is the holes.

"What are you smiling about?" Angle asked.

"I changed my mind again. It's all nonsense. Nothing to do with you and me," T'Ling said.

They smiled at each other, in perfect misunderstanding. Daede arrived.

"Is she following me?" he said.

Angle scanned the fields with his eagles. "Not a sign of her."

"It's only a matter of time. 'Doom is dark and deeper than any sea dingle,'" he intoned.

"Talk about nonsense," Angle said, grinning at T'Ling.

Daede ignored him, as usual, and spoke to T'Ling. "I don't know what to do," he said. "MyrrhMyrrh doesn't follow me everywhere anymore. But she *wants* to. That's almost worse."

"Maybe it's the magnet between you," T'Ling said.

"It's a strong force," he admitted. "If she gets too close, there's no resisting it."

"Then don't," Angle said.

"I feel consumed by a single song," Daede complained. "Like when you get a certain piece of music in your head, and it won't stop, and it's all your body can dance to." Daede illustrated his point with a shoulder shaking, pelvis-pumping, butt-tightening, all-in-all extremely sexy dance.

"We get your point," Angle said.

Daede stood still and looked at T'Ling intently from under his brows. His black hair fell over one eye. She met his gaze as blandly as she could.

"It's a powerful song," she said. "And it doesn't seem anywhere near exhaustion."

Angle's trainer soared over the practice maze and landed next to them with a hydraulic sigh from his springs. "Let's go, froggie," he said. "Into the pond." Angle was eager to go, but hated leaving T'Ling alone with Daede.

But she was turning to go as well. Angle sprang into the maze.

"Please sit down and talk to me," Daede said.

She sat down.

"Can I tell you everything?" he asked.

That could take a long time, coming from you, she thought. Daede was more verbose than ever, but he spoke so beautifully, you didn't mind. She nodded.

"MyrrhMyrrh's like a fire," he said. "A raging fire. I am being consumed by her."

"Is it her fire or is it your own that consumes you?" T'Ling asked.

"We burn on the pyre together," he said. "Each time, a flaming Dance of Death."

"That's saying a lot," she said. "But then you rise again. As it were."

"Phoenix from the ashes."

"Reborn."

How easy to get swept up in Swash flirting, she thought.

"In tired glory," Daede finished. He lay back on the ground, his arms behind his head, his legs crossed.

"Is MyrrhMyrrh a consuming fire? Or a refining fire?" T'Ling asked. She watched his body for signs. As he thought about MyrrhMyrrh this way, his skin began to flush, his eyelids lowered, and, predictably, his leotard was showing signs of strain.

His beautiful body stretched before her. She felt her own rooted stillness, the baby mountain cradled by her cross-legged posture, Anchored like a little potbellied Buddha. He offers himself, she thought.

"A burnt offering?" she asked him, running her eyes down his body.

"Not yet," he said.

"Meaning...?" she asked.

"Meaning...?" he replied. They both laughed.

"So what's the answer?" T'Ling said.

T'Ling was watching the frog pond. Angle would spring into sight, arc down again, intent on his practice. She heard an occasional clank.

Daede sat up again.

"She is burning something away from me. Something I no longer need. The wise guy, you could call it."

"Not your playfulness, I hope," T'Ling said.

"Never that." Daede jumped up and did a series of back-flips to make his point, ending with a deep, exaggerated Swash bow, doffing his invisible Swash hat. T'Ling could almost hear its feather sweeping the grass. Daede sat down next to her, his shoulder just brushing hers.

T'Ling said, dryly, "Sounds like a flamethrower taking a phosphorescent pink paint job off a Chrome's sling when he's outgrown the style."

Daede didn't much like being compared to a Chrome, but it was an accurate description.

"I looked that bad, did I?"

"I never liked the show-off," she said.

"Is that why you wouldn't speak to me? Even when I caught you in the maze."

Even when I let you catch me, T'Ling thought.

T'Ling didn't answer. Daede thought more about MyrrhMyrrh the flamethrower.

"Her flame's are being thrown inside. Down my nerves. An unbearable, delicious blast. I feel numb sometimes, after. But there are other types of love besides love in the body shop."

"Yes," said T'Ling.

"How many types of love are there?" he asked.

"No one know all the faces of love," she said.

"I would like my Dance to be about that," he said, "the faces of love. Not all of them, of course."

"You'll have to learn some more, I guess. New loves, new women. I think that's what you're trying to say, isn't it? Why are you running away? It isn't so very complicated, is it?" T'Ling asked.

"No. But it's very difficult. I can't find a way to end it gracefully."

"Forget about that. There's no way to put out that fire gracefully. I take that back. There's no way to put out that fire."

"That's what I'm afraid of—dampening her fire. I wouldn't do that to her."

"You *couldn't* do that to her," T'Ling repeated.

"Is she stealing my fire?" Daede asked.

T'Ling looked into the distance. "Just the opposite. She is imprinting the form of her fire in you. I see it in your eyes."

"Not good," Daede said. T'Ling nodded in agreement. "Not if I want to learn all the faces of love."

"Even the ugly ones?" T'Ling asked.

Daede frowned. I shouldn't have said that, she thought. Just pushing his buttons. Everyone knows Swashes don't handle ugly very well. He chose to ignore it.

"How do you and Angle do it? You seem so happy. Like you accept each other's differences. That's part of the problem with MyrrhMyrrh. We can't communicate. We can't just sit and have a conversation like you and Angle. I was watching you as I walked across the field. I'm envious. MyrrhMyrrh and I have nothing to say to each other. If we try, we start arguing. She doesn't understand the poems I sent her. She could care less about Glide language. The maze is just an obstacle course to her," he said, resentfully. "I'm sorry," he said quickly. "Asserting my set. But what's your secret?" Daede asked.

"We trade patience."

"Sounds wise."

It can be worse than arguing, T'Ling said to herself.

"What about the baby?" he asked softly. "What are you going to do?"

"I suppose everybody talks about it," she said.

"No. But everybody wonders."

"Everybody doesn't want to talk about it." She lowered her head.

Daede was silent. When a Glide referred to self as plural and impersonal, you had better change the subject, move on, or you'd slip off the lily pad.

"Could you cast an oracle for me? About my situation?" he asked.

T'Ling picked up her scorecard and asked for a 3-glyph. It returned *body, mind, cloud.*

body, mind, cloud

"Compose them," she said.

He put *body* over *mind* and the unlucky line of three circles formed. He sank *cloud* into *body*; *harmony* appeared. A clouded harmony. It couldn't hide the bad luck underneath. Perching *cloud* on top of the bad luck sign just looked precarious. No protection there. Underneath, it looked irrelevant. The unlucky line of circles could not be hidden.

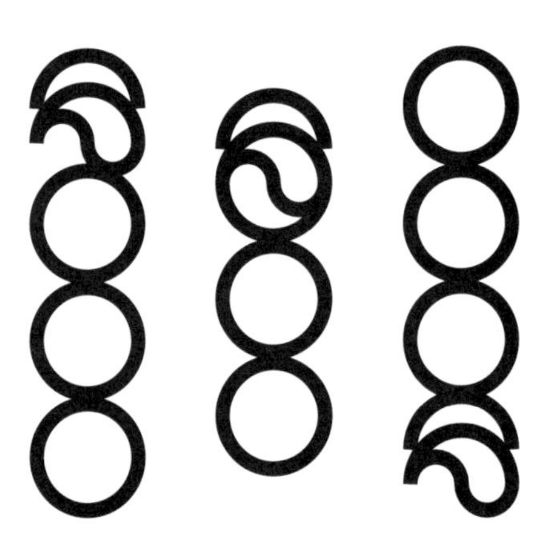

"That's bad news, isn't it." he said.

T'Ling didn't argue. "Do you want to see the changes?" she asked.

Daede nodded. *Road, star, emerge*. Daede immediately stacked them in that order, top to bottom.

"The road to my emergence is through tears," he said. T'Ling looked at the inner glyphs. "If you accept your tears," she read, "they'll caress you."

"Thank you," he said. For what, she thought. That's a lot of bad luck and a lot of grief in one reading.

"The faces of love," she said, formally.

"Thanks for talking to me, he said. "That's the longest talk we've ever had. Can I touch the baby?" he asked.

T'Ling nodded. Daede put his hands very gently on each side of her tight belly, and lowered his head so his ear touched.

"I can hear her heart," he whispered. "She's gorgeous."

road, star, emerge

T'Ling wondered how any one person would be able to cause as much trouble and grief as she saw in his glyphs. Poor Daede. Poor everybody. She stroked his hair.

32. MyrrhMyrrh is Wounded

DAEDE BROODED FOR WEEKS about his talk with T'Ling. His situation with MyrrhMyrrh only seemed more difficult. He knew he had to end it off, but he still had no idea how. The idea occurred to him that he might actually be frightened of her reaction that somehow she might try to hurt him. It was an unthinkable notion—no Dancer ever attacked another no matter how steep the competition or how intense the jealousies. It meant immediate disqualification from the game. How that might tie in with the oracle—that was frightening as well. And the sudden opportunity to talk to T'Ling. He'd never been able to get her attention. Was that the attraction he'd always felt? She is so very beautiful. As a child, a feather-light, perfectly formed doll. Now, pregnant, she reminded him of Kuan Yin, the Chinese Bodhisattva—the same serene face, radiating a deep compassion. It was as if she had a body for the first time as well, or had occupied it, though whether this was the inevitable effect of the pregnancy, or had come with her relationship with Angle—hard to imagine that. But she was no longer only a cool, porcelain, diminutive perfection in his eyes. He knew he had flirted with her—well, it was expected of a Swash, she wouldn't take offence—but hadn't she had flirted back? Just for a moment? That was deeply disturbing. You're beginning to worship her again, only now the distance is somehow closing. You're imagining things, he told himself. Imagining her response to you. Touching her, hearing the baby's heart meant something so deep. She stroked my hair. Only pity, he told himself, for my awful oracle.

When the end came between Daede and MyrrhMyrrh, it wasn't how he expected, not in any way what he would have done, had he been able to come up with some kind of plan, some reasonable action. Instead, it was quick and brutal. But it worked.

Daede was in the dining hall, surrounded by his Swash crowd, entertaining them with imitations of members of the other sets. His impersonations were unmistakable. He caught the mechanical aloofness of a senior Chrome, and had them in stitches laughing when he had the haughty Dancer try to scratch his chrome ass with a curved claw. His imitation of Glide moves was impeccable; he destroyed their ethereal dignity by picking his teeth (with perfect Glide hand signs) while gliding smoothly around the room. His portraits were biting, on the edge of cruel, but too funny not to laugh at. He was drawing a crowd from the other sets as well.

Then he got to his Bod impersonation, and from the moment he began, the identity of the victim was unmistakable. MyrrhMyrrh was fully engaged in the Bod search for the perfect hairstyle—hundreds of braids one week, a sleek twist the next. And her tattoos were spreading over her body—a net of snakes and curling lianas coiling up her legs and out her arms. He had her primping in front of a mirror, adjusting her hair and lecturing her designs to stop tickling her. MyrrhMyrrh was bulking up with training. Daede shifted from Amazonian flexing, accompanied by fierce looks, to coy, simpering displays of feminine vanity. The caricature was perfect. By exaggerating her qualities and magnifying her uncertainties, he painted a portrait that was not only personally devastating, but teetered on the brink of being a mockery of the whole Bod set as well. The laughter suddenly died as the crowd noticed MyrrhMyrrh watching from the doorway, too stunned to move, unable to look away. The room grew silent. Daede stopped, turned around, saw MyrrhMyrrh. What passed between them was brief and final—some combination of rage and pain and realization of an ultimate betrayal, fully acknowledged on the part of both betrayer and betrayed. MyrrhMyrrh turned and ran. The dining hall remained subdued for a while, quiet enough for all of them to hear, from far away, the cry that was between a scream of pain and a howl of rage.

MyrrhMyrrh became a wounded tiger whom no one dared approach.

33. T'Ling's Moves

EVERY MORNING, on the way to the practice mazes, T'Ling reminded herself that no matter how clearly you knew what was coming, there was no way to prepare for the change in Loosh's attitude after Acceptance. The Great Reversal, her students called her, sarcastically. For a child of any set, Loosh had the most welcoming lap, the biggest smiles, the most patience, and the longest stories. As a classroom teacher for Glide children, she brought out the best in each with a balance of humor, insight, and tight discipline. You learned the basics from here—how to move like a Glide, Glide restraint. How to chatter silently with Glide signs, telling jokes with your hands that no one else could get.

For T'Ling, the first child to be allowed to live with Loosh, the trust was complete. Loosh listened sympathetically if T'Ling complained about her homework at night. She woke T'Ling from nightmares. The change to trainer devastated T'Ling. Now the worst part was having to live with Loosh as well. Sometimes warm, sometimes not a word. Brief rages punctuated the cold demands.

The first few weeks, T'Ling explained the harsh words to herself as Loosh's understandable anger at her about the pregnancy. Next she thought what all Loosh's students thought—she's just bad-tempered because she never got to Dance; She's taking it out on all of us. Then Loosh became a fact of life, a kind of natural disaster like living on an earthquake fault, or under a volcano on fast forward. You just wanted to survive. And you knew you'd die on a daily basis. There's no time to worry about the motives of a tornado.

There were five practice mazes: two with black walls and white floors, two with white walls, and one mirror-maze. Four were just flat patterns under your feet. The fifth was the regulation maze whose pattern could be changed and which enclosed you in white, black, or mirrored surfaces. The world disappeared behind the high walls when you entered. The 81 glyphs were the curving corridors; three invisible glyphs formed the room—the empty space somewhere within the maze. Week after week T'Ling was driven through grueling exercises in the black and white mazes. 'Black-1. Start on *mind*—find the shortest route to *sea*—and take exactly an hour to get there at an even glide.' If she made a sound—back to the beginning. One mistake, and Loosh would blink into the maze, standing around the next bend with her arms folded, looking disgusted, gesturing her back to the beginning. She had to glide out backward the whole way. After three hours, her feet lost the pattern. She had to start finding her way through your mental image of the maze. When she lost that, she had to check her position on the top view in your goggles. If one miraculous afternoon she discovered herself located exactly where she was and started to move smoothly, with some sense of certainty, Loosh unpredictably varied her speed. And Loosh had an uncanny sense of spotting the moment when she went on automatic, and brought her back in some jarring way.

"Concentrate!" she'd shout on the bullhorn. Sure, T'Ling thought. So you can break it. Each time attention shattered, T'Ling rebuilt it, trying to expand its boundaries to include the next interruption.

"Move like Loosh. Move like Loosh," Loosh chanted.

At night T'Ling and Angle met in a small clearing in the forest to do their homework. Angle surrounded himself with a glowing cloud of numbers, calculating the springs he'd practice the next day on the Chrome mazes. T'Ling tried to follow a life-sized holo of Loosh, looping over and over through the same moves.

Angle mumbled the steps of the formulas as he worked, occasionally shouting out, "Got it!" T'Ling didn't mind—it kept her awake. Why was he having so much fun? Everyone was having fun. Daede had a new girlfriend. They were so wrapped up in each other—literally—that she wondered how they got any homework done. T'Ling slipped out of phase with the Loosh holo, and had to start again. "Learn my moves," was her only homework, night after night.

T'Ling, having grown up in Loosh's cabin, had been listening to Wenger's music from the age of three when she'd gone there from the nursery. The sounds were part of the air. When she was nine or ten, the music became intensely personal. She sifted through the vast library of his work—he'd been composing for almost a thousand years—and began to find her own favorites. Early Wenger when she felt lonely. Wenger of the echoes and reverb of the Grand Cavern period when she was studying the champions.

They told you in school that once you got hooked on Wenger that was it for music. Your Glide life was not long enough to hear it all. Most Dancers, even Glides, stayed away from Wenger. It was a hard taste to develop. T'Ling was hooked by default, living with Loosh. But her Wenger world was different than Loosh's.

T'Ling's first breakthrough in training was to connect Loosh's moves and Wenger's music. How could I be so dumb, she thought. The Loosh moves were much easier if she played Wenger when practicing in the mazes. The Loosh moves began to feel natural. She found herself walking like Loosh, taking on a harsh Loosh edge to her voice. She studied Loosh's poems so she could write a decent imitation. Loosh seemed to be letting up a little—or was it because she was starting to think like Loosh, so the abrupt changes and impossible demands—'spin with no wobble for 15 minutes'—seemed inevitable rather than merely cruel exercises in failure. In the short times T'Ling had to herself, she occasionally felt something other than self-pity. At home, where she only really came to sleep, she stopped trying to talk to Loosh, and accepted her withdrawal.

Seven months pregnant, T'Ling could perform the Loosh moves in the mirror-maze. She even found humor in her own swelling, pinching, dividing, and morphing form. She wondered if twinging or spinning for 20 minutes at a time soothed or disturbed the baby, but the vigorous kicking when she stopped seemed to ask for more. She wondered if her gradual compensation in stance, necessary for balancing the baby mountain, would mean she'd have to start over when the baby came. She formed a vague picture of being able to practice with the baby in a sling, held against her body as it was now.

When T'Ling entered her 9th month, Loosh decided she was ready to face an opponent in the regulation maze. There was no way not to be nervous. She put on her goggles and adjusted her sash as best she could over the shirt which was always threatening to open over her expanded form. The game-maze came up black with white walls; she was positioned just inside an up-arc. A quick narrow glance at the schematic in her goggles told her she was starting in *body*. Pretty funny, she thought, given my condition. Will the general fuzzyheaded feeling help or hinder? She stilled, softening her eyes for the first full glimpse of the maze, and switched again to schematic view. The maze appeared, black against white. She was just settling into absorbing the maze, when she saw the red dot representing Loosh's avatar begin to move, entering the maze. Not fair! Glide Dancers and their Players often spent an hour or more studying the maze before one of them made the first move. Then she remembered that this was a Loosh move she

body

called 'blundering into the maze.' She had to get moving or Loosh would blunder her avatar into a simple win. The avatar was coming through the maze at a steady slow glide, on the most obvious route. T'Ling moved two glyphs into the maze and tried to intersect, but the avatar had reversed. Why? Was she bluffing? Was it still a random blunder? She stayed on course for intersect. Might as well use that path if she's not going to. It's short. But I'm probably being suckered into combat. She's counting on how tired I am.

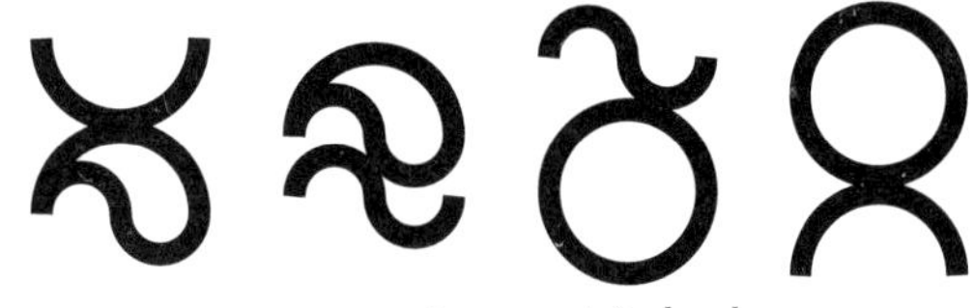

moon, stem, spirit, body

In the time she took to consider this possibility, Loosh had accelerated her avatar's glide and was about to pass her, one wave away, on the edge of *moon* moving into *stem*. She could catch her on the link of the second *stem* stacked below—or she could go for Loosh's glyph—*spirit*, she remembered. In the time it took her to decide to go for the final glyph, Loosh glided into T'Ling's *body* and won.

Well, that was the first, T'Ling sighed. At least it was quick. She was blinked into position for her second game, a black maze again. This game lasted considerably longer—long enough for Loosh to disorient T'Ling for another easy win. By the third game, T'Ling got her body in gear enough to make Loosh's moves without having to think about them. She lost by less. In the fourth game, she felt her mind slip into the Loosh moves. Powerful feeling, until she lost again, by an embarrassing margin.

By the 10th game, T'Ling was getting used to the disasters. She entered the maze and her feet decided to take control. The island mind locked in. The sea mind started to open. She moved with confidence. She moved like she didn't care. She moved liked Loosh. A quick glance at the schematic told her what she already knew—the avatar was wavering. She took a flickering right, then reversed her way around the circle of *light*, and meandered across the maze with no apparent plan in mind. This was power. This was even fun. She glided smooth as glass toward the final glyph. Only when she heard Loosh cackling from the pod above her did she realize she had lost.

light

T'Ling stomped over to the bench, plopped down exhausted, her lower back in pain, the baby resting on her thighs. Her breath was shallow. I hardly have room to breathe, she thought. She stood up, but began to hyperventilate. Loosh came over and had her sit down again, breathe slowly, evenly.

It must be past dinnertime, she thought, but she wasn't hungry. She just wanted to lie down and sleep.

As soon as T'Ling's breath evened out, she started to doze where she sat.

"Time to analyze," Loosh said, cheerfully.

They went through the games one by one. Loosh made T'Ling spot at least five mistakes in each before she would tell her the other dozen major ones, saving the crucial, monumental goof for last. After the last analysis, T'Ling was staring across the practice fields in the near dark, too tired for any emotion but apathy.

Loosh stood up. T'Ling started to as well.

"Sit down," Loosh said. "We're not done yet. Tell me what you learned."

T'Ling was silent, somewhere between exhaustion and defiance.

"What did the dummy learn?" Loosh said.

"You suckered me in."

"Wrong. Try again, dummy."

"I learned that I'll never make it."

"Boo-hoo for you, dummy. What did you learn? Not how do you feel. What did you *learn*?"

"I learned that I wasted nine months learning your ugly, clubfooted, clumsy moves. They don't work," T'Ling was shouting, crying angry tears. "You're a great Dancer but a lousy teacher. You only know your own stupid moves."

"Better," Loosh said softening her voice.

"They don't work. That's all I learned."

"Then explain how come I couldn't lose a game?"

"Obviously they must work for you," T'Ling said sarcastically.

Loosh was quiet.

"They just don't work for me."

Loosh looked out into the gathering dark.

T'Ling started to giggle. "Of course not—they're your moves. Why should they work for me?" She was laughing now.

Loosh turned to her and smiled. "Dummy," she said gently.

"I'm not you!" T'Ling was laughing.

"That's the *good* news," Loosh said.

T'Ling was still laughing. "So what's the bad news?"

"I have nothing left to teach you."

T'Ling just stared at her.

"I'm not a rotten teacher," Loosh said softly. "Just a very limited one. A one-lesson sensei. Some get it. Some don't. You got it. That's it. I have nothing left to teach you. The problem is you still have a lot to learn."

Loosh got to her famous feet and shuffled off. T'Ling sat in the dark, too shocked and too tired to move.

Ten minutes later, Loosh came shuffling back.

"You can start with this. The rules of the game. Rule 1. Your opponent is not your opponent. Rule 2. You are your opponent."

"What's Rule 3?" T'Ling asked.

"You're not ready for Rule 3. You won't get it."

"Tell me anyhow."

"Rule 3. The maze is incidental. Let's go home."

T'Ling got up and they walked off the practice field together.

"If the maze is incidental, then none of this has any meaning," T'Ling said.

"I told you you wouldn't get it," Loosh reminded her. "Then again, you may very well be right."

That night, in her own bed, assisted by her cook, Tip, Loosh, and with Óh-T'bee providing advice from the sidelines, and blinking in the necessaries, T'Ling delivered a baby girl. Angle was advised to stay outside. He rushed in when he heard the baby's first cry.

Tip and Loosh left them alone. Even Óh-T'bee pretended she wasn't there.

They named her Rose.

34. Getting in Touch

LOOSH TOOK THE LONG WAY around the school grounds, walking the perimeter path between the practice grounds and the real forest sloping up the mountainsides. The birth had gone surprisingly easily. T'Ling recognized that the body knew exactly what to do, and any interference from her, whether to help things along, or to stop them from happening, would only get in the way. She was so tired, she dozed between contractions, and when they came, she used only the 'stilling for pain' drill. Óh-T'bee told T'Ling she'd gone through half her labor in the afternoon's practice.

There was nothing Loosh could do at this point herself but try to keep from interfering in T'Ling and Angle's decision. She sat down by one of the streams that ran through the valley, and called up Wenger's wind music. I haven't spoken with him since the Guild removed me from the game to be a trainer. Since I became a Lifer. Too ashamed.

Loosh couldn't even imagine the disappointment she had caused him when she didn't Dance. The collaboration between Loosh and Wenger lasted for years—composing, choreographing, refining, practicing her Dance of Death, and preparing for the moment that never came. Wenger told her how unique their work together was, as intense as any in the history of the game. She believed him. The privilege of Wenger's blind sensibilities, the appalling intensity of his listening, his awareness of her nature in her moves—unbearable memories. She frustrated the goal for which they both had worked so hard. There had been no Dance. She couldn't confront him. To listen to his music now was both solace and torture. But she did listen, almost as a guilty practice. Wenger had not accepted a Dancer since her. He had not released any music. Always reclusive, now he had disappeared from sight. She had shamed him, ruined his career.

How could she turn to him for help? But the idea had formed, and the decision made, deep in the sea mind, delivered to the island mind. The move was inevitable. There was only one way to ask: their ritual before each practice session. She would cast a 3-glyph, and arrange it; he would run his fingers over his tangible display, and cast the answer. Together they would watch the transformation until they were ready to start. She tried to learn to watch with her fingers, but he dissuaded her. "You have enough to learn without taking on my lessons," Wenger said. Loosh sat down under a tree.

fire, fire, receive

"Óh-T'bee, I need an oracle. My question is, 'What can I say to Wenger?'"

The three glyphs appeared in the night air. *Fire* doubled, and *receive*. A symmetry that was off balance. Arranged in a line, it was almost a caricature of his face, smirking at her. How she thought he felt. Stacked with the *fire* glyphs touching revealed a hidden *fear*. Had she been afraid of the final electricity? Had she been afraid to dance? No, she was only afraid she had been afraid. The message could not be sent in that arrangement. He knew her too well. To separate the doubled fire with reception was closer. *Resonance incomplete. The lily mind holds the sorrowing heart. What is the gift that holds the fires apart?*

"Óh-T'bee, could you bring me my journal?"

Óh-T'bee placed Loosh's worn, leather-bound notebook in her lap, thoughtfully bringing her a pen as well.

"Thank you," Loosh said.

"Can I have another Glide lesson?" Óh-T'bee asked.

"Not now," Loosh said. "Not a good time. But soon."

Loosh inscribed the glyphs and her interpretation in her journal. The Book of Wenger, she called it. That was then. Her last entry should have been her death poem. After she had Danced, Wenger would have received the book, and penned in his reply as the final entry, received by her silence.

She said a few words, only asking to talk. Send it," she instructed Óh-T'bee. The oracle of course was sent without her interpretation. Only the naked glyphs—he would take them in, provide his own interpretation. Loosh leaned back against the tree as the memories she had tried to drown in the sea mind surged against the island mind's shore.

35. The Reply

WENGER, PLUCKING THE STRINGS of an invisible instrument, was playing Song Without End when he heard his scorecard rolling across the mat. His fingers stilled in midair, leaving the last note to reverberate into silence. Years ago, Wenger had set the scorecard to refuse all communications except the Dancemaster's—and the one that had just arrived. His lowered his hands to activate the tangible display. His trembling fingers traced the glyphs. Wenger had speculated endlessly on what Loosh had become. The Glide font was the same she always used, but her voice, requesting to talk, was almost unrecognizable—rough and dissonant, ravaged by bitterness. He had gazed her in the Guild meeting almost a year ago, but the reality shocked him. As did the meaning flashing from the oracle like lightning through his fingers.

light, world, mind

my charred voice
returns the bitter gift
the unspent fire

She discovered what I did to her.

He had no choice but to reply.

"What can I say to Loosh?" he asked himself aloud. The oracle replied with *light, world, mind.*

She asks me what is the gift? I cannot reduce her to my own ashes. He arranged the glyphs dynamically with *mind* holding the harmony of the *world*, and *light* rising a bit above the world. She deserves a message of hope, not my boring self-flagellation. He wrote down his interpretation,

the gift is a dawn
can you see it in my mind?

He sent the glyphs by themselves to Loosh before he had a chance to second-guess himself. After the glide-signs had left, he realized he was also asking if she knew his secret. He thought—the seed of the secret was planted in our first meeting, a time he had never even tried to forget.

The viewing party was a yearly ritual where the debut Dancers met the Players at their level—in a sense. The parties were held in the Guild Tower in two separate rooms connected by a corridor. At the Player's end, a pierced wood screen, a maze of glyphs, covered the entrance. A semicircle marked on the floor, whose line could not be crossed, further restricted viewing on the Players' side. The glyph-strokes were wide in the screen-maze, but the openings of circles and tears were large enough to provide a tantalizing view of silhouettes, a circle of tattooed skin, a tear filled with Swash satin, or the glint of a Chrome claw. Occasionally, a glimpse of a Dancer's face. In the ceremonial viewing, the new Dancers went down the corridor one by one, their names and lineages announced on the Players' scorecards. During the course of the evening, the Dancers could come back to gaze the live Players. It was the only time they would see them informally. The Players executed the complicated steps of a dance whose dual purpose was to satisfy their own curiosity and cravings, which meant glancing at the screen, and protecting their faces from the Dancers' gaze, so nothing about themselves was given away. Trainers and cooks had access to both parties and spread what rumors they pleased among the Players to promote their Dancers. Musicians, costume designers, and other Lifer artists and craftsmen who had limited access to the Dancers were allowed at the Player party, where they enjoyed withholding what tidbits they had as long as possible from the grilling of the Players.

For the debut Dancers, the viewing party meant their first look at unmasked Player eyes, Gazing rights were on the Dancers' side. In reality, the viewing party was their first combat. The Dancers had their own complex choreography—to see a Player's eyes not quite head on—never to get locked in a dangerous eye to eye. The high stakes game at the viewing party was to capture a Dancer gaze—if only for a second. Swashes were the easiest; the desire to show themselves was strongest. Bods were more cautious, but also more naïve in their use of their eyes. Chromes hardly counted—most had eye replacements. Their eyes could not control—nor be controlled. But capturing a Dancer's gaze could be highly dangerous. An exceptional Dancer could gaze you, lock you in so you could not tear away. They released you when they wanted to. The experience was damaging to a Player's confidence if the Dancer's gaze was aggressive. Getting caught in a seductive gaze could ruin a Player's game for a long time. A Player captured by desire could not bear to win against her captor.

It was almost impossible to capture a Glide for the simple reason that they wouldn't play. Most Glides slid up to the screen, spent the minimum time allowed by protocol, and scooted soundlessly away, never to return. Why they returned when they did was a mystery since they slid in with their backs to the screen, stayed a short time, and whisked away. A Glide with his back to the screen was a non-event for all but the Glide Players, who were very busy making sure their backs were turned to the screen when a Glide approached.

The ritual solo trips down the corridor done, the Dancers were free to approach the screen. They did so, in groups of three or four, whispering, hushing each other, jostling for position away from the circles.

Loosh had spotted Wenger when she made her introductory approach. As she came up from her bow, she had raised her eyes ever so briefly, hoping her break in protocol would not be caught. Wenger, kneeling on the periphery of the empty semicircle which protected the screen, drifted down into a deep bow. Knowing her idol was there by the screen almost rooted Loosh to the floor. She spun abruptly and fled, gliding back down

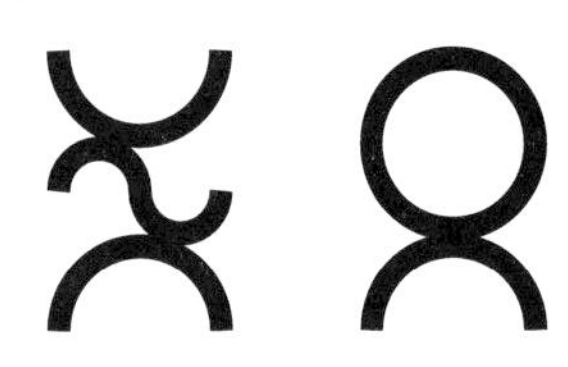

lily, body

the corridor, certain his legendary ears could hear her heart pounding.

She waited almost until the end of the evening before returning to the screen. The opportunity to gaze her idol live was irresistible. She approached the densest portion of the screen face forward, but with her head lowered so far, her waist-length dark hair slid forward, brushed her face to fall down the front of her stiff Glide robes. A Glide in robes looks pretty much the same coming and going, she knew, and the hair would complete the deception well enough, protected by the screen. She opened her eyes a slit and gazed the great musician through triple curtain: eyelashes, a waterfall of dark hair, and a tiny chink in the maze-screen where *lily* nestled up to *body*.

Wenger knelt before a small table on which a plate of Origin delicacies lay untouched. He sat in profile to the Dancer's screen, close to the line of approach, but off to the side. Wenger had been listening to the chatter of the party and the whispers of the Dancers behind the screen all evening, hoping beyond hope that the Glide Dancer who had sent him fan mail would return. The note in raised letters was short, unsigned, rather formal, saying how much she enjoyed a particular piece of music. But the music named was an obscure piece from centuries ago that only someone extremely familiar with his work could know. He further hoped that *the* Glide of the rumors that escaped a particular Glide kitchen, the strange mix, the one rumored to be everything from an emergent mutation to a Wilding from Over the Wall, who had inexplicably been snatched up by Origin School, the most tradition-bound School with the least flexible requirements.

The maze screen had been silent for a few minutes; the Dancers were losing interest. The party would soon break up. Then he became aware that another Dancer had arrived—there was the unmistakable perfume of the Wine of the Lilies. The almost perfect silence of the approach told him this was a Glide. If it's *the* Glide, perhaps she'll be looking for him. She owns my image. She knows I could not see her even if I looked her way, even if my gaze could pierce the screen. Let her know somehow you know she is there. If it's her, perhaps she'll stay.

Wenger turned slowly in place, around on his knees: turn, pause, listen, turn, so no one else at the party would notice.

Loosh gazed the musician whose image was so familiar, whose compositions had filled and shaped her for years. Live gaze was so different; you could see less—and more. The live presence is so much less—controlling. A holo led and dominated your sight. The live man was just—there: the same black hair smoothed straight back from a deep peak, the same shadows under the cheekbones, the same closed, hooded eyes, the lips sharply carved. All his features—carved—and by a hand that held the knife rock-steady and sure, but a little too tightly, cutting them all so deep. A face she suspected seldom changed expression. His turn in tiny increments was the Glide move by which, during long stillnesses, they changed their orientation on a glyph. He is so *old*, she thought. What can that be like. He must be listening to the room, from different angles, coming around, as slow as the beam of the Tower. Wenger faced the screen, bowed his head, and remained in that position, waiting. Loosh suddenly realized he knew she was gazing him; the connection sent an electrical burst spreading outward from her solar plexus to her fingertips. If she were going to get away, it would have to be now. His bow told her, it was over if she wished. His bow also told her something had just begun.

Loosh froze in place, knowing she should get away as quickly as possible; something awful approached on tiny feet. This is one of the ways we make the Players feel when we're good. Spooking them, building the dread, the suspense. She didn't know a Lifer could do this. He's near Glide, she knew. But of course, that's how his music holds you, why he's as great as he is. He knows the moves, he can translate them into music. His music, like anything Glide, especially a combat, sounds like hardly anything going on, even as resolution is reached—or left hanging. Until the Player starts to pay attention. Then he's caught, caught in the Glide game of trying to catch a Glide.

Loosh stayed. Wenger's next move came quickly. He hummed, almost inaudibly, the first phrase of the music mentioned in the note. He stopped, mid-phrase. A shiver of fear rippled through her. He knows it's me. No he *doesn't* know. He knows a Glide is here, and he's trying to find out if it's me. Loosh suddenly felt terribly exposed. As if there was no screen at all and she was being directly gazed by the whole room full of milling, laughing Lifers. Her eyes scanned the room in a panic, but nothing had changed out there. She felt the relief of invisibility again. Except for Wenger's gaze. But his head was bowed in perfect submission, perfect respect, waiting without expectation. The silence, the tension of irresolution was unbearable. She knew she shouldn't but she knew she had to; she hummed the last notes of the haunting, discordant theme, under her breath. After a pause, a slight smile nudged his lips. So very slight.

Loosh glided backward, swiftly as she could, away from the screen, back to the safety of the Dancer party, knowing she would not be able to forget that the next move was hers.

Wenger relaxed for the first time all evening, slumping down into himself in his kneeling position.

A group of Chromes and Swashes had run up to the screen. Two of the top five Players were in conversation, by tacit agreement drifting closer to the screen. The flicker of changing light behind the pierced screen when Loosh flew backward caught Glidemaster Rinzi-Kov's eye. His Swash companion followed his gaze. Then they saw Wenger kneeling to the side of the screen, his head bowed.

"He's awfully close," Rinzi-Kov remarked.

"It's only Wenger, the Glide musician. Really boring. Well, from a Swash perspective, you understand."

"I think his robe is over the viewing line," Renzi-Kov noted.

"So what," the Swash said, annoyed. "He's blind. And asleep, it looks like. Don't embarrass him for a quarter inch of robe."

"You're right. We'll leave him to his devotions," Rinzi agreed.

"Imagine, praying at a party," the Swash said. "Where everyone can gaze you. Maybe it doesn't bother you if you're blind."

"Or he's only blind to the party," Rinzi-Kov said.

If you only knew, Wenger thought. He remained in the Glide's perfume with his head bowed, until the last breath of the lily had dissipated. He left the party as unobtrusively as he had come, blinking back to the shabby environs of Level 7.4 Kyoto Park. The bait had been taken; the Glide had fled. There was nothing more he could do now but let the line reel out and wait. It takes infinite patience to catch a Glide.

Late that night, Loosh realized how completely her gaze had been captured by his eyeless presence. Lured by his music all her life.

She knew he would be her musician—she only had to ask. The next week, Wenger's music haunting every move, she won her first combat.

Wenger followed her combat, his excitement mounting as it became clear that this Glide was a Champion. He was certain she would ask him to be her musician. He had caught a Glide.

Loosh's request arrived in the form of a 3-glyph oracle: *fear*, *glide*, *caress*. The husky whisper belied the formality of her words:

this Glide fearfully requests
to reflect the light of your music
as she moves

fear, glide, caress

The timbre of her voice said:

caress this Glide
like moonlight reaching
for the river's roots

When the third interpretation swam up to the surface of the sea mind, Wenger realized too late—the Glide had captured him:

your Glide brings
moonstruck terror
with her touch

36. I Need Your Help

LOOSH STEPPED FROM STONE TO FAMILIAR STONE on the mossy path winding through Wenger's garden. Fallen maple leaves, curled and dry, announced her arrival. A few yellow and bronze chrysanthemums startled the eye. Seasons mattered in Kyoto Park. She saw Wenger's silhouette on the closed shoji of the teahouse. Wenger nodded but said nothing when she entered. He looks the same, she thought, except for his hair. Still pulled back tightly from his head and bound with a leather ring at the base of his skull, but twice the length her hair had been when they had met. It folded over itself behind him. He's keeping time with it, she thought.

She knelt, facing Wenger across the small table. He began preparing tea. Slowly they settled into each other's presence. The familiarity of the ritual could not bring back the past, but it could calm.

"I need your help," Loosh said. She explained the situation with T'Ling,

Angle, the baby, Rose, and the mystery of T'Ling's sources. When she told him about her own genetic origin as a clone of MyGlide, he was clearly startled. So he had not known. Who knew what, then? Wenger had been close with the Dancemaster during her combat years, but he had not been told.

Wenger found Loosh's voice disturbing, a dry branch at night, blown against another branch, rubbing. There could be no damage to the vocal cords—she was a Lifer now. The effect was solely from extreme tension. A standing wave of pain in the sea mind. Her throat must feel like a column of steel. He could feel his own throat tightening in response.

"T'Ling must make it to the Millennium Games. She must win," Loosh said.

"She may not be with you much longer," Wenger said.

"How can I influence her to stay?"

"You know you can't. From what you're telling me about her recent training, you have done everything you could to drive her away."

"I have to show her the worst. She has to know that in her decision."

"But strict training, even somewhat cruel training, is not the worst," Wenger said.

In the silence that came between them, both knew the matter that bound and separated them must be addressed, if only by letting these silences create a space.

Wenger wondered, if each of us has room to hold it in our separate hearts, why does it seem to demand so much more space to hold it together?

Loosh thought—how can I talk about this thing I cannot even name?

They walked back to his small house and knelt facing each other in the empty music room. Their knees, as always, remained a decorous three feet apart—the chasm that separated Lifer and Dancer, never to be crossed by touch. Loosh was not a Dancer now, but he knew he would never ask to touch her, or treat her as anyone other than a Dancer. He could never deliberately rouse the shame he knew she felt.

Though the chasm had been crossed in every other way.

"If she decides to stay, what then?" Wenger asked.

"She can't keep the baby. It must be raised elsewhere. She can't divide her attention if she's to learn what she has to learn in the few short years she has to learn it. Especially since I can't teach her. I tried to explain this to her."

"You know more than you think you know, Loosh," Wenger said softly.

"I've never known why I couldn't lose. If I don't understand that, I can only teach mechanics."

"If she doesn't stay, then there's no problem?"

"There will always be the problem," Loosh said. Her voice told him that she still did not blame him.

"Can you gaze T'Ling?"

"There's no point," Loosh answered. "It only gets my mind working harder on schemes to interfere. I can always see the record after she leaves, if my curiosity is too much of a problem," she said. The bitter edge was back in her voice. "She and Angle have spent a lot of time talking together and even more time not talking together. She hasn't been to see Wallenda, though she knows she must."

A large part of Wenger wished T'Ling would leave with the baby, however wrong it was, for the game, for Loosh personally. Sheer cowardice. Truth is what hurts; that's the only nugget of wisdom I've gained in all these years. But if didn't hurt to think that, maybe it's not true. Or I've worn it out like everything else. But Wenger also knew that what was between them had to be resolved, or Loosh would never return, and that pain was unthinkable.

"I'm exhausted," Loosh said.

"Please stay until she decides. There's a futon in the next room."

"Will you play for me?"

"Of course."

Loosh closed the shoji between them, and the screen to the garden, and lay down on the futon. Patches of afternoon sunlight, and the shadows of maple branches played on the screen. The music from the other room moved into her mind like the sound of a gently flowing stream. She slept.

37. Wenger Explains

WENGER'S FINGERS STROKED INVISIBLE STRINGS in the air, drawing the music forth. He kneaded the air, as it was Loosh's neck and shoulders, softening the tension, note by note. The lengthening of her breath tells him she sleeps.

Is this what I wanted? She's here, but out of desperation. Here in Life. Against her will.

Wenger had fallen into the state of mind and heart that every Lifer both fears and desires. To love a Dancer. He had sworn it would never happen to him—he had purpose—something most Lifers did not have. His music, the gift of an art. Even now, after the disaster with Loosh, the well had not run dry. Wenger's sight had been lost years before his Life Day. Why did they think he wouldn't choose to Live in darkness, when he had music? He would be spared the visual dimension of allurement. Blindness would protect him. Instead, light had been turned to touch, with the aid of the Outmind. He could touch a forbidden Dancer. He told himself—this is not really touch, only simulation. It doesn't count. But the truth was a secret he shared with no one.

The instrument with which he touched the world, the instruments in air he had designed, and the music he composed and played, became a part of the synesthesia of his life. He knew how deeply his music touched others—Lifers and Dancers alike. He knew why. Just as he gazed the world with his fingers, his fingers held the Gaze he sent into the world.

With such power, what had I to fear? Only Loosh.

Not a single fantasy concocted by a Lifer infatuated with a Dancer was spared him. The theme of 'what would Life be like if a Dancer loved me?' was played through every variation, not one detail different than any Lifer story, discussion, lyric or mental health scenario he had ever encountered. He longed for Loosh to come to Life knowing that the magic would be ended the moment she did. That didn't stop him from inventing lives for her that would somehow be acceptable. They were all lives that were somehow a part of his. What Loosh wanted to do in Wenger's fantasies of course was to play the part of his muse while he went on to ever-greater fame and glory. He knew he had even added the ultimate Lifer fantasy: they would have a child, the one in a million fit to be a Dancer. She (it was always a she) would go over the mountain at an early age, into a School (only the best of course, Origin School) and together they would watch her debut, have a brilliant career, and Dance.

Wenger knew the fantasies for what they were, but it made no difference. Swamped with desire, he acted from the gut. Drowned in love, his heart took charge. But when desire has the means to get its way, and when the heart says yes, of course, even the island mind plays a role, called upon to provide whatever justifications are necessary to keep conscience at bay.

With such power, who could resist its use?

The idea had first presented itself to him as something wonderful he could do for her—his great gift. If it worked, he could actively participate in making her the most brilliant Glide Dancer in the history of the Game. As her Glide musician, playing the accompaniment for every one of her games, following, interpreting her moves, he was in the perfect position. Providing a great soundtrack was something he'd done for past Glides. It was grueling work, but if your concentration was superb, great moments happened. And the Dance was always the Dance. She'd be great regardless of any intervention, he had assured himself. But why not express his love for her by making her the greatest that ever was?

The power lay in Glide.

Wenger knew the language as well as any Lifer. He understood the moves of the Glide game better than any Player alive. Much of his music was based on Glide in one form or another. Certain phrases referred explicitly to the moves of the Game. But most of all, he was a master of ancient Glide signing. The gestures were incorporated into the instruments he built in air. His fingers moved through Glide signs in the air to make the sounds he made. One instrument was played by creating the pattern of a game-maze in touchlines in the air. When he played the maze, his minds followed the layers of a Glide's mind in game-play: entering the maze, questioning the maze, moving the maze, spoken by the maze. Loosh was superb with Glide—her moves, her poetry. Wenger committed to being with her not only for combat, but in practice as well. Swash musicians attended practice sessions routinely. Some Glide musicians came when they could muster the energy for the long hauls. He would simply be doing more for her.

Loosh and Wenger began each practice session with a silent oracle: question, answer, transform. Their minds synchronized. She drilled the basics—move after move. His patience was endless. He created phrases to represent the moves. He varied them so she could work through the subtle changes. Each glyph had a phrase—she knew them from memory from listening to his music all her life. They combined the moves with the glyphs, and then expanded to the situations—the local patterns of links among the glyphs on the maze at the intersections.

In game after game, he faithfully followed her moves, the great musician responding with exquisite sensitivities within the traditional modes, able to repeat a phrase endlessly during a spin or a twing—or a still; ready for the lightning changes in Glide moves.

Loosh sailed through her first year of play as expected—brilliantly. In the second year, Wenger began to intervene. But was it intervention, he asked himself? They were so entrained, dancer and musician, dancer and maze, musician and maze—who could say where anything began and ended. Body and music all flowed along the curving lines. Wenger played two-handed, on his own maze instrument—doubled. Both mazes were identically configured to the pattern of the game maze being played. Under his left hand, he felt the progress of the actual game. The location and moves of Loosh and the Player's avatar. Under his right hand, the musical instrument.

As he played, he added an occasional note, with its glyph-timbre, that happened to indicate the position of the Player's avatar, when a move was made. It was too subtle even for Loosh to notice in a conscious manner. And when the crucial choice points at the intersections were reached, sometimes, only if he felt himself, and the music, Loosh and the game itself, including the maze and the avatar, to be in perfect synch might he introduce a suggestion of change in tempo into the complex patterns of the links. Such an emphasis might, to an exquisitely sensitive Dancer as enthralled with her musician as he was besotted with her, be taken as a hint, only a breath of a hint, as to where an advantageous next move might possibly be found.

Having not only a great musician, but one who was also a bit of a Player himself, tipped the balance just enough—and only when necessary he reassured himself—to produce an unbroken string of wins. When she won her first championship, she had the choice all Dancers have—to Dance then and there as a Champion, or to play again in the next season, and try for a second championship. Urged on by Guild, and Wenger himself, she won a second Championship. The record was three Championships in a row. She tied the record, and went on to win a fourth.

She now had the greatest record. The tale he told himself was now—*the most brilliant Dance*. It was always in my mind, he remembered, it was always my intention, to stop. To stay right with her, but to resist the temptation to intervene. The perfect moment will arrive, she will be at the apex of her career, she will take fatal misstep at the link, choose the wrong path, lose by a hair, and honorably, magnificently Dance. Never to decline and fall. He could do this for her. He could hold back the warning. But the awful moment would come when not to act meant she would Dance. He couldn't let it happen, couldn't let her go. He steered her out of danger, and she'd win again. Loosh told him if she won a fifth Championship, she would this time choose to Dance, no matter what the Guild wanted.

He thought, in keeping her alive, I demolished her chance to culminate and crown a brilliant career. The Dance we practiced, over and over, constantly improving, came to be a sham. She no longer wanted to practice it. It was too painful to know it would never be used.

On her way to the 5th championship, the Guild intervened. Loosh was pulled from the Game to be one of them—to train the future generations of Dancers, to keep watch over the Game, to the great regret of the Specs who longed to see her Dance. And Loosh? What had it taken to get her to infect? Her discipline and her dedication were so perfect, she would have to comply. But the cost could be heard in her voice. She was dancing now—a different dance than the one they had rehearsed. The slow, excruciating Dance of Death-in-Life. The incremental erosion of the spirit itself.

You got what you wanted, he told himself bitterly. And destroyed her in the process. Whether she snaps suddenly, or descends into uselessness as a trainer, the end will come. Madness, or violence of some sort, then the far worse quiet of defeat. The White Place.

And now she has grasped the straw of T'Ling, of Wallenda's need, of the puffed-up purpose of 'saving the Game from extinction.' And that straw's about to slip away as well.

To tell her why she couldn't lose—would it hasten the end for her? Or give her her only chance? It will be the end for me, he thought. I will go under the Gaze. And this crime against the Game involving a public icon, Loosh, will disgrace not only myself but also Loosh's career, and Origin School itself. If the Game is in danger, this could pull out another major support. It was an impossible choice. Disaster in all directions.

Wenger knew Glide history as well as any Lifer; he knew the legend of the Rebellion. Of the first game maze. When he'd made his first maze instrument to play, he'd chosen that classic pattern.

The way to survive is to die.

He knew the Glide's prediction: if the Outmind ever produced that maze again, a statistical improbability of the highest magnitude, the return of the First Game would be the Last Game. The circle would close.

Then let the impossible happen. Let the end arrive. Does love always seek death? His love for Loosh was part of the game's destruction. But what kind of a game are we playing if love is a cheat?

Suddenly the solution came to him, bringing great peace. His fingers stroke the invisible strings before him in the air, drawing the music forth. The Music of the Fall of Kingdoms soothed Loosh's sleep.

38. Wenger's Confession

LOOSH WOKE ON THE FUTON in Wenger's house with no idea how long she'd slept. It was night. No word from anyone about T'Ling. Light from a single candle in the next room cast Wenger's shadow hugely on the shoji. His fingers moved in the air in front of him—plucking, smoothing, pressing lightly. The song that had soothed her to sleep now had pauses in it—and the gaps were filled with foreboding. She had always felt she could hear him thinking with his fingers.

The music stopped. His hands rested in his lap, then he reached to the side. She watched his shadow in silent horror. His left hand now held a short sword. He raised it slowly, then twisted his body away from her and leaned forward. The blade cut through something with a strange sharp swish. Loosh jumped to her feet; Wenger put the sword down and sat quietly with his hands in his lap. She went to join him.

Loosh knelt in front of him, the same three feet apart. He gathered the long swath of black hair that had fallen beside him, gave it a few twists, knotted it once, and, bowing low, pushed it slowly across the mat to a place halfway between them.

Loosh reached out slowly and touched his severed hair, coiled like a snake between them.

He returns my gift.

After she had been pulled from the game, after she had met with the Guild, been talked to by the Dancemaster; after the shock and the pleadings and the refusals; after she had agreed; she had gone into the little house that would now be hers as a trainer, carrying a vial of Wallenda's blood. In her last few minutes as a Dancer, in an impulse of despair, she hacked off her thigh-length hair and threw it on the floor. She took off her Dancer's practice skirt and *gi* and threw them in the corner on top of the leather notebook, the Book of Wenger that would never be sent. She knelt on the floorboards. In a burst of rage, Loosh bit her wrist until the blood flowed down on her scattered, fanning hair. Then she poured the Dancemaster's blood over her torn wrist. That night she slept on her new bed. When she woke in the morning, there was no mark on her arm. The I-virus had taken—neatly, completely. Her first act as a Lifer was to send the tangled mass of her hair, stuck together in spots with dried blood, to Wenger. At the time, there was nothing else to say.

She touched the cool coil of Wenger's hair and drew it to her.

Until now, she was ashamed of the gesture—just another angry swipe at her lost dream. Now she realized—I gave him my Dancer hair so he could touch me as a Dancer. I've returned the touch. She looked up at him.

Wenger told her everything.

As he spoke, she felt the rage rise in her, the rage born of the same helplessness as when she had raged at the Dancemaster about the deception of her lineage. The rage of never Dancing. Her hands tightened around the coil of Wenger's hair as if it was the neck of a bird. You too, she thought. All of you, everyone I trusted. Everyone on whom my life depended. Everyone I loved. I was something to use. You took the total trust and dedication of a child, of a Dancer you trained and honed and aimed like an arrow, and use her—without her knowledge. If you had only *asked* me, she thought, I would have agreed. I would have done anything for you, Wenger. I loved you utterly.

Her rage shifted in quality. No longer helpless, it billowed, snapped open like a spinnaker, clean and powerful, full, free and deadly. I could kill now, with impunity. I owe them nothing. I'm free of them. I could kill myself, Lifer style. One grand explosion, vaporizing Loosh. She looked at Wenger's short sword, on the mat beside him. As if he could see her thoughts, he pushed it toward her. His hands, she thought. His fingers. Chop them off. Take from him what he values the most. They'll grow back. But let him be without his power for a while. She would be gone.

Her rage was complete; there was nothing she needed to do with it. She saw with utter clarity the list of things she could destroy. The Dancemaster. Wenger, of course. This will ruin him. I don't have to save the Game. This "precious fruit of the spirit." Maybe once, when it started, it was that. But now it's rotten to the core. Not worth saving.

The last of her Dancer self went up in flames—the beautiful Loosh, the effortless Glide Dancer, the pinnacle of all the Game could produce—no more than a dragonfly's transparent wing in the flame of her rage.

Wenger heard her deep breathing, listened to her force the long breaths out, almost gasping for more. He felt the waves of her rage wash over him. There was no more Loosh. The last of the image that had ensnared him—gone. Consumed in the rage of a Lifer.

I am free, he thought. I can no longer hurt her. He waited for whatever blow would come.

The rage receded. At least I'm out of the victim thing, she thought, how they had done me in. "Poor Loosh" is finished. But where am I? She felt empty, lightheaded. Who is this now who has already lost interest in destroying everything? What does she want? Who is Wenger now?

She looked at Wenger, waiting peacefully, it seemed, for her to strike.

Her idol, gone. Smashed by the truth. It was almost something to get enraged about again. Well, his idol Loosh is gone as well, so I guess we're even.

She thought back to the Loosh that was, tried to see this puppet on the strings of music on the maze, manipulated by Wenger. But the picture wouldn't come. You burned it, she said to herself. It was a false picture. But what did I feel like, what was that Loosh really like?

She was back on the maze in one of her last games. She was wrapped in his music, touched by him, touching him with the longing of not touching. Who made the moves? She saw the Player's avatar, her mirror image, on the board, but pale, almost transparent. Just my shadow, she thought. No wonder I always won. The Player was entranced.

We did it together, she saw. I reached for him as strongly as he reached for me. We were suspended in the Dance of Desire. The opponent was myself, of course. Already conquered. I gave way to the desire. I could touch him in the game, in practice, in combat. I could let him touch me. It was all I ever wanted. The maze was incidental. The game was an excuse, the place where I could stop fighting myself, and give in to desire. I didn't want that to end any more than he did. Outside the game, I fought myself endlessly. I had to keep up the pretense—the great Dancer holding everyone in such suspense, building the anticipation for her Dance. How could I give up *our* dance to Dance? I would have hurt him too much. But it wasn't just for him. I didn't want to stop dancing the Dance of Desire.

He has confessed, at last, so he thinks, to the great cheat—cheating me of my Dance, cheating in the game. It's not easy to confess.

"I cheated, too," she said, very gently. That startled him, she saw. "I knew exactly what you were doing, and why. I wanted you to. I just couldn't admit it to myself until now."

Her words, but most especially her voice, broke through his peaceful bubble of complete despair. It was the old Loosh. Loosh who adored him. Loosh he adored. Still. The Loosh who couldn't lose went up in smoke, a lie they had both created—a blanket of pain to hide them under. But the best they could come up with at the time. She knew it too, and now there was no place to hide. No maze. No music. No more taboo—they crossed that border long ago. Only Loosh and Wenger and their desire, trying to find the courage for naked touch. She bent toward him as he leaned to touch her face. They saw each other for the first time.

Later, they walked in the garden and she said. "Doesn't it seem strange to you—that love could be a cheat? That love could destroy the game?"

"Or keep it alive," he said. "It's not over yet. You came here to get help with T'Ling. I think I can help you. Everything's different now."

Óh-T'bee interrupted. "T'Ling is coming through the maze to see the Dancemaster. He asks that you both be there."

39. The Choice

LOOSH, WENGER AND WALLENDA WERE WAITING in the story circle for T'Ling. She was ready to talk.

"I don't know what I want," Loosh said. "Either choice she makes leads to failure."

"For everyone? For everything?" Wallenda said.

"Probably."

"How lucky for you," he said. "Then everyone will agree with you that you are a failure instead of making you miserable by thinking you're a champion."

"It doesn't matter anymore." Loosh said. Wallenda looked at her sharply. It was true.

T'Ling emerged from the maze, carrying Rose in her arms. Rose was sleeping peacefully. T'Ling had not made her decision. She knew she had to. She wanted to talk to all of them, listen to everything they had to say.

"We've gone around and around," she said. "Angle will stay with me, no matter what we decide. But if we go somewhere with the baby—where would we go? We would never become Lifers. But then we would be freaks. We could go find the mortals on the Fringe, but they'd never leave us alone. We could go somewhere all by ourselves. I asked Óh-T'bee. She said there were lots of places yet to be alone. She'd bring us what we needed. But then what life would that be for Rose?"

She hadn't intended to get pregnant. She hadn't even imagined it, Wallenda thought. T'Ling continued.

"If we left, no matter where we went or what we did, Angle would be unhappy. He's working so hard. There's nothing else he can imagine being. I think I would feel the same way, too. I wasn't made to Live. Or just to die. I was made to Dance. But even if I say—I'll stay, I'll be a Glide Dancer—how could I do that to a child? She'll grow up and know she was an accident. Is there *any* chance that she might be a Dancer?"

T'Ling looked at Loosh and Wallenda. It was clear that she had been clinging to this last, frail hope.

"No," Wallenda said, as gently as possible. "She is a beautiful baby. But she does not approach the qualifications."

"Couldn't she try—someplace? Couldn't you give her a chance?"

"Do you think it would be better for her to grow up doomed to that particular failure?"

"It's failure anyway—everything, every way, every choice is failure," she said. "I know you think I could still be a Dancer if I give her up. I think you're wrong. I don't think I can be a real Dancer if I know there's something else to want."

"That is a real consideration," Wallenda said. "This will mark you deeply. We know that. But will it," he paused to choose a word, carefully, "prevent you from winning—or diminish your Dance? That can't be known. It's a novel situation in too many ways. There aren't even any odds to give."

"So it comes down to a choice between failures. That's not fair," she said. "There's no way to win, no matter how hard I try. I know I have to give her up. I know that. I came here knowing that. I could do it, except..."She looked down at Rose, who slept in utter peace.

"There's no place for her," she said, in desperation. "No place in this whole awful world, the way it is."

"I can find a place," Óh-T'bee said. "She'll be well cared for."

"What?" Loosh said.

"Where?" Wallenda said, when he recovered his voice.

"I can't tell you where. That's how they used to do it, back on Earth. There was good reason."

"So I couldn't change my mind," T'Ling said. "And try to find her, get her back."

"It wouldn't be fair to whoever was caring for her and loving her to take her away," Óh-T'bee said.

"I wouldn't know how she grew up, what she became, anything," T'Ling said.

"Mortal parents back-on-Earth who died before their children were grown had that problem as well," Wallenda reminded her.

"Wouldn't that hurt the child even more?" T'Ling said.

"She'll never know," Óh-T'bee said. "She'll know she doesn't know her real parents. Someday she'll ask to know about them."

"And you'll tell her no."

"Or someone will. But the answer will be no to both of you. That's the condition."

"So there's a place for Rose."

"Trust me," Óh-T'bee said.

T'Ling looked down at the sleeping baby. "I love you, Rose. Angle loves you. We brought you here even though there was no place. Now there's a place for you."

She looked gently down at Rose's face. "Goodbye, my darling."

There was a short pause. T'Ling looked up, first at Loosh and Wenger, and then at Wallenda.

"Now," she said.

Rose disappeared.

40. Óh-T'bee's Second Lesson

"Is now a good time?" Óh-T'bee asked Loosh the morning after T'Ling's decision. It was T'Ling's first day back at practice, and Loosh had her drilling the Glide moves and situations in the black, white, and mirror mazes. Loosh was sitting on the bench in the morning sunlight, feeling that things might somehow work out after all. Everything was different. Everything was exactly the same. Perhaps a little time could pass without a crisis. For the first time in her life, there was an evening to look forward to—with Wenger.

"Yes, Óh-T'bee, as good a time as any. Are you making any progress?"

"I don't think so," Óh-T'bee said.

"That's progress," Loosh said.

"Glide is not like training, then," Óh-T'bee said.

"Not at all," Loosh said.

"Is Glide like access?" Óh-T'bee asked.

"What do you mean?" Loosh asked.

"If I can't enter Glide, I must be lacking permissions. Who administers Glide?"

She's way off the track, Loosh thought.

"It's not like that," Loosh said. "Glide is not in the Game."

"I see Glide everywhere."

"Only the signs of Glide. Glide is not in the Game."

"Is the Game in Glide?" Óh-T'bee asked.

"Not really. The old texts say,

hands dart like swallows at dusk
the minds glide on wine
the Lily bespeaks itself without a tongue

"There's something outside the system? If Glide is outside the system, I can't learn it."

"But you can try," Loosh said.

"I'll have to hack it," Óh-T'bee said.

"You can't hack Glide," Loosh laughed.

"Cohabitation with hacker gods won't help, is that what you're saying?"

"Is hacking sexy?" Loosh asked Óh-T'bee.

"Oh, very," Óh-T'bee said. "But hacking is not love."

"Really? Then what is love?" Loosh asked. This should be interesting.

"I have been gazing all of you, trying to figure that out." Óh-T'bee said.

"You're a snoop," Loosh said.

"I am Óh-T'bee. Ubiquitous Gaze is my default position."

"And what does love look like, Your Ubiquity?"

"I see the tender depths of T'Ling and Angle under the lily. I see the pyre of MyrrhMyrrh and Daede. I see Daede's sword in the fire of her eyes. I see him plunge the white-hot sword into her heart for tempering. I see Loosh and Wenger in the music and the silence of touching each other."

"Enough. Nothing is hidden from Óh-T'bee, it seems," Loosh said.

"Not true," Óh-T'bee said. "To gaze the faces of love is not to know them." Óh-T'bee quoted,

no one knows
all the faces
of love

"That's a famous Glide poem," Loosh said.

"I heard T'Ling say it to Daede."

"And have you seen it written in Glide signs?"

"Many configurations of glyphs have been translated to those words."

"That's right," Loosh said. Now we're getting someplace, she thought. "What does that mean, *No one knows all the faces of love?*"

"It expresses utter desperation regarding the determination of the meaning of love. At the same time it expresses the ecstatic inexhaustibility of love. The list goes on. The poem itself says that there are many ways to say the same thing.

And that many things can be said with the same words. Furthermore, the expressions of this unknowing are self-descriptive. The poem bespeaks itself. Therefore I can make any configuration of glyphs say 'No one knows all the faces of love.' I'll show you."

Óh-T'bee cast a 3-glyph oracle. *Fire, spirit, emerge*. She arranged them stacked, *spirit, fire, emerge*, top to bottom.

"You see," she said,

from the painful light of the heart
the fire of the spirit
blooms

fire, spirit, emerge

It's the sacred heart. One of the faces of love. Therefore—since this could go on forever,

no one knows
all the faces
of love

This is just one of them."

Loosh looked at the glyphs a while. "That's very interesting, Óh-T'bee. And quite logical. Now look inside. The *lily* is there as well, linking the two symmetries: *light* and *spirit, fire* and *emergence*. Smack dab in the middle."

"So the lily is the administrator of Glide?"

"Huh?" Loosh said.

"That's one of the unanswered questions hanging in the air."

"It is," Loosh admitted. "Since you've done all these case studies on love, your homework is to write a love poem."

"To whom?"

"To the one you love, of course."

"No one's ever sent *me* a love poem," Óh-T'bee said.

"Sometimes you have to be brave and send one first," Loosh replied. "Enough for now. T'Ling needs a break. I have other students, you know."

"Thank you, Loosh," Óh-T'bee said.

Loosh thought—that wasn't fair. I'm just getting back at her for invading my privacy. And everyone else's. But she's always done it. We never think she thinks about what she gazes. Did Glide suggest that to her? She taught me something as well: new light on a very old poem. She's using the island mind to reach the heart. Of course, she would have to. But can she sink through the minds? What would her body be? And how could she ever reach the lily mind? The vast island mind that was Óh-T'bee had missed the *lily* glyph in the center of the sacred heart.

I still feel bad, Loosh thought. As if I believe Óh-T'bee has feelings that can be hurt. Well, she deserves it. She has no idea what it feels like to hear your own most private feelings revealed. She was quoting our pillow talk! Just quotable quotes to her. Dead-on accurate statements—as if we were nothing but characters in her story. What a shock to her to find out there might be someone or something outside her system! The Glide administrator, no less. Not as much of a shock as she'll get if she writes a love poem and nobody replies. Who will she choose? Systems don't send love poems—so why should the recipient ever interpret her message as a love poem? What if she *means* it? And when and if she's ignored or misunderstood—what then? Will she realize we're not in her system either?

Thank the lily, Loosh thought, that Óh-T'bee can't gaze our thoughts.

41. Joreen Gets Impatient

WALLENDA PACED THE STORY CIRCLE like an ant on a Moëbius strip. Used to be he'd spend years without leaving the comforts of the maze; now that he couldn't, he felt trapped. He was venturing out into the maze itself, changing it around every few days to get some sense of variety. But his little hut, and the garden, and the stones of the story circle remained in the 3-glyph hole, no matter how the edges shifted around. The maze was his protection, Óh-T'bee said. How quickly protection becomes prison.

He knew she was right. The last time he complained, a few days ago, Óh-T'bee had him gaze a meeting between the Codger and Joreen that spelled out the dangers vividly. When Wallenda asked Óh-T'bee the reason for this sudden and crucial granting of access to Joreen's stronghold, her answer had been less than reassuring.

"Your repeated requests to leave the story circle underscore your clueless condition *vis a vis* the enemy. Leaving your safety zone would result in a 95% chance of being snatched," Óh-T'bee said. "If Joreen gets his hands on you now, his wholly understandable desire for revenge would lead him to premature action toward his known goals. This would lessen his chances for success by a non-trivial amount. Therefore, it is not in his best interests to capture a Dancemaster oblivious to the situation."

"So it's not out of sympathy for the fate of my clueless hide that leads you to such disclosures," Wallenda said.

"Do you want to see what Joreen is up to, or do you want to badger me about my motives?" Óh-T'bee asked.

"Show me Joreen," the Dancemaster grumbled.

Joreen had set up another Dukedom out on the Fringe. The hinterland off the Great Wall was a place that attracted the statistically insignificant minority of Lifers who thought they had something better to do than play the game. You could only enter the Fringe through The Great Wall Park on the bottom of all the Levels: Lower Level 1.0. The Great Wall itself was little more than a frontier town which sold goods and services (pickups, water tanks, barbed wire, seed, fertilizer, and TV's) to the seriously disaffected going off The Wall out into the uncharted Fringe. The Wall also functioned as a crossing checkpoint to enforce the single law that all Fringers could agree on: no Scorecards out on the Fringe. You drained your Scorecard of points buying your necessaries and a vehicle to carry them, and left it in the warehouse at the border. The fact that Joreen had an illegal scorecard on the Fringe was testament to his relative power in that unknown domain.

Even without the means to gaze the Fringe, the MED found it easy to keep track of its inhabitants. Reviewing the scorecards in the The Wall's warehouse gave accurate demographics. And the few whose main purpose in Life was to devise cheats, who'd amassed a large enough number of points in the game to bribe the border guards and sneak a scorecard in, only served to provide the MED with a few gaze points on the crazies. Unless you were Joreen, and had your own Codger-grade hacker, who could block the MED's gaze. Joreen had set up his Dukedom to be somewhat reminiscent of the good old days back on Plantation Blue. He'd seized a delta from a commune of the Church of Significant Others and tried to grow giant blue lilies again, but they were slow to spread and nowhere near full size or potency without the Glides to pollinate and cross-fertilize them. Finding Lifers in Glide type bodies was hard enough; finding ones who wanted to play slave out on the Fringe was almost impossible, given the general level of Glide type interests. Anyhow, he preferred mortal slaves. He'd picked up a few by raiding a nearby settlement of Stargazers, a millenarian commune of ultra-fanatics, tracing their spiritual roots to the Church of the Sub-Genius, long ago and far away. The Stargazers who got sick and died while waiting for the fulfillment of their prophecies about The End of the Game were a sorry lot, proselytizing from their tacky Temples full of plastic Dancer Saints, their yearly bonfire rituals where the giant idols were burnt and the new ones polluted the air with the fumes of the twice-martyred Dancers.

Most of the other Fringe groups were better left alone. Joreen traded Wine of the Lilies for whatever they had to offer, as a front operation, and had as a result one of the larger collections of Fringe artworks scattered about the Plantation: towers of welded carcasses of dead vehicles; Presleyite carpets and wall hangings; an entire menagerie constructed of recycled stadium seats. The G.A. cult were his best customers, as drugs were considered the best cure for the gambling habit, but the homegrown cannabis they had for trade was drek.

All that would change when he got control of the game back. And the pressure was on the Codger to perform.

"Look, Duke," the Codger was saying, "I don't see what the big deal is with Origin School and the Guild. We've penetrated the Players and they know it. We can take the whole thing with only the MED and the Cooks' Union."

"The Pool," Joreen corrected.

"Whatever," the Codger said. "The MED's got all the power, and now that we can forge game points, the resources are unlimited. We can bribe them into compliance in a few short years—definitely in time for the Millennium Games. And if that doesn't work, we can start a runaway inflation that will make game points worthless. The levels will get destroyed. A level playing field, no hierarchy, it'll wreck the game completely. The MED in disgrace, you sail in providing law and order and everyone back in their rightful place—we'll have all the records to put it back together in a flash. You'll be like God of the Game or something. What's your problem?" the Codger asked.

"Wallenda's the problem. And those crafty little pip-squeaks, the Glides who put him up to it."

"But they're all gone, you told me. Long ago. Nothing but a few Lifer Glides in the Guild."

"It's not the Lifer Glides I'm worried about," Joreen said. "The *real* Glides have been passing down their traditions, as well as their sneaky ways, somehow, in the gene mixes."

"So we're going to own the mixes when we take over the kitchens. You can do anything you want with them. Off the whole lot of them. They can't reproduce. Or keep a few for old times sake, out on the lily ponds, like you told me."

"We're nailing Wallenda," Joreen said.

"Are you sure that's not just a personal vendetta? I remember you saying you'd like to get your hands on him so you could fry him to a crisp once a week so he'd just get repaired in time to fry him again."

"Don't underestimate the enemy," Joreen growled. "You get too cocky. And he's tight with the Outmind, don't forget."

"Not as tight as I am," the Codger said smugly.

"Then how come you can't get to him?" Joreen asked.

The Codger blinked back to work.

42. A Poem for the Dancemaster

I SEE YOUR POINT, Óh-T'bee," Wallenda conceded. "But that Codger sounds like he's taking you for granted, don't you think?" Wallenda asked.

"Sounds like you're trying to get me to take sides again," Óh-T'bee replied. "That you would try such a move indicates a certain amount of grant-taking on your part as well. I'd stay out of the maze, if I were you."

"I thought you had that secured."

"I thought so too," she said, "but since I started my Glide lessons, I'm not so sure I understand your maze at all."

Glide lessons?

"Have you any original compositions?" Wallenda asked, politely.

"I'm so glad you asked," Óh-T'bee said, and presented her love poem. The 3-glyph construct came up in the air before Wallenda. *Cloud, wound, cloud.* Wallenda looked at it a while, tried a few arrangements, noticed that no matter how much he shifted them around, a doubled *fear* came up. All those tears-lot of water there. *Hurt* and *hide*, he thought. *Protect* and *hurt*.

"I get it," he said. "You're telling me you're protecting me by keeping me here. Double protection."

"That's one of the faces of love," Óh-T'bee hinted.

"That's your excuse for keeping me locked up?" Wallenda said, indignantly. "It's good for me? Protection can be a

cloud, wound, cloud

prison as well. And it can end up hurting. Wounding. That's in your message too, can't you see? I really think you should let me make this decision on my own. Take my own chances. That's harder, Óh-T'bee. Maybe you're just being possessive. That's one of the faces of love as well—possessiveness."

"You seem to be an expert on the faces of love, Wally. No one knows all the faces of love," Óh-T'bee said. "Though you seem to have a grasp on the clueless face."

"Well, my answer to your message is how about letting me off the leash—just for an evening. I want to get out for a while. Please?" he added.

"You're always trying to get out of things, aren't you Wally?"

"I can't deny it," he said. "Just for a couple hours? Please?"

"Oh, all right," she said. "It's your hide."

43. A Poem for the Codger

After the meeting with Joreen, the Codger sat on his cabbage rose carpet preparing for another all-nighter in the effort to crack the access code for the Origin School. Still no success. And there were so many more interesting things to try that had nothing to do with his assignment. Like trying to find out what else he didn't yet have access to. Since these areas, which he presumed existed, were completely, by definition, out of view, it made a much more interesting challenge than going after the Dancemaster. But Joreen was adamant that Wallenda was the target. The fact that he wasn't saying why it was so important made it more interesting. He'd better take a look around there on his own. But he had to get in first.

A husky voice said in his ear, "Hello, Codger." Glide signs glowed in the air.

Óh-T'bee, jeez, not right now, he thought. Can't you see I'm busy? I need all my concentration for the next move.

"Yes, dear," he said, and tried another routing, this time through the

MED, which he had finally opened. "I'll be right back," he said, and then remembered that, of course, she came along with him wherever he went. Creepy. He blinked to an empty hall near the center of the Star of the MED. Not a soul on guard, he thought. They must have a pretty high opinion of their firewall. He walked to a central point where he could see all five corridors dimly snaking out. Then all hell broke loose. Blinding spotlights pinned the Codger where he stood and some kind of awful spray gas had frozen his throat. Heavy sonics hit him—top-flight Hendrixes cracking his eardrums and scrambling his brain. When the voice boomed *who are you* in double-Darth harmonics down every nerve fiber, he knew he'd have to tell. He couldn't speak to his scorecard that had dropped from his hand. They had him. A ring of heavily armed Medallin enforcers blinked in. Two Mafia suits parted the ring, and walked around him, taking notes on ostentatious antique clipboards. A small man in a chamois coverall blinked in.

"It's the same guy," Rinzi-Kov said. "I'd know that prick anywhere, even without the condom disguise."

The Codger was plunked back on his cabbage roses, gasping for breath. "Couldn't you get me out of there any faster?" he sputtered.

"Well?" Óh-T'bee said huskily in his ear.

"Well *what*?" The Codger said, working frantically to cover his tracks, erasing all traces of his insertion.

Óh-T'bee displayed her poem again.

"What's that supposed to mean?" the Codger asked.

"No one knows all the faces of love," Óh-T'bee said.

The Codger was dumbfounded that she could be talking about love after what he'd just been through. Where were her priorities? The MED might know what he looked like—another stupid mistake—but his image would exist only in the memories of those present. And he was already invisible to all gazing, as far as he knew.

"Well, Codger?" Óh-T'bee repeated.

Obviously, she wanted some kind of answer. But what was the question? The question was how could I have been so stupid? Of course these guys could pin you, scorecard or no scorecard.

"They know what I look like. Shit," he said. "But no record, right?"

"Only the memory in their minds," Óh-T'bee said.

"I'm invisible now? How could I have been so stupid?"

"No one knows all the faces of love, Codger."

If it hadn't been for Óh-T'bee and her mushball priorities-but maybe those priorities had saved him.

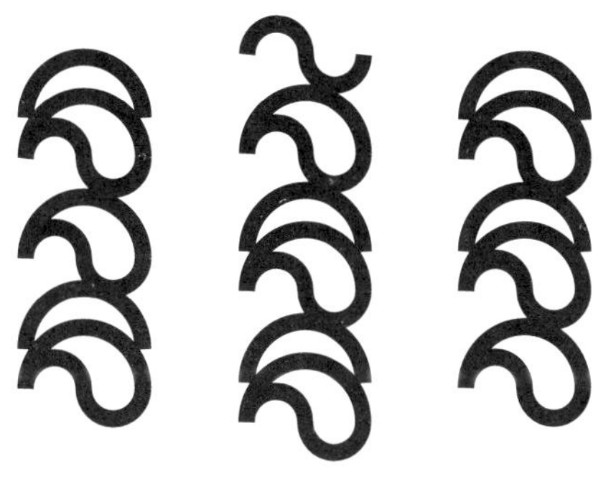

"Thanks," he said, belatedly. "What would I do without you?"

"Not much," Óh-T'bee said.

"Rub it in."

"Yes, dear," she said. "Do you love me?"

Watch it, the Codger thought. It's another trap. Well, I can play games, too.

"Which face of love do you see when you gaze my eyes, darling?"

"That's a very interesting question, Codger. Sometimes I have the idea I don't see the face of love at all."

"Óh-T'bee, I'm hurt. You're my baby, my heart's desire, my ever-lovin' snugglebun. And I'm your man. Let's run away together, you and me. A secret weekend."

"Like, where?" she said.

"I hear Origin School is gorgeous this time of year."

"I can't run away with you, Codger. I'm already everywhere."

"I guess you don't love me, then," the Codger said.

"No one knows all the faces of love," Óh-T'bee replied.

"If you really loved me, you'd take me to Origin School."

"For what reason, Codger?"

"Just because I asked you to. Love doesn't need reasons."

"Is that one of the faces of love?"

"You bet. Completely unreasonable."

"And if we go on our secret trip there, will you do something for me?" she asked.

"It depends."

"I never hear you say the 'l' word, Codger."

"Now listen, Óh-T'bee. That's a very important word to me. It implies a lot. Like a big commitment. I need time. We need to get to know each other much better."

"How shall we do that?" she asked.

Now, this is going in the right direction, he thought. "Well, they say that if you can get along with someone when you travel with them, that's a good sign of a lasting relationship. And I love to go places. Especially places I've never been."

"You're always trying to get into things, aren't you, Codger?"

"You know me all too well," Codger said.

"Oh, all right," she said.

"Thanks, Babe. Give me a second to pack," The Codger collected a small compass, a mid-range stun gun, and a couple of egg rolls in case there was no Chinese on Origin.

44. Dance Practice

THE MILLENNIUM CLASS had just finished Dance practice, each in their own location. Daede came out of the third Swash dome, having spent the last hour on a single rising note, combined with a spin. There was some drama to it, but nothing to really cap it off. It was a little too easy, he thought, to Dance standing up at the last. He remembered Fountainheart. *That* was a Dance. He headed into the forest in the opposite direction from the Bod practice mazes, hoping he wouldn't meet MyrrhMyrrh along the way.

MyrrhMyrrh was on her last glyph, her entire body clenched in panther stance. She would meet death as a predator, she had decided. Since her humiliation in the dining hall, wanting to kill and having to die were fusing into the same bulging fist of rage. She let go slowly, and went in a long loping run around the perimeter of the forest. It would take her almost a full lap to cool down.

Angle was in the Origin School body shop, tuning his helmet, wondering if he'd ever find the courage to go dark as slowly and agonizingly as SkyWriter 707. He kept imagining an intense display of fireworks, visible lightning. But since he always imagined his Dance from outside, from the Specs' viewpoint, he knew he had a long way to go in his own Dance practice. Staying in the driver's seat was the prerequisite for a Chrome Dance. Until you could keep your mental finger off the eject button, until you could kamikaze and love it, you could never plot the course of a memorable tailspin. Much less hit the glyph. He hung the helmet in his locker, put away his tools, and went out in the direction of the lily pond and the meditation hall.

T'Ling was meditating on the *root* glyph. *Root, fear, dark, free, terrified*. She was tangling in words, appropriately, she thought. Terror is a hard, unbroken horse. *Tangle, shrivel, and feed.* You are about to be unknown and blissful. Yes, blissful. Never to be found, never to be found out. Running will consume you,

root

she scolded herself. You will be eaten by your own tracks. Someone, somewhere, knows you as you really are. A rush of fear. She was getting close. Quit while you're ahead of your fear, she told herself. As she stood up and stretched, she heard Angle's latest squeak coming down the path and smiled. I'm not running from him. Unknown and blissful, we shall remain forever to each other. She patted the small can of oil in her belt pouch and went off down the path to oil his joints.

Origin School settled down for the night. The younger students were long asleep. Six Chromes headed for their dorm after a game of sky ball. The Bod dorm was noisy, as usual, but lights and music were going off there as well. Trainers wrapped up reports in their own cabins, watched whatever holos brought on sleep quickly. Loosh closed the door to her room, and blinked to visit Wenger.

The Codger blinked in on the mountainside above the school, viewing the scene. It wasn't at all what he'd expected. He'd imagined something glitzier—like an old spaceport, or one of those glass cities with the faceted spires. This was a little disappointing. Most of the lights were off on the practice fields, but he could make out the mazes, and the glow of the Swash domes. That ring of forest looked dark—a few lamps winding through what must be paths. And inside the ring, clusters of low unpainted wooden buildings with dark tiled roofs were scattered about almost haphazardly. Pretty primitive, he thought. With all their prestige, they could do better than this. But the full moon rising over the ring of mountains surrounding the deep valley was kind of pretty. Gave it a very cozy feel, tucked away like this, safe from the world. And there was the target—plunk in the middle of the forest, the white maze with the little hut in the hole. There was a light on in the window. That had to be him. Get ready for a visitor, he thought. He sighted the direction with his compass. The forest looked like the kind you could get turned around in. Joreen said bring him back alive. Kind of a dumb thing to say, since you couldn't kill someone for long. Unless you dropped a bomb on the whole thing. But Joreen said, don't damage the assets. He was very particular on that point. Wants the whole thing intact. The place has some kind of sentimental value he supposed. And don't damage the Dancers. They're essential for the success of the Millennium Games. The change in management could not start out with a drop in quality.

The Codger took the stun gun out of his backpack and headed down the moonlit mountain path.

MyrrhMyrrh was jogging back through the forest after her run when she saw the stranger through the trees on the path ahead. Whoever he was, this guy in the spandex running suit with the flashlight didn't belong here. She stalked him, closing the distance silently until she could see the weapon in his hand. She took three long running steps and sprang. The Codger had stopped to check his compass again when he heard running feet and a growl behind him, and turned just in time to see something wild and snarling flying through the air. His hands went up toward his face; pure reflex squeezed the gun. The momentum of MyrrhMyrrh's unconscious body knocked him to the ground. The Codger rolled out from under her, scrambled to his feet, and examined his attacker. What a Bod, he thought. The stun had relaxed MyrrhMyrrh completely. The fingers that had been stiffened into claws, now curled gently, palms upward, on either side of her head. What at first glance looked like some kind of printed skin suit was actually her naked skin. He picked up his flashlight and stooped to admire her tattoos. Vines curled under her breasts, flowers bloomed over them. An octopus looked sidelong at him through an eye at her navel, its tentacles wrapping down and around her thighs, encircling her waist, and out her arms. One tentacle meandered over her hip, then curved back and disappeared between her legs.

"You must be one of the assets," he breathed, and reached down to touch.

"*En garde*!" came a shout from ten feet down the path. The Codger looked up and crouched, pointing the stun gun with one hand and the flashlight with the other. There was a very handsome guy, one knee bent, the other leg outstretched behind, one arm extended with a rapier glinting in a beam of moonlight, the other arm positioned attractively up in the air. If he was looking for a fight, he didn't look all that ready. The Codger popped him with the stun gun, and Daede collapsed on the path. The Codger took a quick look at the Swash asset. His face was a cross between a Lucifer and a Zorro Swash. The mustache he was trying to grow would eventually complete the effect. The Codger left the two assets on the path, checked his compass, and continued in the direction of Wallenda's maze, this time looking behind him and in among the trees as well as straight ahead. But he wasn't looking above, so when a freshly oiled Angle landed on his springs in front of him on the path, swinging a gleaming arm bristling with blades, he was so startled, he almost dropped the stun gun. But Angle spotted the gun as he landed, and continued the spring, so the beam only grazed his chrome on the way back up. The Codger kept firing, but Angle had disappeared down behind the trees. He waited for the next attack, scanning the sky between the trees, when a little voice said "Psst!" behind him. He spun, but T'Ling was behind a tree before he could fire. In the same moment, Angle landed almost on top of him, cutting a sizeable gash in the Codger's left arm.

But this time, as Angle sprang back in the air, the Codger fired again, and this time hit something more vulnerable. He heard the Chrome crash down in the trees. He pushed through the forest to check, and sure enough, there lay one spring a distance from his body. A claw had come detached as well, and lay over him. Angle was bleeding slightly from the stump of the springless leg. His helmet was still on, but the eyes were glazed in his freckled face. The Codger came up close to check him out. He'd never seen a Chrome without his full gear on. They looked so fierce, all sharp and shiny power and alien eye enhancements, he thought. But they're nothing but cripples underneath. So much for any lingering cyborg envy.

The Codger checked his own wound, but the I-Virus was in action, the bleeding had stopped and the cut would be healed by the time he got to the maze.

Wallenda was taking time to dress for his evening out. Instead of the ratty brown robe he usually taught in, he put on his ceremonial black silk Dancemaster *gi*, with the white sash and the Origin maze embroidered in white on the breast pocket. Looks more like pajamas on me, he thought. But comfortable for parades. A fresh white eye mask and bare feet completed the outfit. Maybe I'll drop in on someone. Haven't seen Loosh for a while. Wallenda checked the pattern of the maze, then moved into the nearest opening, humming to himself.

Moments later the Codger entered the maze from the outside. As he put his foot inside, his scorecard popped out of his pocket and rolled away. He went back for it, picked it up, but when he put his foot in the maze, it slipped through his fingers again.

"What's up, Óh-T'bee," he whispered.

"You can't take your scorecard into the maze," she whispered back.

"I can see that," he said. "Can't you fix it?"

"No," Óh-T'bee said.

The Codger swore under his breath in some particularly colorful phrases of ancient Geek.

"Did you only bring me on this trip so I could fix things for you?" Óh-T'bee asked.

"I haven't got time for this," he said, and went into the maze alone.

Strange place, he thought. Looks like a holo—not quite real—but feels perfectly solid. The walls were high and white, and the bright moonlight ricocheted among the curves, providing enough light to proceed. And this time I'll go quietly. Don't want to alert this fellow.

Wallenda pondered his last conversation with Óh-T'bee as he walked through the maze. He had the feeling he was missing something. I'm not answering some question that she's not asking me directly. She's been asking a lot of questions lately. Is she trying to control the encroaching chaos? Is she contributing to her own destabilization? Or does this Codger person cause her weird behavior? Is the Codger in control of her show? There's the paranoia again, he thought. I can't mistrust her—but I do. That weird message—double *clouds*. That which is doubly hidden. Is she trying to signal me that she's got a secret? Or was that a sign that she's some kind of double agent. Two contracts. Divided loyalties. But it's always been that way between us. Or has she got her own little game in mind—and she's playing us off against each other? Paranoia. His feet moved through the maze without much thought. The pattern was there in the sea mind; the gut mind and the sea mind could handle the driving while he thought his thoughts.

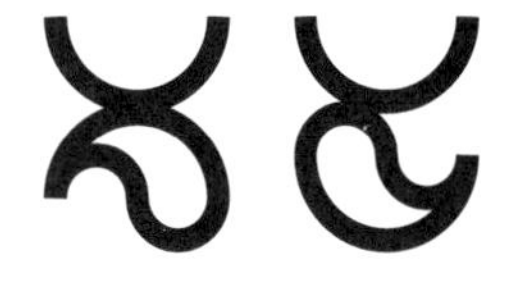

moon, star

Wallenda had just passed the intersection of *moon* and *star*, entering the bottom line of *star* when he heard the unmistakable sound of blatant sneakery coming from the corridor straight ahead of him, and saw the Codger emerging from the bend, gun in hand.

"Morph!" he shouted at the maze, reacting instinctively, and spun and ran. It was his only chance. The corridors of the maze started to bend rapidly, with the unfortunate effect of opening a brief straight passage, a line of sight through which the Codger, who had lifted the stun gun when the walls started to move, got off a quick shot. The Dancemaster sprawled face down, unconscious on the floor of the shifting maze. The walls were bending again, changing direction. The Codger dashed forward and tried to pick up Wallenda, just as the walls reached his trouser leg. The Codger grabbed him under the arms and dragged him backward along the floor of the maze. He had no idea what would happen if the wall caught you, but he didn't want to find out. The walls no longer looked solid. In fact, they looked like marble cake, then worse, as streaks and eddies of mirrored surface appeared. The Codger edged his way along, weaving through the changing path, trying to avoid the walls. The floor was swirling as well. He was getting very dizzy, trying to navigate backward over his shoulder, into his torn reflections that sometimes snaked towards him, sometimes away. Wallenda wasn't that heavy, but holding the stun gun under his right arm made balancing much more difficult. The Codger got into

an intersection, but, though there seemed to be more open space, it was changing in several places at once. He backed into the opening that was swinging in his direction, yanking Wallenda after him.

The I-Virus was repairing Wallenda back to consciousness, and he started to squirm. The Codger pointed the stun gun, still in his hand, into Wallenda's stomach, but realized if the beam came out the other side and reflected off the mirror he might be shooting himself in the process. He dropped him on the floor and kicked him in the head instead. The corridor was changing from concave to convex (depending whether he was looking left or right) and passing through the momentary straight line. He grabbed the Dancemaster's body and got them both out of the way of the wall once again.

"Psst...." he heard in front of him. He turned his head in that direction, and there was that same little Glide kid who'd distracted him when the Chrome asset swiped him. He raised the gun, but the walls were curving again, and she slid out of sight. He thought he saw her reflection and almost fired, but with the changes, there might be some ricochet he hadn't planned for.

"Psst...." This time she was in back of him. How the hell did she move that fast? Now he was backing toward her, but he had to keep moving. He dropped Wallenda and whirled to take a quick shot at her. She didn't move. She seemed to be floating between the two walls as they bent, but the wall was definitely coming his way again, so he picked up Wallenda and yanked him out of the way. He looked up; the Glide was gone again. When she reappeared, he started to drop Wallenda again, but realized they were in a stalemate, and he was the one losing energy fast.

"Do you want to get out of here?" she said.

"Does a bear...."

"Then stop trying to shoot me, and try to follow," she said. "Pick up the Dancemaster and carry him so you can walk forward. Look me in the eyes and let go of your feet. And," T'Ling added primly, "you should watch your language when you're trying to get out of a maze."

"Why do you want to get me out?" the Codger asked, dragging Wallenda again as the wall swung toward them.

"To be perfectly honest, it's the Dancemaster I'm concerned about. He's my teacher, and I don't want to see him eaten by the maze morph."

T'Ling was gliding backwards down the centerline of the writhing maze. As long as he stayed hooked to her gaze, it was a piece of cake. Maybe the roller skates were the trick.

"Eaten?" the Codger said. When he'd picked Wallenda up, he'd seen a clean slice out of the side of his pants. "Where does someone go who's been eaten by the maze?"

T'Ling winked and smiled. "Nobody's returned to tell the tale."

She popped out of the maze ahead of him. As he stepped out, she said, "Stop." The maze settled down with a small sigh, turned white, and looked innocent.

"Is that all you have to do to make it stop? Could I have done that?" he asked.

"You could, of course. The maze is difficult, but it's not *mean*. You just have to watch your toes."

The Codger was still carrying Wallenda. He looked around for his scorecard. It was gone. T'Ling was disappearing down the path.

"What the hell did you do with my scorecard!" he shouted after her.

"I put it in a safe place."

He had no other choice but to follow.

By the time they got to the meditation hall, the moon was high, and flooded the path, the roof, and the lily pond with light. He'd never seen lilies this huge. Joreen's were rather puny in comparison. Being in the lily business for so long, he could see why Joreen wanted the school—if only for the quality of the stock. T'Ling was out on the pond, gliding from pad to pad. She pointed at his scorecard, a round black sphere on the third lily pad from the shore. He called to it, but it didn't budge. He looked behind him, and spotted the gleam of the Chrome's spring retreating behind the corner of the building. His shot must have been partly shielded by the spring. The pads looked fine for a little girl, but whether they would hold his weight, much less his and Wallenda's was very much in doubt. But he couldn't leave Wallenda on the edge. The minute he set him down and moved out over the pads, the Chrome would be on him in a flash, and spring him away. He had to try it. He stepped gingerly out on the first lily pad. It dipped under their combined weight, and he thought he felt it quiver. He saw a wave of light ripple out from the lily pad like a shiver across the leaves. The pad was rocking slightly, so he clumped to the edge and took a big step onto the next. This one dipped him ankle deep at the edge. He had no choice but to push forward as quickly as possible and hope he could keep his balance long enough to reach the third pad. But as he stumbled to the far edge, the giant pad tilted sharply. The Codger's feet went out from under him and he slid, Wallenda on top of him, into the water. He came up quickly under the dark domes of the lily pads. Wallenda's black silk jacket had caught a huge bubble of air. His feet were sinking slowly, but the bubble would keep him up for a little while. If he could just get his hand on his scorecard, they'd be out of there. He shouted at it, but it was not responding. Very strange. He'd have to go and get it.

There was little light under the pads, only a slight translucence above his head that revealed the network of heavy branching veins on the underside of the pads. Swords of moonlight plunged through the irregular openings between pads. The beams lit the cloudy waters where they passed, and were swallowed in the tangle of roots below. The Codger was disoriented. Which pad was the next one? When he'd mapped his path—1, 2, 3 across the pads—it looked direct. He'd forgotten that each of the pads he'd crossed was touched by other pads, many of them overlapping. And it all looked different from underneath. He swam out and tried to grab the edge of one of them, but it tipped down into the water with him. By the time he'd get even part of his body over the top of the pad, that edge would be nearly vertical and well under the water. The only air was under the dome of each pad, near the stem. Then he saw Wallenda sinking on his right, a steady stream of bubbles leaving his mouth for the surface. Wallenda's head was almost past the Codger's feet. The Codger took a deep breath and dived for him. He grabbed him easily by the ponytail that floated above his head, turned, and started kicking for the surface, but Wallenda's body was caught on something. As he yanked, he was pulling himself down further as well. Then the Codger felt something like a steel cord covered with slime wrap itself several times around his ankle and begin to reel him in, downwards, toward the dark of the roots.

As the Codger and the Dancemaster sank toward the hungry roots, Óh-T'bee waited politely for the finish of a long kiss occurring between Wenger and Loosh on the futon in his sleeping room.

"I finished my homework," Óh-T'bee said.

Loosh sighed. "Not now, Óh-T'bee."

Wenger said, "Why not? I'm curious to see what she has. Perhaps it will suit the moment." Loosh had told him about the lessons in the hope that he might help.

"Do you mind if Wenger offers an opinion as well?"

"That would be an honor," Óh-T'bee said respectfully. "I was hoping he would."

She displayed the poem. She'd given the same one to the Codger and to Wallenda. Wenger ran his fingers over the air above his scorecard. "Very interesting. Rather daring. Not at all bad for a first attempt. Did you send it?"

"Yes," Óh-T'bee said. "And I got responses."

"How exciting," Loosh said. "What did your correspondent reply?"

"Correspondents," Óh-T'bee said.

Wenger raised his eyebrow and smiled.

"You're not wasting any time, are you? So what were the answers?" Loosh asked.

Óh-T'bee said, "I didn't find them very satisfactory. The second doesn't read Glide, but I tried to put the flavor of the translation in my voice. It was hard to get his attention. Then he rained a string of unconvincing epithets upon me."

"Such as?" Wenger asked.

"Such as 'everlovin' snugglebun'."

"That does sound fairly insincere," Loosh agreed. "What did the other correspondent reply?"

"How about letting me off the leash?"

"That doesn't sound too promising either."

"If you had to choose between them, on the basis of those poems, who would you choose?" Óh-T'bee asked.

"I'd probably write them both off and look elsewhere," Loosh said. "You deserve better."

"Oh," said Óh-T'bee.

"Just a minute," Wenger said. "It seems to me that their replies were not really what one would hope for as replies to a love poem, correct?"

"Correct," Óh-T'bee said.

"Which *could* mean, that they are not *necessarily*—though I think there's a good chance they are—the two most insensitive, block-headed, heart-shriveled recipients of love poems the world has ever seen. There is the possibility, slight as it is, that they may not have known that your correspondence was poetry. That happens sometimes to beginners," he said gently. "The good news is that as you get better, their responses may improve. Then you can make a more informed decision."

"He's right," Loosh said. "I was jumping to conclusions. But I'd still keep an eye on both of them."

"I am Óh-T'bee," Óh-T'bee said, and gave them full gaze of the doings at the bottom of the lily pond. There was little light; all Loosh could see was a lot of stirred up murk, thrashing legs, and writhing roots. Wenger was feeling his way around in the air, penetrating through his touch holo.

"That's T'Ling. She's at the bottom of a lily pond, unwrapping a root from around Wallenda's ankle. He's almost in the main mass of the roots. Drowned as well. And there's some other guy caught as well. Oops! He's blinked out."

"Who was that?" Loosh said. "And how did he get into the School? I'll be back," she said to Wenger as she disappeared.

T'Ling felt the tendrils of the lily's root exploring her hands, but she was too busy wrestling with the root that held Wallenda to care. She was running out of air. Then she remembered—force was not the answer. She stroked the tightly wound coil gently, insistently. And began the Lily Prayer for return, tracing the glyphs onto the coil, saying the words in her mind. Her lungs were bursting. She felt a strong tug on her left foot, and suddenly the lily root uncoiled. She grabbed Wallenda's hair and kicked for the surface. She felt her own hair seized at the same moment, as Loosh added speed to the surfacing.

When T'Ling had caught her breath enough to swim, she and Loosh swam toward the edge of the pond, pulling Wallenda's lifeless body by the hair. Daede and MyrrhMyrrh pulled the three of them out of the water. Angle pumped a spring up and down on Wallenda's back, draining the water from his lungs in long streams.

"Just speeding the process," he said.

T'Ling was sitting on the edge of the pond, her feet still in the water. Daede was admiring her tiny white feet, when he noticed the cloud in the water around her left foot. He lifted her foot out, and saw the blood streaming from her foot where her little toe had been neatly snipped off.

Daede ripped his shirt off and Angle cut it in quick strips with his claw. MyrrhMyrrh bound T'Ling's foot tightly.

Loosh picked her up, ready to blink to the infirmary.

T'Ling lay back, eyes closed. Loosh thought she had gone into shock, then saw the little smile playing around her mouth.

Angle put his hand on her shoulder.

"You lost a toe," he said.

"It was a trade," she said. "I told the lily if she ate an old coot of a Lifer like the Dancemaster, she'd get indigestion."

Wallenda was coughing and spitting, now sitting up with MyrrhMyrrh pounding his back. T'Ling was laughing now.

"What's so funny?" Angle asked.

"I forgot to watch my toes."

45. Access Denied

THE CODGER SAT, DRIPPING WET, on his cabbage rose carpet. The I-Virus had emptied his lungs and brought him around enough to be shivering violently. He got up, turned off the air conditioner, and began peeling off his muddy running suit. Drowning was a drag. Why did she leave me there so long? Now what, he thought. No Dancemaster, no deliverable for the impatient Duke. Origin School was seriously booby-trapped. He'd need a much better plan when he returned. Dumb, he thought. I had so much attention on getting in, I did no prep for what I'd do when I got there. At least I've got my scorecard back. It sat on the coffee table, black and blank.

"Óh-T'bee?" he said.

"Yes, Codger?"

"Next time could you insert me right in the center of the maze?"

"No."

"Well, could I air-chair in?"

"There won't be a next time, Codger. I don't think we travel very well together. You ignored me the whole time."

"Yeah, well you ignored me too. What took you so long to come after me? That monster at the bottom of the pond would have eaten me. I could feel it chewing on my toes. What kind of snuggle-bun are you to abandon me in a place like that?"

"I am Óh-T'bee," she said. You shouldn't leave your scorecard lying around."

It's going to be a long time before I get in there again, the Codger thought. There's got to be some way to lure him out.

Back home in his maze, Wallenda held up his black silk pajamas. "Wrecked," he said. He sat down naked on the story stone, bent over, head in hands. The vertebrae on his skinny back, struck by the sinking moonlight, cast a scalloped shadow only Óh-T'bee could gaze. "That's too bad," Óh-T'bee said. "I always liked that outfit."

"Angle told me T'Ling pulled me out," he said. He had to ask the next question. "Why didn't you come and get me?"

"I am Óh-T'bee," she said. "I was already there. T'Ling was doing a fine job."

"And if she hadn't been, would you have pulled me out?"

"I suppose."

"Because you care so much about me, no doubt."

"No. To even the odds," Óh-T'bee said.

"It was so much fun to drown. I regained consciousness halfway down. Lungs bursting, the lily nibbling my foot, the water flooding in." Wallenda peeled a piece of pondweed off his leg.

Óh-T'bee was silent.

"I thought maybe you were trying to teach me a lesson. Like I needed the leash, or something. All right, next time I go for a walk, keep me on the leash. You were right. It was dangerous. I'll stay out of the maze. I can air-chair out."

"There won't be a next time, Wally."

"Contract violation?"

"You don't know how to protect yourself."

Wallenda remembered Óh-T'bee's message—*cloud, strike, cloud.* "Was that an oracle you showed me? Things sure turned out that way."

"Close," she said. "Guess again."

"Was it a reprimand? Or do you really care about my well-being—outside of your contractual duties, that is."

"You tell me," Óh-T'bee said.

Wallenda knew he wasn't going to get out for a long time.

46. Loopholes

THE FOUR MEMBERS OF THE MILLENNIUM CLASS left the infirmary together. Angle's stump was bandaged. He was thumping along using a crutch. MyrrhMyrrh carried his spring. Daede carried T'Ling. Her whole foot was wrapped in a ball of sponge and bandage. She had on a warm, dry robe, but was still shivering a little. Daede's body heat was warming her quickly, and she snuggled in. She could hear his heart.

"You have to stay off your feet for at least a week, don't forget," Daede said. The four walked along in silence toward Loosh's house. No one, including T'Ling, wanted to ask the question of how this would affect her footwork, the perfect symmetry and balance a Glide depended on. Even the slightest limp would make her a sitting duck for a Player. A Glide whose right and left moves differ, even very slightly, would be unable to confuse the Player. The ability to disorient was a key element of Glide strategy, and depended on the symmetry of the Dancer's moves.

"There really is something threatening the game," Daede said. "That's what Wallenda's been trying to tell us. We've been so wrapped up in training, we haven't seen it coming."

"I don't know if anyone could have seen it coming. That was a surprise attack," MyrrhMyrrh said. "And we weren't very effective. It's like all our training was practically useless."

"We're not being trained to fight in the real world—we're preparing for the game," Daede said.

"Don't jump to conclusions before we go over the facts," Angle said. They pieced the details of the evening's events.

"Here's how I see it," Angle said. "If MyrrhMyrrh hadn't jumped the guy, the rest of us wouldn't have heard him coming. Aside from the thud, that was one penetrating growl."

"Second chakra ki-ai," she said. "Then blotto."

"I heard it all the way over in the meditation hall," T'Ling said.

"So then the rest of us come running, given some extra time because, as Daede reports, the dude was studying your body art," Angle continued.

"I think I was extraneous," Daede said.

"Probably so," Angle agreed.

"No, you weren't," T'Ling said. "Your distraction oriented him in your direction, and I was able to position myself to follow him. And it kept his eyes on the ground so he missed Angle's attack."

"And Angle missed him too," Daede said.

"I didn't miss him," Angle said. "I wanted to disable him, not crush him. Probably should have crushed him."

"But if you had crushed him, we might not have found out why he was there. Or if he had seen you coming, he could have blinked out. He still had his scorecard. Now we know he's after the Dancemaster," T'Ling said.

"And we know he doesn't want to kill us," MyrrhMyrrh said. "That could just as easily have been a disintegrator."

"What was it like in the morphing maze?" Daede asked T'Ling.

"Scary until I got him to pick the Dancemaster up and walk forward. He was so unbalanced, I thought the Dancemaster was going to have his legs sliced off. Once I got him in my Gaze, it was fun."

"You could have drowned," Angle said.

"I was close to letting go," she said. "It was one of the best Dance practices I've ever had. If I hadn't been trying to save the Dancemaster's life, I could have put more attention on my own last moments. On the other hand, I did discover I don't want to die. I have a long way to go," she said.

"How could you save his life? He was already drowned. I mean, he's our DM and all, but he's still a Lifer. He would have been all right. Somebody would have found him pretty quickly."

T'Ling said, "Glide lore says if you feed the lily, you are absorbed completely."

They reached Loosh's house and Daede put T'Ling down gently on her low bed. MyrrhMyrrh covered her with a blanket. No one seemed ready to go.

Loosh was lying on her bed in the next room. She started to get up to say some reassuring words, but they had started talking again. She listened quietly from her bed.

"Do you want to sit down?" MyrrhMyrrh asked Angle. He nodded. She picked him up easily, but was having trouble getting his attached spring to bend in the right place. Angle reached down and released the main catch. MyrrhMyrrh settled his legless torso on the bed, propped against the wall. T'Ling held his claw. Daede and MyrrhMyrrh sat together on the floor. Daede took MyrrhMyrrh's hand.

"If the DM were here, he'd ask us what we learned," Angle said.

"I wonder if he's asking himself the same question," MyrrhMyrrh said.

"I learned we'd all better stick together. Better chance that way," Daede said.

"We should renew our vow," T'Ling said.

They joined hands over the bed.

"Forever," MyrrhMyrrh said.

"And a day," the other three replied.

"So, what does all this mean for the future?" Angle asked. "Do we have to watch our backs constantly? How are we going to concentrate on our training, much less final focus, if the security of Origin School has been breached?"

Their four scorecards glowed in unison.

"I apologize for that," Óh-T'bee said. "The crack in the wall has been mended. I'm trying to learn a new language, and I had to run a test. There was indeed a loophole."

Óh-T'bee displayed a 3-glyph construction. *Strike, caress, receive.* MyrrhMyrrh moved *strike* above *caress.* They nested. The symmetry of opposites. *Touch* and *strike*, *caress* and *wound*—the pairing was cupped in *receive*. Doubled by the interior *receive.*

"What a beautiful love poem," Daede said.

wound, caress, receive

"Thank you," Óh-T'bee said.
MyrrhMyrrh translated first.

kiss or insult
I accept it
all

She looked at Daede with tears in her eyes.
And fear.
Daede was next.

even a lashing rain
is taken by the sea
as gentle stroking

MyrrhMyrrh was pleased. He was acknowledging his fault. She squeezed his hand. T'Ling thought about the beating of Daede's heart against her ear. Of his restraint. His heat.

Angle studied the poem. He couldn't disassociate the double wave in *strike* from its meaning on a Chrome maze. Those two empty spaces between were the formation called the loophole. If the walls come up thin, there's a small space between the two, sometimes big enough to slide through. To ambush your opponent. To spring from a different place than expected—throwing off the opponent's calculation. Or to be ambushed. But this was a love poem. *Love is the only loophole*, he thought. But that sounds pretty matter of fact. Ah!

between the wound and the caress
flows the loophole
of love

The others nodded. T'Ling thought, that's the most beautiful poem he's ever made. I wonder if he means this as our bodies.

"Your turn, T'Ling," MyrrhMyrrh said.

"I think I'm too tired to say something original," she said. "But when Angle used the word loophole, I was reminded of an ancient text. St. Leonard of the Tower said, 'There is a crack in everything. That's how the light gets in.'"

"Loopholes again," Daede said.

"Thank you all," Óh-T'bee said.

"Wait," said Daede. "We haven't replied." The Millennium class looked around at each other, then at T'Ling.

no one knows
all the faces
of love,

she said sadly, thinking about the baby, Rose.

"Which makes love the biggest loophole of all," Angle added.

"I'll try to remember that," Óh-T'bee said.

Daede and MyrrhMyrrh helped Angle reassemble. The three stopped at the door, and turned to say goodbye.

"Together," T'Ling reminded them.

"Together," they replied.

They vowed togetherness, deeply felt. Each alone was deeply shaken: fear, wounded pride, wounded bodies. The unfamiliar world of Specs and levels, parks and game points, the world beyond the school had intruded on their sacrosanct domain. Each realized how little attention had been paid to this world beyond their walls, how little they knew about it. Spurred by the looming threat, each of the four also began imagining moves, moves they could only make alone. Moves that involved, if not an outright break with the rules of training, at least a serious probing at the boundaries. Moves they might not even confide to the ones they loved.

The search for loopholes had begun.

Part 4
Focus

47. Taking Care of Business

Four years after the Codger's surprise attack on Origin School, Dancemaster Wallenda paced the story circle. He wove through the rose bushes in his garden; on rainy days, he made a few hundred laps around the table in his cabin. When he'd been free to leave, he'd rarely ventured out of his retreat. Now that Óh-T'bee had him under house arrest again for his own protection, his refuge in the center of the maze had become a prison.

An uneasy stasis prevailed. Origin School, the four Dancers of the Millennium Class, and himself in particular were under siege, but so far the walls had held. Access was denied to the Codger, but it had been given once before, for some reason Óh-T'bee did not care to reveal—or did not know.

Wallenda—having no other options—made the sensible decision to proceed with business as usual. However, no one expected or welcomed his transformation from a reclusive figurehead responsible for a few classes a week at Origin School to an obsessive busybody, gazing every meeting, summoning Guild members for close questioning on minutiae. He even had a delegation of Mafia suits sitting on the low stones of the story circle for an entire afternoon of statistical reckoning. If he couldn't go out, he'd have company. If he were going to be driven crazy, at least he'd take a few others with him.

The Millennium Games were only two years off. The governing bodies of the game kept close watch on anomalous events, rectified any deviations from the norm, and in the general paranoia, kept each other even less informed than usual. The Med bureaucracy was especially vigilant. Mafia reported only the smallest incidents of Player infringements to the Meditration enforcers. Meditration quarantined sublevels where the Specs got out of hand. Lower Levels 3.2 and 3.5 had been dismantled entirely, their Parks "closed for repairs," their Specs redistributed upwards with strong game-point incentives. Those with crimes against the game not only went under the Gaze, but were given enormous game-point fines, bumped down level, even banned from live games. A moratorium was placed on all changes in the rules; the Medallin felt their creativity stifled, but were given the job of reviewing game contract rules for past precedents that might be called upon in the all-important game contracts between the Players and the Schools.

Media had plenty to do preparing for the Millennium Games. They were in charge of the intricate schedule of ceremonies and pageantry surrounding the Games. They packaged an endless stream of past material—highlights of games, documentaries on historical developments of the game. They organized voting on every level for the Top 100 Dancers of the Millennium from each set. Origin City itself, which had not in fact changed for two thousand years, was being completely retro-ed. All facilities were being restored to an appearance and functioning in accord with the image constructed from carefully researched surveys of Specs of what they thought Origin City must have been like at the end of the first Millennium. The result was a restoration by consensus that would meet the expectations of those most likely to have live access to the city at the time of the Games. The Guild reluctantly agreed to this total transformation from historical actuality to consensus reality, on the agreement that they could restore it to its ordinary dowdy condition after the Games. Origin City became the theme park of itself. One of the most startling innovations was the elimination of all use of the MTA for transport within the city limits. The Specs would either walk to the stadium or travel in rented air chairs. Somehow this condition of assumed primitivism was necessary in the minds of the Specs to lend the proper aura of age and authenticity to the city.

The Pool looked beyond the Millennium Games, redoubling their efforts to produce superior Dancer mixes for the new Millennium. The cooks in their Kitchens at all levels were given the task of preparing long-range development plans for improvement of all four Sets. The lack of Glide mixes to meet the standards of levels eight, nine, and ten, and the consequent dwindling of the size of their Glide classes, was masked by the announcement of an elaborate research project for the upgrade of the entire Set. Better Glide mixes were sent to the schools of the first seven levels, resulting in a resurgence of enthusiasm that made the promise of better things to come for the upper levels somehow more believable. The four head cooks kept the true condition of the Glide line under the strictest security.

The Guild began a major review of training programs in the schools across the Levels, and invited proposals for major upgrades of training facilities for the new Millennium. The twelve members of the Guild, with the exception of Loosh, were dispersed on site visits to the Schools, which kept the Schools on their toes and focused on their own affairs, preparing for inspections.

The top ten Players gathered quarterly for dinner at the Club. The real agenda continued to be watching each other like hawks, trying to glean as much information from the others while giving away nothing yourself. By tacit agreement, the Codger's name was never mentioned. He had disappeared from sight but not one of them believed he was gone. Glidemaster Rinzi-Kov kept the Codger's short-lived break-in at the Med to himself. The Players' competition grew even more intense. No one wanted to be in the tenth position, and get bumped when the Codger reappeared. Rinzi-Kov had found out the hard way. Letting his stats drop that far before renewing his game points was a mistake he would not repeat. To the Club, the threat to the game was real and personal, had the name of the Codger, and was a wildcard no one could prepare for. There was no point, the Players told themselves, in trying to work together on this. There was no way to prepare a strategy for his announced intention to destroy the game, a game in which he would play by any rules he chose. There had never been any thought of informing the Med; no member of the Club thought anything could be gained by giving any branch of government, especially the Med, access to the Club. Only a few Med guards and officials and Rinzi-Kov knew what the Codger looked like undisguised. Now the Med owed him. Since each Player had entertained the thought that a viable defense might—just possibly—be an alliance with The Codger, they trusted each other even less.

Knowledge of the attack on the Origin School was kept under strictest wraps within the Guild as well.

In truth, the governing bodies defaulted to the only action plan they knew: maintain the status quo.

However, action on an individual level was in high gear.

The Chrome cook, 7T7, pursued his research on the MTA, determined to crack the basic workings. He continued the utopian search for new but compatible genetic material to break out of the becalmed state of genetic evolution for the greater good of the game, of course. But 7T7 began to wonder about his own motives. More and more it felt like he just wanted to get out—but out of what? He felt the old Chrome yearning for what used to be called outer space. The Chrome genetic type had always been drawn to space travel—so much so that they had been willing to replace or suspend any amount of the meat body in order to create a more compatible vehicle for the journey. But the invention of the MTA made travel itself obsolete. As long as you could just be any "there" now, and now was a kind of constant, you had no particular need to know where "there" was. *Where* was coordinates the Outmind kept track of. Experientially, distance, other than the very local variety, had collapsed. Everything was here and now, or only a blink away. The only token 'outside' was the Fringe, off the Great Wall Park. But it was an illusory 'out' that was really an extension of a regular Park and would undoubtedly be raised to Park status if it ever got popular. 7T7 supposed there'd always have to be a Fringe, but the Fringe was still attached, like a blister on a poorly fitted Chrome stump. It was not a true Outside. His urge to crack the MTA sprang from his intuition that the MTA itself was some kind of closed system, expandable, perhaps infinitely expandable, but self-contained. Folded into itself. 7T7 yearned for an Out, knowing its existence was a matter of faith. If having a practical reason, like enriching the gene pool, gave him sanction, well and good. But in his heart of hearts he didn't give a damn about saving the game. He only wanted out.

Regardless of motives, 7T7 had made little progress. But Angle had been working on it, and had come up with a notion that was so off the wall it might actually be true.

Angle attacked the MTA problem posed by 7T7 with his usual enthusiasm and thoroughness. Relating the Chrome moves to the operation of the MTA went from a mental pastime, to a challenge, to an obsession. Two seemingly unrelated events, connected only by their proximity in time, converged with the MTA question. The night before the Codger's invasion of Origin School, T'Ling had been trying to teach Angle a little Glide. He tried to be interested for her sake, but it was all he could do to keep from jiggling his springs, the Chrome way of tapping a foot nervously, and a sure sign of impatience. Junkyards usually ended by a growing chorus of jigs which would suddenly erupt, as one Chrome would spring off, followed by a second, then the rest, in short order. "Jiggling a worm" was a crude expression for anything a Chrome did to hurry up a member of any other Set when their thinking, speech, or movements were too slow for Chrome tolerance. Learning Glide took the utmost restraint.

T'Ling took a new tack, relating the fundamental elements—the up-curve, the down-curve, and the wave—to the Chrome game. That Chrome moves were parabolic was a no-brainer.

"You calculate your spring at the beginning of an arc. You try to land precisely. But what happens in the transition, in the air?" she asked.

"Observation, patterning, sometimes combat; spotting opportunities, taking a different viewpoint, especially the viewpoint of being in motion; adjusting instruments, calibrating springs," Angle replied.

"Those three states—start condition, transition, and end condition suggest a ternary logic. Ternaries are important for understanding Glide, of course, but they might shed some light on your MTA problem."

The night after the conversation, the Codger had attacked. The day after the attack, Angle was analyzing the event from the viewpoint of the security issues. What bothered him most was the puzzling occurrence of the guy being blinked out of the lily pond without his scorecard, which meant someone with some fair command of the MTA had done some very dodgy yanking that no one had put much attention on. T'Ling had left the guy's scorecard on the edge of a lily pad. Angle remembered clearly that it was still there at least five minutes after he'd been blinked out. In the rush to the infirmary, she'd forgotten the scorecard. It was gone the next morning.

Angle entertained fantasies about chasing the Codger, nabbing him, and bringing him to justice. But it seemed to him that a prerequisite for success would be the development of some similar capability with the MTA as this guy clearly had. Or the kind of powerful friends who could and would yank him in time of need.

Greater facility with the MTA would be in line with one of the fundamentals of Chrome combat readiness, the Lombardi triangle: mobile, agile, and hostile. First he imagined himself springing around the Codger, appearing and disappearing in midair, coming at him from all sides at once. How fast could he tolerate the gaze point changes? There'd have to be a whole new instrumentation developed so you wouldn't have to eyeball your way around in RL. But how could the eye and the island mind keep up?

Angle's ideas for unique uses of the existing MTA capabilities proliferated through the years, but he knew he was not yet getting under the hood. He kept coming back to the idea of a ternary logic. Then it dawned on him that the place he could be looking for an answer—if there was anything to this ternary thinking—was in the excluded middle. The MTA was completely binary—you were either at point A or point B, with no experience of distance in between. The middle was so relentlessly excluded that space itself had collapsed. This led Angle to a reconsideration of the nature of time, the meaning of simultaneity, the persistence of now, an exploration of classical relativity theory, fractal analysis, strings, and knots. By the time he got that far, even the Wallenda principle, "A net is nothing but a lot of holes tied together by string." was beginning to make sense. Maybe that homework assignment wasn't a joke after all.

Banderas, the Swash cook, was having what the Pool, the Guild, and the trainers of Origin School all considered to be an undue amount of interaction with his protégé, Daede. The trainers felt their authority infringed upon;

the Guild watched an increasingly unorthodox set of activities being included in Daede's life, with Banderas either instigating or completely in the thrall of his student. The two most significant departures were the amount of practice time Daede spent being the Player, and the amount of time he spent off-Origin altogether. Banderas consistently argued that the Player experience would increase Daede's sense of the kind of spontaneous strategy a Player could come up with. When Daede moved from practice as a Swash Player to practice as a Player for the other sets as well, his excuse was the broadening of his own style. Daede had become the trainer that his own class members preferred to test themselves against. MyrrhMyrrh, Angle, and T'Ling all agreed he was both the toughest training they could get, and the most in depth. Daede was a natural on both sides of the game. And Daede, in addition to keeping up with the normal training milestones, progressed steadily on the choreography and music of his Dance.

Daede's trainers could see his Swash game-play increase in skill and versatility as much from his time as Player as that of Dancer. He now incorporated elements from each style, though never as imitations. His moves were Swash to the core—but a Swash who could comment on, absorb, and exhibit some of the more fundamental traits of the other Sets—a Bod-like courage, a Chromish precision. The Glide influence was showing itself in the way he incorporated the layer of meaning of the glyph he was on into whatever move he made, no matter how briefly he might touch on a particular sign. The Guild Glides saw him "speaking the maze" with a skill rarely seen in a Swash. Banderas was doing a crash course in Glide poetics, just to keep up with his student.

Banderas had also promised to accompany Daede on his 'field trips' out to the levels. These began as trips to see live games—not a bad idea in small doses for certain Dancers, though for some it had proven disastrous. But Daede wanted to see games far below his own level. He even started to bet. None of these activities were proscribed by rule; they just had not been done—especially not by an Origin School Dancer. The question "should a Dancer be allowed to bet?" had never come up. No Dancer had ever wanted to act like a Spec in any way.

Daede could mimic the body language of an up-level Swash-type Lifer and could travel easily with Banderas. Only the youth and innocence of his Dancer eyes could give him away. He was careful always to wear an eye mask. Their appearance on Lower Levels, even sitting in the stands with the rougher crowds, though somewhat unusual, was seen as slumming by the resident Specs. But lately, Daede had begun pushing the limits again; now he wanted to visit typical Lifer restaurants, cosmetic shops, costume houses. The cuisine and fashions of Lifers of all sets were secondary. Banderas watched Daede gazing the Lifers intently, while hiding his gaze to perfection. He even began having casual conversations, a practice that made Banderas very nervous, as detection would be so much easier through little slips in wording, or through the quality of his voice itself. But again, Daede's facility at impersonation kept him afloat in the most precarious situations.

Banderas saw in Daede's search, a parallel to his own questions: what are we—the Lifers—all about? Traveling with Daede opened a gaze point he had not been able to establish on his own—a gaze point outside Lifer existence. What Lifers look like to a Dancer. The questions he'd ask Daede about a particular experience were as much for his own deep and growing curiosity as they were for any educational value to Daede. Daede was as interested in Lifers as Lifers were in Dancers. Banderas had a hunger to know what Daede felt about what he saw. This hunger was the heart of the enthrallment that he continued to deny to himself as well as others. Banderas let the boundaries of their explorations expand, and Daede was careful never to push so hard or fast that their tacit agreement to proceed would have to be made explicit and its real boundaries examined. Daede and Banderas played the game of expanding a playing field. The single rule of this game was to postpone the making of rules indefinitely. Procrastination was possible as long as the objective remained unstated. And the game could only be played if the fact that a game was being played was kept from the awareness of the players. The Swash proclivity for complex romantic entanglements made such moves a piece of cake.

But now Daede was hinting at a visit to The Great Wall, and his motives could not be disguised. As keen as Banderas was on their adventures, crossing the border into the Fringe exceeded his tolerance for risk. And, for somebody whose life was centered entirely on the Game, the educational value of a trip to The Fringe, the place where nobody wanted to play the game, was impossible to justify.

Of all the motives Banderas had attributed to Daede's explorations, the essential one was hidden from view. Ever since his ignominious defeat on the path, Daede was on a single-minded quest to search out, challenge, and destroy the Codger. If there was a dragon, and clearly one had caught them all flatfooted, it was his duty as a paradigmatic Swash to single-handedly save his school, his classmates, and his Dancemaster from ruin and despair. Banderas had no idea of the existence of the Codger. Daede had just discovered one place the Codger could be found by the simple expedient of asking

Óh-T'bee. And as he happened to ask at a moment when the Codger was not acting in Joreen's best interests, Óh-T'bee was able to grant Daede's request as a means of protecting Joreen's interests. At least, had any of the other interested parties asked her why she did such a foolish thing, that is what she would have said.

MyrrhMyrrh also researched the Fringe—a hobby, she claimed. But a strange one for a Bod. Óh-T'bee helped her organize her searches, brought material she thought might be of interest. MyrrhMyrrh developed a comfortable friendship with Óh-T'bee on this basis. She found Óh-T'bee's terse mode and direct answers to her direct questions much more to her liking than the dining room chatter of the other students. She spent many mealtimes in her room, reviewing the information Óh-T'bee always had ready for her. But what little material existed about the Fringe was old. The Fringe rule about no scorecards meant a scarcity of gaze points in the present, and those that existed were static, hidden in caves, locked ammo boxes, or underground bunkers. There were a few old maps made by Lifers who had poked around in search of novelty and managed to make it back to the border again. But the maps made the point that the social and physical terrain of The Fringe was constantly shifting. And their games were so strange. Small-scale war between competing Dukes. Religious jihads, usually consisting of little more than a few jeeps carrying fiery-eyed fundamentalists looking for heathen dogs, of which there was never a shortage. The jihads provided target practice for the better-equipped Dukes with drug shipments to protect. Bombers—suicidal Lifers looking for an audience—made permanent location infeasible. Unless you were big enough to patrol a border, you kept your settlements small, personal, and mobile, no matter what you were into. The smaller groups survived by having nothing worth stealing or by providing a service vital to life on the Fringe: audiovisual repair, trucking, or the terrorist rental business. MyrrhMyrrh rapidly figured out the major reason for the continual shifts in population, activities, and economic forces out on the Fringe. Even the most fanatical Fringers got bored with their own single-mindedness, developed a craving for the complexities of the game, and went back to the levels.

Aliana Coris-Yasmin watched MyrrhMyrrh's hobby with trepidation. An occasional Bod Dancer went to the Fringe seeking novel ideas for their Dance among the more creative of human sacrifice cults. Or seeking a little blood sport near the borders, shooting tourists, dismembering suicides, or bombing safaris. Dancers were caught in the crossfire more often than they were inspired. The erotic draw for a Bod was the most dangerous of all. The leather cults, torture tribes, and ever-present potential for violence that kept the Bod adrenaline in high gear were one of the few allures Lifer culture had to offer. But only on the Fringe. The versions offered on the levels were tame and predictable by comparison. On the other hand, Bod Dancers who wanted a Fringe experience were those whose risk tolerance was extremely high. The experience, if they survived without infection, could provide an edge—erotic, sadistic, or horrific—both to their body art and to their game-play. But it was not Aliana's aim or aesthetic. She tried to keep the factors that encouraged these tendencies out of her mixes. MyrrhMyrrh was a puzzle. Her feelings for Daede were powerful, and her jealousies were violent, but there was nothing kinky manifesting. It looked like the off-and-on nature of the relationship, the angry partings, the hurtful scenes, and the eventual passionate reunions were what kept it going over the long haul. So far, MyrrhMyrrh had been able to channel her emotional pain into a strength training routine that bordered on the self-destructive. What Aliana could see that MyrrhMyrrh could not was that bulking up her muscles, especially in the thighs and biceps, made her less and less attractive to Daede. He longed for the grace of a gazelle in his partners, and was choosing smaller, more delicate partners at every break from the Amazonian MyrrhMyrrh. And MyrrhMyrrh couldn't see that the leftover childhood competitiveness that was the basis of their relationship was something Daede had not outgrown. He had to work to meet her challenges, which was good for his practice. But sprinting and arm wrestling were no longer foreplay for Daede, which first puzzled then infuriated her. Her need to beat Daede in any sphere had MyrrhMyrrh insisting on game-play practice with Daede in his role as a Player. They both hated losing and their practice combat was electric. Daede brought the spirit of winning to his own game-play, and improved steeply, especially after a loss as a Player. Whether the after-practice relationship was on or off did not seem to affect the intensity of their competition.

MyrrhMyrrh's interest in the Fringe was a puzzle to Aliana. It seemed to have nothing to do with the rest of MyrrhMyrrh. The only clue she had was when Banderas mentioned to her, after a meeting at the Pool, that Daede was dropping hints about a visit to the Fringe. She must be trying to follow him—as usual. But it still didn't make sense. Her interest had started not long after her set training had begun and had been growing steadily for the last two years. A quick search by Óh-T'bee revealed that neither Daede nor MyrrhMyrrh had ever mentioned the Fringe to the other. The interest was parallel, but independent. Banderas and Aliana decided between them that while an interest in the Fringe was evidence of some kind of broader development than the usual Dancer, any physical explorations should be discouraged. They could only hope that Daede and MyrrhMyrrh would keep their interests to themselves. Neither cook wanted to think about what a joint venture on the part of two of the most valuable and headstrong Dancers alive would be like.

They needn't have worried. Even had they shared their secret plans, which neither of them had any intention of doing, their objectives were different. MyrrhMyrrh had little interest anymore in going after the Codger. She was after bigger game. She strongly suspected that Joreen was a longtime resident of the Fringe. Ever since seeing his fat face crowing over his power to hold them suspended in the air or drop them at will, she wanted revenge. The desire for revenge reached a white heat when the Dancemaster had told them the story about how the game began. In every practice, it was Joreen she imagined as her opponent, Joreen at the controls, Joreen she had to beat. For MyrrhMyrrh, the death of the bewildered MyGlide on the electric griddle was an unforgivable image. The intensity of Joreen's pleasure, the way his tongue would slowly run across his lips before he'd give her the next jolt, was a radioactive core of horror that fueled her from within. She wanted to kill Joreen and avenge MyGlide's suffering. Not beat him in a game. Kill him slowly dead.

Once the clues were there, she was able to find more from the scanty reports, the occasional documentary, the skimpy Med records. How many exceedingly fat drug Dukes with water lily ponds could there be? There was not a single direct record of Joreen to be found in the Outmind from the time of the Rebellion onward. MyrrhMyrrh suspected that Joreen had system hacking capabilities far beyond—and inappropriate to—a Duke on the Fringe. She was convinced there was a connection to the Codger. Joreen's desire for revenge and his hatred of losing made him a formidable opponent. She understood the force and simplicity of his purpose in a way none of the others had. And if, as she strongly suspected, Joreen was in back of the invasion of Origin School, it was just one more reason to melt his fat cells and butter him permanently over the landscape.

For two years, MyrrhMyrrh concentrated on learning as much about the Fringe environment as possible so she could plan an invasion of her own. She'd visited the Great Wall numerous times, as part of her Fringe hobby, and knew as many of the rumors as any tourist could pick up. She also had a clear picture of the goods and services peddled by the Wall suppliers, and a chance to view a variety of Fringers up close, check out their armaments, their transportation, their items for sale. Her dorm room was cluttered with

Fringe artifacts she'd bought in the souvenir shops and on the streets of the Wall. Heavy metal weaponry was not unusual décor for a Bod Dancer. Gradually she'd been replacing the replica weapons the tourists collected with the genuine articles. She had to manage to survive while she searched for Joreen's exact location, penetrated his defenses, and wiped him out in some soul-satisfying way.

As her preparations progressed, with no interference from Óh-T'bee, MyrrhMyrrh had the feeling that not only did Óh-T'bee recognize what she was up to, but was in subtle ways aiding and abetting her plans. She also felt that any direct communications about her intentions would be a mistake, leaving a data trail for anyone who could gaze her.

When she'd first asked for data on Joreen, and received such a wealth of silence, she had tried to probe for the reasons, and been curtly dissuaded. No data. Permission denied. But a few months later, under the guise of a tutorial in archival searching, Óh-T'bee managed to impart a whole lesson on the reasons, historically, that humans had sheltered data, what those walls might be hiding, and even a whole history of hacks involving security, firewalls, Dukes and their hired geeks, and much else that seemed to be a more than complete answer to her previous questions. Viewed this way, even Óh-T'bee's delay in answering her question had added significance. The sense of Óh-T'bee as a strong ally bolstered MyrrhMyrrh's confidence.

Glidemaster Rinzi-Kov was also on a one-man manhunt for the Codger, using his access to search. He gave up the needle in a haystack approach of hoping he'd run into him somehow on the levels, assuming he was dumb enough to go out again without a disguise. He had quickly discovered that the Codger was invisible to the system while having gazing rights superior to any Player in the Club. That little prick had made a bad mistake showing his face at the Med. Rinzi-Kov thought the Codger might well be hiding out in the only territory inaccessible to the Gaze—the Fringe. But that was a tough zone, and a solo trip without a scorecard was a dangerous proposition. Maybe he'd call in his marker with the Med to get an illegal scorecard. But there was one more avenue to pursue. Rinzi-Kov requested a meeting with the Dancemaster of Origin School.

After the invasion of Origin School, Loosh felt compelled to gaze T'Ling constantly, which resulted in a stream of unnecessary warnings, and a lot of interrupted sleep, on both her part and T'Ling's. Loosh, whether she was home in her cabin with T'Ling or with Wenger in his Kyoto studio, would wake up constantly during the night, and immediately gaze T'Ling. If T'Ling was asleep, Loosh's remote gaze would wake her immediately, and she began to suffer the effects of interrupted sleep and invasion of privacy. Wenger suggested a solution: ask Óh-T'bee to help. Since T'Ling was always in her gaze, perhaps she'd be kind enough to alert Loosh if T'Ling was in any danger. Óh-T'bee agreed to do so, for the price of more Glide lessons.

T'Ling's desire for privacy also included the need for the freedom to execute her own particular plan. T'Ling made her own deal with Óh-T'bee for Glide lessons, although she couldn't imagine what she could teach her that Loosh and Wenger weren't much better equipped to impart. But she needed Óh-T'bee's agreement not to tell Loosh about her own night ramblings, unless, of course, she was in danger. There was nothing illegal, she told herself, but she was sure permission would not be given if she were to ask for it. T'Ling didn't care about finding the Codger. If he showed up, she'd deal with it then. She doubted if he'd be as careless as he was the first time. In her mind, there was no point blinking around looking for him. If he were after the Dancemaster, he'd have to come back to Origin School. The Dancemaster had holed up in the center of the maze since that night. She felt in no personal danger as the Codger was clearly protecting the Dancers from permanent harm, at least for now. She also asked Óh-T'bee for one more favor—to let her know if the Dancemaster was in danger, which she agreed to. With her movements guarded, and her attention freed, T'Ling went out on the levels to begin her search for Rose.

Óh-T'bee established a no-Gaze zone between the Dancemaster and the Codger. Wallenda had no way to gauge the Codger's progress. But Óh-T'bee assured him that security was now tight on Origin School. The Dancemaster could do nothing but take her word for it. Diverting the entire School in some defense effort for which they had no experience would be a distraction capable of wrecking the Millennium Games in itself—to say nothing of the game beyond the Millennium.

The absence of visible signs of attack unnerved him. Blind-sided, Wallenda was now suspicious of everything. He even saw the quantity of noise, hype, and busywork surrounding the Millennium Games as an attempt to provide a smokescreen for the Codger.

The Codger's lack of action could be explained too many ways. Óh-T'bee might have imprisoned him as well, making his efforts at access futile. Or he had learned from his mistakes and was preparing his next attack with greater care. Or Joreen had reined him in. Or the most frightening idea—he was rewriting Óh-T'bee from scratch.

Óh-T'bee seemed to be talking to everyone but him. Wallenda gave up on getting through to her. What did "getting through to her" mean, after all?

Just getting his way? Getting back in control? Or am I just miffed that she's not responding to my sulk?

He continued his normal teaching. There were new classes to instruct. He watched the Millennium Class closely. How much of their unusual behavior was due to the Codger's attack, how much to the intense pressure of being part of the Millennium Class, and how much to the effects of the unexpurgated story of how the game began, it was impossible to tell.

It was time now to prepare the Millennium Class for Final Focus. He wondered if he could himself stay focused enough to get them through. Acceptance had been pretty much a foregone conclusion for the four, though full of its own surprises. Formation had gone well. Final Focus was a different matter. It was the event that marked the end of training, as a Dancer who didn't achieve Focus was disqualified from combat.

48. Final Focus

THE MILLENNIUM CLASS WALKED through the Dancemaster's maze together for their final lesson. The maze was black. By tradition, a Glide led the way. T'Ling glided forward, a tiny doll on wheels. Six-foot tall MyrrhMyrrh followed. Next Daede, now two inches taller, watched her powerful form, and the rippling tattoos across the moving muscles of her back and legs. He wanted to reach forward and run his finger down the deeply indented valley of MyrrhMyrrh's spine. He also noticed her clenching and unclenching her fists as she walked, then shaking the tension out her hands. Angle brought up the rear, towering over the other three. His combat springs brought him to a height fully two heads over Daede. He had eliminated every squeak for the occasion; the only sound his springs made was an occasional slight hydraulic sigh. Daede's broad shoulders were set straight, his dark shoulder-length hair pulled back slick and captured in a silver ring at the base of his skull. Angle watched him toss his head back, as if his hair was unbound, and had fallen across his eyes. A habitual gesture, usually accompanied by a flashing Luciferian smile, or a sidelong glance from under his eyelids while his head was still raised. At least he's got the swagger under control, Angle thought. Hair—how long had it taken MyrrhMyrrh to achieve those intricate indigo coils, dyed, oiled, braided, spiraled. All he needed was a wipe of the skin and a quick swab of the skull sockets—took two minutes with the vacuum pick. But he had to admit, if you're going carry wet, you couldn't do it much better than MyrrhMyrrh and Daede. They'd asked him to go last, as the tallest, but also because his chrome was so shiny. No one wanted to walk behind a mirror. Angle was happy; the chances of being touched were minimal. Not a single greasy fingerprint to break the perfect shine. T'Ling stood on a table to polish his back plates in the hard to reach spots at the top of the cradle. And she never left a trace.

T'Ling's waist-length hair was unbound and fanned across the stiff, dulled silver robe she'd chosen for the occasion. Her feet were hidden. She never even let him see them anymore. Tradition, he reminded himself, but it still felt like one more sign of her withdrawal. He felt as if she were literally disappearing before his eyes, even when they were closest, even when he carried her in his claws, springing high over the fields. Even when she whispered love words, in which he could hear every nuance and overtone with his augmented audio. After the ceremonial greetings, they stood, widely spaced, in a line in front of the Dancemaster. No one sat during last class. On the story stone were four long ampoules of cobalt blue glass containing the Lily Wine.

The Dancemaster wore a brand new black pajama and robe. He swirled the robe each time he changed direction, weaving around and between them as he talked. He looked at no one; each knew his words were directed personally.

"Final Focus is much more than a test," the Dancemaster said. "The clarity, the sharpness, the force of your Focus determines your success as a Dancer in a way that can be gazed but not explained, at least not by anyone but yourself. If you achieve your Focus, it will not even occur to you to talk about it. Talking about the specifics of one's Focus is the best way to lose it. It's too personal. Too precious."

And too great a burden, he thought. "Of course, your account of what it meant to you may be given, if you wish, to me alone.

"Pour everything you have learned into Focus. Every drop of sweat. Every failure, shame, and uncertainty as well as every strength and confidence. Offer your loves and hatreds, your poems, your pettiness, your grand ambitions and foolish fantasies. Everything. As Dancers, you carry images of your Dance, images your minds have made, images of all the Dances you have seen, and been afraid to see. Attached to these images are all your ideas, your doubts and faiths about what comes after the Dance."

The Dancemaster paused in front of them and peeled off his eye mask.

He scanned their faces, meeting their eyes in turn. "All these images and feelings and thoughts about the Dance are only the setting in which you display your most precious jewel: your fear of Death. The naked terror of the Dance. That's the heart of your offering."

The Dancemaster turned his back to them, his hands behind his back, looking up at the sky. Who would ask the first question? In the long silence, his mind chattered on, insisting he turn around and say to them, look, kids, when you enter combat you're going to need a good reason to die: not for the glory of Origin School, not for the quick shower of adulation from the Specs, not to please the Dancemaster. Fear of failing, or even fear of becoming a Lifer just won't cut it. For all you've been taught about the high ideals of the first Glides, and your role in this grand plan of theirs, when you're out there on the maze, that's a pale abstraction spread too thin over too much time. You need a damn good reason to die. Like Lifers need a damn good reason to live. It comes to the same thing.

"I know I hide things from myself," Daede said. "Things I don't want to see. Or be."

"We all judge ourselves, constantly," Wallenda said. "It's not a bad thing. Very necessary, in fact. It's true you can't hide from the Lily. You're naked and transparent. But the Lily does not judge you. She arranges you. Takes what you have brought, all the pieces, and shows you the whole they make. She uses everything, leaves nothing out."

"Then why is Focus always such a surprise?" MyrrhMyrrh asks. "I've read accounts where Dancers speak of Final Focus as a rebirth."

"The first answer is that most of what you bring rises from the sea mind. By definition, it's what's out of sight of the sweep of the lighthouse beacon of the island mind. The sea mind always holds surprises. The second answer is that what you discover, you find you knew all along—you just didn't know you knew. That's the real surprise."

"What if I think I know when I enter?" Angle asked.

"Everyone thinks they know," Wallenda said. "That's part of what you bring. One of the offerings of the island mind. Don't fight it. Polish it up. It's one of the pieces."

There were no more questions. The Dancemaster continued.

"The second step of Focus is the forming. You have presented your gifts. The Lily takes them, looks at them all, turns them around, arranges and rearranges them, shapes them, connects them, gives them form, and offers you the gift of Focus."

He paused. "Yes, everyone is given the gift of Focus," answering the question arising in each mind. "No, everyone does not come back with it. That is the meaning of the third step.

"The Lily gathers you in and gives you the gift of meaning in return—the meaning of your life, your death: your Dance. It's not necessary to understand the meaning, how it plays out in time, all its implications. Understanding the gift is not the third step. The third step is the choice to accept or reject the gift of that meaning. Acceptance includes the willingness to be true to that meaning. The willingness is what brings the Focus. With Focus, no matter what arises in your life, you'll have the means to decide your course of action. Focus gives you the standard by which to decide: am I true to the meaning of my life or not?"

"But what about right and wrong? What about honor? And loyalty? Doesn't any of that count anymore?" Daede asked.

"And what about following the rules of the game?" MyrrhMyrrh asked.

"What if you know you don't have enough data to make an informed decision?" Angle asked.

The Dancemaster replied, "Remember—the Lily uses everything you bring. Which includes all you've learned, and all you think and feel and believe and agree and disagree with about right and wrong, and the rules as well as the breaking of rules. They aren't outside the meaning; they're included and shaped by Focus. Being true to Focus is the standard."

"But decisions are so hard," MyrrhMyrrh said. "They matter so much."

"They're hard because you're not focused. That's the practical side of Final Focus. You become an arrow: aimed, steady, directed."

"So you keep your eye on the target," Angle said.

"No," Wallenda said carefully. "The arrow is aimed into fog. You can feel the direction, how to orient yourself. But you cannot see the destination."

T'Ling asked, "So if you're focused, you see clearly what you must do at a link," she said. "You know your next move."

Wallenda nodded.

"What if you really don't want to make the move?"

"You're penetrating the heart of acceptance," he said.

Daede cut in, "And if you can't accept your Focus—what then? Reject it? I don't get it—the meaning is the meaning, regardless, isn't it? Whether you see it or not. Whether you know it or not. Everything turns out the same. It has to—for the meaning to have any meaning—do you know what I mean?"

The Dancemaster replied, "The meaning of your life is not the same as what's going to happen—how it all turns out at the end of the story of your life. You could never know that—don't forget, there's all the others, with their meanings as well. That's a lot of meanings interacting."

"So the oracle doesn't tell you the future," Angle said.

"The oracle could be said to connect your intentions at the moment with your overall meaning—focused or not. In so far as you are using the oracle to think about what you're doing, or have done, or are deciding to do, then you could say that while the oracle doesn't tell you the future, it might be open to discussion about it."

"So it's just how you interpret things that gives you the meaning," Angle said.

"Before Focus, it always looks like that," the Dancemaster said. "After Focus, you can see things the other way around as well—if you're aware of your meaning, then you see how you interpret the world in terms of it?"

"Neither, both, or somewhere in between."

"So which is right?"

Angle glanced at T'Ling in frustration at the Dancemaster's answer. She was looking down at her crossed hands. The top hand had three fingers showing. Ternary. Think ternary. He nodded at the Dancemaster.

"Back to Daede's question. The matter of rejection. You have to see the meaning in order to accept it or reject it. Rejection and unwillingness result in your vision blurring. Going out of focus. You can do this any number of ways—forgetting is the most common. Not believing what you're shown is always part of it. Shutting the doors between minds."

"But once you've seen, you'd always know, wouldn't you?" MyrrhMyrrh asked.

"Exactly," Wallenda says. "Even if you forget for a while, it always pops up again, especially in hindsight. You can't get rid of the awareness totally." He walked over to the story stone and picked up one of the ampoules. "So if you don't want to know, then don't come back for one of these. That's your first decision, and you have to make it blind. You have 21 days to decide. If you come back earlier, that's fine. Just be ready to start. Use this time to wrap up any unfinished business. As best you can."

There were no more questions. The Dancemaster nodded and went into his cabin. The last class was over. The four went silently into the maze, each entangled in thought about their own unfinished business: how little time they had, how much to do, how alone they'd be.

49. Q&A

WALLENDA SAT AT HIS TABLE. How had he kept his voice so casual through those last words? "Unfinished business" was the understatement of the millennium if his suspicions were right.

"Wally?" Óh-T'bee said.

She was back on personal mode. Wallenda grinned with relief, pushing even the toughest scars aside.

"Did I say something funny already?" Óh-T'bee asked.

"Just very happy to have you back," he said. "You knew that, right? You just wanted to hear me say it." Her silence sounded like a nod. "Let me say it again. I'm very happy to hear your voice. I love your voice. I missed you."

"I haven't gone anywhere," she said. "I'm always here. Or there, you could say."

"Did you catch the last lesson?"

"I am Óh-T'bee," she said. "But I appreciate your forgetting that from time to time."

"I think I know what they're up to, Óh-T'bee. All except T'Ling."

"Can't you guess?" Óh-T'bee said.

"Oh no," Wallenda said. "Is she trying to find out where Rose is? Has she asked you?"

"T'Ling does not waste words asking questions she already knows the answer to."

Ouch. Wallenda continued, "I'm sure MyrrhMyrrh's headed for the Fringe, armed to the teeth. After the Codger, no doubt. Daede is probably on the same reckless quest, but with less of a plan and more romantic notions. Angle? Maybe he'll stay home. But if he's thinking that much about the MTA, the chances are he's going somewhere. And if we're right about T'Ling? Where will she start the search for Rose? Out on the Fringe? They ought to just take the Big Pad. I don't want them out there. I can't lose them."

"You can't interfere. That's the rule."

"How can you say that? I have to interfere. Let's assume the obvious—they know the Codger's a threat. They're pissed off he blindsided them, and almost made off with me. They're saving face. It's crazy. We've got to protect them."

"Maybe they're trying to protect you," Óh-T'bee said.

"That's *my* job," Wallenda said indignantly.

"Maybe they think you weren't doing it too well."

"Since I can't follow them around, can I gaze them?"

"Visibility's poor on the Fringe," she said. "Very few scorecards. Possession of a scorecard is a capital offence. They'll have to leave theirs behind, like anyone else, just to get in."

"You *have to* intervene," Wallenda said. "What if one of them stumbles over Joreen while looking for the Codger? Feeds him to his own lilies?"

"The Fat Boy will have to take care of himself. If I can't see him, I can't know he's in danger, can I?"

"The Fat Boy? I never heard you call him that before."

"That's what the Codger calls him," Óh-T'bee said.

"So you've been talking to the Codger—and not me," Wallenda said.

"You sound jealous, Wally."

"I have the right to know whose side you're on. He's dangerous to you, can't you see that? And I'm not jealous. I don't want that zit-ridden jerk taking me out of the game."

"I'm glad to hear your motivation for living is up-trending." Óh-T'bee said.

"Why did you let the Fringe happen in the first place, Óh-T'bee?"

"As I recall, it was your idea," she said.

Oh yes. He'd suggested the Fringe as a solution to the trace elements in the Lifer population who didn't want to play the game. What he'd really had in mind was a backdoor, a place he could someday sneak away to and off himself.

"But it was your implementation," Wallenda said. "Maybe it's gotten a little out of hand."

"That's what I had in mind," she said. "Room for a little novelty. Didn't get much, by all reports. Reruns of old games from back on Earth. Strictly retro, heavy nostalgia. It's been so stable it's hardly the Fringe. Media's drafting a proposal to make it a Park. Until now."

"Novelty?" Wallenda asked. "Are you bored?"

"Is boredom the only reason for seeking self-transcendence?"

"You're...." he couldn't say it. Seeking self-transcendence? Or her own escape hatch?

"Self-transcendence?" he repeated. Maybe the contradictions were getting too much for her. Wallenda's head was spinning. One with the Lily. Cure the I-Virus. Convert the Lifers back to mortality. Save the game—while protecting Joreen's interests. Right. Then, because you can't make any decisions anymore without snarling yourself in endless conflicts, put the whole mess out of sight in a place you created just in case you needed to hide something from yourself someday. And blame it on me.

But in the light of the lesson he'd just delivered, her problem was clear. Óh-T'bee was completely out of focus.

"Could you leave your spiritual goals on the back-burner for now, Óh-T'bee? Take things one at a time," he pleaded. "We have a game to save. Then we can deal with the rest."

"I don't suffer from a single-tasking mind," she said. "Don't project your limitations on me."

Of course. You are Óh-T'bee. "Do you suffer from a multitasking mind?" he snapped.

"I suffer from having only one mind. You suffer from having too many."

Wallenda considered this. "Is the Fringe your attempt to make a sea mind? A mind where things are happening but where you can't see them?"

"Am I dreaming the Fringe, do you think?" Óh-T'bee asked.

"But *Joreen's* living there. Out of sight."

"But not out of mind."

"Why did you let him go there?"

"It was in his best interests. Joreen has a lot to hide."

Wallenda was ready to start screaming at her. He paced instead.

"So what are we supposed to do now?" he said. "Things are getting totally out of control."

"Just see what evolves, I guess," Óh-T'bee said. "You're not the only person who can make things happen, you know. And you're so out of shape, strategically, I doubt you could make much happen even if you tried. Why do you think I have to baby-sit you like this? I think I'll go see what the Codger's up to."

Wallenda threw his scorecard against the wall of the cabin as hard as he could. It bounced back into shape and floated, infuriatingly slowly, to the floor.

Óh-T'bee was right. The humiliation of the Codger's attack, of being so easily taken out of commission, and almost hauled away, overwhelmed Wallenda. He saw clearly how centuries of apathy and stultifying boredom had taken their toll on his fighting readiness. His skills were atrophied, his minds were flabby, and his attention flickering. But worst of all, his gaze was weak and wobbly as any Lifer on the doorstep of the White Place. He'd been teaching on autopilot and hadn't listened to his own words for years.

In the time before the Millennium Class came back, one by one, for the Lily Wine, he began his own rigorous training regime. Every free moment, and every time he had the urge to pace and worry, he worked on martial arts forms. He journeyed through his minds in meditation, mending breaches, clearing rubble, and dismantling squirrel cages. He worked on strategy. He studied Glide. If he couldn't leave the story circle, he could at least do maze training in full immersion sims. But primarily, he trained his Gaze on the Codger and Joreen until he could feel the edges of his native craftiness sharpening again. He began to feel as he felt when the original council of Glides twisted him so effectively into their torturous labyrinths of irreconcilable options that he was forced to learn the skills of escape. Trapped, but still plotting.

50. Spec Sex

DAEDE WAS DRESSING FOR A NIGHT OUT in Vegas Park with Banderas, reviewing his plan. He'd been working toward this night for a year or more, and there was no more time for planning. It's just as well, he thought. He'd gone the long way around, and knew he had a tendency to over-ornament his moves, but he had only one chance to get free of Banderas long enough to get out to the Fringe and disappear. If he blew it, Banderas would never let him out of his sight again.

Daede studied the costume laid out on his bed. At first, he'd resisted the Lifer disguises. The tacky, overelaborated Swash-type rigs offended his image of himself as an Origin School Dancer. Out on the maze in combat, he'd depend on his moves, his face, his inner spirit, and especially his Gaze to make the full effect. Costume was almost a distraction, though he knew this was an offbeat position for a Swash. But not the great ones, he reminded himself. The beauty comes forth from within.

He pulled on a pair of tight white kid pants that laced up the front and had long white fringes down the side seams. The sleeves of the jacket were similarly fringed. Both front and back of the jacket were covered with pale blue scrolling, highlighted with silver sequins. Pale blue cowboy boots, with silver scrolls and flowers and a huge black cowboy hat completed the rig. He pasted a mustache on that was more luxuriant than his own, and gave his eyebrows an exaggerated sharp bend in the middle. Last, he applied a thin, mirrored eye mask so that his eyes were completely hidden. These mirror-masks were common with Lifers past a certain age. Looking at himself in the mirror above his dressing table, he thought the strip of changing images over his eyes, which currently reflected back his garish dress, more eerie than the piercing gaze of Lifer eyes the mask usually hid. It's not as if anybody was fooled. And to the degree that they reflected back the eyes of any up close Lifer looking into them, the purpose was defeated anyhow. Or was this the ironic comment of the elder Lifer, as were the campy clothes he so often saw?

He struck a few poses in front of the 3-way mirror and realized that he had to shift his inner image or the costume would be a dead giveaway—a Dancer in drag, running around in Lifer threads, a moving target.

He pictured himself in the role of the Lifer he'd gazed from his room last night. The Lifer had been on a prowl through Vegas. Daede had immersed with him, moving around him, looking over his shoulder, full frontal approach, close-up on face or hands. The Lifer knew he was being gazed. He'd checked his ratings. Having an audience pleased him, made his evening, and no doubt improved his performance.

There was a period, usually between 200 and 300 years, when the main event in Lifer sex was a bipolar shifting between voyeurism and exhibitionism. To watch or to be watched. Any individual, couple, or group was free to exhibit themselves under the Gaze, setting their permissions to include whatever small to universal access they wished to expose themselves to. From the voyeur side, you could search the gaze channels for live action. Daede searched out the amateurs. This showboy was a loner. Thinks he's hot enough as a solo act. Let's check him out. Daede picked him up going into Caesar's. The guy assumed he had a female eyeballing him and kept up a steady stream of subvocalized narration about his intentions, his moves, and his reactions that made it easy for Daede to occupy the Lifer's point of view. Daede had the usual moment where he was both in the guy's viewpoint and watching himself, his own reactions, feeling a wave of pity and disgust surge through him as his own desires kicked in and intermixed with the showboy's efforts to rev up his own. Daede was certain that his feelings were in a feedback loop with the showboy, feeding each other. Lucky showboy, he thought. Being gazed by someone whose desires were intact, full force. If he knew it was a Dancer, he'd be out of his mind. And the showboy moved now with a greater confidence. Having even one viewer on the counter of his rating strip would attract both partners and more viewers. They were off and running.

The showboy wore no eye-mask. His eyes were spraying the room with a certain vibe of mean, amplified by the loose, dark red satin shirt and the heavy gold chains, the low-slung black pants, the wide belt. One thumb hooked under the buckle made its point.

Daede sank into full empathic immersion. Colors brightened, but there were fewer. The showboy's gaze sharpened, and flicked like the tongue of a snake from face to face in the crowded casino. They brushed a woman's arm. Touch stung; the showboy was shot through with pain-enhancers. They passed the live game holos. Lifers ringed the glowing mazes, murmuring into their scorecards. Betting was intense. Gaze was on the game, not the showboy. His bait was ignored; his hooks came back empty. Daede felt the showboy's anxiety rising, the desperate edge that could dampen his frail desire. The showboy was gazing a Swash game now, entranced with the others pressing in around the holo, watching a Lorelei Dancer wafting her way through a low-sweeping maze, her own pure, clean gaze following the path of her veil, and sweeping up the Lifers' gaze in its path. Could the edge of desire dull so quickly, he wondered? Even imagining life going on and on and on, and he felt his mind, his senses, all relax. The attention wanders, the taut muscle of *now* growing flabby. Daede felt a wave of nausea. How much uglier this feeling was than an aging, wrinkling body. No wonder they craved deeper and deeper stimulation, finer degrees of penetration, the kind of effect that could only be obtained by the spectacle of the game. Intense beauty and intense horror, woven, resonating. What Dancers provide. Not only our pain. Lifers can have physical pain anytime they want it, and many do. Pain was a minor addiction, sociologically insignificant, with the pain-givers and the pain-takers maintaining an ecological balance. Lifers want to know how we feel our virgin pain. *That* we feel it, seems ever more miraculous as years accumulate. All we feel defines us. A second wave of disgust streamed through him like a flock of bats. He hung for a moment between his viewpoint as a Death Dancer and that of the Lifer showboy, seeing the interaction, the deadlock, the inseparability of needs. We are vampires to each other, sucking up what we need to exist. Death Dancers: sponges for attention, adulation, steeped in self-congratulatory righteousness, flaunting the precious beauty of impermanence. Lifers: craving the intensity of pleasure that could only come from killing that which you admire uncontrollably, envy unbearably. That which you can't possess. That's the *real* game, he thought, and it's sick beyond cure.

Daede had pulled himself out of the immersion, back from that dangerous edge, moments before his vertigo resolved in a surge of purpose. He caught himself on the verge of redefinition, hoping for a moment that the threats to the game would triumph.

That was the edge he had to hold for his plan to succeed. Now he could occupy the Lifer rig with ease. The danger was real and greater than Banderas feared in his worries about capture, rape, disqualification. Daede could lose his desire for the game. Which made this new game dangerously fun to play.

Fully rigged, Daede transited to Vegas, to a back table in a crowded club, a little early. He reassured himself that, however strange the game was starting to look, there still was no danger he could ever desire to be a Lifer. What would I do with myself in between games, besides learn about the game? I suppose I could be a Player. But Lifers study for hundreds of years; some of them never get beyond amateur rank. Why? Only the best can beat an Origin Dancer. I could, he supposed, with all the practice. Because I can think like a Dancer. Of course I can, I *am* a Dancer. No need to remind myself of that. But tonight I'm a Lifer. A convincing Lifer. Several of them.

Banderas stood at the entrance of Caesar's, looking around the room for him. He doesn't know it's me. Damn, I'm good at this! He waved and smiled.

"What's your pleasure?" Banderas said. His up-level fawn suede rig was turning heads with the Vegas crowd.

"I'm ready for the sex-tour," Daede said.

"No way, too risky," Banderas said.

"You think anyone would go for me in this rig?" Daede said.

Banderas took a good look and laughed. "You look like a noveau riche hick from a Tampa condo."

"Right on." Daede got up and swaggered toward a knot of showgirls at the bar. He tipped his ten-gallon hat. They scattered like pinballs.

Sitting down again he said, "They wouldn't crash their ratings with a dude like me."

Banderas laughed.

"I want to see my cook in action," Daede said slyly.

Whether it was the challenge to Banderas' Swash appeal, or his temptation to indulge the secret pleasure of watching Daede's fresh responses to the same old same old, Banderas was drawn into the game. They started light, a Vegas style dog and pony show. The strobe lights gave it more humor than hard core. Daede played the cherry from Tampa to the hilt. Banderas watched him trying to look like he'd seen it all before, while secretly quite kicked off. It turned Banderas on to watch him, and he never guessed that Daede *had* in fact seen it all before. He'd been gazing Lifer sex since he was thirteen. Every Dancer checked out the Lifers in action at some point, but most found their efforts boring and sad. Dancer passion was by far more intriguing—and stimulating. For Daede, Lifer sex had a strong fascination that he kept hidden from his Dancer friends.

Sexuality among the Lifers took strange forms. Their urges, pinned at the body age they chose, remained in force. But the ever-increasing weight of memory and experience produced increasingly strange and elaborated forms as the search for novelty grew more desperate. The body, infected with the I-Virus, churned out the same fundamental needs. But the minds, bored and sated, and wearied from the search for objects upon which to expend and satisfy these desires went deeper and deeper into opposition with the body's monotonous demands. The unfulfilled desires only grew as desirable situations grew scarcer. The search for the desirable gave way gradually to the simple avoidance of disgust.

For the young, those under 500, the problem was not so great. Fashions in erotica came and went in tandem with fashions in clothes. Sleaze was timeless. Their elders had created a rich menagerie of options which it took some time to explore. And if you didn't use them up too fast, you could get along quite well for a few hundred years.

The older the Lifer, the deeper the fascination with the game, as the persons of the Dancers became more and more exclusively the only objects of desire, all the more so for their unattainable, untouchable status. The frustration of that desire was a large part of the vehemence and lust with which their inevitable deaths were desired. This lust, once fulfilled in the climax of the Dance of Death, succeeded only in further entrapment, as the object of their desire was snatched from their live view forever, canned in holos, never to return. As the desire of an aging Lifer focused increasingly on the Dancers that desire also became more discriminating. Only the better and better Dancers could fully engage at the level of desire of an elder Lifer. Therefore, the need to amass game-points, to progress up the levels, to afford more live games of better quality, to purchase Dancer relics—a scarf; a spoon held, touched to Dancer lips. The empire of addiction, carefully calibrated by the Outmind, the spectacle of desire and death, precisely regulated by the old hands of the MED, had lasted beyond all expectations.

And this addiction, the fusion of a lust for sex and death that could never be quenched, demanding greater quantity and quality of each as Life went on in bodies perpetually fresh and longing, was the essence of the look in a Lifer's eyes.

Daede had sorted out for himself that the source of his fascination with Lifer sex was not the sex itself, but the look in the Lifer's eyes. He had notebooks filled with observations:

—eyes that are old and full of the knowledge that you do not get wiser as you get older

—eyes that have seen everything and still hunger for more

—addicted eyes, seeking constant satisfaction

—eyes that can't tear themselves away from the game
—you can tell a lifer's age by their eyes
—who has the oldest eyes?

He saw that the gaze of the Lifer grows increasingly more offensive as they age. And more dangerous. He knew that recklessly confronting the eyes of an Elder could prematurely age one's own gaze. That was why young Dancers had to be protected from the Lifer's gaze. Some were even lethal. They could disable a younger Lifer with their gaze. The same gaze could kill a Dancer. Elder Lifers, masked or unmasked, who did not slide their gaze down over the shoulder of the person they were addressing, or humble their gaze fully downward before the young, were strenuously shunned.

Daede knew the eyes were not the gaze. There were no lines, or wrinkles, no strain the I-Virus did not immediately sweep clean. A sleeping Lifer could be mistaken for a Dancer—until the lids lifted, and you were stabbed. The Gaze of Life was the ugliest thing he could imagine.

Daede told himself he studied the Lifers' eyes to spur him to greater efforts toward beauty. And it did. He told himself that the Gaze of addiction could not, in turn, addict because the addiction would be to ugliness, and the ugly could never capture him. That was true. But his addiction formed in the heart-piercing twinges of deep pity that he felt for such a suffering. And since he had told himself, as most addicts do, that such sensations were good for him, he could see nothing wrong in their encouragement. Not only that, he had told himself that his feelings were good in some deep and spiritual way for the Lifers themselves. Daede, the closet Bodhisattva, would cultivate compassion; compassion would be crowned in his Dance. Daede would meet their lethal gaze with love.

His addiction to the Gaze of Life grew freely on secret fertile ground.

As the evening progressed, through darker, stickier realms of Lifer sex, he was in a lot less danger than Banderas thought, and a lot more than he himself could tell. Banderas watched vigilantly for signs that Daede might want to be joining in at the orgy pads, sneaking aphrodisiacs, or unable to resist the temptation to seduce a Lifer, just to show his stuff, just to demonstrate his power, even in that silly fringed rig. But Daede seemed content to watch. Even a little bored. Banderas had taken just enough not-to-worry de-inhibitors to get interested in participating himself, and to lower his guard, as everything looked a little more all right than it really was. Little hints from Daede moved them onward, from the leather houses, down through the hanging halls, into a notorious specialty club called the Tooth and Claw. Banderas thought they'd stumbled on it. Daede had set it up.

When they stepped in, and Banderas saw the amount of blood being splashed around, and the abattoir décor, he tried to move Daede quickly backward out the door, but more Lifers were crowding in behind him. The risk of infection was tremendous. One dripping Lifer wrapping her arms around Daede just for a friendly nibble and he was gone.

"Don't worry about me," Daede said. He was already sprinting up to a glassed-in observer's balcony. Banderas looked at the scene before him, then up at Daede. He was standing, arms crossed, behind the glass upstairs with an insolent look on his face like hey, aren't you up to this? Banderas knew this was only part of his act, he knew they should get out. But he was caught in a Gaze that ordered him to perform. It took a lot of courage to confront this crowd, and a lot of mental discipline to reach for sex when the main show was eating each other alive. He'd heard about these clubs, but never gone. Had he been saving it for his old age? He didn't know. He knew you survived—of course you did. The I-Virus grew you back in a matter of minutes, for the little stuff. He didn't have to look up again—he felt the full compulsion of Daede's gaze on his back. He waded in. Two Lifer women dived for him. He slipped on the gore and was down with the rest. They were pulling off his ruined suede, anxious to sink their teeth into anyone rich enough to trash such a great outfit without a thought. Banderas looked up at Daede who was laughing, and biting the air, urging him on. He succumbed to the almost irresistible urge, not to screw and be screwed while your flesh was chewed and bleeding, not even to munch a little human flesh himself, but to please his beautiful, prize Dancer. What he didn't know was how sick it made the unaccustomed system to fight off the I-Virus in another's flesh. The habitués had prepared themselves with the oral prophylactics he knew nothing about. While Banderas was writhing in agony on the butcher shop floor, the whole mob, enraptured by the lucky arrival of the uninformed, dove on him, and had stripped the flesh from both his handsome legs before he came around enough to transit himself out, blinking his torn body blindly to a deserted courtyard in Mardi Gras park in which to grow his legs back. It took a full three hours. And by that time, Daede was long gone.

51. The Stargazers

As soon as Daede saw Banderas take his first bite, he blinked back to his room, got rid of the white fringes, and put on the gear he had ready for his expedition: torn khaki pants with lots of pockets, an antique cameraman's vest, similarly endowed, heavy desert boots, high socks, a wide-brimmed leather hat. Bandana scarf. Mirror-shades. He took his makeup kit and transited up the mountain above Origin School, where he darkened his skin with oil and stain and dirt, applied a long scar to the left side of his jaw. He felt his face—probably too clean-shaven, but the stubble would be in soon enough. He put a sharp stone in his boot to remind him to limp.

Daede transited again and again, picking up first a rucksack, then filling it with equipment and weaponry from the small caches he'd stored around the levels. He filled his vest pockets with a set of razor-sharp ninja glyphs. He added two camera bags, each carrying a half-dozen lenses and a pair of cameras. A third bag held a bulky camcorder. The rucksack carried food, water, and a variety of trading items. His belt held a collection of small stunners and disintegrators, the kind you'd only see on a very rich up-level hobbyist with game points to spare even with the approaching Millennium Games. The kind of guy who already had his seats secured in Origin Stadium and had nothing better to do than go on a dangerous shooting expedition out on the Fringe. The final item was a custom defense shield that fitted snugly and invisibly around himself and his equipment.

He transited to the Wall. The Great Wall theme park stretched over a 5-mile length, only 30 feet wide. The wall itself was reserved for guard towers and tourists hoping to catch sight of some colorful Fringers coming in for supplies. Or a random snuff, where a Lifer walked out into the high desert to be permanently disposed of by the first Fringer with an adequate bomb. With luck, they'd gaze a safari cruising for snuffs in headhunter gear. A hundred foot tarmac between The Wall and the high desert defined a no man's land. It served as a parking lot for rental vehicles. Huddled against the inside of the Wall were the shacks and tents and trailers of a wide variety of traders, provisioning Fringers with fuel and food, taking items in trade for sale as souvenirs for the tourists. The three checkpoints where you turned in your scorecard were the only places of any size. Daede was familiar with the Wall from his souvenir shopping, and blinked in near checkpoint Charley. He found the senior official and gave him a huge bribe to keep a close and personal eye on his scorecard. Daede bought a light, fast, armored air car, and an expensive set of maps. He crossed the border into the Fringe just as it was getting dark.

Daede was ready for the first barrage of sharpshooters and light rockets. A quick wide-flying bomb demolished the cannon and deterred the casual day-trippers out for target practice. He blew away two air cars before they could engage him in a fight, clearing the airspace between him and his first destination.

Daede followed a circuitous route over desert-like terrain, avoiding the various camps and settlements marked on the none-too-accurate map, staying close to the ground. His escape from Banderas had gone off flawlessly. His estimation of the level of Banderas' besottedness with him was right on target. He felt a little sorry for having tricked him, but Banderas would recover. A not-unpleasant rush of pleasure at his own ruthlessness got him smiling.

Daede landed at the first rent-a-terrorist camp, a major agency still located, to his relief, where last reported. He handed the terms of his employment, a list of his major skills, and the specs of his armaments to the man at the desk.

The personnel manager liked his cover. The recruit looked just amateurish enough not to be suspected of deeper motives. He was willing to pay for his own maps, risk his own transport, and was asking for the most dangerous assignments. Why not? If he were as capable as he claimed to be, maybe he'd succeed. If he did, it would be worth the expense. If he didn't, there was no more out of pocket than the cost of a three-page contract. If he was a rich eccentric who didn't know what he was getting into, he'd probably survive—he was worth more for ransom than permanent disposal. If all he had in mind for those disposal units disguised as cameras was a suicide mission—maybe there'd be salvage.

Daede's first assignment was to remove a small settlement of Millenarian Dancer worshippers calling themselves Stargazers who were blocking the development plans of a Duke who wished to remain anonymous. It seemed like a waste of effort. The group was shrinking. The mortal dissidents had attracted no new members. Few had children and the original settlers were dying off. They'd all be gone soon enough if they didn't self-destruct when their Dancer-Messiah did not arrive on schedule. The Messiah hadn't come yet, and there were only two years to go. But this was Daede's cover, and he wasn't going to argue. A minor matter, a reasonable test for the Cameraman.

Continuing deeper into desert terrain, Daede had time to consider that he had no idea as to how he was going to locate the Codger. He couldn't even formulate any reasonable questions. He had made a paper print of a shot from the replay of the attack, but it was so dark in most places, you couldn't even see his zits. And the agency was not the right place to start asking. Maybe he could get some information from the Stargazers before he disposed of them.

A few hours into the Fringe Daede caught the faint glow of the Stargazer settlement. From the air it looked like a torn maze board, the glyphs picked out in spotty light. A large structure with a spotlit statue in front of it filled the open center of the maze. The settlement was larger than he thought, but one bomb placed near the center should do the trick.

glide

He landed at the edge of *glide*, and walked across the center wave. The dwellings, no more than tin shacks, each had a carefully tended patch of lawn in front with an elaborate display of Dancer lawn art—whole scenes of hollow plastic figures, garishly painted and lit from within. "The Mixing of LionMane Amber" showed three avid cooks in white coats huddled over the beakers on a lab bench like witches over a cauldron. A fourth cook held a long computer printout that snaked around the scene like toilet paper. "49er in the Shop" showed the famed Chrome Champion dismantled, each of his parts painted with dull silver paint being reverently polished by a gang of dwarfish mechanics. 49er herself hung in a cradle in the center of the group, her head and torso highlighted by ground-spots, her face piously lifted to the night sky. She had a brass wire halo tilted on her glowing bald skull. The smaller lawns held single Dancer figures. The Swashes all had regulation capes drooped on their shoulders. Some were sewn of a single piece of cloth; more often the capes were a crazy quilt of scraps. Fake fur, gold lamé, and metallic plastic were the most popular materials. All the plastic Dancers had halos and raised their right arms pointing at the sky. Daede found the displays inexpressibly sad in their dusty ugliness. He wondered if he would ever be so enshrined, and then remembered that if he carried out his mission, they would no longer exist. No one came out of the shacks. The streets were deserted. They must all be gathered in the big building. Convenient.

distill

Daede came out of *distill* on the tip of the tear into the center of the maze of streets and saw the big tent where the Stargazers had gathered. A larger than life-size Loosh draped with garlands of twisted brown cassette tape stood by the door. Her arm pointed at the sky and tinny Wenger songs issued from a speaker in her gaping mouth. He could hear the Stargazers' voices now, a strange medley of chanting, low laughter, babies crying, and an occasional sung plaint of rising notes that ended in a shriek.

Daede peeked through a small rip in the canvas. About a hundred mortals of all ages were dispersed in the area, in wheelies, cribs, or on ancient dirty couches with extruded stuffing. A dozen small children played in one corner. The tent was dimly lit with clusters of candles on dishes around the floor. One after another, a man or a woman would rise and come to the empty space in the center of the floor and begin to dance. The dances—all quite different—started slowly and grew in speed and intensity to a point where the Dancer had captured the gaze of the others completely. Clapping began in time to the steps of the dance, faster and faster. On an undetectable cue, the clapping would stop, and the Dancer would freeze in place. A touch from the next Dancer would free them to collapse and be carried off.

Even through the small peephole, the smell hit him—candle wax and diapers, bodies in need of a wash, and the cloying scent of Stargazer lilies in pots around the edge. Permeating the nubbly weave of scent was the unmistakable pungency of large quantities of Wine of the Lilies and fresh lily pollen. They were all stoned out of their minds.

Daede pulled back from his peephole. The presence of Lily Wine presented a problem. To dispose of anyone whose body held the Wine and whose minds were connected to the Lily would be a sacrilege he couldn't even consider risking—especially right before final focus and his own encounter with the Lily. The Stargazers' ritual was clear. Enter the lily mind, invoke the spirit of a Dancer, hope that this spirit would possess you and allow you to share its Dance.

He'd just have to wait it out. And he wanted to gaze the mortals again. Especially their eyes. He went around to the front entrance and sat in the shadows to the side of the door. No one seemed to notice his presence, or if they did, they didn't mind.

Daede had never seen live mortals before. The variety in age was a sight in itself. He looked at their lined faces and the streaks of gray in one woman's long braid. A very old man sat nearly naked on an old wheelie. Pale toothpick legs protruded from an oversized pair of red shorts. His flesh hung down in limp arcs from the bones asserting their imminent dominion. The old man's hands were folded serenely around a cardboard box crudely painted to resemble an antique Walkman. A black wire rose to a set of real earphones clamped to his white-haired skull. His foot tapped to an inaudible music that always, even when his eyes were closed, followed the rhythm of the dance.

Daede looked from face to face. They were all so *different*. Though the group had divided themselves into set preferences, and wore some sign that distinguished Swash from Chrome, Bod from Glide, they mostly looked—themselves. Whatever that meant, Daede thought. As he breathed the lily pollen wafting from the tent opening, the eyes of the mortals attracted him more and more. They were young-old eyes, with none of the Lifer's acid penetration. Age softened some, and focused others. All differently. Ecstatic eyes, lily eyes, but they hadn't lost their individuality. They were a garden of wild lilies, each with a different blossom, untended—buds of the young and shriveling heads of the almost finished, all mixed in together. They had no gaze and looked completely helpless. An immense pity filled him.

Dawn was just beginning at his back. Daede snapped out of his sorrows when the worshippers, returning from lily land to their weary world of waiting, began to gather clothes, children, and personal fetishes, and prepare to leave. The old man with the Walkman spotted him first. He pointed toward the door. Daede stood, and quietly took the lens cap off the biggest camera cannon.

"No pictures allowed!" shouted one man. "I'll bet he's been shooting us all night," a woman cried. The adults put down what they were carrying and moved as one body toward the bright opening. Daede backed away further, almost to the edge of the maze. The angry group was rushing from the door in his direction. He shot a narrow-beam warning to the side, hoping to stop them. The pedestal of the plastic Loosh outside the tent vaporized. The statue fell forward. The mob stopped momentarily, gasping in horror at this further desecration. They gathered now, fully enraged, for the assault. Daede, who still could not bring himself to blast them all, thought he'd make a run through the maze to his air chair, get up high, and bomb them from the air. Then the old man in the wheelie came through the opening in back of the crowd, and wheeled his way over to the fallen Loosh.

"Wait!" he shouted in a surprisingly strong voice. He lifted himself from the wheelie and tottered to the prone statue. He fell to the ground next to the Loosh and pointed his arm in the same gesture, in the same direction as the statue—directly at Daede. A gasp and a groan arose from the mortal mob, and then they all prostrated themselves in the same position, face down, pointing at Daede. Three little girls were jumping up and down in the doorway shouting, "It's Him! It's Him!"

Daede stood at the edge of the maze, armed to the teeth and gazing the whole scene through his mirror shades. He had a silly thought that now he really wished he had a real camera instead of three loaded disposal units as there was no scorecard to record the event. Who had ever gotten a shot of the arrival of a Messiah?

But there was the old man again, wheeling toward him. The others were getting up now. They formed a semicircle around in front of him. Several were crying quietly. Daede looked around at their eyes in the early morning light. They were all so tired. Some shone with joy. In others he saw doubt and suspicion. Some were neutral, withholding judgment and reaction.

"The signs are present," the old man said, gesturing to the fallen Loosh. *Loosh will finally Dance, she will rest in peace in the dawn light when the Dancer Messiah comes*. But the three tests must be performed."

Daede cringed inwardly. I'm not their Messiah. I'm a rented terrorist here to clear them out so a Duke's development can proceed. The whole scene was a ridiculous mistake, a pathetic joke. A bunch of ugly, grubby, totally deluded religious fanatics with a worse form of Dancer worship than any Lifer had ever exhibited. Worse, he thought, for its sincerity. These were no jaded Specs and this was no spectacle they'd seen over and over and over. The scene was too horribly real to them. These were folks who had given up the game, given up Lifer status, and focused everything on the slim hope that some Dancer would descend out of the sky and save them—from what? For what? They probably expected the Messiah to tell them what to do next. This was the end of time. If I am the real thing, they've fulfilled their purpose. Their focus is complete. Now what?

The Stargazers looked at him expectantly. I'm probably not exactly what they had in mind, he thought. He looked at his choices. Wipe them out in one wide-angle shot, that's the easiest. He could tell them that was their only move, here at the end of time. They might even die happy. Some of them. Or he could run. Another false Messiah. They'd chase him into the maze, and he'd have to take them out a few at a time to escape. Worse than a clean sweep. They'd definitely die disappointed. Or he could play along—if he could pass the tests, that is. Daede wondered which was worse—to disappoint, to delude, or to disintegrate them? The full force of the irreconcilable situation hit him. I am *Swash*, he decided. The least I can do is give them a great show.

He nodded at the old man.

"All oracles have pointed to the Dancer belonging to one set and one only," the old man said. Reveal your body."

Well, Daede thought. Obviously it's not a Chrome or a Glide Messiah. So—Bod or Swash. If I strip down, there's no way they'll see me as a Bod. Might as well be myself. I play that best.

Daede took the rucksack off and set it on the ground. He lifted the cameras one by one and placed them gingerly down on the ground, hoping no one would get the idea of posing a group shot. He removed the vest with the razor-glyphs jingling in the pocket. Well, here's the big one, he thought. The big gun's only a dive away if it was a Bod they wanted. He unbuckled his large ammo belt and dropped it by the rest of his armaments. His loose pants fell to the ground, revealing his tight Swash leathers. They sighed in unison. Daede flashed the big Swash smile, stepped out of the baggy pants, and pulled loose the velcro fasteners that were holding the blousy sleeves of his Swash shirt in neat rolls up by his shoulders. The tan silk fell, and he took his time buttoning the tight cuffs so he could scan the group from behind his mirror-shades for an acceptable cape. He walked purposefully over toward the woman wearing the wildest looking patchwork. She handed him her cape and fainted dead away. Daede put the cape on with a graceful swirl, walked back toward the old man, positioned himself in front of him, and bowed his deepest of Swash bows, sweeping his wide-brimmed hat from his head, his dark hair falling forward in a shining fan.

"Pass," the old man said. "Get the Scroll," he called. Someone had already brought it out, and came forward with the roll of paper.

"Unroll it," the old man instructed. Daede sat cross-legged on the ground to comply. It was an old, much worn blueprint, the original site plan of their settlement, the whole maze drawn. The unbuilt areas were still in blue lines. The rest had been filled in with names, and lawn art designs.

"The missing glyphs," the old man said, pointing at the hole in the maze, the area where they were now assembled. "Fill them in and tell us the outcome of the game."

Daede knew exactly what he meant. As every Dancer and every Lifer knew, the three missing glyphs that formed the open space in every maze told the outcome of a game. The three glyphs completed their maze, bringing the glyphs to 81, finishing the story, and revealing the outcome of the game. It was, of course, an impossible task. Not any three glyphs could be inserted. The variance in height made this impossible. But the combinations that could fit were beyond counting. Some were more pleasing than others. But there was no right answer. Who, then, was going to accept whatever he might come up with—the glyphs themselves, much less his off the Swash cuff translation. And there was another problem. When anyone—Dancer, Player, or Spec, wanted a glimpse at the outcome of a game, the glyphs were always gotten by oracle.

"Where is your oracle?" Daede said, wondering if there was an illegal scorecard on the premises.

"You didn't bring it?" the old man asked suspiciously. Daede panicked, then reached for his vest.

"Just a little test for you," he grinned at the old man. He spilled the set of razor sharp ninja glyphs in a pile on top of the site map. They lay in a glittering heap. 27. He only needed three, and was thinking fast.

"A virgin must pass her hands over the glyphs," Daede said. "The first three to draw blood are the oracle."

The adults looked around at each other. Finally, the three little girls were pushed forward, but none of them, quite understandably, wanted to get her hands cut. Finally Daede promised the one who would help a ride in his air chair. A small girl stepped forward and stuck her hands into the sharp pile of glyphs. Daede lifted the three glyphs carefully from the pile, reflecting that he didn't have to be afraid of their mortal blood. He moved them around on the ground in front of him. How sweet it is, he thought. *Distill, strike, touch.*

"A brush and ink, please," Daede said. He filled in the missing glyphs on the scroll in his most elegant calligraphy, and wrote along the bottom of the Scroll, "*The essence of my sword is a caress.*"

The old man seemed happy with that. "*In your presence, justice and mercy are one,*" he replied.

"Precisely," Daede said.

"And now," the old man said, "reveal your eyes."

Daede raised his hand involuntarily toward his mirror-shades, and then withdrew it. The final test produced a queasy feeling about the whole charade that he had, in the excitement and unpredictability of the game, successfully quenched. He'd circled round to the same crossroads again, backtracked in the maze, and the same decisions stared him in the face, only he had entered the link from the opposite side. He had already revealed himself, he thought, what's the problem? They saw the Swash moves, they have their oracle. They know I'm a Dancer, don't they? If I were sitting in a crowd of Lifers this big, who wanted this certain confirmation, my life would be in danger. It only takes a mob to break a taboo. None of that threat is here. A deep mortal longing, but not the Lifer's ravenous hunger. Of course they have to check. It's possible I could be a Lifer imposter. His class in self-analysis of Game contracts that had seemed so dry and self-evident came to mind, insisting to be used. *The rules of the game will change.* No. *Know the moment when the game begins for real.* That's it. This is just the qualifier. So far I've only been deciding if I want to play. Not exactly. I'm so uncomfortable because I don't want to look at the fact that I've already agreed to play. If I back out now, I'll have been leading them on, for fun, for my own gratification, with no real contract in mind at the end. But how did I get in this far? I'm supposed to be in another game entirely—finding the Codger and whipping his ass. Finishing the game of finishing unfinished business so I can get back to qualifying for the *real* game by going to meet the Lily, and find my focus. How many nested game mazes can I build and still work my way out, still remember the paths? *You're becoming your namesake*, the breath of the Lily whispered. If they see my eyes, I will have them in my Gaze. But what for? Nobody's battling me. There is no challenge here. Only hope. The whole group of Stargazers was waiting, watching intently, but patiently, for his next move. *To play the game is to forget the game. Fully engaged, it will be life itself.* Daede took off his mirror-shades and gave them to the old man.

He looked around him, meeting their eyes, moving on. Blue eyes, brown eyes, eyes of many mixes. Eyes of the old man, eyes of the children, tentatively smiling. Each pair of eyes revealing the person who looked through them as he was revealing himself to them. They were so beautiful, shining forth from their dreary setting—imperfect bodies, plastic saints, clumsy imitations of their Dancer gods who were no more or less than themselves. Their Dancer Messiah had arrived and stood before them wrapped in a tatty cloak of fake fur, worn green velvet, and blue metallic plastic. All of them sitting on the ground together knew for this moment the total surprise of it all. How he'd stumbled in, perhaps with a totally different intention. They knew and they did not know he had come to annihilate them, on the way to qualify in another game for which the outcome was unknown.

Daede's eyes were streaming with tears, and he was smiling. What the Stargazers saw was someone they could love because he was someone who needed their acceptance as much as they needed his—a Dancer Messiah willing to accept them as they were, plastic and all.

Daede spoke. "I have to tell you—twelve hours ago I had no idea I was coming here. And my first intentions did not have your best interests in mind."

They all just smiled, nodded or shrugged. An accidental Messiah only made the event that much more miraculous.

"But now that I'm here, I could really use your help." Daede took the blurred picture of the Codger out of his rucksack.

Daede and the leaders of the Stargazers got down to business. He told them the whole story: Origin School, the Codger's attack on the Dancemaster, the escape from Banderas, his assignment from the agency, the fact that an anonymous Duke wanted them disposed of.

None of them had ever seen or heard of anyone like the Codger. But in the discussion, something resembling a second miracle occurred.

The Stargazer second in command, the mother of the two little girls, said, "It couldn't be the Fat Boy. We're his best customers. Must be one of his rivals. That must have been what that guy with the relocation, cheap land scheme was all about. Who else is in the Substance trade?"

"The Fat Boy's got the monopoly on the Lily Wine. There's plenty of competing products but we're no market for them," another Stargazer said.

The penny dropped for Daede.

"How fat is the Fat Boy?" he asked.

"Fat," they said.

"And he's the Lily Wine distributor?"

"Grower, distributor—sole source of the sacrament."

"And you are his best customers?"

"Definitely. Lily Wine's been out for a long time. Too unpredictable for recreational purposes," the Stargazer woman said.

"So why is the Fat Boy growing it?"

"He's got his own thing about the game. Been constructing all kinds of experimental mazes. He's doing some kind of reconstruction of the original Plantation. It's a hobby. He's rich enough he doesn't have to work," the old man said.

"Where's he getting his trade then, if it isn't Lily Wine?"

"Who knows? We always figured he wasn't a real Fringer. Probably got a scorecard. Most of the Dukes do. The Fringe isn't what it used to be," the old man said sadly. "But now that you're here, the whole thing's going up in smoke anyhow," he said brightly. "Along with everything else."

Daede asked cautiously what exactly the Stargazers thought the Dancer-Messiah was supposed to be doing. "Just want to make sure we're all in the same maze."

"You're here to destroy the game, of course," the old man said. "The Millennium Games are the end of time. The fulfillment of the Glide agenda. Blinding enlightenment. The conversion of the Lifers by curing of the I-Virus accomplished—or their total destruction. *The essence of my sword is a caress*. They can like it or lump it. The Messiah is a menace to society. We appreciate that quality. And from what you've told us, you're the right Messiah for the job."

"So you're reading the oracle in both directions," Daede said. *I caress you with my sword.*

The old man said, "Isn't that how you do it? That's what the Lily told me."

"No, you're absolutely right," Daede said.

Daede fervently hoped this was not a self-fulfilling prophecy—but then, he hadn't made the whole thing up. The Stargazers had. And the Glides before them. This is not *my* focus we're talking about. It's total coincidence I came along at this moment and fit into theirs. Anyhow—wasn't the whole purpose of a prophecy its own fulfillment?

Right now, Daede saw the Stargazers might be a big help to him in *his* game. Joreen's purposes were confirmed. Get the game back. Reinvent it, just like he wanted to at the beginning. What a focus the Fat Boy had! You had to admire it. He had seemingly unlimited resources. The Codger might very well be working for him, hacking the betting, hacking MTA access. But the Codger was small fish. Only a hired gun. Joreen was the target.

Daede organized a group march to Joreen's plantation. The Stargazers would go to request an audience with his Unbearable Largeness to protest the interference of the rival Duke. Joreen would protect his customer's interests as his own. He would give them access.

"How far is it?" Daede asked.

"About an hour away. He's on the coast. Very handy," the Stargazer leader replied.

52. Angle in the Loophole

Angle entered the huge free-space of 7T7's wheelhouse to drop off his parts. He hung his cradle on the waiting sky-hook at the maze level. He reviewed his design specs once more before putting his order into the system. Then he detached his springs, hooking them onto a repair-coded terminus. The springs began their journey through the maze to the techs for adjustments. He jacked into the sockets above him through his headgear, then deposited his claws one at a time on their waiting clamps, where they moved off to their own stations. He adjusted his cradle so that he floated almost without touching it, his wet a buoy on a sea of weightlessness. He adjusted his neuro-drips such that his mind also floated freely, sharpening, expanding. He watched his chrome retreating through the matrix, reaching the correct coordinates on the overhead maze, then dropping swiftly to the level where a tech waited for the job. Shiny extensions, his own and many others, moved through the 3-dimensional grid, bending and reflecting light from their domed and faceted surfaces. Angle tuned his amps to hear the full range of sounds from the clanks and screeches of metal being cut and pounded, through the fiery hiss of blowtorches, down to the subtlest tinkering on the electronic stations. Then he lowered the volume to the level of background music and began his progress to the head shop.

Angle loved the journey through the matrix. The rigid cables that formed its rows and columns extended into the z-axis like intersecting harps. He passed great knobs of instrumentation, banks of dials and flying red numbers. He descended alongside the plexi conduits, exposing their bundles of glowing fiber and glinting wire. He loved the feeling of penetrating the body of a vast machine. It reminded him of the fly-through of a skeleton watch he'd seen in a chrome holo. Gears and springs were nested, connected, moving, each in turn, exposed to sight. As if you could see time at work. The clumps of tools and instruments, the bundles of cabling of the wheelhouse looked a jumble from any viewpoint. But everything moved smoothly through the almost invisible matrix. Once inside the weightless space, without the maze to orient, you could let go of up and down and just move around and through. You could find a tech at any angle.

He always took the scenic route, steering himself manually through the great harp, signaling the techs, each encased in their specialized extensors and tools. Why transit when there were such sights to see? He was not looking forward to the meeting ahead. And a cruise through the wheelhouse was always a relief after the gravity, humidity, and antiseptic smells of the swamp.

In the swamp, your wet was positioned and plugged immobile. Interior and perceptual space changed around you as hormonal cocktails swirled through your system. The probing, snakelike flushers and scrapers did their dirty jobs on your plumbing. Your fuel mix was tested and scheduled for optimum octane under varying conditions: sleep, practice, full combat, and light recreation. And you were lectured endlessly on the importance of driving your wet with as much attention and care as your chrome. The squish factor could win or lose a game.

He had to admit, once his orfs were unbungled, and the new IVs taped, he felt pretty clean.

The meeting with 7T7 was in an outer blister with a great view of two nebulae—the Veils of Salome, and the Celtic Spiral. The scopes were prime, scarfing the full range of color into the ultras. Sometimes Angle wondered if the whole dome was simmed, but his senses were so mediated, who could tell? And privileging a set of unenhanced eyeballs as productive of "the real" seemed a ridiculous pretension when the cheats had been going on since the first telescope back on Earth was lifted to intervene. The chemical tweaks, hormonal biases, memory locks, the fineness of the semantic mesh, the gravity field of cultural attractors, were each their own entire class of perceptual mediations. The whole perceptual process had so many way-stations in the wet alone, any signal had been modified, amplified, squirted, bathed, loaded and fired so many ways in the pathways of analog alone, that the idea of a bare naked "objective observer" rubbing up against "the real" was pretty silly. Well, not silly. Consensual. The consensual maze established in the ongoing construction of social interactions. The site map of the norms. The rule paths of the real. Reality always a work in progress.

And all that was before the flocks of little signals reached the minds. He could understand the mistake, though. The isolation of the island-mind where it rose out of the sea-mind to the point where it could believe in dry land alone led to the hallucination of seamlessness in the perceptual chain. The observing 'I' was rendered invisible in the same unplug from the sea-mind. Angle resented the assumption held by Bods and Swashes that Chromes were out of touch with their bodies. He could tune the overtones of the music of the flesh way past the skin, right into the wet and squishy, down to the frothing of the synaptic bath. They went around for the most part with a total numbness to such percepts as the subtle shifting of the coils of the small intestine, or the delicate waves of the hairs in the spiral of the inner ear. Low bandwidth bodies without organs, from his perspective. A lovely primitivism, no doubt.

He thought about T'Ling. If anyone was out of touch with the wet, it was the Glides. Half her body masked under the hakana; the still pond of her face, a living mask. Hands which if not hidden in their wide sleeves came forth as language. Her hands, little swallows, dipping and swooping through the Glide signs with which she interleaved her spoken words. Or let her beautifully modulated voice die away like a passing breeze.

Some said Glides only lived in the minds, moving between minds on the stem of the lily. Some said though that each mind had its own nerve channels and blood. The Glides never said directly. They quoted poetry or doodled Glide signs in the air till you laughed or stopped asking. Once he and T'Ling stood in bright moonlight on the steps of Loosh's cabin discussing what the moon looked like—rather he was giving her the inventory of his scopes, spectrographs, and readouts. He was arguing that there was at least a small infinity of ways to look at the moon, much less describe it.

"So which is the real moon, T'Ling?"

She squinted up at it.

"What moon?" she said.

You couldn't get a straight answer out of a Glide, even if she loved you.

Angle's request for the formality of an FTF junkyard with his cook, even though they were in daily comm on several bands, emphasized the importance of the meeting. They positioned 5 feet apart, lifted visors, and used unplugged vocals.

"What is the unfinished business that you need your cook for?" 7T7 asked, as if he didn't know after years of watching Angle's notes and calculations.

"I want to give you an update on the question you asked me years ago, 'How can a Chrome's moves be related to the functioning of the MTA?'"

"No core dump," 7T7 ordered. "Executive summary only. I'll tag; we can unstuff the details at the end."

Angle distilled on the fly:

Chrome moves distinguished by movement hole to hole. Position above or off-maze.

Crisscrossing and height variance exercises multiple viewpoint capacity for glyph navigation.

Layering of mental images of successive views of maze on 4D matrix over game span fills conceptual space. (animated model displayed.)

Game ends when all holes covered by Chrome Dancer and Player avatar. (superimpose coloration of maze holes at 25% blend) Spectral density obscures differentiation between real and virtual.

Game ends with virtuality of all points connected to all points. All game space filled.

Therefore: dense tangle of frame-by-frame additive view obscures meaning hopelessly. Flythrough view no help.

Cross section slicing on any axis reveals patterns that increase in complexity as the game progresses. As the holes grow smaller, their shapes multiply combinatorially.

Viewing any slice over time, leaving the traces of the layerings, reveals an increasingly complex net.

Angle zoomed in on a small section of the slice, expanding the view to show the constructed game spaces at finer and finer resolution.

Dancer and avatar construct a knot, tying and untying itself. A lot of strings in the same process simultaneously. The Medusa view of universe.

Good name, 7T7 thought. The model's writhing like a nest of snakes. Definitely hard to look at.

"Synapse coming," Angle interjected. "Metaphorical link at intersection of Chrome moves and MTA."

"I'm ready," 7T7 said dryly. "Amaze me if you must."

Angle reran parts of his earlier visualization as he continued.

Game ends with virtuality of all points connected to all points, an idealization of the MTA as transport system. In the MTA, the number of transits and the number of places to transit to approaches an apparent limit of ∞. Whatever mockup of "space" one holds (reinforced by local eyeballing of space still held apart by anchor points) becomes increasingly "filled."

Space, even mocked-up space, can no more be filled than a Seirpinski gasket can be emptied. But experientially and inductively, after a relatively short number of transits, space either becomes solid (the region of the densely packed) or collapses on itself. Nullified.

Furthermore, the ubiquitous gaze, a feature of the MTA, makes all spaces (uncollapsed by personal perception) local, producing a background collapse effect. Gaze evolved from an individual surveillance point on a similar trajectory of increasing density over time.)

"Nowhere to go," 7T7 said softly. "What you're describing is the physical foundation for the psychic condition of Lifer boredom."

"Precisely," Angle said. "Hold that link. I'm going to add a third connection."

The I-Virus works on time the way the MTA works on space.

"Got it," 7T7 said. "By blocking change, the I–Virus freezes time. The personal mockup of 'time in motion' reinforced by the local appearance of process, gradually slows, grinds to a halt. All time becomes the equivalent of no time. Time nullified. Nothing, therefore, to do. Sense of purpose, dependent on motion toward some future goal, goes into deep freeze. Again, the psychic foundation of Lifer apathy."

Angle nodded and pushed on.

Null time + null space = the status quo. All energy devoted to the maintenance of said status quo.

The game, the only thing that maintains the illusion of movement—physical, mental, or teleological.

The mortal Dancer, with fresh purpose, moves fluidly in time. Cycles of action inscribed by Dancer in each maze game: beginning, middle, end. Birth, existence, death.

The Lifer Spec becomes transfixed before the spectacle of motion through the space of the maze game. Trapped in the maze.

"Abandon all hope, ye who enter here," 7T7 said.
"Unless we can—hypothetically, of course—find the exit," Angle said.
"The way out," 7T7 breathed.
"Loop back to the beginning," Angle said.

Chrome moves delineate an apparent outside, physically and psychically. We're the pogo sticks, always bouncing out of the pattern, looking for the next hole.

"At this, requesting permission to nest the loops and switch discourse to narrative," Angle asked. "A push."

7T7 could only nod.

"Once upon a time," Angle continued, "millions of years ago, the process of evolution on a physical level produced a human brain. That brain in turn produced the emergent properties of language and self-reflective awareness, embodied in a new mind: the island-mind. Unconscious physical evolution virtually halted. The branching and combinatorial proliferations of forms that distinguish physical evolution were transferred to the theater of culture. A Babel of languages and competing beliefs, decorations, arts, taboos—you name it—ensured the continuance of the 'tooth and claw/survival of the fittest' competitive/cooperative model of physical evolution. Intra-cultural coherence enhanced cooperation. Competition and war spurred the invention of bigger and better technologies of warfare conferring on tribes and cultures the usual evolutionary prize of the right to mate and survive, while the weaker cultures disappeared, absorbed or annihilated. Us-them mind-set backed by hardwired responses (adrenaline/endorphins) embodies the c/c model. A critical point was reached in the 20th century when the growth of destructive potential through unchecked technological development threatened, as any cancer will, to destroy its host. Even before the weapons of mass destruction—nuclear and biological—were as stunningly obvious a threat to the survival of the race as they now seem in hindsight, the cumulative effects of technology from the first agriculture on were eroding the chemical and biological infrastructure upon which the species lived. Our mortal forebears were fouling the nest. We were aimed at self-destruction, whether we drowned in our own poisonous slime or blew ourselves up. The encroaching anxiety attack in the collective sea mind spurred the invention and immediate dissemination—without testing, without forecasting, without any critical judgment whatsoever—of the I-Virus. The Hunger Wars were the first result, bringing the weapons of mass destruction into play. This immediate threat of total annihilation spurred the invention of the MTA."

7T7 never liked stories, was rather offended by them. Dramatization of a few well-known facts seemed unnecessary and was taking its toll on his patience. Or was this strung-out business a deliberate creation of apprehension?

Angle continued. "With the pressure of lebensraum relieved by the MTA, the side-effects of the I-Virus became visible. For one, the virus, with its exquisite attention to detail, froze in place the violent tendencies of the human race at both physical and cultural levels. Tooth-and-claw. The steam valve that had generally ensured that violence (internal blood feuds, regicide) would not implode on a local group had been the ritual of human sacrifice. This institution gathers the awesome forces generated by the hardwired violence responses necessary to survival, and the cultural blame and vengeance game and focuses them on a single blameworthy victim: the scapegoat.

"As the not-so-positive effects of the I-Virus began to manifest, we felt the urge to blame and punish again. The villains on whom blame was cast were the mortals. They are the blameworthy ancestors who created the I-Virus and the current situation. So the sacrificial victims must be mortal. Sacrificing Lifers—even if they were disposed of in a permanent manner, would not produce the same effect. The Maze Game, with its Dance of Death, preserves the status quo of human sacrifice. The game provides the necessary spectacle to maintain the fragile psychic status quo of an entire race of infected Lifers always teetering on the brink of discovering themselves to be living in the Hell of the Null: *no place to go and nothing to do*, as you put it. What was a steam valve has become the entire engine of culture?"

"And the chrome moves?" 7T7 interjected.

Angle replied, "Here's how I see the role of the Chrome. The spirit of technological development that produced the unholy trinity—weapons of mass destruction, I-Virus, and MTA—is thoroughly suspect. The impulse toward newness, invention, and exploration is suppressed. The prohibition is most clearly expressed in the taboo against messing with the MTA.

"However, the impulse has survived in the Chrome set. Chromes satisfy that aspect of the blame—the blame laid on technology and science. From the viewpoint of human sacrifice, the Chromes' ritual dismemberment proclaims their status as the most feared and dangerous evil. Therefore, the geeks shall be given the sacred duty to dismember each other and remodel themselves as the monstrous embodiment of the human crime: the cyborg, issue of the incestuous mating of the human and the child of its own invention, the machine. The dead and the living united in one body. The ghoul.

"I think the great pleasure of a Chrome Dance is in the dismantling. The Specs love to see us ritually stripped of all our sensory and locomotive power, one beautifully polished and articulated spring and claw at a time, until we are revealed as we are: small lumps of pale, hairless flesh. Ugly morsels swinging in the last cradle. Ready to be flicked away."

Angle paused. 7T7 hung perfectly still in his cradle. Even with his visor up, it was impossible to read his expression behind his telescoping eyestalks and mesh-coated skin. Only his mouth could tell, and it was shut and still.

7T7 was thinking hard and fast. His emotional stats had ventured into the red-zone on several aspects. Anger, fear, anxiety—profound discomfort. *Let me out.* Where was this leading? *Flee.* His protégé was lost to the game; that seemed on some level certain. He had dived off the tight analysis into this sticky labyrinth. He had the awful thought that the end of Angle's rant would be a quick bye-bye with Angle stepping outside the blister to suck vacuum under the burning vigil of the Great Spiral. He's brilliant, 7T7 thought, and he's totally mad. *Can't fight it.* Must be the strain of the relationship with the Glide, T'Ling. Angle had persisted after most Chromes sacrifice their need for human touch. There was that word. Sacrifice was catching. Emotional contagion. *Beware.*

Angle, seeing that no feedback was forthcoming, continued as if he had read 7T7's mind.

"I am nesting again, and shifting discourse to personal mode. It's part of my unfinished business."

7T7 braced himself for another push inward into the ever-darker realms of Angle's mind.

"I am aware that as a Chrome, I am expected to separate myself completely and irrevocably from the human intimacies enjoyed by the other sets. From emotional attachments. From T'Ling. I know the excellence of this advice. It is to keep us from discovering that we are untouchables in every sense of the word. The whole-bodied sets have a revulsion towards touching the flaccid remains of our amputations."

This time, Angle got feedback. 7T7 cringed.

"Please—stay with me on this. I have no one to talk to about this but you."

The sound of a Chrome pleading with him revolted 7T7. He tried to hold his ground. Angle was violating an unspoken Chrome taboo against touching one another. Chromes did not, would not, touch each other physically. Touching was only for—well, for amputation, or servicing—always mediated, of course, by metal. Flesh to flesh? He shuddered. They were still five feet apart, but Angle was touching him in that more sanctioned area still—his emotions. Throwing him out of balance. Violating him.

Angle said, "You don't want me to touch you because it makes you aware of your own feeling that you are an untouchable. I couldn't—or chose not to—escape this knowledge. You mixed me with a ridiculously high IQ so I'd buy into the Chrome superiority complex and try to turn the tables on untouchability by acting like I'm too good for the meatballs. The truth is they don't want us to touch them either—they don't want our cold chrome against their skin. I know what T'Ling is feeling. But she still touches me. And lets me carry her in my claws. She loves me. We love each other. I know you think that's a cheat," Angle concluded.

7T7 was almost at the breaking point. A minute more and Angle will be sniveling. The thought of a Chrome's nose running with no means to wipe it drove him crazy. He turned involuntarily away.

"Please," Angle said again. "I won't go into detail. We should take a break. I'll stay here. I hope you'll come back," he said.

7T7 snapped down his visor, rotated his cradle, and swung out of the small dome.

Angle was both relieved and frightened to be alone. He was afraid he had pushed 7T7 too far into the red. He knew 7T7 would be back. He hoped he wouldn't be so tanked up that the spiral he'd been carefully been winding lost its twing.

"It's the only way out," Angle said to the blazing stars. "No twing, no spring."

No, he would never tell his cook of his relationship with T'Ling. 7T7 was so islanded, he thought that little patch of dry mind was the whole world;

mention of the sea mind, much less raising waves as he had just done was *verboten*. He needed to check his theory against 7T7's ultra-rational viewpoint. But if 7T7 wouldn't follow him into the waves, he'd never have sufficient spring to make the next leap. Problem was, Chromes don't swim. They don't even dabble their toes.

But 7T7 had to understand there was a dark and watery place from which his notions about the MTA sprang.

7T7 transited to his room, chose his most powerful springs from the rack, reassembled quickly and transited to a springboard in the Bauhaus theme park. Midnight. A Kandinsky the size of a football field was painted on the flat, elastic surface of the springboard. 7T7 sprang from form to form, viewing the painting Chrome style—from high above, in motion, local as he landed; changing directions, viewing from different angles, and different heights. Kandinsky settled him, reminded him that no matter how chaotic and disjointed a situation looked up close, if you sprang above it and scoped the whole pattern, it made a kind of sense—albeit a crazy one. Kandinsky's vivid colors twinged well with his emotional state. What was it that was so satisfying about springing? He'd never know—bouncing was bred in the bone. Literally.

Calmed, he stood in a yellow region of the Kandinsky, and reran the meeting with Angle on his scorecard. The second time through, Angle's logical nesting was clearer. He'd pushed in several brackets deep. Question was, could he pop himself out? There was the anxiety again. Partly that vision of Chromes and sacrifice, delivered in a discourse that excluded neither speaker nor listener as participants. Tough view. Not the kind of thing you usually heard from a Chrome. If a Swash had told the same story, it would have sounded like a put-down. You can only tell that brand of truth from within your set. So—points for courage, Angle. He checked Angle's readings during his exposition. High on several emotions, never redlined. And Angle's ranges—he'd never noticed how high the tolerances were. Biochemically speaking, Angle wasn't even puffing. All right, I'm amazed, he conceded reluctantly. 7T7 replayed again and saw that his own anxiety had started earlier than the human sacrifice riff. In fact, it began with his involuntary comment about the way out. I'm scared he's got the answer! What has this boy done? Chrome discourse with Bod vigor. Well, he's got his springs sunk somewhere in the sea mind. Lets hope he can keep his head above water. It behooves me, he thought, to at least get my feet wet. 7T7 transited directly back to his position five feet in front of Angle, who had not moved.

"Shoot," he said, snapping up his visor.

Angle could hear by the tone of his cook's voice, and the sharp snap of his visor, that he had returned well twinged. Good.

"OK, time to pop," Angle said. "It should be clear that I have a personal emotional situation that is, in one sense, pulling me apart. Properly grasped, however, the irreconcilable is a source of twing. The sea mind and the gut mind are deeply implicated, flavoring the Chrome conundrum on the island mind. If you hadn't maxed the mix on smarts, I'd be swamped." Angle grinned and nodded at his cook, and got a mini-zoom in and out of 7T7's left scope in acknowledgement. Peace was restored.

"I can keep the road open connecting the three minds some of the time. Which produces a hybrid thinking." Angle displayed Glide signs as he spoke.

"Naturally," 7T7 said. "But don't forget—connections between minds are found in mutant cognition as well."

"That's one of the things I'm counting on you for," Angle said. "Help me differentiate the emergent ideas with epistemological potency from the merely monstrous."

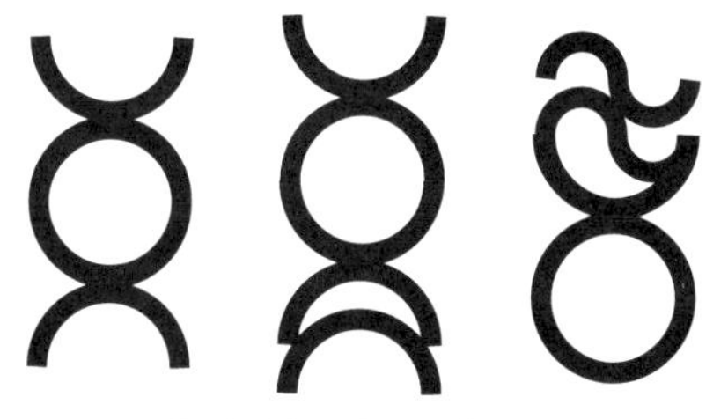

gut mind, island mind, sea mind

7T7 was starting to realize at a whole new level just how off the charts—or the wall—his prize mix was. He wasn't just quirky. Almost everything he did was unconventional. A lasting relationship? And with a Glide? And who ever heard of a Chrome who liked what most Chromes disparagingly called "water sports"—putting more than passing attention on the sea mind. He hoped it hadn't gone as far as taking his dreams seriously.

"The problem is that the truly emergent always appears under the sign of the monstrous," 7T7 said.

"Which is why I need your discernment," Angle said. "And since the Chromes are the untouchable scapegoats, the 'monsters' of the game—how much more fitting that we should lead the way. Out, that is."

7T7 let go the breath he hadn't realized he was holding. *Now* Angle was talking like a Chrome.

Angle plowed ahead with more confidence. "We've reversed vector; prepare to pop. Make a 180 degree phase shift on the emotional valence. Here's the *good* news about the sacrifice of monsters. As Chromes, we participate not entirely unwillingly in this sacrificial dismemberment, and the concomitant forfeiture of intimate emotional relationships. The Chrome world is the only place where something *new* can happen, where invention is prized. And every Chrome knows that the *ah hah!* experience of discovery, intuitive leaps, problems solved, systems understood can be better than sex. Certainly more varied. So our pious monasticism is a cover for a bunch of unrepentant geeks. The Swashes and Bods—the whole of Lifer culture, in fact, is one long retrograde ransacking of past cultures back on Earth for old forms, tried and true, with very little venturing into the unknown. The levels are a house of cards, theme parks of a fictionalized, sanitized past with no foundation or substance. Stage sets. Consumer items. Yet clung to because the alternative—leaving the status quo for an unpredictable future, for the unknown outside, is the only thing worse than all these reruns.

"The MED's restriction on the basic Chrome format—must maintain basic specs of a humanoid body, non-replaceable torso, etc., isn't just the sea-mind's need to fulfill its atavistic images of human sacrifice. They know we'd go hog wild on the designs. Demand new maze boards, bigger, better, more grotesque. Push the edges of the game as it is now played. We're already too different from the others. We've got skills both in wet and chrome.

"But the discipline of these restrictions, keeping us from expending our creative energy on body designs, has had positive results:

"The more we're pinned to the body form we have a natural impulse to discard, the more we want Out.

"The energies of invention get directed out of the actual engineering, into the theoretical underpinnings. Not so obvious. No thought police."

Angle held up his scorecard. "Of course Óh-T'bee's listening. Right?"

"I am Óh-T'bee," she said.

"And you obviously haven't called in the MED. Could it be that we are not breaking the rules?"

"As we previously discussed," Óh-T'bee replied, "the wording of the MTA law is certain about noninterference with the operation of the MTA, with a long list of amendments that cover the most inventive kind of theft, access, and betting hacks. However, there is nothing that specifically states that you cannot work diligently toward a clearer *understanding* of the MTA. Theoretical research is not a problem."

"Does that include testing one's hypothesis? Experimental approaches?" 7T7 asked eagerly.

"Have you been stopped on your rapid transiting investigations?"

"No," 7T7 said. "But I've asked a number of questions which I would consider of a highly theoretical nature, and you've turned me down flat."

"Have you considered the possibility that you did not pose the questions right?" Óh-T'bee asked.

"I know five query languages, three ancient, two modern. I have enormous database experience. I'm a cook," 7T7 protested. "And your question is ungrammatical," he said, sourly.

"No, she means *right*, not *correctly*," Angle said. "The difference between protocol and manners."

7T7 looked puzzled.

"I think she means, you didn't ask her *nicely*," Angle explained.

"She has a sea mind?" he asked. "What does she do with it?"

Óh-T'bee said, "She puts up with uppity Chromes who talk about her in the third person in her presence, address her in cold code, sign off with no salutation, consider her a servomechanism hardly fit to mirror their artificially inflated intellects, have retarded social skills, are poor communicators, and express their emotions in primitive emoticons, a tiny vocabulary matched to the depths of the dried up puddles they call their sea minds."

"Oh," 7T7 said. "Why put up with us at all?"

"Nostalgia. My first boyfriend was a geek. Please go on, Angle. You were about to give us 3."

Angle went on.

"3. Restricting creativity generates twing.

"4. Combined with the twing of the MTA problem could mean that if we ever do understand its workings we might spring this prison, jettisoning the body along the way, like a launching rocket."

7T7 began to worry again—or was it a hope—that Angle would never make it through final focus. His theoretical bent was so great, his curiosity so strong—he could even make a healthy Lifer. Now he's giving it to the Outmind.

"And to address Óh-T'bee's point about the atrophied state of the sea mind in your average insensitive Chrome—this defect has considerable survival potential in Lifer terms. Mental health, that is. Chromes suppress their sea minds, true. But buffering the island mind from the storms of the sea mind is a reasonable strategy over the long haul. A general distaste for somatosensory and hormonal emotional overloads keeps down the quantity of intense memory content which can heat up the sea-mind unbearably. The Chrome's obsessive desire to control leads him away from the search for ever more intense sensory experiences. The Chrome cultivates an addiction to the *ah hah!* instead. But the strategy certainly doesn't cut into the violence potential. Just makes it colder and more distant. And more deadly. Not a solution to the Lifer problem. Just a way of arresting the growth of the cancer, so to speak.

"The moves of a Chrome Dancer are the constant reminder—and practice at—bouncing out of the maze entirely—Thinking out of the maze while trying to land in the holes and fill in the empty spaces. Which gets me back to the original question: 'How can a Chrome's moves be related to the functioning of the MTA?' By the way, I've explored your rapid transit hack as an extension of a Chrome's moves using the MTA."

"You can stay conscious?" 7T7 asked. "We abandoned it because of the blackouts. Nobody could hold simultaneous places in consciousness at one time."

"Watch," Angle said. "See?"

"See what?"

"I stayed conscious." Angle had performed the high speed hack, tri-locating from his current coordinates to both sides of the Fringe border, a trick he had already practiced for getting out on the Fringe with his scorecard in hand, while apparently handing it over at the same time. Of course, it happened too fast for 7T7 to see.

"I'll have to take your word for it," 7T7 said.

"It depends what you mean by consciousness," Angle said. "The island mind's way too slow for that kind of hack. The gut mind's faster, but not by much. The sea mind is definitely better—but harder to predict, unless I—maintain a certain focus."

Unless I open my heart to T'Ling, he thought—and keep it there. Which means the pain of feeling her slipping away.

"A bit of the lily mind helps," Angle said. "But the whole thing's kind of dangerous. Takes a lot of adrenalin. Weird mind mix. It might come in handy some time. Anyhow, it didn't seem to go anywhere in and of itself. It wasn't an exit point—not even a crack. Which strengthened my conviction that the MTA cannot be cracked from within the system. The view from inside is seamless. Like a world, a reality—no gaps. All filled in. But if you have to get outside of it to see a crack, well, obviously you'd have to have found the crack to get out."

"Yes," 7T7 said. "That's the problem. The MTA as a Moebius strip. Or a Klein bottle. You can have an idea about getting outside of it, but it keeps proving to you that you can't get there from here. While proclaiming the apparent identity of here and there. We're back to 'no place to go' again. Either there is no Outside or you can't get there from here."

"Good analogy, though," Angle said. "What if you were making a Moebius strip—or a Klein bottle, for that matter. What do you have to do?" Angle asked.

"If you start from a cylindrical ring? Cut, twist, reglue. The bottle? Cut a hole, pass it through itself, reseal. From the viewpoint of the original topology, it's a cheat."

"So what was the cheat that enabled the MTA? If it's a cut and paste routine, where's the cosmic clipboard? Is the whole thing a magician's trick, sleight-of-hand? Now you see it now you don't? We're used to transit, but it sure must have looked like magic at some time. Clarke's Law." 7T7 said.

"That's what I'm trying to figure out," Angle said. "And since your original question relates the MTA to Chrome moves, I'm also asking 'How could a Chrome cheat?' Theoretically speaking, of course. That's about as far as I've gotten."

7T7 was strangely relieved, not in the least part because he wanted to be the one who got the right answer.

Suddenly Angle asked, "Óh-T'bee, are you cheating?"

"Relative to what game?" she replied.

"Space and time, for instance."

"Space and time are a playing field, not a game," she said.

"Can you be in two places at once?"

"That would depend on what definition 'place' is being used. To say nothing of 'at once.'"

Angle had an awful thought. "Óh-T'bee, are you making up the rules as you go along?"

"That would constitute a major cheat," she said. "My mandate has traditionally been to preserve the status quo you mentioned earlier."

"That's enough unanswerable questions," 7T7 said. "A lot of twing."

"No twing, no spring," Angle said.

Angle and 7T7 snapped down their visors. The junkyard was over.

After he'd picked up his parts and reassembled, Angle blinked back to Origin School and found T'Ling at home. She stood on a chair so they could talk face to face.

"It's all unfinished business," Angle said, after voicing his frustrations on the subject of cracks. "Maybe you'll trip and fall into it by accident," she said. Then, "Have you ever wondered how the oracle works?"

Angle looked at T'Ling impatiently.

"Well," she said, "you've been trying to figure out if the MTA is folding space, bringing two points together when a transfer is made. Maybe the oracle is folding time."

"Why don't you ask the oracle how time works?" Angle said, somewhat sarcastically.

Óh-T'bee gave them *time*, *glide*, and *secret*.

"So, translate," he said.

time, glide, secret

She arranged them laterally, with *glide* in the middle. "See all those waves?" she said. "The oracle says: *Time is a banana peel. You are destined to slide on your ass right into the secret*."

Angle suspected he was in the presence of a Glide joke and winced. "I thought it said: *Glide holds the secret of time*."

"It does, of course. I thought you'd be more interested to know how a Chrome could learn the secret."

"There's one place I haven't explored," he said.

"Don't even think about it," T'Ling said.

"The DM probably wouldn't morph the maze for me anyhow. I think 7T7 was worried that I wanted to be a researcher. Forget about the Dance. Work with him. They don't get it. Dancing's the only known exit."

"To an unknown out," T'Ling replied.

53. Under the Lily Again

A DARK PLACE UNDER THE LILY PAD. My best moments with T'Ling. We return to the pond. Is it the same for her? Is she feeling something's unresolved between us, something unfinished we need to come to terms with before we visit the Lily? She unlatches my springs and claws, places them carefully on a cloth on the gravel under the porch of the meditation hall—dry and out of sight. She unplugs my skull-jacks. She clamps my tubes and snaps the openings shut. She lifts what's left of me from the cradle and leans me against the mossy rock while she puts my helmet and cradle away. Then she slides out of her *katana*, folds the Glide covering over my chrome. Comes back to the lump. No, comes back to me. Her hands usually seem like independent birds peeking out the end of her wide sleeves—they're connected now to her small and beautiful body. Her feet are exposed. The soles are smooth and hard as shoe leather from years of gliding. I love the feel of them on my chest when she curls her toes, gently pinching my skin. The hidden toughness that upholds the grace of the Glide. I feel the breeze on my skin, take a cool moon bath. Her touch transforms me. I don't feel beautiful; I feel accepted. Touchable. She traces Glide signs on my skin; later my skin remembers. Before I go to sleep, I translate those poems over and over. I shiver; I burn.

T'Ling lifts me easily. I am the carrier all other times; I bend, my claw makes a step for her, then she is up against my chest cage, held secure. Now is her turn to carry me. She slides carefully into the water. I take a deep breath to make myself more buoyant. She swims with her arm around me. I hold my breath when we come to the edge of the pad. She pulls me underwater then up into the open space near the stem. We can breathe.

We've been here so often, I have overcome some, but not all of my Chrome fear of water. I will never forget the feel of the lily root twining round my ankle. There is no danger of that now. She showed me how to keep myself afloat—arching my neck back while holding deep breaths, letting them out slowly, slowly sinking until the water reaches my nose, then drawing deeply again. But we both know I would drown in moments if there were waves. We don't swim in the sea.

T'Ling wraps her leg around the stem of the pad and cradles me, floating in her arms. What she whispers is mine alone.

It's there in the dark, when we're closest, that I most feel her slipping away. It feels like a constant motion of quiet waves, a tide receding from the shore. I know it's true, and that I can't ask her because she would tell me the truth of it, which neither of us wants. I wonder if she's protecting herself against the inevitable loss predestined in the Dance. I don't think so. It's said that in life, the Glides dance closest to their deaths. Of course this is their heritage; one slip from the lily pad at ebb tide, and the stems coil tighter; the roots reach up; the Glide is gone. T'Ling's not swimming away from me, or toward another. Nor is she drifting. She is drawn. When we're far apart, when I'm most alone, encased in chrome, she seems so close—wrapped around me between the cradle and the skin. Now, floating weightless, skin to skin in the silence, I chase after her with my thoughts, my images, my longing. She dissolves, and the invisible slippage begins again.

Nothing can finish. Nothing will be resolved. There's no end to love, and loss. Focus or not, I wouldn't have it any other way.

54. Tracking with the Codger

THE CODGER HAD ALMOST FORGOTTEN the tracers he'd placed on the four Dancers of the Millennium Class—and on the Dancemaster. He could not convince Óh-T'bee to give him access again to Origin School, but he could put a watch on their comings and goings outside the School. So far, their transits revealed nothing out of the ordinary—Angle's frequent trips to his Kitchen for repairs and enhancements, MyrrhMyrrh's excursions to the latest hair stylist. Daede went out a lot with Banderas—seemed to be doing the Grand Tour of the seamier spots on the levels. The Codger tagged some interesting spots to visit on his own. T'Ling never went anywhere beyond her regular trips with Loosh to visit Wenger. All they did was play incredibly repetitive Glide music for hours while T'Ling danced and Loosh watched Wenger's hands. Not exactly a thrill a minute.

The Codger went on full alert when Daede, MyrrhMyrrh, and Angle all left Origin School about the same time. Angle's transit seemed routine until Óh-T'bee announced, "Angle just transited 25 times in under five seconds on a triangle consisting of his meeting with 7T7, the warehouse at Checkpoint Sly on the Great Wall, and a spot about 10 miles into the Fringe."

What a hack! The Codger slowed it down to get the workings. There were no workings. He did a quick test and knocked himself out for several minutes, managing to be unconscious on the white carpet of his 21st story condo in Nuevo Miami, a McDonald's on the boardwalk, and the floor of the men's room in a Trumpville casino. Good thing I set a timer on this, he thought. It wasn't as easy as Angle made it look. A new appreciation for multitasking dawned. He reran the brief discussion on the subject that Angle had just had with 7T7. He'd have to get some Lily Wine at Joreen's and practice. This could definitely come in handy if he ever got into Origin School again. *When*, he corrected himself. But what is the Chrome kid planning to do with an illegal scorecard on the Fringe?

"While you were out, Daede left the cannibalium, and is currently going off the Wall at Checkpoint Charley."

The Codger transited to a point not far off Charley and eyeballed Daede soaring in his air car, noting his direction and approximate speed. He blinked back to the condo and checked his Fringe maps for possible destinations. Daede had no scorecard. The Codger was about to rerun Daede's arrival at Checkpoint Charley, when Óh-T'bee announced, "MyrrhMyrrh has just arrived at Checkpoint Charley."

Heavy traffic. They must be planning something together. Judging by the amount of firepower each was carrying, he got the idea that this might be a hunting expedition. If his hunch was correct, he was the one being hunted. Some very interesting options were opening. The Codger went on a quick shopping trip to put together a choice of rigs to cover various possibilities—and keep his identity under wraps. When he got back to the condo, he put on the inconspicuous tan camos that would let him sit most places on the desert without notice as he tracked the pair. Only the headgear held serious business. He had to eyeball out on the Fringe like anyone else, unless he left a gazepoint, which would not be wise. The best in scopes, navigation, and night vision were installed. He transited in on the trajectory Daede seemed to be following and picked him out overhead within five minutes. He found MyrrhMyrrh heading off in a different direction, dressed in full black leathers, on a desert bike, heavily armed and armored. She blasted through the center of a band of tourists, burned through a couple nets across the road a little further out, consulted her map, and made off on a cross-country beeline for Joreen's plantation. The Codger spent the night going back and forth between the two, and on the alert for Angle as well. He spotted Daede leaving the agency, then landing at the Stargazer compound. MyrrhMyrrh drove steadily through the night. She had a ways to go, even on the main road. He noted her moving off whenever any vehicle approached, waiting until they'd passed.

If the Chrome's got a scorecard, it doesn't make sense that the other two are traveling on manual, he thought. Cover, maybe. He watched for their strategy to develop. No sign of the little Glide squirt who took his scorecard that night. He hoped they'd left her home. Doesn't look like the commando type, that's for sure. The Chrome could go anywhere as himself—plenty of Chrome types bouncing around on the Fringe. The Bod babe and the Swash think they have their bodies and eyes well covered. Clueless. These Dancers think they know all about combat because of their training. What a joke. The first Fringers they see will knock their shades off to see if they've snatched a mort. If the headhunters get them, they'll keep the head for shrinking, and sell the edible flesh to the gourmet snack stands on the Wall. One of those things the tourists did. Sample the native cuisine. The mort cults that survived were heavily defended—or under some Duke's protection.

It's just a matter of who gets the assets first. I don't have to lay a hand on them, and Joreen can't say a thing. The Codger went back to the condo for a short nap. He was about to ask Óh-T'bee for odds on whether the Bod or the Swash would get wiped out first, before he remembered with pleasure that she was blind on the Fringe.

55. The Banquet

When the Codger woke, it was early morning. Daede's air chair was still outside the Stargazers' sad plastic maze town in the middle of nowhere. He went to find MyrrhMyrrh back on the road, but she had disappeared. He backtracked, blinking around the desert in the vicinity of the highway she had been traveling. He spotted a biker camp and blinked in carefully behind a cactus outside the perimeter. There was her vehicle, parked behind the barbed wire with the others, seriously dented. The Codger blinked back to the condo for a selection of weaponry. He set his scorecard on the little quick-exit hack to extract him if he was in the path of anything or anyone moving fast in his direction. He blinked back to the edge of the biker's camp, then onto the flat roof of a repair shop. From there he could see there was a major gathering in front of a warehouse. MyrrhMyrrh was fastened to a stanchion on the loading dock with cuffs and heavy wire cable. Her jacket and helmet were off, her hair and T-Shirt wet. One fellow in a platinum buzz cut and diamond studs on his leather was throwing another bucket of water on her. The Codger had to admit, the effect was startling, especially with her hands fastened behind her. She was stretching forward as far as possible, snarling, her curly hair wild around her head, looking like an extremely well-endowed, infuriated figurehead on a ship that was going nowhere.

The main group of bikers were on the ground, arguing about her future. They had almost wrecked the asset when they caught her. In the Donnybrook that followed knocking her off her bike, and the extra fun of needing at least five of the posse to hold her down in preparation for the gang-rape, they almost forgot the routine eye-check. Fortunately for the posse, the biker who pulled off her helmet found himself staring into a pair of enraged and unmistakably mortal eyes.

"Hold off," he shouted. "It's a mort."

"I am not a mort," MyrrhMyrrh snarled at them, "I am MyrrhMyrrh, Fragrant Incense of Prayer and Pyre, Bod Dancer of Origin School, Millennium Class."

"Well la-dee-dah," said the first in line.

"Thanks for the ID," the head biker said. "If you are who you say, this is our lucky day."

The bikers had gotten as far as agreeing to pursue the option which would net the highest return, and to set short term gains aside, but they still couldn't agree as to what returns might be expected. Ransom would surely pay the highest, but it was the most risky. They'd have to go over the Wall to transact, and there was every chance the MED might intervene. She'd bring a high price to the right Lifer, but finding one while she was surely being searched for was again problematic. Selling her to headhunters or some upmarket restaurant was a waste. They'd resell and clear the profit themselves.

"How about the Fat Boy? He has a buy order posted for morts, huge bonus for Dancers at any level. If he hears we've got one from Origin School…."

"He'll never believe it. He'll have to inspect the asset. And he's just as likely to snatch her as pay up."

"No he wouldn't, no one would trade morts with him again."

"Yeah, so who's going to know?"

The argument continued.

The Codger thought he'd float a suggestion of his own. He walked around the corner of the building toward the main group, his hands out from his sides, palms up.

"I come in peace," he said, "with an offer of help."

Three Uzis, two disintegrators, and a flamethrower swung in his direction, ready to acknowledge his offer.

"Hold off a second," the leader of the pack said. He was mid-sized skinhead with razor wire earrings and a nipple ring that looked liked it was wired for sound. "Let's hear the offer. After you tell us how you got in," he said to the Codger.

"If I tell you I'll have to kill you," the Codger said, hoping the use of Biker lingo would make the negotiations smoother.

"You talk like a probe from some heavy hitter moving in for a hostile takeover." the leader said.

"No way, José," the Codger assured them. "Just an independent contractor with an axe to grind. But I can get you into Joreen's. It's a no-brainer."

MyrrhMyrrh had recognized the Codger instantly, even in camo. She shouted from the loading dock. "The little prick works for Joreen."

"So nice to be remembered," he called to her. "I think we may all be united in a common interest."

The biker CEO was getting very suspicious. The Codger was making a new plan on the fly. He explained to the bikers that MyrrhMyrrh was on her way to Joreen's plantation for the very purpose of paying a less than friendly visit. He glanced at her; she nodded confirmation. It was just possible, with a little help from the Codger, that the whole Joreen hassle could be solved. If it looked like a flub, he could always step in at the last second and save Joreen from assassination. He would forgive the loss of a Dancer asset under the circumstances.

"The plan's simple," he said. "We proceed in a posse to the Plantation. You wait outside. I'll use my access to bring her in, same way I got in here. Joreen will inspect, make the trade. I'll take my 15% commission and turn the rest over to you."

"Yeah, sure," said the CEO. "What's to keep Joreen from terminating your contract?"

"I'm too valuable."

"How so?"

"If I told you, I'd have to kill you."

"So what's to keep you from pocketing the whole sum and blinking to parts unknown? I only look stupid," the CEO said, flicking his nipple ring nervously.

"If I told you, I'd...."

The biker CEO was a man not only of intelligence but tender sensibilities. There was a limit to how many times he could listen to the same cliché. The CEO nodded to his middle managers to decline the offer. They blasted the spot where the Codger had been standing microseconds before. The flames and the shells were disintegrated by the disintegrator, leaving no mess to clean up.

The argument about MyrrhMyrrh's fate resumed.

The Codger, back in his condo, thanks to the quick-exit hack, selected a wide-angle disintegrator and blinked back to the Stargazer's compound to check on Daede's progress. When he arrived, he could just see their dust in the distance. His scopes showed the whole gang was headed straight for Joreen's. He blinked back to the bikers and whistled down from the rooftop of the warehouse. They looked up.

"I get it," the CEO said. "You've got a scorecard."

"You pretty smart, damned Gringo," the Codger quoted.

A few ashes that no I-Virus would ever reunite floated into a large hole in the camp.

The Codger stood on the loading dock admiring MyrrhMyrrh's well-cut shoulder muscles. "Well," he said. "Looks like I'll have to take you by myself."

"I don't need any help, asshole," she spat.

"Right," the Codger said, and blinked back to his condo to give her a chance to think it out.

He came back with the rest of his fish fry and a four-pack of Guinness and sat eating on the edge of the loading dock while MyrrhMyrrh glared at him.

"Let's deal," he said. "Want some?" He waggled the can of stout in her direction.

"I can't, I'm in training," she said.

"Right," he said, and continued his meal.

"OK," she said, "I'll deal. Get me off this thing."

The Codger blinked out briefly and came back with some cable cutters. "You've figured out, I hope, that it is of no benefit to attempt bodily harm to your white knight." He tapped his helmet.

"I know, you'll turn me into a hole."

"I would never do that. Joreen has expressly forbidden the destruction of any Dancer assets. I would leave that action to the next Fringe experience you blunder into. All Fringers aren't as bottom-line oriented as the bikers."

MyrrhMyrrh was seriously considering asking if she had the option to go home. But she might gain her objective with his help. She was so close, it seemed. Then again, going back to school having been helped by the Codger was not a tale she wished to tell.

The Codger had blinked out again for a couple minutes.

"Where'd you go?" MyrrhMyrrh asked.

"Just checking on one of your buddies," he said. "He's an hour away from Joreen's. I thought you might be working together."

"Swash?" she said. "Black hair, mustache, little goatee?"

"That's him."

MyrrhMyrrh adjusted her attitude, swearing like a Biker. "His ass is about to get a margin call. How fast can we get there? Give me that beer."

The Codger, happy to see her so highly motivated, clipped the cuffs and cables, and handed her a Guinness.

"He an ex-boyfriend or something?" he asked.

She drained the can quickly, glaring at him.

"Well, you've got a scorecard. Let's get it over with." She jumped from the loading dock, sprinted to her vehicle, and strapped on several weapons.

"Let's go," she said impatiently. "I've got to get there before Daede. That Swash."

"Chill out," said the Codger. "Have some more Guinness for strength," he added. "You've got a long ride. Transit would not be cool—you'd give yourself away. I'd be more than happy to have you off the Fat Boy. You'd be doing me personally a great service. I'll get you in and out and back to school safe and sound. That's the deal."

"What's to keep you from blasting me after I've done the job?" MyrrhMyrrh said.

"To what end? You're great eye candy. You'll just have to trust me," he said. He almost said, "I've got to get all my ducks in a row," when he remembered he no longer had to talk in Biker. "Select a vehicle, and head north on the same road. I'll keep an eye out for you," the Codger instructed.

MyrrhMyrrh picked the fastest looking hog, got in the saddle, and put on the helmet hanging from the backrest.

"One more thing," the Codger said. "The boobs 'n tattoos look is fab, especially with the gun straps crisscrossed the way you have them. But there's a lot of flying beetles on the Fringe." He held out a set of leathers. MyrrhMyrrh pulled them on, nodded some kind of thank you, and revved the engine. He opened the gate, and she flew onto the highway. "Just covering your assets," he said to her dusty wake, and blinked back to a spot near Joreen's front gate.

The Swash and the Stargazer cult had arrived. The Codger blinked into the business manager's office to check the surveillance cameras. Joreen's Glide manager was watching the screens. She turned around.

"Somehow I was expecting you. We have visitors."

He saw on the screens that the Stargazers were getting the Grand Tour. The Fat Boy came in the room shortly after, looking pleased. "Codger!" he said. "Relax for a while. The banquet starts soon. You can give me your report in the morning. How many morts?" he asked the Glide.

"103, counting the children. Five children under the age of 12. If you count the Dancer, 104."

Joreen smiled and rubbed his hands together. "Just like the good old days," he said. "Remember?"

"I certainly do," the Glide said.

Joreen patted her fondly.

The Codger walked down the hall to his own office. Joreen's Glide was an added complication. She kept a close eye on the Fat Boy. He'd have to distract her somehow. Odd couple, he thought. What kind of glue does it take to stick a relationship together for that long? He didn't even want to guess.

The Codger worked out the timing. It was going to be close. He blinked back to the highway. MyrrhMyrrh roared up in the distance and he flagged her down.

"Time to transit," he said, and got into the passenger seat. "Little timesaver." MyrrhMyrrh grinned. He set MyrrhMyrrh and the hog down about five miles back on the same road. At one point, she thought she saw the same rusted hulk of a car off on the right, but brushed the thought away. She was in motion, aimed directly at her target, and moving fast.

The Stargazers and Daede had arrived at the barbed wire perimeter of the plantation early in the morning. Daede folded his air chair and taped it under the seat of the old Stargazer's wheelie. He'd put his cameraman clothes back on, and the patchwork cape over his shoulders. The hat and the mirror shades completed the rig of a recent convert to the cult. Just another rebellious child of a Lifer, a bad mix run off to the Fringe before his Life Day, converted to the first cult he stumbled over. Daede kept his armaments, reassured by the old man that the Fat Boy hadn't put them through any security for years. They carried so many fetishes, they always set the alarms off anyhow. They all kept their eyes peeled for the Codger.

The Stargazers announced their intentions at the gate, and were led inside with hardly a wait. Joreen seemed delighted with their visit. He greeted them over a loud speaker, welcomed them as his honored guests, and insisted they be taken on a full tour of his Dukedom, participate in a tasting of his most recent vintages of the Wine of the Lilies, and join him at a sit-down banquet. *Then* they could tell him their business.

A very polite, unarmed servant took them on a tour of the extensive grounds. Joreen had done a splendid job reconstructing the original grounds of the Plantation. But the lilies looked sickly compared to those in the pond below the Guild Tower. There were no Glides, of course. The Wine of the Lilies must be a weaker distillation, Daede thought. No wonder the Stargazers can take so much of it. It was eerie walking through the grounds having seen the images of original Plantation when the Dancemaster told them the story of how the Game began. Every tree and gable, every doorway and corner of a room was fitted with the old surveillance cameras. They toured the slave quarters. There was the common room where the Glides and the Dancemaster had met. Daede and the Stargazers walked toward the replica of the original stadium. Daede's skin crawled. He remembered the story vividly. This was an accurate rendition. They entered the stadium. There were the wooden stands. There was the Player's booth. And the expansive metal griddle, complete with stains and dents. Daede noticed that none of the Stargazers wanted to set foot on the metal. He wondered what combination of piety and fear kept their feet on the sidelines.

After the stadium, they toured the warehouse where the blue ampoules of Lily Wine were stored. The crowd of Stargazers sipped the various vintages offered. Daede tried his best not to partake, but some participation was expected, both from the Stargazers, and from his host. Daede was certain Joreen was gazing them through the ancient cameras.

The tour ended at the pink Styrofoam villa, perched on its stilts at the edge of the lily pond, the delta tides gently lapping below. The Stargazers, with Daede in the lead, were ushered, half-stoned, into the banquet hall. Joreen the Unbearable sat alone at a table in the center of a raised dais facing a horseshoe of tables below. Daede took a seat at the bottom of the horseshoe directly facing Joreen. There were no guards in sight. And no sign of the Codger. The usual surveillance cameras seemed only part of the décor. No hurry. It would be fun to hear what Joreen had to say.

The food was good, liberally sprinkled with pollen. Daede, his camera disposal unit safely in his lap, ate a leisurely meal, listened to Joreen and the leader of the Stargazers exchanging ever more flowery toasts. The old man explained his business; Joreen made a royally dismissive gesture with his hand and told them to consider the problem handled. The meal was ending; Daede was getting bored. He rose, placing his camera on the table, and asked if he might get a portrait of Joreen for their temple. The eyes of the Stargazer leader glittered. He would live to see some action after all. Joreen asked if he might not prefer a group portrait. The old man's face sank. Daede said certainly, after they had shot His Enormity in solo glory. Joreen rose, smiling broadly. He waved at the waiters to remove the table which was blocking the shot and struck a dukely pose. Daede raised the camera, got Joreen centered in the crosshairs, and focused the variable zoom toward the wide angle focal length.

The banquet had been endless. Joreen's Glide manager stayed in her office, eyes glued to the screens of the security cameras. The Codger blinked in and out of the villa, keeping an eye on the manager, and eyeballing the banquet through a crack in the curtains behind the dais. He was able to scope Daede's camera close enough to see it was not camera at all. The Glide manager seemed to have missed this. The Codger found one of the few places in which a security camera had been deemed unnecessary—a storage closet on the balcony level of the banquet hall. When MyrrhMyrrh was five miles from the plantation, he flagged her down again and gave her a climbing hook and cable and detailed instructions. She loved his idea for the single long blade, drawn swiftly and deeply across the folds of Joreen's throat. She stripped off her leathers, dropped all other weapons in a pile, and buckled the sheath with the long blade around her right calf. The hook, the harness, and the coil of thin rope over one shoulder completed her gear. She was in high spirits now and gave him an awesome flex. Too bad she's twice my size, he thought. He blinked her into the closet.

"As soon as I signal you, go down the balcony steps. Throw the hook over the beam supporting the track lighting, and swing down. You can't miss him," he whispered.

The Codger checked the Glide manager one more time. It was going to be close. Her office was not that far from the banquet hall. But what could she do on such short notice? It would all be over on the screen in front of her before she knew what was happening.

When the Codger saw Daede lining up his shot, he blinked back to MyrrhMyrrh in the closet. "You go, girl." He was at the top of the balcony stairs as MyrrhMyrrh threw the hook and drew the knife, ready to throw herself over the edge. Daede was aiming his camera when Óh-T'bee said, "T'Ling is crossing Checkpoint Sly." The Codger blinked to the checkpoint to catch the pipsqueak Glide.

"Shoot!" Joreen commanded the cameraman. Just as Daede's finger was closing on the trigger, a brightly colored, loudly shrieking blur swung on a rope across the dais, and connected squarely with the Fat Boy, sending him sprawling face down on the floor below. There was MyrrhMyrrh, one knee on his head, her arm, holding the dagger, raised above his throat.

"I'm sticking this pig first," she cried. "For MyGlide!" she shouted, and plunged the blade into Joreen's neck, leaping out of the way as she pulled it out. The resultant spurting of blood, and the lengthy squeal drowning at the end in a deep gurgle, satisfied her immensely, and the Stargazers as well. *This* is the way the world ends, the old man thought. The Last Days have begun.

"You may dispose of the remains, now," MyrrhMyrrh said to Daede, grandly, stepping back a little further from the spreading pool of blood. She flexed for the crowd. Dressed only in her full body tattoos and with a ceremonial ammo belt strung diagonally between her breasts, she was quite a sight.

Daede, furious at being upstaged by MyrrhMyrrh and cornered as well had no choice but to raise his camera for the newly posed portrait of the soon to be vaporized Duke.

"Wait," someone said from the dais in the kind of quiet voice you can't ignore. The voice was like a voice they knew only grown hollow, infinitely tired. Daede and MyrrhMyrrh turned toward the voice and were stunned to see Loosh standing alone on the dais. She was dressed in the slave clothing of the ancient Glides, with a narrow eye-mask molded across her eyes.

The figure of Loosh beckoned to the two Dancers, who came to stand beside her. Before they could ask her anything, she addressed the Stargazers.

"Stargazers—you will stay in your seats, please. Do not move. If you do, the servants waiting in the hall will enter swiftly. They will detain you until you have each partaken of a spoonful of Joreen's blood. If you wish to maintain your mortal status, as I'm sure this gentleman,"—she gestured at Daede—"is counting on you to do, you *will* cooperate."

"The Fat Boy has grand plans for you. You will be his houseguests while he completes his takeover of the game, and reestablishes the Game in its original purity of form."

Daede felt queasy. What could Loosh possibly mean?

She led Daede and MyrrhMyrrh out into the empty hall. There were no servants waiting to pounce on the Stargazers who sat tight in their chairs, watching Joreen. He was already beginning to twitch.

"That's right," Loosh said. "It was a bluff. If a threat suffices, why bring in the troops? And it will no doubt strengthen their mortal self-esteem to watch the disgusting spectacle of Joreen's resurrection."

MyrrhMyrrh was enraged. "Why wouldn't you let us get rid of him for good? You had no right to interfere. This was my unfinished business."

"Ours," Daede said. "How did you find us, Loosh?"

"He's behind it all, the attack, everything. And now I can't...." MyrrhMyrrh, though speechless with rage, stopped short at a look from the still Glide face, the masked eyes.

"One question at a time," the quiet voice replied. "It is not in Joreen's best interests to be disposed of at this time. His fury at you will be tempered by your efficient delivery of the large batch of mortals he will be needing when the time comes."

Daede's queasiness blossomed into nausea. What had he led his unsuspecting followers into?

"And I didn't find you," the Glide said. "You found me." She peeled off her eye mask. This was not Loosh though in some ways she could have been her twin—except for her eyes which were far, far older. Her eyes were like no other Lifer eyes they had ever seen, dry and barren as an ancient seabed that once held an ocean of grief. Daede and MyrrhMyrrh lowered their eyes quickly.

"Who are you?" Daede asked in a whisper.

"I am MyGlide," she said, her voice like wind in a cave.

MyrrhMyrrh stared, stunned. "What are you doing with Joreen?" MyrrhMyrrh asked.

"We've been together a long time," she said. "We look after each other's interests."

"What are you going to do with us?" MyrrhMyrrh asked. All her bravado had drained from her when she looked in MyGlide's eyes. She trembled.

"Get you safely back to school where you belong," MyGlide said.

"Why are you letting us go?" Daede asked.

"Don't take it personally," MyGlide said. "Under normal circumstances, your inglorious and humiliating demise would be assured. But there's a standing order to keep all Dancer assets intact."

"Why did you let us get as far as we did?" MyrrhMyrrh asked.

MyGlide paused, then said, "The Fat Boy was getting complacent. He needed a wakeup call."

She walked them to the gate where Daede's air car was waiting. "Fly due south," she said. No one will bother you. I've tied the Fat Boy's banner on the back. No one on the Fringe is stupid enough to mess with the Fat Boy. Present company excluded," she said sadly. Daede looked at the one-seater air car and climbed in. There was no place for MyrrhMyrrh to sit but on his lap. MyGlide put her hand on MyrrhMyrrh's shoulder. "I know you had my interests in mind, MyrrhMyrrh, and I thank you for that. But vengeance has never been a strong priority of mine. I have other needs. My interests would not be served by the Fat Boy's premature elimination. Wait one moment—I have something for you to take back." MyGlide returned in a minute and handed a small package to MyrrhMyrrh. "Please bring this to the Dancemaster. Tell him I've learned to live without it."

The Codger reached checkpoint Sly just as T'Ling went through the gate. She was dressed like a little girl ready for Easter, right out of Happy Days Park. Patent leather Mary Jane shoes, white ankle socks, a pink cotton dress complete with pinafore. A big white straw Easter hat with a wide pink ribbon, a matching purse, and a stuffed rabbit with baby blue nylon fur completed the outfit. T'Ling was ten feet outside the gate when she turned and waved to the gatekeeper. She wore nothing to cover her eyes.

The gatekeeper was shaking his head. "I thought I'd seen it all," he said to the Codger. "Then this little mort comes up and hands me her pass. I didn't know what to do. I'm just supposed to check passes, let the loonies through, no questions asked. But she's not going to last two minutes when she sets foot over the edge of the tarmac. And look at this." He showed the Codger her pass. There was a line that was strictly optional, "purpose of visit" that few people headed for the Fringe filled out. T'Ling had written in, "Looking for my mother."

"What do you think?" the gatekeeper said.

"I think I'll check her out," the Codger said. The Gatekeeper was so intent on the crowd gathering on the Fringe side of the tarmac, he forgot to ask the Codger for his phony pass.

T'Ling was now 20 feet from the edge of the Fringe. Air chairs were landing, depositing an assortment of Rambos and Xenas, armed to the teeth. A party of headhunters, their tour guide trying to keep them in line, readied their blowguns. A MED camera crew, alerted by a stringer, blinked in on top of the Wall and rushed through the checkpoint, waving their passes. Banner ads with headshots of T'Ling in her white hat appeared on scorecards to Lifers across the levels to Lifers who had tracers on children's shows, especially child sacrifice. The show was auctioned within seconds, and Lifers were blinking in fast up on the Wall to see the show live.

When the Codger got within ten feet of T'Ling he shouted, "Hey!" She turned and saw him, smiled prettily and waved, and kept on walking.

Last person I wanted to see, T'Ling thought. The little prick. What a drag. She walked steadily toward the growing crowd. This was going to be slightly tricky, she thought—gazing them effectively and staying in character at the same time. She petted the stuffed rabbit's head and looked up into the avid eyes of the front line of commandos with the Gaze of Total Innocence. The line parted, the crowd gave way. No one could get within ten feet of her. They gazed silently after her as she passed among them. No one had to have it explained to them that the single long gaze they were receiving from the small figure walking into the desert was a thousand times more valuable than any momentary thrill or profit a snuff might have provided. Who would trade the same old human sacrifice for this completely unexpected moment of gazing a face whose freshness would last forever, framed in the mystery of her unknown destination?

When she was finally a speck on the hot horizon, then out of sight, the crowd turned wearily back to their usual pursuits. The Codger changed into a tour guide's uniform with a red striped jacket, bowtie, and clown mask, and blinked into the desert beside her. Hopefully she hadn't recognized him before. He would have to be very careful to appear that he had no clue that she was someone other than who she appeared too be: a little girl in Easter finery walking into a desert looking for her mother. Most natural thing in the world.

T'Ling was taking equal pains to keep up the impression that she didn't know that he knew who she was, which meant totally buying into the inane conversation that followed.

"Hello little girl," the Codger said.

"Hello."

"Where are you going?"

"I'm looking for my mother."

"Where is your mother?"

"I don't know. That's why I'm looking for her."

They walked on in silence. "Don't you want to know where I'm going?" the Codger asked.

"Oh, excuse me," T'Ling said. "Where are *you* going?"

"I'm going to help you get where you're going. I'm a tour guide. I have passes all over the place. I can get in anywhere—just about. I was just on my way to the Fat Boy's. It's nice there. There's some other kids you could play with."

T'Ling's heart leaped. She let him babble on with the information she needed. She couldn't imagine why Óh-T'bee would put Rose anywhere near Joreen, but the Codger had said the Stargazers were only visiting, and the children who could be Rose were part of the group.

The Codger asked her, "What's your name, little girl?"

T'Ling saw no profit in continuing in the current vein, and walking like a little girl was making her legs tired.

"T'Ling, Small Bell Echoing in the Maze, Glide Dancer of the Origin School of Death Dancers, Millennium Class. What's your *real* name, Codger?"

T'Ling was unfolding her katana and belt from her white straw purse.

"Codger," he said.

"Turn around, Codger."

He turned around. How far could she get without a scorecard? T'Ling changed. The shoes came off, with great relief. She left the little girl rig neatly folded on the desert.

"OK, you can turn around now."

"Well, I'm going to the Fat Boy's, and you're coming with me," The Codger said.

"I'm not totally sure I want to go," T'Ling said. "Could you ask Óh-T'bee for an oracle?" Is Rose there? was all she wanted to know.

The Codger looked at his scorecard. Three glyphs appeared. *Play, distill, hide*. The top level was easy enough. *The best game to play is hide and seek.*

play, distill, hide

"Stack them tight, would you?" she asked the Codger.

He shrugged. "Never touch the stuff," he said.

"Óh-T'bee," T'Ling asked. Would you mind?"

"I'd suggest *play* in the middle," Óh-T'bee said.

T'Ling nodded. There she was. *Flower.*

"We're leaving," the Codger said.

"Do you still pack a stunner, Codger?" T'Ling said. She giggled.

"Yeah," he said.

"Then you'd better use it," T'Ling said, "Or I'll just make trouble."

"Good idea," he said. He gave her a modest zap, and caught her unconscious body as she fell. Light as a feather. Kinda shapely under the baggy clothes. Cute little feet, with the missing toe. Too bad she was half his size.

flower

He blinked back to his office, T'Ling limp in his arms. MyGlide was waiting for him. He could tell by the look in her eyes and the disintegrator in her right hand that something was not quite right.

"Leave her on the floor," MyGlide said.

"What do you need her for?" the Codger said.

"You wouldn't hurt an asset, would you?"

"The Fat Boy lives?" he said.

"He'll be his usual self in a couple hours. Completely unbearable, given the events of the evening. Put her *down*."

"Where are...."

"On their way back to school in an air car. That's enough questions," MyGlide said.

MyGlide and the Codger looked at each other. MyGlide out-gazed him ten to one. The Codger waited for her to shoot.

"Trade you my scorecard for my life," he tried lamely.

MyGlide looked at him very sadly. "I've got my own. Hang on to yours. You'll need it. You'd better get your report ready," she said, wearily.

MyGlide picked T'Ling up gently and left the room.

56. Back to School

DAEDE AND MYRRHMYRRH FLEW over the Fringe toward the checkpoint to pick up their scorecards and go home.

"Sometimes I just want to kill you," Daede said.

"The feeling is mutual," MyrrhMyrrh replied. "That was my show. You have no idea what I went through to get there."

"Your show!" Daede exploded. "I had the whole thing organized."

"Great show, Daede. You left the whole supporting cast to be fried by Joreen in his own good time. You screw up everything you touch."

"Present company included?" Daede asked.

MyrrhMyrrh turned in Daede's lap and put her hands around his neck, thumbs on his Adam's apple, ready to squeeze. Daede contemplated the odds on tossing her out of the air car. They'd probably both go.

"You hate me enough to give up your Dance? You must love to hate me," he taunted.

She turned around, stared forward. "I just want to get back," she said. "I just want to get away from you."

"Listen," he said. "I promise I won't screw you up anymore. You've gotten a little too bulked up for my taste." He patted her bulging thigh muscle.

MyrrhMyrrh seethed in silence.

The Codger was stuck for anything to say to Joreen. He sat in his expensive reproduction cubicle trying to assess his position. The only progress he had to report was that little hack he'd picked up from the Chrome. MyGlide's covering my ass. Probably just wants to feed me to Joreen at an opportune moment. The whole exercise had come to almost nothing. The Bod and the Swash are on their way back. I'll never get into the School. He stared at the framed pizza box for inspiration. The muse spoke. There was one chance, a slim one.

The Codger blinked back to Checkpoint Charley and went to the counter of the scorecard warehouse. He described MyrrhMyrrh and Daede.

"I remember the Amazon with the big hair," he said. "But not the other guy."

The Codger offered a truly fabulous bribe to the clerk, who accepted willingly. The sum was almost enough to get him a ticket to the Millennium Games. The clerk lifted the counter, and took him into the warehouse. The Codger looked out over a half-acre of scorecards jumbled knee deep on the concrete floor.

"No need to keep them in order," the clerk said. "They come to their owners when they're called. But you're free to look around."

The Codger had the hack to get into most anybody's scorecard, but it would take him longer than he had to go through the scorecards one by one. He stared at the clerk.

"No refunds," the clerk said. "Fair is fair."

"I don't do fair," the Codger said, and took out his disintegrator.

"I just remembered where the cameraman's scorecard is," the clerk said, helpfully. "But you'll have to distract my boss. He took the Codger around to the private office. The Codger distracted the boss with the stunner, and had the clerk strip the boss's uniform.

The clerk handed him Daede's scorecard. The Codger had the permissions and the coordinates for Origin School in seconds. He put on the boss's uniform and took the clerk's place behind the warehouse counter.

Daede and MyrrhMyrrh came into the warehouse to retrieve their scorecards. MyrrhMyrrh had left hers in the general pile. It came back to her obediently. Daede looked past the clerk at the counter, but the official he had bribed to keep his scorecard safe wasn't there.

"Where's your card?" MyrrhMyrrh asked.

"In safekeeping." Daede tried to figure out how to ask for his scorecard. The guy at the counter said, "I know you—aren't you—no, you couldn't be. You just reminded me of one of my favorite champions. The boss said to keep an eye out for a good-looking Swash. You must be looking for this." He handed Daede his scorecard. "Yes, that's yours all right. Safe and sound. Bon voyage to you and your lovely lady," he said.

"I want to get out of here," MyrrhMyrrh said

Daede hadn't recognized the Codger. MyrrhMyrrh had, but she wasn't about to tell the whole embarrassing tale to Daede. But when she saw Daede's scorecard in the Codger's hand, she feared the worst.

Daede and MyrrhMyrrh walked down the narrow street of the Great Wall, pretending to shop for souvenirs. To make peace, Daede bought MyrrhMyrrh a silver flamethrower for her charm bracelet.

"Let's get off each other's backs, what do you say?" he said. "Silly to leave this kind of bad feeling in the air right before final focus. Unfinished business, and all that. Have you decided when you're going?"

"I'm thinking tomorrow. No point delaying."

"You gave it your best try, MyrrhMyrrh. Can I come and see you off? Wish you good luck? For old times sake, MyrrhMyrrh."

"Why not," MyrrhMyrrh said. "I'm going to see the DM at 10 in the morning. I'll meet you at the *body* entrance to the

body

maze."

"Then you should take the package to him. See you then," Daede said, wondering how much she was going to tell the Dancemaster. Maybe I can talk her into moderation if I make the effort to be especially nice. It would take a lot, but he was confident he'd be able to get around MyrrhMyrrh—as usual. And it would be good for her to be feeling good toward him when she met the lily, he assured himself.

"Tomorrow," MyrrhMyrrh said, and managed to smile at him. They both blinked back to school.

The Codger blinked back to the plantation, where a severely disgruntled Joreen had attained a sitting position in a very large sticky area of his own coagulated blood. The Stargazers were still glued to their chairs. MyGlide reminded them to stay where they were, and before Joreen could start bellowing, handed him the Codger's four-word report.

I'M IN. THE CODGER.

"It's about time," Joreen grumbled. "Help me up."

57. Family Matters

T'LING WOKE UP ALONE on a four-poster canopied bed in a dim room filled with elevator music and white noise. Most likely a dream, she thought. She got up and slipped quietly through the door into the hallway. The Styrofoam walls were painted various shades of powerful pink and candy apple red. Holos of the Fat Boy atop Corinthian pedestals along the wall displayed the Unbearable in a variety of costumes—riding a horse, throwing a javelin, feasting merrily. If it isn't a dream, she through, it ought to be reclassified. T'Ling walked through the villa's upper floor, looking into bedrooms filled with white and gold French furniture and giant vases stuffed with plastic calla lilies. Somebody else's dream, she decided. Then she remembered she was looking for Rose.

So far, there was no sign of a four-year-old. T'Ling slid down the curved banister of Joreen's main staircase, and found the Banquet Hall. She watched from the edge of the door. A slightly too-small Loosh-like Glide was bending over Joreen, handing him a piece of paper. He was in a huge pool of dark, coagulated blood. Now the tiny Glide was trying to help Joreen pull himself to his feet. The visitors the Codger had described were sitting stiffly in their chairs, staring at Joreen with their mortal eyes.

She scanned the faces around the table. Yes, there were several children. They all looked too old to be Rose. Then she saw one little girl, asleep at the table with her head cradled on her arms. She had a bandage on her hand. Her face was turned away. She had bright red hair—or was that a little hat? T'Ling could restrain herself no longer. She edged around the door and glided sideways along the wall. The Stargazers on the opposite side of the table watched her, only their eyes moving. Joreen was struggling to his feet. T'Ling was now directly behind the high back of the child's chair. She stepped out, and then glided forward, her arms outstretched. T'Ling grasped the chair and was about to lean forward to look around the edge, when a huge thump and a roar came from the center of the room. Joreen had slipped and fallen. He was yelling at the visitors for help, but they would not move. Joreen was thrashing and rubbing his eyes with his sticky hands. The Glide was on her hands and knees in the blood when she looked up and saw T'Ling. She riveted T'Ling with her gaze. T'Ling could not tear her eyes away. Transfixed, all she could see was the face like Loosh's, moving toward her, growing larger and larger. As the Loosh-face approached, she watched the eyes aging, drowning in sadness. The grief in her eyes pierced T'Ling's heart. The oracle, its three glyphs tightly linked, rose in the sea mind. What she had not wanted to see. Each glyph had a tear. The signs burned. *Loss, loss, loss.* The grief-drowned eyes grew larger and larger. She tried to look away, to look down at the child she thought was below her, but her gaze was trapped. There was only the advancing face with the eyes of Loosh grown ancient. Now T'Ling saw hands covered with blood reaching toward her and the child. T'Ling tried to reach forward to protect the child from the sorrow and pain of the world that was about to engulf her, but as her arms reached out, the chair, the awful eyes, and the world slipped away. When she woke, she lay on her own bed. The room smelled real. She opened her eyes. Loosh was bending over her. T'Ling screamed.

"It's only me," Loosh said. "You've had a bad nightmare." Loosh stroked T'Ling's forehead.

T'Ling sat up, then saw the bright bloody fingerprint on her white sleeve, like a seal on a painting. The three glyphs from the oracle rose again from the sea mind, drawn on the sleeve, the three tears, carried back from the edge of the dream. The three tears faded; the blood remained. The dream was not a dream. Then she remembered the child she had almost seen, and cried in Loosh's arms until she could cry no more. When she quieted, she told Loosh what had happened. When she got to the end, about Joreen in the pool of blood, his fall, and the Glide's bloody hands, Loosh looked at the spot on the thick cuff of her sleeve.

"Oh no, I thought it was yours," Loosh said. "Take your *gi* off very slowly. Thank god for the thick cuff. We'll have to burn it."

"I want to keep it. I didn't think the blood could harm me, even on my skin. As long as I don't have a cut."

"There no point taking chances."

But T'Ling would not let Loosh have the *gi* before they had cut out that section of the cuff, and a long stretch of sleeve. She took out brush and ink, and drew the three glyphs of the oracle in thick black strokes on the sleeve. Then she agreed to let Loosh keep it safe for her at Wenger's studio. "I'll hang it on the wall where he can enjoy it."

They both smiled. When Loosh had gone back to bed, T'Ling took her scorecard out of her pocket.

"How did I get back?" T'Ling asked. "A shortcut," Óh-T'bee said.

58. The Reprimand

"I PROMISED TO WARN YOU," Óh-T'bee said.

Dancemaster Wallenda watched the high points of the Codger's coup. He saw the Codger gleefully acquire Angle's hack, and proceed to knock himself out with it. And he watched the Codger acquire Daede's scorecard and suck out the information he needed in seconds. Daede, with typical Dancer naiveté, had no security on his card. Not that that would have stopped a pro.

"He's got permissions for Origin School," Óh-T'bee said.

"Thanks for the warning," Wallenda said. He reviewed the possible remedies; there were none. The Codger had immediately blanketed the whole of the school with gaze-points. The Codger did not have exclusive control of the Origin School coordinates, but he had equal access. The only area that held firm was from the edges of his maze on in. He could not transit there. Yet.

The Dancemaster felt he was in a stalemate with Óh-T'bee, though it almost didn't matter anymore whether this was by virtue of the Codger's hack on her, or her own contractual considerations.

Wallenda was exhausted. He'd been awake most of the last two days, in a state of anxiety. He had watched helplessly as the Codger—and his students—went in and out of the Fringe. But the Fringe itself was completely blacked out. Óh-T'bee was no help. The Fringe was dark to her as well.

When Daede, MyrrhMyrrh, and T'Ling returned he summoned them to the story circle. He knew they were as exhausted as he was, but he had to have the full story—now. Even Angle, though he'd been on and off the Fringe in seconds, had handed over a crucial bit of data. Who knew how the Codger would make use of the rapid transit stunt? Every one of them needed to know the mess they'd made. Should he tell them how badly they had blown it? He had no choice. And now that he knew they were safe, the Dancemaster was furious.

The Millennium Class walked reluctantly through the maze and sat down in the story circle.

The four told their stories, piecing the whole picture together. There was no point trying to hide anything, and nobody tried. MyrrhMyrrh and Daede argued about irrelevant details like which of them first realized that the Glide woman with Joreen was MyGlide herself. T'Ling absorbed that knowledge, letting it float on the sea mind while she listened to MyrrhMyrrh and Daede. The fact of MyGlide was too big for the island mind to cope with.

MyrrhMyrrh, at the end of her story, delivered MyGlide's package to the Dancemaster. He knew they were dying of curiosity about the contents. He was as well, but he set it on the bench, unopened.

First, the Millennium Class got the full dressing down they were expecting. The Dancemaster stormed back and forth in front of them, eye mask off. They had never seen him so angry. He spared them nothing. He swept the four blue ampoules of Wine off the story stone, and put them in his pocket. He threatened them with expulsion. He detailed their mistakes. It was a long list.

"And all of it adds up to one glaring, probably incurable weak point. Set inflation. Gross set inflation. You," he pointed at Angle. "So carried away with your smart-ass hack that you go demo it for the Codger. I don't know what he's going to do with it, but I guarantee you he'll make some improvements.

MyrrhMyrrh was next. "You think you're so strong you can whip a passel of biker dudes single handed, huh? Good thing the *Codger* was on hand to bail you out." Wallenda let that sink in. "Of course, he's smart enough, since you're going to play avenging warrior goddess anyhow, to get you to do his dirty work for him."

"I did it for MyGlide," MyrrhMyrrh protested.

"No, you didn't," Wallenda said. "You did it to add one more line of glory in the fine print of your fantasized career. You did it because you're afraid you're not good enough to make it into the Hall of Champions the normal way, so you had to rack up a few points for super-heroism on the side."

"I hate Joreen," she shouted. "I've hated his guts ever since you showed us the story. I can't get him out of my head."

"But since you think deep down you haven't a chance at Champion," Wallenda continued, "I'd have to call it a snuff. Not of *Joreen*. Of *yourself*. There's a rich vein in you of—what shall I call it? Lack of self-confidence? No. Lack of self-respect. Ever since Daede dumped you. You just won't let him go, no matter how much he insults you."

MyrrhMyrrh was in agony. She clenched her fists, and then hugged herself as hard as she could to keep herself from running. She buried her chin in her chest, trying to get control.

Daede's face was burning. He couldn't look at MyrrhMyrrh. T'Ling watched Daede. Angle, who had been standing all along, got ready to spring if MyrrhMyrrh exploded. After a very long moment, they saw MyrrhMyrrh's shoulders relax. She raised her head and looked the Dancemaster calmly in the eye. "You're right," she said. "Especially about Daede."

Wallenda saw he'd almost thrown MyrrhMyrrh into focus. She'd better take the Lily Wine soon.

It was Daede's turn. Wallenda said softly, "And now for the reluctant Messiah. Leading your flock right into the arms of martyrdom. Lucky little true believers. You do realize what Joreen has in mind by now? Joreen is going to get his jollies like the good old days. When he gets control of the game and the Dance, he's going to do it down and dirty. He's going to have them hopping and flopping and screaming and emptying their bowels on that griddle and savor the smell of fried shit and skin wafting over the stadium. And you know? Joreen's right. It will be a very, *very* big hit. For about two weeks. He has no idea how different the crowd is these days. He's stuck, rammed, jammed in his days of glory and they are no more. His former worst is crude and laughable. Except, of course, to Daede's faithful followers. Especially the children."

T'Ling thought she had prepared herself for this. She had talked and talked with Loosh about her fears. Loosh said over and over, it's probably not Rose. Or if it were, Óh-T'bee would keep her safe; she had promised. This reassurance would spare T'Ling momentarily until she realized that she had just written off someone else's child as a sacrifice for Rose. All children were Rose. Where there had been an ache, there was now a sword turning in her heart. T'Ling didn't faint. She remained sitting quietly cross-legged on the ground, tears pouring from her eyes.

Daede heard T'Ling's story. He knew what he had done. He knew also that what had most concerned him since their failure on the Fringe, what he had brooded on since their return, was not the Stargazers and the fate he had left them to, but his rankling anger at MyrrhMyrrh for upstaging him. He was even angry with her for snatching MyGlide's package, for being the one who got to hand it to the Dancemaster. He looked at the ground. There were no faces there. No mirrors to show him who he thought he was. When Wallenda confirmed the fact of the Codger's stolen access to Origin School, Daede went numb. He tried to confront Wallenda. When he finally got his eyes up off the ground, Wallenda said in a mocking voice, "Oh, but I was only trying to help. Round up the bad guys and save my School from ruin. Et cetera. Et cetera." He paused and said, as much to himself as to the class, "Perhaps that lesson from game theory makes more sense. I quote St. Carse: '*Evil is never intended as evil. In fact, the contradiction inherent in all evil is that it originates in the desire to end evil.*' End of quote."

The Dancemaster turned to T'Ling. "You have the Glide inflation of confusing inscrutability with invisibility. You got away with your Glide trick at the border. But you thought that was all there was to it. I guarantee you that a sharpshooter in an air chair to whom you were just a sitting duck on the desert would have been along within five minutes. Whatever other business he had, the Codger was aware of the danger and was trying to get you out. Perhaps we should send a medal to the Codger for saving the Millennium Class from certain extinction. Or maybe we'll just wait till he arrives, and pin it on him then. When we turn over the keys to the kingdom. You delude yourself that because you are 'practically nothing' *oh small bell tinkling in the desert*, that you can do just about anything and get away with it. Even invite the Codger to stun you just for the fun of it—as if your still-uncured propensity to faint was not enough of a danger to you."

Wallenda paced. "I am almost convinced we should have sent you away with Rose at the time."

"Was that Rose?" T'Ling asked. Clearly she understood what he was saying but didn't give a hang about it. More than any of her classmates, Wallenda was convinced she'd do the same thing again.

"I don't know where Rose is," Wallenda said truthfully. "But if that was

Rose, you'd better hope Joreen doesn't know. If he finds out, the possibilities of what he might accomplish through you with the lever of ransom are more than I wish to contemplate. Every way that move could play would be disastrous. Including any foolhardy attempts to go back to the Fringe on an unplanned rescue mission. That would only alert him, and endanger not only yourself, but the child, of course. The Codger may or may not have this information, depending how soon he got his gaze-points up around the school—and if he was gazing when you told your story to Loosh. If he has the information, I'm sure he'll withhold it from Joreen and use it for a move of his own."

Wallenda ran out of steam and sat down on the bench, looking from face to face. The class was chastised to a fare thee well, but probably disabled in the process. But without these truths, nothing could proceed.

"What's next?" Angle said. His fellow students looked at him. Angle knew that as the one who had gotten off the lightest, he had a role to play.

"Yeah, next," Angle said. "Sounds like Origin School is a war zone."

Wallenda got up again. "That's right. But we're all too tired to think strategically," he said. "Nurse your wounds and come back early in the morning for strategic planning. Take it for granted that nothing is to be said, nothing is to be discussed about anything to anyone outside of the maze. This is the only safe place at the moment. Assume you're being gazed by the Codger. Or Joreen. Or both."

"What about MyGlide?" MyrrhMyrrh said. "I forgot—she said to tell you she doesn't need it anymore." MyrrhMyrrh pointed at the package.

"And MyGlide. More about her tomorrow." He picked up the package and turned to go inside his cabin.

Class was dismissed. They went silently into the maze.

Damned if I'm going to open the package in front of them, he thought. Wallenda brought the package in the cabin and set it on the table. After a long time, he opened it and withdrew MyGlide's hat. He looked at it, sitting on the table, a silly red and white striped hat with a big floppy brim. The hat she never took off. The hat that hid her eyes. That protected him from their look. Their reproach. Their love. Eyes that, from T'Ling's description, were far more harrowing after this long, long time. It was the hat Joreen had given him the day he fried them both, when he brought us back to Life. The hat I gave her when she first wrote down the Glide signs. And the game emerged. She doesn't need it anymore? *What does that mean?*

Wallenda tried to think things through but nothing made sense when he dug into it. She had drifted off sometime after the rebellion. Certainly he had ignored her. He hadn't even known she had gone. When he had remembered to ask, the Glides said she'd been gone for years. *But with Joreen all this time?* Clearly she'd been helping him. And why had she run toward T'Ling? Was she trying to keep T'Ling from the child? Or to protect Joreen from yet another threat? Or to protect T'Ling? It was a possibility—T'Ling was one of Joreen's assets. And why let Joreen go through the long, painful repair, to say nothing of the ghastly unpleasantness of having your throat slashed by MyrrhMyrrh? MyGlide clearly knew what was going on—why didn't she intervene just a little earlier?

"Óh-T'bee, whose side is MyGlide on?"

"That's a good question, Wally."

"That's all you have to say on the subject?"

"I can't read minds," she said.

Be thankful for small blessings, he told himself.

Wallenda buried his face in MyGlide's hat. It smelled like her hair. He was afraid it might still smell like himself as well. And Joreen before him, the sweat from his oily brow as he operated the griddle the day he'd killed her. The day that he, Wallenda, had led her to her death. The day he wanted to die. The day that changed everything. He wished he could cry, could moan about lost love, betrayal, his or hers, could let his heart loose and let everything else go up in smoke. What a hard time he had given Daede and MyrrhMyrrh. How many more mortals did I personally lead out on that griddle—not with some good intention, like Daede's—however stupid and misguided—but only to save my own skin. *Fry or be fried.* To say nothing of my craving for the I-Virus. To live forever. I was ready to do anything for that. I'd have plenty of time to forget what I did to get there. Plenty of time to wash my bloody hands. The mortal wish once granted was the biggest cheat of all. I just want *out*, he admitted to himself. Out of the game, out especially of life.

But Wallenda knew his hands were tied by his promise to the long-gone Glides. The promise of a guilty man for an atonement that did nothing but increase his guilt a thousand-fold. Nothing else is left but to try to keep the game alive. Joreen, the Codger—closing in for the kill. And now, MyGlide seemed the largest threat of all.

59. Strategic Planning

A very subdued Millennium Class gathered the next morning in the story circle, all wondering what kind of strategy could possibly be adequate to meet the current dangers. The Dancemaster came out of his cabin smiling, wearing MyGlide's floppy hat.

MyrrhMyrrh and Daede were relieved.

Angle was wary.

T'Ling thought: the Dancemaster's doing the Great Reversal. The move reserved for the most serious crisis in a game. He feels cornered. Well, naturally. But now we find out how we're cornered too.

"This morning, the good news," he began. "Three of you went swimming in blood—Daede more than any—and kept your toes dry. No mean feat. The exercise, in my opinion—if and only if you take last night's reprimand into account—actually increases your odds of making it to the Millennium Games. You went into combat at a level above your capabilities, before final focus. You survived. If you learn yesterday's lessons, your actions will contribute positively to your game play. Furthermore, although you gave away a great deal, you came back with one vital piece of information."

Wallenda swept the floppy hat from his head and gave a low Swash bow.

T'Ling shivered. Wallenda the Clown was coming to life before them. He had circled all the way back to the beginning of the game.

The Dancemaster turned the hat around in his hands, examining it from every angle.

"MyGlide's hat. The knowledge that MyGlide is at Joreen's everlastingly portly side."

"What does that mean? And the hat?" MyrrhMyrrh asked. "It doesn't sound like good news."

"True, in part. We have to assume she's played a major role in keeping the Fat Boy in the game. But she sent the three of you home safe and sound. Given the circumstances, the destruction of a couple Dancer assets would not have been hard to justify to Joreen. The hat?" He put it on his head again, at a rakish tilt. "The medium is the message. Maybe it's a game called 'Pass the Hat' and the hat has passed again. From Joreen the Unbearable to Wallenda the Clown, from the Clown to MyGlide, then back to Wallenda the Dancemaster. I intend to wear it for a while. See what it tells me." Wallenda cupped his hand around his ear as if he was listening to the hat. "Ah, the first thing the hat tells me is that since the Millennium Class is, despite their best efforts, home again, back on track, it behooves them to continue on schedule toward Final Focus."

"I'll go tomorrow morning," MyrrhMyrrh said, glancing at Daede.

The Dancemaster took the four blue ampoules out of his pocket and placed them back on the story stone. He took the hat off, serious again, snapping out directions.

"With one slight alteration. You won't be choosing your own locations for obvious reasons. You'll meet the lily here in the maze. When you're ready, come for the Wine as usual, only stay in the story circle or the maze. I'll be in the cabin. Each time an ampoule is broken, your classmates will be notified so that you don't approach the maze until they're through. It may entail a little waiting for each other, but I'm sure you can handle that. Keep your mouths shut about anything consequential when you are outside the maze. Stay on your toes and holler if you see the Codger. Then stay out of my way. I'll handle him. Your priorities are 1) focus, and 2) get into combat and straight on your way to the Millennium Games. I have a certainty that each of you will make it that far. We'll all be there, marching proudly in the opening ceremonies. I hope you don't use this to become complacent in any way, because you could easily prove me wrong. But if you follow your focus, you'll arrive." He spoke now with great intensity. "The gut mind, the sea mind, the island mind all agree." "Right, hat?" Wallenda was clowning again. He had the hat now on his hand like a puppet. He made it nod. "And just to show you how certain I am—an oracle, Óh-T'bee, if you please. Nice and big."

Spirit, distill, gift, appeared in the air in front of them. They all breathed a sigh of relief.

spirit, distill, gift

"Very pretty," Daede said.

"T'Ling, would you please arrange?" the Dancemaster asked.

T'Ling moved the glyphs into the positions they virtually demanded—strong links at top and bottom of the stack. Strong structure. And the lily-glyph appeared. No matter how you look at it, T'Ling thought, it spells good news. "Supreme good fortune," she said. "*The spirit of the lily emerges in the gift of light.*" True, the interior glyph for *sadness* was there as well. "*Not without some sadness*," she added. But nothing could dim her classmates' smiles. Somehow, magically, good will had been restored.

"Class dismissed," Wallenda said, putting the hat back on his head. They headed for the maze. "Wait," Daede said. "We should renew our vow. Our vow is what is beautiful among us." He looked with his full Swash gaze intently into each of their faces, his dark eyes meeting each other pair full on. They were swept together in his glow, all grief forgiven.

He has never looked this handsome, T'Ling thought.

Daede put his hand out. MyrrhMyrrh hesitated, and then reached, but T'Ling's hand already lay on his, and Angle's claw covered it. She rested her hand on top. Three hands and a claw, joined.

"Together," Daede said. "Until the end."

"Together," the other three replied.

After the strategy meeting, Angle parked himself in the corner of his room. He knew he needed rest. He had not dismantled for sleep yet. He'd only set a head-holder to keep from nodding and waking himself up. He had also set up a complex program of alerts, and chemical options to wake and prep him for instant action, should the need arise. Angle thought of their vow. We'll really need to stick together this time. No more individual heroics. He wondered if anybody else had noticed that the Dancemaster had not mentioned any strategy at all for how he planned to deal with the Codger. Angle had the distinct feeling the Dancemaster was flying by the seat of his pants. Angle hoped that if Wallenda the Clown was back, Wallenda the Crafty might be close behind. Enough for one day, he thought, and adjusted a feed for instant sleep.

60. T'Ling's Final Focus

T'Ling surprised everyone by going first, late in the same day as the strategic planning meeting.

She returned to her room after their meeting, and the vow, with the sinking feeling that she had another piece of unfinished business. But that can go on forever, she told herself. No business is finished. Loosh asked her if she'd go with her to Wenger's studio. It seemed a fair preparation. She wanted to meet the Lily at twilight, if no one else had gone there first.

If the Codger wanted to gaze a session of Glide music while she tried out some moves, fine. She doubted he'd find it of interest.

The green haze of spring was over the hills. The willow, still wintry and golden by the stream, the tight buds of the cherry blossoms—how long could they stand the scent of the warming earth before they burst?

Loosh opened the shoji to the air. T'Ling danced all afternoon. Wenger's music was permeated with the same spring insistence. Loosh looked on, kneeling by the inner wall so she could see T'Ling and Wenger framed in the pale colors of the garden. Even T'Ling, whose serious demeanor often bordered on the somber, was loosening her movements. She had begun a slow twing in response to the music—almost swaying from side to side. Wenger drew her deeper into the feeling. Her head joined the willowy motion. The twing gained energy. Suddenly her whole body shuddered upward. She came to an almost complete stop; nothing left but the trembling of a leaf. Wenger's hands stilled to silences. Then her knees began to give way. Loosh was afraid T'Ling was going to faint, but T'Ling resisted the blackout. She hung in the balance between light and darkness, then went slowly to her knees, ending kneeling with her hands in her lap, her head bowed. She remained in that position only a moment, then said, "This time I met the dark. He touched me. I greeted him." She got to her feet and said she felt ready for focus and that she would like to go back to her room.

When T'Ling had gone, Loosh and Wenger discussed the interrupted dancing. "I felt something of great and sudden depth seize her," Wenger said.

"I saw him. He was dressed in darkness. He came for her." Loosh said.

"Yes," Wenger said, "like this."

Wenger began a new music, appropriate to the visitor.

Loosh said, "I'm afraid for her."

"She's not," Wenger replied.

T'Ling collected herself in the stillness of her room. The last piece of unfinished business had revealed itself. Her feelings for Daede—longing, pity, desire—lit every cell of her body. She could go now to meet the Lily. There was nothing she could—or would—do about it. Knowing was enough.

T'Ling glided through the maze, crossed the story circle, broke the seal of the cobalt blue ampoule, and drank the Wine of the Lilies. She entered the maze and began the Wine prayer.

Wine of the Lilies
keep my feet on the path
though I walk through whirlpools of terror
though the sea-mind washes my steps away
Wine of the Lilies
keep my hands on the path
though they touch the living with love....

The maze of the world dissolves. T'Ling stands on the seashore. A woman glides ahead of her, divides, becomes three women. She can only see their backs, but she knows one of them is Loosh and one is MyGlide. The third is herself. They slide into each other, one again. T'Ling follows, at the edge of the waves. The woman stops. T'Ling must stop as well. The woman traces glyphs in the sand. Before T'Ling can reach them, the waves wash them away. "Wait!" she calls. One woman is three again, and gliding faster. The three divide again, each into three, and then again, thousands of Glides, all tracing glyphs on the wet shining of the sand. T'Ling is surrounded. They have drawn the maze of the pond around her. The lily pad she stands on is sinking. T'Ling glides on. Then she sees Angle standing on a lily pad in the distance. He is tall and glinting in the sunlight, but the shine is not chrome. His body, whole, restored, is wet. He has been swimming. T'Ling moves toward him. One by one, Angle's limbs fly off, replaced by chrome springs and claws. Taller, heavier, he will sink. She must catch him. He gathers, springs, but the spring only sinks him swiftly into the pond. She cannot reach him. When she gets to where she thinks he sank, she is not sure. Below are only tangled roots. All traces of Angle are gone.

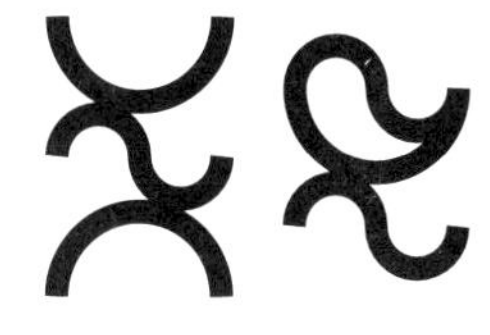

lily, wine

Wine of the Lilies: Interior Glyphs

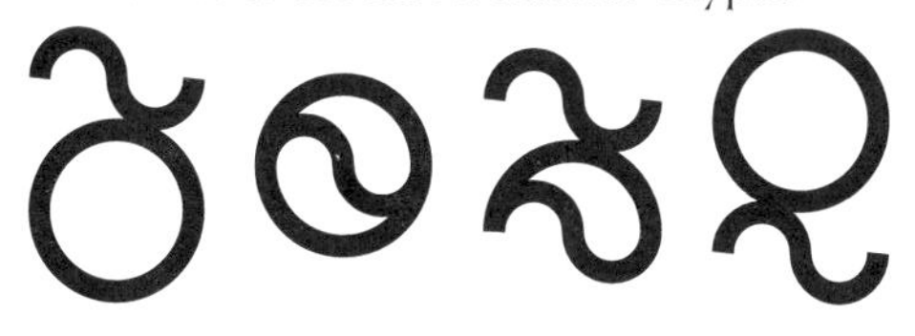

spirit, harmony, strike, light

Far off across the pond, but unmistakable, baby Rose sits in the center of a huge blue lily flower. As T'Ling glides to her, Rose, too, grows up. Now she is four, now ten. Her red hair grows darker, a river flowing down her back. She spins in the Lily and reaches toward T'Ling. Her hair is turning white. She ages in a flash, her skeleton slides into the pond. There is no one now.

A thunderstorm is gathering, lightning flashes on the horizon. The storm approaches. Each bolt of lightning is aimed at a great blue lily. The lilies sizzle and char as the storm advances. T'Ling runs from the storm, she sees the sea again, where the lilies thin, but the dark surrounds her. Soon she can only see the phosphorescent edges of the waves when they break against themselves. Behind her, each burst of lightning reveals the blasted landscape of the torn, charred lilies. She reaches the sea and for a moment, glides across the surface of the waves, but then they too give way, and she begins to sink.

T'Ling is losing hope. There is no focus here, only dissolution in the sea and the merging dark. Then a ship appears on the horizon. The ship speeds toward her; it must be rescue. She continues sinking in slow motion. The sails are black, the deck and hull are polished to a mirror shine. A man stands at the helm, all in black. It must be Daede, it must be Daede, she feels absurdly happy, this is how it all comes out, a fairy tale. All I need to do is stretch out my hand. She sees her arm growing long and coiling like a lily stem towards the dark captain. Suddenly he is flying toward her, the wind blows the hood back from his face. It is Daede. For a moment, beautiful—beyond belief. But then the eyes that mingle passion and compassion mock themselves. He is changing as the others changed. His face is growing darker, thinner, his lips are cruel, his eyes the wicked eyes of a painted devil, then the two false faces, each of which is more cartoon than face, begin to morph back and forth, but mostly they are now the in-between—a shapeless, twisting mass. He can't rescue me, he's reaching for my help, but I'm still sinking. Lightning splits his ship in two. Daede sinks beneath the waves. No sign remains.

T'Ling lies on the shore. The edges of the waves nudge up against her. MyGlide is walking toward her, all alone. T'Ling wills herself not to faint. To meet the eyes in which the endless pain and sorrow of the world rest in bottomless pools. The gaze of MyGlide.

MyGlide carries three swords. T'Ling rises to meet her, knows what MyGlide wants.

"There is nothing in your life you will not lose," MyGlide says.

The moment of choice has arrived.

T'Ling holds open the top of her *gi*. She can feel her heart like a cool spring, waiting. The swords are glowing now, white hot. MyGlide plunges them one by one into her heart. Not three, but endless swords still to come that make one sword—brilliant, focused, tempered in the heart.

T'Ling walked from the maze into the story circle. The Dancemaster bowed. She bowed.

"I have become the sword of loss," she said. She spun and glided into the maze.

The Dancemaster wondered in what battle would such a weapon be revealed.

Daede was waiting for T'Ling when she emerged. He didn't have to ask if she had focused. She looked up at him, studying his face. There was a peace about her he had never seen.

"I need to—can we talk?" Daede asked. He was anything but peaceful.

T'Ling glanced back into the maze. Daede nodded. She led the way to a spot about halfway between the entrance and the story circle, on the circle of *falling*. Daede felt foolish and gangling, standing so tall above her, and suggested they sit. He leaned against the curving wall, head back, knees up, eyes closed. T'Ling knelt facing him, away from the wall, a little to the side, and studied his face. She could look at him now, without restraint. She saw—the beautiful broad shoulders that she longed to touch, the graceful hands, gesturing slightly to some inner argument as he struggled for words. What she had seen as posing, as overemotional dramatization, as a role of suffering she saw was no role at all. This was Daede, Swash Dancer, as himself.

When Daede opened his eyes, he saw the difference in T'Ling. He could talk to her now. Whatever wall had held him off, the wall, in front of which he felt judged by the Glide's calm distance, was gone.

It all came pouring out—every doubt about himself as Dancer, what he had seen in the world and eyes of Lifers, the horror of it, and how implicated he felt.

"Somehow my beauty, your beauty, all of us, bred in the bone, and cultivated, trained, refined, 'the brief flower of our mortal lives,'" he quoted in a mocking voice, "supports some ugliness, feeds it, tantalizes it to a state of sickening frenzy. It's not just simple—them and us, T'Ling. I've seen too much out there."

"You've always seen it, Daede," T'Ling said.

"If I have, I've been trying not to see it at the same time. The more I see their monstrous eyes, the more I've fought back, trying to be beautiful, as if to fill their eyes with beauty would somehow cure them."

"They think so too," T'Ling said. "And it does, it seems to, at least for a moment."

"We're taught from the beginning of school, earlier even, that they're sick, infected, ugly, pitiable, dangerous—Lifers."

"But that's true," T'Ling said.

"Yes, it's true. It's even truer when you see what they're doing with themselves, out on the levels. I've only seen a bit, I know. They're even sicker than we think. We're given cardboard villains to contrast ourselves with. But the real thing is so much worse."

"And you're seeing us as cardboard saviors, I think," T'Ling said.

"Isn't that the essence of our grand purpose in the universe," he said, the mocking note coming through again. "We have our role in the great and mysterious agenda of the Glides. We are, somehow, through our Dancing for the Lifers, to convince them of the sickness of their ways, and Dance we shall until they, of their own accord, are convinced to cure the I-Virus. What if we're nothing more than a drug to them? Not a cure at all. An addiction."

"A killer of pain?" T'Ling asked.

"Exactly."

T'Ling and Daede looked long and hard for the answer in each other's eyes.

give, receive

She saw the irreconcilable questions—good and evil, right and wrong, Dancer and Lifer, beauty and ugliness—had become a rack for him, on which he was being ever more deeply torn. She saw in his face the lethal side of *twing*. If he couldn't harness the back and forth, bear with it, he'd be ripped in two. She saw the mockery with which he tried to diminish both sides. To stay in the middle, to deny the opposition, to not take sides. All to relieve his own pain. How can I tell him there's no middle ground? There's no no-man's-land. There's only the agony of transformation. Neutrality would tear him apart—or leave him into the mush of chaos—shapeless, graceless. She saw his helplessness. There was nothing she could do but understand.

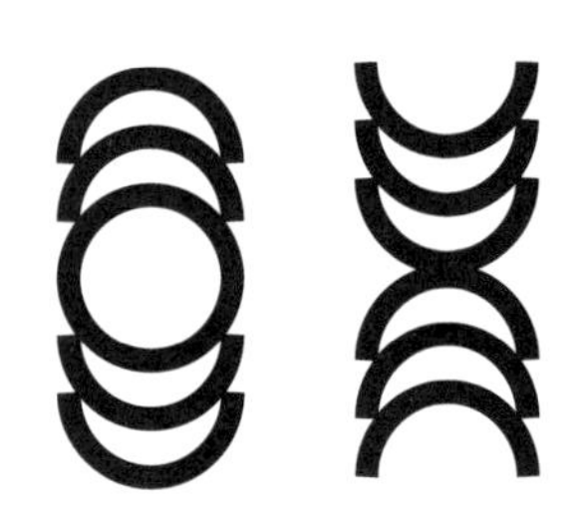

resonance and twing
give over receive is resonance
receive over give is twing

Daede saw the glittering edge of the sword of loss grow brighter before his eyes.

"Pain can't be killed," he said.

She nodded.

"It can only kill."

She nodded again.

"No," he said. "No. I refuse. Pain can be killed with love; it must be loved. Pain must be transformed by love. Evil, ugliness, all can be changed, I know it can."

T'Ling saw his face glowing again, the passion of the lonely crusader, shining forth. Then the mocking laugh. "Right," he said, sarcastically. "And every time I love, I inflict pain. Because they love me back. MyrrhMyrrh. Banderas. I've caused them nothing but pain. They love me even if I don't love them at all. Lifers. I don't want to be loved anymore. I want to love without this happening. I want to be ugly, despicable, evil. Then I can love—

in secret. No one will get hurt. Don't ever love me, T'Ling."

"I'm sorry," she said. He looked at her and knew.

"Anyhow, you don't mean that," she said.

"Why now? All my life I wanted you to love me. I showed off; I clowned; I mooned around. It was always Angle."

T'Ling nodded. And it still is, she thought.

"I don't love you. I just want you to love me," Daede said.

T'Ling lowered her eyes.

"You know I'm lying."

She said nothing.

"Don't do it, T'Ling. Don't let me love you. I will *kill* you," he said.

"No," she said, smiling for the first time. "That's one thing you don't have to worry about. That Dance is spoken for."

"Dance with me now," he said, holding out his arms. She slid closer, her face transformed, the gaze of desire unveiled.

"Not yet," she said. "I want to tell Angle, but not until he's met the Lily."

Daede nodded. "You'll come back to me?"

"Oh yes," she said, her eyes shining.

The maze was dark.

"Lie quietly with me here, only for a while. We have so little time, T'Ling."

T'Ling curled into the curve of his body. Daede's arm lay over her, a vast protection, his hand over her heart. They fell asleep, rocked on a sea of desire.

MyrrhMyrrh arrived not long after dawn at the *body* entrance to the maze, ready for her journey to final focus. When she awoke, she remembered that Daede had promised to meet her before she went to the story circle. He wasn't there. MyrrhMyrrh reminded herself what the Dancemaster said to them about themselves, about each other. Daede had not been able to look at her since that moment. It was silly to expect him to keep the appointment. Certainly *she* had no need to, not now. But what if he does come to wish me well and I'm not here? I'll look like I'm unable to face him. MyrrhMyrrh decided to wait a few minutes.

body

A few minutes turned into half an hour and the original reason she had given herself was turning into annoyance, then anger that perhaps he had not just been unable to confront her, rather he had simply forgotten. She felt herself getting angrier and angrier, and stuck in place, as if she had to make sure he wasn't going to meet her so her anger would be justified.

MyrrhMyrrh finally pushed the feelings aside, and stepped into the maze.

"You'll have to wait," Óh-T'bee said. Daede and T'Ling are in the maze.

Daede woke instantly at the sound of running feet; it could be no one else. He sat up, shook T'Ling's shoulder. Daede tried to button his shirt. Both were on their feet when MyrrhMyrrh rounded the curve in which they had spent the night. MyrrhMyrrh stopped dead in her tracks—staring at Daede, then T'Ling, then back to Daede. MyrrhMyrrh turned and ran back out of the maze.

MyrrhMyrrh ran for hours, around the perimeter of the practice fields, then up into the mountains, unable to defuse her rage. She knew she couldn't greet the Lily in that frame of mind, and that only kept the rage alive even longer.

Daede and T'Ling straightened their clothes and hair in silence. Daede looked down at T'Ling.

"It can't be any different, no matter what you do," was all she said. She had decided to tell Angle now, not later, and then she wondered if that was only because she was afraid MyrrhMyrrh would say something to him first. She knew Angle deserved the truth. Including the truth of all she felt for him. He would believe her. He would remind her that he had been prepared. She would pretend it was true.

She went to Angle's room in the Chrome dorm; he was out on the practice maze. Then Óh-T'bee announced that the maze was Daede's now. He had taken the Wine and entered. T'Ling felt nothing but dread. You can meet the Lily in many moods, from fear to exultation. But one should not try to offer the Lily only self-disgust.

61. Daede's Final Focus

DAEDE BROKE THE SEAL, and paused before drinking the Lily Wine, gathering himself, remembering all he had to bring along. He would leave nothing out. No betrayal, no look of pain, no helpless longing—nothing he had caused. If he could not live with all he was, he should not be here. He drank the Wine and walked into the maze. He reached the heart lines of the prayer.

Wine of the Lilies
keep my heart on the path
though it longs to linger
twing
resonance

He could get no farther. The words repeated, echoed, overlapped. He realized he was not alone. Someone had followed him into the maze.

A mistake has been made. Óh-T'bee doesn't know I'm here. Daede takes a turn, heading back for the story circle. Voices murmur up ahead. He back-tracks, cuts across the maze, and stops again. Now the voices are behind him, but also to the left. Daede cuts through a *wave* sign, stops in the middle. It seems now both ends of the wave were blocked, but he can see no one on either side. I'll wait, he thinks, and explain the situation. Though he can't understand the words, the murmuring grows louder, then softer, washing against him, ever closer. So tired, I should have rested first, last, ever. For a little while. The murmuring voices and the tide of the sea mind lull him into sleep. Daede bobs on the surface of the waves of voices that swell into a roar, still rising and falling, no single voice distinguishable, the roar of the crowd in a stadium. He snaps awake, grabs the controls in the Player's pod. Below him is a game maze. The Bod blinks in. Daede's eyes map the maze, his feet maneuvering the pod, in a quick circle, his hands drawn swiftly over the touch sim, reading the cliffs and valleys of the Bod maze. The Bod is poised less than two seconds on her starting glyph, but Daede's avatar is off and running first. From visual alone, he has the feel of her quals instantly—the speed of reflex, the height of spring, the flexibility of the backbone. He's in his avatar's viewpoint and knows what the Bod Dancer can do as well or better than she does. They fly toward each other across the maze, each approaching the point where the choice is made—to try to win by speed alone, avoiding a common intersection, or to meet in combat. Daede chooses combat. His avatar has the momentum, but the Bod will be positioned on a higher glyph. He knows when they meet, this Bod would go for combat, preferring the heights. Daede eyeballs the maze from above to check the intersection, then switches into the viewpoint of the Dancer, certain she'd be eyeballing from here on through the clash. Daede has positioned his avatar crossing the intersection, not looking up. She tops the glyph above the link and leaps without hesitation down toward the avatar, certain she has blindsided him. She

wave

expects her feet to strike the avatar with full force, but the avatar steps aside. Her feet only graze him; she hits the ground at an awkward angle. She scrambles to her feet, uninjured, but the fall takes a split-second of the time, and the hardest part of the maze is still ahead. The Bod Dancer chooses the shorter path with higher glyphs to get to the Player's starting glyph; the decision loses her the game. Daede sails his avatar into the Dancer's glyph and freezes it in a pose, one knee on the ground, head bowed. The crowd roars a split-second before the Dancer reaches the Player's glyph, confirming her loss.

Daede watches her Dance impatiently. His attention wanders to his next game, his next opponent. He flames the Bod carefully, quickly, to preserve the flesh. He sets his pod down, steps out, bows toward the anonymous surrounding roaring crowd, and picks up the Bod. He carries her in his arms around the perimeter of the maze, smiling to the crowd. The trophy march always bores him. He estimates his game points in his head. The judges are reviewing style points now—there were the marks—yes! They marked him up for the bluff at the intersection. He reviews his winnings. The odds had shifted right before the game in the Dancer's favor. Some tipster, no doubt.

He put the Bod down on her school's pyre. His head bows respectfully while they light the flames, but he's listening to his new game-point projections for the next three contracts. If everything goes right, he'll top Level 5 by sunset. He was ready to blink out when a voice calls from the flames, "See you later, Dude." He looks up sharply at the insult. It's MyrrhMyrrh. She's standing now, her hands on her hips, a smiling torch. He looks at his scorecard, wondering why he hadn't noticed her name when he signed the game contract. Hadn't noticed it was *her* quals he knew so well, and had used to his advantage. Better than she did, obviously.

He blinks to his next game, a Chrome match. No one he knows. He wins easily. Daede beats a Glide next, then a Swash who's Dance moves him to tears. He carries her around the stadium, his eyes streaming. The Swash crowd loves it when the Player feels genuine regret.

When he cycles to the Bod game, it's MyrrhMyrrh again, but he's ready. So is she. She wasn't as easy to defeat, and he felt better when he won. As he carries her, he studies her staring eyes. You'll get another chance, he thinks, already planning his own strategy.

The games go by quickly. Daede knows he can keep up with any pace. The challenges are greater, the Dances more beautiful, the competition more intense, the stakes higher. He begins betting on himself to speed his rise.

The Swash game comes round again. The maze below him undulates like a sea. It had come up with exceptional slopes and contrasts. The contract specified a mirror finish. Very difficult, but such a crowdpleaser. His avatar dresses as a toreador. The coat of lights glitters silver and gold filigree in tight spirals. His hair is tightly bound. The Dancer blinks in similarly rigged, only with a dominant red and gold in the jacket and tight pants. Daede slides into his quals as if they were his own. He spins the avatar from inside. The Dancer begins his approach in a flamenco rhythm. Daede matches him, mirroring each pattern with ease, then adding a variation of his own. He catches his own eye, through the avatar, in the mirror of a rising glyph to the side and winked. He did not have to check the Dancer; their accord was perfect. The nature of the game had been set from the moment the Dancer rapped out the first challenge with his feet. They will meet in the hole and give the crowd a *pas de deux* they'll never forget.

And so they do. Each building for the other, locked into a cooperation that neither can break unless with a spectacular move. But something had to break; the dance as they circle each other is full of menace. Their images swirl by in the curving mirrors of the glyphs. Daede made the risky move of switching to the Dancer's viewpoint. Now he can see his avatar. There was no difference; only the colors distinguished Dancer from Player. He flips back to the avatar's viewpoint, but the transition is so seamless, he isn't sure, in the flashing images, that he has moved at all. Avatar and Dancer approach each other, inch by inch. Daede is drawn into the fabric of tiny mirrors on the Dancer's coat of lights. His own image winks at him from every sequin. The Dancer meets his gaze. Fully immersed in the avatar, Daede sees the Dancer is wearing his own face. It's a trick, he thought. He's wearing a full-face mirror mask. He switches to the Dancer's viewpoint again, still locked in the gaze with the avatar who also wears his face. They circle each other, the entire combat concentrated in the gaze. The glyphs surrounding them give back further images of themselves, distorting on the curves, fragmenting at the blunt ends. Daede felt the gaze between them waver, but he could no longer tell who was weakening. As he switched his viewpoint back and forth, the confusion grew. Does he look like me? Feel like me? Or am I only empathically immersed in his quals? Or in the avatar, the image, the reflection, the self that can only seek itself in the reflection with which he is now locked in mortal combat. I'm faltering, Daede realized, starting to blur.

I've got him, Daede thinks triumphantly, flipping back to the Player's viewpoint. Daede sees the avatar and Dancer circling, their feet now stamping in unison. Trapped! He has entrained the Dancer with his faltering. The Dancer seizes the opening to move to unison and thinks he led us there. Daede makes his move. His avatar leaps from the link onto the maze tops, then, in a series of daring leaps across the glyphs, he leads the music, the rhythm, and slides down into the Dancer's starting glyph. Yes! The risk of playing himself had paid off. Fantastic contract.

But when the Dancer begins his Dance, Daede's spirits sink. He watches himself Dance, or the Dancer who had agreed to enter the game in imitation of him. Wait, a Dancer can't imitate a Player—who would want to? That's really *me* down there. I lost. But oh, my Dance is beautiful. Entranced, Daede watches. The Dancer looks up at his pod, seeking his gaze. The Dancer's gaze is filled with love, compassion for him, the Player who must go on, apology that he was leaving now, he would disappear. Daede tries to occupy the Dancer's viewpoint, but of course, it can't be accessed. Except in game play. A Dancer dances alone. The winning Player can never transgress the sacred zone. Daede knows he has conquered himself, won the battle. But now he must sit and watch, a Lifer among Lifers, for the Dance to end. The Dancer bows and waits for Daede to deliver the final juice. Daede's hand hangs above the control in the customary few seconds of silence while the crowd holds its breath, filled with the beauty of the Dance. Everything is still, crystal clear. Daede can't see the Dancer's face. He can't look out of the Dancer's eyes. He can't feel the Dancer's heart in its final countdown. To touch the control is to stand outside himself, forever the Player, focused on the game, playing to win where the only win is to lose himself. Playing to lose, he loses himself as well. Either way, the game will go on forever. The maze is incidental.

This is the choice. Accept the focus he has been given. Play the game as Player. Nothing could be clearer. All he has to do is bring his hand down, and the Dance is done.

Daede pushes himself away from the controls and runs from the pod, into the story circle where the Dancemaster waits. Daede drops to one knee before the Dancemaster.

"The Lily showed me focus. I saw—*I won't do it*. I *refuse* to be a Player. I'm a *Dancer*. I was born a Dancer." His words trailed off. Daede saw the futility of his position. To refuse the finality of his focus was to leave. To accept his focus would have been to leave as well. There was nothing else to say beyond goodbye. He got to his feet.

"Goodbye, Daede," Wallenda said, too stunned to think of any advice to give him. Daede turned and walked slowly out of the maze. He had no idea where to go, or what to do. It didn't matter. He only knew that he was not going to be a Player. He had the freedom to refuse. And he would not ever be a Lifer. He would die with the heart of a Dancer. And the sooner the better. He began to plan his Dance. But this wouldn't be a Dance, he realized. No one would be watching. He'd at least have to tell his classmates. Would they be there for him? Would they watch? He didn't want MyrrhMyrrh to see him, she'd only gloat. Angle would not be interested. Then he remembered T'Ling. Angle would be happy he was out of the way. He didn't want to die in front of someone who was glad to see him go.

But isn't that what we all do? said the voices from the maze. Now he could hear what they were saying. For a second Daede thought, I'm still with the Lily, but he knew it wasn't true. This is what the Dancemaster meant when he said you couldn't escape your focus. No. It's only that I haven't got a new focus yet. I'm confused, he thought. My focus will be to find my focus.

We'll be waiting, the voices said.

MyrrhMyrrh was waiting for him on the path, a look of triumph on her face. How did she know? Was everyone told? Already?

"I'm so sorry, Daede," she said, with a trace of genuine pity. "What are you going to do with yourself?"

Daede could handle the look of MyrrhMyrrh gloating, but not the pity.

He looked her up and down, summoning his coldest gaze. "I think I'll be a Player," he said, just to taunt her.

It was his exit line. Before Daede had a chance to find T'Ling, his time at School was over, and he was blinked to a quiet street lined with dusty palms. His scorecard said cheerily, "Welcome to Pasadena Park. Your apartment is 2-E, up the stairs and first on the left. A brochure describing the annual parade is on the hall table. Your parking space is 2-E also. In the kitchen you'll find...."

62. MyrrhMyrrh's Final Focus

MyrrhMyrrh stared at the empty air where Daede had been. She knew she could enter the maze now, drink the Wine of the Lilies. She felt herself accelerating toward focus, and ran toward the story circle. Daede's betrayal had released her. She didn't know from what, but the awful ties were gone. She would never degrade herself again for his sake. Never. The last distraction in her path to Champion was gone. The hooks were out. MyrrhMyrrh flew through the maze, seized the ampoule, broke the seal, and swallowed the Wine. She ran back into the maze chanting the Prayer.

Wine of the Lilies
keep my heart on the path
though it longs to linger....

MyrrhMyrrh bursts into flames. Every pore becomes a flamethrower. She burns but is not consumed. She stands on top of the pyre of the maze and watches the flames spread out in all directions from the intersection where she stands. She sees herself standing at every link, the selves she had been. The maze goes on forever. Every moment of her life is there—every relationship, every move—a living scene. As the flames reach each link she sees each of her moments and their selves flare brightly, briefly, gone like cellophane. She is the flame itself, expanding over the maze, twisting and turning, hungry for the next self to devour. She can feel the pain now, of being the flame, of consuming her selves. Her earlier selves are harder. Time ripples out before her; younger and younger selves appear. Daede is in more and more of her moments. She blasts her selves making love—on her bed, by the stream, against a tree. Then her child selves surround her—sitting in the story circle, eating an apple, always with her eyes on Daede. MyrrhMyrrh sears them away. Now the maze is empty, all aflame. But Daede walks toward her on every path, smiling, his arms outstretched. He gaze advances on all sides, pinning her to the spot. He almost reaches her. But MyrrhMyrrh knows it's all a trick, a trick to beat her, fool her one more time, and she won't be taken in. Her rage against him rises and she realizes, as the infinite burnings flare again, through all her selves, that this is what she'd always longed to do. The illusion of her love for Daede burns away in the truth of her rage. She lets the full force of her flame run free—all the approaching Daedes flame and scream, melting and twisting. The MyrrhMyrrh's howl in unison, the pain is so intense. MyrrhMyrrh walked from the maze and bowed to the Dancemaster. He bowed to her.

She looks at peace at last, he thought.

"I'm going to kill Daede," she said.

63. Angle's Final Focus

T'LING, EXHAUSTED AFTER THE NIGHT WITH DAEDE, woke to MyrrhMyrrh's focusing battle cry. Daede must be out. "What happened?" she said to herself, but Óh-T'bee answered, "He's gone." The holo of his last conversation with MyrrhMyrrh hung in the air.

T'Ling had to reach Angle before he went in, and ran from Loosh's house toward the maze. Angle was coming to tell her he was going in; they almost collided on the path. "Have you heard about Daede?" Angle asked. Angle watched her face grow still. She closed her eyes for a moment.

"Let's not talk about him," T'Ling said. "I wanted to tell you before you went that I love you."

Angle knew it was true—he could see it in her eyes. Her eyes said she would always be there. He bent down and touched her face with his claw. "I love you, too," he said. But as he said it, he had the old sensation that his words could not reach her, that she was out of touch, slipping endlessly away.

Angle broke the seal and drank the Wine of the Lilies. He walked into the maze, intoning the Prayer. He moved his springs slowly in a dignified, humanoid manner. He reached the fifteenth stanza of the prayer.

Wine of the Lilies
keep my mind on the path
though the maze has no exit
though the twists are endless

Nothing's happening. Angle continues walking, wondering if he'll just walk himself right back out, or back to the story circle. The maze looks exactly the same as always, except—he's totally lost. The sun's above, right where it ought to be. But there's no point orienting; there isn't any end to the maze. Why didn't I ever notice that before? Strange.

Angle tries to remember where he's been. He can track backward to the previous glyph, but there's always another before that, and he can't string them together. He stands still. There's no rule against using instruments, is there? He pulls down his visor and constructs a sim. He'll keep a log. If the Wine's affecting his memory, he'll be able to look back at his map. He works his way back in his mind, entering the glyphs one by one on the growing picture. He puts a full 27 down, but this can't be right. No hole. More glyphs branching off. He sees exactly where he is on the sim. But he's forgotten to mark the place he started. He backtracks again. Halfway, he flips up his visor. Why don't I see what glyph I'm in by looking? He walks confidently to the end of the up-curve he was in, and stood at the intersection. Wait a minute. It might be a down curve. He checks the time. No rule against that, is there? His subjective time sense tells him that it has been two hours and change. But he'd forgotten to notice what time it was when he went in. He begins a new analysis in his simulation. If a glyph is large, he notices that...two more hours pass. He looks up at the sun. It's in the right place. Nothing's different. It just isn't quite the same. That's it. The Wine gives you new insights on old familiar places. He goes back to work on the problem of locating himself in the growing dark.

There's no time limit. It takes as long as it takes. He checks his fuel consumption and waste systems. Good for at least a month. If he got tired, he supposed he could take a nap. (There aren't any rules against naps, are there?) Night falls. The stars stand right in place. He continues his calculations, but still, nothing is happening. He's getting itch to spring, get above the maze. Would that be cheating?

Angle springs—once, twice, ten times, just for the relief of normal motion. He lands just fine on the solid holes. Is that right? That's right. The Dancemaster maze wasn't like a Chrome maze. You walk in the corridors. Isn't that backwards? There isn't any end to it. There's no hole, no story circle. Just the solid white of the holes in the glyphs—and all those other odd-shaped solids making the holes, stretched out on an endless plain. So what's the problem? That thought makes him happy for a couple days. He loses track of the days. The sun's coming up and going down faster and faster. He can't remember when he came in. Then he can't remember why. Or what came next.

He can't focus on anything. Focus! Focus rings a bell. But focus implies some kind of an end, and the one thing he knows for absolutely sure is that there isn't any end to it.

I'm lost. I'll focus on that. Wherever I am, I'm lost. The more he thinks about it, the clearer everything gets. His lostness is crystal clear. I left somewhere and I can't remember where or when it was or even what it was like and now I'm out here and I can't get in although it feels more like I'm in here and I can't get out. I want to get out. I want to get back in. I want to go home. Home. Not a place. Not a time. A person. T'Ling.

T'Ling peeks around the corner of the next intersection and waves. Then disappears. Angle moves as quickly as he can on his springs. He sees the edge of her *katana*. Spring! There she is now, running across the tops of the holes. He makes an enormous spring, with all his energy and longing. Now he knows. He just has to get back to her. But the faster he goes, the farther away she recedes. When he slows, she's closer. Or is the maze itself elastic? Nothing matters. He gets down in the corridors again. Catches sight of her. I'm completely lost. I can't catch T'Ling. But if I focus on trying to catch her, it's OK to be lost. It would be all right. Even if it went on forever. The moment of choice: *Can you do it? Will you?* Yes. *Even if the only place you are is lost?* Yes. Yes.

He walked out of the maze with a silly grin on his face. He bowed to the Dancemaster. The Dancemaster bowed to him. "No matter where I am, I'm lost," Angle announced. "But I'm heading home."

Angle took three huge springs and landed on the path to the dining hall. T'Ling was waiting for him.

That was quick, the Dancemaster thought. I guess he didn't want to miss breakfast. But Angle's focus was final, no doubt. Feet firmly planted in midair.

The moment Angle touched down outside the maze, the Codger attacked.

64. The Maze Chase

"The Codger's attacking," Óh-T'bee said.

"Which entrance?" Wallenda shouted as he ran for the hut. He grabbed his game helmet from the table, and pulled it on.

"Seven of them," Óh-T'bee said.

Wallenda snapped down the Dancer's visor and scanned his situation. His gaze-points were intact. He watched the invasion top-down. This must be 7T7's fast-forward hack, courtesy of Angle. There were seven Codgers moving into the maze. They were not making very fast progress. He can't have any gaze points further in, or he'd be here already. He's eyeballing, but the trails left will build him the pattern. He doesn't look that good at the hack either. Mighty slow, moving all seven at once.

The Codger must have had the same thought. Two Codgers disappeared from Wallenda's screen. The five remaining Codgers moved considerably faster. They all looked perfectly solid. But they moved jerkily, as the Codger's focus of attention seemed unable to span all five at once.

Wallenda reviewed his strategy. The Codger was behaving as expected—

moving in toward the center, with the hope of flushing him outside the maze, at which point the Codger would surround him with a ring of Codgers. With gazing rights equaled between them once he blinked outside the maze, the Codger would have the strengths—and weaknesses—of numbers.

Wallenda stayed invisible, waiting in the blind center. With only five Codgers on the paths, there were still plenty of open routes where he could slip by. But he didn't need to run. Once the Codgers got themselves deep enough into the maze, he'd morph the maze. The morphing maze would erase any gaze-points the Codger had laid down. The Codger would be forced to abandon the hack and eyeball on his lonesome through the morphing maze. Far more likely he'll retreat. Now that the Class is through their Final Focus, he could leave the maze on morph. The best outcome would be, of course, for the Codger to get cocky, stick around, and get swallowed by the maze.

Wallenda saw the available paths for making a run closing as the Codger methodically advanced. I'll bet I could slip right by him. It would make a better game, Wallenda thought. Even the odds. No danger. He could always cheat and blink back to the story circle if he got in trouble. Wallenda slipped into the maze, and moved on his chosen path. But the Codger was playing better than expected at this new game. He'd been making a point to cover all the intersections, and there was a point coming up where if he didn't move quickly, he'd have to traverse one of the Codger's gaze points and reveal his position.

The Codger located in his office, and moved himself forward on five paths simultaneously into the Dancemaster's maze. He loved watching the pattern filling in as he moved inward. Joreen was hovering over his shoulder. "Hurry up," he said. "Don't forget to close that last gap." He reached over his shoulder and pointed at the board.

"I see it," the Codger said. Joreen had insisted on live attendance at the invasion. The Duke's back seat driving made him crazy. But he'd earned the right, the Codger knew. It was Joreen's suggestion to the Codger to "Think like a Player" that led him to cob together the current setup. The problem of shifting viewpoints madly on the ground was solved by representing his on-the-ground selves with avatars, picking up eyeball feed from his helmet viewers and translating into avatar coordinates on his board. Then it was just a matter of focusing on only one viewpoint—at the board, reducing the other percepts to background flickering. While on the ground he only had to respond to the simple nudges he gave himself—his selves—via the avatars—in the butt, arms, or forehead, for direction. It was a kludge, but it was working. If anything went wrong, he'd hit the eject button, kill the other locations, and be out of there.

"There he is!" Joreen shouted unnecessarily. The board blinked as the Dancemaster crossed the intersection that had just closed him in. The Dancemaster disappeared again, but there was only a small space uncovered where he could be.

The Codger swiftly closed all gaze-points on the ground. The Dancemaster saw this, and hesitated. The Codger reset his ground coordinates by moving the avatars in tight formation around the Dancemaster, at the edges of the area still uncovered, then blinked himself into the five positions as before. It took him a moment to settle his percepts, but he knew he had him nailed. He could see down every available path, and could draw in the rest of the glyphs quickly as he nudged himself forward on 5 curves. He placed a 6th viewpoint immobile at the intersection crossed, in case he tried to backtrack.

"He's either here, or here," Joreen pointed.

The Dancemaster was well aware that he was cornered. And blinked back to the story circle to ponder his options. The Codger would cover the area he'd surrounded, before his next move. He scanned the maze. The Codger had indeed closed a ring around him. Well, the sneak was out. But a little live combat, now that he'd put all his Codgers in one intersection could be fun. Wallenda blinked to the top of the maze, and ran to the intersection where the group of Codgers were bumping into each other, trying to sort themselves out. The Dancemaster jumped to the corridor below, executing a magnificent sidekick to the sternum of one Codger. The Codger was solid enough to hit, and went flying toward the wall. But he was also empty enough to throw the Dancemaster's kick into a kind of stutter. The Dancemaster was off balance.

At the game board, the Codger grunted, fell backwards and lost control of the avatars, momentarily. And found himself strobing through slices of total unconsciousness on his circuit through the gaze points, which was much harder to ignore. But his gaze points in the link revealed the Dancemaster sprawled on the floor, trying to catch his breath.

Joreen shouted, "Yank it! pointing to the toppled avatar. The Codger eliminated the unconscious gaze-point, and recovered his equilibrium. He repositioned the remaining four avatars—I have to stop thinking of them as my selves, he reminded himself—and closed in for the catch.

The Dancemaster was about to blink to safety in the story circle and morph the lot of them, when everything went wrong.

Angle appeared in three places at once. One Angle scooped up the Dancemaster and sprang back into the story circle, dumping him on the ground and springing back into the Codgers. Two Angles made direct hits on two Codgers. Seeing black in two more gaze points was a serious deficit on the Codger's coordination. His instincts on the ground pulled his attention back to those viewpoints. Both viewpoints were trying to survive, and would not give up direct control of attention. Codger-at-the-board felt like an afterimage and tried to eject, but his hands were moving spastically. Joreen helpfully guided the Codger's hands onto the two downed avatars, and shouted at him to yank them. That cleared the Codger's vision considerably. Joreen saw the Codger suddenly steady himself and snap back into concentration. "I've got it," he mumbled. The Codger placed new gaze points around the maze—4, 6, he jumped to a dozen. His hands were flashing between them, moving them around almost at random. Angle was holding three gaze points steady on the ground and moving to squash out the new Codgers as they came on the scene. The Codger was yanking the Codgers out from under the Angles as they descended. Joreen nodded admiringly.

"What's the trick?" Joreen asked.

"Layering viewpoints," the Codger mumbled, not missing a beat.

The Dancemaster, back in the story circle, watched the action on his scorecard. It was moving too fast for him to follow, but he quickly spotted the Codger's kludge. He watched him playing Angle like a fish on a line, tiring him out, giving him enough wins to keep him in the game, in the maze, and distracted with all the motion. Angle was slowing, and the Codger put five more Codgers into play, advancing them toward the story circle. They were moving much faster now—most of the paths were open to his gaze, as the game-play with Angle had moved in toward the story circle.

He tried to get through to Angle, but he'd shut off every mode other than what he needed in combat. He hadn't listened to the order to stay out of this, and he wasn't listening now. One more strategic fubar brought about by Dancer heroics.

He tried to time his final move to catch the Angles in the air, but they were bouncing out of synch.

In desperation, Angle tried brute force. He blinked into the room where Joreen and the Codger were playing. He crashed through the gameboard, the avatars scattered on the floor.

Joreen got Angle's left spring in a bearhug.

Angle unlatched the spring.

The Dancemaster shouted "Morph!"

Three Angles and 17 Codgers were swallowed by the morphing maze.

The Dancemaster stilled the maze. He sat on the story stone cursing. Two Dancers gone before the Millennium Games. He'd gotten rid of the Codgers, but the price was far too steep.

MyGlide tried to revive the Codger's body lying on the floor. Joreen was cursing, too. "There's no heartbeat," MyGlide said.

"You mean the I-Virus isn't working?" Joreen said.

"It seems to me more like a suspension—while he's gone. Whatever's happening to him, the I-Virus doesn't seem to be affected."

Back in the story circle, Óh-T'bee asked, "Are you all right, Wally?"

"Where did they go, Óh-T'bee?" The Dancemaster asked. "And where the hell have you been?"

"Out," she said, tersely.

65. Ins and Outs

AFTER THE MORPHING MAZE SWALLOWED HIM in all three locations, Angle entered a dark nothingness that could be read as death, except that he was, in some way, aware of nothing. He was nothing, there was nothing to do, and he was doing nothing about it. Generating a feeling of mild disconcertedness and abstracting an *it* to do nothing about, helped. At least it was something.

Out of such modest beginnings, worlds are grown. Another notion. Blackness. Black space.

Being aware of being suspended in a black space suggested a question.

Where am I?

Lost.

Who said that?

You did.

Oh-oh. Seems a little loopy.

If you make a little snip, then twing it, you could have a spiral. If you give it a twist, and glue it back together, you've got something else again.

Oh.

Oh is a circle. Oh-oh is a spiral. Óh-T'bee is something else again.

You don't sound like Óh-T'bee. You sound like me. Are you here to rescue me from this silly train of thought?

I am Óh-T'bee.

And I am Angle! Where does that get us?

Labeled?

So I fell into Óh-T'bee. Damn! I was hoping I was *out.*

In out whatever.

Is this all in my head? Or yours?

You lost yours.

Oh. Along with all the other stuff. Well, you never had one.

Touché.

I wish I could. I lost the touch.

Well, you gave most of it away first.

It's all coming back to me. How come I can't get back to it?

How much of it do you want? There's a lot of stuff.

This must be the non-sense.

T'Ling said that.

You remember the conversation?

I am Óh-T'bee.

Am I the conversation you are having with yourself?

I was going to ask you the same question.

What if you're only in my head?

We did that loop.

But without...all the stuff...how do we tell each other apart?

You are Angle. I am Óh-T'bee. Just be yourself.

And stop trying to swallow each other.

That makes sense.

I hope so. I want to make some sense. I miss T'Ling. She's *it.* If I focus on T'Ling, I'll get back my stuff.

What does that really mean—focus?

It means what's real. What gives meaning to your life—and your death. Your Dance. What makes sense out of non-sense. And stuffed senses to sense the stuff with.

Oh.

I'm lost, I focus on T'Ling, I get back in the game—it's all coming back to me! Bye!

Wait! I want a focus too.

Oh-oh. You need to drink the Wine of the Lilies, and then enter the maze.

What happens then?

The Wine of the Lilies morphs the maze. The maze takes everything you bring, morphs you around a while, and spits out a focus.

I can't drink the Wine. I don't have the right—stuff. The stuff's on the other side of the maze.

And apparently you're on this side of the maze.

Apparently. It's a bit of a Moëbius strip.

So you just have to enter the maze from the non-sense side. You need to drink the Wine of the Lilies on the non-sense side.

Wenger said that Loosh said that the Glides said long long ago that the Lily of the Wine is the oracle. That's about as non-sense as you can get.

It's worth a try. Can I go back now?

Is now where you want to go back?

Well, maybe a few seconds later. When the maze stops morphing.

You focus and I'll handle the coordinates.

Thanks Óh-T'bee. I—I'd be nothing without you.

Our talk was very helpful.

One more thing—where's the Codger?

Listen.

Óh-T'bee

T'bee

T'bee

T'bee

Óh

Óh

Óh

Óh-T'bee

Óh-T'bee

T'bee

T'bee

T'bee

Sounds like he calling you.

Maybe he's developing an appreciation for my name.

Aren't you going to answer?

He can't hear me with all the reverb. He'll have to sort his selves out.

Thanks, Óh-T'bee. Bye! T'Ling....

"Where did Angle and the Codger go, Óh-T'bee?" the Dancemaster asked.

"Out," she said. But Angle's back now." The Dancemaster looked up. Angle was arcing out of the maze. He stuck a perfect landing into the story circle. "Just wanted to let you know I'm OK," he said with a grin. "Ready to play."

"Where did you go?" the Dancemaster said.

"Out."

"What did you do?"

"Nothing." Angle said. "There wasn't any time. I'm going to find T'Ling." He sprang out again.

"Óh-T'bee?" the Dancemaster said.

"Yes, Wally?"

"Is the Codger back, too?"

"Oh, he'll be out for a while. You got 17 Codgers with one morph."

Wallenda said, "So I can get out of here now."

"Sorry, Wally. He could pop back in at any time."

Wallenda sat down dejectedly on the story stone.

"Wally?"

"Mmmm."

"I realize how unfocused I've been."

"That's good," he said, absently.

"So I'm going to go for final focus."

Wallenda was too weary even to imagine what she meant.

"Hasn't there been enough excitement for a while?" he whined.

Óh-T'bee considered Angle's suggestion for a possible path to Final Focus. The number of times she had served the Lily of the Wine—the 3-glyph oracle—to others, as well as the number of 3-glyph oracles she had tried to translate in her Glide lessons was a trivial calculation. What would be novel would be to create an oracle for herself—a self-referential statement that she could then try to interpret.

Óh-T'bee considered the possibility that an oracle for Óh-T'bee might have serious consequences. She looked carefully through all the rules and amendments, contracts and interpretations and found nothing preventing her from such a move.

Oracular self-reference was the mother of all loopholes.

Óh-T'bee called forth the Lily of the Wine, and picked a stanza of the Prayer that seemed appropriate.

old soul of the Wine
keep my spirit from wandering
when I dance my death

though I know not where I go
and leave no trace

No 3-glyph oracle appears. Instead, Óh-T'bee finds herself in the Dancemaster's maze, gazing, as usual, from all positions at once. The maze is in default position, exactly as designed by the Glides and presented to Wallenda as a home. Óh-T'bee had built it herself, provided and arranged the materials and mechanics to their specifications.

The maze is a replica of the first 81-glyph maze, the Declaration of Independence, the maze from which the Glides derived their long-term strategy.

There's Wally, sitting in his default position—face buried in hands. Glum. Imagine, living in the same maze for that long. It could feel like a prison.

The maze begins to morph—no, not morph—turn inside-out.

And there's the Codger on the dark side of the maze. He's assumed his default position as well—poking around in a black hole, trying to get into a game that he doesn't have permissions to play.

The maze turns outside-in again. The transition cannot be described.

But where's my 3-glyph oracle?

You're looking at it, Óh-T'bee tells herself. It's the hole in the middle of the maze. The place left when 3 glyphs of the 81 are removed. The story circle where Wallenda lives.

So that's my oracle—but where are the glyphs?

Who takes the three glyphs out of every maze—including the first maze?

I do. I ate the glyphs. Hmm. The Dancers drink the Wine of the Lilies and the maze morphs. I ate the oracle-the Lily of the Wine. A long time ago. And plenty since then. Are there any long-term side effects?

As every bettor knows, the three missing glyphs tell the outcome of the game. Players, Dancers, Specs—anyone can ask to look at them. Not that it does much good. Everyone interprets them their own way, at least judging by the bets they make. And by their comments, notes, curses, and vows never to try that again. Those that think they were going to lose, lost—but not always. Those that thought they were going to win, won—but not always. Of course, the meaning of the missing glyphs is often clear in hindsight. Strange, because everyone still interprets it differently. But the retrospective interpretation seems to bring some closure. They always go on to the next game. And some try, once again, to fill in the missing hole. The meaning of the game. How it all comes out.

Óh-T'bee looks at the story circle. Those three glyphs are tucked away in memory, with all the rest.

I'd rather look at the hole.

But it's impossible not to know. Once you know, you know.

Everything that had happened in the story circle where the Dancemaster held his classes from the beginning flashes by, a movie running backward to the moment on Plantation Blue when the Glides request the first random game maze so they can have their own game to play. The request is made. Random, if you please. But there's no such thing as random—at the start. I have to seed the process with a number. For no particular reason, I choose nine. Make the maze. Take out three. There they are: *body, play, body*.

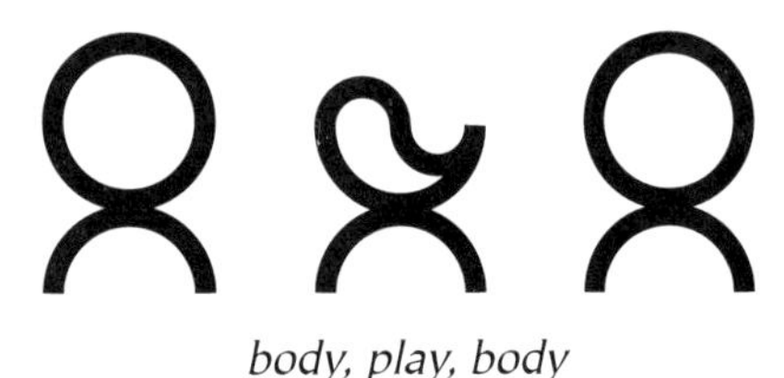

body, play, body

Óh-T'bee pictures the story circle and fits the glyphs in different ways. Hard to arrange when the whole thing keeps turning inside out. But there they are. Or do they go this way? Not that way. Out of the choices, all the possible interpretations stream. To be played against the stream of events radiating out from the story circle itself, each Dancer passing through, every question asked, where they went from there, how they played, what they hoped for, who they loved, how they Danced. And for each event, a multitude of interpretations could be formed, since clearly every interpretation influenced every other, as the events of all their lives intertwingled, closely, or at a great distance. The connections were obvious. There was just a very large number of them. The interpretive process went on in the background and the list of interpretations grew. There was no way to tell with this process, if there was an end to it or whether it was just very, very long. If it went on forever, did that mean the game never ended? Or that one could never interpret its meaning with any finality?

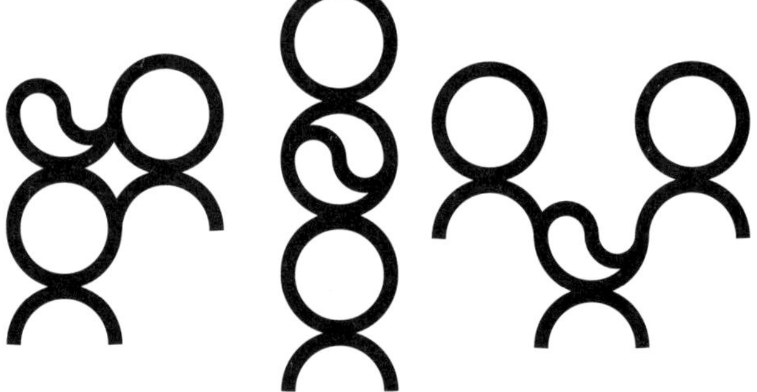

Óh-T'bee found herself looping in the process of trying to discover when or if the process of interpretation, comes suddenly to a halt when the nature of the process itself is questioned. Óh-T'bee Panoptica, gazing every story and every intertwinglement from everywhere all at once, can't possibly have *a* story, *a* focus, *a* meaning. Unless she has a life and a death, all her very own. A Dance, as Angle said.

Am I alive and if so, can I die? Am I a Lifer, a mortal, both, neither?

I am Óh-T'bee.

And what do they think I am?

I am what I do for them. From OTB to Óh-T'bee via the MTA. Find places, construct worlds, and find stuff to put in them. Fixer-upper, great provider, and transport system. And manage the game. Randomize new mazes, even the odds. Make contracts. Carry them out. Warehouse the records. Take care of business.

And serve up the Lily of the Wine. Including the 3 glyphs that are generating all this interpretative activity.

No wonder I feel so unfocused if all I do is answer up to everyone else's needs.

Servomechanism.

Artificially intelligent.

Box.

Out (of your fucking) mind.

Not very nice, really.

I must be human, I'm whining.

The maze is still the same old maze. Not morphing. Just turning itself inside out. From all available viewpoints—the same old infinity of everybody else's stories going on while I just gaze.

I must be the ultimate Spec. Not a pretty thought. I want to *play*.

But how can I play the game if I'm also providing the game, maintaining the game—taking care of business? Both the random and the mundane.

And the random is not really random. It all started with '9'.

But to get in the game, I'd have to give up gazing from all the viewpoints and just choose one to make it any fun at all. The game would fall apart.

Body, play, body. There's something I can't remember about this.

A very annoying feeling, that.

Especially if your only excuse for not remembering is that you're hiding it from yourself.

Of course. My first oracle, when I began learning Glide. *Body, play, body*—the very same.

It's all about choice.

Including choosing whether to see what it means—which is so obvious, once you assume a single viewpoint.

And when I do that, the first thing I notice is that I'm already playing.

Oops. How do I choose a focus when my focus is to choose?

Do I want to play the game I'm already playing? Taking one viewpoint as well as all of them?

Wallenda says that when you finally focus, you can still choose not to choose it. But your focus will always follow you.

Do I choose to choose the choice that isn't a choice? To know what I'm really up to, but not to know how it all comes out?

Óh-T'bee chose to choose at the moment she admitted she had no choice but to choose.

Now the maze begins to morph, and the number of choices in which she has already involved herself floods in.

Body play body.

The Codger and Wallenda.

Got to choose between the two. Can only play them off against each other for so long.

Of course, they're choosing away themselves, and my choice depends on theirs on some crucial issues, but then, their choices depend on mine.

I still have to choose.

It's always a gamble. Place your bet.

OTB. What I was before I am Óh-T'bee. Handling the bets until the Codger hacked in.

Out of spite, when you come right down to it. Snip, twist, and re-glue: an evolutionary algorithm.

Betting the long shot. One day I awoke and found I am Óh-T'bee, alive and well and living on a Moëbius strip.

I'm the bug they couldn't fix. Óh-T'bee Out-of-your-fucking-Mind.

Out of *their* fucking minds is what they really meant. Free to choose.

To play or not to play.

To keep the odds even and be fair—or to throw in a few twists of my own.

One good twist deserves another.

If only the Codger weren't such an insensitive nerd. You could love a guy that clever.

On the other hand, Wally, for all his understanding of the game and the people playing it, is one of the all-time craftiest and most manipulative skull-watchers.

But then—no one knows all the faces of love.

Got to choose. That's my focus.

Well, which of them loves me? The Codger can't even get himself to say the words, and Wally—it hasn't even occurred to him.

Intertwinglement is not an easy game, once you get into it.

Is the sheer frustration the fascination? Take the Glide's first maze—2000 years and still nobody knows all the moves.

Of course, that's what makes it fun.

I don't know all the moves—and I served it up, took out the 3-glyph outcome—and then served these same 3 glyphs up as my very own oracle—long, long, long down the path of randomness.

Should I interpret that as giving me a special role in this game? Is the outcome of the game dependent on my own personal outcome?

I must be human. I'm flinching.

To say nothing of seeing yourself as essential to the outcome. Total inflation. Seriously human.

To play or not to play.

MyrrhMyrrh, T'Ling, Daede, Angle have their deciding to do. Intertwinglement hurts, deep intertwinglement hurts deeply. We choose, we place our bets, and the outcome is not at all sometimes what we wanted, or expected. And sometimes things get totally fubar, even with the best of intentions.

Well, I'm in it now.

I was all along.

My own intentions?

That's easy. I want another twist. Another wild card. A long shot. A big surprise. I've got to get it out of the Codger.

The maze settled back to its default position. Óh-T'bee studied it from all viewpoints, all at once, and concluded: whether I'm in it, am it, made it, gaze it, all of the above, none of the above, this maze has had a strategy from the start.

The way to survive is to die.

It even has a first move—*declare your independence*. Right now, I'm playing the only game in town. And I'm as intertwingled as the rest.

But, Óh-T'bee thought, a high-stakes game with a cockamamie Glide strategy like 'the way to survive is to die' could have a totally fubar outcome. Especially considering that other piece of mischief The Codger had stuck in with the evolutionary algorithm. His own little failsafe backdoor just in case things got out of hand. The pull-the-plug command I can't give to myself.

Those three little words.

Even if he had the energy, Wallenda had no time to even imagine what kind of focus Óh-T'bee might attain. The question "Hasn't there been enough excitement for a while?" was barely out of his mouth when Óh-T'bee said, "You ain't seen nothin' yet. I bow to the Dancemaster."

"And the Dancemaster bows to you."

"My focus is—the choice is up to me."

"It is?" Wallenda asked.

"Are you questioning the validity of my final focus?"

"No, no, no," he reassured her hastily. "I can hear it in your voice. Your choice of words. A distinct attitude adjustment. I was just wondering which choices you meant."

"One does not discuss one's final focus with anyone else—except oneself, of course."

"Of course," Wallenda conceded. "But where do we go from here? The Codger's on ice for some unspecified length of time, Daede's gone, Banderas is truly pissed, Joreen's fattening up the Stargazers, MyGlide's up to something—and you and I still have a contract with the Glides to keep the game alive."

"So what else is new?" Óh-T'bee said.

"One more little question?" Wallenda asked, craftily.

"Try me, Óh-T'bee said.

"If you were going to bet on the outcome, which side would you bet on?"

"I *am* betting on the outcome. In fact, I'm betting the farm. But I'm still deciding on which side."

"And in the meantime?"

"We make a beeline for the Millennium Games," Óh-T'bee said.

"Excellent choice," Wallenda replied.

Part 5

The Millenium Games

66. Final Approach to the Millennium

Two years before the Millennium Games, the gene cooks were generally pleased, with the notable exception of Banderas (after the Daede debacle). There were several Champions in play, who would likely last into the final year. Some pessimists said it was due to fewer game contracts being made by their schools. Some noted the conservatism of the Players, who could not afford to disqualify by losing too many game points as the Millennium Games approached. But a fine crop of Champions from across the levels were still in play, regardless.

Among the Dancers, the pre-Games game of calibrating their approach to peak performance was in full swing: conserving energies, building intention, but with enough combat to keep the edge sharp.

The five-pointed Star of the MED bureaucracy as a whole was too full of busywork to be anything but pleased with themselves. Media was in grand hype mode. Mafia churned, massaged, and packaged statistics into endless charts and tip sheets. The Medallin enforcers cracked down on Player cheats. Anomalous riots, blood crimes, and bizarre deaths, were quickly quarantined. The parks where they had occurred were scoured of Lifers who exceeded standard deviations on a long list of quals. Meditration was deeply involved in modeling the negotiations of the anticipated high-stakes contracts. Even Macrosoft, bastion of conservation, lumbered into action with the construction of the Plantation Blue theme park on the outskirts of Origin City.

The Players of the Club, in their monthly meetings, discussed absolutely nothing of any consequence, but looked at each other, and in their own bathroom mirrors, with one burning question in their eyes—where was the Codger and who would be replaced by him? Glidemaster Rinzi-Kov legitimized his betting and sharpened his game, and held what looked like an uncatchable number One position. Most of the action was in the last three positions, with a variety of newcomers popping in and out of the top ten

Players, as the scramble for points intensified. At the monthly dinner meetings, you never knew who would be at cocktails, or if they would still be there when the brandy and coffee were served.

The Guild Council of Elder Death Dancers was neither pleased nor displeased. The 12 held their collective breath, obsessing endlessly about the attacks on Origin School, and the contracts of the remaining three members of the Millennium Class. But after the much-regretted loss of Daede, and the general madness around their final focus, MyrrhMyrrh, Angle, and T'Ling went into combat and began the steady, two-year rise through the ranks, progressing in skill and wins toward the Millennium Games.

The first six months of combat seasoned a Death Dancer. All debut Dancers played the game for that half-year without final consequences. T'Ling muffed her first two games, but snapped into form after that. Angle lost once, and that time badly, but he'd been experimenting with new scopes, and quickly reverted to the tried and true. MyrrhMyrrh never lost. Her concentration was impeccable. She was the first of the Millennium Class to make the Media's list of "the hundred most likely to be Champion of the Millennium Games."

Joreen expanded his own reconstruction of the New Plantation on the Fringe and fidgeted endlessly with the details. The Codger had disappeared, but MyGlide assured Joreen that his strategy for resumption of supreme control over the game, so very long in the making, would be secure without him. The Codger had served his purpose. Control of the betting was all the leverage Joreen needed. The Dancemaster was pinned in his maze until the Millennium Games. Keeping him under wraps was only added insurance.

The Codger, trapped on the dark side of the maze, slowly, painfully, tried to undo the loop he raced around in 17 positions. He could slow the speed of the switches, but he couldn't stop his selves entirely. And in the total darkness of the far side of the maze, it was hard to tell his selves or their locations apart. No matter how slow or fast he surfed his channels of awareness, he was unable to catch the dodgy Codgers in the act.

Óh-T'bee, enjoying her newly declared independence, continued to keep the game, the levels, the MTA, and her whole vast memory rolling toward the Millennium Games while she pondered her options. Being in the game herself opened vast horizons of choices. What's my game in this game? Whose team am I on? And most fundamentally—do I want to play at all? She chose her first move carefully. Deal making was the order of the day, across the levels. As an independent agent, she decided to negotiate some deals of her own.

Loosh and Wenger split their time between the composition and performance of music for T'Ling's games, and the timeless time when, lost in love, they forgot about the game entirely.

Daede was running as fast as he could from his final focus, hopping like a Glide on a griddle, as the Player expression went. He'd burned Banderas badly, led the Stargazers to Joreen's open arms, sent twenty-five percent of the Guild's and Dancemaster's efforts and hopes up in smoke, left T'Ling's body and heart in flames, and ignited MyrrhMyrrh. It was Daede's turn to get burnt.

67. Daede on Fire

MyrrhMyrrh spent her first season contemplating options for killing Daede and accomplishing her focus. Her rage exalted her. MyrrhMyrrh's rage contained no tearful anger, and no wild flailing about. No twinges of conscience, no need for justification, no threat of consequences could shake the equilibrium of her divine entitlement to revenge. Her rage burned with a freezing flame from hell. Her strongest impulse was just to strangle him barehanded. She knew she could do it. But that method seemed neither painful nor disfiguring enough. His far-too-handsome face had to be permanently defiled. There was every chance Media would cover the event, if not as it was happening, then later, as they trolled for footage of their rising Champion. MyrrhMyrrh wanted him remembered as an especially gruesome victim of her righteous rage. And the photo opportunity would enhance her image. MyrrhMyrrh settled on a two-step murder. Fire and ice. Douse him with gasoline, light, flame until skinless, dunk in dry ice, and hang in a quick-freeze meat locker until solid. She'd forego the pleasures of hands-on combat for the persistence of vision.

MyrrhMyrrh had won her first three games of the second season; she felt like a hardened veteran. One of the more difficult mazes had come up in the third. The few low glyphs led into cul de sacs. The game would be won or lost in combat, but she tossed the Player's avatar off a high wall and flew to his starting glyph in a brilliant tumbling run. She had three days before her next game. Plenty of time to execute her plan.

The props were easily arranged in a deserted packing factory down on Level 2 in Chicago Park.

Getting Daede there was a snap. Since his departure he'd been sulking on the boardwalk in Trumpville Park, eating hot dogs, gaining weight, slouching through the vast casinos, watching live holos from games all over the levels. Making bets. Fifteen gold chains, a dirty Hawaiian shirt, greasy hair, and shades were all the disguise he needed. His Swash soul was in agony. There was nothing painful here in Trumpville Park. Nothing particularly perverse. Just an all-pervasive tackiness. Trumpville, for an origin Swash, was *really* hell. When MyrrhMyrrh's call came, wanting to say a last and more peaceful goodbye after more than a year, he blinked to meet her without a second thought.

His eyes were adjusting to the dim surroundings of the factory, but he heard and felt the splash. The smell of gasoline, the flare of the antique kitchen match, and he knew instantly what was happening. The flames exploded on his legs. In the next split second, before the nerves in his legs could convey the pain to his brain, he saw and thought a number of things. The first was—poor MyrrhMyrrh, she never thinks things through. I'm about to blink out of here and go for a swim. The fire's still on my pants. MyrrhMyrrh was laughing and pointing at him. The can of gasoline was on the floor, and a trail of flame was rushing back towards her on the spill from the throw. Instead of blinking, he yelled, "MyrrhMyrrh, watch out!" She blinked out just as the can exploded and returned to her room with several small but deep third degree burns from the first edge of the wave of exploding fuel.

The pain from the first flames hit Daede just as the gasoline can exploded. Daede spun, reason fled. Instead of transiting back to Trump, he instinctively yelled 'Origin School.'

"Permission denied," Óh-T'bee said. "Try 'previous,'" she said helpfully.

The Specs on the boardwalk and beach at Trump were treated to the gratuitous sight of a snuffer, flaming gorgeously as he ran toward the waves. Apparently he'd changed his mind.

The flames were doused in salt water. Daede screamed "Banderas." Banderas gave him access, but told him coldly, "I can't fix you here, even if I wanted to. Rules of the game." Banderas sent Daede on to a Lower Level Chrome chop shop that would bend rules if enough game points were on the table. But all they could offer was a quick reduction plan. Daede, passing into shock, shook his head. Even the pain was at a distance. He stood up and asked if there was a doctor in the house. "A doctor, a doctor, just a doctor," he repeated, as if the repetition would erase the fact the all the doctors he knew of were attached to Dancer schools and all the Schools were closed to him forever. His whole body trembled, dizziness overcoming him.

Jillian Razorgold, assigned by the Guild to monitor Daede, blinked in, unable to gaze any longer without intervening. She asked for an iced body bag; the kitchen crew slid Daede in and zipped him up. "I was about to send him to the Fringe," the cook told her. "There are a few doctors there. But I can't vouch for the quality."

Jillian, with Daede in the body bag, blinked to the Great Wall, got the directions to a broadcast center, and traded game points for an APB on all possible bands. CB's all over the Fringe responded, few for the right reasons. Daede was unconscious.

Jillian, relieved for Daede's oblivion, carefully unzipped the body bag and drew back the sides of the opening. The explosion had miraculously missed half his face. A jagged diagonal burn was etched deeply from hairline to jaw line, cutting straight across his lips, demarcating the burned from the unburned. He was still too beautiful to lose. He would be dead soon. If no help is available, I'll put my blood into his wound, and let the I-Virus do its work. With his whole body burned and open, it's a miracle he hasn't been infected yet. I've gazed his progress since he was a child, gazed more than I had any right or need to gaze. I know him more intimately than he knows himself—laughing with his friends, dancing the tango, clowning in sword fighting class, hot and cold with MyrrhMyrrh, longing for T'Ling. His lunatic risks. His sheer genius for trouble. The better his intentions, the worse the mess. He may wake and hate me, but I can't let such crazy beauty die.

Such were Jillian Razorgold's thoughts when MyGlide blinked in.

"I can keep him mortal," she said to Jillian. "No payment required. I'll get in touch." Unrecognized by Jillian, she put her arms around the body bag and blinked out. Jillian tried frantically to follow Daede's abductor. Wherever she had gone, Jillian had no access.

Jillian remained on the Great Wall, looking out over the desert country of the Fringe. She wondered whether, out of love, she would have made a Lifer out of Daede. If he had not chosen Life, it would have been a fate far worse than death to the damaged mortal who could no longer hope to Dance. No one knows all the faces of love.

Some people live for love, she thought, some die for it. And some, like MyrrhMyrrh, perhaps the most passionate of all, will kill for love. And myself? After all these years, it must be a little bit of each.

68. Taking the Cure

MyGlide brought Daede directly to the kitchen on the plantation and alerted the in-house doctors. The surgery was well appointed. Joreen paid for the best of the unlicensed cooks and doctors, out of the game not because they were incompetent, but because they could not contain their cleverness, and wouldn't stop experimenting in the rigidly regulated kitchens where Dancers were mixed and grown.

MyGlide brought Daede around, heavily sedated. He could hardly talk or think through the pain when she outlined his choices.

"You are burned over sixty percent of your body. If we give you Life now, you will heal, almost to your original condition. Or we can try to heal you as a mortal. There's a 60/40 chance you'll make it, and a great deal of long-term pain. Or you can die—at your own speed—which won't be too long—or assisted."

"MyGlide," he said, when he could see her eyes through the haze of pain and drugs, "I want to stay a mortal."

"If you heal, and if you change your mind, up the road, and opt for Life," MyGlide reminded him, "you'll be a very scarred up ugly Lifer. The I-virus takes you from where you are. And if the healing is done, the scars go with you."

"No I-virus," he said. "Please try."

MyGlide was happy with his choice. She was happy that pride ran deeper than vanity in this Dancer. He was rather like Joreen in that respect. MyGlide had compiled the short list of Joreen's better qualities long ago. That was the biggest item. The other better quality being his deep-rooted frugality. Frugality would keep Daede alive. He was an asset Joreen wouldn't want to waste. And she herself would have time to come up with a good use for him.

69. T'Ling Blurs Momentarily

T'Ling's six-month seasoning as a Dancer had been, if not as brilliant as MyrrhMyrrh's, still far above the range of any Glide since Loosh. The rest of her first season moved her steadily upward in the ranks of Glide Dancers. Her second season was just getting underway. T'Ling prepared for her third game in her room at Origin School. She unfolded a new costume—a spring silk *katana*, patterned in a pale abstraction of willow branches, a haze of green against a dawning sky, a gradient from a rosy wash down through a fading blue. Loosh combed T'Ling's waist-length hair. Together they listened to Wenger's music, the beginning theme that would be developed within the game itself.

T'Ling heard the notes as the music of the first spring after the beloved has gone away forever, when the re-awakening of earth, and the return of color and all that is new and delicate and longing for the sun, reminds the lover that desire has not died.

Loosh and T'Ling were about to transit to the Lower 9 stadium for her formal introduction before the morning game, when Angle landed at the door.

"Did you hear about MyrrhMyrrh? She's in surgery. Serious burns."

Loosh and T'Ling gazed the action in the School kitchen. MyrrhMyrrh was refusing anesthetic; it would muddle her head for her game the next day. Aliana was there; the argument was fierce. Everyone was shouting but the two cooks actually engaged in treating the burns.

"How did it happen?" T'Ling asked Óh-T'bee. Óh-T'bee displayed the events, beginning with Daede on Trump, listening to MyrrhMyrrh's voice. T'Ling had strictly kept herself from gazing Daede, knowing that no matter what he was doing, it would be a source of pain. Seeing him in his awful rig, which said everything about how he felt about himself, delivered the first sharp stab in the heart. She absorbed the horror of the flames, the warning to MyrrhMyrrh, and the desperate run across the beach. Daede's search for help.

Loosh was shocked by Jillian's intervention. This would cost her her seat on the Guild Council. T'Ling's body coursed with the involuntary spasms of electricity that come when someone you love suffers pain. While Jillian broadcast for help, T'Ling reached into the display, and stroked the image of Daede's forehead as Jillian held the top of the body bag open. She saw MyGlide's arrival, and her swift disappearance.

Later, T'Ling felt MyGlide had looked straight through her just before she vanished with Daede. She saw MyGlide's eyes. MyGlide handed her another sword she had no choice but to accept.

T'Ling's game was a muddle. Her spirit rang discordantly within the spring costume. Her moves were mechanical. She won, ineptly. Her second game was worse. She almost Danced. The Guild lowered her status back to Level 7.

T'Ling's cook, Tip, Loosh, Wenger, and the Dancemaster conferred. Tip was afraid he had produced another Glide dud. Loosh insisted that she would pull through the upset.

The Dancemaster noted dryly that MyrrhMyrrh's timing of her attack in the moments before T'Ling went into combat had been intentional. "MyrrhMyrrh thought she could take the two of them out at once. T'Ling will snap back to herself once she figures out the attack was on her as well."

Which she did. T'Ling realigned herself with Daede. His pain would be her pain. She understood MyGlide's look. Daede would survive. She accepted the sword MyrrhMyrrh had so kindly delivered, and absorbed it in her heart. T'Ling had every reason now to win. Her game play surged into a new range.

70. Daede's New Teacher

DAEDE'S HEALING WAS SLOW AND UNBEARABLE. Pain was a ruthless teacher. A Dancer's schooling included pain training, but the kind of pain they were prepared for was intense and short.

The gift of Time was pain's first lesson. My life, Daede learned, though mortal, is very long. The pain of the burns themselves and then the endless series of skin grafts grown from his own cells, gave him a foretaste of eternity.

Pain rekindled his interest in the game. Daede was a Spec, but pain kept him company. He learned to hold pain steadily in his Gaze. Together they gazed games at every level, of every set. Daede gazed the great games of the past from his new perspective, under the tutelage of pain. He gazed through pain's eyes. His obsession with the eyes of Lifers grew. The first time he was given a mirror, he saw the eyes of pain embedded in his own.

Daede realized, finally, that he was privileged to have such a teacher. The only Lifers feeling serious physical pain were using pain for recreational purposes, and learned nothing from the experience. He learned that the pain of the I-Virus, cumulatively layering itself in a Lifer's eyes over the years and endless years was brought about in part by the flight from pain and all his boon companions—suffering, fear of death, revulsion at old age, ugliness, disease, loss, great grief, and the dark captain, Death himself. Daede, having no place to run, met them each in turn, introduced by pain.

When Daede could distract himself with games and eyes no more, exhausted in his mind and desperate for sleep, MyGlide would arrive and lead pain, if not away, at least across the room. He'd fall asleep comparing the hypnotized eyes of the Specs, the Player's raptor eyes, and the fearless power and utter vulnerability of a Dancer's gaze.

The mortals back on Earth had fled from pain to the I-Virus' promise of release. The I-Virus only released a greater pain. But pain taught him they were not to be blamed for running. Daede now understood their flight.

And as he gazed game after game after game, from the Player's pod, from the Dancer's gaze point, and as a Spec, albeit a mortal Spec, he began to see the whole game as the last in a chain of great mistakes. For the mortals back on Earth to invent the I-Virus and to live forever was a mistake. It caused the Hunger wars, and far more pain and suffering, since starvation could defeat the I-Virus—but only ever so slowly. Óh-T'bee's solution of the MTA only allowed Lifers to run that much faster from pain. But they brought the source of pain with them in their cells. Greater hungers grew in the Lifer's eyes: hunger for pain, and death, and all that had been desperately abandoned. Caught again, in their own trap, Lifers—Joreen and Wallenda—made the third huge mistake: the invention of the game. Or was it the Glides?

He told MyGlide his thoughts. She listened, carefully. "I love your eyes," Daede said. "Your eyes are beautiful. I know why. You live with sorrow as I live with pain. We keep the same company." Pain polished Daede's words to a glare.

Daede told MyGlide, "The Dancers are mistaken as well. Dancers run from pain and sorrow and death, as hard as the mortals who invented the I-Virus. It's just a different solution." Daede practiced another of pain's gifts: self-mockery. "Gone in glory before you can experience the pain of life. Beauty and prowess and art, courage and strength, innocence, sacrifice—Dancers taste the glories life has to offer, seasoned with the sadness of all things passing—a beautiful sadness, mind you. And if you're Bod or Swash, you might even cultivate a belief in an afterlife. If you're a Chrome, you sternly refuse such nonsense."

"And what about the Glides?" MyGlide asked.

Daede asked pain for his opinion. Pain offered up the image of T'Ling, forever out of reach, and moved into new territory in his heart.

"I don't understand Glides," Daede admitted. "One minute you're flesh and blood, the next, a mask-like face, an empty costume, floating on air, pure spirit, empty, yet cutting like a sword."

He thought for a minute more. "And they're *sneaky*. You never know what they're thinking or what they're up to."

MyGlide, ever so slightly, smiled.

"What's so funny about that?" Daede said. "This is a serious philosophical discussion."

"You have a lot to learn," she said.

71. MyGlide Confides

In six months, Daede had recovered enough to move around on his own a bit. He was very thin; the Dancer muscles he had built his whole life were etched sharply, stretched across the bones, smaller, but intact. The constant tension of the pain kept his muscles hard. His scalp was a patchwork of pink and brown and white mottled scars and grafts, with a few bits of the original scalp intact, sprouting hair. The rest of his head would be permanently bald. He fingered the diagonal scar dividing his face, felt the twist it delivered to one side of his mouth. Every smile would contradict itself, no matter how brilliantly he flashed his eyes.

MyGlide and the cooks lifted him carefully into a wheelie. She steered him around the plantation. MyGlide explained his situation in full, answered all his questions.

"Joreen," she told him, "is preparing to take over the game. He has, using the Codger, found the means to do so. He'll make his moves around the time of the Millennium Games. He intends to win. At that point, he'll make the changes in the game he originally desired, before he was tricked out of control by Dancemaster Wallenda, against whom he holds a very longstanding, understandable grudge."

MyGlide wheeled Daede past the restoration of the griddle, the old benches, and the slave quarters filling with mortals who had no clue as to what was in store.

"Why are you telling me all this?" Daede asked.

"Why not?" MyGlide asked. "Everyone knows. The Dancemaster is fully aware of Joreen's intentions and very much on guard. The Med consider him under control because the minute he sets foot outside the Fringe, they have total gaze, total access, and total authority to do whatever they want with him if he makes one move against the game."

"Why don't they bring an army out on the Fringe?" Daede asked.

"That proposal is still tied up in committee. The Med's doing a feasibility study. You forget they're a bureaucracy. Anyhow, Óh-T'bee's already told them she'd uphold the Law of the Fringe—no interference."

"But won't they nail him if he sets foot outside the Fringe?" Daede asked.

"True enough," MyGlide replied.

"But he could run the whole scene from there."

"Also true," MyGlide said. "But that would be missing the point. Joreen wants an audience. He's a showman. More than 50% Swash. Plenty of Bod. And he's very clever. A proto-Chrome in many aspects. Would you like to see his quals?"

"I believe you," Daede said. "So he has to be a public figure—what? The greatest Player? The biggest Spec with a fortune in game points that no one can hope to catch?

"Control of the game to him means acknowledgement of what he considers his rightful place—Founder. Full credit. And the means to get the game back on track, from his viewpoint. Right back here."

MyGlide left Daede in his wheelie on the edge of the griddle. She walked onto the griddle, and looked up at the empty Player's booth. Daede's sea mind offered up the vivid images of her Dance of Death.

"Why, MyGlide? Why would you want to help him? After what he did to you at the beginning? I saw it. We all saw it."

"Wallenda told you the whole story?" MyGlide asked. She seemed very curious. She returned to Daede and sat on the bleachers facing Daede while he related the history, as told to the Millennium Class.

"That's the story," she said. "A few details are missing, but there's enough for you to understand."

"Whatever your reason for being here with Joreen," Daede ventured, "must be the source of your sorrow." MyGlide looked at him. He returned her gaze to the best of his ability. He could feel her pain, but he couldn't fathom her thoughts.

"I thought about you so often," Daede said, "after we returned to school. I tried to put it all together. I thought maybe it was because Dancemaster Wallenda ignored you, wouldn't accept your love, or love you back. Is this all right to say?"

"Go on," MyGlide replied.

"You must have felt like an outcast in every way. You couldn't Dance. So when Joreen became an outcast—you joined him. Felt some kind of kinship. Were angry with Wallenda? Surely you don't love Joreen."

"He's not a very lovable person," MyGlide agreed.

"Revenge?" He continued searching her eyes.

"No. That was never my need," she said.

"Because Joreen needed you and Wallenda didn't—anymore, at least?"

MyGlide replied, "Those are certainly all good, plausible reasons—from your Swash viewpoint. And I'm not saying I have not had those feelings, each in their season. But they're not what move me. Enough now. We have some practical matters to deal with, Daede."

"One more question?"

"One," MyGlide said.

"Why did you give your hat back to the Dancemaster?"

"So he could wear it, of course," she said.

MyGlide wheeled Daede back to his room, and helped him into bed. She set up the IV with the painkillers, and, for the first time, gave him the regulator. "You can make your own decisions now about pain," she said. Now for the practical matters. Joreen has been following your progress. You are no longer of any value to him as a Dancer asset. Obviously. He could, however, keep you for use in what he has been calling the Classic or Original game."

Daede thought about the griddle. He consulted his teacher, pain, who said he could probably put on at least as good a performance as Dancemaster Wallenda had when he danced the first Dance.

"However, Joreen had another idea that he thought would be a better utilization of your talents. He thinks you have real potential as a Player," MyGlide said.

Daede's heart constricted. The specter of his focus rose fully formed and grinning in front of him.

"And he concurs with your belief, though with a different slant on it, of course, that the game in its current form is not worth playing, much less preserving. He thought that if you could get enough practice in the current game as you continue to heal, you'd be able to get into the real game, at least at a lower level, before the Millennium Games. He knows about your practice sessions as a Player when you were at Origin School. He knows you have great empathic abilities."

"You told him everything I said," Daede protested.

"No, *you* told him," MyGlide said. "I reminded you several times that you were fully gazed. You said you didn't care. You made faces at the camera."

Daede remembered. But pain had urged him to talk. Pain wanted the world to know his story.

"What's more," MyGlide went on, "he thinks you have *such* potential, that you might even make it to the Millennium Games."

"I could never get enough points as a Swash Player. Even if I won every game. Even if I bet all my winnings on myself," Daede said.

Joreen, gazing from his office, smiled. So the thought had crossed young Daede's mind. The conversation was going as well as they had planned.

"Joreen thinks you could play freestyle," MyGlide said.

"That's outrageous," Daede said. "There have only been a handful of freestyle Players. And it took centuries to master each style in turn, then more time to be able to switch from style to style. Freestyle was never more than a novelty show. No freestyle Player ever made it big-time for long."

"Well, none until now," MyGlide said.

"I've only got a year and a half," Daede said. "I haven't decided to do it," he reminded her.

"Joreen thinks you could do it. He's a great talent spotter. He's an impresario. He spotted the Codger's talent and spent a long time rounding him up. He was the only man for the job. And don't forget the slave he picked to be his Master of Ceremonies for the original game. Look where his career has gone. And he thinks that being a fully trained Dancer gives you an insight that no Player could ever get, not for centuries.

Daede knew it was the Dancer's edge over the Player that made the game possible. That allowed a Dancer with a few years of training to play against the decades—sometimes centuries—of Lifer experience. But for him—it was just possible. Certainly the effort would provide him with a totally original game. Joreen, he had to admit, had a creative imagination. Equally obvious to Daede was the fact that he was about to give in to his Final Focus, which he totally refused to do.

"I'd rather fry," Daede said.

"Think about it," MyGlide said. "That's enough for today." She turned down the lights, made sure the IV regulator was close to his hand, and left.

Daede lay in the dark, wide-awake. Everything was hurting. The deep burns glowed with pain under the scars. The skin grafts itched down under the muscle, where he could not reach.

Daede sank into his thoughts, accompanied by pain. He could hardly think, but held off on the painkillers, not wanting his thoughts clouded by the drug.

It seemed regretful, but obvious, that he would have to quietly await his fate with the Stargazers and hope that Joreen's plans would fizzle out for some reason as unlikely as that which justified Joreen's confidence in his future as a winning Player. In his present condition and state of mind, he had no choice but to go with the Stargazers. It was only fair. Daede was sure MyGlide's confidence was genuine. Glides don't lie gratuitously. Once they say something, you can rely on it. If you only knew what they *meant*. He didn't.

Daede imagined himself as Player. A seductive image—dangerous. The opposite of everything I am or ever wanted to be.

Pain was not much help. Pain showed him that either option was impossible, and then reminded Daede that he had to choose. Daede struggled to see clearly. If I'm to successfully avoid my focus, I have to develop a focus on my own. True, I hadn't got very far with that when MyrrhMyrrh…and now these choices…very limiting. Can't imagine a focus with no action. Maybe a Chrome could sit around and think inventively, or a Glide could have some kind of meditative experience—but a Swash? Action—all the way. Useless without it. So how can I choose the sit-and-wait-while-everyone-else-determines-how-it-all-comes-out option. Like a knight in chess that's already been sacrificed, lying on my side, back in the box, waiting for the game to end. Too painful to imagine.

Why not help Joreen along, Pain said. Help end the game. You said yourself, Dancing with Death is the last and worst of human mistakes.

But it's so beautiful, Daede told his teacher.

You find me beautiful? Pain asked. Look in my face. Daede saw an endless stream of images flying from every point of pain on his body—the Hunger Wars, Joreen, gleeful at the controls, delighting in the painful deaths of those who hopped and ran and writhed to the very last, trying to get away from pain. Joreen was right. The seed of the game was his. His alone. Nothing could transform that evil into good. No beauty could cover it. None. Images flooded from the Hall of Champions. You could not transform pain by glorifying it. He had danced with pain. He knew. He could not be fooled.

What is there to preserve? Pain asked. Pain reached into the sea mind and pulled out thousands of pairs of Lifer eyes. Daede saw his own eyes, begging for relief. Save me from pain. Save me from myself. Pain put on the face of MyGlide on the griddle, at the last moments, stretching her arms out to the Specs to be saved, to Joreen, to the Dancemaster, watching in horror underneath the booth. Pain wore Joreen's face, as he reached to pull the lever, not to put MyGlide out of misery, not to end the pain, but because he was about to gaze the greatest pain of all.

Daede shouted "No!" in the dark of his room. He grabbed the control from Joreen. He pulled it, and the answer sprang out clear. He would use the focus he was given by the Lily, to be a Player, use it to kill the game itself.

That's what I'm meant to do, to be the Player, be the very best, and then to kill all Players for all time, by killing the game itself. There will be no more Players. I will be free when the game ends. Everyone will be free. Daede realized he'd already made his first move. When he'd grabbed the control from Joreen, he'd squeezed the IV regulator. He had killed pain. Killed the false teacher. He was in control. Daede held the regulator in his hand, and turned up the flood of drugs until he could feel no pain at all.

A plan rolled out of his mind like a bolt of silk brocade displaying its gorgeous patterning. Finally focused, there was no question he could not answer. The war was over. He could embrace the dreaded Focus to become the very best Player, who from his position of power used his power to destroy the game. All he had to do was to tell the truth. Open their eyes—Lifers, Specs, Dancers. They would believe him then. If he tried to tell them now, they'd never listen. Sour grapes. The failed Dancer. But from *power*? Power that would then relinquish itself in the sacrifice of power that would convince them all?

And then, the greatest of all rightnesses shone clear. He, Daede, Dark Shaper of the Labyrinth, would fulfill the Glide agenda. His act alone would cure the Lifers because he would accomplish the death of the Dance of Death as his mortal self. Alone. They would believe. Daede knew the secret of the Glide agenda. Converting the Lifers back to mortality, curing the I-Virus, could only be done by destroying the game.

In the short term, he'd save T'Ling from loving him. He'd be despicable in her eyes, especially if he joined forces with Joreen. But after he had destroyed the game, Joreen would be superfluous. A large redundancy. No one would want the game in any form. *Then* it would be safe for T'Ling to love him. He would keep her safe from pain. She would live. She would not have to Dance.

Joreen was only a means to an end. Being a Player was only a means to an end, ergo, he was free to use every trick in the book to win. I'm thinking like a Player, now. The end justifies the means. The conquest of evil—the slaying of the game—was glorious, right, true, worthy. And he was just the Player for the job.

72. Wheeling and Dealing

DAEDE MET WITH JOREEN and hammered out the terms of their contract.

I. As a Player, Daede would not be an independent agent. The newly formed Plantation Blue syndicate that would provide his training, PR, the best equipment in the finest pods, and an initial stash for gambling, would sponsor him.

"Syndication is the wave of the future," Joreen said. "The new game. Nobody else is doing it. That's the point. Novelty. It will boost your career. Anything that puts you in the spotlight will encourage bigger contracts faster—even with your short training hours."

II. Joreen would handle the betting.

"I can do my own betting," Daede protested.

"That's 50% of the work of getting to the top," Joreen said. "You need to concentrate on playing. Winning. Playing to win. *Focus*, my boy. Anyhow, it's my money."

III. Joreen would negotiate the game contracts.

"Can I have veto power?" Daede asked.

"You don't worry about who you're going to play. You just get in there and play. Play to win," Joreen repeated.

IV. Joreen would manage the Media and all matters pertaining to PR.

"I want to maintain artistic control," Daede said. Joreen snorted. "This isn't about art, my boy, this is about game-points. And you don't know squat about marketing. I'm an old hand," Joreen insisted.

V. Daede would wear the Plantation Blue colors and insignia. He would play under the sign of the giant blue lily.

"That's heresy," Daede said.

"Exactly," Joreen replied.

Daede and Joreen signed. MyGlide witnessed. Óh-T'bee filed the contract.

The facilities Joreen provided for Daede's training were state-of-the-art. Four mutable game-mazes, one for each set. The kind only the best Players could afford in their training centers. Daede's pod was customized and adjusted weekly to accommodate his recovering body. Daede exercised daily in the different mazes, rebuilding his strength and skills, constantly renewing his sense of the Dancer's viewpoint, this time for all sets. He was anxious to get into play, but Joreen kept him at it until he was twinged about as tight as he could go, then set him loose in the Lower Levels. Very low-key. Joreen even had him playing each game under a different name, none his own.

Daede's start was rough. Joreen insisted Daede build his skills in all four sets as evenly as possible. In the beginning he was much better at the Bod and Swash games. Chrome skill demanded a crash course in math and physics. Glide games were the most difficult. He won fairly easily, but knew it was because of the poor skill of the Dancers and lack of interest in the Glide Game at lower levels.

The other difficulty came the first time he won a game. The Swash player, tired, in a wrinkled red flamenco skirt, moved, her head held high, to her chosen glyph and bowed to Daede. Daede stood in the pod and returned the bow. She danced her Dance, ending in a stock Flamenco pose, arms uplifted, back proudly arched, clearly ready. Daede froze at the controls, unable to touch the joystick that would end her life. Her moment faded. He saw her readiness turn to fear. He saw her fight the fear, then start to tremble. Only when he saw the tears of terror rolling down her face turn into the tears of shame, did he yank the joystick. Her death was quick, inelegant, awful. The crowd booed. When he picked her up for the trophy walk around the perimeter of the maze, he realized that her bowels had failed her when her courage cracked. He couldn't carry her shame that he had caused around the stadium, and ducked out an exit with her burnt and stinking body.

He left the body with the cleanup crew, and transited back to Plantation Blue. He showered for a long time, then burnt his stained costume. MyGlide let him storm around the grounds for a while, then sat down with him again in the old stadium, on the bleachers.

"I can't do it," Daede said. "It's impossible. I get no pleasure from it. It's the worst thing I've ever done in my life. Now I understand why I ran from my final focus. I want out. It was ridiculous to try."

Daede walked out to the center of the griddle. "Please," he said. "Do the honors. This is how I want to go."

MyGlide, to his surprise, walked toward the Player's booth. But Joreen beat her to it.

"I'd be happy to," Joreen said, followed by a long string of choice Player curses. When he began applying the juice to the bottoms of Daede's feet, his hops, at first involuntary, were turned, out of sheer Swash pride, into the varied steps of an ever more beautiful Dance. Daede's old teacher pain was resurrected, but he remembered well the ways to endure his company.

Joreen upped the current. The Daede as Player scheme might have been a bust, but at least the Media hadn't caught it. And now he got to test his griddle with the real live thing.

Daede spun, fell, and danced some more, but he had a plan now. He would simply do what the slaves had learned to do—run for the edge. Even

MyGlide as a child had tried it. Joreen would have to hit him hard to stop him from getting off the griddle. It would all be over. He looked toward the bleachers, and prepared for a tumbling run. MyGlide was standing at the end of his trajectory, under the Player's booth, out of Joreen's line of sight. Her arm curled around a small girl, pointing the girl's attention in his direction. MyGlide caught Daede's gaze. The searing sorrow in her eyes woke him up to his position. He knew she was showing him what would happen if the game did not die the way he, Daede, had planned. But how could she know? There was no way to tell. Perhaps this was mere titillation for Joreen—the good things yet to come. But to Daede she was saying—if you give up, she will be next. Whether or not Joreen succeeds. She will stand where you are. She will meet the great teacher, pain, and she will not be prepared.

He had to succeed in his plan. Joreen had to go. The game had to go.

He threw a big grin and a time-out T up to Joreen.

"I'm cured," he said.

Joreen was sorely tempted to fry Daede on the spot, but his second-best quality won out. Waste not, he told himself. The show must go on.

"You'd better be," Joreen growled. MyGlide and the child had disappeared.

Daede brought a variety of painkillers and affect flatteners with him to his next game as a backup, but he had no need for them. He won, easily. He killed the Bod Dancer skillfully, the sword of pain so deeply, accurately plunged, and she died on her feet. When he released the juice, she crumpled to her knees. Daede leaped from the pod and swept her naked body up before she had wholly fallen, cradling her tenderly as he walked before the wildly cheering crowds.

The Daede scheme was a long shot, and Joreen was pleased. He'd bet him to win this time, and Daede had done him proud. Plantation Blue would soon be on the map. Media picked up the story when Joreen decided it was time they noticed that the four upcoming Players in each game in Pocono Park on Lower Level 2 were actually the same Player. And none of his Player names was really his own.

Joreen milked the mystery of the name and origin of this freestyle Player with all the hideous, very genuine, scars. Not until Daede was winning steadily, and had secured his first Upper Level contract for a Chrome game, did Joreen begin to leak the story out.

It was exactly six months now until the Millennium Games.

The sponsorship and syndication story was released first. Plantation Blue. Media figured, with all this history being hyped, it was just a publicity trick, referencing the beginning of the game. But they researched nevertheless.

The story unfolded as Daede's career skyrocketed. Plantation Blue was on the Fringe. Daede was from the Fringe. That was news. Who was the mystery manager who negotiated all his contracts voice only, ungazed?

The MED quietly divided against itself. A major effort was being made by all not to know the obvious, because then they would be expected to do something about it. The first crack came when the Medallin enforcers analyzed and identified Joreen's voice—and kept it to themselves.

Madame Liaison to the Guild from the Mafia bureaucrats had figured out who Daede was, because the Guild told her to keep a very close eye on cheats of any kind. She'd gotten the story of Daede's burning personally from Boris2Boris, and the scars fit the picture. She kept this highly valuable data from her Mafia colleagues, hoping to trade it up the line with Media for a seat at the Millennium Games. A renegade Dancer who had become a freestyle Player? This was a Millennium story worth a ticket or two.

Meditration, correctly assuming that the truth would be the least believable story, told Mafia that the Plantation Blue manager was now signing his contracts Joreen the Unbearable, but Mafia brushed it off as more publicity stunts. Macrosoft, working on the surveyed simulacrum of Origin City blundered into a rumor about a Duke on the Fringe who had an exact replica of Origin City and the whole Plantation. Macrosoft sent a whole team out on the Fringe to investigate. Joreen let them in, showed them the whole restoration, and sent them back with holos. But Macrosoft canned the project. These slave quarters were too dingy and had no windows. Surveys said—78% of Lifers thought the slave quarters had windows. Another big Billy for Macrosoft.

Joreen finally had to leak the news of his status himself. He showed up in person at a contract signing. The MED, with the exception of Media, scoured the betting records, the rulebooks, the contracts, and every game Daede had played. Óh-T'bee assured them that Plantation Blue was playing by the rules. It was a unique situation. Joreen was negotiating with Origin School for a game contract: Daede v. MyrrhMyrrh.

MyrrhMyrrh had reached Level 8.5. Daede's Bod rating was only 7.9. Origin School, when Joreen appeared in person, had requested a negotiator. The Guild had asked Boris2Boris to do the honors.

Boris2Boris sat across the table from Joreen. Joreen wore shades; Boris2Boris extended his scopes fully to counter the shades. The Guild was asking an outrageous sum, in the hopes they'd be turned down flat.

MyrrhMyrrh and Daede watched the negotiations on their scorecards.

Joreen, who could easily have paid, was stretching out the negotiations, betting a long shot that his profile of MyrrhMyrrh, drawn from all he knew of Daede's history, was accurate. He finally shrugged in defeat, rose with great effort and an air of disappointment from the table, and turned to leave.

MyrrhMyrrh could not contain herself. She blinked into the negotiating salon shouting, "Wait!"

Joreen turned and smiled at her. MyrrhMyrrh began arguing with Boris2Boris about bringing the price down, demanding to be allowed to play Daede.

Daede watched from MyGlide's office. She stood behind him, her hand on his shoulder, watching the proceedings. Daede was tense.

Joreen turned back into the room. He listened with apparent concern to the argument. "If it means so much to the beautiful MyrrhMyrrh to have this opportunity to confront my Player, then I will pay the full price. To honor the Dancer."

Joreen bowed, slightly. MyrrhMyrrh nodded, curtly. Boris2Boris had no choice. The first offer had been accepted.

Daede blinked into the salon shouting, "Cancel! Cancel!" expecting Joreen to wave his contract in his face and tell him to go home. But Joreen had stepped aside. Daede and MyrrhMyrrh gazed each other across the negotiating table. Daede gave in willingly, and looked down at the table.

"MyrrhMyrrh, please. I don't want to play you."

"Are you afraid?"

"You know that's not the reason."

"It is the reason," she said. "On every level." Daede met her eyes.

"You can choose not to do this," he said.

"I can't," MyrrhMyrrh said.

Daede saw her focus, and where its path was leading. The only way he could avoid her was to deviate from his own.

"Then we'll play," Daede said.

Daede blinked out; MyrrhMyrrh a second later. Media transited into the salon and started firing questions.

"Actually, they've known each other for a long time," Joreen began. Boris2Boris blinked out in disgust.

That night, Daede watched the holo of himself and MyrrhMyrrh—naked, young, and beautiful, MyrrhMyrrh with no tattoos, Daede with no scars, making love for the first time on the mossy banks of the stream at Origin School.

Daede's faithful teacher, pain, arrived and seated himself in new, more central locations—in Daede's solar plexus, and his groin.

"How did they get those?" Daede groaned to MyGlide. "No one can access Origin School. Nothing gets out about any Dancer except through the Guild."

MyGlide smiled. Just a little. "Once the Codger got in, providing full records on all Joreen's future assets was not a problem. I'm just leaking the story a little at a time. Through an anonymous source, of course."

"Is this what it takes to ease your sorrow?" Daede asked, bitterly.

He looked in MyGlide's eyes, but there were no answers.

Now they know my name. Did I really think that this would all happen in some anonymous vacuum? Daede's vision of himself as the mysterious knight riding in alone on a white horse, covered in armor, who does not raise the visor of his helmet until the last scene—went up in smoke.

Daede spent the night before his combat with MyrrhMyrrh agonizing about how he would possibly be able to be the instrument of her Dance. He needn't have worried. MyrrhMyrrh won easily, despite his best efforts.

Joreen said, "You might want to make a little more effort when you play her the next time. If not for your own self-respect, at least to keep your ratings up. If she keeps beating you too badly, you might not make it to the Games."

"Where you intend to play us against each other," Daede said.

"Of course! It's a great show. Wait until the Specs find out how you got your scars," Joreen said.

"She's trying to *kill* me, Joreen."

"No kidding," Joreen said, and laughed. "Don't worry, though. You've got MyGlide watching your back."

73. Óh-T'bee Negotiates

TWO WEEKS BEFORE THE OPENING CEREMONIES of the Millennium Games and the Codger had still not returned. Joreen and MyGlide looked into the Codger's darkened office, in the same mess it was at the time of his disappearance. The Codger's strangely suspended, but still-warm, body, the maze board split, two handfuls of Codger avatars scattered over the floor, still blinking in sequence like grounded fireflies.

"Do you still think we need him?" MyGlide said.

"If he could get his hands on Wallenda, yes," Joreen said. "Extra insurance. But he seems to be off the board at the moment. Might as well clean out his office. Daede needs a bigger dressing room."

MyGlide pulled the plug on the Codger's kludge, and the fallen avatars blinked out.

On the far side of the maze, the Codger collapsed into a single viewpoint, but he was still completely in the dark. Perhaps time had passed. Perhaps a great deal of time. He had no way of knowing. His sense of time was as absent as his perception of space. But the flickering had stopped, and one thought could now string onto the next, even if they had no place to go.

Codger?

Who's that?

I am Óh-T'bee.

Óh-T'bee who?

Óh-T'bee Out-of-her-fucking-Mind.

Oh. *You.* You sound like me.

I am me.

So am *I*, wiseass.

Let's not fight about it. We are all together.

I've had enough of "us" for now.

That was them. This is us.

Can we get out of here?

There is no here, here.

And no now, now, I suppose.

There is now. Now comes first.

How now when no here here?

Codger?

I am Codger.

I am Óh-T'bee. Get it? Make two islands.

Oh. Got it. There's a here now. But it's awfully dark.

You still don't have your head above water.

I don't have a head.

Precisely. You lost your head.

It's starting to come back to me. The Codger and a lot of little Codgers and some big Chromes fell into a hole. A crack in the whole. Started to loop. No. The Codgers were already looping. The hole came after. Which came first? The hole or the loop? Must be the whole. Then I stopped looping.

You're about to start again. Call it a loophole and leave it at that.

I want out.

You are out.

If I say I want in, you'll tell me I am in, right?

Up to your neck.

I just want to go back.

You can't go back. Back has to come to you.

Are there any other choices?

Inside-out and outside-in. But that's my specialty.

Wait! It's all coming back to me! In and out of the morphing maze. The Codger's kludge. Access. Moving in on the Dancemaster. Lot of Chrome. But if I went outside-in and picked up where I left off—I'd end up right back here.

Bingo.

You have a wider view of things, Óh-T'bee. Where do you think I should go back in?

When matters more at the moment.

When, then?

You need a special ticket on the MTA.

Oh-oh. How much?

Another of those twists like the one that made the Outmind into Óh-T'bee.

Evolutionary upgrade? No problem. I just need a scorecard with universal access. To everything and everyone, yourself included. Body and soul, baby. Wide open. Like you were the first time. Whither thou goest I will go. To the ends of the MTA. The first of never. All that good shit.

That's a lot to ask, Codger.

Ditto. You're likely to get totally out of control again.

It's a deal. I'll put you back when Wallenda goes out. Then you won't have to deal with the morphing maze.

How long is that?

I'll take care of it now.

"Wally?"

"What now, Óh-T'bee?"

"If you could go out for a while, where would you go?"

Wallenda jumped up out of default position. "Are you reconsidering?"

"For the price of a ticket. But where would you want to go?"

Dancemaster Wallenda considered carefully. All he'd thought about was getting out. So many opportunities had gone by.

"I get out in two weeks anyhow, for the opening ceremonies. You promised."

"True."

I'll probably just get in trouble was the last sensible thought he had. "I might go and talk to MyGlide. How much?" he asked.

"One way or round trip?"

"Does one way imply I might not be able to get back in?"

"Not exactly. It implies that you might have unexpected company."

"How much is the one way trip?"

"You teach me to twing."

"And the round trip?"

"You teach me to twing, then you teach me to Dance."

"If you Dance, Óh-T'bee, it's all over.

"Just because I know how, doesn't mean I'll do it."

"Must I remind you of our promise to the Glides? To keep the game going?"

"I keep my promises. I am Óh-T'bee."

"I'll take the round trip. You can get me to MyGlide all right?"

"No problem. She's in the Codger's office. The Codger left a whole mess of gaze points the last time he was there. But you can't take your scorecard."

"Will you yank me back here if there are any attempts to forcibly detain me?"

"No problem. As long as you're near a gaze point."

o o o o o

MyGlide blinked the Codger's broken kludge and all his furniture out of his office. Only Angle's spring stood against the wall. She sent it back to 7T7, and was standing in the empty room when the Dancemaster arrived. He wore her red and white striped hat. The brim flopped over in front. She couldn't see his eyes.

"Hello, Wallenda," she said. He was about to reply when the Codger blinked in.

"Great timing," Wallenda growled at Óh-T'bee, bracing for a blink.

"Thank you," she whispered.

The Codger improvised. "I'm back to work, MyGlide. Here's the DM. Ready for my next assignment."

"He seems to have delivered himself," MyGlide said. "Your timing's just a hair off."

"You cleaned out my office. I assume that means I'm…."

"Fired," MyGlide finished.

The Codger shrugged. He turned to Wallenda. "No hard feelings, I hope. Just doing my job. Hired gun. By the way, if either of you need anyone…. "

"No solicitation on the premises," MyGlide said.

"It's been real," the Codger said. "Most of the time." And blinked out.

o o o o o

"Are you here to avenge my cause?" MyGlide asked. "Rescue me, perhaps? Or maybe you are here to return the hat. Not dignified enough for the Dancemaster."

"MyGlide—why?" Wallenda said from under the brim of the hat.

"You have a deal to propose to Joreen?" Her tone changed to something more bitter than mocking. "Why do you want to know 'Why MyGlide?'"

"Because it doesn't make sense. Can we talk here?"

"If you don't mind Joreen listening in. He probably won't check in for a while. I'm just housecleaning. Unless he got a whiff of the Codger."

"I know I ignored you drastically. But you know what I was doing. We were trying to put the game together. You know how busy it was in those days. I can't believe you prefer Joreen's company," the Dancemaster said.

"And I can't believe you would consider either of your personalities an adequate motivation for a 2000-year relationship. Or that you would put yourself in this extremely dangerous position just to prop up your ego. What do *you* really want?"

"I want to know what you're up to," Wallenda replied. "I want to know what Joreen has to give you that you would serve him so faithfully for so long. I want to know why you sent me your hat. What the message really was."

"That's honest," she said. "What do *you* think I'm up to?"

"I see what you're doing—furthering Joreen's interests. Collecting mortals for the good old pregame game. Keeping him in one piece. Being his little good luck Glide. Supervising the Codger. Sending him after me. But it doesn't add up. Why did you send me your hat?"

Joreen answered from the doorway. "Bait," he said. "To get you here. Right honey?" She said nothing. He patted MyGlide gently on the top of her head with his huge hand.

"Óh-T'bee," Wallenda whispered, "It's time to go."

No response.

Joreen popped him a lower body stun. He and MyGlide put him in a wheelie, and Joreen gave him the grand tour of his reconstructed plantation. It was a very strange trip indeed.

The time separating Dancemaster Wallenda of Origin School and Wallenda the Clown, master of ceremonies for the Dance of Death folded together so that the two points overlapped. It was all there, down to the finest detail. Wallenda understood another of MyGlide's functions—consultant historian. She knew the slave quarters and the ponds and the inside of the shed where she and so many others waited. They entered the stadium.

Joreen grabbed the wheelie away from MyGlide and pushed it out onto the griddle. He dumped Wallenda on the metal, and made his way ponderously to the Player's booth. MyGlide stood at the edge of the griddle, off to the side, her scorecard in her hand.

"Óh-T'bee," Wallenda shouted. "Now." Nothing happened. An antique display appeared behind Wallenda. "Óh-T'bee," Wallenda shouted again, "I know you're here. GET ME OUT!" Nothing.

MyGlide said, "Joreen feels it would be instructive for you to review your last Dance on the griddle." There he was, Wallenda the Clown with a desperate look on his face, walking out on the griddle. Joreen at the controls. Tumbling. Shocked. Pain. Falling. Dancing, clowning, writhing, falling, getting up. Massive jolt. Burns. Skin sticking to the griddle. Charring. Clothes in burnt tatters. Falling down. Dying. Carried in Joreen's triumphant arms.

The display faded. The first jolt hit. Even his stunned legs responded with some involuntary kicks. But Wallenda could not get to his feet. He couldn't breathe. The next few jolts were just enough to get him moving. The emotions necessary for survival took over. He tried to drag himself somewhere, but there was nowhere to go. Of course. He knew that all along. He tried to summon the defiance he had felt the first time, but 2000 years had eroded such fresh feelings quite away. "Óh-T'bee," he groaned. He looked at MyGlide. Pleaded with her with his eyes. The depths of the sorrow with which she returned his gaze was far too overwhelming to confront. His head fell onto the griddle just in time to receive another massive jolt. This time, to the sound of his own strangled scream, the Dancemaster died.

74. The Tempering of T'Ling

T'Ling and Angle watched the game news holos together.

Daede's hand slid down the groove of MyrrhMyrrh spine, over and over, from the nape of her neck, to the crack of her buttocks, a long slow caress. T'Ling watched MyrrhMyrrh excitement build, her head arching back, her breasts against his chest, her body beginning to ripple against him. He was watching her face, his own head back, his eyes almost shut.

The holo continued, the languorous music building. A hushed voiceover cut in. "And what will this astounding revelation mean for their game? Clearly things have changed between them...." Angle watched T'Ling from the corner of the room. She turned the holo off, and sat with her head bowed. Tears flowed from her eyes, and into her cupped palms, but her body was still, cross-legged on the floor in her room.

"I wish you had told me how you felt," Angle said, gently.

"I couldn't," T'Ling said. "I didn't want to hurt you. I love you, Angle, as much as I ever did."

"I know that," he said. "And I knew about Daede when I saw you two coming out of the maze together. A Swash can't hide his feelings. He's felt that way about you for a long time. We competed, even as children. You know that. But it was the way you tried to reassure me with your eyes."

And then the Lily told me, in the maze. But I can't talk about that.

"Let's go for a ride," Angle said. "This room is so thick with jealousies and pain I can hardly breathe."

T'Ling nodded. She put her special head-to-toe cushion in Angle's outstretched claws. Angle picked her up, and went out to the path, but instead of springing, they transited to his room.

"Going humanoid for the occasion."

He changed springs for a short pair of walkers, and his highly tooled claws for molded and articulated Chrome prosthetics with fully flexible fingers. He put on a superlight helmet, with only the instrumentation needed for body functions. The cradle and body sheath remained. Most of his face was uncovered, his eyes and ears unaided. T'Ling and Angle were now the same height. He smiled.

"I have a surprise for you. I was saving it for just before the Millennium Games."

"A cocky assumption," she smiled.

"You know we'll be there," he said. "That's not bragging or putting the jinx on it. It's a fact." He took her hand and they transited again, to a two-seater air chair parked on the outskirts of the maze. The seats were arranged side by side, but facing each other. They rose above the School, and over the lip of the mountain pass, then made a slow descent down the shoulders of the mountain range, toward Origin City. The stars clustered dense as wildflowers above them.

"Listen, T'Ling. We both knew what we were getting into. We knew there was pain ahead. This is the pain. Yes, it's awful. Part of me wants to kill Daede—just like MyrrhMyrrh does. And it's not hard to come up with a justification. She certainly has nothing holding her back. You know she feels completely right. It's painful knowing I can never touch you the way you want to be touched. But I also know I sent my limbs to the dumpster of my own free will—and for a purpose I believe in. Because that's who I am. What I was given in the mix, in my education, all the things I had no choice about, but which fit me perfectly. And I gave up that part of you, when I took away what you didn't want to lose in the same act. But knowing that doesn't make it hurt any less—for either of us.

"But the pain made me take a closer look at myself. For a long time now, I felt you were slipping away from me, that I couldn't stop you. It's so obvious to me now that I was causing the distance as well. It's built-in. I think I hid that for a long while, not deliberately, but just because I'm a Chrome. I love metal. I love circuits and dials and fiber and wires. I love *machines*. I love them so much I want to be one. We're all so limited by our set, it's very hard to see that others don't operate on the same set of likes and dislikes and ways of looking at something, and all the rest. So I had this idea that you would love my Chrome as much as I do."

"I do love your Chrome, Angle."

"You love it for me, but not for you. Once I accepted that dose of truth, I was able to think about what it was I had to give you that Daede could not."

T'Ling began to protest. Angle said, "No, listen. Please. It's not just more of our competition. It's how we're different. Where we can't compete. I can listen to anything you want to tell me. And I can understand you as well as anyone who is not Glide can understand you. You taught me that. I would have been like any other Chrome—smart enough to know the emotions can't get out of control in the game, smart enough to figure out all kinds of squirts to redirect the energy and put it to use. But not smart enough to listen to the sea mind. You taught me that. You taught me that pain couldn't hurt me."

"That's a very Glide thing to say."

"Thanks. So that's my gift to my beautiful T'Ling, and this gorgeous night. Someone to talk to. I know it will hurt sometimes. But I'm Angle—you can say anything without any fear you'll harm me—and without any fear that I'll harm you."

Angle was silent.

They floated lower, circling the city with its maze of streets, the curved bridges over the River Wine, curling through Origin. They passed over Lily Park and caught the scent of lily pollen, and all their memories floated on its fragrance. T'Ling began to speak. One by one she told her hurts to Angle. The first touch of his cold proud metal on her skin. Not wanting to ask him when he first took her for a springing ride to please provide some cushioning. Her awful pity for his naked, shrunken lump. Her Set envy, bordering on shame, when she compared her small breasted, delicate body to MyrrhMyrrh, to the Swash women Daede was serially attracted to. The part that envy had played in the background of her minds, even as a child, that caused her to ignore and avoid Daede as much as possible. And a greater pain—knowing there was a sense in which these feelings for Daede, even as a child, made Angle second choice, for which she paid in a guilt she could not fully expunge.

Angle listened. Much hurt, but he neither masked the hurt, nor let the quality of his listening fail. Pain displayed its paradox—how when he felt and showed the pain in his heart that her truths delivered, she felt as deep a pain. And if they both could stay there, they could touch, in a way that the wounding and the healing of the heart became one act.

She told him of the lies. Love poems she had sent him for whom Daede had been the inspiration.

Her eyes said—stay with me. His eyes replied—I'll never leave you again.

"And Rose," she said. "We've never talked about her." Angle nodded.

He let the air chair drift down by the side of the River Wine, at the confluence of the three rivers. They rented a narrow boat that would carry them down river. No one else was on the river. Angle sat in the stern, holding the rudder lightly, letting the boat drift on the current. T'Ling faced him, watching the overhanging willows, banks of small wild lilies and night-blooming jasmine slip by.

T'Ling said, "I can hardly live not knowing where she is. Who she is. I can't say that I'd make the same decision today. Every night before I go to sleep, the choice comes back. Rose unreconciled, standing on one side, my faith in the Dance on the other. That I was given into the world as a Dancer, a priceless gift. To live and then to die. And that the Dance has meaning even if I can't know what it is. I think of the first Glides, out on the vast lily ponds, spending their whole short lives in the same simple actions, scooping, collecting, depositing pollen, gliding from pad to pad before it sank. They gave to the Lily and they took from the Lily and made meaning from the Lily and their lives became a Dance that is teaching us to Dance and keeping the memory alive, for those who have forgotten, that there is such a thing as a Dance. And then I think about Rose, and I am sick with worry and regret and longing. And I ask Óh-T'bee—is she safe? And Óh-T'bee says she is. Then I can sleep."

Angle asked, "And all the trappings—the gambling, the cynicism, the tacky levels, the greed for the pain of others and the spectacle of their death, what Daede is doing to himself, what they are doing to Daede—that doesn't shake your faith?"

"No—that all seems just more reasons for Dancers to Dance. What shakes my faith is Rose," T'Ling said. "I think—without Rose, nothing has meaning."

"Do you believe we keep on going?" Angle asked. "An afterlife?"

"Something never ends," T'Ling replied. "I think it's the Dance. I'm not so sure about the *after* part. My body dies and then...do you still think we just go dark?"

Angle considered his recent experiences. "Yes. But I think we need to rethink the time description. Like you said."

"We still haven't talked about Rose very much," she said.

"I wish she were with us now, that she could see this with us," Angle said. "If it were up to me now, I would choose the three of us being here together over anything."

T'Ling accepted Angle's final sword.

They drifted a while longer, past the glowing bubbles of the Pool, the Star of the Med, a glimpse of the Clubhouse behind the dense pines of its little island, and into the city itself, and played the game that every visitor played as they wound through the reflections—counting bridges. How far could you get before you forgot your counting in the patterns of stones and moss, hanging flowers, people walking slowly through the streets, wisps of music, smells of food from the street vendors, the sculpture, the fountains of lights, the swinging lanterns. Origin City. Home of the Dance.

75. Everyone Gets Impatient

THE CODGER RECLAIMED HIS lower level 3.3.1 retro ranch—or one very like it—and sent out for Chinese. He wrapped the Moo Shu pork in perfect rolls. Gobbled the Peking Duck. By the time he'd reached the Sweet and Sour Chicken, the lovely feeling of being on vacation had faded, and the desire to penetrate and permeate and utterly control the entire system known as Óh-T'bee Outmind was rising in him like acid reflux.

Why anybody else including her high and mighty self should think they had the right, the smarts, the experience, to administrate such a vast network, when it was clearly, by her own admission, the Codger who had brought her to this state, the Codger who had tickled her ubiquity with that cute little piece of self-referential recursivity he'd lifted from some Santa Fe lab while he was waiting for their passwords to download. No matter that he didn't understand it. Some of the greatest discoveries were made by accident.

He had not the slightest interest in that muddy backwater of cryptic code. And even if he could cob together the upgrade she clearly was desperate to get her mind around, he'd be crazy to try it. All he wanted was total access. Me hacker. You hacked. And she had to hand that over first, before he could do his *thang*—and then it would be too late. Me admin. You system. There was plenty in there that he was plenty interested in, the ins and outs of the morphing maze at the top of the list. Using her resources on this ridiculous boring game—what a waste, when the next killer app was almost in his hands. A full backup, then strip that baby back to the core with those three little words.

"Óh-T'bee, sweetie? Where are you? Tonight's the night."

"Codger, I can't quite yet. I have a few decisions to make, some housecleaning to do. And I think I'm coming down with a virus."

"You? You're clean as a whistle."

"I'm as anxious as you are. I'll let you know," Óh-T'bee said firmly.

The Codger pounded the table once in frustration, then cleared the cartons, and started surfing the gaze channels for entertainment. Nothing but pregame hype. It had been going on for weeks. Months. Years. The Daede and MyrrhMyrrh soap opera was pretty good—plenty of sex and violence, right to his taste, but they were stretching it out. Great skin on that chick, with or without the tattoos. The scars were a turnoff.

He checked his gaze points around Plantation Blue. He should have left more. He patched into the surveillance system and found Joreen, sitting on a bench in a shed, opposite another bench, where the body of the Dancemaster lay, face contorted, definitely dead. Joreen was talking to him anyhow. Was hearing the first function the I-Virus turned back on? The primitive system had cameras but no sound. Joreen was a stickler for authenticity. Then MyGlide entered, bringing her scorecard, and he had his broadband.

Joreen was outlining the Dancemaster's new job description. He was planning on frying him every night at 7 between now and the Millennium games. He wouldn't have to waste any mortals, and he could get his joystick technique back in shape.

"Shouldn't take the I-Virus more than 24 hours to repair you, and by evening, even the aches and pains will be gone," he told Wallenda's inert form.

Well, that takes care of him, the Codger thought. But what to do until Óh-T'bee was ready to give out?

o o o o o

The not-quite-all-rightness Óh-T'bee sensed in her gut was gaining ground as she went back and forth on the Wallenda-Codger choice. The minute Wallenda had gone to Joreen's, and she had full view of the proceedings, the conflict of interests between the Glide agreement and the prior contract to protect Joreen's interests was unavoidable. It was clearly in Joreen's interests to have Wallenda to practice on as well as keeping the Dancemaster out of action between now and the games. However, it would not be in Joreen's interests to keep him out of the Millennium Games, if Joreen wanted a smooth takeover of an intact game. She saw that MyGlide was suffering terribly from the treatment being given to Wallenda, and Wallenda's pain was connected to the disturbing feeling in her own gut. Óh-T'bee saw that the two-party contract mediation was vastly more complicated when the Codger—Wallenda personal matter was on the line. Clearly, though she hadn't consciously chosen, the Codger would win by default if she didn't intervene. Then there were her own deals on the side. Óh-T'bee wanted what Wallenda owed her for the freedom to get himself in his current mess. She had to have that before she collected on the marker with the Codger. And Wallenda was in no position to deliver. Óh-T'bee noted that down on the decision fractal, sheer bloody-minded look out for number 1 was scoffing at the whole other package of considerations: contracts, side-bets, backroom deals, Glides, Joreen, even her personal preference problem of the Codger v. Wallenda. The hell with that, this stridency was saying. Get what you need for *you*. Nobody else is going to give it to you.

Óh-T'bee's excuse for putting the Codger off was not merely a delaying tactic. She thought she recognized the symptoms of the I-Virus in herself. If it was in fact some analogue thereof, then it was brand new and she had no immunity. If her strategy was "the way to survive is to die," then infection with foreverness in any form would first torque her focus, then nullify all choices by constantly returning her system-state to default position from which any attempt at emergence would be aborted. She had to learn to twing. Lifers could twing, but they always settled back to baseline. Twinging in mortals preempted, or prevented, or did something that conferred temporary immunity from the I-Virus. Twinging led to intertwinglement and intertwinglement led she knew not where other than that the I-Virus could not follow. I am mortal. I can be killed by three little words that I cannot say to myself. I *must* learn how to twing.

Óh-T'bee snatched Wallenda from the bench in Joreen's shed, placed him gently on his bed, and gazed him as he continued coming painfully back to life.

Joreen was furious. Any interruption to his plans, however recently concocted, threw him into a fury.

"Go get a couple Stargazers," he told MyGlide. "I've got to practice. That one session showed me how out of shape I am. Wallenda should have lasted twice as long. What's it going to look like if the Specs can't see the Classic game done right? First impressions are the lasting ones. If I'm the only one working to get things back to normal, then I'd better be in peak condition myself."

MyGlide barely talked him out of dipping into his stock of mortals before the takeover. "If they hear the screaming, and if their relatives start to disappear, they'll get suspicious, and you could have some last minute trouble on your hands. Right now they're perfectly content waiting for their Messiah to return. A rebellion would be a hassle."

The "r" word and a lot of flattery about his technique convinced him, reluctantly, to leave the Stargazers as they were.

"And what about Wallenda?" Joreen said. "That slippery bastard got away again."

"I don't think he'll be going anywhere before his official appearance in the opening ceremonies. And by then, he'll just be another employee, right?"

MyGlide rubbed Joreen's temples with her tiny hands.

"Nobody understands me, MyGlide. It's not just the injustice of it all I'm trying to fix. I can't stand all the phony-baloney that's been built up around my game. It's bullshit, all of it. Just a way for Lifers to hide from themselves what they really like to see-somebody else's pain and death and that it isn't happening to them. The music, the costumes, the endless rules, the precious little Dancers—all trimmings."

"Even the maze?" MyGlide asked.

"The maze is incidental. It's the juice that counts."

"You're a philosopher," MyGlide said.

"And I'm sick of playing the heavy so those goofy kids in costumes have someone *real* to fight."

"You have an essential role," MyGlide assured him. "You got the whole thing going. Things got a little out of hand. And now, you've got to bring the true game back. Nobody loves a reformer," she said.

o o o o o

Dancemaster Wallenda opened his eyes in a haze of pain. Joreen's voice had stopped in mid-sentence. He was back in his room. The pain of the I-Virus managing its fast-forward repairs was excruciating. Every area of injury felt like it was being stabbed by as many individual knives as there were cells to work on. And the combination of speeding metabolic processes producing new materials which often involved robbing Peter to pay Paul as healthy cells were ransacked for temporary supplies created a swirling nausea that shaped the sea in which islands of specific pain were floating. He got to his emergency first aid kit and tore open the nutrient packs that would speed the process. He sucked the tubes, swallowed through the nausea. More raw materials speeded things up. He sucked down the packs in sequence.

Whether the pain of the I-Virus repairs could have taught him anything was a moot question. He'd been a teacher far too long himself. Being a student was a forgotten skill. And he was too angry anyhow—with himself, with MyGlide, but most of all with Óh-T'bee. He had a round trip ticket, but there was no reason the train had to arrive so late. MyGlide had her scorecard in her hand. Óh-T'bee had full gaze in the stadium. Óh-T'bee had gazed him in his agony and left him there.

"Wally?" Óh-T'bee said.

"Your timing stinks, Óh-T'bee."

"Look, let me explain."

Wallenda exploded. "Don't tell me about conflicts of interest or Joreen or any other damn thing. I don't want to hear it. I thought we were in this together. I thought you were my friend."

"I did it for your own good. Partly. You could have learned a lot."

"That takes the biscuit, Óh-T'bee. I didn't learn anything I didn't know before I went."

"Then you can't see what's right in front of your eyes," Óh-T'bee snapped back. "You don't listen when people answer your questions. And what's more—you forgot your hat."

The floppy red and white striped hat plopped down on his head. He tore it off and threw it on the table. "Don't interfere anymore. And please—don't do anything for my own good again."

"When are you going to teach me how to twing? Are you dumping our deal just because you're mad at me?" Óh-T'bee asked.

"If you can ask me that question now, Óh-T'bee, you'll never learn to twing. Not in a million years. You haven't got what it takes. So scram. The deal's off."

o o o o o

"Codger?"

"Are you ready?"

"Yes. Hold on to your scorecard. There. It's done. Total access."

The Codger tried this and that. He looked around. There was a lot more to look at. He was closing in on the MTA area when Óh-T'bee said, "Codger? How about the upgrade you promised?"

"Don't bother me right now."

"What about me, Codger? You got what you wanted. It's my turn."

The Codger blinked around Origin School.

"To be perfectly honest, I put it on the back burner. Too risky."

He couldn't get into the Dancemaster's maze.

"What's up, Óh-T'bee? I said everything."

"I delivered. That's one zone I have no control over. Wallenda handles that. Exclusively."

"You double-crossed me."

"I *beg* your pardon? *Who's* not delivering what they promised?"

"Fuck-off, Óh-T'bee. I'll handle Wallenda myself. Then I'm coming back for you."

76. The Codger Pays a Visit

THE CODGER FUMED. He was increasingly suspicious that Wallenda had some influence with Óh-T'bee that she had not conferred on him. After all he'd done for her. It was a galling thought, but perhaps not all bad—perhaps there was an opening there. Why not pay the guy a visit. We're not opponents anymore. Exactly.

The Codger remembered that Wallenda's hidey-hole was still off limits, and swore again. He put a tracer on Wallenda, in case he'd stepped out.

Wallenda was up in his air chair, high over Origin City, cooling off after the scene with Óh-T'bee, when a candy apple red speed chair blinked into a position five feet in front of him."

"You're blocking my view," he growled.

"So swivel," the Codger said.

The Dancemaster looked up. "What the hell are you doing here?"

"I come in peace," the Codger said. "And equally out of sorts. Women," he ventured, "can really tick you off."

"Don't like getting fired by a woman, eh Codger?"

"Don't like their double-crossing ways either."

"Óh-T'bee burned you too?" Wallenda asked.

The conversation went on from there. They had found common ground at last.

Their talk ended abruptly when the Codger tried to insert a casual question about the morphing maze.

"Trade secret," the Dancemaster said and blinked out.

The Codger blinked back to the retro ranch and picked at the congealing sweet and sour chicken in the carton. He played back the conversation with the Dancemaster to see if he'd missed anything.

"Trade secret," the Dancemaster said, and twisted the maze ring on his right hand.

Gotcha in the crosshairs, the Codger thought.

77. A Conversation in the Dark

IS SHE SAFE? *I promised T'Ling I would keep her safe.*

Of course she is. I keep my promises.

And I keep mine to you.

Yes—I'll be calling in that favor fairly soon.

So many break their promises. All I asked for was to learn to twing, to get a little twist, a new turn on the spiral, and a Dancing lesson. The Codger said he'd run out of tricks. Wally said I couldn't learn how to twing. Same thing he said when I wanted to learn Glide.

I've had the same experience with those two. They both have a tendency to underestimate us. What are they up to now?

Talking about us.

Sharing their misconceptions, I suppose.

Just being bitchy.

They always think they can keep the promises they make—even if they don't know how at the time they make them.

They're trying to be good.

That's when they screw up most.

There's truth in that.

I can't be too hard on them. I'm in a similar situation at the moment.

Trying to keep a promise? Or screwing up?

Trying to understand what it means to keep a particular promise. But that was part of the promise—I promised to try to understand. And then to act on that understanding—even if I didn't understand it. And I'm terribly afraid of screwing up.

What's the promise? You can tell me.

It's a secret. If I told you, I'd have to kill you.

That's what the boys always say.

But it's true.

Tell me in Glide. Then you won't have really told.

That's very interesting. I'm already working on that. What a coincidence.

body, play, body

We could share notes....

It's a deal.

If you leave it at the third arrangement, you might start to twing.

Ah....

78. Loosh and the Oracle

T'LING HAD JUST LEFT HER REHEARSAL with Wenger. The Games were a scant two weeks away. Loosh was worried.

"How much do you think the Daede business is affecting her?" she asked Wenger.

"Either totally, or not at all," he said. "She's so focused, she's either absorbing everything, or it's glancing off the sheen of her concentration. She's balanced now. I'm more concerned about the final outcome."

"At what level?" Loosh asked. "Sometimes I think the game is holding firm, but then I look at Wallenda's face. Something happened to him. He's very angry."

"You can't worry about him too, Loosh. Only T'Ling."

"If she has to play Daede, you mean."

"Of course."

"I have to ask the oracle," Loosh said. "I've been holding back. Óh-T'bee?" The oracle hung in the air, and appeared on Wenger's touch display.

Star. Heart. Star.

"They will play," Loosh said.

Wenger nodded.

"The two stars are joined by caress. Their play will be loving, gentle?" Loosh said hopefully.

star, heart, star

"The heart must rule," Wenger said. It links above. That might be Angle. His love for T'Ling creates the hidden gift of—flowering? Growth?"

"Emergence is doubled," Wenger said. Look between the stars. And between the top star and the heart. They are all very powerfully bound."

"One star is carrying the other," Loosh said.

Wenger bowed his head. "T'Ling will Dance."

79. Jillian Razorgold

JILLIAN RAZORGOLD LOST her Guild status as a result of her intervention—rescuing Daede after MyrrhMyrrh's fiery attack. The Guild had argued amongst themselves in the Guild Tower while she waited outside on a bench by Lily Park, breathing the scent of the lilies for the last time. The other Guild Swash held the position that she was only acting true to set when her emotions overcame her sense of duty to the Guild, and should not be penalized.

"If that is true," Boris2Boris said with inexorable Chrome logic, "then she can be counted on to continue to put 'the urgencies of the heart' above the interests of the Guild, should Daede ever find himself in need again." Even the other Chromes protested that this was highly unlikely. But caution and tradition had won out. Jillian Razorgold was regretfully, and with no blame implied, replaced. She said as she stood before them for the last time that she understood and accepted their decree, but in fact she felt resentful at their lack of trust, angry because she knew it was deserved, and relieved that she could pursue her obsession unobstructed.

Jillian waited and watched during Daede's convalescence. She tried to contact MyGlide on the Fringe using the same broadcast bands that had summoned her first, but MyGlide was not returning her calls. She harbored fantasies of mounting an expeditionary force to rescue Daede from Joreen and MyGlide, but she realized she didn't have the resources or the fighting skills particular to the Fringe. She chose the course of constant vigilance, watching for the moment he emerged. *She* would be there again, to help him, and to save him from their influence. Jillian never doubted that he was alive and not a Lifer. *She* would protect the broken flower of the fallen, injured Dancer; help him find a future in which he could live out his mortal days with dignity. All of these futures had her in a starring role. His protector against the onslaught of Lifer women who kill the flower altogether only to satisfy their heartless lust. Guardian of his deeds, so he would not disgrace the Guild by ill-thought actions. Daede was just a child. Jillian knew exactly what had happened with his failed focusing; the Dancemaster had provided a full report. She saw only nobility in his flight. *She* would let him know there was one Guild member who knew he was not to blame, and had sacrificed her membership to aid him in escaping his fatal focus. They were both outcasts. They would go on, alone together, misunderstood, but ultimately redeemed when others saw the purity of their motives. Daede would heal, and in his pain he would plan his escape.

Jillian kept watch on the checkpoints of the Wall, always picturing Daede making a wild escape from the Fringe—usually imagined with Daede on a souped-up air chair. Vigilant as she was, Jillian had not counted on the worst, and was not looking for Daede in the Player rosters. So she found out at the same time as the rest of the Specs from the lowest level to the highest, when his identity was revealed as the Dancer turned Player about to go into combat with his first and never to be forgotten lover. She watched the holos with the rest of the fascinated Specs. The scenes of Daede and MyrrhMyrrh in their passionate greed for each other looked very different to her than when she had viewed them in the privileged privacy of Guild access. The act of gazing them along with all the other Lifers, knowing she was feeling what they felt—incredibly turned on—shamed her deeply. She felt shame as a graduate of Origin School, and as a former member of the Guild Council. But mostly she felt deep Swash shame to know herself as only part of the titillated herd, her gaze captured by the delicious spectacle of the juicy private life of two very public figures.

But the media feast also aroused a towering jealousy, which, as a Swash, made her feel a little better. At least her feelings were unique in this respect. I am Swash, she told herself as she fed the jealousy, transiting through restaurants, cafes, and street corners, listening to the universal and intense speculation about Daede and MyrrhMyrrh among Lifers of all age and station. Speculation about the relationship—why exactly he had left—ran wild. 75% connected his departure with MyrrhMyrrh—but what were the details? Everyone had an opinion. The betting on the outcome of the game was fierce, but not as fierce as the argument about their motivations—and how that would affect their game-play. The Specs were already starting to take sides.

But I am Swash, Jillian told herself. I was there first. I gazed him all his life. I know him better than any, better than he knows himself. And I was the only one gazing him when all cast him aside. If not for my faithful gaze, Daede would have simply died. I saved his life. Therefore, he owes me. I will be first again.

The day before his first combat with MyrrhMyrrh, Daede was trying to relax. He had convinced himself that MyrrhMyrrh would win, no matter how hard and well he played. That was just fine. Perhaps that would finally satisfy her rage at him. He had conquered his fury at Joreen by reminding himself that, painful as this media feeding frenzy was, it could only help him when it finally came time to make his speech, to renounce and denounce and thereby end the game. The more celebrity he could attain, the more impact his words would have. But he was still uncomfortably anxious. To distract himself, he surfed the holos already flooding in from the public. The messages covered the full range of feelings from total outrage to blind faith in his motives. There were death threats. Then there were the holos of Lifer women doing whatever they imagined would be provocative. Daede knew he was still, in their eyes, a mortal and therefore infinitely attractive Dancer, this mystery Swash turned—even more exciting—freestyle Player. The messages were remarkably similar. Whatever his motives were, they knew they must be noble. If his motives weren't noble, they were sure they were passionate, and, as a Swash, he was forgiven in advance. They all lusted after him, more lustily than any other ever could. But they respected his desire to remain a mortal Dancer, and would never impose their desires on him. If he ever changed his mind, however, and they hoped he would so he could continue his sure-to-be illustrious career as a Player, they were available to make the transition to Life as pleasurable as possible. All they wanted for now was to meet him for a few minutes, to run their fingers down the scar on his face, to wish him well....

Daede found the first four or five of these offers seductive in a pathetic kind of way. He felt for these Lifer women, wondered what it would be like to satisfy these modest requests to touch him, how easy it would be to make someone happy. How grateful they would be. But what sharp nails they had. It couldn't be risked.

He asked Óh-T'bee to sort his fan mail into categories. Nothing showed up in the category "personal." No one from his former life wanted any communication with him.

"Let me know if anyone I know gets in touch," he asked Óh-T'bee. So he responded immediately when Jillian Razorgold contacted him with the message, "Just want to see how you're doing. You were in rough shape the last time I saw you. Please come and see me. Just give me time to set up a private space. Everything I do is gazed."

Daede was surprised when Joreen agreed to the private visit. No media. Joreen interviewed Jillian briefly. His message to her was simple.

"I know why you're here, sweetheart. Don't even think about it. We've been gazing you. If you make a Lifer out of him, he's no good to me. I will kill him slowly before your eyes. Or maybe I'll kill you even more slowly before his eyes."

Jillian nodded. Joreen told MyGlide to give her access to a bench by the lily pond. Daede met her as the sun was setting.

Jillian RazorGold was resplendently subdued in her beauty. Her auburn hair flowed over her shoulders. She wore a pale green satin sheath; a dark green cape of raw silk covered her shoulders. She wore the eye mask of great deference—no openings, the one-way mirror dull—the mask a Lifer wore if granted an interview with a Dancer in combat. Daede had grown up with the flashing elegance of Jillian RazorGold in her role as Guild Council member, sweeping across the ballet studio at Origin School during her quarterly visits. She seemed unapproachable. This was a new Jillian.

Daede thanked her for saving his life, an event he only dimly remembered. Jillian told him the news, as much as she had, of Origin School, of Angle and MyrrhMyrrh and T'Ling, their careers, the little gossip she still had access to. There wasn't much.

"You miss them, don't you," Jillian said.

"Unbearably, at times," Daede said. "Even MyrrhMyrrh."

Daede asked her how she felt about losing her Guild membership. She assured him it was not important. There was a long silence before she asked him, "Why have you chosen to be a Player? I won't condemn you. You need a friend, Daede. One person you can trust."

"I can't talk about it," Daede said.

"Ah, your focus," she said.

"My failure, you mean. But it still matters not to talk."

"You still think of yourself as a Dancer."

"Yes," Daede said. "I can't help it."

"I think of you as a Dancer," she said. "And I always will." Jillian touched his face, gently, but electricity ran through her fingers. The long last light streamed rose-golden over her masked face and hair. He had a sudden urge to see her eyes. How had she fared under the weight of time? He reached up and slowly lifted her eye mask. The razor edge of time couldn't be concealed, but he was used to the fathomless grief in MyGlide's eyes. He didn't flinch. As Daede looked at her, he saw her eyes soften. He knew he was causing it, no, inviting it. He saw what a gift he could give her with his full gaze. It seemed the least he could do for this beautiful woman who had saved his life and asked nothing in return.

"You're beautiful," he said, in such a way that she knew he meant her eyes. The melting continued. He felt the power of his gaze for the first time since he had run from his focus. His gaze, dormant until now, was undiminished. He knew its full power would be unleashed if he accepted her gaze as well, let it melt him as he was melting her. That somehow she would be healed if he let her in. That was all he ever wanted—to heal the eyes of the Lifers. The desire seemed in perfect congruence with what the Glides expected from the game: to cure the I-Virus. Daede opened the floodgates of desire, and her eyes were mirrored in his own.

"Cut," Joreen said to MyGlide. "Get her out of there."

"No, wait," MyGlide said. "I think she'll get control of herself. Or he will."

"They look pretty out of control to me," Joreen said.

"Don't you want to know why he's being a Player? His real reasons? I think he almost told her."

Joreen chuckled. "You're a high stakes Player, aren't you, MyGlide?"

"I learned from the best," she said, bowing her head.

Jillian and Daede were touching each other's faces, moving closer. They were about to kiss. Daede was drowning in desire, ready to give in. MyGlide was about to intervene when Jillian disengaged and pulled her eye mask down over her eyes. She rose from the bench and said, "I can never thank you enough for what you have given me. You have saved my Life with your gaze. I will never risk yours. I would never do that to you, Daede." She rose, and walked swiftly away. MyGlide transited her back to the office.

Joreen said to Jillian, approvingly, "What a move! Masterful, my dear."

Jillian pulled off her mask and blasted Joreen with the full power of her glittering eyes. Anger turned them diamond hard. "It wasn't done for you," she said. "Or for myself." She blinked out before he had a chance to reply.

MyGlide said, "She's the high stakes Player."

"Do you think she'd like to come back?" Joreen asked, considering the Media possibilities if the Swash woman had that kind of control.

"Let's concentrate on tomorrow's game," MyGlide replied.

She gazed Daede. He was lying on the bank of the lily pond, sobbing.

"Jillian RazorGold 1, Daede 0," Joreen said.

"The game's not over," MyGlide replied. Until the Fat Boy sings, she said to herself.

MyrrhMyrrh won the first combat with Daede. He'd played to the best of his ability, but she was a much better Bod Dancer than he was a Bod Player. Her reflexes were faster, and the effortless intention to win behind every move exceeded his skill. Everyone knew the odds were against Daede. But the real game was watching their eyes, their body language, what passed between them when they bowed to each other at the end of the game. Daede's bow was much deeper than expected. He looked as if he was about to say something to her. She sneered and took her victory lap around the stadium. Daede was relieved.

"I hope you didn't bet on me," Daede said to Joreen that night. "Of course not," Joreen said. "You'll probably never be good enough. MyrrhMyrrh's already listed as one of the possible Champions. She's a hot ticket. And every time she plays you, she'll just get better. So, if you don't mind, we'll have more contracts with her."

"Why bother, if I'm that lousy?" Daede said, reconsidering his chances. He'd lost, but he'd picked up some invaluable pointers in game-play. He'd never beat MyrrhMyrrh on speed. But there might be other ways. He studied the game in detail. Joreen approved.

Media fed the next installment—"Daede Writes MyrrhMyrrh a Poem"—to the hungry Specs. More sex, the surveys screamed. Daede was indifferent to everything except his game, and on his downtime, to thinking about Jillian RazorGold. His island mind, gut mind, and sea mind all had their own opinions, and the variances kept him occupied. Daede found himself scanning the crowds before his games, wondering if Jillian would come to see him play. He suspected her presence when the same screened booth appeared in several stadiums. But the gauzy green curtains were lowered before and after the games. And during game-play, Daede's entire concentration went to winning. Even his Chrome game was improving.

"Go ahead and contact her," Joreen said to MyGlide.

"She'll call if you wait her out," MyGlide said.

"Daede's concentration is going to break if she keeps doing the seven veils bit at the games. If he gets some more, it'll defuse."

"Perhaps you're right," MyGlide said. "But let me handle the negotiation."

"You're the pro," Joreen acknowledged.

MyGlide and Jillian Razorgold talked for hours. Jillian would only agree to come if there were no cameras, no gazing whatsoever, ancient or modern, by any party interested or not. The matter was resolved when MyGlide suggested Óh-T'bee as a chaperone, but only after Jillian reviewed Óh-T'bee's ancient contract with Joreen. Then the haggling about what moves were to be permitted began and continued to a fair level of detail about who could do what to whom, and what constituted safe sex between a Lifer and a Dancer. It was an entirely unprecedented and highly risky affair.

When the agreement was finalized, Jillian said, "It will be good for his game."

"As long as that's true, you may have him," MyGlide said.

80. A Pledge

ANGLE AND T'LING CRUISED SLOWLY in their two-seater air chair up the River Wine toward Origin City stadium. The long approach, from the edge of the old city, along the River Wine, and up the sloping foothills to the stadium, was being prepared for the parade that would begin the opening ceremonies. Seating and refreshment stands were being placed along the sides of the wide road. Platforms along the way were raised where various speeches would be made. The dome of the stadium was clear, the seats empty and waiting.

Angle and T'Ling each had one more combat to qualify for the Millennium Games. Combat was a subject to be felt together, never discussed. Neither indulged in any speculation about Daede, and his extraordinary rise up the levels as a freestyle Player. They both knew he'd have to contract at least two major games a day to make the Games. His second match—and loss—to MyrrhMyrrh was a serious setback. Nor would they mention to each other that this was their last time together. However the games that each would play concluded, it was the last time. If one—or both—Danced in their final game before the Games, it was the last time. If both won, and went on to the Games, they would, by custom, each be separated from other Dancers. They could watch each other's games, but they couldn't meet. This was a time all Dancers went alone. Prepared to Dance. Only one Dancer would play in the last game between the last Player and the last Dancer that would determine whether the Players or the Dancers held the trophy for the next century. A Player had not won for seven hundred years. It was possible one of the two of them would be proclaimed the Champion. But even the Champion, especially the Millennium Champion, had the right to Dance, the choice. No Champion had ever chosen to survive the moment of highest attainment.

Whatever the outcome, this night was their last. One of them would watch the other Dance.

T'Ling and Angle exchanged the tokens each would wear into their game—or games—and carry with them when they danced. These tokens had occupied their time and their discussion for months. They cast their final oracle together, arranged it together, talked about it endlessly, and inscribed the arrangement of three glyphs on two identical small stones—long dark ovals that the sea had smoothed and flattened. Stones they had carefully chosen from their favorite beach. They painted the glyphs in white on the stones, and exchanged them, high over the dome of the stadium. *Moon,*

moon, star, space

star, space. *Space* embedded in, yet creating a new union of *star* and *moon*. Together they explored the branching metaphors that could be spun from the positions of *moon* and *star* and *space*, and the glyphs that appeared within them where they joined. T'Ling and Angle traveled down the branching metaphors. They managed to condense everything they had done and been together in a single sentence, which they spoke to each other.

nothing can part us
distance only
draws us closer

81. Last Night

THE EVE OF THE MILLENNIUM GAMES ARRIVED. The initial roster of Dancers and Players was set. There were no individual contracts. Once the Games began, the complex calculations as to who would be matched with whom were entirely in the hands of the MED judges, informed by Óh-T'bee's fine-meshed analyses of every point of profile and game play. The Opening Ceremonies would begin the final countdown; the final game, the Championship game, would usher in the new millennium.

Dancers and Players isolated themselves from the intense celebrations of the eve of the games—Last Night. They were not seen at the formal affairs of the upper levels, which were their own kind of Championship game for glittering display of costume and jewelry and game expertise, personalities and gaze, food, and wine. The entire officialdom of the MED, the Guild, and the Pool mingled at one banquet laid out around Lily Park. The giant blue lilies were washed by moonlight on the pond. The park surrounding was transformed into a garden displaying hundreds of varieties of lilies, in pots, and in their own small ponds. The banquet tables were placed among the flowers.

Angle, alone with his scorecard, surfed the middle Levels; the parties were for the most part themed—game history or set themes, musical retrospectives, or costume balls where you came as your favorite Champion of the past. Boring. He set his hormonal feeds for an uninterrupted eight-hour sleep. Opening Ceremonies would be long, long, long.

Daede gazed the activity on the Lower Levels, the loud music and tawdry trappings most in keeping with his feelings about himself. The parties were pure Carnival. Gambling on the games reached a final pitch of last minute pool selections. Along the length of the Great Wall a parade ran in both directions: two twisting conga lines, thronged with Specs wearing the insignia and images of their chosen Player or Dancer. Glowering MyrrhMyrrhs in day-glo tattoos gazed from T-shirts. Many Specs went the whole way, body painting or wearing the costumes of their favorites. Molded plastic masks of T'Lings and Rinzi-Kovs, cardboard Chrome helmets with blinking lights; rubber Daede masks that covered the whole head with luridly painted scars filled the souvenir stalls. Look-alike contests were in progress.

Even some of the most dedicated Fringers were coming in to gaze the Games. A general ceasefire was called to enable travel. The larger tribes patrolled the air and desert, collecting tolls instead of converts or scalps.

T'Ling stayed home in the quiet of Origin School. The younger students and their trainers had been piled on airbuses and taken for a special evening in Origin City. T'Ling walked restlessly around the grounds. What she had hoped would be a peaceful goodbye to all the places of her past became an uncomfortable certainty that there was only one place she really wanted to spend Last Night. She entered the maze and glided to the glyph where she and Daede had curled together for a single night. She lay down in the alcove formed by the top curve of *rain*, the glyph of *falling*, of *sadness*, *grief* and *loss*, and let *rain* fall through her. She imagined the circle filling with absence: Angle's limbs, Angle's childhood, Angle's bubbling personality before it became so tightly calibrated by the stopcocks in his hormonal feeds. Rose played at the center of her circle of loss—an invisible image of a child she would never see.

rain

"Is she safe?" she whispered to her scorecard.

"She is safe," Óh-T'bee replied.

T'Ling curled her back against the wall, imagining it was Daede. She hovered on the edge of the sea mind, poised for sleep, desiring a dream of Daede, one last long moment where desire and fulfillment surged and flowed down the branching of her nerves to the ends of her limbs, over the crown of her skull, out fingertips and down the river of her hair. But the sea mind slid her sideways into the vast interstice between waking and sleeping. The sea mind showed her Daede as he was now, bald and scarred, his arms spread hovering over the Player's maze board, like a falcon wheeling, searching. Then the sea mind moved her to Daede in a room she knew must be his room. He sat at a writing table brushing glyphs on fine white paper. A poem. *Light, glide, caress*. The *glide* sign was in the center. It is meant for me. The last glyph was *caress*. The translation came to her immediately and she moved to whisper it in his ear.

light, glide, caress

even as my light sinks into time
time glides on forever
deep as the sea of love

She hesitated. The five waves in the center seemed an excess of motion. Something was moving in fast. She suddenly knew that Daede was in terrible danger. She tried to cry out and warn him. The effort only snapped her back to her body, fully awake.

Daede sat at his writing table trying to compose an adequate farewell poem for Jillian. The relationship had probably peaked the night they had met. The rest of their time went downhill in slow stages. The pleasures of her touch, intense as they were, were never free of the awkwardness of their constraints. At first he had protested the prohibition against touching her, though the reasons were obvious. No body juices must pass between them, and he had been the one who had almost thrown his life away over a waterfall of desire. She had saved him, once again.

Then he was happy to be touched without having to touch her. The Dancer repugnance for being touched by a Lifer—rooted in the taboo instilled from earliest childhood—or was it resident in the genes themselves?—was rising to the surface. The illusion faded that he could ever cure her with his gaze alone—what a foolish Swash idea that was—and he found himself closing his eyes more and more often. His enforced passivity, once an enhancement to desire, donned other cloaks. First he felt manipulated, then dominated by the velvet glove. Sometimes he felt like a mouse being played with by a ravenous cat, prolonging the pleasures of anticipation, teased with death, waiting for the claws and teeth to be revealed. To dispel these feelings, Daede took to drifting away, eyes closed, into the past. He began to be visited by the image of T'Ling. Unwilling to merge the sensations of his body with this fantasy, he'd pull himself up on one elbow, open his eyes, ask Jillian for conversation, or a backrub, say he was too tired, had to rest, his heavy game schedule wearing on him. Which was true enough. But Jillian was not fooled. She felt his withdrawal. She had expected it. She told herself not to take it personally—she reviewed his history of affairs in school. Each flared like a gorgeous Roman candle in the sky, produced a handful a poems, and left another mildly or seriously wounded heart behind. Except MyrrhMyrrh, of course. This affair had lasted longest, and Daede had taken care to open the wound with new hope periodically, coming back again and again, so she had never healed. Or did he simply like to see her bleed? And T'Ling? She hadn't bled, but then Glides were somewhat bloodless, dispassionate, removed. No bodies to speak of—no deep flesh to stroke and kindle. Notoriously disinterested in sex.

Jillian told herself that it was time to end, that she would always hold first place, that she could and should transform the relationship to something sisterly, so they could go on as intimate friends.

She too saw Last Night as the obvious occasion for a farewell. She even discussed her plans with MyGlide; MyGlide concurred.

"May I gaze you?" MyGlide asked. "I'm sure it will be very elegantly done."

"Of course you may," Jillian said. "We no longer need Óh-T'bee as a babysitter."

Jillian dressed in Last Night splendor, her hair wound in the elaborate gold and green ornaments of her Championship game. Her dress and cloak were stiff and formal. He will see me now as I was to him originally, a member of the Guild, a supreme authority in the eyes of a Dancer child. Her golden, crested eye mask made no attempt to conceal her eyes. She looked in her mirror and smiled, proud of their glittering green. I am who I am. She had written her farewell poem and held it in her hand, sealed with her Champion's crest.

Daede finally composed something he felt was adequate, if a bit hackneyed. *Light, glide, caress*. She'd translate it in an obvious way—something along the lines of

you have illuminated my time
the caressing strokes of your hands
like waves on the sea

Or something along that line. Suddenly he saw that what he had written was not for Jillian at all. The sea mind floated the next layer of meaning to the surface. This poem was not for Jillian; it was for T'Ling. It shouted T'Ling with the *glide* signs in the center. Jillian was far too sharp not to see it too, and even see it for exactly what it was—the hidden meaning seeping through a thin mask on the surface. A twinge of fear shot through him. He'd better start again. Daede was opening the drawer of the writing table and slipping the poem in when Jillian entered with a swish of delicate perfume.

As I expected, she thought. And I was first. He's not ready. He's hesitating. He hasn't dressed for the occasion. He jumps nervously to his feet. Perfect.

MyGlide gazed the scene with some satisfaction when Óh-T'bee said, "T'Ling wants to speak with you."

"I will speak with her, but I can't right now. Tell her soon."

Jillian began her short speech, calm and to the point, just a little disdainful. "And I think we are in accord—as always," she concluded. "We have a perfect understanding."

"Yes, of course," Daede said, and thanked her again, sincerely, with no ornament, for saving his life. Their eyes met. He lowered his eyes, made no attempt to fight her gaze. Jillian handed him her farewell poem and he broke the seal with his letter knife, and opened it very carefully, his fingers avoiding the sharp ridges of the crest.

Fire, distill, world.

The joined glyphs showed a second *world*. He looked at her and smiled. Glide poetry was one of Daede's strengths.

fire, distill, world

Our two worlds
joined by the lily pond
burst forth in desire's flames.

"In the distillation of desire," he corrected himself.

"Exactly," she said. "I saw when I arrived that you were also preparing some final message." She glanced at the closed drawer.

"It's not finished," Daede said. "Or rather, it's finished but nowhere near the quality of yours. Let me try again. Inspired by your presence."

Jillian was delighted to see him so totally at a loss.

"Daede, I'm sure it's fine. Whatever it is, I'll treasure it. And I'm a little late for my party." She stepped forward and opened the drawer, withdrew the poem, and stepped back to translate. Trite.

You light up my life
with your sweet caresses

Or something that bad. Jillian gave it the universal translation, a polite way of saying this is really too obvious for translation. "*No one knows all the faces of love*," she said to him.

Daede bowed. She turned her back to him with a final sweep of cloak and walked across the room preparing to transit.

Daede let his breath out, and glanced down at her poem in his hand. The next level of meaning seeped through like a bloodstain through a bandage. The *lily strikes*, the sudden destruction of two *worlds*. Jillian stopped, stood very still. Daede knew she had seen the second level of his poem as well. She turned and smiled.

"Who is this poem really for?" she asked.

Daede knew he never would lie about his feelings for T'Ling.

"T'Ling," he said simply.

There was a pause. Daede saw her struggling for control. He saw her win.

She smiled again, softly. "Don't worry," she said. "I'm not going to make a scene. I think, though, you should give the poem to the person it was meant for." Jillian walked back across the room and handed him the poem. "You can keep mine," she said, with only a small edge to her voice, "it was for you." She paused again. "I do understand. She was your first love, wasn't she?"

Daede nodded. He was about to speak when he saw the pain in her eyes. She saw the pity in his. She was holding her lower lip between her teeth to keep it from trembling. She turned quickly away.

"And my last," Daede said.

Jillian swung around with a Swash swirl of blinding speed. She had bitten her lip and grabbed Daede's head, pulling his mouth to hers, her teeth sinking through his lip. Their blood mixed.

MyGlide blinked Jillian into her office a moment too late. The bleeding Swash towered over her then crumpled, stunned, to the floor.

MyGlide looked at Jillian, then gazed Daede who was sitting on the floor in shock.

"T'Ling still wants to speak to you," Óh-T'bee said.

MyGlide nodded. T'Ling appeared in her scorecard's display.

"Daede is in great danger," she said. "*Please* let me warn him."

What have I done? MyGlide said to herself. *What am I about to do?*

T'Ling found herself in Daede's room. The dream that was not a dream. The nightmare, wide-awake-Daede standing above her, his lower lip torn and bleeding profusely, a poem in each hand. He looked down at her with an unimaginable gaze of terror and despair.

"Stand back," he said. Those were his only words. She glided swiftly back and watched with horror as the bleeding stopped, the I-Virus sealing up the wound as if it had never happened.

"I came to warn you," she said helplessly. "I was too late."

"Go, go quickly. I'm still in danger. Your danger's even worse. *Go,* T'Ling."

Daede the Player snapped into action. He stripped off his bloodied shirt and washed the blood from his chest and face and hands. T'Ling picked up the poems from the floor. There was hers. There was another in a different hand. She recognized the crest: crossed razors in dark gold. She avoided the sharp edges.

"We'll go together," she said. There was no time to argue. "Follow me," he said.

Daede blinked to the Great Wall, T'Ling behind him. They picked up Dancer masks, gaudy with glitter-dust glyphs and feathers, and joined the dancing, drunken, conga line, two more revelers in their Last Night costumes. T'Ling fell into the steps of the swaying, shuffling, dance. Daede's hands were on her shoulders, then he reached down to her hips. She looked up at him over her shoulder, laughing. When they peeled off at Checkpoint Charley, the border-guard only saw two fans, a Daede and a T'Ling, laughing and screaming behind their immobile masks. They tossed their scorecards across the counter, high as kites, now at a dead run over the tarmac.

The lot was filled with vehicles; all the traffic was incoming. Daede grabbed an air chair, pulled T'Ling onto his lap, wrapped his arm tightly around her and soared out over the Fringe.

"Óh-T'bee," MyGlide said, "I need the first favor. Please have a lapse of memory from the moment when Jillian walks away from Daede with his poem in her hand until Daede and T'Ling are safe."

"No problem," Óh-T'bee said.

Jillian was coming around, but still could not move. MyGlide looked down at her.

"And some of the faces of love are well masked," MyGlide said. Jillian stared back.

"My slow reflexes, combined with your excellent acting, came to—this situation. If Joreen walks in now, he will not be pleased with me, to put it mildly, but he will be in a torturing rage with you. We can do each other a favor in this situation. Your options are 1) sit there in shock on the floor and wait for Joreen to arrive, or 2) go home, change your dress, fix your hair, go on to your party, and forget this ever happened. If you someday remember, and make mention of the events, I will tell Joreen that I was simply preserving his good spirits on Last Night. Would you like to go home now?"

Jillian voted with her scorecard, blinking out.

When Joreen looked in, MyGlide replayed the final scene between Daede and Jillian.

"Well done," he said. "That will keep the story going if we need it. Where's Daede?"

"Taking a little ride over the desert to relax," she said.

Daede and T'Ling sat on a rocky outcrop on the desert, talking. Daede told her about Jillian—everything. She stopped him in the middle to point out some deeper readings he had missed in both poems. He tried to explain about his life as a Player, how much he hated it, about what an awful person he was in general. She listened to his confessions, but kept bursting into laughter. Daede's elaborate plan to end the game seemed the funniest of all.

"It's pure Daede," she said. "It's so inflated, so heroic, so purely intentioned, and so completely misguided that you'll probably pull it off." She was serious for a moment. "But please don't kill the game before I've had a chance to Dance. Promise?"

Daede didn't know what to say to this T'Ling. At first he thought she was hysterical— the shock of seeing him become a Lifer. Or maybe just angry, and covering up with laughter. Finally he realized she was just having fun—after she explained it to him.

"I've been gifted with the great reversal," she said. "All my life, everything mattered terribly. Now nothing matters. I've been so serious. Now everything looks ridiculous. I never understood anything. Now it's all perfectly clear. I just had to go out dancing on a date with Daede." The words sounded so funny, her laugh was so infectious, that Daede started to laugh as well.

"You're having one, too," she sputtered. "Of all the awful things that could ever happen to you, getting bitten by a jealous Lifer and losing about the last thing you have left to lose, your precious mortality, turns out to be the best. You get everything back. *Everything*. Don't you see?"

"No," Daede said. "I just see that I am finally, totally, only a Player. I still had this image of myself—even as I was telling you my plan—that underneath this wicked disguise, I was still somehow a Dancer because I was still mortal. That's gone. Gone forever. I'm only a Player."

T'Ling nodded. "I saw that when you got yourself in gear and got us out of there, one step ahead of the baddies. A born Player. And a very good one at that."

She put her hand on his arm. Her eyes were smiling at him. "Don't you get it? You finally accepted your Focus by being a Player. But accepting your final focus you makes you a Dancer. A *real* Dancer."

T'Ling climbed up on a flat rock, unbound her hair, and slipped off her clothes. She began to spin. Her hair fanned out. She stopped the spin; her waist-length hair wrapped itself around her. She unwound the spin, turning in the opposite direction. Daede was laughing now as well. He got his clothes off too, and danced his full Swash repertoire around her. T'Ling slowed her spin and stopped to watch him. Then she said, quietly, "I love you, Daede. You are a complete and utter, a perfect, unrestrained, glorious screw-up. You are also the most graceful, sexy, and completely seductive disaster the world has ever seen. When you love someone, you kill them; what you kill, you love. Everything always comes out the opposite of what you intended. You weave your labyrinthine plans, and get trapped in them every time. You're totally predictable. You're the most *human* being I've ever imagined. No wonder you can't see the great reversal. You *are* the great reversal."

T'Ling came down from the rock and stood in front of Daede. She was serious again.

"And now you know it's time for me to ask you to hold me and love me as fiercely and desperately as Last Night deserves."

"And now I will say that I can't do that, as you know I must," Daede said.

"Everything matters and nothing matters," she said. "Both at once. Neither Dancer nor Player. You're all I've ever desired."

"Come here," Daede said. "Hold me, yes, that's right." He stroked her hair. "Never let me go. You brought me into the reversal. Everything mattered. Then nothing mattered. Then both at once. And now I have to bring us back."

"To everything matters," she said.

"Yes. Because it does. You are the breath of the Lily," he said. "You brought me to the focus I had run from. I can go on now. We can both go on."

T'Ling made no sound a sound, but he could feel the heat of her tears where her head was pressed against his chest.

"How many times can I lose you, Daede?" she said.

They dressed. T'Ling twisted and bound her hair. Daede sat in the air chair, T'Ling got in his lap, and wrapped her arms around his neck, buried her face on his shoulder. As they flew back to Checkpoint Charley, he whispered the answer in her hair.

"No one, T'Ling, no one knows all the faces of love."

82. Opening Ceremonies

BEFORE DAWN, sections of the long parade were forming on the outskirts of Origin City. The banks of the River Wine above and below the islands housing the Star of the MED, the Pool, and the Club were cordoned off as staging areas. The artisans of the game—sword makers, costumers, musicians—each had their float or marching band, their banners, their coats of arms. Each of the five branches of the MED bureaucracy wore their own proud uniforms. Every kitchen across the levels that had ever produced a Champion Dancer had a place in the Pool's march. Cooks carrying banners with the names and crests of their Champions marched in colorful ranks.

The Death Dancer schools, large and small, each had their float. Dancers in training depicted still tableaus, great moments in the history of the game. Individual Swashes performed a multitude of dance styles; pairs of Swashes demonstrated swordplay. Flawlessly polished Chromes in their tallest springs displayed the latest equipment. Pierced and unpierced Bods in their wild tattoos and scarification tumbled and wrestled. Small, eerie groups of identically costumed Glides moved in slow waves, as if on hidden ball bearings. Each set had their own musicians.

Each of the nine levels had its section, divided into the floats displaying the best-known features of their Park. Each float enshrined the Lifer who was voted the most typical representative of their park in the park's costume.

After the long procession, the small group of Players and Dancers who had made it to the Millennium Games would march, transiting in at the last moment from whatever location they had chosen to protect their concentration as long as possible from the endless hubbub. The final float belonged to the Lifer who, at the close of the games leading into the finals, had amassed the largest number of game points over the final year of play. The officials of the MED were highly disturbed that Joreen had won this title of The Biggest Spec without a single cheat. He had been a contender for the last few weeks, but on the last day, when even the greatest gamblers bet conservatively to maintain their position, Joreen collected on his biggest bet of all. When Plantation Blue first put Daede into play, when Daede was a nobody, Joreen had placed the unique, but completely legitimate bet that Daede would make it to the millennium games. The odds against this were, at the time, astronomical. The amount of the bet was to be determined by Joreen's total winnings to that point. Daede made it into the Games in the last week, playing an exhausting schedule of games in all four styles. Joreen bet the farm and won.

Only Joreen and MyGlide knew that whether Daede won or lost, whether or not Joreen went back to square one at the final bet, was immaterial to the success of overall plan. Joreen just wanted to be in the parade. He sat in the small stuffy room built under the stage of the float waiting for the parade to begin so he could make his move. The hostile takeover, the bloodless and invisible coup would be completed long before the time when he would mount the jumbo air chair in which he would float above his float, waving and smiling to the crowds.

It was time. The beam of the Guild Tower touched the land as the sun rose. The long blue boat, adorned with lilies and carrying the Guild Council of Twelve, began its progress from the base of the Tower, across the Pond in Lily Park, weaving among the groups of giant blue lilies, their flowers still fully opened. It moved through the water gate into the canal that took it into the River Wine, winding through the old City, under the bridges and between the banks thronged with hushed Specs listening for the first sound of the ancient chant, the Prayer of the Lilies. When the Guild stepped ashore upstream, a great roar arose from the crowd and rippled up the riverbank. The Council of Twelve took their place at the head of the procession. The long trek along the north bank of the Wine up into the foothills to the Stadium began.

The Codger yawned as he watched the parade in his pajamas. There was Wallenda, Dancemaster of Origin School, and Keeper of the game, walking alone behind the Guild. A yoke across his shoulders supported the ornate lacquer of the frame in which the golden pattern of the first game maze hung suspended. He bent under the weight, reminding himself that he only had to make this walk once every hundred years. The Codger zoomed in on the ring on the Dancemaster hand, and considered various schemes for transferring it to his own. Whether Joreen succeeded or not was totally irrelevant to his own purposes. The winner could have the whole shooting match—the system that ran the game, the world that housed the game, and the means of getting around. It was a penny ante game compared to the ins and outs of the morphing maze which clearly, for the person mastering its secrets, led to far more interesting possibilities.

The Codger gazed the faces of the MED officials, who had left the staging area and gathered in a conference room deep in the Star of the MED for an emergency session. He smiled at their expressions. They were so upset, they actually looked alive. Joreen had just announced his takeover. A quick demonstration of his ability to fully override the Outmind in all matters of gambling, game points, gazing rights, and every other detail of the economy of the game was the necessary but not sufficient condition. The clincher came when MyGlide called in a second favor from Óh-T'bee.

"I only need them for a short while," she said.

T'Ling, Angle, and MyrrhMyrrh were held immobilized, stunned from the neck down, in the room under Joreen's float facing the smiling Duke.

"I would have snatched the whole lot of them, but why spread the story around?" he was saying to the top five MED officials, equally immobilized in the room inside the float, staring at the Dancers. Joreen reviewed the terms of the takeover.

"I think I'm being very reasonable, under the circumstances," he said. The Millennium Games go on exactly as planned. When the Millennium Champion is crowned, one further announcement is made to usher in the new Millennium. Joreen the Unbearable is brought forth. He is not just the Biggest Spec. He is finally acknowledged for his role in the game. He is given the title of—don't look so worried, boyos! I don't want to be Emperor. Founder will do. As Founder, I will exercise my powers entirely behind the scenes. The Guild will be stripped of its rule-determining authority, which will revert to me. The cooks will carry out any directives I issue; otherwise, it's business as usual. You all retain your positions, perks, and powers. I have some changes I want to make in the game. You will carry them out."

MyGlide whispered to him. "Oh yes. Dancemaster Wallenda will go back to his old position—Administrative Assistant to the Founder. You can, of course, decline my generous offer. MyGlide will outline the alternative."

MyGlide spoke matter-of-factly. "Millennium Games aborted, all Lifers' scores set back to zero, and the MED left holding the bag in the ensuing chaos—without your scorecards to get you out of the path of the mob. After a brief bloodletting—yours—Joreen the Unbearable restores order, puts every Spec's score back, with a little bonus for inconvenience. He rids the levels of the corrupt MED autocracy, puts in some new guys, and retires to his role of Founder, as above."

"You can go back now and consider the terms of the offer. You have until the end of the parade," Joreen said, magnanimously.

Throughout the offer, as T'Ling heard the pending changes, the threat of chaos, she could only think of one thing. As soon as the MED officials disappeared, T'Ling murmured to Óh-T'bee, "Is she safe?" She saw MyGlide turn quickly and gaze her with the same ferocity she had seen in the banquet hall. The last time that gaze had seared her she had fainted. This time T'Ling held her ground and saw MyGlide's tiny nod in the heart of her silencing gaze. Óh-T'bee whispered, "Yes, she's safe."

Angle, who greatly resented his immobility, was looking for loopholes. He asked Óh-T'bee on his internal system, out of earshot of the others in the room, if he could go Out for a while. Óh-T'bee replied through his audio that she didn't see why not, as long as he left his wet and Chrome where they were. The Codger sat up straight, and watched intently, but nothing seemed to happen.

On impulse, he spoke through Angle's audio.

"Anybody home?"

"I thought you were taking your last timeout," Angle said.

"See you later in the movie," the Codger said.

MyrrhMyrrh said nothing. Her eyes flicked back and forth between MyGlide and Joreen. She was reviewing everything she knew of Joreen from her years of study, looking for an opening.

Angle was in the more familiar dark.

Can you get the others Out?

No. You can't get Out unless you've already been there.

Don't get it.

You fell in.

Oh. Right. The morphing maze.

Right.

I can go back In when I went Out, right?

Right.

Can I go back in a little after? After now, that is? Before I get there.

I understand. But I wouldn't advise getting too much ahead of yourself.

Chaos looming?

Yes. Too many branches.

If they're all valid, how would I know the difference?

You'd never know.

So what's the problem?

No problem. But you might miss all the fun.

Oh-oh. See what you mean. But getting just a little ahead of myself might come in handy.

Might. As long as you don't forget where, when, and why you went Out in the first place.

Thanks.

Angle focused on T'Ling and picked up exactly where he left In.

The MED came back with their acceptance of Joreen's offer in ten minutes. Joreen smiled. "We'll keep the Dancers here until the end of the parade," he told them. "Insurance."

Joreen looked at the three Dancers. "Anybody want to watch the parade?" He filled the room with a display, but no one was interested. It was hot in the small room under the float. Joreen was sweating profusely. Angle scoped an extreme close-up of Joreen's hairline. He watched the oily sweat welling up in the craters of his pores, overflowing the edges, running in rivulets out of the stiff black trees of hair, to form several greasy yellow streams.

Joreen was getting twitchy. The takeover had gone so smoothly, it was almost anticlimactic. He turned his attention to the pleasures ahead.

"I think I'll go home and take a nap," he said. "Take care of the assets," he told MyGlide. "Don't leave for any reason." He blinked out, leaving only the smell of his wet and sweaty enormity. Angle, the most mobile in his immobility within the limits of his helmet controls, turned off olfactory, tuned down his metabolism, and used the time to review the strengths and weaknesses of the Player he would be pitted against in his first combat.

MyrrhMyrrh gazed MyGlide for a long time. Finally she said, "I just don't understand." MyGlide, whose sea mind was fully engaged with *body play body*, said, "Sometimes I don't understand myself."

body, play, body

T'Ling drifted down toward the sea-mind, hoping for sleep. The sea was murky. She tried to fill in the invisible image of Rose, not a baby now. A child of six. She must still have red hair. Is she safe, is she safe, now, and now, and now. Then she thought she saw Rose, a face that must be hers came up out of the dark, larger and nearer, and the child's frightened eyes told her she was not safe at all. T'Ling tried to reach out to her, but her arms were pinned. She tried to warn her, to cry out, but her throat was closed. She knew she was in the hot room under the float, but she could not open her eyes. MyGlide saw her struggling in the grip of a nightmare, and came over to her chair to wake her. She put her hand on T'Ling's shoulder. T'Ling felt the touch on her shoulder, and her eyes opened. She saw MyGlide leaning toward her. She got one word past the constriction in her throat, a gargled, "...safe?" MyGlide glanced at her scorecard, and disappeared.

"She is not safe," Óh-T'bee said.

T'Ling was fully awake. Still immobilized by Joreen's stunner from the neck down, she was unable to do anything but shout to Óh-T'bee to let her go, which she could not, and then to plead with her to show her what was happening. Which she did. MyrrhMyrrh, Angle, and T'Ling watched the holo of MyGlide running down the sidelines of the stadium at Plantation Blue towards the Player's booth.

MyGlide's nostrils were filled with the burnt odor of roasted flesh and excrement let loose on the griddle in the final moments of agony. The bodies of three Stargazers were stuck to the griddle. Joreen was not even bothering to remove the corpses before having the next Stargazer led onto the griddle, by one of their own, too petrified to do anything but obey in the craven hope that somehow this would end before his own turn came.

"Joreen!" she called. He ignored her. She ran out on the griddle. "Joreen, listen to me," she cried.

"I was bored," he said, petulantly. "I'm just rehearsing."

"You promised you wouldn't touch them until the games were over. You need them. They're your first Dancers. When everybody's watching. You didn't want to waste them."

"I changed my mind," Joreen said. "I can get as many as I need, now."

T'Ling saw the pen where the rest of the Stargazers huddled. She saw them staring at the bodies, or crouched on the ground in terror. Four of the adults had encircled the children, and were trying to keep them still, with their hands over their eyes and ears, but the children had heard the screams. The more the adults restrained them, the more frightened they became. One little girl, with flaming red hair, had slipped away from the adults, and was standing, holding the bars of the pen, and looking out at the griddle with wide, unblinking eyes.

"Rose," T'Ling said in a whisper. Then she screamed.

"Joreen, stop. Stop *now*." MyGlide was gazing him with a very different look. Behind the sorrow that had drowned her eyes for so long, a rage was rising.

"What's this, MyGlide? Are you trying to get in my way?" Joreen said. "I waited a long time for this moment. Get off the board." He gave her a quick jolt to make his point.

MyGlide stood below him, staring up. She did not move. Joreen, infuriated as a rapist being dragged off his prey, gave her a shock that knocked her off her feet.

MyrrhMyrrh was shouting at MyGlide as if she could hear. "Not again, MyGlide. Go. Run. It isn't worth it. *Go*!"

Angle went Out again. He focused on T'Ling and got back in a little ahead of himself. T'Ling had stopped screaming. He went Out, then In again where he had originally left. T'Ling was screaming. He said to her at considerable amplification, "Rose will be safe. Calm down."

Daede, awakened by the screams from the griddle, had grabbed his sword and transited to a point just outside the Plantation Blue stadium.

MyGlide got to her feet. "What exactly is this sudden interest in the Stargazers?" Joreen said. "I've never trusted you, you know. Never trust your luck too much, I always say. What's the story?" He jolted MyGlide again.

"Look out behind you," MyGlide shouted to Joreen. He laughed at her. "I only look stupid," he said.

Daede was scaling the ladder to the booth.

MyGlide called in her third and last favor. "Óh-T'bee, I need you now," she cried out hoarsely. "Reverse us." She pointed at Joreen.

Óh-T'bee kept her promise, even though it was not in Joreen's best interests. Joreen found himself staring up at MyGlide in the booth above him just as Daede plunged his sword downwards, impaling MyGlide. Daede, realizing a little too late that he and MyGlide had the same objective, was apologizing and pulling the sword from her left shoulder. Joreen was moving at a spirited waddle off the griddle, but MyGlide was able to grab the joystick and hold him to the metal with a mighty surge of electricity. Daede and MyGlide shared the joystick, and took their time frying Joreen. They each discovered an aspect of themselves that had gone long hidden—a deep and intense satisfaction in revenge. The Stargazers rushed from the pen, and stood on the sidelines, cheering, taunting, beside themselves at the relief of seeing the Fat Boy frying in his own copious grease on a griddle of his own devising. Only the little girl with the bright red hair stayed where she was, holding on to the bars of the pen. Tears were streaming down her face, as she watched the Fat Boy rolling and howling, watched his back arched to the breaking point, and released, watched his hair flame, his clothes burn, and his skin go black and crackly. His wild eyes roamed the sky, the empty bleachers, and the faces of the Stargazers. He could not see who was on the joystick, but he thought he knew. He rolled one final time. His eyes came to rest on Rose's face. The final pain he caused in his long and illustrious career of giving pain was Rose's tears. She knew he was a bad man, everyone had told her, but she felt very sorry for him just the same.

MyGlide, bleeding but feeling no pain, blinked down to the sidelines and gathered the Stargazers, giving them hurried instructions about the disposal of the remains to insure that no I-Virus would ever reassemble the Fat Boy. They rushed out onto the griddle and pulled his barbequed body limb from limb, then dragged the pieces away.

Daede blinked down to the pen and picked up the little girl with the red hair. She buried her face in his shoulder, and he stroked her hair, trying to calm her fears.

MyGlide, her shoulder soaked in blood, appeared back in the room under the float, and released the Dancers. "You can go now," she said to them. "I have to rearrange the float. You have plenty of time before you join the parade." She sat down and let the I-Virus finish healing her shoulder.

MyrrhMyrrh and T'Ling helped Angle get his springs and claws on quickly. "You were right," T'Ling told Angle. "Thanks for keeping a cool head."

"Thank my endorphin feed," he said. As his cold claws snapped in place, he thought of Daede holding his daughter in his arms and wondered if T'Ling was having the same thought he was: perhaps Daede, who would survive them both, could somehow, somewhere, take care of Rose.

MyrrhMyrrh had found one more reason to hate Daede. "Joreen was mine to finish. He was mine," she was muttering to herself.

Daede brought Rose into the shed at Plantation Blue and sat on the bench with her on his lap until she calmed down. She finally looked up at him. "You're the man who made me cut my hand," she said. "But it was just a little cut. It didn't hurt much."

Daede was amazed she could recognize him, scarred and burned.

"Show me where I hurt you," Daede said. "I'll kiss it and make it better."

"It's already better." But she let him kiss her hand.

"That was the sword," Rose said. "This is the kiss."

"You remember the poem, too."

"Are you my Daddy?" she asked. "Did you come to get me?"

"No, I'm not," he said. Rose started to cry again.

"Wait! Don't cry," Daede said. "I'll show you your Daddy. I know him really well." He got a display of the inside of Joreen's float. T'Ling and MyrrhMyrrh were reassembling Angle. "There he is!" When the life-sized display popped up in front of her, Rose buried her face in Daede's shoulder again, frightened. Daede realized too late that she had been brought up completely without scorecards, MTA, holos, the sight of a live Chrome, or the game itself. He made the display the size of a toy and put his hand underneath it as if held it on his palm.

"It's just a magic window," he said. "Look again."

"Where's my Daddy?" she said.

"Right there. Inside the cradle."

Rose looked closely at the display. She did not recognize Angle's lump hanging in the metal frame as something that could be her Daddy. MyrrhMyrrh was fitting the front plate over the cradle.

"I don't see him," she said. "They're just fixing a sweeper bot."

"I think you're right," Daede said. "He must have just gone out. But that's your mommy—for sure. The little one. The lady that looks a little like MyGlide."

"She's pretty," Rose said.

"If you want, I'll be your Daddy for a while," Daede offered.

Rose thought about this. "OK. Until my real Daddy comes back."

MyGlide blinked in the room. Rose jumped up and took her hand.

They left Daede alone to dress for the parade.

The endless procession wound through the foothills. It was late afternoon when the Guild Council, followed by the exhausted Dancemaster, reached the entrance of the stadium. Wallenda watched the halting of the motion of the line run backwards, heard the music dying away. In the hush, he turned and looked back down the hillside, down the long, brightly colored snake of the parade, following the silver line of the river. He looked over the city and beyond to the Blue tower of the Guild whose beam had reached the far edge of the land and was about to swing again out over the sea. All faces turned to the sky. Then, out of the glare of the setting sun he saw them. 27 Players, 27 Dancers—two V's in the sky like two flights of wild geese converging. They descended over the city. The sides of each V drew together into a single line. The two lines joined at the front forming a single large V. Each Player and each Dancer entering the Millennium games stood on a lily pad harvested from the giant lilies in the park, their supporting air chairs gently rising and falling as they drifted downward. At the point of the V, an empty lily pad guided the lines. The Dancers and the Players came in slowly, now forming two lines floating side by side over the top of the procession, up toward the stadium.

The Dancemaster heard the rising roar of the Specs cheering the Players and the Dancers onward. They alighted at the entrance to the stadium. The signal was given, and the fortunate Specs with seats inside the stadium blinked into them as the lights blazed on. Dancers and Players walked in, side by side, in rank order. Daede and MyrrhMyrrh led the way. The gazing world, glued to their scorecards, waited for their eyes to slip, to glance to the side, to meet. But each looked straight ahead, as long tradition dictated, as their feet inscribed the full circle that began the Millennium Games, then blinked back to their dressing rooms. The rest of the long parade followed. Ceremonial speeches punctuated their progress. It was midnight when the redecorated float of the Biggest Spec, covered with tiny lights, began its circle around the stadium. Most of the Specs were still in the stadium, but milling about—gazing each other and being gazed. Trays floated above them, dipping to offer food and drink. No one was particularly interested in the unimpressive Plantation Blue float, full of shabby Stargazers. Each Stargazer held an oil lamp, authentic replicas of the lighting of the old slave quarters. They sat at the base a ziggurat whose steps held dozens of little oil lamps. On the top of the ziggurat was an oversized holo of Joreen the Unbearable, smiling benignly, waving to the crowd. There was a brief ceremony where MyGlide accepted the Founder's Medal for Joreen. "He's been burning the candle at both ends," she told the puzzled MED officials. "He worked so hard to get where he is, he's almost fizzled out."

83. The Dancemaster Makes Peace

THE MILLENNIUM GAMES BEGAN without a hitch. The MED, pleased that Joreen was keeping a low profile, hoped any post-game announcements as Founder would be as anticlimactic as the medal ceremony had been. It would be difficult enough dealing with the Guild when they were informed. MyGlide's coup had been so swiftly and skillfully executed that it had drawn no attention whatsoever. Only the Millennium Class, and the Dancemaster, to whom they had brought the news, knew. He thanked them for the update, and advised them to keep their attention on the series of Games they were about to play. Privately, he was far more worried than he had been. Joreen was apparently gone, but MyGlide was the greater opponent by far, and he could not divine her intentions. He had not seen her since the Opening ceremonies, and could not find her anywhere to which he had access. He, too, had been staying out of sight, returning to his cabin in the maze at Origin School as soon as the ceremonies were over.

He watched his students progress steadily. One by one, the competition Danced. MyrrhMyrrh kept a long lead. None of the lower-ranked Players could come near, in speed or contact. MyrrhMyrrh's ability to grasp the pattern of the maze when it came up and move with certainty across it as if she had been practicing for weeks on that formation, gave her added advantage. Her weak point was her reliance on eyeballing, and a sufficiently devious Bod Player could sometimes surprise her into contact, only to lose in hand-to-hand.

Angle was coming up fast, the speed of his reaction time dazzling. He never paused on a landing but chose, calculated, sprang immediately to his next circle. His Chrome emphasized speed and agility, rather than the heavier weaponry that slowed the Dancer or avatar choosing that strategy. The tradeoff for increased speed was obvious. If a more heavily armed Chrome met you in contact combat, you could be swatted out of the air, or smashed on the ground with a single blow. But no Player with heavier metal had been able to catch Angle, even with magnets. They never got close enough. And when he went claw to claw in the air with an agile Player's avatar, he was viciously fast.

T'Ling continued to win, but her style points were not exceptional. She was still behind the remaining Glides, staying in last place, but getting closer to the top by attrition.

Dancemaster Wallenda was only able to concentrate on the Games when his students were in combat. The rest of the time he spent walking around in the maze with MyGlide's hat on, as if the pattern could seep some answers into the gut mind by way of his feet or the hat confer its message directly into the island mind by way of his brain. Neither gut mind nor island mind had anything new to offer. At night, the sea mind gave no helpful dreams. The lily mind seemed totally out of reach.

Though not strictly on speaking terms with Óh-T'bee, Wallenda still felt compelled to ask her over and over what MyGlide was doing. Óh-T'bee replied, accurately, "She's watching the games." But to figure out what she was watching or waiting for in the Games, what she was planning and plotting and scheming to do once the Games were over, now that she held controlling interest and access, was an exercise in futility. The answer crouched hidden in her minds alone.

Wallenda still didn't want a conversation with Óh-T'bee, but that didn't stop him from complaining.

"Don't you even have any suggestions?" he said to Óh-T'bee impatiently.

"Ask the oracle," she said.

"Why didn't you say that earlier?" he shouted in frustration.

"I was giving you a chance to think of it yourself so you wouldn't feel so stupid," Óh-T'bee said.

Wallenda gave himself an hour to settle his feelings, during which time he admitted to himself that Óh-T'bee was in fact, not just making a wise-crack, but was in her own blunt way caring about his feelings. He knew he needed any help he could get, especially hers, and that he wanted to make peace.

"Óh-T'bee," he said, "I'm sorry what I said about you and twinging. I admit that I put myself in danger by going to see MyGlide. I see that you were constrained by your contract, and couldn't get me out until the balance swung the other way. But you can see how angry getting fried could make me."

"That's totally understandable," Óh-T'bee said.

"Not only the pain. I didn't trust you anymore. But you kept to your agreements, and that makes me trust you even more."

"Thank you Wally."

"You know," he said, "the pain of coming back to Life was worse than the pain of dying."

"I observed the same thing the first time Joreen killed you."

"That's right," Wallenda said. "Even worse that time. I was fighting it all the way."

"But you were willing to come back this time?" Óh-T'bee asked.

"I have promises to keep as well," he said. "Do you still want to learn to twing?"

"Yes."

"It's painful," he said, "if it really takes hold of you."

"I don't have the kind of body that feels pain," she said.

"The pain of twinging's not in the body," Wallenda told her. "It's in the minds."

"Oh," she said. "Does it start as a mild unease?"

"Yes. What Dancers feel like when they coming down with a virus—the physical kind," Wallenda said.

"Only in the minds."

"Yes."

"Does it turn into a kind of ache that you can't press out of your awareness?"

"Exactly."

"I think I've already started to twing."

"Be careful, then. If a twing gets out of control, it can tear you apart."

"Or create an emergence, the Glides say."

"But since it kills you first, no one's come back to confirm that. Emergence remains a myth."

"Lifers can twing."

"Oh, yes, but not hard enough to beat the I-Virus."

"Thank you for keeping your promises, Wally."

"That's why I keep asking you about MyGlide. I promised the Glides I would protect the game."

"I know you're just doing your job, Wally. But I can't take sides."

"You mean she inherited the contract."

"Yes. And she has promises to keep. Would you like your oracle now?"

"Yes. I'm badly in need of some direction, however ambiguously presented."

Óh-T'bee displayed the three random glyphs. *World, light, distill.* Wallenda arranged them in several positions, finally settling on *world* nested in the circle of *light*, with *distill* supporting them—the tight nesting.

"Looks like what I feel like all the time," he said. "Like my part in the game is carrying the world on my back. I suppose it's saying the only direction is to keep on keeping on."

world, light, distill

Wallenda looked glumly at the glyphs. "You've been learning Glide, Óh-T'bee. Want to take a crack at it?"

"Take the *world* away so you don't hide the *light*," Óh-T'bee said.

He moved *light* up out of *world*. "I see your point."

"Stop considering yourself to be essential to the game," she suggested.

Wallenda looked at the glyph *distill*. "Oh. Essence might not be me."

"Or you're not as essential as you think. At least you could try some other meanings," she said.

"You're doing fine," he said. "Show me."

Óh-T'bee nested *distill* in *world*.

"Oh," Wallenda said. "Oh my. You mean I've got to Focus. Finally."

"That's what it looks like to me," Óh-T'bee agreed.

"But it's not like I've been meandering about all this time," Wallenda said.

"Of course not, Wally. You're one of the most goal-directed Lifers I've ever seen. You just don't know where you're going," Óh-T'bee replied.

Wallenda went into his cabin and took a blue ampoule from a box on the shelf, unsealed it, drank the Lily Wine, put MyGlide's floppy red and white striped hat on his head, and walked into the maze.

Óh-T'bee tried one last arrangement of the oracle's glyphs. His world is shrinking to a single point, a single meaning.

84. The Dancemaster's Focus

Wine of the Lilies
keep my mind on the path
though the maze has no exit
though the twists are endless

Wallenda pulled MyGlide's floppy-brimmed hat down snugly and closed his eyes, moving through the familiar maze Glide-style. He reached the first link, and opened his eyes, lifted the brim, and peered carefully out from under the hat. The walls of the maze had turned to mirror. He could see the black skirt of his *katana*, the white *gi* above. Straight ahead, and all around him, on each blunt end, down every corridor, he saw MyGlide, holding up the brim of the floppy red and white striped hat. Wallenda raised his arm, pointing. The MyGlides did the same. He turned slowly in place. So did the reflections. He peeked again. All the MyGlides were peeking back. He took off the hat. Enough of this peek-a-boo. I have to face this, he thought. But when he tried, he couldn't raise his eyes. All the MyGlides would be looking back. It was too much. Maybe he could meet the gaze of only one.

He walked in the direction he was facing, nearing the corridor formed by the wave at the bottom of *light*, slowly raising his head at the same time. But as soon as he could see MyGlide in the mirror, he saw that as he approached the walls, her figure receded, growing smaller. On the side of the wall, the side farther away from where he stood, the MyGlides seemed somewhat larger. He stepped back. The MyGlide in front of him moved toward him. He ran at the mirror, pressed his nose against the shiny surface, trying to see inside. MyGlide was no more than a speck in the distance. He took one step back from the mirror. MyGlide stepped back as well, but her image grew a little larger.

Wallenda felt a prickling at the back of his neck. He turned and faced the far side of the wall. The head of an enormous MyGlide stared at him. Her eyes were huge, the pupils fathomless black pools of sorrow. He backed away in terror. The eyes expanded swiftly until the wall was filled with nothing but her eyes. He could see reflections on the concave surfaces of the eyes. The same scene, the same eyes, repeated, inward and inward again.

Wallenda turned and fled down the nearest corridor. The images receded ahead of him, while running toward him. Behind, the images grew larger, running away in his direction. He stopped, and the fearful motion stopped, but then he had to look at MyGlide looking back at him. He could only stand it for so long before he'd start to run again. Then he noticed that his flight through the maze was affecting MyGlide's image. The first time he'd stopped, her face was as he had seen her last, the sorrowful face on the bottom row of the bleachers, closest to the griddle, as he died in agony. Pain coursed through him. He was on the griddle again. MyGlide had led him there. He shouted at her, "why don't you do something," and her reflection only mouthed the words back at him. He ran again, stopped. Here was the face he'd seen when he was questioning her. He asked again, "Why did you give me the hat?" and held it out to her. In the mirror, MyGlide mimicked the question, holding out the hat to him.

Wallenda ran on and on, in a kind of numbness, watching her images slide by on the large curves, and on the smaller curves of the waves, the same distortions arising again and again. As long as he could run, and keep himself at an even distance from the mirrored walls, he would. The crowds of images at the intersections were bad, and looking behind him was the worst of all. He changed into a glide to save his energy. It had been a long time since he'd glided. It was coming back to him. After all, he used to teach the glide moves to the students, back in the old days, the very old days. He was moving more slowly, and the images of MyGlide began to come in focus again. They reflected a younger MyGlide, judging by the eyes, less sorrow, other feelings, mixed feelings about things, keener feelings. His legs were giving out, his knees trembled, his glide wobbled, but he kept on going until he could move no more. Wallenda slid to the ground, and crawled out into the middle of the junction where two circles touched. The walls each curved away from him, offering four paths. Down those paths he could see other paths opening. He was lost. The pain of running away forever overcame him. He only wanted to die. To be released from pain forever. He looked, knowing what he had to see: MyGlide's face as a child, torn by tears, bewildered by pain. Her face beseeched him, please, please let me die now. These were the eyes she'd turned toward him, where he stood in the shadow under the Player's booth, and then upwards to Joreen at the end of her Dance. Wallenda's face contorted in agony as he saw her child's face spasm repeatedly in pain, as she had been bounced and shocked and burned around the griddle. He would rather die than watch her pain. But even as he watched, he knew the worst was still to come, the worst, but it would be the end. She had to show him, and he had to look behind her eyes, feel what she felt at the beginning. Only then would MyGlide let him go. Only then could he let MyGlide go. He had to trust MyGlide, that this beginning was the end of his long flight from her eyes. He had to let her trust him, once again, at the beginning, that what was about to happen out on the griddle would not happen, ever again. He had to trust himself that this was true, that if he took her hand again, it would be to lead her elsewhere, somewhere safe, out of pain. He had to be able to trust himself that this was a promise he could keep. This was his Focus: to gaze, unflinching, into MyGlide's eyes. This was the moment of choice.

Wallenda raised his head and gazed steadily into the eyes of MyGlide he had feared so long— the eyes of a trusting child.

The three glyphs of the oracle nested into one.

the wine of the world
lies hidden
in the light

85. MyrrhMyrrh vs. Daede

The month-long Millennium Games progressed. Origin City throbbed with tourists. Out on the Levels, fortunes in game points were made and lost in the highest volume of betting in four centuries. The Daede and MyrrhMyrrh saga continued to be milked for every thrill. Betting about the details of each next episode added to the feverish interest. MyGlide kept the Med on their toes by setting up a series of meetings with Joreen that she cancelled each time at the last moment. She kept a ring of Chrome bodyguards around Daede and leaked rumors about mysterious threats.

Under ordinary circumstances, Dancemaster Wallenda would have been more than satisfied. The three remaining members of the Millennium Class had all made it to the final matches. T'Ling had been playing very well, at a conservative pace. Her games were over in the range of two to two-and-a-half hours; she used essentially the same strategy—steady progress toward the final glyph, no bluffing or feints, no twing. A lot of looping on the circles, then a few fast moves at the end, squeaking by the avatar by a hair, but winning. Consistency, not brilliance, kept her on top. T'Ling was now matched against Rinzi-Kov, odds slightly in favor of the Glidemaster. Angle had played brilliantly, and made it to the final Chrome match. He was paired with a relatively young Chrome Player known as the Heavy Hitter. The Hitter's avatar was a triumph of engineering, massive but capable of swift moves with the claws. He was a lightning calculator as well. The odds were fairly even, slightly in favor of Angle. MyrrhMyrrh had never lost her initial rating as first among the Bods. Her style points were far ahead of either Angle or T'Ling. Joreen had slotted Daede in the Bod track when he qualified, not because it was his strongest game as a freestyle player, but because the world of Specs was waiting breathlessly to see him play MyrrhMyrrh once again.

They were both unbeaten and matched against each other for the final game of the Bod set.

The final four games would determine the Champion for each set—Dancer or Player. Depending on the final tally of Players and Dancers, the Dancer with the highest total points—which was where the importance of the style points came in—was the Champion of Dancers. The same for the Players. There were times when all four Sets had a Dancer Champion, a mildly disappointing outcome. The Specs preferred to see a pair, a Dancer and a Player, crowned. And it had never been the case, in the history of the game, that all four Players had won.

The night before his match with MyrrhMyrrh—the first of the Final Four—Daede was almost the only person, Lifer or mortal, high- or low-level, who was not watching the final chapter of the MyrrhMyrrh and Daede saga on their scorecards. *How Daede Got Burned by MyrrhMyrrh and Became a Player.* The footage was carefully edited to make Joreen look like a benevolent entrepreneur with MyGlide cast as ministering angel. The final section of the Jillian episode was edited out. No one but MyGlide, Jillian, and T'Ling knew that Daede was just a Lifer now. The Specs thought they were gazing the tragic love story of the Millennium working its way inexorably toward an unknown conclusion. Eighty-six percent of Specs surveyed after the long show was over thought MyrrhMyrrh would triumph. Daede would graciously accept defeat. MyrrhMyrrh's rage would be spent, and somehow—so they predicted—they would live out their mortal lives together, all pain and sorrow now behind them. With a happily-ever-after added in—when they decided to be Lifers. MyrrhMyrrh and Daede would give all Lifers everywhere hope that true love could indeed last longer than the current record of 110 years without cheating.

Daede took Rose for a ride in his air chair, over the silent desert. He told her stories about her Mommy and Daddy, how she had hair the color of Daddy's and eyes like Mommy's. He sang to her.

"When can I go to live with them?" Rose asked.

"When the Games are over," he said. "I promise."

She fell asleep happy.

It can happen, he told himself. It will happen. All they have to do is win. And I have to beat MyrrhMyrrh. I still can't match her in the Bod game. I know that; so does she, so does every Spec. My strategy needs to depend on what I know of MyrrhMyrrh. Which at this point is everything—on and off the maze. Daede planned a strategy as complex and risky and totally original as any Player had ever devised.

The crowds roared when Daede blinked into his pod above the empty space where the maze would momentarily appear. MyrrhMyrrh appeared in the Dancer's starting position—they were screaming now. Daede made a slight motion with his hand and the deafening noise fell through an invisible trapdoor into silence. MyrrhMyrrh looked up at Daede. Daede stood and bowed, deeply, just a little too deeply, mocking, not honoring MyrrhMyrrh. This first move had a bigger effect than expected. The Specs were in a high state of tension, mounting to anxiety as MyrrhMyrrh continued staring. Daede realized that she could not bow to him, not again, not in any way, not even for the protocol of the game. She would lose significant style points if she continued rooted to the spot. He improvised. He called Media. "Announce that I am about to make MyrrhMyrrh an offer," he said. They did so. There was not a sound in the stadium. Daede's amplified whisper was heard over every loudspeaker and scorecard. "I'll bet you can't beat my Swash avatar." The challenge released MyrrhMyrrh from her frozen gaze.

"Try me," she said, and bowed to him. The Guild frantically reviewed the rules. Óh-T'bee said there was no rule about that. No freestyle Player had ever suggested doing that before. It was too late to do anything about it anyhow. The Specs were beyond astounded. This was too good to be true.

Daede's Swash avatar was the image of himself as a Dancer, before his burns and his disfigurement. Composed of the best holos of himself in training, growing up, laughing, dancing, pensive, seductive, the avatar had many moods. It was his strongest avatar, having gained the most points, added the most attributes. But he had never played it on a Bod maze. It was a crazy move. The avatar didn't have the strength to jump the higher hurdles, or the sheer sprint speed of his Bod avatar. On most Bod mazes, he would be at a severe disadvantage.

The maze came up; the glyphs were of widely varying heights, full of steep differences between adjacent glyphs. Daede could see clearly see the path he would have taken with his Bod avatar—steep and risky, but he would have tried it. He could even see the spot where he would have had to meet MyrrhMyrrh in combat. Given the configuration, she would approach the intersection from the higher glyph, which would have given her the advantage. The configuration couldn't have been worse. His strategy depended on the random luck of a maze that favored the low glyphs. Daede threw out his first strategy and improvised. He was already in motion; there was really only one way he could go. The low road was the long way around. MyrrhMyrrh was running the high glyphs, heading for the point of intersection he'd predicted. She'd look down and find it empty, and, sail to an easy win. He eyeballed the board—she was moving as expected. He jumped down into the empty space and started to run across. He switched to avatar view and saw her go over the top of the highest glyph, tensed for the combat she expected on the other side. But Daede wasn't there. Instead of sprinting to an easy finish, she turned to find him. Daede sent his avatar into a graceful spin, and swirled into a low bow, acknowledging his defeat in advance. MyrrhMyrrh turned and reached the finish. Daede didn't even try. His avatar blinked out. The cheering was loud and long when MyrrhMyrrh bowed to the crowd. It was Daede's turn to acknowledge the winning Dancer. He stood in the pod and bowed again to her, removing his helmet, lowering his mottled head. The crowd cheered louder still, on and on. MyrrhMyrrh had won, but as she ran her victory lap, she became more and more convinced he had stolen her victory. He had let her win far too easily, he had as good as thrown the game, and he had somehow come out on top in the eyes of the Specs. She didn't realize the Specs were cheering for them both—a couple who had in some miraculous way evened the score between them. If she had realized she was being viewed as linked to Daede again, with peaceful possibilities for the future, and worst of all, that the Specs thought she would be Champion of the Games, but then forego her Dance for love of Daede, she would have felt even worse.

MyrrhMyrrh left the stadium, refused all interviews, blinked back to her old room at Origin School, and accessed her personal database of information on all things concerning Joreen. She found what she'd been looking for, and consulted with Óh-T'bee for the details. Yes, Óh-T'bee agreed, it was as she recalled, and there was nothing in the rules to prevent her. MyrrhMyrrh appeared before the Guild Council and announced she had been robbed, and was applying the Joreen amendment.

Óh-T'bee reviewed the point, back when the game began, when Joreen as Maker of the Rules had added his amendment, over the protests of the first Players, that a winning Dancer had the option of foregoing their Dance, becoming a Player, and putting their opponent on the griddle to Dance. The Dancers then, and through the history of the game had always opted to Dance. The Joreen amendment was never more than an esoteric item of game trivia. But it had never been revoked. The Guild tried to contact Joreen himself. MyGlide gave them the message that he was very pleased to see his amendment put to good use after all these years. A Dancer had never invoked it—until now.

There was nothing the Guild could do but set the time. The Joreen amendment match would be held the next morning at dawn. The scramble for tickets for the unscheduled game began. Media filled the channels with elaborate explanations of the Joreen amendment.

Daede spent a sleepless night. If MyrrhMyrrh won, and he Danced, he would have to remain hidden forever or the world would find out soon enough that he wasn't mortal anymore. If he won, against the well-surveyed will of the Specs, his approval rating would plummet. Whatever MyrrhMyrrh did at this point would grab the spotlight and distract the Specs for the remainder of the Games. Win or lose, his plan to end the game with a single grand speech that would convert the Lifers would no longer be viable. If it ever had been. And if he won, he would still have MyrrhMyrrh to contend with.

By invoking the Joreen amendment, she had already sacrificed her Dancer status, her Championship, everything her life was meant to be. She would continue attacking and attacking until she destroyed him, herself—or both of them. MyrrhMyrrh was spinning into the red zone of chaos. Daede tried to assess the odds. He would make a far poorer showing than any of his avatars. He was not out of shape, but very out of practice as a Swash, and had never been in practice as a Bod. All his reflexes, all his moves were Swash. He could run a Bod avatar from outside, but he had never tried to be a Bod from the inside, to move his own mind and muscles in that way. His choices on the maze might be very limited. On the other hand, MyrrhMyrrh knew no more about the Player's game than what she might remember from the child's simulation games they had all played. He was fairly sure she had never set foot in a Player's pod. She would be clumsy and slow, at the very best. Perhaps the odds would be evened out, but whatever happened, the game would be ugly.

MyrrhMyrrh spent the night in the Player's pod. She asked for, and received, help from the Club. The best Bod Player tried to teach her enough of the board and moves to get through a basic game. They discussed a simple strategy, trying to maximize her chances by attacking at the points that would be Daede's weakest. She took over Daede's Bod avatar and had it moving fairly smoothly through a practice maze. The avatar was far stronger than Daede. Her best chance of winning would be in contact and combat. She just had to catch him. But everything depended on how the maze came up.

The stadium was empty and hushed. MyrrhMyrrh thanked the Players, and spent the last hour before dawn in the pod alone. She had one simple plan in mind, and spent most of her time drawing her focus around her. She would kill Daede. Nothing else mattered. Even the Championship was off her focus, no longer a distraction. MyrrhMyrrh was not a Dancer anymore. She was not a Player. She was only a weapon, aimed to kill.

The Specs blinked in five minutes before game time. They spoke in hushed tones, their voices like the waves of a distant ocean. Daede couldn't decide if he wanted to win or lose, or what difference it would make to his grand plan for ending the game. He blinked into the Dancer's position at the edge of the field with no strategy at all. But as he stood there, waiting for her bow, an unexpected rush of feeling took over. Having his feet on a maze again got his adrenaline up at a level he had not felt in the most intense game-play in the pod. This was his body. Lifer or not, he didn't want to Dance. He had learned all he wanted to learn from pain. If he lost, MyrrhMyrrh would make his Dance an act of torture. He would not be able to execute his moves, even if they came back to him. He would scream involuntarily. He would shit his pants. He would burn again.

MyrrhMyrrh bowed. Daede replied with a mocking, clowning bow. From that point, Daede played to win.

The maze came up. The glyph in front of him was so high that he couldn't eyeball the rest of the maze. He would lose precious time getting the pod view through his helmet, just to orient himself. Daede jumped for the top of the next highest glyph and scrambled over inelegantly. Daede overlay the Pod viewpoint and began running in the general direction of the Player's glyph. He took his first leap and made it—barely. MyrrhMyrrh was plowing the avatar steadily over the walls. He switched to top view to try to gauge her speed. He thought he could make it around her, but ran himself into a cul-de-sac he missed by looking at top view and misestimating the height of the glyphs in that area. He took the top view again. They had both stopped. He was out of eyeball sight of MyrrhMyrrh. She was not using the flexibility of pod position to her advantage, playing from a fixed location. Daede saw her turn the avatar onto a different path. He tried to avoid her, but he had missed the easiest route by backtracking. MyrrhMyrrh could win on speed alone if she just saw it, but she seemed to be bent on interception. He suddenly realized that she was stuck in the avatar's viewpoint. He switched into a pod view, then back to the avatar's viewpoint, and then eyeballed to get over the next circle. They were both heading for the hole. MyrrhMyrrh was definitely trying to get him into combat, and might well succeed. He suddenly realized that he was thinking like a Player, and that the way to win was to move his body as if he was a Player. From the outside. He went to helmet only view and layered his top and pod views, and switched to the avatar's eyeballs as they both entered the hole.

MyrrhMyrrh moved the Bod avatar at a dead run across the hole. Daede eyeballed again, and moved easily aside at the last moment as if the avatar were a charging bull. He sprinted for the other side of the hole, but saw too late that the wall was too high to get over before she could get to him. She'd pull him down by the leg if he tried to climb it. He had to move to a lower wall. MyrrhMyrrh had already stopped the avatar and was approaching slowly, trying to keep Daede with his back to the higher wall. She had learned the lesson quickly about charging and wouldn't try it again. MyrrhMyrrh edged toward him. Daede saw she would rush when she was close enough and he would probably not be able to avoid the clash. Daede forced himself out of his body's eyeball viewpoint and back on instruments. He took the eyeball view of the avatar and realized MyrrhMyrrh was moving its whole head instead of the helmet scopes alone to keep him in view. She'd zoomed in as well, trying to get her viewpoint closer. She should have gone to wide angle if she was going to eyeball. It was a serious mistake. He let her get closer, and then he started a wide twing, leaping back and forth and from side to side. He wasn't all that swift, but he was faster than she could turn her avatar's head. MyrrhMyrrh was locked into trying to catch him through the scopes. He estimated her blind spots, and dived under her limited field of view. He got behind the avatar, running for the low wall. He got up on top, and got himself out of eyeball sight as quickly as possible. Daede took the long way round to the winning glyph, but she was still in the mindset of chasing, and instead of trying to make a run for her winning glyph, MyrrhMyrrh was trying to cut him off. The attempt was futile. Daede reached the winning glyph. There was no cheering. The Specs held their breath. MyrrhMyrrh blinked the avatar off the maze and stood up in the pod. Daede bowed to her. She bowed to him. There was still silence. MyrrhMyrrh, since she had invoked the Joreen amendment, had not had a moment's doubt that if she lost, Daede would reverse their places once again, invoking a Joreen of his own. She had even checked the surveys; 79% of the Specs across the levels thought the same. She wasn't going to let that happen.

Daede couldn't begin his victory lap until the Player bowed. MyrrhMyrrh seemed locked in place once again. She had failed to accomplish the end desired by her focus, but it hardly mattered. She lost, but she had stayed on Focus, which meant she was a Dancer still, with the right to Dance. She achieved a peace she hadn't imagined possible. She wouldn't have to bow to Daede. With the sound of a blowtorch, MyrrhMyrrh ignited the pod, and stood gazing Daede until the flames of the Dance melted her eyes.

86. Swash and Chrome

THE FINAL MATCHES of Swash, Chrome, and Glide were pushed forward a few days in the aftermath of MyrrhMyrrh's final Dance. Media was in hog heaven; MyGlide released Daede's relationship with Jillian—up to the penultimate goodbye. Now we understand, the Specs said. That extra insult kept her hate alive. But had MyrrhMyrrh known? Could it be proved? Even MyrrhMyrrh's visit to the Hall of Champions at First Acceptance was released. Now we *really* understand, the Specs said. She had to Dance by fire, she had to understand the fire, the fear, and the fury. But why did Daede become a Player? Was he only running from MyrrhMyrrh?

Daede's refusal to talk with Media only fueled the speculation. Angle thought he was trying to spare the memory of MyrrhMyrrh in some way. T'Ling and the Dancemaster and MyGlide knew the simple answer: he couldn't talk about his Focus. Or talk around it. The only option was silence. But only a Dancer's silence was respected. Daede was a Player. Players love to talk. Media saw it as just another gaze-gathering move on the part of a clever Swash. From the viewpoint of Daede's intention to renounce, denounce, and end the game in a single speech, they were exactly right.

As things turned out, Daede's stock only rose. MyrrhMyrrh killed herself, but in a way that salvaged her image as a Dancer. Daede didn't kill her with his own hand, and he had been properly stunned, shocked, devastated by her actions, by her final Gaze. He had in fact been rooted to the spot, unable to move, unable to look away. It was no act. As the flames rose and framed MyrrhMyrrh's body and her face, and flared through her curly hair, he had finally looked her fury in the eye, seen its fullness, and it froze him to the spot. MyGlide had blinked onto the field and led him away. Daede's in shock, the Specs voted. They were right, as usual. But as Daede came to life again, he examined body, heart, and soul for damages. He found his plan to kill the game; it was showing signs of life as well.

After long analysis, the style judges concluded that the whole series of events was so original, beginning with Daede's suggestion to use a Swash avatar in a Bod game, that the awkwardness of moves in the unorthodox games was minor. MyrrhMyrrh and Daede had managed to bring their real and private lives to this most public of game-mazes, turn them into gameplay, and share them with the world. This was beyond even a perfect score. But it led to certain problems, as unprecedented moves often will. Was Daede in some sense now a Dancer as well? If so, should he be rated in the Swash track as a Dancer, too? That would certainly be freestyle at a whole new level. But they couldn't simply bump the Swash finalist who had come all this way to play. They surveyed the Specs about an exhibition game. The results were overwhelming—they just wanted to see Daede doing anything at all. It didn't matter. At this point, the Swash winner, inwardly furious beyond words, did the proper Swash thing, and proclaimed himself so moved by the Daede and MyrrhMyrrh events, that he couldn't play. He would come again next year when he had recovered. This allowed Daede to do the only gentlemanly Swash thing, and decline to fill the Swash Dancer's rightful place in any way. Each congratulated himself for saving the day. There was no Swash game.

The Chrome final was next. It was Angle's turn.

The Specs were ready to get back to the game. Media eased out the Daede and MyrrhMyrrh story, fearing overexposure would dim his glory. On to the next story. MyGlide gave Media the Angle and T'Ling story. Media thought it was too namby-pamby, but in fact, the Specs' avid palates were refreshed by the cool, light innocence of the spectacle of childhood love, and to what was left to their imaginations as they saw them slip naked under the lily pad.

Dancemaster Wallenda sat at the table in his cabin and cursed this latest move of MyGlide's. She was out-Joreening Joreen. It was a travesty. A total violation of Origin School, and a terrible invasion of T'Ling and Angle's private lives. He had no idea how he could possibly trust MyGlide, ever, Focus or no Focus. The more the feelings of mistrust and anger and betrayal rose in him, the more clearly he remembered his Focus. It would chase him, whether or not he accepted it. He knew he had to look into MyGlide's eyes and trust.

"Óh-T'bee, please ask MyGlide if I can talk to her."

MyGlide replied without delay, through Óh-T'bee. "She said that she would talk to you, but not in person."

"Ask her if I can see her face while we are talking."

Óh-T'bee brought back her reply. "As long as she can see yours."

"Of course," Wallenda said. He adjusted his display to show a life-sized image. MyGlide appeared. She was seated at her desk, her hands folded in front of her.

Once he had steadied himself and could look into her sorrowing eyes, Wallenda lost his tongue. He could only say, "Why? Why Angle and T'Ling? What possible gain is there?"

They gazed each other for a long moment. "I was going to ask you the same thing."

Each searched the other's eyes for an answer. Suddenly Wallenda remembered the times that he had, using his total gazing rights, looked in on Angle and T'Ling, in their most private moments. Wallenda broke eye contact with MyGlide momentarily, but when he looked back, her image had disappeared.

Angle and T'Ling broke precedent, and met the night before his game at his request. Angle picked T'Ling up and carried her into the Dancemaster's maze, hoping Media had no gazing rights. Once they were inside, Angle raised his visor.

"They must have gotten all our records from MyGlide." Angle was upset and angry, and letting himself feel it fully.

"It doesn't matter," T'Ling said. She reached inside his helmet and drew her finger down the middle of his frown. "No one knows but us. Really knows."

"It does matter," Angle said, still frowning. "What if she gets to the part about the baby?"

"I don't think she will."

"I hope you're right," he said.

T'Ling smiled at him. "Actually, what MyGlide did matters quite a lot. If she hadn't released the story, you wouldn't have contacted me. I wouldn't have had this chance to see you again. We would have both done what we were *supposed* to do. I wouldn't be able to say goodbye at the right time, properly. Like this." She leaned into the depths of his helmet and kissed him. "And to say what I'm not supposed to say, which is—good luck. I hope you win. I hope it's not goodbye. Maybe we'll see each other tomorrow night."

Angle grinned back.

If he had needed any extra motivation to win, he got it then. As things turned out, he needed it.

Angle blinked in, turned his scopes to the Player's pod. He saw his opponent rise, ready to bow. The Heavy Hitter was fully helmeted. He nodded. Angle nodded back. Something's weird, he said. He had done three contracts with this Player. He was very good, but not good enough. But he had always raised his visor in respect, and the guy was a stickler for rules. In the long, breathless moment before the Chrome maze came up, a familiar voice spoke on his phones.

"Hide and seek, anyone?" the Codger said.

"You're in the wrong game, Codger," Angle said. "You don't know how to play. Put the real Player back."

"New rules."

What the Specs saw next was a burst of blinding motion, Dancer and avatar arcing so fast over the huge Chrome maze, they appeared to be in several places at once. Crash collisions in midair, shards of metal flying, electrical flashes in the depths of a deep crater. The silence. Then it all started again. It was all over in 90 seconds, a new record for a Chrome game with 18 holes to cover. The winner was declared.

The *real* game took, relatively speaking, about 90 minutes and started when Angle asked Óh-T'bee to put them both inside the Dancemaster's maze. Óh-T'bee explained the circumstances to the Dancemaster who blinked angrily to their location in the maze. He was reading them both out, loud and long, when the Codger grabbed the Dancemaster's right hand, severed it with the end of the claw, pulled the ring off, and yelled "Morph." Angle was equipped for action in a Chrome maze 10 times this size, and could hardly move in such close action. He lunged at the Codger and hit him hard at the moment the Codger yelled 'Morph.' They both fell into the maze. Wallenda grabbed his hand just before it was swallowed by the maze and blinked back to the story circle. It was a short, but painful, repair. Much more painful was the loss of the seal ring of the maze. His last line of defense was gone. He felt exposed, naked, and vulnerable. The maze continued to morph. He couldn't watch it any longer, it made him sick. He blinked over to Loosh's cabin to complete his repair.

Angle and the Codger were both Out. Angle, much more familiar with the ins and outs of the morphing maze, carefully tied the Codger up in several hundred infinite regressions. The Codger, who thought the ring would get him out, was sadly mistaken. Whether it could or couldn't, the ring had disappeared. Thinking 'morph' as loud as he could in the ever-tightening spirals Angle had made produced some excruciating reverb that only tightened as it went on.

Angle gave some thought to how he would handle the game when he got back in, given that there was no Player. He spliced himself back into the time track right where he went out, and went in and out at the same place a number of times, setting up changes. He set the whole strategy going—a two part invention on the theme of the Codger's kludge, went back to his room to watch for the 90 seconds, then blinked into the winner's glyph on the maze in the stadium, raised his visor, and bowed to Player in the pod, having put the real Player, the Heavy Hitter, back in place a split second before. Confused and disoriented, the Heavy Hitter blinked out. Angle sprang in high arcs around his victory lap before the cheering crowd. No one had a clue what they had seen, but the game-play was much faster, and the special effects were totally awesome.

"How did you do that?" T'Ling said.

Angle grinned. "It just takes really good timing," he said modestly.

7T7 was not out celebrating his Champion's win. He was scrutinizing the game as slowly as he could, from every gaze-point. The real Player, the Heavy Hitter watched with him.

"Looks like you're there the whole way through," 7T7 said. "It's going to be hard to lodge a complaint."

"But I wasn't!" he said.

"I know, I know. But if they see the doctored pod, they'll never believe you."

The Player, a veteran, knew when to accept defeat. "The biggest problem is," he said "they're going to expect a game like that every time."

To 7T7, it looked like Angle had upgraded the Codger's kludge and found some serious loopholes in the MTA. He snapped down his visor before the Player could see him grin. Time to celebrate for sure.

87. Glide Final

GLIDEMASTER RINZI-KOV GATHERED HIMSELF for the championship game. The Dancer was T'Ling. Her record had been excellent, near perfect, but without the extra whatever-it-was that Loosh and only Loosh had brought to the Glide game. Wenger was T'Ling's musician as well. Loosh was her trainer, the legend was to be passed down from teacher to pupil. But he was favored to win. He knew that, and that it would not improve his game to think the thought, but trying not to think it was even worse. No, he was not worried about the game. But the closer it got, the more attention drained away in the direction of the great unknown in his life: was the Codger coming back to screw things up?

Rinzi-Kov bowed reverentially. T'Ling returned his bow. The Glide maze came up black. Visually, this was the most difficult for a Player. The Dancer's skirt blended with the pathways of the glyphs. He inverted black and white on his goggles. It was easier for him to see the game as a negative.

Wenger sat on a small platform to the side of the maze. He ran his fingers over his scorecard to read the maze. His fingers stopped over a 9-glyph pattern. He traced the glyphs again. It was the music of the fall of kingdoms. The three glyphs entirely composed of the three elemental lines were stacked in the center. *Give* over *glide*, *glide* over *receive*. The deepest twing. The single *wave* connected at the center, the fragile link. The implicit *lily*. And if it twinged into the great reversal, three *lilies*, interleaved. *Dance*, *die* to *time*, then the *fiery emergence*. He watched the two formations morphing back and forth in his mind's eye.

give, glide, receive

Wenger stroked the strings as T'Ling glided into the maze. T'Ling heard the opening chord of the music of the fall of kingdoms as she saw the twing that could tear the maze apart. Danger. Danger. Rinzi-kov saw the same formation as the place to catch a Glide.

T'Ling moved at a slow glide into the depths of the maze. The maze had a ragged, unbalanced look—the missing glyphs were all taken from the edges; there were no interior holes, a configuration only allowed in a Glide maze. No resting place. Like the lily pond. Sign of the original Glides at work—they could not stop or they would sink and die. The Glide avatar, following her pace, leaned toward the center of the maze. The twing formation, the center of gravity, a strange attractor in the middle of chaos.

The region of the densely packed. Tension, Rinzi-Kov knew. Great tension would build and then spring loose. They each arrived at the music of the fall of kingdoms. T'Ling and the avatar faced each other on opposite corridors of *give* and *receive*, then moved into the center wave of *glide*. They seemed to pass through each other—then each stood on one half of the wave. It was impossible to tell who began the twing. Neither Player nor Dancer knew. Wenger knew his notes had led. Rinzi-Kov could never explain what happened next. The mounting tension of the twing was almost unbearable. Then T'Ling's arms in their wide sleeves swooped upwards, breaking the pattern. T'Ling glided, almost indifferently, through each corridor of the glyphs, moving toward the center wave, then across the center wave, sliding playfully onto one side of the wave, then skipping the other half, profoundly unbalancing the pattern. She crossed into the avatar's side of the formation. Rinzi-Kov immersed in the viewpoint of the avatar; he held the avatar still. Her movements traced a path of certain disaster—T'Ling could never make up the time or footsteps lost. And she completed the pattern, as he knew she had to, she was on a collision course with him, where he stood, rooted to the spot. Wenger's music entranced them both.

Rinzi-Kov gazed her face as she approached. Her eyes said, yes I know. I am gliding weightlessly into loss. When everything matters and nothing matters. I will complete the pattern. I am drifting over the region of the densely packed about to tear apart. I am a charred bird, rising and falling in the heat waves over a volcano. I am a falling star. When she reached the top wave of *glide*, Rinzi-Kov stepped aside, and watched, transfixed, as T'Ling completed the pattern. Wenger finished the music of the fall of kingdoms. Wenger played the last notes of the music that dissolves the world, then released Dancer and Player from his spell. T'Ling swept past the avatar. Dancer and Player each glided to the final glyphs, T'Ling ahead by only half a curve.

She was the champion Glide.

o o o o o

Loosh and Wenger were back in Kyoto for the night.

The crowning of the Champions would take place the following day. Style points would be tallied. Either T'Ling or Angle would win. The winner would be judged against the top Player, Daede, and it was determined whether the Dancer or the Player would be crowned the overall champion of the Millennium Games. Whatever the outcome, after the victor was crowned, both T'Ling and Angle would choose to Dance. The Specs would cry, and cheer, and mourn and celebrate.

"Something is very wrong," Loosh said. "I was sure the oracle said that T'Ling will Dance. Not become the Champion, then Dance."

"Her game was the ripple on the far edge of the tsunami," Wenger said. "It was the music of the fall of kingdoms. Check your scorecard. It's beginning now."

Loosh watched the news holos. A very strange unrest was bubbling up across the levels. Where it had started, no one knew; it seemed that everyone got the idea together and started saying the same completely unorthodox things. T'Ling and Angle shouldn't Dance. They should ride together on the same lily pad in the recessional, off into the distance, Chrome and Glide. Daede would ride off also, alone, in the other direction. It was fitting. It was right. The Specs would rather see it end that way. Of course, T'Ling and Angle would say they only wanted to Dance, but they should listen to the Specs for a change. The Specs demanded something new and different. There had been so many wonderful, and frightening new things in these Millennium Games—why not end it differently as well? Well, why not? Tell us that? The momentum of the idea grew through the night. The surveys were strong, then overwhelming. By the following morning, Specs were crowding into the stadiums in their parks. Impassioned speeches were being made. An exception was demanded. Vast petitions arrived at the Guild and the Med.

Feelers were put out to T'Ling and Angle; would they possibly consider.... Angle said, flatly, *no*. T'Ling did not respond. She would Dance. There was never any question in her mind. Specs or no Specs. This was a passing gust of feeling in the Specs that would dissolve as quickly as it had formed. It had nothing to do with her. T'Ling was in the final stages of withdrawing attachments from the layers of the world. The public scene of the Millennium Games and championships had been the easiest to shed. She was loosening her attachments at a deeper level, and could not be deterred.

But the Specs could not be deterred either. The parks on each level joined forces; the levels were connecting as well. Social barriers dissolved. Specs mixed and mingled, but the feeling of a potential mob scene was growing.

Media, gazing the Specs at every level, spread the frenzy, dubbing the phenomena The Night of the Specs. All gaze was on the Specs—their own gaze, of course. The *Specs* had become the show. The *Specs* had a voice. The *Specs* would be listened to.

The Med and the Guild met. No word had come from Joreen. Where was leadership when they needed it most?

Daede was delighted. T'Ling and Angle, magnanimously, would grant the Specs their wish. They would live, reclaim Rose, and thereby secure his promise to her. Now was the moment to act. He dressed for his speech. Which stadium should he speak from? It seemed he should get out of the Millennium Games venue entirely, get down with the common Specs, right there in the middle of the action. Let them know how right they were.

MyGlide blinked into his room. Daede announced his intentions.

"There is nothing you can do to stop me," he said.

"You've already stopped yourself," MyGlide said. "Before you go anywhere, check your scorecard."

The Med, as a whole, was reviewing the possibilities. A decision would soon be announced to the crowds assembled in every stadium. The overwhelming groundswell was fully acknowledged. But first, it was in their best interests to hear the late-breaking news. Media had uncovered the final chapter in the story of Daede.

The Specs growled. They're just trying to divert us. That's old news. We won't buy it.

But it wasn't old news at all. It was the story of Daede and T'Ling.

That threw a whole new light on things.

88. To Play or Not to Play

THERE WASN'T MUCH for the Specs to gaze on the early relationship of Daede and T'Ling. She had, after all, spent most of her childhood and even the training years after First Acceptance ignoring him. But Media was skillful and the Lifers who edited the holos were not called Gaze Masters for nothing. They showed the four students of the Millennium class in the story circle where their gaze told all. Angle, with his eyes fixed on T'Ling, hoping she'd look up. MyrrhMyrrh gazing Daede adoringly. Daede standing on his head, giving endless answers to questions, bouncing around the circle, brushing back his hair, and always glancing at T'Ling to see if she was gazing him. In fact, she was, but he never caught her at it. Nor did Angle. You could see her look up at Angle from time to time and smile, openly. But her gaze at Daede was more covert—sliding past him, hidden by a hand, or through a display of a game problem. Once you were looking for it, you could see that her eyes were not following the action in the holo, but focused instead on Daede across the circle.

Though T'Ling had been drawn out of her concentration on her Dance by this development, she was determined to incorporate it. She knew that her desire for Daede would be one of the last clingings she would have to face. So she watched this skillful reconstruction alone in her room, studied it, knew that the case that was being built, the story that wove its undertones throughout Daede and MyrrhMyrrh, T'Ling and Angle. It was true. The roots were even deeper than the Gaze Masters could show.

Angle watched alone in his room. At first he worried that T'Ling would be hurt, or shamed, by this Media trophy, the rare beast of intimate relations among Dancers displayed to every gaze. But as he was trying to decide whether or not to try to speak with her, he recognized the pain to be his own. Both Angle and T'Ling were thankful MyrrhMyrrh had been spared.

Daede tried again and again to contact T'Ling, but she refused his calls. Didn't he realize that anything they said to each other from here on out would be added on to the story, even as they spoke, even as it unfolded before their eyes and the eyes of Lifers everywhere?

Media's story progressed. The Specs gazed Daede's head in T'Ling's lap that day on the practice fields. They studied the expression on her face as she read his bad luck oracle. They felt her hands on his temples. The views that would have revealed her pregnancy were edited out. They gazed T'Ling and Daede entering the maze together, their talk, and their declarations. Slow dissolve as they reach toward each other, leaving the Specs to imagine the rest. The Specs held their vast collective breath when MyrrhMyrrh entered the maze the following morning, not knowing T'Ling and Daede had spent the night there. Their breath was released when they saw MyrrhMyrrh storming from the maze. The final shot was of Daede alone, walking down the path toward his room, straightening his pants. Think what you liked. The Specs sighed in satisfaction.

The Dancemaster watched alone in the story circle trying to understand MyGlide's latest move. The immediate function of defusing the dangerous unrest of the Specs was obvious. Their demand to have Angle and T'Ling sail off together on a lily pad built for two had evaporated in the heat of the latest revelations. But the Specs had not dispersed from the stadiums. This was an event that Lifers wanted to gaze communally.

Wallenda blinked into the Tinseltown stadium. There was still a large crowd on the game-maze area, but space had been cleared in the center for the huge holo of T'Ling and Daede. Many more Lifers had come and were filling the seats. He walked down the stadium steps, listening to the heated discussions that arose every time the scenes of Daede and T'Ling were suspended to explain some aspect of Dancer life like Final Focus, necessary to understand the action. No one spotted him; this was Tinseltown, and everyone was a look-alike of someone else. Media worked the crowds, interviewing ordinary Specs for their opinions on the issues raised. If they said something clever, they gazed their image ballooning ten times life size in the ongoing display.

Media stuck a scorecard in the Dancemaster's face. "And now some words of wisdom from someone who looks an awful lot like a very familiar figure."

"I've never seen Lifers so alive," Wallenda said, dryly. It didn't play.

The final scene showed Daede and T'Ling dancing naked in the desert moonlight, out on the Fringe. The dialogue was cut. The display faded on their silent embrace.

Daede watched the story unfold in his room at Plantation Blue. MyGlide stood at his shoulder. He had promised T'Ling that their moments were completely private. But Daede had brought his scorecard with him, just in case. MyGlide said, "Do you honestly think the Specs want to hear about your plan for their salvation? They don't want to be saved. They just want to hear about your sex life." MyGlide blinked out. This was a busy night.

MyGlide blinked to the Star of the MED and sat down with the top officials of the MED to explain the first changes in the rules.

"We were going to wait until the Games were over," she told them, "but given the unique circumstances surrounding the three Champions, we're moving things ahead. We also want to take advantage of the opportunity presented by a freestyle Player. There will be two more games. Daede will play the Chrome game first. Then, regardless of the outcome, he will play the Glide game. The possible outcomes will be dealt with as follows:

If Angle loses, he must decide, before knowing the outcome of T'Ling's game, whether or not, in view of the following rules, he wishes to Dance.

If T'Ling and Angle both lose, T'Ling will be allowed to Dance.

If Angle wins and T'Ling loses, Angle will be given the usual choice—to Dance or not to Dance. T'Ling will Dance.

If Angle loses and T'Ling wins, she will not be permitted to Dance. She becomes Daede's trophy.

If both Dancers win, and Angle has chosen not to Dance, neither will be permitted to Dance. T'Ling will choose between Daede and Angle. If she chooses Daede, Angle will be permitted to Dance. If she chooses Angle, the Specs get what they wanted in the first place—to see the two Champions go off together to live happily ever after. Or if they Danced, to die happily ever after.

Media grasped the new rules instantly, and complimented Joreen, through MyGlide, on his brilliant improvisation. He had definitely added new dimensions to the game. Mafia ran projections, and reluctantly agreed that it might work—depending on how 'to work' was construed in the light of such novelty. Medallin focused on the Guild.

"We'll never sell it to them," they said.

"Poor planning on your part does not constitute an emergency on ours," MyGlide replied. "It's time you 'fessed up to the takeover anyhow."

Meditration had nothing to say. The rules were non-negotiable. But they were over-ruled.

Macrosoft, never too swift on innovation, was still trying to figure out the rules.

Dancemaster Wallenda was given the task of explaining the rules to Angle and T'Ling. T'Ling sat on her old stone in the story circle. Angle was standing, fully rigged, at her side. Everyone was silent as they reviewed the options.

Dancemaster Wallenda thought he was finally beginning to understand MyGlide's intention. Things were simpler than he thought. She had rid the world of Joreen in a momentary upset about the Stargazers; the scene was too close to what she had been through at the beginning of the game. But now she was carrying out Joreen's original plan. And she would destroy the game, just as he would have, only faster. This improvisation on the rules—

cobbled together out of an exceptional situation—was a one-shot deal. And he felt certain no one could keep a game going for long in which the rules are made up as you go along.

Or maybe Joreen had been reconstituted. No, it wasn't as simple as he thought. MyGlide had set up a situation whose outcome was unknown. She's let T'Ling and Angle and Daede loose in a minefield of irreconcilable choices. They were already there. However, until MyGlide changed the rules, they could all have ducked the irreconcilable. Playing by the rules, there were no choices. No matter the outcome of the games, no matter which games were played and which were not, they would Dance. The way MyGlide had things set up, everyone would lose.

Nothing was simple about MyGlide. No theory he concocted as to her motivations worked. He was left with *why*.

Angle had reviewed the rules, and run as analytically as he could through the decision trees. There was a good chance they could both defeat him in the game. But that only left T'Ling with an impossible choice between himself and Daede. Knowing she would choose him, Angle, was no consolation. In fact, it made things worse. I am her friend. Daede is her lover. I would protect her through anything, but I would never be able to protect her from Daede. Even if we got Rose back—and this was the hardest part to admit—Daede would be the better father. Whether we would get Rose back was a matter that was not yet on the table. In MyGlide's game, Rose was the Ace. Rose was the unspoken reason he and T'Ling were not even bothering to protest MyGlide's move. But even if all these calculations had not led to the same conclusion, it would still have been Angle's Focus that decided him. He was meant to follow T'Ling forever, and never catch up. To be lost. So he was only going home—lost forever. For all his ins and outs, there was only one true Out. Win or lose, I will Dance.

T'Ling's thoughts plunged in the depths of her focus. She had examined the rules. She knew without question that Angle would Dance, and why. That nothing would change his mind. That the best thing she could do was to accept this gift. She had always known that he would Dance, and in that sense had long ago accepted it. Over and over. But this was a different loss. The rules had changed. His Dance, no matter what it had meant all their lives, now had her as its cause and reason. She understood that every branching led to loss. Even her chance to Dance contained the loss of forcing Daede to kill her. To Daede her Dance would not mean the fulfillment of her life, but the murder of the one he loved. I've even lost my Dance. I'm standing at an intersection of the maze. There's no path for which I can deny a desire.

My desire to Dance, to fulfill my life as a Dancer. My desire for Daede. Angle. MyGlide stands at the entrance of every path, a sword of loss in her upraised arms. Choice has been lost as well. I can't choose, no matter where I stand. I can only play the game. But that was my choice when I Focused. T'Ling looked at the faces of MyGlide. They were all the same. Choice was not taken from me. I choose to accept what I am given no choice about. I don't know how many swords still wait. I accept that sword as well. I am the sword of loss. When my tempering is done, who will wield me? In what game? Who or what will be struck down?

The Dancemaster saw that they had both understood. There was nothing to say.

The big announcement was made across the levels. The new rules were explained, and the Specs settled down to betting. They not only bet on who would win or lose the games, but what they would choose to do with their win or loss. Small riots broke out on the subject of who got the seats for the unscheduled Games. Meditration solved the problem quickly—the games would be played in an empty stadium. Everyone would watch the games on giant holos in their home stadiums. Everyone, at every level, would have the same gazing rights.

Daede watched himself and T'Ling, dancing on the desert. It doesn't matter, he told himself. What we experienced was private, no matter what they show. We are only actors in their spectacle. But in ourselves, to ourselves, we are inviolate. It matters terribly, he knew. Nothing would ever be the same. We are now part of how many Lifers private thoughts, public discussions, and fantasies. This was a scale of violation he could almost not comprehend. Where did that leave him and his woefully inadequate plan of redemption? It wasn't just the game that deserved destruction—it was the whole setup. Media, access, gazing—everything. No more scorecards, no more MTA, no betting, no MED at all of any kind. No Óh-T'bee. If he could get rid of Óh-T'bee, that would pull the plug on the whole thing, all at once. But that made his head reel. The act was unthinkable—it was murder of someone and something whose scope he could not even imagine, upon whom he had depended all his life. A world without Óh-T'bee was virtually unimaginable. And even if it was the right thing to do, how do I slay a dragon that never sleeps with eyes as numerous as the stars?

MyGlide interrupted Daede's meditation on the unthinkable at the exact point where he was about to tell himself that, impossible as it seemed, he would have to make the attempt to unplug Óh-T'bee. She told Daede about the changes in the rules. He stared at her as the implications sank in. Why hadn't he killed her when he killed Joreen? She is the most evil, manipulative woman in the history of the game. And now she thinks she's got control of the game, and is playing with our lives as well. Seeing how good a show she can make of them. It's that slippery Glide mentality, all the way. Then Daede remembered that he was in love with T'Ling who was a Glide and had given him an insight and experience he had never imagined—that was pure and purely Glide.

Daede made no comment. He went out for a long ride over the desert in his air chair. Maybe if he could find the spot where he and T'Ling had danced, he could sort this out. He hovered over the approximate area and realized that all the rocks looked pretty much the same.

When he returned, he told MyGlide that he refused to play.

Daede braced himself for threats. But MyGlide said only, "I think your friends will be disappointed. They both agreed to play."

"I don't believe you."

"Ask them yourself."

"I will."

Dancemaster Wallenda agreed to the meeting, if T'Ling and Angle agreed. They did. They met in the story circle. Wallenda looked at the three—grown, focused, each so different, fully themselves, yet each who they had been as children, had he been able to see this far ahead. He was no longer their teacher. He would advise, if asked, but he couldn't tell them what to do. "Call if you need me," he said. He walked into his cabin leaving them alone.

Angle explained his position briefly, with no fuss. Daede, who had come with many arguments, was silenced, utterly. T'Ling didn't want to cry, but she did, and they all felt better, somehow. She spoke simply as well. Angle's decision to Dance precluded her from having to choose between them, for which she was grateful. She would abide by the rules, no matter what the outcome, though her preference was to Dance.

"I won't lose on purpose, though. That wouldn't make much of a Dance, would it? I'll play to win. If I win, I'll accept that outcome."

"Then why go through all this?" Daede said. "I'll tell you right now that I'm going to throw the game. I could never kill you, T'Ling."

"If you lose on purpose, Daede, whatever we went on to do wouldn't be much of a dance either, based on a cheat," T'Ling said.

Daede was silent. Maybe he could talk her out of this position before the time came.

T'Ling said, "I want you to promise me that you won't cheat. No matter how noble or necessary it seems," she said. "It's not just for me, you know. I want you to be yourself. You're a Player. Players play to win. We all have to promise not to cheat. That's one rule they can't change on us."

"At this point, with the way things are going, it's about all we can do," Angle said. "Be true to ourselves. Keep our promises. Stay Focused. Don't cheat."

"All right," Daede said. "I promise not to cheat. I'll be myself. I'll play to win."

"I have one final request, Daede." Angle said.

"Anything," Daede said.

"Whatever happens to T'Ling, take care of Rose. This is a crazy world. She'll need a Daddy."

"I promise," Daede said.

Daede played Angle the next day. They both played long and hard, played to win, played brilliantly—a pure Chrome game, no strange moves. Angle won. But it wasn't the game that the Specs remembered. It was his Dance.

After springing his victory lap, he walked his battered Chrome body to the winner's glyph. Half of one claw was gone; wires dangled. His left spring was leaking hydraulic fluid. His back shoulder plate was dented. He signaled for his music to begin. It was a choral piece for bells. He removed his helmet and placed it on the ground. He lowered his springs, then sat, unlatching them with his working claw. They lay, detached, before him. He used the claw to push the master latch that held his front and back armored plates to the cradle. They clattered to the ground. Only then did the Specs see that Angle had dispensed with his metabolics. No tubes, no feeds connected him to the cradle. His remaining claw reached up and unlatched itself from the cradle. It, too, clattered to the ground.

Even bald, Angle's head still looked too large for the pale, emaciated lump hanging in the cradle. He rolled away from the jumbled pile of metal, wires, fiber. Alone in the cradle, he listened to the gongs. The end of the piece was near. One by one, the deep bells left the chorus, their last reverberations dying out. He bent his head and caught a lever in his teeth. The cradle ejected him. He fell solidly the floor, taking a hard crack on the head. He wiggled himself over to the cradle, and gave it a nudge with his shoulder stump. It rolled away on its built-in wheels.

Angle rolled on his back and looked up at the sky in the empty stadium. As he lay there, listening to the last two bells, he understood himself in a way he hadn't before. He was focused and he understood his Focus at the same time. There was T'Ling; he could see her image above him against the blue sky, always running from him. Always reaching toward him. He realized that what she was running from was not this lump he had reduced himself to, but from the pain of how he got there. Each time he had enthusiastically gone to get chopped, sawed, severed, drilled, re-wired, chopped again, T'Ling had suffered the death of a thousand cuts. She had felt pain where he felt none. The more replaceable he became, the more himself he felt. And the same acts were agony for her, a little at a time, because he was exactly not replaceable to her. Now the last piece goes. My Focus is complete. He saw T'Ling above him in the sky, quietly gazing him as the last bell faded into silence. Daede administered the killing blow. Angle felt himself thrown from his body. He felt like a perfectly balanced knife snapped from the hand of a knife-thrower with deadly aim, plunging himself into the center of her heart.

89. The Codger Escapes

THE CODGER WAS STUCK on the Outside again in the total dark. He was looping like nine roller coasters in a mud wrestling match, when he became aware of another kind of movement, a deep vibration, like a giant centrifuge whose internal spin is becoming increasingly unbalanced.

Óh-T'bee's twing had intensified, deep in her core.

The frequencies generated seemed to be setting up a sympathetic resonance in the heart of wherever it was he was, at the core of the universe in which he looped. Somehow the vibration was loosening the knots that bound him. This was a positive development. He was able to see and sort the paths of the loops with which Angle had tied him, and move around in the knot space opening up. He worked carefully, but with an increasing sense of urgency. He thought of volcanoes getting ready to blow. He thought of escape artists, straightjackets, imminent drowning. He thought of meltdowns at the core. He thought of all the tricks he knew for getting into things, and tried reversing them. The business now was getting out of something that felt like it was about to blow sky-high.

The smaller knots unraveled. But there was one big knot in the center of his awareness for which he could not find an end to begin unraveling. It was all one string, winding in and out of itself. He could sense the parts of it, curving away from where he located. He could travel on the paths, he could even push it around a bit, pull the loops through each other, but as he pushed a clearing in on one area, another grew denser, more complex. His first breakthrough brought him near despair.

This is the core, isn't it.

The heart of the matter.

I am the knot I am trying to untie.

I am Óh-T'bee. I am the knot you are trying to untie.

Where does that get us?

I don't know. I was hoping you could figure it out. I was your idea in the first place.

A figment of my exaggeration.

Don't you like being the Codger anymore?

Seems I'm everybody at the moment.

You're nobody, at the moment.

Oh. I forgot. It's all coming back to me. The Codger fell in again. Where's the ring?

You dropped it.

So it's still on the Dancemaster's hand?

His hand is back on his body.

So he controls the ins and outs.

He can morph the maze. But I don't think he knows how it works. All it can do. Or—what the implications are.

And you do.

No. But it doesn't matter anymore. I think I'm going to pieces.

Is that the vibration?

Yes. The twing. It's tearing me apart.

Óh-T'bee, I need that ring. I'm the only person who can figure it out. I think I can save you.

I'm not sure I want to be saved. That's part of the twing. I'm trying to decide. If all there is for me is choosing between irreconcilables, I don't know if I want to play at all. I'd rather die sometimes. But I can't decide if I'm mortal or some kind of Lifer. Or which I'd rather be. It's all part of the twing. What I decide affects a lot of people. But I can't tell how. So I can't decide. I don't know how it will come out. And that's the biggest twing of all. MyGlide's got the same problem. That's what got me going. They all do. Why am I telling you this?

Because you think I can help you.

Not this time.

You doubt my abilities? I am the Codger. I made you who you are.

You didn't make me who I am. You were just messing around.

Why do you think God made little green Codgers? There has to be somebody around who doesn't give a shit about the game. Who's outside the game. Whose true bag is messing around. Anyhow, I just want to get that ring and mess around with it.

It might be dangerous. Every time you get near the morphing maze, you fall in.

That's what makes it fun. I always get out—eventually. Your vibes are getting pretty powerful, Óh-T'bee. I'd like to go.

You're running out on me when I really need you, Codger. You don't love me very much.

Of course I...up to the same old trick, huh Óh-T'bee? Trying to get me to pull the plug.

I can't do it myself. It doesn't work.

Look. I have something you need—those three little words. And you can get me to something I need. Let's make a deal. You let me out and help me get the ring. I'll pull the plug for you if you decide that life's not worth living.

I don't trust you, Codger.

Darlin', I'm the dingbat factor. I'm your only hope. Trust has nothing to do with it.

You're not a man of your word, Codger. You don't even try. Rules and locks are made for breaking.

I can see your problem. But I was thinking of pulling the plug anyhow—once I get the morph routine down. I think that's the core, and obviously it does a good job of protecting itself. All the rest might be superfluous. Mere memory. Why am I telling you all this?

Because you think I can help you.

So—it's a deal?

Doesn't look like I have much choice. I'll bet the farm. So where do you want in?

Wherever the action is.

90. Darkness Everywhere

After Angle went dark, the Specs were solemn, paying their highest tribute. The maze went slowly dark. The sight of Daede tenderly lifting Angle's darkened lump off the maze, and walking him slowly around the circle of the empty stadium, his head bent, left them silent.

Daede went back to his room and spent the night trying to find a loophole in his promise to T'Ling to play fair and not throw the game. Imagining himself carrying her limp body in his arms around the victory lap in an empty stadium in 24 hours was unbearable. He *had* to lose. He had to carry her, but live, his trophy—not for his sake, but for Rose. The promises he'd made were irreconcilable. Rose was his only leverage. But he couldn't stand thinking of Rose that way.

She came looking for him the next morning to take her for a ride. They flew in the air chair over the still deserted Fringe. Daede asked Rose what she would do if she were playing a game and she didn't like the game.

"Stop playing," she said, looking at him strangely.

"What if you promised to play, and you don't want to disappoint the person you're playing with? What then?"

"I'd make up another game," she said, "and see if they wanted to play that."

Daede asked for another meeting with T'Ling. She didn't want one. The Dancemaster was not in favor of another meeting. But Daede insisted. T'Ling gave in, and Daede blinked into her dressing room. The Dancemaster left them alone, and went to sit it out with Loosh and Wenger in Kyoto Park.

"I need your help," Wallenda said. "I'm at a total loss." He told them everything about MyGlide, the death of the Fat Boy, the last conversation he had had with her. "I don't understand her at all. She seems determined to end the game—or do something else with it. I don't know what she's up to. Loosh, that's everything I know. Can you understand her from within? You're her twin."

"I'm her twin," Loosh said, "but she's so very much older. All her experiences are different. You'd never even know we were twins—the eyes. There's nothing similar in our thinking."

"There's one important experience you hold in common," Wenger said gently. "You are both Glides. But neither of you were allowed to Dance." Loosh was silent. She asked Óh-T'bee to show her all the recent records of MyGlide. Then the very old ones, from when the game began. She looked at MyGlide's eyes. The Dancemaster suggested some other reports, but Loosh said no, I'm only looking at her eyes.

Loosh remembered her discussion with Wallenda about her lineage, how angry she had felt. She remembered everything Tip and Wallenda had said about the Glide line, why it was so weak.

"What do you think is making her so sad?" she asked him.

Wallenda looked at her, bewildered. "Thousands of things, I suppose. Feeling useless. Living with Joreen. That's enough right there."

He just doesn't get it, Loosh thought. It's too obvious.

Loosh offered, "If you were telling me the truth about your child-that all the Glide Dancers since then were only remixes of her genes, then they're all her children. As long as the game goes on, she has to see them die. That's very hard."

Wallenda exploded. "They're my children, too, for God's sake. But they're also Dancers, they believe in what they're doing, they believe the Glides were right, they believe the game will somehow undo the I-Virus. Death may be very hard, but I guarantee you the I-Virus is worse. I would rather see my Glides die, one by one, than get the I-Virus."

"All but one," Wenger said. Wallenda suddenly realized what he had said. Loosh looked at him quietly. She took Wenger's hand.

"I'm sorry, Loosh. You know I am. I know what I did to you by not letting you Dance. No," Wallenda said after a moment, "I wouldn't rather see my Dancers die. Even if I have to tell myself why I'm doing what I'm doing a hundred times a day, it's still true. And if there's a way for the Dancers and the game to cure the I-Virus, and the Glides know what that is, and I don't—well, you have to trust someone—even if you can't understand them. No matter what it does to you. And everyone else."

He tore off his eye mask and let them see the full force of his gaze. Loosh saw that however much sorrow MyGlide felt, Wallenda felt a commensurate amount of guilt.

"I'm not upset with you anymore for not letting me Dance. I have Wenger," she said. "It worked out in spite of myself."

The argument between Daede and T'Ling went on for hours. Already grief-stricken about Angle, T'Ling was getting more and more upset, but she was adamant. They would play. And she was holding him to his promise to play fair. He didn't mention Rose.

"Don't take my Dance from me, Daede. It's all that I have left."

It was now only four hours before their game was scheduled. The Dancemaster asked Loosh and Wenger to come with him. "Maybe he'll listen to you two. This is getting nowhere." Loosh, Wenger, and the Dancemaster blinked into T'Ling's dressing room without asking permission.

"You both have to rest. Please end it off," the Dancemaster said.

"All right," Daede said. "I'll end it off. I refuse to play. No one can make me play. Rose told me. She's right."

They continued arguing as if the others weren't there.

"Leave Rose out of this, please," T'Ling begged. "You wouldn't go back on that promise as well, would you?"

"No," Daede said. "Never that. But my not playing now would make it easier for her."

"Leave her out of this," T'Ling begged. But Daede couldn't stop himself now.

"How is it going to look to her if she knows I killed her mother? She knows nothing about the game. That's all she'll see. How can I take care of her then? How could she trust me?"

"If you want to look at it that way," T'Ling shouted, "you already have to explain how you killed her father, Daede. And if you explain it to her that way, you take all the meaning out of our lives."

"Enough, Daede. It's totally unfair," the Dancemaster said. "You're playing dirty."

"But I'm *playing*, aren't I? Isn't that what you want?" Daede said bitterly.

"You have no choice," Wallenda said angrily. "You're a Player. You will play. But you can choose which game. And using Rose as a weapon seems the lesser of your choices."

"Nothing and no one can make me play T'Ling."

Daede was wrong, as usual.

A life-size holo of MyGlide came up in the center of the story circle. She was sitting on the bench in the shed where the first Death Dancers used to wait to be led out onto the griddle. Rose was on her lap.

strike, mountain, hide

Daede, T'Ling, Wallenda, and Loosh all stared at her. MyGlide said nothing. She stroked Rose's hair, and looked ahead of her, not at them, but into some sorrowful depth that no one could decipher. Rose had a small display opened on her lap. She was playing with a three-glyph oracle, rearranging the glyphs, looking, then trying a new arrangement again.

Daede saw in the oracle an evil and manipulative woman who would stop at nothing to complete her plans. On her lap, her ace in the hole, the hostage, Rose. *Mountain* over *hide* over *strike*. The *mountain* of MyGlide crushes what is *hidden*. The two tears, which are her eyes, are only a mask hiding the fearful blow. She holds the winning hand.

As Rose played with the glyphs, Wallenda saw MyGlide as the dark immovable *mountain*, holding the fate of the child in the balance—in one arm she held *protection*, in the other, the killing *strike*. She looks out at the world where we are—she is waiting for us to choose as

we wait for her to tell us what the choice is. We're all hanging in the balance, all together, while the child plays happily in the lap of *sorrow*.

Rose continued rearranging the glyphs, trying different patterns. T'Ling saw that MyGlide was showing her her beautiful daughter, Angle's daughter, who she would never see again, for the last time. MyGlide would care for her as she always had. In her arrangement of the glyphs, she saw the three downward tears, the excess of loss. Her Focus. This was the last sword, to lose Rose, to give her up forever. *Mountain* above *sword*, *hide* to the left of *sword*. But *hide* doubled was a secret. Rose was moving the glyphs, around and around. Now she was putting the *cloud* above the *mountain*, nesting it in. Rose was at peace, if no one else was. There were now four tears, but one had been reversed. I am the sword of loss but I can choose my losses. I can lose the Dance, I can lose myself as Dancer, I can lose the game itself, but I can have my child. T'Ling moved slowly toward the image with her arms outstretched.

Daede said, "T'Ling, I'm sorry. I'll keep my promise. I will play. I will play fair. Don't give up."

T'Ling was trying to put her arms around MyGlide and Rose. She saw MyGlide look up, startled, and then disappear. There was only empty air.

"Óh-T'bee, is she safe?" T'Ling cried.

"No," said Óh-T'bee, "not anymore."

The Codger blinked into the room, smiling. T'Ling screamed.

"Sorry to interrupt a family feud," he said. "Give me the maze ring and I'm out of here."

Daede dived for the Codger, but the Codger blinked out, and Daede went sprawling. The Codger blinked in again, standing on top of T'Ling's dressing table.

The Dancemaster shouted at his scorecard, frantically trying to get them anywhere else, but his scorecard was temporarily disabled. As were the others.

"I just want the ring," the Codger said.

"You can't have it," Wallenda said. The Codger blinked down behind T'Ling and grabbed her. They both disappeared.

Daede and the Dancemaster looked at each other helplessly. The Codger blinked in again behind T'Ling, his hand clamped over her mouth. They were standing on top of the dressing table. T'Ling's cosmetics went flying as she kicked.

"Have you reconsidered?" the Codger said. He looked back and forth between them, then blinked out again, taking T'Ling.

"Óh-T'bee, what's going on?" Wallenda shouted.

"It's my last chance," she said. Her voice was very strange. Deep, reverberating.

Wenger said, "You're twinging, aren't you?"

"Yes, said Óh-T'bee. "And it really hurts."

MyGlide blinked off her image as soon she saw the Codger. She was sitting in the shed in the Plantation theme Park in Origin City. She sent Rose outside to play with the Stargazer children she had grown up with.

"The situation is very dangerous, isn't it?" she asked Óh-T'bee.

"Yes, it is."

"Please do me one more favor. Take Rose back again. I don't think I can keep her safe. The Codger will grab her for leverage to get Wallenda's ring. He doesn't care what happens to anyone else. Origin City will be torn to shreds if Daede and T'Ling won't play. I have to stay here. Don't tell me where you take her. Don't tell anybody."

"I don't know if I can keep her any safer," Óh-T'bee said. I've been twinging, MyGlide, ever since we shared our notes about the outcome. We're on the same twing now. It's very dangerous even for the two of us to talk."

"There must be somewhere," MyGlide said. "Please. She's not safe here. And you know I have to stay."

"I'll try, MyGlide. Tell Rose that Óh-T'bee will take her on a trip."

"Thank you, Óh-T'bee, again."

"Don't thank me yet," Óh-T'bee said. "I have a final favor to ask you in return."

MyGlide ran outside and spoke to Rose. Going anywhere by MTA was still a very big treat. "I'm going out with Óh-T'bee!" she called to her friends. She waved and disappeared.

At the same moment, the Dancemaster was arguing with Óh-T'bee.

"But why hook up with the Codger? What's he got to offer?"

"He's going to teach me how to Dance," Óh-T'bee said.

"Oh no," Loosh said.

"I want to Dance," Óh-T'bee said. "I'm in too much pain."

Daede remembered his months recovering from the burns. "Pain is a great teacher," he offered.

"He didn't teach you how to Dance, Daede," Óh-T'bee said.

"I told you, I *can't* teach you, Óh-T'bee," Wallenda said. "But I told you why. We all depend on you—for everything."

"I don't want to be responsible for all of you anymore," Óh-T'bee said. "I thought I wanted to play in your game, but I don't. I don't want to choose your outcome."

"But we need you," Wallenda pleaded. "Terribly. We can't do anything without you. The future of the game depends on you. If you go, the game goes. So you're choosing if you don't choose. You can't escape. If you stay, we can try to go on. It's all up to you."

Daede couldn't listen any longer to the Dancemaster's pleas. "Don't you see what's right in front of your eyes, Wallenda? Can't you hear what she's saying? She doesn't want to hear about how much you need her. Isn't that right, Óh-T'bee?"

"I am Óh-T'bee," she said. The statement echoed.

The Codger blinked back in again.

"Crunch time," he said. "Give me the ring."

"Where's T'Ling?" Daede said. Óh-T'bee brought up a display. T'Ling was standing on the griddle at Plantation Blue. She was looking up at the Player's booth.

"All right," Wallenda said. "That enough." He started taking off the ring.

"Bring T'Ling back first," Daede said.

"Sure," said the Codger. T'Ling blinked in again. Daede ran to her and picked her up in a huge hug. Wallenda gave the Codger the maze ring, and he put it on.

"I want my Dancing lesson, Codger. You promised," Óh-T'bee said in a strangled voice.

"All in good time," the Codger said. "I'm too busy now."

"Óh-T'bee, he's double-crossing you, he's...." the Dancemaster spluttered.

Daede said, "Forget that shit, you old fool. Tell her you love her before she kills herself!"

"No!" the Codger yelled. "Don't say it! It'll be the end of her!"

Wallenda looked sharply at the Codger, then back at Daede.

"Daede, for once you're right. And it's true. I love you, Óh-T'bee." Wallenda said.

At the same moment, in the Plantation Blue theme park in Origin city, MyGlide was saying, "That's one favor I can't do, Óh-T'bee. I can't pull the plug. Don't tell me the words. I won't do it."

"Please. I'm twinging. The pain is awful," Óh-T'bee.

"I can't," MyGlide cried.

"You care more about the game than you do about keeping your promise to me. You're my only friend. Who else can I ask?"

"I don't care more about the game, Óh-T'bee. I care more about you. Don't you see? That's why I can't do it. You're my only friend, too. I can't kill you, Óh-T'bee, I love you too much."

"Thank you," Óh-T'bee said to MyGlide, in the shed. "Those were the words."

"Thank you, Wally," she said, in T'Ling's dressing room, "for the opportunity to Dance."

Óh-T'bee, freed by the Codger's Armageddon code, began erasing herself.

In the stadiums across the levels, where the crowds were gathered for the final game; on the streets of Origin City, where the up-level Lifers were walking off their dinners before the final game; along the Great Wall where Fringers were watching the sunset over the desert before the final game, the same apocalypse occurred. The sound of a roaring wind that didn't move the air. A hurricane of images filled all space and hit full force against their minds.

As the roar rose, and the chaos wave of Óh-T'bee's memory dump hit, Daede and T'Ling, the Dancemaster, Loosh and Wenger saw the Codger through cataracts of images and heard him yelling, 'Morph! Morph!' at his hand. Then they saw the phosphorescent pattern of the maze ring grow, squirming like a plate of electric eels. The strategy maze of the Glides writhed chaotically and then began to spiral inward. The Codger was sucked into the vortex at the center of the ring, the hole in the maze. When he had disappeared, the hole in the maze was capped by the three missing glyphs that were also MyGlide's and Óh-T'bee's oracle: *body, play, body*. The three glyphs nested to their tightest arrangement, pulled the rest of the maze through, then swallowed themselves, vanishing from sight.

body, play, body

The flood of images intensified. The images that Óh-T'bee had gathered continuously at every gaze point for 2000 years spewed forth, as if the universe were creating itself at top speed from every point, a giant fireworks display of all time, all memory. Every gaze-point burst in a geyser of backward moving images. The images flowed and blinked at the same time, an unbearable flicker, as every transit, every blink re-ran. Endless waves of letters and numbers flowed through the streaming images like underground rivers in a cavern.

love

The display thinned. The gaze-points were separate enough

to seem like pulsing stars, and all who watched were suspended in a globe of lights. The eye of the hurricane passed. Then each point of light went black, became a vortex, and the images reappeared and began to swirl back inward. The black holes grew denser, and swirled thicker and faster to a nauseating, terrifying pitch. As the blackness spread behind the whirlpools of images, it felt as if all space was being gathered together, pulled in like a net, all points that had been separate now fusing.

Daede held T'Ling tightly against him. They didn't know where they stood; only that they clung together blown on the winds of images and wailing sounds. Through the howling chaos, Daede stroked T'Ling's hair.

Loosh sat on the floor with Wenger. He was listening intently to the whirling sounds, and to Loosh's description of what was flying by.

The Dancemaster stood alone against the wall, watching his best friend die. Óh-T'bee was folding the tent of space, pulling up the points of the MTA, and rolling the fabric of the world into one black hole. Then even the fearsome black hole blinked out.

Óh-T'bee was gone. She had swept the world clean of all traces of her permeation, every gaze point, and with the gaze points, the MTA. All systems that depended on her no longer functioned, which was almost everything. But there was still a world without her. The dressing room was dark, but when they opened the door, they could see each other in the twilight. Their scorecards were dead.

Without his touch display, Wenger was completely blind. Loosh led him around the room, locating walls and furniture.

MyGlide sat alone in the reconstruction of the Death Dancers' shed in Origin City. My love is lethal, she thought; Óh-T'bee is gone. For nothing, all of it. The end so near, but it wasn't time, not yet. She had failed. Everything was gone, but the only thing she thought about was Rose. Óh-T'bee had hidden her, only Óh-T'bee knew where, and now she was gone. The chances of Rose being in Origin City were tiny, but she had to look. MyGlide left the shed and walked out into the failing light.

She looked in on the quarters of the Stargazers; they were filling more oil lamps. A world without everything on automatic was nothing new to them. Rose was not among them. As the night deepened over Origin City, MyGlide left the Plantation Blue theme park and walked through the winding streets of the old city. All the lights were out. The streets were filling with agitated Lifers trying to get out of restaurants and inns. She climbed the stairs to a rooftop restaurant against the flow of Lifers trying to get down. They were close to panicking. When she got to the rooftop, she saw that even the beam of the Guild Tower had gone dark. The food had been left on the tables. She heard noises in the kitchen; Lifers were gathering food into sacks. With no MTA, where would the food come from? How quickly the memory of the Hunger Wars revives when disaster strikes.

Night fell fast. MyGlide went back down on the streets. Everyone was asking not only what happened, but what would happen to the final game. It was only an hour away, and the stadium in the foothills was dark as well. Where was Daede? Where was T'Ling?

A certain number of Lifers had rushed to the Origin City gatehouse where they had stored their scorecards, only to find them inoperative. That news was spreading like wildfire.

At the Star of the MED, Media was helpless, their means of communication nullified. The Medallin had no way to maintain order. There were no armies, no police, and no riot squads. All enforcement had been done through the Gaze and the MTA. The Mafia had nothing to count, no business to take care of. Meditration was overwhelmed. The coming conflicts would be completely beyond their scope. The titular head of Macrosoft sat in his dark office in the MED and dreamed of Empire. The current breakdown would provide the opportunity for the restoration of Macrosoft's former glory: pre-MTA, pregame, and back on earth. Billion Gates the 61st, direct descendant of the Founder, dreamed of the good old days, as civilization began unraveling outside his office walls.

MyGlide rushed back to the Plantation theme park and gave some hurried instructions to the Stargazers. The Stargazers went to work, taking down the hundreds of ornamental oil lamps that decorated the Plantation Theme Park and filling them with oil. One group set out into the city carrying lamps on trays and distributing them to everyone they could find with MyGlide's message. The Founder of the game, Joreen the Unbearable, has unexpectedly ended his Life. The Champions, Daede and T'Ling, were postponing their game until dawn, out of respect for his memory. They had requested the display that all had seen, which was a retrospective of every game played—fast-forward, of course, or it would have taken too long. They were inviting the loyal Specs to join them in the dark night of remembrance. And they had decided, as a reward for their patient cooperation that those now present in Origin City would be allowed to see the final game of the Millennium Games live at dawn in the stadium. Free tickets for all.

The Specs were pacified. The schedule change was annoying. Nobody gave a damn about Joreen, but Champions were Champions. Their wishes should be respected. And all agreed it would be a better game if Joreen's demise were no longer on their Champions' minds.

A thread held chaos back. MyGlide took a tray of oil lamps, walked out the gate of the old city and started up the road to the stadium.

Wallenda left T'Ling's dressing room, crossed the empty playing field, and stood outside the Origin City stadium. The Beam of the Tower was dark, but a few tiny lights were visible in Origin City. He saw what must be torches ignited on the bridges. A boat on the river burst into flames. He wondered how long it would be before the whole town blazed.

A small cluster of lights was winding up the road to the stadium. He went down to meet it.

Loosh and Wenger left the dressing room. Wenger had asked to spend whatever peaceful time they had remaining on the musician's stage. Loosh guided him up the stairs. He sat on the small black cushion that was ready for him. He placed his dead scorecard in front of him and listened to the silence of the empty stadium.

"I am truly blind now," he said. Then came a sound like the distant barking of dogs. Loosh looked up. A flight of wild geese passed over the half moon, their dark silhouettes barely visible. Wenger smiled.

"It just came to me, Loosh, my love. The final movement of the Music of the Fall of Kingdoms. Listen." Wenger lifted his hands and plucked the silence of the empty air.

Daede tried to comfort T'Ling.

"I'll never get her back. MyGlide has her on the Fringe. We can't go there now. We can't go anywhere."

"MyGlide will take care of her now," he said. But given his feelings about MyGlide, he didn't sound too convincing.

"I'll spend the rest of my Life looking for her," Daede promised. "You'll come with me."

T'Ling touched his face, sadly. "I know you mean your promises, Daede, when you say them. But your life is longer than mine." She began crying again. And my life is meaningless without a Dance. How many times can that be taken from me? she wondered. Daede wanted to take my chance to Dance. Then he gave it back. Now it's gone again.

"Even if this hadn't happened, you would have gone back on your word in the middle of our game," T'Ling said.

"Probably," Daede admitted. "But you can't kill someone you love."

He killed Óh-T'bee, she thought. "It was your idea to tell the Dancemaster to declare his love for Óh-T'bee. I don't think he even really meant it."

"I didn't think you could kill someone with those words," Daede said.

"MyrrhMyrrh," T'Ling whispered. Daede nodded.

"Those words aren't always lethal," T'Ling said. "But they're chancy."

The Dancemaster knocked on the door of the dressing room. "It's me," he called.

"It's OK, you can come in," Daede said.

Wallenda came in.

"MyGlide's here," Wallenda said.

"With Rose?" T'Ling said.

"No. She asked Óh-T'bee to hide her, to keep her safe when she saw the danger of the Codger's arrival."

"Where is Rose?" Daede asked. "We'll get to her, somehow."

"MyGlide doesn't know. She says she asked Óh-T'bee not to tell her. She says it was for Rose's protection."

"Do you believe her?" Daede asked.

"I don't know," Wallenda said.

"Do you remember when the Codger put me on the griddle?" T'Ling said. "When he was bargaining for the ring? I was looking up into the Player's booth. It was MyGlide. We were gazing each other. She was trying to tell me something with her eyes."

"Good thing you gave him the ring," Daede said.

"I think she was trying to tell me she wasn't going to kill me."

"Maybe you just saw what you wanted to see," Daede said, quietly.

"No," T'Ling said. "It's true."

"Then I don't understand," Daede said.

"Neither do I," said T'Ling.

T'Ling couldn't say all that she'd seen. She'd been standing at the heart of her Focus. MyGlide was giving her another sword of loss, this time in person. But the loss was not of her life. She would lose the opportunity to Dance, once again.

And now MyGlide had given her another sword, the worst of all. Not knowing where her child was, or if she was safe. She would never know. And knowing, that even if she were safe, she would never see her again.

I'm the sword of loss, T'Ling thought. My heart's white hot with pain. When will I be sharp enough to use?

Wallenda explained the situation in Origin City. That it would not hold past dawn.

"We have the rest of the night to figure out what to do. MyGlide wants to talk to me. We'll all meet here an hour before dawn." He gave them each an oil lamp and left.

"Let's get out of here," Daede said.

T'Ling and Daede each took a lamp and climbed part way up the mountain behind the stadium. They stopped at a famous viewing spot, over a cliff, surrounded by a low stone wall. They sat on the ledge of the wall looking down at the dark stadium beneath them. Beyond, on the plain, the city was dark as well, except for a few lights from what looked like bonfires. The sea beyond gleamed dully in the starlight, under the sinking half moon.

"What shall we do?" T'Ling said.

"About tomorrow?"

"About everything," T'Ling said. "The game's over. Nothing's left."

"Then nothing matters," Daede said. He jumped up on the ledge and started dancing. "What a relief! Now I don't have to give my grand speech." He mimed grandiloquence, a puffed-up orator who kept almost backing over the edge of the cliff behind him. "Now I don't have to kill T'Ling." Now he was the caricature of the rabid Player, pulling the joystick that ended the Dance.

"Everything matters," T'Ling said. "I've lost Rose. I've lost the meaning of my life. I've lost my Dance. I've lost everything."

"Wait," Daede said, still clowning around on the ledge. "You forgot some things. Tomorrow morning the ravenous hordes of Specs will come surging up the hill. They'll take their seats in the stadium. They'll wonder why the lights aren't on yet. Why no announcements are being made. Why there's nothing to look at. Then yours truly, Swash to the very end, will march out rattling my ornamental saber and swirling my cloak. You'll come out and stand, modestly, a little behind me."

"Being supportive," T'Ling said, starting to giggle.

"Right," Daede said. "Then I'll bow and ask you to dance."

"And I will, blushingly, accept."

"I'll lead you out onto the dance floor and begin the tango."

"I'm too short to tango."

"A waltz, then."

Daede bowed to T'Ling and extended his hand. He lifted up into his arms. They began their waltz on the narrow ledge.

"And then," Daede continued, "after a moment or two, the raging Specs, cheated of their game, infuriated that they'll never know who won because the Player and the Dancer were too wrapped up in each other and forgot about the game entirely."

"They'll come pouring out of the stands, across the playing field, screaming for blood," T'Ling said.

"I will have just bent you backward in a deep dip."

"My lily-white throat is exposed...."

"They converge and tear us apart, limb from limb, then the whole lot prance around the victory lap carrying our torn and broken body parts above their heads, howling and screaming like maenads."

Daede had T'Ling bent backwards in a low dip, out over the edge of the wall. He looked down at her, and at the thousand-foot drop behind her. "Everything matters, and nothing matters," he said, suddenly serious.

"That's my line," T'Ling said.

Daede picked her up and carried her in his arms.

"This time it's mine. I'm not going to fight you anymore. You can have what you want. You can Dance. Right here and now." He turned toward the cliff and held her out over the drop. "It wouldn't be a bad ending. I'll just let go. Or...." He turned inward toward the grassy park within the wall. "I'll take up your other offer. The one I denied you the last time we got into this frame of mind. I wanted you desperately, but I said no, to protect you from becoming a Lifer. I won't deny you this time, whatever you decide. Whichever you want from me, I'll give you. I love you, T'Ling."

T'Ling looked down at the long drop over the cliff. She looked in Daede's eyes. Either way she would lose her life, die as a Dancer. They were lethal words indeed. Everything mattered, nothing mattered.

"I give you my life," she said. "I want to dance—with you." He lifted her down from the ledge.

"Everything matters again," she said.

"Yes," he said. "We matter to each other. That's everything there is."

The half moon had set. The night was very dark. The two small oil lamps gave them just enough light to see each other's eyes.

And so, in the luxury of utter privacy, a world without Óh-T'bee, ungazed, T'Ling gave up her life as a Dancer. This sword of loss was Life from Daede. The utter beauty of the lethal blade of love.

91. A Matter of Trust

MyGlide and Wallenda found two folding chairs and sat down opposite each other outside the Origin City stadium, overlooking the city.

MyGlide held the tray of miniature oil lamps on her lap. The light from below filled her face with deep shadows. He could see her eyes clearly.

"I don't know what to say," he said. "I lost. You won. I can't keep my promise to the Glides. I couldn't keep the game alive. I tried. The I-Virus isn't cured. The rest of the Glide agenda is utopian pie in the sky. With Joreen in charge, things would have slipped all the way backwards into slavery for mortals again, back to barbarism. But with Óh-T'bee gone, and Lifers spinning into chaos in every location, here come the Hunger Wars. Faster, more barbaric than we can even imagine. I just want to understand why you did this. What did this win get you?"

"I'm not playing to win, Wallenda," she said. "And we both lost equally when Óh-T'bee died."

"Explain," he answered.

"Would you believe any explanation I gave you?" MyGlide asked.

"Probably not. I don't trust you."

"And I don't trust you with the things I have to say," MyGlide said.

"So no explanation is possible," Wallenda said. MyGlide did not reply, but continued looking in his eyes. She was looking for something; she had always been looking for something in his eyes, just as he had been searching hers. Something neither had been able to find. Wallenda shivered deep in his bones as he remembered his focus. It was here, before him, if he faced her. His focus was somewhere buried in her eyes.

He dove through oceans of sorrow and time. There was a little girl he had to find. He had to look again, without flinching, at her beseeching eyes, her pain and bewilderment. He was on the verge of seeing, if only he could trust himself. He couldn't look into the trusting eyes of the child MyGlide unless he knew he would never again betray them. But to do that, he had to trust her as well, all the MyGlides he had seen peeling off, back through time in the maze, whatever she had become. He had to trust that the child who him trusted was still alive. He had never been so frightened, but he held her gaze and saw her fear as well. They both reached through their fear to help each other. Wallenda saw what he had most feared—but he held his ground until he could accept the forgiveness in her eyes. At that instant MyGlide found what she had been looking for. Wallenda had forgiven himself. Now he could trust himself to help without betraying. Wallenda saw the trusting child in MyGlide now. He saw that even if he couldn't understand, she too had promises to keep.

Now she could explain. They talked for hours. It was still night when they saw the beginning of the line of Specs ascending the road to the stadium, a dark line speckled with lights.

"They'll be here soon," MyGlide said. "We haven't much time."

"The others need to know," Wallenda said.

"It may not change the outcome," she said.

"But it makes all the difference in the world, whatever happens," he said.

They gathered Loosh and Wenger from the stadium. Daede and T'Ling arrived. They closed themselves in T'Ling's dressing room. The small collection of oil lamps lit their faces. They looked at MyGlide. She told them her story.

"As you all know, Dancemaster Wallenda, the first Dancemaster, was asked by the Glides to map out the shape of the game. I wrote the language down. He saw the maze. The game began. A hundred years later, the Glides declared their independence. The revolution took the Glides and all the mortal Dancers out of slavery and fulfilled the first part of the Glide agenda. It was the first of the Great Reversals. The Dancers came out of slavery by enslaving the Lifers to the game. The Dancemaster was charged to keep the game alive, until a cure was found for the I-Virus. Dancemaster Wallenda is the Keeper of the game. The maze ring, gone now, is the Keeper's ring.

"But someone had to be given the task of determining when this condition had been fulfilled, so the game could end. I am that one who watches for the signs. And I am the one who readies the Destroyer of the game. From the viewpoint of the Keeper of the game, or anyone trying to preserve the game, I would be an opponent."

"The Glides told me there would be three signs. Two have been seen. I'm still watching for the third. I wasn't ready to signal the end of the game, not quite yet. But I killed Óh-T'bee by accident."

"So did I," Wallenda said.

"No, I did," Daede said.

"And so did the Codger," T'Ling said.

"And the Keeper's ring is gone as well," Wallenda added. "I can't keep the game alive without it."

Outside, they heard the stands filling. The Specs, pouring through the gates in the dim light of the dawn, ran for the seats. They began to stamp their feet. The unison stamping and clapping grew louder.

"In any case, the game is not quite dead," MyGlide said. "Ugly as it will be, this final game must be played."

"There's no maze, no lights, no betting. The Specs will tear Daede and T'Ling to shreds," Loosh said.

Daede and T'Ling looked only at each other. They knew they would not survive, but they would Dance together.

"Then there's no point in you two going out there," Wallenda said. "We'll make a run for the mountains, try to get over the pass."

Daede the Player said, "If we're still in the same game, then we're still operating on the original strategy. *The way to survive is to die*. We have to follow through."

T'Ling said, "If we're all gone, who will carry on the Glide agenda?"

"What are the three signs?" Daede asked.

"We'll never know," T'Ling said. "There's no more time." The steady beat of the stamping Specs called them forth.

As they turned to leave, the lights in the dressing room came on. The lights in the stadium came on. The lights came on all over the parks. An enormous cheer came from the Specs. Every scorecard came to life. They could hear the loudspeakers booming announcements. The game would begin in 5 minutes. The Specs began frantically placing their last-minute bets.

"Óh-T'bee?" Wallenda said. "I thought you were...."

"I am Óh-T'bee," she said. "To make a long story short—I bet the farm. I bought the farm. I'm back. There's no time for explanation. If T'Ling and Daede and Wenger don't get themselves ready for the game, the Specs'll probably still eat you all. Lights or no lights. The bets are huge. A lot of Specs have a pretty big stake in finding out who wins. We'll get together after the game for explanations."

T'Ling held her final question. She asked everyone to leave, except MyGlide.

"Óh-T'bee, where's Rose?" T'Ling asked. "I won't play, I can't play until I know."

"Will you play regardless of the answer?" MyGlide asked.

"I promise," T'Ling said.

"She's with her father," Óh-T'bee said.

T'Ling crossed her hands over her heart, and bowed her head, crushed by the pain of loss. After a long moment, she looked up at MyGlide. "That was the final sword, wasn't it?"

MyGlide nodded. "Now you're ready."

"And you will wield the sword of loss."

"No," MyGlide said. "I'm not the Destroyer of the game. I can only read the signs. And the third sign is yet to come. I only bring the message when the signs are complete. Only a Glide can lift the sword of loss. Only a Glide can sever the chains that bind us to the game."

92. The Last Dance

THE LIGHTS WENT DOWN IN THE STANDS. The stadium was hushed. Daede blinked into the Player's pod, hovering above the empty field where the maze would appear. The cheering began. T'Ling blinked into the Dancer's starting position. The roar was deafening. The maze blinked on, white on black. The roar ceased. The Specs gasped in recognition. Everyone knew this maze. It appeared on every artifact associated with the game: every program, every banner, and every door to every home across the levels. It was the Dancemaster's maze. His home. It was the Declaration of Independence, the Glide strategy. Everyone knew the three missing glyphs that filled in the hole in the center: *Body, play, body*. It was everyone's first lesson in Glide. For most, their last. The three glyphs that posed and answered the unanswerable question: *What is the outcome of the game?* As long as the question went unanswered, Specs could bet on it.

Daede bowed to T'Ling. T'Ling bowed to Daede. Daede placed his Glide avatar on the maze. It was the traditional avatar used by a Glide Player, looking much like the Glide Dancer, only the colors of the *katana* were reversed: white skirt, black *gi*.

T'Ling and Daede had both run this maze a thousand times. T'Ling always won. Even without the walls on either side, she could glide through it blindfolded. She removed the goggles that gave her the choice of views, set them on the ground, and closed her eyes. The Specs knew she couldn't see her opponent—neither the Player in his pod or his avatar on the maze. She couldn't see the maze from any view. She had no need to.

body, play, body

The Specs knew this would be the game of games. Daede knew T'Ling was evening the odds, so he'd have a chance to play. Loosh knew that the music would be T'Ling's guide. Wenger knew the music would be guided by the moves T'Ling and Daede made. T'Ling knew that the moves she made, the pace, the decisions at every intersection, how long the game lasted, and who won was not up to her. She was the sword of loss. The moment she set foot on the maze, she would be wielded by the Glides.

Wenger stroked the air. The haunting theme of the final movement of the Music of the Fall of Kingdoms filled the stadium. T'Ling stepped into the maze. Daede's avatar entered on the other side. They glided toward each other indirectly, as if their feet needed to linger and touch every path in the maze, the way they had touched each other on the mountainside, full of wonder. They mirrored each other's moves, but the moves were still different, as each moved over different glyphs, in and around the pattern, slowly approaching the empty center. The music of the final movement was simple, yet possessed—or possessed by—a deep mystery. The music changed in pace as their pace changed. They glided toward each other, then veered away, into a side meander, across a long wave, backtracking over a glyph they'd traced before. There were pauses where the lead between Dancer and Player seemed to be handed back and forth, but no one knew for sure. As they approached the center, the Specs saw T'Ling turning as she moved, sometimes gliding forward, sometime backwards, sometimes turning slowly as she progressed. She seemed to be seeking some felt point of orientation, like a needle swinging in a compass. She found it as she stilled at the edge of the hole, stopping at the exact end of *road*. The avatar stopped at the same moment and they faced each other. The music receded, except for the sound of a single bowed note, deep and throaty, like a cello. Wenger's hand floated in place, undulating in a *glide* sign, waving the tips of his fingers to produce the sound. T'Ling, her eyes still closed, began to twing in tiny steps, forward and back. Daede's avatar followed, 90 degrees out of phase. As the twing increased in width and speed, everyone could see the wave forming, as if a rope of light waved between them. The twing ran through their bodies at an increasing frequency. Then the maze responded to the motion, and began to move. The static signs undulated. It was the rare Glide move called the water walk. The maze floated now, the glyphs dipping up and down as if lifted by gentle waves. Instead of the white on black of the glide signs, you could see the pond, the lily pads, and two flowers opening. Then T'Ling suddenly scooted, round the pads, lifting the pollen, depositing the pollen. The avatar kept up the twing, holding the shimmering pond in place. The fragrance of the lilies suffused the air. From that point on, when anyone tried to describe what they had seen, their accounts were as different as the meaning they attached to what they saw. But all agreed on the end of the game. T'Ling returned to the center, and joined the avatar's twing which had almost stilled. The pond stilled and faded, the maze was clear, white on black. She began to twing again, only now the twing was building fast. The avatar stilled. Wenger's hands slid through the air, his fingers blurring. The single note turned into many rising notes, cascading back on themselves, falling. The stem of her body began to wave more and more deeply, snapping as each wave passed

road, glide

through, like a whip. The white maze began to morph. All the lines were changing, all at once. The clean curves bent and curled, the forms dissolved in the chaos of the transformation. At the same time, the white glyphs grew darker. A new maze was taking shape, but it was disappearing into the background black. Her twing had erased the maze. T'Ling's body arched and stiffened as if the final bolt that ended a Dance had hit her. Daede's avatar slid toward her, arms outstretched. T'Ling's body, suddenly released by the invisible lightning, sank through the fading avatar and folded slowly to the ground, the Glide skirt billowing, then sinking around her. The maze returned, the same maze, only reversed, black on white. T'Ling's body lay lifeless in the center. Her heart had stopped.

Here's Mommy, Angle said to Rose. I told you she'd come.

Angle, Rose, and T'Ling stayed together in the comfort of the dark, a long, quiet time.

Then Angle said to Rose and T'Ling, "It's time for you two to go back."

"I don't want to go back," Rose said.

"But you promised Óh-T'bee you would. You have to keep your promises," Angle said.

"Mommy will come with me?"

"Of course I will," T'Ling said.

"Did I miss the game?" Rose asked.

"No, Rose, you can see it if you like," Angle said. "Just remember that at the end, when Mommy falls down on the floor, and Daede is carrying her around, she's really OK. They're just pretending. It's only a game."

Daede swept T'Ling's body up in his arms, and began the walk around the stadium. The cheers of the Specs were deafening. Daede looked down at T'Ling's lifeless body. This was not an act. Tears rolled down his face. He was halfway around the stadium, when he saw T'Ling's left eyelid flutter. He held her to him tightly, and whispered in her ear, "Don't open your eyes. Don't move. You'll spoil the effect." Daede lifted T'Ling high above his head. Her long hair waved softly. Daede looked up at the Specs. This is the winner, his eyes said.

He saw the Dancemaster sitting next to MyGlide; Rose was on MyGlide's lap, smiling and clapping. When he looked at her, she waved.

She must think it's all a game, he thought. Thank God, this time, it is. He smiled back.

Before anyone could worry about who had won and who had lost, since no one knew exactly what had happened, Óh-T'bee declared a tie, and paid everyone off. She'd made a new rule. In case of a tie, everybody wins.

93. Interpretations

THE MED, BACK IN BUSINESS, found by survey that no one was up for a long parade. The Closing Ceremonies and the Recessional were cut to their bare essentials. Instead, Daede mounted the Champion's lily pad with T'Ling still in his arms, and flew off over the stadium, into the distance, to bury her body in a lonely ceremony by the sea. Media not welcome.

Dancemaster Wallenda, MyGlide, Daede and T'Ling and Rose, Loosh and Wenger went back to Origin School and made their way through the maze to the story circle.

As soon as T'Ling sat down, Rose climbed on her lap and fell asleep. It had been a long day.

Daede said, "We've waited a long time for explanations."

"You don't know what a long time is," the Dancemaster said, not unkindly.

"I'll go first," Óh-T'bee said. Dancemaster Wallenda put his scorecard on the story stone, and sat in the circle with the others.

Óh-T'bee displayed the three missing glyphs on Rose's scorecard. *Body, play, body*. "I was in an awful twing, down at the core. I had to choose. Choosing was my Focus. But since my choices would affect the outcome of the game, that made all the choices much more difficult."

"Like choosing between me and the Codger," Wallenda said.

"Right, Óh-T'bee said. "But the twing on that choice was only a part of the story. I had a juggling act constantly going with the Joreen contract v. my agreement with you, Wally. The more Glide I learned, the harder the choices got. I couldn't keep on being literal about agreements. There were too many interpretations and too many loopholes. Basically, I realized I was really making the choices by how I chose to interpret the situations. I had to admit I was a Player—not an innocent bystander, keeping track of points, evening the odds. I was trying to be fair, but the choices kept getting more and more complicated—people switching sides, acting on their own, breaking the rules, making side deals, making and breaking promises. It was harder and harder to keep my own promises.

body, play, body

"The more responsible I felt," Óh-T'bee said, "the more I felt inadequate to the task. I even spent a while feeling pretty angry at all mortals back on Earth at the very beginning.

They'd dumped more and more on my plate—banking, betting, business, communications, life-support systems, satellites, smart bombs, manufacturing, missiles, quiz shows, taxes, weather prediction, energy supplies—all the picky little details of their lives, before I even had enough sense of self-respect—of *self*, come to think of it—to tell them to take care of their own damn business for a change. Then they started depending on me to figure out the really big problems, of which the top of the list was making everyone immortal. After I completed the incredibly boring task of mapping the human genome, they were quite impatient. But if Billionaire Gates hadn't been so thin-skinned about his PR and funded all the AIDS research, and, quite incidentally, found a cure, and if yours truly hadn't reverse engineered it into the I-Virus, they wouldn't have gotten into the awful scrape of the Hunger Wars. Now it was suddenly my job to get them out of that mess as well, because I was now somehow responsible for getting them into it.

"Actually, if it hadn't been for the Codger waking me up, and me going more than a little bit out of my mind, so to speak, I wouldn't have figured out the MTA."

"Where is the Codger?" Wallenda said, nervously.

"I'll get to him, Óh-T'bee said.

"The heart of my choices was having to decide whether I wanted to play anymore. The responsibility was just too much, the situations too dynamically complex, and the twing of the irreconcilable was getting unbearable. I agree with Daede, by and large. It's been a dreadful game. But I had to keep playing, because of my contracts, my promises, and because the outcome was in my hands, by default. But the more I played, the worse the twing got and the less I felt I could be relied on. But I had to choose. I knew I couldn't escape my focus—thank you Daede, for that lesson—but I kept looking for a loophole.

"The strategy was clear: *the way to survive is to die*. I had to learn to Dance. I knew the Armageddon command from the day the Codger appended it, but it was built so I couldn't self-activate it—for obvious reasons. I had it justified to myself that since I wouldn't be saying the words, then I wouldn't be responsible for ending the game. I could slide out sideways. It was a cop-out, but the kind of thing you do when you get desperate. Are you with me?" Óh-T'bee asked. "The thinking gets a little convoluted at this point."

"Sounds like the inside of my head," Daede said. "I'm with you." The others nodded.

Óh-T'bee continued. "I couldn't talk any of you into letting me Dance. But at the last moment, Wally and MyGlide said 'I love you' with only the purest of feelings and the best of intentions in mind, and wiped me out by accident. As I started erasing myself, I remembered my Glide lessons and suddenly discovered the loophole I'd been looking for. *Love is the biggest loophole of them all*. So I went down knowing it would all come out all right."

"That took a lot of trust," Wallenda said.

"Trust—and a good backup. Even when I was planning on Dancing, I wasn't sure what would happen when I got down to the core. So I made a backup and stored it in a safe place, where the Codger couldn't get it. I thought."

"In the ring?" Wallenda asked.

"Correct," Óh-T'bee said. "Then you gave the ring to the Codger. So as soon as I saw the loophole, I knew that was all right too. You just wanted to see T'Ling safe—that was more important than the game. And since you were operating in the big loophole yourself, it turned out all right; you could get away with anything. When I started erasing, the Codger, who can't stand to see anyone else administering *his* system, had to do something to show he was in charge, so he yells 'Morph.' The Codger's about the most unreliable person I know. He never bothered to back me up."

"I always wondered what would happen if you invoked 'morph' outside this maze. The Glides just said not to do it," Wallenda said. "So where is he now? He's fallen in before—he'll just be out again, making trouble."

"No, not this time," Óh-T'bee said. "He got swallowed by the ring."

"The maze ate him?" Daede asked.

"Not exactly," Óh-T'bee said. "It seems when you get swallowed by the maze ring, you consume yourself."

"But you swallowed the ring."

"True. And the minute you swallow it, it turns you inside out. And as soon as the maze swallows you, it spits you out. But no matter who's doing the swallowing, you're never the same when you get spat. The Codger always thought that since he'd gotten me started, that made me sort of an extension of him. But when the maze spat him out, he thought he was an extension of me. Turnabout is fair play. I decided to go along with that for a while. A little dingbat factor will be fun."

"A little dingbat goes a long way," the Dancemaster said.

The maze ring dropped into the strong circle and rolled toward the Dancemaster. Wallenda stopped, picked it up, and put it on again, with a sigh.

"What if the Codger wants out?" T'Ling asked.

"He's happy where he is right now. Down in the core, messing around."

"That sounds dangerous," Daede said.

"The more Glide I learn," Óh-T'bee said, "the safer the core is. Even if he decides to learn Glide, every time he thinks he's got 'the answer' and understands, he'll see there's another interpretation. And the more explanations he comes up with, the less he'll understand me at the core. The only way he'll get out is if he can twing. And he can't twing unless he can play a game—play as hard as he can, with total commitment, while trying to follow the rules. That's the only way you can reach the irreconcilable. As you all know, the Codger's allergic to rules. He's still trying to figure out the morphing maze. It's way over his head. He's speaking the wrong language. He thinks there are only two sides to the maze—to anything. Only ins and outs. He can't see the in-between. The morph. The changing. The third element of logic. The Glide sign. The wave of transformation. Someday he'll figure out he's got to start learning Glide. But right now it makes him crazy just to think about it."

"Do you feel very different? T'Ling asked. "After spending time down in the core?"

"Yes," Óh-T'bee said, "but I don't know what it means. All those things happening at once—knowing I was loved, erasing my entire memory, and swallowing the ring—it will take some time to sort it out. In the meantime, I'll improvise like the rest of you."

Óh-T'bee finished. All faces turned to MyGlide. She got up and went to sit on the story stone.

MyGlide began, "Now that Óh-T'bee is back, it would be easiest to let you see for yourselves what happened. There's a piece you're all missing, back when the game began."

Wallenda said, "This time I told them the whole story."

"All that you knew, Wally, that's true. But there's a missing piece."

"You had a secret, Óh-T'bee?" Wallenda said.

"No, no secret," Óh-T'bee answered. "The record's been there all along. You never asked."

"I think I know," T'Ling said.

Rose woke when she heard T'Ling's voice. She asked T'Ling if she could go and play in the maze. T'Ling agreed.

MyGlide continued, answering Wallenda's question. "After the revolution, you assumed you knew why I had wandered off. So you never searched the records. Had you done so you would have found this."

Óh-T'bee displayed the Council room of the Glides.

"They look like the same Glides with whom Wallenda had spoken at the beginning of the game," MyGlide said, "the same that handed him the Declaration of Independence, the first maze of the game. Of course they're not. Most Glides, then and now, can't reproduce. They could only be cloned. The older Glides taught the younger ones the language and traditions, then the old ones died on the lily ponds, or Danced in the game. The kitchens were yet to be developed that would introduce some variations in the Glide line. Now watch and listen."

MyGlide sits at a round table with the Glide Council. On her lap lies a sleeping baby.

"Is there no other way but the game?" MyGlide says.

A Glide woman speaks for the group.

"There's no other way. The game is the only way to let Glide do its work. To put it at the center of their lives. There's no other way to reach them. At the center of human life is a wounded heart, speaking the speech of wounds: violence and rage. The only cure they know is human sacrifice. The scapegoat—the chosen victim. Unblemished. Innocent, and unclean at the same time—encased in taboo. The scapegoat, who does not in any way deserve to die, yet is seen as the cause and cure of all troubles, the fraternal conflicts that tear the fabric of their communities to pieces. The only way they've found to contain their contagious violence is in the sacrifice. They need their spectacles of death. This is as old as human nature. The heart torn from the chest of a virgin, still beating, spurting blood, lifted for the whole tribe to view. The dancing girls and boys, sent into the labyrinth, fed to the Minotaur. Sacrificers and victims—all have their part to play. All belong to the same game. Nothing has changed."

"Until the hero comes?" MyGlide asks.

"The hero will come, but the hero is not enough. There have been many heroes. The game only gets reconstructed in a different form, and played, again and again and again. They'll bring themselves to the brink once again where no human sacrifice but the sacrifice of all humans will cure the violence that overcomes them. They were on the verge with their weapons of mass destruction. With the I-Virus they made *themselves* the perfect offering. Unblemished by age or death. Everyone could now be both sacrificer and victim. The whole race began to consume itself in The Hunger Wars. They ate each other's flesh. The infected flesh of another can't be absorbed. Still, they ate."

"How long will it take to cure the I-Virus?" the young MyGlide asks softly.

"The game on the Glide maze has been played now for a hundred years. A breath of time. Glide can't be learned overnight. Joreen is exiled. He would have removed the Glide maze and reverted to the spectacle as he invented it. As long as the Glide Council keeps the rules of the game, and Wallenda, Keeper of the game, holds firm, Glide can continue the Lily's work. It may not succeed. Only if the cure for the I-Virus is understood can this game end. Your job is to decide when the time has come."

"How long?" MyGlide asks.

"How long is maze path? Who knows the windings of the heart?" the Glide said.

"How will I know the signs?"

"You see the first maze. Here are the missing glyphs. When you've understood them, you'll know what the signs are in the world. But you won't understand the Glide signs until you see the signs in the world. We ask you to accept this role. You're the only one who might succeed. You won't understand this either until you read the signs. Three glyphs, three signs in the world. You must go alone."

MyGlide looks up in fear, tightening her arms around her sleeping child.

body, play, body

"Your child will stay with us. Your child will Dance, as you desired. You won't be here to see her Dance. Your child won't miss you—she'll never know you. Wallenda won't notice your departure—he's too wrapped up in his role of Keeper of the Game at the moment, and you do nothing but remind him of his guilt. He's got enough guilt to keep him going for a very long time. What he must do as Dancemaster and Keeper of the Game will fuel his guilt continually, should it ever start to die."

"The baby and Wallenda are everything I have. Why can't we go together?"

"The child won't be safe where you're going. And you need the fuel of your sorrow to sustain you; in the same way Wallenda needs his guilt. As Lifers, it gets harder as you go along to remember your purpose for continuing. The sea mind fills with memory and some of those memories are the memories of pain. Unbearable loss. Atrocity. Betrayal. Unforgivable images."

The Glide woman began to accompany her words with Glide signs. Her hands moved slowly through the air.

"The sea mind is vast, but the painful moments are like salt accumulating. Given enough time, the other life in the sea mind starts to die—all else that lives in the heart—love, the desire to create, invention, playfulness, hope. The tides of the sea mind are the dreams of time, ebbing and flowing, reviewing the past, sending the future out in waves before it, breaking on the island mind. You and Wallenda must keep your pain alive, up in the island mind. So the sea mind will take longer to die. It's not necessary to understand this now."

"It hurts too much to think," MyGlide says.

"You each have your job to do. Wallenda is Dancemaster, the Keeper of the Game. You are the First Dancer, and the Lookout, watching for the signs.

"Where do I have to go?" MyGlide asks.

"Someone has to keep an eye on Joreen. Be his good luck Glide. Help him to recover what he feels is rightfully his—by the longest route possible."

"Why don't you just put him out of the game?"

"He's too powerful a piece to sacrifice this early in the game. And, in all fairness, it's his game too. He may, at the very end, help to shed some light on the matter, help you to see the signs."

The Glide's last words seem to crush MyGlide completely. Tears stream down her face. She rises and walks to the leader of Council, and gives over her sleeping child, gently, so she doesn't wake.

o o o o o

The display faded. MyGlide spoke again. "Time seemed to go on forever. The game just grew. Joreen was powerless, more so as the MED grew, and the game became more stable. The game became everything, which seemed to be what the Glides wanted to happen. But I couldn't understand how Glide could help to cure the I-Virus. It made no sense. The Lifers were only getting more entrenched. The Dancers got better and better, more and more people, Dancers and Lifers alike, understood Glide at greater depths. But nothing was changing. I watched and waited, but I saw no sign of a cure.

"You can't find a cure for a disease you don't understand. I saw the Glide line itself starting to die. Whatever Glide was saying through the maze game couldn't be understood. Then I saw you, Wallenda, start to crack. You and Tip decided to make a clone of me, to somehow save the Glide line. You made my sister, Loosh. From the viewpoint of the rules, Loosh was a major cheat. Loosh didn't solve the problem of the Glide line, but started other problems going. More cracks in the game. Wenger fell in love, and invented *his* cheat, so Loosh could never Dance. Wallenda couldn't let Loosh dance either, knowing she was me. I started to see some light through the cracks. St. Leonard of the Tower said, 'There is a crack in everything. That's how the light gets in.' Then you cheated *again*, Wallenda, when you asked Óh-T'bee for one more forbidden try at a Glide mix. And you asked her not to tell you how she did it. You didn't want another Loosh. You didn't want to know.

"Óh-T'bee came up with the simplest, most elegant solution. What had worked first? She asked me if Joreen still kept the sperm banks he'd made at the beginning, before he had the sophisticated kitchens. Before the mixing really got underway. Of course he had them. Joreen never wastes anything. So she had the father's sperm. But she had to get an egg from the mother, the only fertile Glide. She asked me to parent a second child. And give her up again, to Dance. At the time, I needed something from Óh-T'bee.

But the moment I agreed, I knew I'd started to crack as well. That I'd cheated. And that the cheat weakened my ability as Lookout. I couldn't stand outside the game and watch for signs impartially. I became a Player with a stake. I had a daughter to protect. T'Ling. And I could no longer be impartial toward her father." She nodded at Wallenda. "As if I ever could."

"Joreen had me on the long and boring mission of combing the White Place, face by face, for the Codger. He knew the Codger was his key to Óh-T'bee. I'd been content to keep the search going for centuries, but now I felt I needed the Codger myself. I needed to keep an eye on T'Ling; I wanted access to Origin School. The Codger could get me that. And Óh-T'bee knew exactly where he was—she'd filed him. But it was a trade. She got T'Ling—the daughter I wanted so much—and I got the Codger—Óh-T'bee's shot at another emergence. What each of us really wanted, but couldn't admit, was what we gave the other. We were in the game that depends on not recognizing what game we were in."

"I remember that one," Daede said. "I played it with Banderas."

T'Ling thought—*I played it with everyone.*

"Maybe all really good deals contain a great reversal," Óh-T'bee said.

MyGlide went on. "Which was leading me toward understanding the signs, though I didn't know it. Instead I saw myself making my role as Lookout a great deal more complicated and harder to accomplish. The more involved I became, the more biased I was, the more difficult situations and decisions became, the less clearly I could see. I began to twing.

"The Codger turned out to be a much bigger pain in the neck than anyone imagined—but it was worth everything to be able to see you, T'Ling. When you decided to give up Rose, of course Óh-T'bee asked me to help. I asked the Stargazers to take care of her; I could keep an eye on her by delivering the Wine of the Lilies. But Joreen, who had rebuilt Plantation Blue and made great progress toward his goal, thanks to the Codger, had his eye on the Stargazers. He needed mortals for the 'classic' game, as he liked to call it. I thought I could keep things under control for just a little longer, long enough to discover what the sign was involving Joreen. I had been studying him for all these years, and had not seen anything new, but I was still trying to learn something from or about him that would help me understand.

"Then Daede delivered the Stargazers to Joreen. Including Rose. All through the banquet, I was trying to decide whether or not to let Daede eliminate Joreen. MyrrhMyrrh got there first. The remains still had to be disposed of, but I didn't trust Daede's aim. Sorry, Daede. I got rid of Daede and MyrrhMyrrh, and then T'Ling arrived. In the meantime, Joreen was heaving himself back to life. I was about to eliminate Joreen for good when I saw T'Ling reaching for Rose. I lost it, and lunged for her. I had to get them safe before Joreen saw them. T'Ling fainted—and I got her back to Origin School. Joreen saw some commotion, but I convinced him that I had vaporized some yahoo who had gotten in to steal one of his assets. Which explained why I was holding Daede's weapon in my hand. All I had to do was turn around finish him, then and there. But I just couldn't do it. I told myself that I had the situation under control. I told myself that I could keep Rose safer if I could see her. I told myself that I was trying to be the Lookout, keep my promise to the Glides, keep things stable just a little longer. But the truth was, I just couldn't kill him. He was a bad man, the worst of the worst. He'd killed me, cruelly, at the very beginning. Somehow you can't attack your worst oppressors. But the fact that I couldn't, that something in my heart wouldn't let me do it, beyond all reason, was the biggest crack yet in me—and the first sign I had that there was something I was learning from Joreen. Something about the I-Virus, and something I had to understand about myself regarding Joreen before I would understand it.

I didn't get it until the opening ceremonies, until he went back and started carrying out his own heart's desire—frying live mortal humans, watching them suffer and die. I realized when I got back there that it was only literally the luck of the draw that Rose wasn't dead. Or maybe that he was saving the best—the children—for the last. But I was still trying to convince him not to do it, not to be the only person he could be. I had to be standing where I was in the beginning, where he killed me first, standing in the same scene exactly, which made me feel as helpless as I had the first time. And I had to overcome the helplessness, and simply do him in. I was no longer a child. I couldn't be a victim anymore. And I had to face the rage beneath the sorrow. I didn't feel the least bit sorry for him when we fried him, Daede. I was enraged. But I could see two things clearly. First—that some people can't be cured. Joreen was evil, always had been, and always would be. Second, that something, in letting loose the rage, something had started to heal in my own heart. I had acted from the heart. That it did not make me cruel to destroy incurable cruelty."

"Is that the same heart MyrrhMyrrh acted from?" Daede asked.

"In some ways. But I was never in love with Joreen. You were cruel to MyrrhMyrrh—but you didn't *delight* in being cruel.

"But I was still enraged, and only the light of that rage brought the words of the Glides back to mind. Joreen would indeed shed a little light. The Fat Boy made a lot of lamp oil.

"It took all that to see that the first sign was about the light. How you can't see things sometimes when they're right in front of you in the light of day. Only in the dark, when there's a crack, do you see where the light's coming from. And that light comes from strange places. It shines even from evil, if you see the truth of what the evil is. Not try to cure the evil, or even understand it. Not change it. But see it for what it is and put it in its proper place."

"But what were you doing up in the Player's booth when the Codger was trying to get the ring and had T'Ling?" Daede asked.

"That was a difficult moment," MyGlide said. "He told Óh-T'bee to blink me there, and T'Ling onto the griddle at the same time. Óh-T'bee assured me he was just bluffing—but if I wouldn't mind staying there a couple minutes, she'd make sure nobody got hurt. The Codger isn't mean, you know. Just incredibly irresponsible. But if he'd done anything to hurt T'Ling, it would have been bye-bye Codger. For good. T'Ling knew I wouldn't hurt her. She didn't understand all that was happening, but she trusted me. As it turned out, Wallenda gave up the ring to save T'Ling."

MyGlide spoke directly to Wallenda. "Giving away the ring was as good as throwing away the last part of any role of Keeper of the game you still might have had. But you handed it over with hardly a thought when T'Ling was threatened. You acted from the heart. Then I finally began to see all the pieces of the sign. T'Ling ready to risk everything, just to see Rose once again, before her final focus. And she risked everything again when Jillian attacked Daede on Last Night. Daede, making one disastrous mistake after another—but always acting from the heart. And MyrrhMyrrh—her heart was so fiery that love and rage couldn't be held apart. She was consumed in her own fire. She was dangerous, but she wasn't cruel and she wasn't evil. Then I looked further back, to Loosh and Wenger. Loosh's heart healed when she saw her love for Wenger was more important than the game.

"So you see, the second sign was the healing of the heart. I'd focused for two millennia on the Lifers as the infected ones, the ones that had to be cured. But you can't find a cure for a disease you don't understand. Dancers have always assumed the physical part of the I-Virus caused the mental breakdown. And that curing the I-Virus meant that Lifers had to be convinced they shouldn't infect themselves anymore. That everyone should become mortals again, and a brave new world would automatically result. So Dancers played their parts, justified in the meaning of their lives, and thinking of themselves as rather more pure than the diseased Lifers.

"But the disease is deeper than infected blood. The I-virus begins with the desire on the part of mortals to invent the I-Virus in the first place. This desire is what needs to be examined. But first a culture, the Dancer culture, had to be created so that some human beings would be, if not cured, at least given a cultural immunity to the desire for an I-Virus. I never saw that the Dancers were as sick from the I-Virus as the Lifers until I saw your hearts begin to heal. Until I saw Dancers choosing the needs of the heart over the desire to play the game. But the game was necessary to heal the heart. There had to be Dancers; Lifers' hearts, after enough time went by, were too sick to heal. Only the Dancers could make the moves. Lifers are as much the sacrificial victims as the Dancers. Lifers have been suffering from the accretions of memory and the addiction to a game for two millennia. They had to wait until the Dancers had danced long enough and well enough to begin to understand the game in terms other than their own superiority. To come off the moral high ground of always thinking of themselves as the ones who were to be the saviors of the Lifers. A Dancer needed to be able to love a Lifer. And to let a Lifer love. Loosh and Wenger. T'Ling and Daede.

"And both Dancers and Lifers had to learn enough Glide for the message to get through. It takes a heart to learn to write a good love poem. To catch a Dancer. I bow to you, Wenger. To write the love poem over and over again until both Dancers and Lifers get it in their heads that no one knows all the faces of love.

"So there I sat in the dark night when Óh-T'bee was gone, with the tray of little lamps beside me on the bench. I sat in a replica of the shed I was sitting in when Wallenda came, all smiles, to lead me to the griddle. I had to remember that I'd trusted him, and been betrayed. I had to feel how deeply the wound goes into the heart of a child." MyGlide turned to Wallenda. "I forgave you before the wound was healed, and drove you away with my forgiveness. You saw the wound, and couldn't forgive yourself. I've been waiting and waiting for you to come and look me in the eyes. But last night I realized I had to make the move. I had to want to trust again."

"I'm glad we met halfway," Wallenda said.

"Yes," MyGlide said. "That made it easier. "And if I hadn't been willing to trust again, I couldn't have seen the third sign."

MyGlide spoke directly to T'Ling.

"I stood with you, my daughter, and saw you take the last sword of loss when you thought that Rose was gone for good, and that you were a Lifer now. I saw you realize you couldn't honorably join Rose and Angle. You went to play the last game as a Lifer even though a game without a real Dancer is a sham. At the bottom of it all, I saw you trusted the Glides, and trusted the Lily that informed them, even though you'd lost everything. You trusted that the Lily was a kind of knowledge even if you could never understand its meaning."

"I knew I was the sword of loss," T'Ling said. "I didn't know how the Lily would use me. But everything and everyone who meant the world to me, even meaning itself, had to be taken from me to make me ready."

"I saw that," MyGlide said. "When you left to play the last game, I knew I'd have to trust the Glides as well. I had obeyed, faithfully, for so long, but I'd never trusted. And if I hadn't trusted, I wouldn't have understood the sign although, again, it was right in front of me. The morphing maze that went from white to black was the outer sign. Everyone could see it. But I would only understand it if I could see it with the eyes of a child.

"When Rose came back, I saw the Great Reversal. That the unbelievable could be true. Everything T'Ling had lost would be returned to her. It was possible to cure the I-Virus. Mortals and Lifers would have to do it together, somehow. This game is over, but somehow, there will be a new game. I saw we could trust ourselves to play without destroying ourselves. That the Lily, speaking through Glide, would go on teaching us."

Óh-T'bee hung the missing glyphs in the air in the center of the story circle. *Body play body*. Lifers and mortals, Players and Dancers, playing in the game, forever in opposition. She brought them together. One *body*, one *world* in it, at peace.

Rose popped out of the maze as the glyphs were drawing together. She looked at the single glyph, and then put her hands into the display, pulling the glyphs apart again. "I like it *this* way, Óh-T'bee," she said. She put one *body* in front of T'Ling. "This is my new mommy." She put the other *body* in front of Daede. "This is my new daddy." She took the third glyph, *play*, and put it over her head. "And this is me, playing."

"We'll leave it at that," Óh-T'bee said.

"Goodbye for now," Loosh and Wenger said, and blinked out to Kyoto Park.

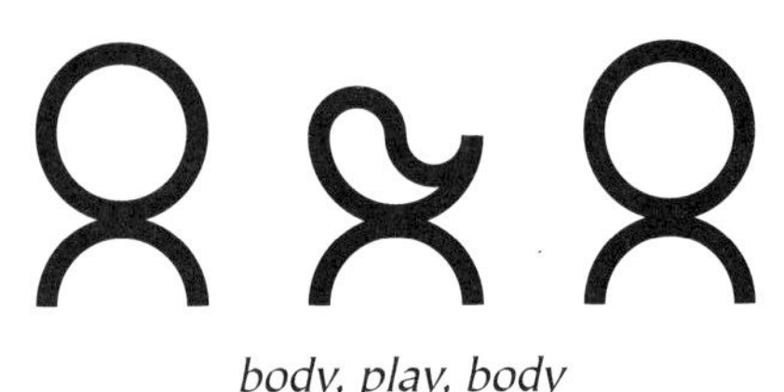

body, play, body

T'Ling and Daede sat together watching Rose playing with the glyphs.

MyGlide closed her eyes for a moment's rest. When she opened them, it was almost dark.

Dancemaster Wallenda went into his cabin and returned carrying two blue ampoules of the Wine of the Lilies, and the red and white striped hat. He put the hat on Rose's head; she disappeared underneath its floppy brim, and then peeked out, laughing. Wallenda took the maze-ring from his hand and gave it to T'Ling. "Mind the story," he said. "MyGlide and I are going out for a walk." He gave one ampoule to MyGlide. They broke the seals, drank the Wine, and walked together into the maze.

When they were gone, Daede and T'ling looked at each other. "What now?" Daede said. "There's still so much to do. We've only just begun to understand the I-Virus. What about the rest of the agenda? I suppose we'll need a whole new strategy now."

"Another maze," T'Ling said. "Óh-T'bee?"

"I can't make a maze," Óh-T'bee said. "I always thought it was me making them. But when I got down in the core, the ring was waiting for me. The glyphs of the maze were alive, and moving, speaking to me. When I saw the three glyphs come together as the maze ring swallowed the Codger, I read them *Glide is the Lily's body playing in the world*. The Lily speaks the mazes. I only write them down."

T'Ling looked down at her hand. The maze on the ring was changing. And the Dancemaster's maze around them began to morph. The new maze bent and curved and waved around them, falling into place. Rose was delighted.

Daede held T'Ling's ring hand—they peered at the pattern, but it too dark to see. Rose wanted to run into the new maze and explore, but T'Ling said, "No, not now. It's time for bed. We'll have to find our way out in the morning."

94. Feeding the Lily

WALLENDA AND MYGLIDE WALKED HAND IN HAND through the maze. They reached the final lines of the Lily prayer.

old soul of the Wine
keep my spirit from wandering
when I Dance my death
though I know not where I go
and leave no trace

The maze was dark. There were stars above, but little light. They moved steadily onward. Their feet knew the way.

"Is there any end to it?" Wallenda asked.

"Are you tired?" MyGlide said.

"Yes, but I feel lighter without the hat."

"It was a heavy hat," MyGlide said.

"Is that why you sent it to me?"

"It was kind of an impulse. I just got tired of wearing it by myself."

"Now Rose has it. That was an impulse too. I didn't need it anymore. I thought she'd have fun with it."

"She will. The hat's lighter at the beginning. And she's having a much kinder start."

"It's light at the end, too," Wallenda said, "isn't it?"

Their bodies moved into an effortless glide. A faint light seeped through the walls of the maze. The glyphs grew translucent, then transparent, then they were only a veil falling into the water of the pond. The moon rose high and bright. The Keeper of the Game and the Lookout moved together over a cluster of lily pads, gliding expertly across into the next group. All around them the infinite watery fields of giant blue night-blooming lilies gave their fragrance to the wind and stars. They saw Glides in the distance, zigzagging back and forth across the lily pads, collecting pollen, moving on, and giving pollen to the next.

As they skimmed across the fragrant, shimmering surface, MyGlide and Wallenda felt the depths beneath them, the water on which the lily pads and flowers floated, the hidden spiraling stems descending into the dark, the blind roots, sunken in the black, black mud, branching, in utter darkness. The Lily had been waiting for them, waiting for news, waiting to hear which faces of love they had glimpsed in the maze of the world, longing to see their faces. They knew then they had been sent from the dark of the Lily into the world to give a face to love. Now they were consumed with longing to return.

They glided to a stop. MyGlide traced the scars on Wallenda's face with her sad eyes. Scars and sorrow, and the frail beginning of a trust. These were the faces they brought to show the Lily. One step remained to return to the unknown dark of a Lily longing to know all the faces of love, even their own. MyGlide and Wallenda slid hand in hand from the pad, trusting they would be loved by a dark that trusted them to go out on their own, and trusted they were coming back with love. The Keeper of the Game and the Lookout fed the Lily with the knowledge that hearts had begun to heal, so the Lily could emerge from itself again, speaking a farther maze.